THE ADVENTURES OF
DEACON COOMBS

THE ADVENTURES OF
DEACON COOMBS

THE CASE OF THE VANISHING VESPER

AMBIT WELDER

IN THE BEGINNING

"Imagine the shock when Earth and its galactic allies finally come to the realization of the destructive power I hold and of the devastation I intend to unleash. All those years of evolution and peace wasted. In Earth years, it is 3533, I believe."

"Yes, Master."

Copernicus, Kepler, and Galileo first unlocked the significance of the heavens. Kepler was branded a heretic for suggesting that man's habitat was not the center of all creation. However, life on Earth survived this shock of discovering that our tiny planet orbited a sun, in a galaxy of suns, in a universe of countless galaxies, where many life forms abounded and where the hunger to travel deeper and deeper into the unknown grew and grew.

Jurgen Peeters first claimed contact with aliens, but subsequent attempts failed as governments grew weary of his claim. Years after Peeters died in persecution, messages were decoded—contact with alien life forms.

Nearly six hundred years after Jurgen Peeters had first spoken to the Aralians, Earth was admitted to the Tetrad Alliance—"Tetrad" referring to the four star systems in which known life existed. Earth's sun was known as Solus. The sun Proximus had two inhabitable planets: Zentaur, the watery habitat of aggressive, scaly, reptilian creatures; and Jabu, a desert planet with a paucity of water. The other two stars were the double star Alpha-Beta Centauri and Barnard's

Star. The Alpha-Beta Centauri system was dated as having the oldest life in known worlds.

Earth and Barnard's Planet were the novices as recent admissions. With newfound friends for Earth, interplanetary trade was established, including the acquisition of Vespering, the technology of interspace travel perfected by the Aralian innovator Luuqus Vesper, who, like Kepler and Peeters, died with his dream.

AND SO THE
BEGINNING ENDS

By the year 3200, Earth had bonded with her allies and found peace in new friends. Earth's ships were admitted to the Union of Space Traders, and Vesper stations were erected on Earth's moon. The grand accomplishments of the Alliance were obvious: space travel, space trade, and, foremost, friendship and peace.

In the year 3533, an Earthman, Landrew of Niger, was elected as the high ruler of the High Council of the Tetrad Alliance. Landrew was the first Earth species to hold such high honor. But Landrew and his people would soon have to confront the supreme challenge. It would commence as a series of seemingly unconnected events in the fourth year of Landrew's reign. It would rise to threaten space trade and then jeopardize the existence of mankind wherever they dwell, until eventually it would lead an innocent Earthling, Deacon Coombs, into the depths of mind and space to confront an unleashed terror witnessed before only in the nightmares of mankind.

"You can trust me. I understand our mission."

The sinister creature towered over him and replied, "Yes, I know that."

"Forgive me, but I feel uncomfortable residing in your space. Do you have any more orders at this time?"

"No." The black-hooded evil glared down at him. "I sense you wish to pose a question about me."

"Yes." He felt afraid to inquire but did so as he wiped his sweaty palms on his shirt. "Where did you come from? Which part of our galaxy, or universe? Where does your kind dwell?"

The creature stood taller, the gaze of its two piercing, glowing yellow eyes impaling the servant below. "It is of no concern to you where I came from." The voice was intimidating.

"Can I ask, please, respectfully, why you do not come in peace? Why does your alien race wish to bring death and destruction and annihilation to the alliance of mankind? And why do you carry the venom and hatred of Earthlings?"

The response was shrill. "You will have many rewards for obeying and following me. It is not your business to question me. It is not your concern to know why bloodshed and chaos must absolutely be forged in the path to victory." The voice expressed anger and irritation. "It is not your concern to understand my ultimate motives. They are completely justified, as you will eventually learn. You do realize what happened to infidels before you?"

The servant stood at attention. "Yes, my Lord. I heard you twisted their minds. You used your powers to render them mentally insane." There was an ominous silence as he recalled the dementia.

The diabolic being now rose to enhance the fear that his follower felt. "It is time. The campaign to assault those I despise has arrived. You will hear of my first triumphs very soon, and when you do, I hope you will feel the elation and confidence of our mission."

"Yes, Lord. I am truly ready to serve."

"Death is also a solution for disobedience and betrayal." The being glanced at the mutilated body of the Jabu warrior beside him, the purple plasma still oozing out of the wounds in the torso.

"Yes, Master." He bowed his head rather than look into those mesmerizing eyes as his lord spoke again. "I must go.

My destiny and the misfortune of all mankind are awaiting me."

"Yes, my Lord." The space was suddenly empty; the creature had fled. He breathed a sigh of relief and then felt a swell of confidence as he thought of his future promised powers and the important role he would play in the new order that the being would establish. He did feel a moment of remorse for all the friendships that would be destroyed. But only a moment.

A PRESENT DANGER

At the Jabu Vesper station

"Quobit!" said Maretz. "You missed an opportunity to navigate the next ship into the disc! You younger generation! I never missed a chance to outsmart the storms!" Maretz had just arrived on the deck of the control tower, where Quobit was focused on the chaos before her. She resented Maretz's comment and crafted a reply.

"Excuse me, Maretz, but the risk is too great. Severe electrical storms have been disrupting the normal flow of space traffic all during my shift. Just before you arrived, I attempted to guide the next in line to the alternate Vesper station on the third moon, but I was unsuccessful. The situation is too dangerous to execute arrivals and departures. Have you not been following the intensity of this ion storm?"

Maretz was blunt. "Of course I have. As senior engineer and today's traffic director, it is my duty. However, look at the consequences. Departing freighters are now lined up twenty deep. Remove yourself from the chair and give me the controls."

"I must exercise what I have learned at the academy, Maretz, which is not to take chances and gamble with human lives. With experience I shall become as proficient as you, but for now, our instructors direct new graduates to err on safety's side. Tempers are flaring as ships awaiting final instructions to enter the Vesper disc are doubly delayed by the fifth departing merchant vessel, which has unexpectedly lost power. You are distracting me. I must communicate with them." She turned away from him and tossed her full head of fiery red hair behind her.

Presiding over operations, the tall Jabu engineer now eyed the sight before her. A stream of ships, lit up in the respective colors of their homelands, stretched out toward the dusty orange planet of Jabu, all awaiting instructions to enter the Vesper disc to travel elsewhere. From childhood, when she had peered into the heavens, she had dreamed of the moment when she would direct traffic at a Vesper station. Her only regret was that Maretz had been assigned as her mentor.

She spied the vessel from Earth and then thought to herself how Vespering had been perfected before the first appearance of man on Earth, just as new electrical flares from the storm lit up the disc and the control center. While the ions flashed in blue stabs, she pondered back to school days when she had first read in her engineering textbook, "A system of trial and error had sacrificed the lives of innocent space pioneers, all of them Aralians. They misunderstood the risks of Vespering; they did not comprehend their chances to meet death. Dismembered or disfigured bodies too frequently assembled at the first primitive relay stations."

Her thoughts were interrupted as Maretz complained. "What are you thinking about now?"

"Just reminiscing on how this process of Vespering has become an infallible everyday procedure, sir."

Maretz had an unusually deep, throaty voice. "Let's keep it that way. That's our sacred responsibility. I have never, in my numerous years at these stations, tired of this spectacular sight before me. In our technology, in this enormous disc, we hold the power of shaping the history of the galaxy with every execution of duty. We hold the power of Vespering. Look at that Earth vessel. In their measurements, this disc is two thousand feet long, nearly nine hundred feet deep. Look, an opportunity! Quickly position the orange and blue thorbee ion particles around the periphery, Quobit. Observe the monitor as the storm is decreasing in intensity."

"Yes, Maretz, I observe the quietude in the signal. You need not remind me of my duties. I know the drill implicitly."

"Then pay attention and carry them out." Maretz scratched his foot-long earlobe, held taut by a bulky black earring.

Quobit, with Maretz leaning over her shoulder, continued to listen to the captain's orders; then she slowly commenced to guide the Earth ship into position as all the precautions were checked to lessen the shock of cellular demolecularization. Maretz whispered, "Even with this scientific technology and modern drug advancement, the life spans of Earthlings are shortened by the biological shock of Vespering. To a nine-hundred-year-old Guillianan, the effects remain inconsequential; to an Earthling, the robbery of life is a disincentive to Vesper."

"Quiet. You are distracting me, Maretz." Maretz fell silent but appreciated the pleasing wafts of aroma from Quobit's hair, recognizing the fragrance of her desert tribe.

The procedure was instantaneous. Quobit watched on her screen as the ship dematerialized to energy, the translucent, frozen white figures suspended inside the ship. Then she threw the frenzied blue and orange thorbee ionic rays into the disc to envelop the package before dispensing the fuzzy beam on its way across the galaxy on a voyage faster than the speed of light, the beam propelled by Vesper particles. Maretz stood behind her at attention, checking her process. "Perfect. Five point five seven from the time you unleashed the energy to the time of departure from the station. You are a credit to our profession, Quobit. I have served you well as mentor."

Maretz eyed her and mused about her. Quobit was very representative of the female species of her tribe—tall, lacking any substantial fleshy parts, her body best described in the literature as nodose. The protrusions of bony material bulging out under her tough tan skin gave the guise of undernourishment to the eye of any foreigner. Females on Jabu required little daily sustenance to survive. However, Quobit's head was uncommonly large for her sinewy six-foot-eight body's frame. Most prominent was her square, protruding forehead, characteristic of all Jabu, which extended above two deep-set ebony eyes. Before her next task, she flexed all of her four arm joints. Then Maretz, in a gesture of what he thought to be respect, rubbed one of his large, bony elbows against one of hers.

Quobit bristled. "I suggest you control your urge to rub, Maretz. I am best noted for my athletic ability, a necessity to survive in the harsh desert climate of Jabu, where I originate from, where a daily battle is waged against nature for land, food, and water. I don't wish to demonstrate my prowess to you. You may outweigh me substantially, but I am a match for you. No disrespect intended, but rubbing by the desert peoples has a different inference than rubbing by metromen like you. You may recall my athleticism has won me awards at the physical tribal games."

Maretz's stocky frame backed away. Then he used his authority to order her out of the control center, seating himself in the command chair and flipping his protective visors down to prepare for the next Vesper, an Aralian freighter bound for its home planet, Aralia. "Perhaps you read my dissertation while training, Quobit, where I captured the Jabu passion for the engineering of Vespering. While seemingly a monotonous vocation to most races, we the Jabu carry a penchant for intricate detail and are compensated handsomely by the Alliance to treat each Vesper as the last—no room for human error, and punishable by death under the Vesper laws of Jabu for blatant mistakes. Thus, we Jabu engineers are recruited at Vesper stations around the galaxy."

Quobit was irritated because Maretz was violating a golden rule—that Jabu engineers be silent while conducting the process of Vespering. She decided not to remind him but instead checked the results as the beam engulfed the Aralian frigate and the ship departed as a taut beam into space.

"Six point six three, Maretz. You are slipping. That performance doesn't deserve a rub. You'd best watch my techniques."

She was kidding him, so he turned and frowned at her. Now the third freighter in line entered the disc, as the ion storm seemed to have dissipated. Quobit resumed her position to maneuver the ship to the proper position by quickly filching the controls from Maretz and sitting in the oversized pivoting chair.

At the Aralian Vesper station

"What is that statue?" the junior engineer inquired.

"It pays direct tribute to all those who sacrificed their lives to make Vespering an indefectible process, to remind those who engage in duty today of this fact. Many a beam missed its target in the early days of Vespering. Read the inscription while I set up."

He stood in front of the sculpture and read. "Where are they now? Where are those Aralian souls who travel eternally as pure energy out of bounds of the Alliance?" Behind him there was a noisy commotion, as a senior instructor had just arrived and was addressing potential new recruits. He knew he must not be caught being distracted by the scene, but he listened to the instructor's comments.

"This station is one of the original six Vespering stations installed in the Alliance, having logged over four plentha entries since inception. The width of the bowl takes into account even the greatest error in coordinates and transmission. For sure the calculation of error will be one of the questions on your final trials. Ah, we have an incoming ship. Move closer to observe, but please remain away from the engineer's guide pod and place your visors over your eyes!"

The students stood at attention, mesmerized as a thin red veil sailed over the top of the disc, warning outbound ships of incoming traffic. In the distance beyond the bowl, the students observed the blue-white frozen land of Aralia. Aralians were well adapted to the environment of extreme bitter cold, and the cold air inside the Vesper station reflected the temperature of their habitat. Aralians were diminutive in stature, fleshy, covered in white fur, standing on average at five foot six on the bare-boned bottoms of their feet.

The beam carrying the first ship from Jabu arrived. In less than ten seconds, the apparition was being metamorphosed back to steel and flesh. The instructor directed their attention. "Look! The ions are aligning on the outside of the disc; soon the final rematerialization will be complete and this crew will signal greetings to the Aralian engineers." The Aralian engineer returned a welcome of "Villya" and then activated the warning system in preparation for the arrival of a second ship.

The instructor continued. "Evolution has provided Aralians with a graceful, calm composure during periods of stress." The Aralian engineer checked and calculated the estimated arrival time of the second ship. Curiously, the ship was overdue. "There must be an error in our calculations; perhaps even erroneous data dispatched from Jabu. No arrival. No signal of an incoming vessel." With the vessel now grossly overdue, the senior engineer said, "Alert the signalmen to scan the magnetic outposts." In a rare moment of Aralian frenzy, ten engineers now huddled, yammered, scurried about, and then cursed the instruments as the new recruits remained amused. Reminiscent of a flock of irate penguins, the furry, squat bodies paced and deliberated in noisy, cackling voices.

Their debate was intruded by signals indicating a new arrival. Silence gripped the crowd. All eyes focused on the red sheet covering the disc. The beam entered, and the ionized package held at the top of the bowl and then gradually lowered and reassembled. The Aralians cheered until they discovered the true identity of this vessel. This was a different ship bound for Aralia, inbound from Glossis. A message was dispatched to Jabu by a Vesper wave: "Crisis: Aralian trade ship *Sleigher* did not reach Aralian Vesper station. Please confirm departure time and route."

A probe was dispatched to seek out vapor trails of *Sleigher* from Jabu. Meanwhile, engineers at both stations played an uneasy waiting game. The investigation determined that the beam had simply vanished. Somewhere, impossibly, in the millions of distant, lonely light-years between Jabu and Aralia, the trade ship *Sleigher* traveled aimlessly, the victim of a perfect process.

On the planet of Aralia

The temperature was twenty degrees below zero, wind gusts driving it lower. Falling snowflakes shimmered in the purple rays of light cast on the governor's palace. Inside, the revered statesman Como rehearsed his speech; outside, the crowd swelled in anticipation of hearing their beloved Como. Few would miss his oration, which would be broadcast live into every home on this frigid evening on Aralia, where the nearest sun, Alpha Centauri, was 150 million miles distant, and Beta Centauri only a glimmer at this time of year.

The Aralians, camped in front of the majestic massive stone structure, were huddled close together. Their shiny, soft white fur, which prevented heat loss, covered their entire body except for their bare feet and powerful lower legs. The first reports ever written on Earth describing Aralians noted that they resembled shaggy dogs found on Earth, because of their small, pointed snouts and beady red eyes. The females had significant white hair growth on their faces, while the males had tough, exposed scaly cheeks.

The glossy bottoms of their feet allowed Aralians to glide at high speeds over the icy and snowy surfaces on Aralia. These nude soles were more effective than the best waxed skis of Earth, while their long, awkward limbs served to steer the body by shifting their weight to and fro. Aralians continued to propel themselves into position in the winter wonderland in front of the palace grounds to pay homage to their leader, Como.

More of the crowd assembled toward a specially installed viewing screen that was currently broadcasting the feats of Como over the background music of the national anthem. The biography recalled how the young general had proved his value to his homeland by saving them from the tyrannical clutches of the planet Zublear.

Aralians reached a crescendo with their yowling and fussing as they witnessed footage of Como trading the safety of Aralian lives for valuable Aralian ores to be shipped to Zublear. Aralia would lose income but be allowed to retain the continuance of their precious individual pursuits. Several years later, as deadly bacteria encompassed Zublear, Como silenced his critics as he delivered the antidote to Zublear in return for an end to the exportation of valuable ore shipments and the cessation of Zublearian military strikes. Both nations praised his efforts. The assembly knew this tale but enjoyed revisiting the heroics of Como.

The protruding balcony from which Como would sermonize tonight was adorned in brilliant crimson and malachite—the colors of Aralia. It was situated on the third floor of the elongated, silky, blue palatial hall, halfway down the rectangular square that comfortably held seventy thousand Aralians.

Como finally appeared on the balcony and on the screen. A thunderous applause reverberated across the square, climbing into the high-pitched shrill of "Co-mo, Co-mo." He savored this moment. Then, to demonstrate his power to himself, he lifted his arms over his head to ask for silence while relishing his frenetic patrons.

His shaggy silver hair betrayed his years, as did his hair loss, which resulted in random patches of bare skin and bone over his body. In place of his usual enthusiastic countenance, the red of sadness prevailed in his eyes.

He welcomed his viewers from around the planet and then dwelled on the economic state of affairs for some time before focusing on his main agenda. In a melancholy tone, he commenced.

"My dear, dear Aralians, I stand before you tonight with the shame of all Aralians, for it is disgrace that I must speak of." Curiosity and attentiveness now gripped the gathering. "For years, the Union of Space Traders has been conducting illegal trade practices." He paused and glared below to silence a group who dared to speak while he orated.

"Corruption among the traders has led to bullying tactics, such as holding precious cargoes for ransom, selling contraband for healthy profits, and providing arms to subversive organizations. The traders' actions have been well monitored by agents of the High Alliance. In an attempt to put an end to these activities, one of our own, Travers of Revonna, was brought to trial. I know that I speak for all Aralians of how relieved we were when the charges against him were dismissed, as Travers hails from a respected house here on Aralia."

He sighed, portending unpleasant news. Leaning over and out of the pulpit, he strained to speak. "Now it bereaves me to inform you that new evidence has been uncovered to prove that the man that we love, admire, and respect, known as Travers, is indeed the foul perpetrator of crimes by the trade union."

The crowd erupted in disbelief, hurling angry shouts across the plaza. The viewing audience across the planet was equally offended. But Como continued undaunted, recognizing the uncomfortable task tonight. "Of all the Aralian traders, Travers is held in highest esteem by our people, serving as a hero to our youth who hope to one day journey into outer space in the name of peace, trade, and friendship. He has been honored on our planet and others for his accredited actions. He is without doubt the best-known Aralian in the worlds outside Aralia."

Como felt that he was losing his audience. "Silence! Please, I ask of you." Como was known for his bluntness. "I know this is difficult to accept, my comrades, but . . . I have reviewed the evidence personally, and it is with a heavy heart that I stand before you tonight to declare that . . . Travers . . . of Aralia is guilty of smuggling, inciting conspiracy, promoting bribery . . . and even . . . abetting subversives." Barely discernible, he theatrically said, "I am so ashamed." The crowd was numb, deadened. The entire planet was shrouded in hush.

Como painfully elaborated on each charge in length, and he then summated his speech. "Aralians have played the most vital role in the colonization of space, have forged the evolution of space trading, have conquered space travel through Vespering, and have formulated and executed laws for safe interplanetary migration. No Aralian has ever been implicated in such a scandal as Travers's. Our record as Aralians was one to be proud of—until today." Como bowed his head as each spectator contemplated the gravity of his remarks.

"I pray as you do that Travers is found not guilty again, but the evidence speaks to another conclusion that will bring pain and shame to us all." A moment of silence engulfed the planet.

"Furthermore"—he waited for dramatic effect—"it is my sad duty to inform you that Vespering has proven impaired today, as the Ministry of Transportation and Vespering has informed me that the Aralian trade ship *Sleigher* has met with tragedy. The ship is now officially declared lost, as it never docked in our port today after dispatch from the Vesper station at Jabu. Its whereabouts are unknown. My sympathies rest with the bereaved families of the crewmen, who were contacted just before our assembly.

"In conclusion, I sorrowfully say to you that everything possible is being done to find Travers and bring him to justice. The sadness in my heart has been shared with you tonight." With that, he turned and disappeared.

Como was tired. He shuffled back into the cool of the main chamber, where his political comrades were lined up to salute him—the normal custom after an official public address. Dreveney approached. "Brief but effective, Como. I know how disappointed you are in Travers, but this had to be done in the interest of sharing what will become public information soon." Como nodded in agreement.

"I am so tired, Dreveney. Please remain to discuss the repercussions of my address with our fellow comrades while I retreat down the hallway to the sanctity of my personal library. I am not willing to partake in conversation tonight." Dreveney was about to place his arm on his friend, but Como turned and departed.

His body ached. An uncomfortable light-headed feeling spun wildly in his head as he shuffled down the dimly lit hallway. Once inside his sanctuary, he locked the door for privacy; crossed the palatial room of desks, sitting areas, and book shelves; and then slumped in his favorite chair to construct how he had grown impatient with these recent Aralian imperfections. He shook his head. Then a smile crept across his face as he thought of the good old days of Aralian pride, leading the Alliance into uncharted frontiers, establishing new trade routes, negotiating new treaties, and achieving victory against Zublear when he planted the raging disease in exported ores and then arrived ceremoniously later with the serum. But times were changing. "The past glories . . . they were the best times," he said to himself.

In his oasis of serenity, he sat in his high-backed command chair and stared to the other side of the room at the glorious portrait of himself as captured upon his triumphant return from Zublear. Then, without warning, it struck him—that uneasy light-headed feeling that had overtaken him before. His eyes throbbed without warning; he rubbed them as he stood. A sharp pang passed across his forehead from side to side. He eyed a razor-sharp pen on a desk across the room whose end gleamed in the soft light like a beckoning razor's edge. While his innards pounded, his eyes opened wide.

"No, I don't want to die!" He could not believe that he had just uttered those words. And why? And for what reason? Quickly he advanced to one of the many mirrors that adorned the four walls, hanging among the many bookcases, and gazed penetratingly at his image. His eyes were still red with sorrow; the hair on his scalp seemed to be thinning more than he recalled. The white hair of Aralians was turning to silver. "Am I going mad?" he stated in both earnest and jest.

More importantly, he wondered if anyone had heard him utter this indignity. He skied across the room on the glossy polished-stone floors and opened the door just a crack to peer back down the corridor. No one was in the hallway, and his associates seemed still to be engrossed in the analysis of the situations outlined by his comments. Their remarks were vaguely decipherable at this far distance.

Breathing systematically harder, he stepped back into his office and sealed his sanctity, leaning his back against the door. As he turned, he found the stylo enticing him again with its glittering sharp edges. In the darkness, it summoned him to admire further its stiletto-like spire protruding from the leather handle. Now sweating profusely, he slowly moved to the desk, placed his fingers around this weapon, and positioned the end of the spire so that it pointed between his eyes. Como stood bewildered by his actions but mesmerized by these events.

As he moved to stand in front of a mirror, the pen began to pulsate in his grip. His limbs involuntarily hoisted the dagger above his body and then thrust it into his chest. His body expelled a torturous shrill that penetrated the halls of the royal palace and sent his advisors scurrying to his library only to find the fortress locked. Again and again he shredded his skin, plunging the dagger deeper into his vital organs, spewing the purple plasma out, staining his dignified silvery fur as he wept and wailed. With each successive stab, he squealed for an end while his comrades valiantly tried in vain to break into the sanctuary.

His friends comforted his body too late. Desperately, they searched for an assumed intruder while perplexed by the locked room. Outside, the fires on Aralia burned lower and lower as the news spread. There grew a feeling of despair. Something evil lurked there on Aralia that night. Laughing it was, in a cold, calculating sneer, as the little statesman Como, his eyes wide open, whispered his dying words to his kinsman Dreveney.

On the planet of Globiana

Geor stood nine feet tall, weighing in at a rotund seven hundred pounds. His six limbs, whether he was standing upright on two or crawling on all six, could serve as powerful deadly tools on defense or attack. He stopped in his tracks and twisted his head to look back into the gardens toward some disturbance. Ripples of green fatty tissue on his neck contorted as he strained to see. On the top of his oblong head, a thick crop of short black hair sent strands over his ominous reptilian face. High cheekbones and fat hid two deep-set azure eyes.

"Did you hear that, Geolo?"

"I heard nothing, Geor, except you rustling about anxiously, as you have been since I arrived here. Come and sit down, my husband. Relax."

Geor, as all Globianans, relied on his keen sense of smell. His upturned piggish nose snorted and sniffed for signs of unwelcome visitors to his estate. He opened his large eating vent under his pink nostrils, flicked his tongue to sense the air, and was satisfied that all was calm in his flowery garden. Then he moved to the round granite table, where he proceeded to position himself close to his mate. He picked up the manuscripts and perused the transcripts of the first trial of Travers while Geolo stared intently at him with admiration and affection. Geolo's chest heaved as she inhaled the fresh fragrances from an arboretum in full bloom. With her middle limb extended to him, she softly said, "Take time out, Geor, and smell the wondrous odors of the blooms."

The table was situated under a canopy of hides but positioned so they could admire the vine-laden walls and the magnificent gazebo, adorned in colors of Globianan spring flowers. Instead of following Geolo's request, Geor slammed his fist in anger. "How could this have happened?" He was angry and vented at her. "I have convinced myself to not read any further. The original trial of Travers was error-filled, blundered by the prosecution, even by myself. If Travers is to receive justice, a clever prosecutor must be personally selected to prepare the retrial. Perhaps even me, Geolo." He hunched forward, his head cupped in his hands, breathing heavily, peering into her huge hazel eyes. "Geolo, I now realize there is a lack of hard evidence to convict Travers. How disappointing." He shook his head. "Where is the evidence we require? Perhaps, Geolo, it does not exist. I know I startle you with this conclusion because of all my tirades against Travers, but I am failing to find concrete facts to commence this retrial. The evidence is circumstantial and leads to not guilty, just as the first trial. I must dig deeper to uncover damning truths."

Geolo was surprised and disappointed. "Geor, I cannot believe you say this."

Geor stood to stretch his aching muscles. The soft, rippled green flesh of his underbelly bounced as he kneaded the twelve fingers on the hands of his upper limbs. The underbelly was the only place on his body where tough scales had not evolved. Geolo stood too, walked beside him, held his arm tightly, and said, "I will retrieve a refreshment for you." She then left, puzzled at his last remarks. As she did so, a branch brushed against the garden wall, attracting Geor's attention. Geor peered to the spot the noise had come from. "Who goes there? Who disturbs my solace?"

He toddled out of the sheltered area. "This is my private time at sunset." He followed the red crushed-stone path to a far corner of the arboretum where the vegetation closed in on him. "It is off limits to all during these hours." There was no reply, yet he was convinced that someone had intruded his privacy, as a scent foreign to him now wafted his way into his vents. He sniffed vigorously to verify, his nostrils ever widening and twitching, his tongue flashing quickly in and out of his mouth in thrusts. The stench disappeared.

"It must have been the moving shadows of the sunset; it must have been the wind," he said to himself. The permeating aromas of the multitudinous flowering shrubs filled his air intake now and pleased his floppy red tongue as he limberly strolled upright. His pleasure was suddenly interrupted by a putrid odor that shattered the pleasantry of the stroll of the evening. The trail led him back to his granite table, where he found a vile liquid in a glass. Immediately recognizing the foul stench as the juice of the chiachia tree, he shifted his head from side to side in quick thrusts to ascertain who had deposited this tumbler here while he was engaged in his momentary pleasantry. Certainly Geolo had not left this liquid for him."

The silence was broken only by the soft breezes. Puzzled, Geor lifted the murky brown contents to eye level and examined their translucent color. While his limbs forced the glass away, his mind became preoccupied with the idea of gulping down this deadly potion. *Why should I entertain such a vulgar thought?* He wondered. *Is this a dream?*

In the next second, his body trembled from the frightening tincture as the contents snaked down his throat and into his body cavity. The elixir, finding its way, cast its enigmatic spell, paralyzing his three hearts. Geor suddenly felt the scorching blaze within. His body convulsed; his mind screamed a too-late note of regret.

Crying for his beloved companion, Geolo, the servants arrived just as his body fell with a thud into a soft bed of soils and foliage. Geor's tearful wife stood at his side as his mouth frothed, his body rejecting the poison too late. In an isolated corner of the garden, an evil creature watched the scene gleefully.

At the Aralian Vesper station

The deaths of Como and his dearest friend, Geor, had cast a cloud of depression and uncertainty over the Alliance. The Aralian engineer making her way into the Vesper station felt this discomfort too, as this state of affairs had touched everyone on Aralia, with Como's funeral having been televised the previous day. It was a rare day that the Vesper station was closed, and now she, as first on duty, plugged her fluorescent card into the coding machine. The machine accepted the card key and then spat it out, and the security laser evaporated, leaving her free to enter.

She stepped down into the hall and noticed the panoramic view before her. Colorful electric particles danced on the disc in the foreground; one of the distant suns of Aralia was blooming in dusty orange, the stars of a million suns twinkling in white, silver, and red behind it. The planet Aralia, partially obscured by the disc, presented itself in shades of spectacular blue and lavender at this time of day. The vastness of space overwhelmed her. Checking her watch, she saw that the rest of the shift would arrive soon, and she had duties to prepare for their readiness.

She felt a prickliness on the back of her neck—the result of her recognition that something was odd. It was only now that she realized a peculiar shadow existed in the far corner of the amphitheater, which by her intuition she surmised should be fully lit by the light of the dancing electrons outside. Cautiously, she spied the rest of the hall. Only in this corner was there an eclipse.

Her body froze. After a moment, she slowly waddled forward toward the blackout. Objects in the corner were faintly becoming visible. Then she saw it—a well-defined demarcated line on the floor inside.

Terror struck her. Something very large and opaque was outside the control windows, blocking light from entering and causing the shadow inside. Whatever it was, it was juxtaposed against the windows of the control tower. Summoning courage, and squinting hard to recognize the identity of the object, she pressed against the skylight. She reached below the panel to flick a light switch, and the engineering control room was bathed in light. In a moment of disbelief, a shriek jumped out of her as four crazed, withered bald heads, their eyes enlarged, enraged, stared back at her. She realized now that she was looking into the byway starboard control of a trade ship that was jammed against the Vesper station outside. She was gripped with terror, constantly looking over her shoulder for the arrival of others while remaining paralyzed in her tracks.

The crazed crew now clawed furiously from inside their ship. Looking closer, she could now see that these were Aralians who had lost all their body hair. Their eyes uncharacteristically bulged from their sockets. Though she could not hear their tormented screams, their faces conveyed their tortured souls. Her Aralian hair stood on end as she dared to move to a vantage point from which she could read the ship's name. Finally she saw it; it was the AKA *Sleigher*.

Long after she ran to summon help, the wily crew hurled themselves against the *Sleigher's* control window, attempting to break free of the ship. In one corner of the deck, an Aralian sat quietly praying for an end for the incessant throbbing in his head, praying for an end to the nightmare that he had lived and wished to forget—a nightmare that was now about to invade his homeland.

On Jabu

How very peculiar, she thought to herself. Quobit was sitting alone in a corner of the stark white room, sipping on a hot, dark beverage of borrow leaves. No one else was presently in the large, isolated cubicle at the Jabu Vesper station. She often sat here during her single daily break, cherishing the brief moments to unwind from her intense duties of Vespering, and sipping her favorite desert teas.

Today was different. From the first time she heard of the *Sleigher*'s return to Aralia and her friend had read to her the disturbing facts about the loss of sanity of the crew, their confinement to the facility on Brebouillis, and the mystery of where the *Sleigher* had journeyed to, an ugly thought had reared itself. Over and over she tried to justify that horrible thought while her mind kept reminding her of its remote probability. She closed her dark, sooty eyes tight. The silence allowed her to walk through the series of events of that day one by one until she arrived at that flash in time.

She opened her eyes in fear first, and then terror. Yes, she did remember the correct sequence. And something was wrong. Out of instinct, she spied the monitor on the other side of the room. Trepidation caused a chill throughout her arms and legs. Was she being watched? Whom could she possibly confide in? Whom could she share this saturnine result with? Maretz? Certainly not, for he would dismiss it. Her close friends? To be laughed at? No. Maretz's supervisor—for her to then be personally investigated because of the outlandish corollary? No! She didn't want to jeopardize her future career. Silence and anxiety—she would live with them.

She consumed the hot tea and was still cold. She reversed her decision; she had to tell someone. She left the break room queasy and fretting, for she knew her conclusion to be true.

MOONLIGHT BRINGS A STRANGER

At Moonbeam

Waves crashed into the jagged rocks below. Deacon Coombs stood more than two hundred feet above the craggy coastline on an overhanging balcony, savoring the rising full moon, which cast intermittent rays of light across the foamy white tide. After a grueling day's work, Deacon found the rhythmic hiss of the waves against the chalky cliffs a tonic to soothe his day's anxiety.

He moved to place his slightly pudgy five-foot-nine frame on a recliner, and then, closing his eyes, he allowed the aquatic fury to penetrate his mind. Moonbeam had been built over eight hundred years earlier on the steep white cliffs of Dover with this isolated spectacular panorama in mind. Deacon ensured that his daily ritual included an hour of relaxation to savor these moments. A cool breeze, coupled with the sounds of percussion, sent him into a deep slumber, and as he dreamed, his right hand released the empty tumbler and it fell to the floor of the wooden carapace, where the final drops of liquid flowed between the cracks of the floor and dripped onto the rocks beneath.

Under the balcony, a sleek orange- and yellow-striped creature slithered over the cold, mossy chalk. As the tumbler hit the floor, the snake reared its head, peering upward to see the presence of the slumbering man through parallel openings between the boards in the balcony. Out of two narrow slits, it focused its luminous amber eyes as its gray tongue rapidly slipped in and out of its mouth. The asp lowered its head and meandered purposefully to the nearest post to begin its ascent.

It wrapped itself around the post, and using its muscles and scales and the friction of the wood to propel itself upward, the three-foot snake wound its way around and around the post until it peeked out from behind the pylon to espy Deacon's motionless but snoring figure. In his state, Deacon was oblivious to anything but the hypnotic sounds of the sea. The viper traveled over the balcony, reached the detective, and slithered over his black boots, eyeing the exposed soft flesh at the base of his leg muscles. Then, holding its head high and compressing its neck so it appeared three times its normal size before striking, it punctured the skin with two sharp fangs, transmitting elixir into the veins of its master.

Deacon's trance was interrupted. "Ah, my dear Miram, I see that you have brought me a treat."

The snake responded by tautening all of its body muscles, standing on only the tip of its tail, bobbing its head to and fro toward him while appearing as if to smile. In his thirty-two years, Deacon's body had suffered little abuse. His only vice was the elixir of the royal viper of Globiana, a harmless, short-lasting pleasure that acted as a sleeping agent. Miram was a gift from Geor of Globiana, where these snakes were valuable treasured exports because of their beauty, rarity, and delights.

As he slept peacefully, the snake diligently and proudly patrolled the deck for her principal, gliding gracefully in repetitive patterns, taking an occasional glance over the deck to the rocks and surf below. Her vision, while blurry at great distances, was complemented by a keen sense of smell. In addition, behind her two harmless fangs were four smaller fangs which housed deadly neurotoxins for which there was no antidote on Earth. Death came instantly to victims, as Deacon had witnessed on the sole occasion that a burglar had been the recipient of Miram's venom.

Hours later, the moon was high but repeatedly blocked from view by streams of angry sinewy clouds racing across the heavens, signaling the first arrival of seasonal precipitation. Miram was disturbed by the sound of a stone falling to the beach below. She wriggled herself into position to see a solitary robed figure climbing adeptly, moving stealthily forward up the craggy slope with conviction. An alarm was sounded.

She hissed into Deacon's ear. He stretched his arms, arose out of the slumber, and then, rubbing his eyes, addressed her. "What has you in a dither? What do you see down there? You are an overanxious sentry. You know that?" Deacon leaned his upper body across the rails, his eyes panning the landscape. All he saw was the usual paradise of surf and stars. As he looked upward, Pegasus became visible briefly between two strands of clouds. Suddenly his thoughts were interrupted by footsteps to his far left, at the end of the porch, where the only access to the cliffs, and eventually the beach, lay.

Miram glided over the dewy boards to take a position behind a beam at the top step, coiled and ready to strike upon her master's command. Deacon possessed no firearms, so he glided to his left to clutch a metal bar used to bolt the doorway to the balcony. Hiding it behind his back, he asked in a commanding tone, "Who is there?"

A deep, forceful voice answered. "Villya, Mister Coombs. I am here to deliver a message to you. I mean you no harm. Please call your snake back or she will surely meet her death."

The confident intruder continued to climb the stairs and now became visible, ascending slowly step by step, his menacing black-robed outline rising higher and higher in the murky shadows. Deacon removed the disheveled brown hair from his eyes with his hand. He saw that the intruder was much taller than he, and very muscular, as the gown was filled. The face was well hidden by the black hood, but as the stranger finally entered the light, Deacon saw two glassy, unflinching green eyes staring out of the shadows—fixated on him. The stranger was soon atop the stairs and stood beside Miram.

"I have a front entry for those whom I call friends." Deacon was firm in his delivery.

"And I have my orders, Mr. Coombs, to deliver an urgent message to you." There existed an eerie silence as they sparred with their eyes, Deacon straining to see deeper into the hood; struggling to guess the intruder's identity and agenda. A motion of Deacon's hand signaled Miram to take her place beside her master, and she did so behind his boot, her eyes fixated on the invader. Her tongue rapidly flicked as she waited for the command to attack.

The stranger spoke again. "I come here as a friend."

"I shall decide that."

The figure took two more steps forward as Deacon clenched the bar firmly. The visitor spoke deliberately. "Mister Coombs, it is indeed a pleasure and an honor to meet you. I bring a message of great importance to you. It concerns a matter of global security with far-reaching implications for the safety of the Alliance and our existence as we know it. The High Council respectfully asks you to attend a meeting—"

Deacon grew impatient and interrupted. "I am not an employee of the Alliance. I do not entertain cases of global espionage or political intrigue. I handle private cases only upon request by local authorities. Surely the High Council knows this if they have investigated my career."

The visitor waited until Deacon had finished his outburst. "Excuse me, Mr. Coombs, for my entry. I shall continue. I have my orders. Your presence is requested in Liberty City, Americana, in two days. If this was any ordinary matter, I would have come to your front door and during daylight hours for all to see. My visitation here tonight must remain a secret, and thus so my message. Here"— the stranger thrust forward discs by sliding them on the balcony to Deacon's feet—"are your travel arrangements, your lodging reservation, and, lastly, codes that will prove you are an ambassador of the Alliance."

Deacon bent down to grasp the orders while eyeing his visitor. "What if I choose not to accept?"

"Then I shall return with new orders that delegate you to the employment of the Alliance." Deacon had already guessed from the tone that the new orders would include coercion.

"I have found that encounters with politicians have been less than rewarding—with the exception of one called Geor, bless his soul. However, I read from your comments that I have no choice." He opened the disc with his handheld. Time passed. The figure stood statuesque at the end of the porch, waiting for Deacon to complete his reading. "Please inform the High Council that I shall reluctantly arrive on time. You will convey the word *reluctantly* in your reply."

"Excellent," the stranger said with a note of elation. "Then we shall meet again in Liberty City, Mr. Coombs. Your departure from your residence has also been arranged, as well as a house sitter for your abode and pet. Follow the enclosed agenda carefully, Mr. Coombs. Do not deviate. Speak to no one of my visit; speak to no one of your absence."

Deacon wished to cross-examine, but the visitor turned and fled down the stairs and into the midnight cover of the rocks. Deacon scoured the cliffs below and spotted the mysterious stranger dexterously bounding from rock to rock. Eventually he lost sight, so turned to open the ticket. One way to Liberty City. Open return. He seldom left his beloved Moonbeam, although inside he was bubbling. "Well, Miram, it appears that I am off to Liberty City, the one place I have always yearned to visit, with its museums of history, its libraries, and its simmering teapot of cultures. I often envision it as a living cultural museum of space travelers where one can learn firsthand of other races and species to further embellish one's own manuscripts and fantasies."

He looked down at Miram. She was the recipient of his feelings. "Sorry, Miram, I can't ignore this challenge." He glanced below, but the stranger had disappeared. In Liberty City he would determine whether his guess as to the identity of tonight's visitor was correct.

"Deacon Coombs, you say?"

"Yes, my Lord. He is quite well known in our worlds as being a great detective."

"You dare to bother me with such bore! He is insignificant in my plans! When we meet, if we do, I shall render him powerless, dismiss him! Go away! Don't bother me again!"

Just as his informant departed, the evil creature smiled and hatched a plan. "Deacon Coombs. You dare to investigate me. So I will play a game with you!"

IN LIBERTY CITY

In flight

Deacon was frustrated as he thought to himself, *Oh, my intentions to shed pounds. This extra weight on my one hundred ninety-five pounds just never seems to evaporate. Always too much time spent sitting in front of the computer, lounging in the library, analyzing in the laboratory, cogitating in the parlor, and deliberating evidence on the balcony. Now I'm suddenly forced to expose my condition of being physically overweight to the general public while I am on this mission.* He knew that his attire would never win him any awards; today he had chosen an innocuous khaki shirt, coordinated with baggy steel-gray pants and black sneakers.

She stared at this peculiar man. He had choppy light-brown hair cropped around his orbicular face. Peering out from above his chunky cheeks were those large, bright blue eyes exuding confidence. *Could this possibly be him—the man that the public has come to know as the Deacon?* She spotted the nickname on a magazine cover staring at her. She turned toward him again and glimpsed two seats over. She recalled reading that those eyes had earned him the nickname Moon Eyes from his classmates when he was younger. They symbolized the eternal hope that he displayed as he confronted new master criminals at every turn. *No. I must be mistaken. This man in dreary garb—so plain, so ordinary looking and overweight—this is not him.*

Deacon secured himself by buckling his ankles, his waist, and then his chest. Taking a deep breath, he swallowed the gooey substance that would aid his body in withstanding the rigorous jounce of takeoff. A soothing feminine voice addressed all the travelers.

"Good afternoon, and welcome aboard *Sleek Stoll Twenty*. Our destination is Liberty City. We will be flying at an altitude of thirty thousand feet with cruising speeds of twenty-one hundred miles per hour. We will arrive in Liberty City in less than two hours from gate to gate. Your captain today is Johann Welders, who will be aided by his Quadro computer system. Remember, Quadro is number one for in-flight navigation and safety. Please consume the milk in front of you. Secure yourself tightly. Sit back and relax. Thank you."

His body was jolted as the tiny, slender craft jerked, ascending vertically off the ground from the gate. At one thousand feet, it turned to face west, the nose slightly tilted up. Then it threw the passengers against their seat backs as it rocketed into the heavens, the synthetic fuel components mixing and combusting while the capsule accelerated and climbed at a sharp angle into the clouds. Johann Welders introduced himself and shared two experiences with the passengers. He then said, "Finally, the Quadro system stands for the four components of computer-controlled segments of our journey: vertical lift-off, cruise control in-flight navigation, fuel blending, and vertical descent." Welders's sense of humor concluded the address as he spun light yarns to the passengers and put them at ease.

But it did not appease Deacon. His heart throbbed; his palms were rich with fresh, sticky sweat as he hugged both armrests. He distracted himself by examining the elaborate menu, entering his selection of fresh salad with his favorite—Menzel fruit juice. *Perhaps,* he thought, *this was the greatest benefit of traveling—to be able to sample the cherished juices of planet Menzel from the Alpha Centauri system.* Since his preliminary glance at the ticket that night on his balcony, he had dreamed of this moment to again sample these rare juices not found on Earth except on all Quadro flights.

As the craft leveled, Deacon poked his head into the aisle to spy the carriage with the Menzel juice heading in his direction, and his face broke into a broad smile. *Truth* magazine had said that "many a female's head had been turned to catch a glimpse of Deacon Coombs's gorgeous, straight white teeth, which so characterized his infectious, innocent schoolboy smile." Flattered, he noticed a lady across the aisle doing just that. She appeared to be examining him.

Deacon sat back to relax, but it was impossible. Behind him, a man reminisced about a lascivious summer's affair with a mistress; two young ladies directly in front of him were both recalling their journey and frolics to Anglo; across from him to the right, a game of Othello evolved into a shouting match between two youngsters; and the woman to his left stole another glance at him. Suddenly, a smile crossed his face. He wondered what would happen if he were to stand up and profess himself as Deacon Coombs. Thieves, murderers, liars, forgers, madmen—all had met the wrath of Deacon Coombs. There was the assimilation of facts, the analysis of matter (soils, skins, excretions), the examination of the crime scene, the astute revelation of motive.

Disbelief, he decided, would be the reaction of this group. "Perhaps I would be labeled mad." He sat back and nestled his head into the headrest, closing his eyes, thinking about how he viewed his isolation at Moonbeam as a blessing since many of his foes had never confronted him in real life. A curious public craved an in-depth exposé of his life. He had never granted it. Instead, there were articles from the gossipmongers that exaggerated his feats and occasional photos.

A buzzer sounded to waken him. The entrée had arrived. The robotic device lifted the fragrant delicacies onto his tray first and then dispatched the salad. Sipping the frigid juice, he realized how his tradition had been broken; he had abandoned Moonbeam to solve a case for wanton politicians. *And for what drama?* he wondered.

Left behind—my library, stretched with books to the eighteen-foot ceiling, with accumulated texts on characteristics of all known human races. The bulk of my cases have been on Earth, infrequently aiding other planetary policing agencies. Once on Globiana, the only other planet I have visited, the police declared my treatise on human races as required reading for all novice agents. He continued his cogitations about Globiana and sorrowfully thought about the untimely death of his friend Geor.

Left behind—my soil laboratory, the site of categorizing all the uniqueness of soil profiles, including associated bacteria. Many a time a crime scene revealed out-of-place characteristics to finger the criminal. The feldspathic sands of Jabu, the bacteria of Aralia, the waxes of

Holtzgghen, and the muds of the Congo delta all aided in exposing recent villains. Oh, how I treasure those moments.

Left behind—my televiewer, which transports me to the 3-D scene of any crime in the Alliance regions. Content turned to anxiety. "And what mystery am I to solve now?" he said aloud, though quietly. "Safety of the Alliance? Huh." One of the girls in front turned her head at his loud expulsion of "Huh" to curiously observe him.

Deacon now became aware of how elegantly dressed the lady across the aisle was. It was his turn to assess her. Her face placed her at forty years, but her wrinkled neck and liver blotches on her hands betrayed her older age. The indentations on her fingers revealed the recent discarding of rings, perhaps the result of a relationship with a jilted lover, or an indication of a recently deceased spouse. Maybe she was luring new possibilities with her extravagant dress and jewelry. Maybe rich jewelry had to be sold because of hard times.

The pitch-black hair, the proud bones of the forehead, the dark eyes and long eyelashes, and the skin coloring all made him believe that she may be of Native American descent. If so, how rare, as interbreeding had long since done away with pure Native American blood. She turned and smiled as if to open a dialogue. This was not a time to make new friends, so he briskly looked away to disappoint her.

He dug into the greens. As he chomped, he recognized how fallible he was. *What possible mystery could the Alliance summon me for? Is it solvable? Any failure will be widely publicized.* He recalled the school yard murders in Euro, which to this day were unsolved. In his quiet moments, as now, he sadly recounted his face-to-face encounter with the killer, Guinez, as he too late recognized his identity. Then there was the conniving Wentee, his own personal Moriarity, who had outwitted constables around the world and universe and was still unleashed, whereabouts unknown, in the Alliance somewhere. Many times Deacon had unveiled him as the perpetrator only to have him elude capture by local authorities. Wentee was a true master of disguise, but on one occasion, he was brought to trial. However, a bribed officer was never seen again after abetting Wentee. Deacon sighed. *Geor was the only politician I ever trusted, the only person to convince me to leave Moonbeam and Earth.* He closed his eyes in a moment of silence and respect for Geor.

Deacon opened his tattered brown-skinned briefcase and stared at *Protecting the Being*, his greatest achievement in publishing. He never traveled without it. This voluminous work cataloged the protective coatings of all living beings. Fur, skin, fiber, hair, secretions, scales, mucous, oils, cutin, and many others were described in infinite, enthralling detail. Deacon had a solemn wish. *I hope this text withstands the test of time.*

In retrospect, he recalled that Investigative Research Adventures had praised him: "His brain rarely shifts into neutral. It always churns, deduces, ponders, learns, and concludes." Candide had written of him, "Once Deacon Coombs is summoned, a criminal's days are numbered." It was clearly an exaggeration, but he had not contacted Candide to correct the overstatement. His ego had talked him out of it.

He sipped the last of the Menzel juice and then shuddered. *What is egging me to recall these triumphant flashbacks? I have authored testaments to my profession; the cases solved are proof of my fame.* He had the undaunted respect of many peers, and those who displayed disrespect did so out of jealousy.

It was I who recovered Queen Btavia's stolen jewels, I who fingered the psychopathic murderer of Indochina, I who caught red-handed the master forger of the Planetary Treasury. And yet where will I be in ten years? Bored? Displaced by some younger hotshot? Someone brighter than me? Relegated to the dreadful position of job share? Just a passing fad? A past curio? Was it these insecurities that triggered this nostalgic justification of talents? Or perhaps this unknown assignment?

He smiled. *Maybe this trip will be the pinnacle of my career! An award. Recognition by the High Council! By the entire Alliance. No! It is as my midnight visitor said—grave circumstances that demand my skills. An awkward consultation.*

The plane bounced. Deacon checked the weather screen to find that they were passing over storms that projected thunderheads up to the thirty-thousand-foot level. The white body raced through the stratosphere to its destiny while Deacon slouched to brace himself for another shot of turbulence. While other passengers were oblivious to the storm and unaware of his presence, a solitary cloaked figure sat at the rear of the plane, intently watching over Deacon Coombs.

The craft commenced a rapid descent. In its path were more unstable air pockets that shook the plane. He considered establishing contact with the lady next to him to take his mind off the bumpy ride, but he was disappointed to find her engaged in dialogue with another passenger. There were those fleeting moments late at night when he longed to feel the affection of someone close. His true friends, few in number, had married and lived distant from him. After the sudden death of his parents a few years previous, he had no family to turn to in his hours of need. Among his close repertoire of friends, there was no confidant. Therefore, this trip brought a hope to him—that he might make an acquaintance that in time he could call a friend.

In containment

The ship docked, the passengers departed, and, as instructed, Deacon waited until everyone else had deplaned. Then he arose and strolled along the busy corridor. He had made it only two hundred feet when his path was blocked by two uniformed Owlers in official blue attire.

"Deacon Coombs, we are instructed to escort you to your accommodations. Please follow us." They presented identification tags to him accompanied by a sealed envelope. Deacon decided to read it immediately and so withdrew the contents, which contained a letter of welcome by the Alliance signed by Landrew. With one officer ahead and one behind, he was led down an escalator and into the subway, and from there to a black metro car with four seats, where the security escorts barked instructions to the Owler driver. As they sped into the wormhole, the robed stranger from the plane emerged from the shadows and watched. He had completed the mission to deliver Deacon Coombs safely to Liberty City.

The metro car wound its way underground, twisting and weaving. Deacon longed for glimpses of the city, but they followed a three-lane trail of dimly lit concrete and steel. In an instant, they came to a halt at an intersection as two vehicles flashed by at high speed through a perpendicular crossing tube. Arriving at the hotel minutes later, the metro car rose vertically up the center of the hotel, skirting foliage that reached skyward in the atrium of the lobby.

Deacon was astounded by the array of multicolored waterfalls that cascaded to ground level. The entire scene was capped by a mirrored dome that gave the illusion that this building was much higher than its eighty stories.

As he stared at the sight, an ugly thought surfaced. His forte was deductive reasoning. Too often people in high places expected him to perform favors for them or let their personal ambition get in the way of his duties. Dearly he hoped that this would not be the case, for he had other clients to satisfy, other duties to execute at Moonbeam.

The thirty-third floor

As he emerged from the cab, Deacon saw that the lobby below as a hive of crawling activity. The circular hotel had dramatic views from all angles. But suddenly the two security guards blocked his vantage so that he was forced to enter his cramped room, which was pleasantly completed in his favorite motif of blue walls and gray furniture. On a night table stood a bottle of Menzel nectar, in a drawer lay some of his favorite writings, and on the table were meat and veggie slices for dinner. The Owler spoke succinctly: "Please be prepared by eight o'clock this evening to depart for your meeting." Here he was, thousands of miles from home, being drawn into a web of suspense.

As the door closed with a chink, he replied, "I'll be ready." No one heard his response. A further thud sealed him inside. He wished to take a stroll of the magnificent lobby and the streets of Liberty City to join the throngs, to be surrounded by people of a million races, but he discovered that the door was locked from the outside. He was a prisoner. He displayed his frustration by kicking the door. It would have been futile to lodge a complaint.

Gazing out the window, he was confronted by towers of glass, with no sight of street level. Every direction was blocked by a skyscraper casting a dull look back at him. So far, this trip was stale. So he sat to read, eat, and sip his precious Menzel nectar, which he savored for the second time on this day. Later he passed time by cleaning his fingernails. He had shaved his blond peach-fuzz quills from his face earlier before departure, so it would not be time for another shave for days. Hours later, after his dinner, a knock interrupted him just as he was about to nap. He checked his handheld device. It was time to meet his summoners.

The metro car descended and, as before, entered an underground tunnel in the pit of the city. After twenty minutes, they emerged in a forested area with majestic low-rise stone buildings dotting the landscape. Suddenly he saw in front of him the revered rows of gargantuan marble structures—the history museums—flanked by fountains and statues.

There were memorials to Donsetter, the great general; the famous Asiatic president Bulgamov; and someone else of long ago, Lincoln. The view was lost as the vehicle turned directly in front of one of the enamel buildings. His heart palpitated as he recognized it as the History Archives Library. It encompassed twenty acres of land, if his memory served him correctly.

After anxiously exiting, he climbed thirty granite stairs. He turned in time to see the sleek black metro car disappear, leaving him alone. He examined the structure. Six pillars, each eighty feet high, bearing immaculate carvings of graceful birds. Through the crack between two columns, he noticed a thin vertical ray of light that guided him to one of the enormous copper doors that was slightly ajar. This building bore the scars of hundreds of years of pollution, which had eaten away at the stairs and pillars, leaving unsightly pitting. Upon closer examination, he concluded that the speckled look was also the result of some of the damaged blocks having been replaced with newer, whiter stone and unoxidized metals. Guards were staring out of the shadows.

On the huge doors were inscribed greetings from all alien life forms in the Tetrad Alliance, including the universal greeting of "Villya" in bold letters. A tingle swept up his spine as he entered a voluminous lobby where circular staircases graced each of the four corners. Four granite columns reached defiantly to alpine heights, each column representing one of the four suns of the Tetrad Alliance.

To his left, one of the staircases was bathed in fluorescent yellow lights, so he took the cue to follow that path, the sound of his footsteps rebounding like a hammer's glance on the polished floors. The air was invigorating. His stomach was ripe with fluttering sensations.

Busts of famous figures from Alliance history greeted him as he ascended. Scientists, philosophers, politicians, philanthropists, writers, athletes, authors, explorers, businessmen—he recognized the majority of the names. In the excitement, he soon found himself at the top of the stairs, realizing that he had not cherished the climb to his satisfaction. Now a long, narrow corridor was in front of him. An open door at the end was obviously his destination.

Deacon decided to linger. Looking into a mirror to comb his hair, he became aware of the figure on the other side. The precautions caused him to relax. To his left, a Vergotti sculpture confronted him. The bust was representative of the works of Vergotti's era. The expression carried an intense look, characteristic of the period when Earth was building a new life out of nuclear ashes. The emerald eyes sparkled; the granite jaw protruded in confidence. He thought from his recollection of history that this bust was probably Yavetnikov, the first leader of Earth's global unity program.

In their presence

"Villya, Deacon Coombs. It is indeed a pleasure to meet you." Deacon turned to recognize Rande, a short, silver-haired, wiry being who served as the private secretary to Landrew and always wore an ever-present melancholy frown. Deacon moved to shake his hand.

"Good evening, Rande. The pleasure is mine."

"I trust everything has been to your satisfaction."

"Yes," Deacon replied affirmatively rather than complaining about his short imprisonment, although he did add, "I do hope that this journey is not in vain."

He was silenced as he entered a large boardroom to stand stupefied before the members of the High Council of the Tetrad Alliance. Never in Deacon's wildest reasoning had he suspected that this assembly was to be conducted with High Alliance members in person. A sweat broke out over his forehead as Landrew moved forward.

"Deacon Coombs—how great an honor it is to finally meet one of the greatest sleuthing minds of our times," Landrew said in a commandeering voice. His handshake was firm. His smile was resilient, just as Deacon recalled from photos.

Deacon felt a twitter in his arms as Landrew's black hulk towered over him. "The honor," he said, "is . . . is . . . I'm sure belongs to me. I'm humbled to be in the presence of the supreme beings that control the decisions of our worlds."

The members sat around an elliptical, polished pink feldspathic table. They all stared intently at him while Deacon surveyed them with eye-to-eye contact of each host.

"Permit me to facilitate the introductions, Mr. Coombs." Deacon stood on his spot while Landrew circulated around the room to identify his committee.

"May I introduce Princess Xudur from Zentaur."

Her intimidating, pensive glare was fixed on Deacon, shattering his short-lived confidence. The muscular, scaly creature nodded her imposing, obtuse green head in recognition. Her snakelike eyes, thin nose with slotted nostrils, and clawed hands typified the reptilian appearance of the Zentaurians. Her mouth, upon opening, exposed bloodred fleshy tissue inside. *How revolting to kiss that*, Deacon thought. Princess Xudur said in a low growl, "Villya, Coombs."

"The pleasure is mine, Princess," Deacon replied.

Her webbed hands were an indication of the fondness for water by Zentaurians, an aspect that had not disappeared through evolution. Razor-sharp platinum teeth, present because of the tough game on Zentaur, gave him a further fright.

"May I now introduce to you Dithropolis, of Jabu. The Jabu live to be the equivalent of hundreds of Earth years. Dithropolis is a mere one hundred sixty Earth years old—far below the age at which Jabu are normally rewarded with statesmanship. But he has earned it."

The multijointed creature extended one bony hand in a Jabu salute. Deacon examined the long, thin facial features with deep, furrowed eyes as he returned the gesture. He knew the Jabu detested physical contact with aliens, so he remained on his spot rather than advance, although he did extend his arm in a return salute.

"This is Raal from Mendalgon. The other members of the Council can tolerate Earth's atmosphere for short periods, but Mendalgons require air cylinders and masks and their own air mixture to breathe comfortably on Earth."

Deacon considered how Raal was typical of her race. The translucent body shifted in harmony every minute, approximating the look of Earth's jellyfish. Multicolored limbs floated alongside her torso. She looked like a character from a pleasing night's dream, but this was no dream and Deacon knew that of all the races in this room, Mendalgons, when provoked, were ferocious fighters possessing natural built-in defense weapons of poisonous and toxic emissions that could be expelled from their bodies with pinpoint accuracy to paralyze and kill a target, or injected by stingers at the ends of their limbs. Deacon became uncomfortable, as he didn't know which pair of eyes to look at in order to return his acknowledgment. He bowed his head as the being whispered, "Villya, and thank you for coming."

"It is a pleasure to meet you, Raal."

"This is Eggu-Nitron, from Barnard's Planet." Deacon recognized the name of the chief security officer, now president. In a system infected with rebellious factions, Eggu-Nitron had somehow remained in control. "The people of Barnard's Planet are the most similar to Earthmen, although Eggu-Nitron, at five foot five, would be considered tall for his race. His thick neck is just as wide as his anvil-shaped head, a characteristic of the race. Eggu-Nitron has been a valuable member of our High Council since joining, with his many voyages and experiences as a trader and soldier to many remote parts of the Alliance."

Eggu-Nitron addressed Deacon affirmatively. "Your assistance will be much appreciated." Eggu-Nitron broke rank and paced forward to shake Deacon's hand and say "Villya." Deacon said, "Villya," and noticed the firm, locked handshake.

Landrew moved to firmly embrace the next introduction. "A newcomer to our group, Dreveney from Aralia, is serving in the painful absence of our beloved Como. Dreveney was the first to find Como's body and stayed with him for hours to mourn his loss. Como's dying words were uttered to Dreveney."

Dreveney's sad pink eyes conveyed his grief as he lifted his furry head, brushed the growth from over his eyes, and nodded to Deacon. "Villya, Coombs."

Landrew motioned Deacon to sit between Rande and himself. Deacon examined Landrew further. He appeared to be a healthy, muscular specimen, his deep ebony skin in contrast to his glowing hazel eyes. His baritone voice resounded in the room.

"A sad and baffled High Council sits before you tonight, Mr. Coombs. In time you will understand our dilemma and why you have been summoned here. We do apologize for any inconveniences imposed by our hasty request. First, this chamber must be sealed." Landrew motioned to Rande, who initiated the universal translator for Raal, Eggu-Nitron, and Dithropolis. Then he pressed two buttons to activate the prevention of any intrusion, physical or remote.

"Mr. Coombs, we have been assembled for hours before your arrival." Small-eyed discs in the middle of the table spun rapidly to capture the minutes of each speaker. Landrew exhaled. "Out there, Mr. Coombs, light-years away from Earth, a danger lurks. After intense investigations, we do not have many clues to its identity, but the unsuspecting populace of the Alliance may be its prey." Landrew had lost his smile. Deacon shuffled in his seat.

"Since Earth joined the Alliance, there have been no interplanetary wars. Indeed, this High Council, until recently, faced the challenge of retaining the state of peace, economic prosperity, and stability that has blessed us. Our achievements have included an increase in interplanetary trade, new mining settlements on moons and previously uninhabited planets, and stable effective government. With the exception of Eggu-Nitron's internal unrest on Barnard's Planet, we have focused on the robust economy of the Alliance. Our track record speaks for all of our efforts." Landrew stretched his thick closed lips in satisfaction, as so often was his pose.

Xudur interrupted abruptly. "I too have been a part of these glorious achievements and have personally been involved longer than anyone else here to validate our success." Her voice had gurgling tones as she barked at Deacon in a threatening, ominous way. "The High Council delivers a lifestyle that its inhabitants expect."

Dithropolis spoke next, without Xudur's permission. "Many are responsible for the stability of our world, Xudur's modesty included." Xudur snarled as the others were amused. "We all know the successes past and present, but recent developments have puzzled us, even cast doubts . . . upon our abilities."

The Zentaurian was quick to reply. "My ability is never in question. He does not speak for me. However, I agree that it is not past glories that cause our anxiety, but a present danger."

Landrew retook the conversation. "It has been policy of the High Council to never engage outside help, since we have our own security and investigative staffs. The mystery of the deaths of Como and Geor, however, are exceptions. The death of Como was a shock to us. Never a more trusted advisor shall we see again in our galaxy." At this, Xudur glared at Landrew with resentment. The others looked toward Dreveney.

"Dreveney, will you please address us, painful as the events are? Please share your thoughts with Deacon Coombs."

Dreveney placed his hands on the table but left his head bowed, his long hair covering his face. He spoke softly. "Aralians are incapable of committing suicide. It is not part of our genetic makeup. Yet the autopsy of Como and the investigation of the site do not lie. There was no way into, or out of, Como's library . . . so . . . Como committed suicide. He alone held the instrument of his death. There is not a shred of evidence to suggest murder." There was pause as Dreveney sobbed, and then sniffled. The others cast sympathetic looks his way except for Xudur, whose body language expressed her distaste at the outburst of emotion by the Aralian.

"As incredible as it seems, Mister Coombs, the single case of suicide in all of Aralia's history is the death of its most beloved citizen, Como." Staring at Deacon, his head erect and proud, his voice now firm, he shrugged his shoulders and said, "I hope that you will prove this conclusion to be erroneous." Deacon nodded to acknowledge him.

"Perhaps," Dreveney said, now speaking in anger, "Aralians are really going mad, as we have seen Como commit suicide and our once highly trusted advisor, Travers, indicted for the shameful sake of power and greed."

"For clarification to all of you, no disrespect intended, I am neither a geneticist nor a psychiatrist," said Deacon. "Madness and genetic imperfections may best be examined and analyzed by someone other than me with credentials that fit the problem."

The Jabu shook his head to disagree with the sleuth. "Mr. Coombs, these are not the sole reasons we have invited you here tonight. Dreveney speaks only to the grief on Aralia." Deacon took exception to the word *invite*, recalling the words regarding new orders if he resisted. He thought too of the escape from his abode, during which he had been carried away degradingly and secretively in a box, and then into an awaiting vehicle; then there was the imprisonment in his hotel. "All this for your security," would be the answer if he complained.

Landrew elaborated on Travers's situation. "Coupled with Como's death are the incessant problems that our Aralian friend referred to with the Union of Space Traders. To now discover that an Aralian is responsible for these crimes compounds our bewilderment, for Aralians have always been the backbone of honesty and dependability in our alliance."

Dithropolis commented next. "Most curious of all is the recent event involving space travel. Vespering has been a part of our everyday life. We, the Jabu, are meticulous people who are proud of our efficiencies. So we too are asking questions about the missing Aralian freighter and the security of Vespering and the subsequent return of the *Sleigher*. These events are so out of character. And when changes happen with this alarming frequency, we need to take heed."

Eggu-Nitron's shrill voice piped up. "The empty chair at the end of this table confirms the sudden chaos. Geor was both comrade and business associate. We are deeply saddened by his untimely death. It too has been described as an accident or suicide! Maybe the cure for madness is out of your area of expertise, Coombs, but the causes are not. That is my opinion." Deacon had to be attentive, as the Barnardian spoke his words rapidly without pauses between any of the words or syllables, his mouth barely open. His coal-black clothing matched his hair and his swarthy, wrinkled complexion.

Deacon spoke up. "I solve crimes on a weekly basis from my home in Anglo for rich and poor, Earthling and Barnardian, utilizing the resources at Moonbeam. I just cannot ignore my current commitments to solve crimes of madness."

Xudur stood, laughing and boldly shouting. "I told you all before this meeting that this Earthling is not the one. He is weak. He is not up to the challenge of this onerous assignment. He retreats already before he has heard all the facts. We need an individual of strength, of—"

"Quiet, Xudur!" Landrew said impatiently, rising and motioning to Xudur to sit down.

Feeling irritation compounded by insult, Deacon leaned into the table and stared up at her. "Princess Xudur, I feel the deepest loyalty to the Alliance; I feel this same deep commitment to whomever I have pledged my services to. Just tell me how I might inform my current clients that I have suddenly abandoned them."

"You will not have to abandon them, for we have already put plans in place to satisfy their needs," said Dithropolis.

"Without my consent?"

Landrew took up the cause. "Yes. You must give serious consideration to our plea. We have not the faintest idea how the deaths of Como and Geor and the charges against Travers and the Vespering tragedy are linked, but this group knows that four simultaneous crises demand an immediate investigation, and . . . we believe there remains the possibility that these four events are connected." Before Deacon could reply, Landrew continued by waving his hand at him.

"The resources of this building will be at your complete disposal, as are the documents on these aforementioned incidents and the principals involved. The greatest known library is for your beckoning. Deacon Coombs, never has anyone been granted this opportunity to have this knowledge for their sole use. We have closed the library and history archives to the public just for you. That is how important a mission this is."

Deacon cast a respectful glance at each member and then said, "And you obviously fear for your lives too. Certainly you must, since your congregation has been diminished by two." Body language confirmed this without a word spoken as he panned the table and made eye contact with each.

Raal offered the confirmation in her soothing voice. "It is a self-centered concern, but our safety must be of concern to all inhabitants of the Alliance, since our deaths in such a short time would bring instability, anguish, and chaos everywhere. It might also provide the opportunity for dissidents to surface and conquer, or aliens to advance unchecked."

"But I am but *one* being," said Deacon. "What can one single human do against this unknown force?"

Xudur snapped back at him. "He is not the one. I've stated this before. He has not the courage! My comments now are officially on record."

"Xudur, please," said Raal, "Deacon Coombs is our guest."

Deacon responded by saying, "I have courage, Xudur. It is sense that I seek. From what you have disclosed, you need someone else. I can't comprehend how my skills suit these problems."

Landrew stood and placed his arm around Deacon's shoulders. "Deacon is correct. It is time to bring him into our complete confidence so he will understand the gravity of this situation. I will accompany him to the screening room myself. The rest of you will wait here. I will convey the imperative nature of our request by showing him the facts. He deserves to know."

Landrew motioned to Rande to breach the security and then motioned to Deacon to follow him. As he did, he caught Xudor flashing disgusting scarlet flesh from inside her mouth at him. She knew that would annoy the detective. It did. The room was silent as he and Landrew departed.

In the abyss of the archives

The two men walked briskly, descending two flights of stairs before submerging in an elevator down into the abyss of the library. Deacon sized Landrew up. He appeared smaller on vidvision, probably because of the angles at which the cameramen captured him. He had read that Landrew never skipped his daily physical workouts. His stout, firm neck and muscular arms were a testament to his exercising rituals.

As the carriage came to rest, Landrew spoke. "We are five to six hundred feet below ground level." As Landrew marched forward, the colorful crimson jewelry that adorned his neck, wrists, and torso provided a brass symphony. He halted. A long, elegant aristocratic nose was his most striking facial feature. His eyes glimmered beneath a high, proud forehead, while his stern chin accented two overly thick black lips, so characteristic of his Central-Africo tribe. They stood before a silver portal. Landrew exhibited the familiar intense look that the public was accustomed to.

He punched a code into a box and then bent to submit retina and skin DNA scans. A red light flashed as it replied, "Villya, Landrew."

"Hello, Bella. It has been three days since I last visited Venus." The computer released the door after performing the voice scan and identifying the code words. The two walked a short distance to a small amphitheater, where Landrew addressed another black box at the open entry. "Please confirm identity of my friend." He motioned to Deacon to move in front of a red scanning beam. Deacon felt as if he were standing naked before the serpentine eye. "Villya, Deacon Coombs." Landrew extended his arm in a gesture that beckoned Deacon to move inside.

The tiny theater had comfortable seating for twenty in recliners facing a wall screen. "This is my private viewing room. The three videos that you will witness have been seen only by the other members of the High Council plus Como and Geor." He entered a code into a panel on the chair's arm and then inserted a disc.

Deacon sat anxiously awaiting. "I hope my role becomes more transparent."

"The first clip was sent to me by Geor's mate, Geolo, whom you may recall spent three years here on Earth as Globiana's ambassador to Earth. Geor, Geolo, my wife, and I became good friends during that period." Deacon fondly remembered his relationship with Geor when Geor was posted on Earth.

On the screen, the puffy red face of Geolo appeared, hardly recognizable to Deacon. "Landrew, my dear friend," she said, "I am sick with grief over the unexpected loss of my beloved partner, Geor." Her swollen eyes were imbued with a pink discoloration. Deacon realized that it was characteristic of Globianans to exhibit swelling in the facial area during times of suffering. Now her small upper limbs cupped her head as her middle limbs flailed.

"He was a great diplomat, and a nobler person did I, I . . . I . . . excuse me. In all our years, he never did anything that I should consider remotely shameful. Our people implicitly trusted his judgment. They followed him wherever he led us. In Globiana's recent bout of economic instability, it was Geor who saw the way to pecuniary recovery. Geor sacrificed his entire life to enhance the prosperity of our people and the protection of Globiana."

She sobbed and sighed. "His death is more unsettling to me than anyone suspects. In confidence now, I send you, Landrew, my deepest-harbored thoughts. As you know, Geor had been wrestling with the Travers case. The chief of the Union of Space Traders escaped our clutches in the first attempt to convict him of treason, but Geor vowed to place him in the celetron prisons since he blamed Travers for holding ransom the medical supplies for Bruu'un during the epidemic there.

"Unbelievably," she said, her voice strained, "I could hardly comprehend it when Geor informed me that the charges against Travers should be dropped. My Geor despised everything that Travers stood for, and now he comes to the conclusion that there is not enough evidence for a retrial, only one day after Como viewed the same evidence and shared with all Aralians that Travers should be charged? There is something wrong here." Geolo broke into a wail as she disappeared from the screen. Landrew paused the viewing and turned to Deacon.

"Geor was evaluating conspiracy charges against Travers. Obviously, we wanted the blaggard removed as the executive of the traders' union to provide for a renewed honest management. Travers escaped our clutches in the first trial, and the not guilty verdict was a huge disappointment to many. With the unchecked power of the Trade Union, Geor was preparing for the retrial with the hope of acting as co-lead or sole lead in the prosecution. I too was astonished to hear Geolo's remarks. Let's continue."

"Wait! Why was Geor personally investigating this?"

"Geor was closest to the original trial. He aided the prosecutors and blamed himself for the poor efforts of the prosecution when we failed to convict Travers. I could not refuse his request when he asked to be appointed to prepare the retrial."

"Surely Geor had other business on Globiana to tend to. It has never been the responsibility of a member of the High Council to personally prosecute a trial. Also, Geor is not a skilled criminal attorney. He does not have the litigation skills. Landrew, this aspect seems out of character."

"You are correct on all counts. But I neglected to tell you that it was on Geor's advice that we hastily moved the first trial date forward. He bore a heavy conscience when we failed in the courtroom. You must also know that Geor held Travers personally responsible for the death of his only son when he was killed in the traders' revolt at Revonna."

Deacon suddenly recalled this incident. "It sounds to me that emotions play a larger role in this, Landrew, than the process of justice. It also seems so out of character, for I too knew Geor. I also wonder why the High Council thinks that one man, Travers, is so dangerous in a world of billions."

"You will soon see." Landrew recommenced the message from Geolo.

"There is more to my story, Landrew. As I said, I knew this man intimately. It wasn't just this case that bothered me. My Geor is dead. He drank a potion that he knew would kill him. The vile odor of the chiachia liquid is clearly recognizable. We all identified its odor as we ran into the courtyard. The acid ripped his innards apart. Ooh, aah, my poor Geor. Ach, it's too late. I feel . . . that somehow evil is at work here; that murder, not madness, is at play. Please do not accept the verdict as it stands. Ach, please, Landrew, help me. Something is terribly wrong. I know it. I know it. My Geor was somehow murdered, and the murderer of Geor is now free." Geolo's face contorted as she spat out the word *murderer*.

The remainder of the tape was a eulogy to Geor, as Geolo recounted his endless feats of bravery and leadership. In a wild fury of weeping and wailing, Geolo ended the recording with yet another plea for help from Landrew.

Landrew stood in front of Deacon. "It cannot be a coincidence that two of our members died under suspicious circumstances. I, like Geolo, have inklings of foul play, except I cannot prove it without facts—facts that I do not have and you must find."

Deacon stood and, with outstretched arms, said, "Hence the arrival of Deacon Coombs." The mild comic relief washed away Landrew's consternation for a moment until he captured Deacon's attention again.

"This second register that we are about to witness is very disturbing. It was recorded six years ago, and the original has remained locked away in a security vault ever since. Let me tell you the background."

Landrew descended into a seat beside the detective. He folded his arms and leaned over toward Deacon. "Six years ago, a space trading vessel was forced off of major passage routes to avoid a severe cosmic storm. The ship did not escape without damage and drifted aimlessly while repairs were conducted. She wandered into an area of space that had remained uncharted by the Alliance largely because of the frequency and voracity of the magnetic storms in the quadrant.

"There she landed out of necessity on a sunless planet. Lured by what looked like fires, a landing party explored the surface. On that lightless planet exists a race so cruel, so violent, and so repulsive that these films have remained in secrecy ever since. The life forms are hideous by any standards. They are a demented, untamed, primitive society living day-to-day in a dark, dank, overpopulated world. There was nothing to be gained by interfacing with these squalid heathens, so it was decided to keep this incident and the planet's location a secret. Contact by the Alliance would only interfere with their evolution and might attract curious space game hunters."

"What about the recollection of the landing party?"

"They were administered a mild drug upon return to erase the memories of this incident. These savages have the minds of children, the physical strength of mature, virile thirty-year-old Earthmen, and the ferociousness of the wildest beasts on Jabu. As with Earth when the Alliance first discovered our planet, the High Council unanimously agreed to let this civilization evolve untouched. So false charts were issued, and trade lanes were redefined to provide a quarantine to guarantee the planet's safety."

Deacon examined a still photo. The beings were covered in matted fur and had two limbs with sharp claws at the end of each finger. Long fangs protruded out of their frothy, drooling mouths. Landrew commenced by injecting the disc into the arm of the chair.

On the large screen, several beings appeared as slimy humanoids with large, cumbersome jaws. In the background he saw one of the traders, so he was able to place the creatures at around six and a half feet tall. Suddenly, two creatures jolted into the group and began to smash other creatures with wooden clubs. This was followed by inane prancing rituals.

"Let's fast-forward. As you can see, Deacon, the planet's surface is very rocky, with only scant signs of erosion, indicating diminished wind action or brief seasons with minimal surface runoff. Large bonfires rage, probably drawing their fuel from mineral sources since there is very little vegetation observed. Primitive signs of tribal life are evolving, as sentries are posted while other savages sleep. There is more of the same—beatings, rituals. Recently, and quite unexpectedly, a second film of these savages came into our possession. Pay close attention."

Deacon did, and with clearer detail on this version, he saw much of the same as on the first tape.

"Watch this," Landrew said.

As Deacon leaned forward to the screen to see some bestial dancing, one of the beings approached the fire. To Deacon's amazement, the savage revealed an instrument from under his cloak. The natives clapped furiously, working themselves into frenzy. As Deacon stood directly in front of the screen to try to inspect what the creature held, a laser gun fired into the dying embers, and suddenly an inferno flared. The film ended.

"We have no idea how a weapon of this nature got into the hands of such savages. There is no record at the nearest Vesper stations of any ship traveling here, or even filing a flight plan to here. So how did a ship get behind our security lines? And for what purposes?"

"I noticed that the weapon appeared to be a recent five-fold model, Landrew, so that rules out someone on the previous expedition from six years ago leaving it behind."

"Very observant of you. Strange happenings on Aralia, on Globiana, and on Nix."

"Nix?"

"Yes, the Aralian word for 'out of bounds.' Hence the inhabitants are Nicosians."

"So these primitive savages have somehow obtained a weapon, or weapons. But, Landrew, these Nicosians are no threat to the Alliance. They have no means of travel and can't be recruited, because of their low mental abilities. They are technically inferior, thousands of light-years distant!"

"Deacon, first the loss of two key leaders, then the betrayal of Travers, then the malfunctioning Vesper beam resulting in the disappearance of the *Sleigher*, the grave problems within the traders' union, then the creation of this tape within the forbidden zone.

Lastly, the laser gun acquired by these savages. And all of this in such a short time frame. Such a plethora of surprises! Coincidence? I say not! And so do my comrades. Please don't ignore our experience and instincts."

"Okay, I am curious. Suspects, please. I'm interested in your opinion, Landrew."

"Number-one suspect is Travers. The traders' union has grown too powerful. They have their own private arsenal, as demonstrated by recent skirmishes. They are shrewd navigators, savvy negotiators, and their union grossly outnumbers all our armies and security forces. Most importantly, Travers has the undying loyalty of all his members. He commands a spell over them. His true headquarters are unknown to us. His influence may have reached into the jurors of his trial."

"You are suggesting that he bribed the jury?"

"With all our precautions we took, yes. The traders have recently incited riots, smuggled arms to the enemies of this government, held cargoes for ransom, and traded for illegal drugs and goods. It is a shame to admit this, but the Alliance has lost control of the Union of Space Traders. They are not capable of self-governance, and we are not capable of wrestling the power away from them. Dreveney recently arrived at these same conclusions in an internal memo about this union. Eggu-Nitron bears the scars of their recent illegal activities on his planet, which he believes may give support to the rebels there."

"I still need convincing. What possible motive could the traders have to murder Como and Geor? To triumph over the Alliance? They can't possibly conquer humanity as we know it. They may be large in numbers, but they are totally underarmed. They are not a military threat! They don't have the weaponry of your high-tech armies."

"Here is a dossier on Travers. You investigate. You report back to me, Mister Detective." Landrew handed him a small chip to plug into his handheld device and then pulled a folder from beside him.

"Number-two suspect is Ochman, the new ruler of Zentaur. Even Xudur is suspicious of his current mobilization of troops for a land at peace. His forces travel off the planet frequently. Where? Xudur doesn't know! Xudur believes that Ochman possesses blind ambition and is mentally unstable. Unfortunately, elections are still distant to replace him. Zentaurians by nature are an aggressive race, and Ochman is the most aggressive leader ever."

Deacon facetiously said, "They are an aggressive race, admittedly." He disbelieved this lead.

"Number three, the Egocentric Rebels. As with every generation, there are discontent malefactors and terrorists. We have this irritation. While they have no anointed leader, they follow a doctrine, and they are spreading their brand of terrorist ideology through attacks."

Deacon stared back at Landrew. The High Council seemed to be leading him down blind paths. *Purposely?* he wondered. "All three of these leads could be routed by galactic forces, quelled by legislation to place these people at huge disadvantages by implementing severe punishments. What chance has a lightly armed space trade freighter against a battalion of Alliance fighters? What chances have rebellious youths to conquer the Alliance and win against Alliance forces? Ochman's army pales in comparison to your Owler battalions. Maybe you suppress the truth to me? Maybe there are no bona fide leads?"

"I appreciate your honesty, Deacon. Let us move on." Now his tone changed as stony features embraced his facial muscles. "Number four." Landrew shifted in his seat. "There is the possibility that these events are a prelude to alien invasion. We consider ourselves to be so damn smart. Perhaps we are being invaded and this is a kind of test to determine how much panic and disruption can be achieved before the main alien forces arrive, a few isolated incidents to ascertain whether we are smart enough to detect the infection. Perhaps this is a test of our mettle."

"Now this is the most believable lead yet." Deacon perked up, but not without his mind filling with uneasiness.

"Unfortunately, Deacon, this is the easiest way out but the most difficult to prove. If aliens are already here among us and have the power to bend Vesper waves, make people commit suicide, hide themselves from detection, and influence trial outcomes, then we are doomed. If they are among us now, you have the impossible task of finding them, identifying them, and advising us on their weakness so we can attack or contain. This will be your greatest case ever!" Deacon sat attentively, believing that Landrew's reference to finding aliens could expose his own weaknesses.

"Finally, for the safety of our people, for the sake of the future of the Alliance, you must investigate . . . the members of the High Council. Maybe Geor and Como were killed for something that they discovered about one of us. Maybe there is a touch of madness among us. Or maybe we are the first targets of an invasion."

Deacon smiled. "Well, this makes my task easier, for I intended to do just that."

Landrew replied, "Have fun with our checkered backgrounds. Deacon, all the information that you require is in the History Archives Library and at your complete disposal, including copies of all of your works. No file is too confidential, no transcript denied, and no request withheld. You have the highest security clearance ever given to a public resident."

"Permission from a potential madman?"

"Correct again," Landrew said with a hearty laugh. "The entire history of all mankind wherever he dwells, whenever he has been documented, is at your disposal. To aid you in your research, we have entrusted to you the top-of-the-line Owlers. They are called Gem and Jim. Their three major functions are performed to perfection. Firstly, they will protect you from all harm and will kill offenders to accomplish this. Secondly, calling them efficient researchers would be an understatement, since they research and assimilate data at light speed. Finally, they are expert navigators to travel with you and protect you wherever your clues lead you—even to Nix!"

Deacon sat rigidly with an astonished glare. "Travel? Nix? I . . . I . . . I will not leave Earth." There was an edge in the room as he rose and stood nose-to-nose with Landrew. Time passed. "Do they cook?"

His query broke the tension. "Best cooks in the galaxy, Mr. Coombs. The next time that I see you, I figure you will have gained twenty pounds."

"Ask them to come in."

"What makes you so sure that they are nearby?"

"Where else would they be if their primary goal is to protect me? I can only presume that they are doing their job; I presume that they are outside." Landrew signaled, and two humanoid specimens entered. They had identical six-foot frames with lifelike hands and faces. They were trim in build. Their stares were expressionless, with glassy eyes peering out from sandy, tanned faces. Their movements were graceful, fluid. One wore a blue strap over the shoulder; the other had a red belt around the waist.

The one with the blue strap, dark green eyes, and slick black hair spoke first. "Villya, I am Jim, the latest of the line of modern security Owlers. Let me take this opportunity to introduce my partner, Gem." Jim's voice was deep and his hands were animated upon speaking. The reply from the other was smoother, with a slightly higher pitch.

"Greetings. I too look forward to service under you, Deacon Coombs. We are equally efficient, here to obey your commands." Gem had platinum short hair and sparkling blue eyes.

"But I was the last one off the assembly line," Jim said.

Deacon grinned and looked at Landrew. "An assembler with a sense of humor." He then directed his attention to the Owlers. "Yes, yes. I am confident that you will perform up to your expectations. Now, I still have discussions with Landrew, so I would ask you to wait outside, please." The Owlers obeyed him without hesitation.

"That wasn't necessary," Landrew said, "as they maintain strictest confidentiality and cannot be influenced. They will be your most trusted allies on this quest. Emotions do not figure into their analyses."

His hand under his chin, Deacon looked at Landrew. "A test of ultimate loyalty. To you? Or to me? They passed the test. You stated that the Owlers do not let emotions interfere with their decisions, yet I detected distinct notes of affection in the one called Jim."

"Human engrams. Engrained in Jim for your benefit, not theirs. A little humor to break up the monotonous chores they systematically perform."

"You said earlier that they are excellent pilots."

"Correct. They will navigate your craft safely, anywhere."

"What craft?"

"The ship docked at space hangar seventeen, the *Heritage*, reserved exclusively for you and Jim and Gem."

Deacon was firm. "There is a gross misunderstanding. I work exclusively from my facilities at Moonbeam. You know that. My laboratory, my library, my scanners, the comfort of my home—these are the tools of my trade." Landrew was patient as Deacon summated and rambled and justified the single time that he had departed Earth to assist Geor.

"My dear Deacon. This assignment may take you elsewhere."

"Where?"

"Wherever your heart leads you. Wherever your brain directs you. Wherever your instincts compel you. Wherever the evidence must be gathered."

"The Owlers can go; I will stay here and direct their activities, await transmissions. My facilities are the best in the world. I will lose time and competitive advantage by departing Earth. To voyage to Nix as you suggested earlier is even more ludicrous."

Landrew replied with a soft "No."

"Then you shall have to find someone else."

"Then I order you on behalf of the High Council."

"Am I to understand that you are coercing me to accept this case?" He pointed a finger at the authoritative figure. "I will bargain with you, compromise, but I will not accept these duties under duress."

"I cannot, in clear conscience, Deacon Coombs, force you to undertake this mission. However, I ask you, I beg of you to admit the gravity of this situation. The Alliance is at risk. Thousands of years of building relationships, an economy, and our future are being tested and threatened."

"Landrew, the Alliance has supreme fleets of fighters, brave soldiers, vast armies of Owlers and deadly robots, intelligent commanders, and technology. I am but one individual. What is my role? How can you be so sure that I can make a difference?"

Landrew was becoming irritated. "We are utilizing all available resources to solve these crimes. As an extension to our efforts, we, the High Council, would greatly appreciate the opinions of Deacon Coombs to act independently of all our other authorized efforts, to take a completely different, unbiased route to the solution, to act with the respected good judgment of Deacon Coombs. Please, Mr. Coombs, once again, I plead with you to do so. Your opinion and findings are important to us, for you act independent of the High Council's other efforts."

"You still withhold information."

"How so?"

"Why the emphasis on Travers? The time is past that a sole mortal could influence history or be a threat to civilization."

"Okay. Sit down. Let us not quarrel. I will put Travers in perspective according to Landrew. Vespering was an exact engineering and science for millions of years, until that fateful day when the *Sleigher* departed for Aralia. The Vesper beam vanished without a trace. The ship's captain was . . . Travers."

Deacon was genuinely surprised. "Could the incident be attributed to faulty equipment?"

"Highly unlikely. One, the next ship beaming outbound from Jabu to Aralia made its destination. Two, the equipment was checked at both stations, and there were no malfunctions at either Vesper station." Landrew motioned with his hands and arms to keep Deacon silent. "Travers was also the captain of the ship that went to Nix six years ago. I told you that we used mild mind-altering drugs to erase the memory of the crew then. Well, Travers was not drugged. He comes from fine, honorable Aralian blood." Landrew sighed in disgust.

"After the recovery of the *Sleigher* on Aralia, Travers and his crew were detained at the medical facilities at Froora. Before his discharge, before we had a chance to conduct an interrogation, he escaped without a trace. No one witnessed him leave. Believe me, Deacon, when I tell you that we have searched everywhere for him in our known worlds with huge resources and we can't find him. Travers has vanished."

Deacon felt cold. "And you . . . want me . . . to go out there"—he pointed to the roof of the theater—"out into the depths of space . . . to find Travers."

"That was the conclusion I hoped that you would reach after your own investigations in the library. Travers seems to have an intersection with these recent events."

"I might very well fail, for it is not my style to travel around the galaxy looking for a missing person with a one-in-a-billion chance of finding him."

Landrew smiled. "I trust you. Don't forget, I previously stated that we have other resources. We simply ask you to act independently of them."

"Disprove two suicides, find the power that bends Vesper beams, investigate the sanities and vanities of the High Council, and find Travers, who is hiding, place unknown, in our space."

"An excellent summation!"

Deacon felt despondent. Landrew continued. "Now for another surprise. The crew of the ship *Sleigher* has been rendered totally insane. Permanent brain damage has been sustained by all these poor souls. They are mindless vegetables, bodies alive. The insane asylum at Brebouillis is their resting place. Oddly, those who spoke to Travers at the hospital before he disappeared say that they felt Travers was not touched by this madness. Somehow he made the same trip on the *Sleigher* but did not suffer the same fate as his now-demented crew. Something is terribly, terribly wrong, Deacon Coombs, just as Geolo stated. In confidence, I will share with you that I am fearful of what the future holds!"

"So Travers is the common thread. Como dies on a night that he blasphemes Travers; Geor dies as he is investigating Travers as the corrupt head of a powerful union; a trade ship under Travers's command disappears from a Vesper station, and Travers does not suffer the same fate as his crew. There is no direct evidence in all of this data to say yet that Travers has done anything wrong."

"Ah, Mister Coombs, this is your challenge."

Deacon felt some shivers. "Travers took that second film on Nix, didn't he?"

Solemnly, Landrew replied, "Yes. Well, probably. We found the film on the *Sleigher* in Travers's cabin after the ship was disposed of at the Vesper station. Can you imagine the scenario? First the *Sleigher* disappears in a Vesper beam. Then it gets directed to Nix, where there is no materialization station. Then the film is taken by Travers, the crew rendered demented, and the ship returned to Aralia—and by whom? No explanation from my other resources pleases me. I need peace of mind about Travers. We need information and facts quickly."

"You have my curiosity. I realize your fascination with the man Travers, but I shall restate that the Owlers can perform in space."

"You are not the only hope, Deacon."

"Can you disclose to me who else has been assigned to this case, so I don't interfere with their work?"

"No. You must work independently. Press the Owlers, Deacon. In this facility you have all the information you need. You will find the logs of all Travers's journeys. Then, when you are prepared, you can depart for Brebouillis to study the demented members of the crew and meet two people who will prove to be invaluable. Brebouillis is a moon that orbits planet Aralia. Patiently, doctors there await you."

"Who are they?"

"Two doctors with ample backgrounds and insights into this investigation."

"I am most curious why Travers did not suffer the same fate as his crew, unless . . ."

"Unless what?"

Deacon remained silent to Landrew's query. Landrew expressed his frustration once again. "We are helpless against this evil. I fear it may strike again soon. The members of the High Council researched you thoroughly, and you are the one. You and I know why you should take this difficult mission."

Deacon shifted uncomfortably. "I'm not sure what you reference."

"You don't need to deny your gift with me, Deacon Coombs. Your scholastic records are impeccable, your intelligence quotient as high as any recorded, and I know that you have the power to receive and transmit energy waves emitted by the human brain at a level rarely documented on Earth."

"I see you too are a sleuth."

"Rudimentary. A little snooping here, a little cooperation there, and suddenly I discover a man whose extraordinary skills are what we might need. You are indeed gifted. I know this is the very reason that you hide, or shall I say work, at Moonbeam. You are uncomfortable interfacing and intruding into the minds of others, receiving unwelcome thoughts."

Deacon was startled. "You are correct in your assumptions. But I do not perform this purposely, and I receive only certain wavelengths that compose a small part of the brain's emissions. I prefer to shut myself away at Moonbeam as you have stated, for I don't wish to intrude on other people's thoughts. It is an affliction.

"Just on this plane ride from Anglo, I was subjected to recognizing the details of an affair by a gentleman, a mental pass from a lady sitting across the aisle, and two girls thinking and recalling their vacations in Anglo in intimate detail. I don't wish to be bombarded with this, Landrew. My mind wants to be left alone."

"Interestingly enough, Deacon, I did not speak of Travers taking the film on Nix. I only sent it to you mentally. And you received it!" Landrew said proudly. "You are the one."

"I find great solace at Moonbeam. I don't want to read other people's minds."

"And will you believe me, Deacon Coombs, when I tell you that this affliction will save your life on this mission? With this so-called disease, you will have to invade the sanctity of the minds of others to save our world. You might discover terror. You might find evil. I don't envy you. But my prayers will always be with you, Deacon. You must do this!"

Landrew's comments frightened Deacon. "You speak as if you know what I might find out there." Landrew gazed sternly back with no sign of affirmation.

"Down the hall you will find your wardrobe. Your library of discs at Moonbeam has been transferred here, and we have constructed a direct link to your files. Owlers visited Moonbeam and made the transfer earlier today immediately after your departure." Deacon resented this invasion of privacy. Landrew continued. "We also have a new handheld device that is more powerful than the one you bear. It straps painlessly onto your wrist and has an immense memory. You can also link into many remote databanks; the Owlers will demonstrate this to you. Consider this a gift from the High Council.

"The Owlers will also insert a microdevice into one of your ears. It is the recent state of technology and serves to translate instantaneously any foreign languages you may encounter. Remember when using it to put the shield plug in the other ear so the speaker does not interfere with the translator. Carry the translator at all times."

"My life is my work. It is the supreme satisfaction that I receive from life. It is the only happiness that I know," said Deacon. Landrew stared back with a poker face. After a silence, Deacon said, "But I guess that I am about to take my show on the road."

"Ah, ha ha ha!" Landrew shouted jubilantly, extending a hearty handshake to Deacon. "I will say good night to you. Good luck from the members of the High Council."

Deacon refused to break the handshake. "Wait! I have other questions for you. And you speak as if we may not see each other again."

"Maybe not," Landrew said, and he barged out of the viewing room and into the hallway.

Deacon presented a barrage of excuses as Landrew gained distance between them. The two men stood facing one another as the elevator door closed. Piece by piece, the body of Landrew disappeared behind the iron curtain. As the doors emitted a resounding thud, Landrew was gone. Deacon strained to hear the last whine as the carriage left, leaning against the door, his ear pressed to the metal. It was completely silent. He was alone in the abyss of the archives, alone with the creaks and groans of the concrete and steel. Dejectedly, he turned to find the two Owlers fifty feet in front of him, awaiting his return.

They were soulless, expressionless, at attention, ready for his commands. Inside, he felt empty. Where to start? How he longed to converse further with Landrew.

<hr />

High above, Landrew exited the elevator. Confidently he strolled down the hall with broad steps in his gait to his awaiting party. He sincerely liked the little man. He had wanted to stay and converse with him further, but he knew Coombs must be not be influenced by even him.

Stepping into the conference room, he discovered Council members all staring at him. He shared their eye contact one by one. Raal spoke first. "Is Mr. Coombs accepting the assignment?"

"Yes."

Dreveney quickly intervened. "And you shared the footage on Nix with him?"

"Yes."

"And he is willing to travel off Earth to investigate?"

"Yes."

"I am skeptical about this Earthling," Xudur said. "He has not traveled extensively throughout our worlds and is certainly not one prepared for any physical combat should the circumstance arise."

"Trust him. Trust me when I tell you that I know Coombs has accepted the mission; for I have firsthand proof; I saw the look of excitement and adventure in Deacon's eyes."

GEM AND JIM

A dream come true

"Dreveney, this is a dream come true for me. Wandering around the catacombs of this magnificent structure, I am inspired to hear that the only human footsteps echoing in the aisles are my own."

Dreveney chuckled. "I haven't had exercise like this indoors in many years. As you know, we Aralians are outdoor creatures. Where are you leading me?" After climbing up endless flights of stairs, and dragging Dreveney through maze upon maze of hallways, Deacon finally said, "Here." The twosome stood stupefied on the great balcony that loomed some three hundred feet above the acres of data and history before them.

"Deacon, I am overwhelmed."

"Me too. From here you can obtain an appreciation of the caves, stalls, terminals, footage viewing rooms, alcoves, and row upon row of archaic manuscripts, all rows lit by resplendent multicolored lights in the floors that serve to code the areas." Dreveney watched Deacon as his large blue mooneyes darted to and fro, feasting on the vastness of knowledge at his disposal.

"It is here on the great balcony that I decided to set up my control center. With this exhilarating view, I am inspired to work. Meanwhile, as Landrew stated, an unsuspecting civilization is being informed that the museum has been closed indefinitely for structural repairs."

"While inside," said Dreveney, "Deacon Coombs is on knowledge overload, his mind tempting hourly to disband this foolish quest and alternatively plow through the original ageless works of past masters. Do you know, Coombs, that there are identical information databases on each of the other planets in the Alliance?"

"No. I did not know. So tell me, Dreveney, what other lucky souls have you and Landrew engaged to scour those bases?"

"Sir, that is confidential," he quietly said. "What form does the data take here? What media do you inspect?"

"Microchips are the common venue of storage for literary works, history, news clips, science, and treatises. I found that the system needs only split seconds at the most to retrieve any entry and project it on my monitor or 3-D screen. Jim and Gem raised an objection to the control site, citing more convenient sites below that provide the advantages of faster retrievals of paper copies, but I ignored them, constructed their chores of investigation, and issued orders that sent them on their way."

"I envy you. Have you found Travers in your files yet?"

"Visual segments take longer to retrieve, although the eye scans thousands of feet per second per disc to locate requested footage." Deacon turned to face Dreveney. "Yesterday, on the big screen,"—he pointed to it behind them—"I found and faced Travers of Aralia, an innocent-looking specimen."

Dreveney's look turned sour. "I am the expert on Aralians, Mr. Coombs, and I advise you to respectfully not think of Travers as innocent."

"I hear you, my friend. I also unearthed the last days of Geor, the rebellion on Valdecon, and dossiers of influential trade officials. A file with blemishes on the record of Travers was very easily stumbled into. Do you think this was conveniently planted? Perhaps to influence me?"

Dreveney changed topics again. "What else have you observed?"

"I discovered a damaging address by Travers to trade members admitting that the trade union was indeed responsible for many illegal activities. In it, Travers vowed to find those responsible and punish them. This file further documented the union's measures to smash smuggling rings and put an end to illegal sales of armaments. I surmise that the Union of Space Traders grew too large too rapidly and too soon with new admittances, and that there are ineffective screening processes for tradesmen, who are issued immense, sweeping powers to conduct trade throughout the Alliance. Travers seems to exhibit and express good intentions, but a poor enforcement of regulations is a persistent theme throughout all the criminal infractions. I had no idea that interplanetary trade was such a lucrative business.

"I concluded that Travers was an honest industrious individual trying to grasp a monstrous out-of-control organization. I truly do feel sorry for the Aralian and the overwhelming task of leading the traders. Landrew was correct in his assessment of the undying loyalty of the membership to Travers. This makes Travers powerful, but only within his domain." To himself he pondered why the High Council wanted him to focus on Travers. Even with the intersections of evidence, it still wasn't clear to him.

"Deacon, I must depart for other business meetings, although you have confused me and I know not what direction to exit."

"I can help with that," he said, and he summoned Gem on his handheld to escort Dreveney. As Deacon and Dreveny waited, Deacon hugged him good-bye, sensing the aromatic, silky white fur.

"I admire you, Deacon Coombs. Don't you ever wonder, or fear, what might be waiting for you?"

"Each evening in my small room, I ponder what horrible fate awaits me when I finally uncover the evil; what beings lurk in space, ready to feast on my cowardice. In this case, courage is a thin veneer masked by the presence of the Owlers. I will have to depend on the Owlers' skills to save me. How easy it is to confront criminals in the virtual reality I control from Moonbeam."

"Are you satisfied with the Owlers' performance?"

"I am very impressed. Gem and Jim assimilate data at full tilt, producing compact, comprehensive, timely reports for me to absorb each evening. So far they have examined the political careers of each member of the High Council, documented the exhaustive problems of the Union of Space Traders, summarized the facts surrounding the deaths of Como and Geor, provided the expert medical evaluations of the crew of the *Sleigher*, and helped me understand the physics and engineering of Vespering in layman's terms.

"However, most difficult of all was reading the excerpts from the trial of Travers. After two days I concluded that the prosecution had presented no direct evidence to link Travers to the crimes that he was charged with. Not a shred of direct evidence. How peculiar. How could they have made him take responsibility for the heinous acts he was accused of? Travers personally had broken no laws. There was only one logical verdict: not guilty. Why had he been brought to trial with such flimsy evidence? And where was this new evidence that Como had viewed that convinced him to blaspheme Travers before an Aralian public?"

"Sadly, I was not involved in the case and so cannot comment on your observations," said Dreveney. "Ah, here is Gem, my escort out of this puzzle." They hugged again, and Dreveney departed. Deacon spied them weaving amid the aisles below, Dreveney skiing on his bare-boned feet, his weight shifting to and fro until they traversed out of sight. It was the first time that he had used the universal translator, and he had found it to be totally efficient in translating Dreveney's remarks.

<hr />

Deacon sensed that the time to depart for Brebouillis drew nearer, and as each day passed, he grew stronger in his resolve to unearth the truth but more apprehensive about what lay ahead. After five intense days in the library, it was apparent to him that he should follow Landrew's advice to journey to the asylum on Brebouillis and directly interface with the doctors and observe the crew of the *Sleigher*.

He had come to relish the company of Jim and Gem. Though overprinted with human engrams, they were too logical, too factual, and too cold to be anything but Owlers. He often admired the technology of their fluid movements, unlike the jerky twitches he had observed in past models, and he never tired of Jim's reference to being "the last off of the assembly line." Deacon drove them to the limit to perform, and they never let him down. At his prompt, stimulating conversation was initiated each evening. On his orders, they spent nocturnal periods scouring files for his perusal the next morning.

He spent two evenings playing the game Vigogg with Gem but tired after three defeats. The Owler's moves were too swift for him to analyze and unnerved him. While Gem was constantly expressionless and businesslike in responses, Jim's regular onslaughts of humor and arrogance amused him. Deacon admired the sense of teamwork and respected their opinions. One evening, while in his dorm, he decided to broach the matter of the Vesper incident.

"Speculate on the Vesper problem at Jabu, Jim."

Jim stepped closer and gestured while talking. "There is the chance of possible interference by an alien technology using methods beyond our detection and comprehension. It is possible that there are physics unknown to our greatest scientists. Secondly, possible human error and subsequent cover-up to protect the guilty party at the Jabu Vesper station. It is only human nature to harbor mistakes, although I must add that the Jabu have never been known to do this and are characterized as a trustworthy race. Thirdly, possible impedance of the Vesper wave by either a collision or interference with a space phenomenon not recognizable or detected by our current technology."

"Space phenomenon? Elaborate."

"Proximity to a pulsating high gravitational pull, interface with a magnetic field, collision with a celestial object, intense unusual ionic or cosmic storm, or perhaps intersection with a rare, naturally occurring positron beam. All space storms are not accurately mapped, and Vesper particles are not immune to these events. However, one must be able to explain the subsequent return by the *Sleigher* to the Aralian Vesper station. Therefore, premeditated interference by an unknown technology seems a logical first explanation."

Each answer had almost human comforting tones, though Jim's pitch was deep. Deacon had instructed Gem to prepare the personal habits and close acquaintances of Travers. "Gem, where should we look to find Travers?"

Gem's response was spontaneous with absolutely no hesitation. "Aralia."

"Why?"

"Aralians cannot sustain long periods of time from Aralia except in Aralian trade ships that are adapted for their particular frigid environment and gravity. With the current ongoing scrutiny of all trade ships by Alliance forces to locate Travers, he would logically not be on an Aralian trade ship. He escaped from the hospital at Froora on Aralia. It would be then easiest to take refuge on Aralia, where he still has a very large and loyal following. Interplanetary security is intense and effective; Travers's closest allies are on Aralia, where security forces may be aiding in his concealment. Travers is still on Aralia, Master."

Jim piped up. "Master, I totally agree with my partner Gem. There are remote locales where he could hide effortlessly. Gem and I reviewed all the states and geography of Aralia last night and came up with a list of regions we should visit. Here is the list for your perusal, Master."

Deacon felt uncomfortable at Jim's reference of "regions we should visit" as he thought of just how vast Aralia was. He decided to force an important issue. "How about we place an advertisement through well-placed individuals on Aralia that states we are attempting to communicate with Travers, and see if he finds us?"

"Out of the question," said Jim. "We are assigned to protect you, sire. The plan you propose prescribes a possible threat to your safety. Since Travers is dangerous, Gem and I cannot support that plan."

Deacon felt a jar at Jim's reference to Travers being dangerous. *What has Jim read? How is Jim programmed?* he thought. He proposed a rebuttal. "I have carefully examined the transcripts of the trial, and they proved to me that there was only circumstantial evidence to link Travers to the criminal charges. How do you know that Travers is dangerous?"

Deacon shivered upon hearing Gem's cold, smooth, calculated response: "Travers is the enemy. We seek him out."

Deacon stared at them. He rose slowly with iciness in his bones, walked away, and then turned to step slowly forward to confront them. He had to verify any preplanned prime directives. The small confines of his room now seemed so uncomfortable. "And what are your instructions once we find him?"

Gem was quick. "To apprehend Travers. To bring him back for questioning. To kill him if he should pose a threat to you or the safety of the Alliance."

Deacon cringed at the expressionless stares of Gem and Jim. Behind those steely faces were the wires and metal and discs that housed the instructions of the mission. He had to trust them, but there was a gnawing in his stomach, a feeling that he and Travers were pawns in a game of much larger stakes. Even so, the only safe pieces on the chessboard to protect him were these Owlers. He continued. "Kill. That's a very strong, decisive order Gem. I don't remember instructing you to kill Travers."

"It will be necessary if he harms you."

Deacon wanted to change the subject. There existed an eerie silence, for Deacon wanted to capture Travers alive for interrogation.

"Aralia is a very massive planet. Some of the remote provinces are one-fifth of Earth's size. How do we commence this search for Travers, Jim? Have you and Gem identified logical starting points?"

"Some Aralian regions are faithful to Travers. Within these regions, his friends will hide him and protect him. Gem and I have composed a prioritized list of areas that include cities, Trader refuges, remote geographical sanctuaries, and certain close Aralian friends of Travers. We also have embedded in us a list of Alliance patriots to Landrew and Como who will help us locate Travers. Additionally, on Brebouillis we shall meet two doctors who will be invaluable in our mission."

Curious, Deacon thought. *Those are the exact words that Landrew spoke.* "We should plan to depart the day after tomorrow. However, I want to leave in secrecy. You two must ensure that we depart before anyone on the High Council knows. Jim, I leave you to make the necessary arrangements and file our confidential flight plans at the port, firstly to the asylum at Brebouillis, then on to planet Aralia.

"Gem and I suggest docking at Froora, which is central to our initial stops on the planet. Froora is also very congested, as it receives thousands of non-Aralian visitors each day; thus we will be just one party of many aliens, giving us a chance of entering in anonymity."

"Okay. Plan our stops with the least risk to our mission."

"Yes, Deacon," Jim said, and with humor he added, "and I will plan an economy Vesper so you will lose only a quarter-year of your life span."

Deacon smiled and said, "I want to reach the Vesper station with all my vital parts."

"Yes, Master, no liver or heart left in outer space as cosmic energy. I'll Vesper all your parts, sire. I have noted your specific request."

Deacon laughed at the comic relief but quickly switched to drama. "I want Travers taken alive at all costs."

Gem said, "Any harm to you means his death."

That was not the response he wanted. "The first directive is to protect me; the second to obey me. In conflict, I want you to obey me and take Travers alive. It is vital to our mission that we question him."

Gem stared back. "When the directives are in conflict, your safety comes first, Master."

"Are those your orders?"

"Yes."

"Reluctantly, I accept them. I must be protected."

The Owlers remained silent. "Are there any other commands for us?"

Deacon stood staring at them until he finally dismissed them, realizing that there could be other instructions that might irritate him. He longed for rest and not to debate this issue any further at this moment. He watched them depart. Jim, ever acting like a gentleman, allowed Gem to go first. He knew from the moment when Landrew introduced the Owlers that Jim had been his visitor to Moonbeam. The visitor had to be an Owler. It was not out of breath after scaling the cliffs. It did not fear a potentially fatal bite from Miram, and the pupils of the eyes were small when they should have been large in the darkness. When Jim spoke five days ago and Deacon witnessed those green eyes, he verified his guess. He didn't dare insult Jim by revealing that he had also noticed him on the flight to Liberty City.

Comes an intruder

Two nights later, Dreveney startled Deacon as he stood on the great balcony. The two embraced, Deacon catching a whiff of the Aralian's aroma, which was pleasant but different from the previous one. He continued to find physical contact with Aralians very agreeable; the feel of the fur was smooth, warm, and cuddly—a totally satisfying experience. The natural perfumes emanating from the fur wafted into his area again.

"Dreveney, do I detect a change in the odor emanating from your fur? It seems different from the smell of previous?"

"Aralians have many odor glands buried shallow under the skin. Depending on our mood, different glands are opened and different fragrances are emitted."

"Sounds like a useful addition to my next volume of *Protecting the Being*. On Earth we have some rare species that emanate foul odors to protect themselves. Can Aralians do that?"

"Sad to say, no. All the glands emit soothing bouquets, some more appealing than others. I came to say that I depart for Aralia tomorrow, Coombs. I wanted to come in person and wish you success and tell you how grateful the High Council is that you have accepted this challenge." His lips were a deep ruby. "Please visit me at my home on Aralia if your travels lead you there. I know that you have been instructed to operate independently, but I extend an invitation of my Aralian hospitality if you should come to our planet. I have given the coordinates of my estate to the Owlers."

"Thank you." Deacon already knew that he would not accept the invite. It seemed critical to operate independent of the High Council.

"I also came to sternly warn you. Travers has many friends throughout the Alliance, so choose your allies wisely. Many Aralians choose to admire him with enormous pride. Aralians are a passive people but are very passionate about Travers, who retains hero status. Travers has served as an admirable ambassador abroad and has been bestowed, as you probably discovered, with many national awards recognizing his accomplishments in new trade treaties, new trading routes, and new friends for Aralia. His father was also a very renowned trader. If you find yourself in danger at any point in your journey, please don't hesitate to summon me. I have given the Owlers my contact information."

"I will keep your gracious offer in mind, Dreveney, but at present I know not where the quest for evidence leads. The days here have been fruitful. Interesting facts have surfaced."

"Ah, very good. Such as?"

"Independence, dear Dreveney, as you have said. I find one of my most powerful tools is my silence."

"I am very disappointed that you cannot share developments with me, but yes, I understand very well what you say." The two discussed Aralian customs, and Dreveney presented Deacon with a guide to Aralia and a chronology on the key historical events in the planet's history, which were self-authored. Deacon in return presented Dreveney with a chip on his most memorable crimes, self-edited. Dreveney again cited the confidence that the Council had in Deacon, bestowed a prolonged Aralian hug on him, and then departed. Deacon thought about what he had just done. He had left Dreveney with the idea that he had made some interesting discoveries. He had planted seeds. He was counting on Dreveney to spread that news to other High Council members. Deacon was engaged by the Council; it was time now to use the Council to his advantage.

Deacon's last day at the library arrived. Jim loaded the metro car and transported their belongings, complete with all their research findings, to the *Heritage* while finalizing flight plans for their departure. Gem remained behind to copy and transfer selected data for Deacon's analysis during the journey, and then store them in the Owler's housing. Deacon ambled around the library amid the towering blocks of information. He stopped at a section on the horrible nuclear wars on Earth, extracted a rare disc volume, transferred the contents to his handheld device, and then retreated to an elevated cave underneath the great balcony that had comfortable seating. He read of the cold wars leading to the crisis, in particular reading excerpts from the frustration of world leaders to resolve religious and political conflicts while wily dictators spoke in doubletalk. As he became engrossed in the escalation of arms, footsteps broke his concentration.

He dismounted from his chair to look over a podium that gave him a view down dimly lit tunnels of data banks. In the dim red light of an aisle, he spied a tall, muscular figure sauntering through the maze, being careful at each intersection to inspect the next aisle. He could tell by the gait that it was not one of the Owlers; nor was it Landrew, nor Dreveney. Not instantaneously recognizing this silhouette, Deacon became fearful. He broke into a sweat as he saw the stranger step into a green-lit corner. He was an Earthling, about six and a half feet tall, with a swarthy complexion, now curiously assuming a crouch on his haunches, listening intently. *Is he listening and spying on me?* Deacon wondered. Deacon slowly bent down behind the rails, fumbling for his handheld device to alert Gem.

Damnation, he thought as he realized he had plunked the signalet on a bench in a distant aisle where he had retrieved the history.

Whoever this person was, he was here without Deacon's knowledge and was now skulking around each data bank. Methodically inspecting each aisle, he was now approaching the sector under the balcony, moving furtively toward Deacon, ever so much closer.

The intruder paused, and the light exposed his facial profile. Deacon had seen this swarthy face before, but in his anxious state, his memory was failing him. Was he friend or foe? He couldn't take a chance. He spied the aisle where he had left the safety control. It would require a leap over the rails, then a dash of fifty yards, and then a sharp left turn, followed by a further run to the bench. It would require him to grab the device while running at full speed, signal Gem, and then outrun the culprit until Gem arrived. But where was Gem? Which direction to run when he had the signalet? *How stupid of me to abandon my safety alarm.*

Suddenly Deacon was terrified. Gem was the security system. Gem was controlling any visitors. How had this stranger entered? With or without Gem's approval? The intruder clumsily knocked into a cart just as Deacon dared to steal a peek and examine him closer, searching his memory unsuccessfully as to his identity. Yet he felt he should know this being. From out of the silence, a door slammed. Suddenly, another being appeared in the shadows on the balcony at the very far end of fourth floor, at least five hundred feet away.

An Owler at last? Deacon wondered. His eyes penetrated the murkiness for a sign of Jim or Gem. The shadows were too deep. The figure above stepped to the front of the balcony and leaned over, surveying the maze below. It was not Gem, not Jim. If either one of these individuals was in honest search of him, why didn't they summon him? Hail him? Determine his whereabouts? The visitor above moved out of sight, but Deacon recognized the whine of the lift, which would deliver him to the same level he was on. But with this new development, the first invader now focused his attention to the door of the lift and started to proceed toward it on tiptoe.

Deacon hid, terrified, and as the prowler passed by, he scrutinized him. He stopped only twenty yards in front of Deacon. There he extracted some wire from his pockets and curled it around his stubby fingers, preparing it; he jerked it to check its tautness. Deacon knew then that to sit and do nothing would result in the murder of one or both of them. *What a tragedy if this new arrival is Landrew!*

As the elevator arrived, the man in front of Deacon disappeared to stalk the recent arrival. As soon as he disappeared, Deacon summoned his courage and jumped from his hiding place. He leaped over the rails, dashed to the aisle where he had left the handheld, and turned left, not daring to look behind. There he grabbed the security device on the run, and he began pressing hard the alarm button to signal Gem as he sprinted down the aisle. As he did this, he decided to scream for help to identify his position for any ally, and also to alert the new arrival of danger. Twisting and turning while galloping at full speed, he made his way toward the portal of the lift. Gasping for air, he was almost there when he slammed into a ladder hidden in the shadows and fell hard to the floor. Behind him he heard footsteps. Around the corner lay the lift. He bolted to his feet, and found the inner strength to hurdle the last twenty yards. He stopped dead in his tracks at the end of the aisle; there was no sign of the recent visitor. When he turned to look behind him, the hulk appeared and proceeded to hurl himself at Deacon in full tilt.

The two hit the floor with a thud, the assassin on top, clearly overpowering Deacon. Gleaming wires sought to cut the flesh of his throat. As air rushed out of his body cavity, the choking commenced, and he felt the gelid grip of the metal. Two fiery eyes drained his confidence as the madman enjoyed the encounter, a grimacing, wild sneer possessing his face. Deacon was engaged in survival; he could not find the breath to expel a plea for help. Suddenly all life was frozen.

With his head now twisted back, he saw a dark figure appear out of the corner of his eye. It stood still in the shadows, slowly raised its arms, took aim, and then fired. A flare hit the thug in the side of his body, driving the assailant ten yards back down the aisle.

Gem moved into the light, while Rande appeared behind the Owler. Deacon felt a tingling sensation in his throat and then turned to prop himself up on his elbows to view the dead assassin. Spying the bloody mess and seeing his own blood-soaked hands, he collapsed.

When Deacon returned to consciousness minutes later, five faces stared down at him. Landrew spoke first. "Deacon, are you cognizant? My dear Deacon, are you okay?"

Before he replied, he looked at each in turn. There was Dreveney, who only the night before had been told that new clues had been uncovered. There was Landrew, whom he felt had misled him about the charges against Travers and who the possible murder suspects might be. Beside Landrew was Rande, who had not announced his entry. There was an unknown medic. And then there was Gem, who had saved his life.

The physician asked, "Can you breathe without difficulty?"

"Fine. I feel revived," Deacon said, although every nerve in his body tingled, every muscle ached, and his throat throbbed in excruciating pain. His shirt was soaked in bloody patches. "Who was the assailant?"

Gem answered. "Morris Mydloan, alias the Wireman, alias Mad Morris."

It was difficult for Deacon to speak. "Yes, I . . . I . . . I testified against him years ago in a felony charge, but that was many, many years ago. How did he gain entry into the library?"

Again Gem replied. "I found this top-level security access eye lens on his body. I checked, sire, and it was reported stolen by Alliance Security Forces weeks ago."

Deacon examined the security lens while laying prostrate as Landrew looked sheepishly down at him. Deacon eyed Rande. "Rande, what were you doing in the library?"

"I came to invite you to dinner, provide a relaxing interlude from your rigorous week. Gem cleared me before I entered. I took the lift to the lower level, and I was on my way to find you when I heard your screams for help. I followed the sounds, eventually running into Gem. I was standing behind Gem when the Owler fired."

Deacon was angry. He stood up with Gem's help. "My testimony years ago provided no incentive for this man to seek me out to murder me. So what does that tell us?" Deacon espied the body. "Indeed, he was after me because of this investigation and not any prior incident." He looked at Landrew. "I don't like the security arrangements."

"I am so sorry," said Landrew. "Are you planning to depart tonight?"

"Why do you ask?"

"I saw Jim loading the metro car as I arrived."

"I . . . I don't know. I do know that I wish to be left alone. I respectfully ask each of you to leave us."

Landrew was concerned and apologetic. "Again, Deacon, sincerely, I am so sorry that security has been breached. I came with Dreveney to just socially provide encouragement and our support for your mission and determine what you have learned to date. We arrived after Rande and the incident and were cleared by Gem previously to enter."

Rande was shaken. "I apologize to you, Deacon. This theft of the lens worries me. I will launch an immediate investigation. We will find out how it came to be in Mydloan's possession, and I will send a report to Gem of our findings."

The medic intervened to provide instructions on caring for his neck wound. Dreveney hugged Deacon once again. Rande abandoned his dinner invitation. Landrew instructed his personal security Owler to alert forces to remove the body and clean up the mess in the library.

"Gem, is he dead?"

"Quite so. As required when your life is threatened, I set my Vishup50 to Kill."

"Gem, do you believe that I was the victim?"

"Yes. Mydloan did not hesitate. If I had delayed, he would have killed you."

"Is it true that Rande had clearance from you? Did he lead you to me?"

"I encountered Rande at the entrance. I gave him clearance and indicated where he might locate you. As your emergency signal alerted me, I ran to your rescue and intercepted Rande. We followed together when we heard you scream. As he stated, he was with me when I fired."

"Does the body have any identification tags? Any ID cards?"

"Absolutely nothing. I searched it thoroughly. We have a record of Mydloan's fingerprints and skin DNA in your data files, which I house. It was those files that provided a match and gave clues to his identity."

"I want to depart immediately. Is everything in order?"

"Yes. I will convey your desire to Jim. The coordinates are set for the Vesper station at Brebouillis. We have the gear packed, except for the last load that Landrew saw Jim loading." Landrew interrupted their dialogue to extend his hand. With a firm grip, he solemnly said, "Good luck. I feel as insecure over this incident as you do. The Owlers will protect you."

Deacon ignored the arriving officials and Owlers and responded to Landrew as Jim arrived. "Landrew, if Gem and Jim and I are to proceed with this journey further, I want our travel plans to remain secretive. Therefore, I order you right now to answer my query. Do Jim and Gem have any implanted devices in their hardware that allow Alliance Security to track our whereabouts at all times?"

Neither Jim nor Gem hesitated as they answered truthfully before Landrew spoke. "Yes," the Owlers stated in unison.

Deacon stared at Landrew. "Then I order you, Landrew, to instruct the Owlers to dismantle the transmitters. Remove them at once."

Landrew shook his head. "Not wise. What if Alliance forces are required to rescue you?"

"Landrew, in light of what happened here tonight, I came within seconds of having your Alliance forces scrape up my remains. Don't lie to me or deceive me or counter me on this." Deacon's voice conveyed his urgency and request. Landrew tightened his lips and squinted back.

"Landrew, you are the one who said that Gem and Jim report to me, yet it looks like the Owlers are awaiting your command to dismantle the tracking implements."

Landrew looked at each Owler and nodded; he then instructed them to remove the devices. Gem first moved behind Jim and opened a hatch in Jim's back and spent one minute, pulling out a small disc. When finished, Jim then likewise did the same for Gem. Landrew was the recipient of both of the mechanisms.

"Thank you," said Deacon.

"Good-bye, my friend. I want to see you again." Landrew clenched his fist around the devices and departed.

Deacon abruptly returned to his room and bent back the swath of skin on his neck, examining the cut that might scar him for life. Through the translucent vanilla cream, the dried spotted blood showed a perfect horizontal break in the flesh from the wire.

"It was too coincidental; you were the target," he heard from behind him. "We won't let this happen again, Master." He whisked around to find the Owlers. Jim, beside Gem, nodded to concur with Gem's comments. He now knew that they were his true friends.

"Let's depart immediately. I'll meet you at the metro car soon."

As Gem and Jim made the last preparations, he took a last nervous walk through the corridors. Guilt surfaced in him as he realized all that he had taken, having left nothing in return. He walked out the main copper doors through which he had entered one week ago, descending the steps after eyeing the activity around Mydloan's dead body. Then he entered the metro car, glancing one last time at the museum and praying for his safe return. The vehicle sped into the black tubes under Liberty City.

After an hour of uncomfortable travel, the *Heritage* came into sight. She was a compact ship, stunning and elegant, 260 feet long. She was bathed in the bright colors of the Union of Space Traders, which Deacon read about: scarlet for aggressiveness, emerald green for courage, and white for purity and honesty. The letters of her name were written in bold gold. Two thin wings housed the rocket engines of the triple-decker. Deacon was impressed with the site of her dangling from the pier.

There was an attractive sleekness about this vessel with shiny curves oozing out of her shape. Deacon ascended up the lift, hustled aboard, and found the cozy living quarters to his taste. In addition to a wall screen that projected the 360-degree view of space into the ship, he had sleeping quarters, a computer room, a small dining area, and countless music selections at his disposal. The controls of the ship were on the middle deck; the lower deck contained fuel tanks, the machinery to operate her, and storage areas. But most of all, the *Heritage* was built for raw speed, and there was not a meter of wasted space inside.

As the Owlers issued the order for liftoff, sadness welled within him. He was leaving Mother Earth, maybe never to return again. His emotions conjured up fear and apprehension. This was not his strength—traveling around the galaxy, a vulnerable, fragile human specimen. He drank a portion of liquid to soothe his nerves as the engines purred.

The ship accelerated suddenly, the pull gluing him into his seat as they first lifted vertically out of port and then rocketed out of Earth's orbit on their way to the Vesper station. It would be an overnight trip. After staying awake as long as he could to witness the last vestige of his beloved Earth, he tumbled into slumber, later awakening to find Gem standing beside him.

"We await your orders, sire. We are in line to Vesper to Brebouillis."

Gem handed him the potion. How he hated the taste. He had endured it once before, when journeying to Globiana. Just before the dematerialization, he experienced a strange drunken feeling followed by a severe bout of nausea. There was no turning back. If there was a force out there waiting to capture him, to transport him to Nix, to bend this Vesper wave, and to render him insane, to even assassinate him, now was the chance for it to do so, and he was helpless to defend himself.

The *Heritage* Vespers

As dematerialization peaked, Deacon's stomach churned, his cheeks were flush and rosy, and visions of pink clouds charged into his retinas. His body floated and then fell into a chasm as his stomach sailed into his mouth. His feet were swollen to three times their normal size, and the gray laces on his black shoes cut bloodily into the tops of his feet. Sharp pangs of pain drove into his fingers as his nails curled and perforated his flesh.

"Sit still. Relax," said Gem. "Keep your eyes closed. Count backward from one hundred to one. Then stand ever so gingerly. Vespering is complete."

"Where are we?"

"Near Brebouillis." It had seemed as if only seconds ago he had been at Earth's Vesper station. The drowsiness. The nausea. The disorientation. The aching. He tried to stand unsuccessfully and slumped back. Gem looked at him with the usual expressionless stare. Jim entered. "Do you have all your parts, Master?"

Deacon pinched his body in various places. "Yes. Yes, I do. What about you, Jim? Do you?"

"Definitely, sire." Jim flashed a brief smile.

"I am human, Jim. There are times when it pays to be an Owler."

"The disorientation will pass quickly if you do not overexert yourself. We shall return to the steering level to assist with docking on the moon Brebouillis."

"No. Not yet." He turned to face Gem. "Please, Gem, help me to my private room, for I think I shall be sick." And after Gem left him in his silence, and for one hour after, he was.

IN THE DEN OF INSANITY

Schlegar

In cramped quarters, three men sat. "Brebouillis is the fourth moon of the frigid planet of Aralia. Like the other cold, rocky, scarred satellites, Brebouillis was at one time a mining colony. However, Mr. Coombs, the ore became depleted and the moon's fate plunged into abandonment. The government later saw that these facilities on this moon could be modified to house an insane asylum for criminals. But Brebouillis is unlike other institutions of its kind because the criminals and madmen here are terminally insane and extremely dangerous individuals. They come from all races throughout the Alliance, where life sentences were rendered as opposed to death. Thus the security system here is entirely handled by machines, some primitive robots, and some Owlers, and even by some computer functions. In addition, this institution often plays host to renowned doctors on sabbatical who find their studies of the insane of vast medical value."

"Yes, while on Earth, I took note of some of the famous physicians who have served here."

"This is the first stop of your capsule, I understand. What a pleasure to host you. I have read some of your cases. I love how you solved the disappearance of Avery Lorrel."

"When all else fails, Dr. Schlegar, one must look to the obvious and operate within the limits of the data. Mr. Lorrel failed to take that into consideration when he planned his own disappearance to escape his punishment for embezzlement and therefore exposed himself to me. However, let us return to observing the crew of the *Sleigher*. I am grateful for the time afforded me by you."

Dr. Schlegar turned away from Deacon. Deacon noted the signs of Aralian aging in him—the loss of hair, the turning of his bones to a light brown color, the slow speech impediment. "Temisori, can you hear me?" The demented, wrinkled face of Temisori stared blankly to a spot behind the two men. Deacon intersected the path of his gaze, leaning over into his hollow fix. Two unflinching beet-red eyes gave no recognition to those who invaded his solitary confinement in the small cell. The muscles of his torso gave a frequent flinch. The body was completely harnessed in the chair.

Deacon asked, "Temisori, if you can hear me, nod your head."

Dr. Schlegar turned to Deacon. "He will not respond."

"But he has not lost his sense of hearing, Dr. Schlegar, for I examined his charts upon entry."

"True, Mister Coombs. He hears us but he will not respond." Schlegar was confident. "His brain does not provide the data that will allow him to formulate a response."

"You're telling me that he has suffered permanent brain damage?"

"Yes and no. On the contrary, the brain itself is in perfect physical condition, except for a small amount of scar tissue at the base of the organ. What I am trying to tell you is that the brain is empty. There is the possibility that there is no information to reply with."

Deacon felt sympathetic toward what had been an Aralian being and was now an empty shell. The skin was withered on his neck too; deep longitudinal furrows scarred along the arms. Most of the beautiful Aralian hair had been shed from his chest area. "Has he ever displayed any feelings?"

"He has wept on occasion, and chanted, but largely he sits in his straitjacket, staring into space. When we release him, he paces the cage."

"What do you suppose created this condition?"

"I don't know. The government wants us to maintain our watch of this crew from the *Sleigher* as top priority. The rest of the crew is just like him, sedate and brooding and unresponsive. Let me, however, offer you three scenarios that may be proved or disproved over time. Come, let us walk back to my office." Deacon noticed guards at regular posts and cameras strategically positioned along the corridors. He slowed his gait to allow Schlegar to keep pace.

"My specialty, Mister Coombs, is illnesses of the mind, no matter what the race. I have spent enough time here to achieve tenure as the senior director." Deacon had already taken an instant liking to this burly, fat Aralian man with a slow, gimpy walk. Schlegar's sense of humor and satire was a gift of compassion in his profession.

The halls of the institution were wide, painted in cheerful colors to offset the morose environment. Owlers were omnipresent, performing chores, escorting patients to therapy, delivering medicines, spying, and escorting residents to and from cells. Schlegar acknowledged each Owler, saluted each doctor. His entire rear mass shifted horizontally from his left across his body to his right side with every creeping step. "One of my current research projects centers on reversing insanity."

"Wow!" Deacon stopped in his tracks. "And I thought I had a tough task."

"Some of the patients have been selected as guinea pigs for my new research, Temisori being one of them." They reached Schlegar's lab. "It could be that all knowledge in Temisori's brain has been removed by an instrument or a power unknown to us. We have devices that can alter brain power, but not this show of extermination." Deacon immediately thought of alien invasion again.

"Secondly, his mind may be possessed with one single thought. Perhaps something terrifying that occurred on Nix. It preoccupies him day and night, and prohibits response functions from reacting; thus the brain appears empty." Deacon gazed up to the monitor into Temisori's room. What horrible thing had happened on Nix?

"Or this may be a psychosis, a disease of the mind, contracted by the crew on Nix. It could be cellular damage without cellular disarrangement. Every planet has different bacteria, fungi, viruses. They may have contracted a host unknown to us that is either feeding on the brain or impeding it."

Deacon broke in. "Any chance that this crew are all good actors, awaiting the triumphant return of Travers?"

"Huh! So you do consider all possibilities, don't you? If this is good acting, then it is the greatest in the Alliance, and these men are wasting their time—they should take up politics!" The two men shared a moment of laughter in Schlegar's crescendo.

On a somber note, Schlegar addressed Deacon's idea. "Mr. Coombs, all of our tests tell us that these men are insane and possess brains that are not functioning."

"You are the expert, so I shall accept your verdict. Do the others suffer from the same symptoms as Temisori?"

"Identical." He proceeded to open a monitor on the desk to illustrate his point using ray diagrams. "See here." Withdrawing glasses from his lab coat pocket and perching them on the end of his pointy, ruddy snout, he indicated a dark patch in the brain scan. "This small amount of cellular damage should not affect the brain's function."

"So is the brain empty or overridden by one dominating thought?"

Schlegar peered over his wire-rimmed glasses. "The conclusions, my dear fellow, are frightening. The brain emits energy, and in front of you are the brain scans of all of the Aralian crew members. However, some of the characteristic energy peaks are entirely absent. As I stated before, the brain itself is in perfect condition, except for these small scars, but the brain is unable to function, thus leaving the subjects as vegetables because there is an absence of information. There is the absence of synapses."

"How much of the profile is absent?"

"Oh, it varies, I would say . . . uh . . . 40 to 100 percent."

Deacon was taken aback. Schlegar was somber. "When the first Aralian dies, we shall remove the brain specimen, dissect it, and pray to discover clues to this perplexing quandary. If the crisis upon us worsens with more deaths of members of the High Council, or future bouts of madness, like bending more Vesper beams, then as grisly as it seems, we may have to end the life of some of these poor souls earlier. I most favor the theory that the brain has some parts that have undergone a brain drain and the rest of the information is suppressed by one engrossing thought."

"What about the missing bands of energy?"

"Well, I believe that certain sections of the brain have been shut down or just don't have the information anymore. It probably is the result of something encountered on their terrifying journey. This seems like an appropriate time to introduce another topic." He rose from his seat by the lab desk to retrieve a model of the Aralian brain.

Deacon furrowed his brow. "Did the autopsy of Como uncover any damage to his brain?"

"Autopsy? Mr. Coombs, in our culture, Aralians do not perform autopsies on any beings that have made significant contributions to society. The family of Como was quite insistent on this. The remains are reduced to ash and then scattered throughout the planet's atmosphere to seed and germinate new life." He directed Deacon's attention to the model as Deacon let that thought sink in.

Deacon took a seat on a stool in the lab while Schlegar planted a model in front of them. "The Aralian brain is much smaller than the average Earthman's brain, see, but admittedly more advanced. On your Earth in the 1920s, an Earthman first measured the electrical potential of the brain. The recordings are called an encephalogram. Earth now uses an Aralian technique to quantify this information. Measuring an electrical profile of the brain is a common practice throughout the Alliance. So commonplace has it become that it can be used as proof of security clearance. The emitted waves are in the form of alpha, beta, delta, theta, and epsilon waves. The terminology varies from planet to planet and species to species, but whether it comes from an Earthling, a Zentaurian, a Phlebite, or an Aralian, the energy is measured in millivolts. Don't lose sight of the fact that we are talking about minute amounts of energy."

Schlegar directed Deacon's attention to the scans in front of him. "Aralians are similar to Earthmen in that we each have five peak energy areas. In this graph"—he pointed with his finger—"Temisori is missing distinct energy levels that should be present in even the lowest forms of life on Aralia. However, you already know much about this, Mr. Coombs."

Sheepishly, Deacon said, "Well, what do you refer to?"

"You can receive brain waves of certain energy packages!"

"And how do you know this?"

"Mister Coombs, do not be angry. There are few who have your gift. The brain is my business. I have access to all the brain scan profiles of the entire population of the Alliance at my disposal. I was quick years ago to notice yours. But I won't mislead you, for Landrew reminded me recently of your capability."

Deacon was irritated. "I am not proud of this trait."

"Please, you have been invited here so that we may aid you on your mission. It is not only important that you view the victims of the *Sleigher* but also that you understand your mental powers." Schlegar decided to rise and slide his stool farther down the lab table to beside Deacon. He placed his arm around Deacon's shoulders. Deacon knew that this was an Aralian custom to signify friendship and ask for trust.

"Schlegar, I did not come all the way to Brebouillis to hear a lecture on brain waves."

Schlegar's mint-laden breath permeated Deacon's space as he leaned into him. "Be patient, my friend, while I address you. You need patience." Deacon felt as though he was a pawn again, in some greater scenario.

Mindor

Schlegar began by informing Deacon about the details of his own medical background. As he did so, Deacon examined the doctor. He had soft white fur, sprinkled with dots of silver on his head and torso. With a small nose, perpetually uncombed disheveled hair, white gowns, and messy lab coat, he played the role of sage physician to perfection. Deacon stole a glimpse at the bare elastic muscles that held his pancake feet in position beneath his furry knees.

Schlegar continued. "When Aralians first encountered life forms alien to them, they discovered that these aliens were not all that much different from themselves. Oh sure, they appeared to be different because of the environment they had to adapt to, but we all require basic organs to survive. Consider, for example, the respiratory system. On Jabu, it is encased in thick membranes to protect itself from the infiltration of miniscule particles of dust. The planet Jabu has concentrations of dust particles that would prohibit you and me from existing there."

Schlegar became animated. "On Zentaur, the body cavity is open to the atmosphere so vital gases can pass into the body by osmosis. Likewise, every specimen has a central organ for intelligence. This organ, which you call brain, comes in various shapes and sizes.

The Bernardians call it *Ioj*; the Mendalgons refer to it as *Jonhonso*. No matter what the race, we have determined that this brain has negatively and positively charged areas. This sets up electrical differentials, measured, as I stated earlier, in millivolts."

Deacon relaxed. Schlegar was enjoying the role of professor. "This energy also produces an associated magnetic field." He produced a pen and pointed to a model in front of them displayed on a screen.

"Here at the base of the brain is the sector that allows one to capture and receive, and then translate, electrical impulses. Think of it as a transmitter and receiver. All brains receive energy. It is the purposeful transmission that has not entirely evolved. In the Alliance, the Medullans are most advanced in the evolution of passing mental thoughts between them and capturing them—but only between themselves because of their frequencies."

"What do the Medullans receive? Electrical or magnetic energy?"

"They receive both. But only highly evolved species can take these receptions and translate the incoming energy to messages. The highest forms of evolution on Medulla communicate by pure electrical thought."

"Are the energy signals transmitted by Medullans stronger? Or are their brains more evolved to decipher the signals?"

"Questions, questions. But very good ones. The brain energy emissions of the Medullans are the highest frequencies known in our worlds—and the strongest. This obviously coincides with the evolution of the species, which is the most advanced. Evolution over time performs the function of eradicating useless organs and evolving more important ones to become more durable. The Medullans retain ultimately only what they need by discarding useless organs and flesh through evolution."

"And you think that I am a higher-evolved Earthling because I have some of this ability?"

"An emphatic yes! An emphatic no! Some parts of your body are behind evolution, for you were born with tonsils and an appendix, bodily pieces long vanished in most Earthmen. On the other hand, evolution has given you and a few others on Earth the power to receive and decipher brain waves from other human beings. Only a very few like yourself can translate these incoming packages." Schlegar beamed. "Deacon Coombs, your gift is not unique, but rare on

Earth. On Medulla, you would be much less than the norm; on Earth you are gifted."

"It is an affliction!"

The doctor raised his voice. "I guarantee you not. You must learn to use your powers. Since medical research first realized the development of the receiver sector in the brain, everyone on Earth, everyone in the Tetrad Alliance, has been tested to record who has this ability. When the Alliance made this decision, it was because we had to know who might misuse this power for personal gain. People such as your father, since the trait is passed genetically, probably passed it to you."

Deacon had never suspected this. He raised a hunch. "Landrew?"

"Yes. He and you deal with it in different ways."

"Do Earth's education systems monitor this gift to prevent criminal usage?"

"Exactly."

"How can you personally be so sure that I have the power?"

"A short while ago, as we conversed, I turned on a machine. It emits thoughts as magnetic waves. It can also receive and translate. A thought was directed to you earlier by this machine—a thought that Landrew had this power."

Deacon smirked. "So you send thoughts to unsuspecting victims via black boxes?"

"If I choose to do so, yes."

"It is trouble enough to deal with humans, so now I have to fend off mind-twisting machines! Machines of this sort could be dangerous if they should fall into the wrong hands."

"My dear Deacon." Schlegar rose to open a small door to expose a small gray-and-black box with flashing dials. "There is only one Mindor." Pride radiated from Schlegar as he spoke. Deacon saw them as master and mentor as Schlegar proceeded to pat Mindor gently on top.

"Does Mindor parallel the power of Medullans?"

"Mindor can be adjusted for any level of mental powers. I just have to know something about the ability of the subject to receive and transmit before I commence."

"What percentage of Aralians have this ability?"

"Like Earthlings, very, very few."

Deacon formulated a bold idea. "I think, Schlegar, that Brebouillis might very well be the Alliance agency for monitoring serious criminal activity and persons who misuse their mental powers for evil. It becomes logical to have a central repository for all brain scans, as you stated—a central library for all who possess the abilities that you have just outlined. Mindor here can actually be present during interrogations to expose any sinister plots of potential violators and, of course, uncover crucial evidence. Brebouillis can serve to study individuals who direct their power toward evil."

"How did you deduce this?"

"It wasn't very difficult. Once Landrew insisted that it was imperative for me to journey here, I searched the travel logs to find if Travers had visited here. Instead, I discovered that many renowned doctors, including you, had served sabbatical here, as you confirmed. Since the occupants here are insane, and their contributions to society minimal, I deduced that brilliant minds here were focused on the security of the Alliance as a first priority and that therefore this is a criminology laboratory. It just made more sense to believe that."

"Carry on," Schlegar said in encouragement.

"The amount of effort being expended here does not support its inmates; it supports a greater cause—the ultimate safety of the Tetrad Alliance, the cataloging and monitoring of all those who have abnormal mental powers, and the discipline to make sure those mental powers are not misused. Mindor is one of the crowning jewels of success, as it can aid in interrogations, as you just admitted."

Before Schlegar could get another word in, Deacon continued. "I noticed upon arrival that Owlers patrol patients in the hallways. Therefore, why the unusually large resident professional staff? I also noticed the Owlers guarding data banks and file rooms. You almost convinced me that it was pure medical research being conducted here, but Mindor changed all that. This place has to be the center of all the records of brain scans with a strong flavor of criminal investigations, with a cover of a residence for the criminally insane. Brilliant cover."

"You have in your summation underestimated the medical research being conducted here. However, Mister Coombs, you are correct in assuming that this is the central repository of all brain scans and that Brebouillis is that place where we analyze who should be monitored. A kind of . . . well . . . yes . . . mental Alliance police station."

"Travers of Aralia must be one of these gifted, or you would not fear him so much. Has he used his power to influence others? Has he planted the seeds of his personal success into the union?"

"I have found Travers to be a great disappointment," said Schlegar. "Yes, Como and I feared that Travers misused his powers to gain control of the trade union."

"And Mindor? Did Mindor do its dirty job at the trial by probing Travers's mind?"

Schlegar became irritated and twitched his nose. "How did you know Mindor was at the trial?"

"Simple! I have a suspicious mind, remember. I read the transcripts of the trial. All the evidence was indirect. I would, shamefully, say that the trial was a fraud, with all the charges having been manufactured by the Alliance." Schlegar slouched in his chair, head down.

Deacon took this as a cue to advance. "My dear Doctor Schlegar, unless you speak of new evidence, then the previous trial against Travers was a deception. In Liberty City, the Owlers summarized the trial for me in depth. I examined the records of the trial closely. I noticed that you were on the planet but not in the courtroom. As soon as you exposed Mindor, it occurred to me that you could have been in proximity, using Mindor to probe Travers's mind and feed real-time information to the prosecution fresh from Travers's mind."

"For what purpose?"

"Let me summate. The Alliance had suspicions that Travers had gained too much power over the Union of Space Traders by illegal means and wanted him replaced. In addition, Travers was to be held directly responsible for these illegal activities of the union. Number three: the Alliance decided to erode Travers's power but needed to get direct evidence to implicate him, so they staged the trial, and by placing Mindor in proximity to Travers at the trial, they hoped to read his thoughts, obtain real-time evidence, and construct a successful real-time trial, as I referenced earlier.

"My observations also account for the disjointed efforts of the prosecution. I was very curious when I first watched and read of the proceedings. Menubou was very conservative in his prosecution when many others I know would have been aggressive considering the stakes. Quickly I saw why Menubou had been selected. His hearing aid! He kept fiddling with it. Touching it. Positioning it. His eyes and mannerisms betrayed him. It occurred to me that the hearing aid may be acting as a receiver for information being relayed to him. The more I watched Menubou, the more I was convinced that someone was transmitting him information through his hearing aid. I admit I was wrong. It wasn't someone; it was Mindor—feeding Menubou thoughts fresh out of Travers's mind, through the machine, and back into the courtroom! Was that how it happened?"

Schlegar sighed. "I confess," he said softly. "Desperate men were driven to these measures for the safety of our all our peoples."

"The people might say that you misused the judicial system."

For the first time, Schlegar became irate. "The trade union has become too powerful. Their problems are all of our problems. We—that is, the High Council and I—wanted to find information we could use in a retrial. It became apparent quickly that Travers was not an easy read. We continued with this hopeless charade for days."

"Tell me, why you could not read Travers's mind?"

"I don't know. It was just that Travers was full of guilt and fear and warned of impending doom. We couldn't get to the truth. His mind was preoccupied with garbled veiled threats. Geor asked Landrew if he could rewrite the script for the next trial. He died constructing it. Is this not evidence enough to suspect Travers?"

Deacon stared ahead without saying a word.

Finally Schlegar lifted his head to speak. "Geor and Como, my two dear, dear friends, are dead. An Aralian trade ship has taken a torturous journey into a forbidden zone where the crew was deprived of their sanity and their right to live. That too is reality. The only character who keeps surfacing is an Aralian who made that trip and has now disappeared. And why wasn't Travers affected? And why didn't he remain behind in the hospital to explain to authorities what happened on Nix—or wherever they journeyed to—if he is innocent?"

Schlegar paced. "Travers is the key. We were wrong to approach the trial the way that we did. I admit it. I express to you my deepest regrets. I owe no apology to the masses. But the mysteries that plague this Alliance are beyond the bounds of using reasonable means. Look at Temisori! He is proof!"

Deacon raised his voice. "You can't drag your damn Mindor around the galaxy to read peoples' minds, delving into their inner thoughts, invading their privacy. So you chose a pawn to do so. He can be protected by the most reliable Owlers in the Alliance. He has multiple passports issued by the highest of Alliance officials; he possesses a naturally suspicious interrogative mind; he travels in a small, high-tech, fast spaceship, undetected, spying for government officials, knowingly breaching the sanctity of the minds of everyone he interrogates; and he can flee quickly upon immediate danger once the truths are discovered."

Schlegar nodded in agreement. "Yes. You, Deacon Coombs, were the most obvious candidate for this assignment. Landrew and I chose you. But your journey here is an important step. I want to help you control your mental skills. You perceive that you are able to receive and interpret only certain wavelengths. Indeed, you may have even greater powers."

Deacon furiously interrupted, now standing in front of Schlegar. "I nearly go crazy being bombarded by extraneous thoughts of others, and you want me to advance this insanity! Why do you think I hide at Moonbeam? I always use the convenient excuse that I don't want criminals to know what I look like. But that is not the truth. I can't stand violating the sanctity of other people's thoughts."

Schlegar rose to his feet. "Deacon, I can help you. Give me this chance. Please." Schlegar and Deacon stood face-to-face, with Schlegar grabbing Deacon's arms, fixing his grasp on his elbows. Schlegar's ruddy eyes penetrated Deacon.

"How can you and Landrew be so sure that I am the one to find Travers and uncover the menace behind the deaths of Geor and Como?"

"As Landrew affirmed previously, there are others. You are but one of the resources committed to this cause."

"Travers's trail dissipates. How long do you expect me to remain here?"

"I have found an excellent teacher for you." Schlegar extended his hand to the detective. It was as if the second union of master and mentor had taken place as he proceeded to hug him. Schlegar, with bent frame, hobbled, tugging Deacon in tow behind while Deacon lamented aloud.

"My work is the mask that I hide behind. It is the drive that allows me to escape the reality of the constant barrage of thoughts. Maybe other Earthmen yearn to invade the minds of their comrades and strangers, but not me. Schlegar, my mind has not rested for years. Even in sleep, I sometimes feel the touch of my neighbors' conscience."

"Just follow me, please." They weaved a circuitous route into a darker arm of the structure, where the cheeriness of the walls disappeared.

"When I was a child, I felt as though I would go insane. As hard as I tried, I couldn't conquer this affliction. I've kept this secret to myself my entire life, not even sharing it with my parents—although I regretted that after their sudden, fiery, tragic deaths."

"I know, Deacon." Schlegar unlocked a sitting room. He motioned to Deacon to situate himself at a table for four in the middle of the small space.

"It was embarrassing growing up. I intercepted lust, greed, dishonesty, deception, lies, hidden anger. During my university years, my class visited an astronomy professor, Dr. Biggs, who resided in a somewhat remote area of Anglo. When I first set eyes on Moonbeam, I knew that I had come home. I knew that I had to save enough money to purchase it or clone its setting. Luckily, now Moonbeam is my personal sanctity, run-down as it is."

Schlegar turned to him. "I know, Deacon. I shall return momentarily. Trust me. Relax." The door closed to isolate Deacon with his painful memories. In five minutes, an Earth woman with a full head of wavy, thick brunette hair stood in front of him.

Lyanna

"Villya," the Earth woman said. Her high cheekbones accented a warm, broad, pleasing smile that prompted Deacon to say, "Hello. Whom do I have the pleasure of addressing?"

"I am Lyanna, Doctor Schlegar's assistant." He admired her dainty, appealing build, her pretty face, her lavender scent, and her sparkling hazel eyes as she bustled about the room, opening and closing drawers.

"And I am Deacon Coombs," he said, on his feet now.

She extended her hand to him. "It is my pleasure to make your acquaintance, Mr. Coombs. We have a common bond in both having been born on Earth."

He had been so enamored by her entry that a prickly feeling raced up his spine, causing him to wriggle when it reached his shoulders. He now realized that he had no inkling of the sound of her voice, for she had not spoken a word! He backed away from her. In awe, he closed his eyes.

"Amazing," Lyanna said with her arms folded. "You captured every syllable that I sent to you. Didn't you?" She giggled in a mousy high pitch; he failed to recognize the humor. Now that she had spoken aloud, Deacon knew that her voice was as amorous as her composure.

She moved closer. "I am very flattered that you believe that I have a warm, broad, pleasing smile." Deacon blushed. He could read her, and she could read his thoughts without a single word being spoken.

Schlegar interrupted them. "Ah, I see that you two have met. Lyanna will be your tutor during your short time here. There is no better expert teacher on the abilities of the mind. She has impeccable credentials in her past assignments. I hope you will become friends." With that statement, he took their hands and sealed them together, looking alternately at them. That both pleased and frightened him.

This side of the moon Brebouillis was in perpetual darkness, and the low gravitational forces could not retain any atmosphere. Deacon examined the weightless workers from his vantage point on the observation deck as they fluently finagled to repair a malfunction on the landing dock. Their motions reminded him of an ancient form of dance that he had witnessed once on Earth called ballet.

It had been an exhausting day between the arrival procedures and the discussions with Schlegar and Lyanna. His role as one of a number of secret weapons was reinforced by Lyanna. In intricate detail, she explained his gift in scientific, medical, and emotional constituents until he grew weary. That signaled an end to the day's teachings, so he retreated to the space deck to locate and admire celestial objects. He sought to forget his mission temporarily by studying the depths of space from this foreign perspective. Making use of the charts in front of him, he identified heavenly objects one by one. His head jounced to and fro as he searched the skies until fatigue strangled his senses and he collapsed onto the sill.

In his dreams, shadowy figures pursued the *Heritage*. As he summoned Jim, Gem, and then Lyanna, he discovered that they were not on the craft. Ships harkened for his surrender. In his hesitance, they fired, hurling him across the deck, his body jostled about as the ship was then rammed from behind. He awakened to find Gem towering over him, shaking him to his senses.

Temisori

"Master Deacon!" said Gem. Deacon wiped his eyes and inspected the serene surroundings. "Doctor Schlegar requires your presence immediately."

His watch was still set on Earth's time; he realized that he had been asleep for three hours. Groggy, still petrified by his nightmare, he stumbled down the hallway with faithful Gem leading the way. Gem's canter was so fluid, the body frame so proportional, that the Owler's walk and physique could have easily been mistaken for a human's from behind. In Schlegar's main lab, he found the doctor and Lyanna intently staring at a wall monitor that snooped into the den of Temisori. The scene was discomforting, as Temisori was screaming like a lunatic, his mouth open and his jaw extended as the word was expelled from his body cavity. A closer examination of the subject showed that Temisori was bobbing his head up and down rhythmically. His red eyes bulged from their sockets.

At the top of his lungs, he screamed, "Ur . . . zel! Ur . . . zel!" The beginning of the scream was a gurgle of "Urrr," reaching a crescendo with a succinct yell of "zelll!"

"What does it mean?" Deacon inquired of Schlegar.

"Don't know. It is certainly not of Aralian derivation."

"Not of Earth, that I ever learned," Lyanna retorted.

The three stood paralyzed as the Aralian ranted. Deacon strained to hear every syllable, lest the figure spurt out another word as a hint to the chant. Now Temisori whispered, falling into a corner of the room where he commenced to weep. Immediately, Schlegar ordered Owlers into the cell to bind him. But his strength was enormous, and from the viewer Deacon saw how he fought the guards with every ounce of newfound force. Eventually he was subdued. The Owlers administered a drug, and he collapsed into a lump.

"Temisori finally speaks to us to utter a single word over and over," said Lyanna, "a word foreign to the three of us." Quickly Schlegar changed the channels on the monitor to view the other crewmates of the *Sleigher*. All were silent. Deacon turned and immediately ordered Gem to search the data files for a reference to this word they had heard—*urzel*. The Owler admitted that it was not in any universally programmed vocabulary.

Schlegar turned on the mind analyzer. A single repeated pattern obtained from Temisori blitzed the screen. Lyanna and Schlegar expressed surprise. Deacon waited for their analysis in suspense.

"He is thinking the one word, the sole thought. No doubt about it."

"Perhaps a word he heard on Nix!" Deacon said.

Schlegar alerted the Owler at Temisori's station. "I want to be awakened again if Temisori starts to chant."

"Yes, sir," was Owler's curt monotone reply.

Deacon moved closer to the screen. He thought, *Could this be the single thought that occupies his brain?* He turned to find Lyanna staring at him. Quickly, he replied to her, "A dangerous habit around here! Thinking to myself."

"What are you mumbling?" she asked. He remained silent. Temisori's outburst had concluded, so the threesome each retired to other duties while Gem and Jim performed their analytical functions.

Upon waking

Deacon was submitted by Lyanna to a series of tests to determine the absolute strength of his mental powers. Passing from headset to obtuse contraptions, to discs glued to his forehead, Lyanna scribbled down copious notes as a printer spit out chart after chart and graph upon graph. Later, at his favorite locale, the observation deck, she confronted him with the day's analysis. "You seem to enjoy fixing your gaze on the heavens."

"My home in Anglo is perched on the precipice of the southern shores, overlooking the straits toward Euro, but it pales in comparison with the panorama stretched out in front of me. Aren't you captivated by it? Look." He pointed. "There is the Donut Galaxy, there the Crab Nebula. These are but specks from Earth. But here . . . well. How incredible! What glorious detail!"

She caressed her hair and then, leaning on one elbow, positioning herself beside him, peered and pointed. "I know that one over there, fourth to the right of that expansive nebula. That tiny, bright whitish-yellow star. Solus. Home."

Home, he thought to himself. *I wonder if I shall ever set foot there again.*

"Yes. You will," Lyanna said.

"Can't you stop intruding my thoughts? That was a private matter."

"I'm sorry, Deacon. I only meant to reassure you. It is just that your thoughts of insecurity reigned strong today and I wanted to provide you confidence."

Lyanna changed the topic quickly. Shuffling her papers, she said "I want to review the test results, which confirm you have an unusually high reception ability that requires little effort. Few Earthmen, if any, have ever approached these scores. Come and take a seat over here, away from distractions." He did so, and she sat directly next to him in his space. "It is time that someone explained to you what we measured today. I have studied the brain for the past ten years. To put a definition on it, I would respond by saying that it is the organ that receives stimuli from the other organs and senses and interprets them to formulate a bodily response. It is the organ of thought, intelligence, learning patterns, and responses; it is the most vital part of the nervous system."

Deacon guessed her age to be in the early thirties. That warm, soothing voice took on impish overtones when she flaunted her intelligence. She had a relaxing influence on him. "The three vital functions, then, are to receive impulses, interpret them, and then respond correctly—sometimes incorrectly, but respond in some manner. As the brain goes about its business, electrical impulses are generated. This in turn creates a magnetic field around the brain."

She displayed images to him on her computer of an aura surrounding his head. "Look, here you are with your energy emanations. This is your personal magnetic colored image."

Deacon scrutinized oblong bluish hues encased in orange and greens.

"The second way that we can measure and illustrate this energy field is by brain scans. Our machine captures the energy packages and then converts this energy back to ideas. The patterns that we witness on the scan profile or in the aura depend on the function being performed. Let me explain.

"Every brain emits brain waves." She manipulated herself closer beside him and then turned inward to him, touching her knee to his. "The amounts are so miniscule that it took even the Aralians thousands of years to devise the machines that we use now to measure this energy. The total field is a product of the functions that the brain is performing at any given time. These emissions are most intense when one is thinking to oneself—that is, when one is focused on a single thought. Look at your profiles." Deacon did not understand the squiggles. Lyanna had marked the charts by writing/speaking, receiving, thinking, reading, and shouting.

"Deacon, I must emphasize to you that the energy from the brain is dissipated in all directions when leaving the body and is a miniscule amount. Therefore, whether you are an Earthling, an Aralian, or a Medullan, you must be in proximity to receive this energy."

"But . . . my neighbors? Sometimes—"

"They must have been trespassing, or on a stroll on your property, or perhaps you dreamed these situations. They don't have to be in the same room, but in some proximity."

"Define proximity."

"Three hundred yards maybe. That would be extraordinary." She moved to the next topic. "On Earth, we have always had those strange instances we explain as telepathy or extrasensory perception or clairvoyance. It was only when we joined the Alliance that we truly understood the complexity of the brain and how to read and measure its energy. It was only then that we realized that in proximity a person can intercept the energy field of the brain of another person and can interpret this energy."

"As man's brain evolves, is the so-called receiver area evolving?"

"Exactly, but at an incredibly small pace. In our brain, this area is named the Uscher zone, after Hergund Uscher, who first recognized it in primitive form. You are an exception to even Uscher's laws on Earth."

"Lucky me!" he said with a hint of sarcasm.

"Our progress toward the development of a receiving area in the brain is the least of that of all the species."

"Is that because we have the ability and don't know how to use it? Or because the organ's physical potential has not evolved?"

"Good question. The Uscher zone has not evolved fully in Earthlings. Oh, some people capture an occasional thought and dismiss it as an intuition. These are early signs of development. Then there are specimens like Deacon Coombs, in whom the gene is well developed and retained. Both your mother and father passed this to you genetically. Pure breeding progresses this trait. You are no fluke. Your father in particular had very strong powers."

Deacon's interest was piqued. "An area in the brain has evolved to recognize energy patterns that it intercepts. Like learning, it stores this information. As genes get passed on, the amount of information builds. Through pure breeding, the information base aggregates."

Lyanna nodded. "Exactly. Only on Zentaur is this gene totally regressive."

"Xudur would be irritated for the rest of her life if she ever found that out."

Lyanna laughed and said, "I have met her once before. She is quite a woman! She doesn't need any more weapons in her arsenal, believe me."

"You haven't told me exactly how this works."

"That's the next step. The brain comes to recognize patterns. It is the changes in these patterns that are stored. Let's do a test. I will send you a well-known tune. Concentrate as I send it to you."

He sat back, eyes closed, and recognized it immediately as a love ballad. It told of two intellects in love. Was she teasing him? She giggled, touching him, and explained that she had no chance of keeping that ballad a secret from a strong mind like his.

"Now I shall change the tune in mid-song to another classic. See if you can recognize it."

Deacon comprehended the first tune; likewise the second.

"Excellent. Let me tell you what functions the brain just performed. You identified the changes so rapidly. Like weight, height, and intelligence, which evolve over time in man, the brain started with the primordial chordal wavelengths. Then it evolved to identify changes in the energy field."

"But I identified the changes as fluently as the initial tune." He answered his own puzzle. "So I must be as versatile in the changes library as I am in the basic knowledge function."

"Correct. The Uscher zone is made up of two areas. The first is where the basic response to external stimuli from other brains is stored. The other area is called the treasure bank; here the mind adjusts to the changes in wavelengths that it is subjected to."

"Lyanna, let me take a guess how it works."

Lyanna nudged him on the shoulder, beaming broadly. "Sure."

"I would say that it takes time for the mind to adjust to the fluctuations in energy and wavelength. By the time the brain reacts, previous patterns have disappeared, so no thoughts are captured. So I would guess that the major difference between me and other Earthmen who have mental abilities is that my mind reacts instantaneously?"

Nodding her head, she applauded him. Deacon asked of her, "Can you teach me to turn off my mind?"

"All in good time, Deacon, but that is highly unadvisable for this assignment."

"How did you ever nurture an interest in the brain?"

Lyanna folded her arms, crossed her legs, and leaned back. "My father died when I was very young. Unfortunately, he left little security for my mother and me. My mother became a professional socialite. She could be very persuasive and talked a good game. She ran a circle of friends obtaining invites to key social gatherings. She was not a con artist. She was, however, a master of self-preservation and became the benefactor of gifts, dinner invites, theater seats, and my education. I promised my mother that I would see my education through and support both of us. Unfortunately, when I made this solemn oath, I promised her that I would become a brain surgeon."

"What!"

"Yes." She shook her head wildly, and her brown hair tossed about while she laughed and touched him on the shoulder. "Instead, after my medical degree, I studied the Uscher zone to master the brain's energy."

"Why the switch away from surgery?"

Her laughter spewed forth. Before she answered, she pulled her full lips taut, raised her cheeks, and, squinting her eyes at him, said, "I made a startling discovery. I detested the sight of blood." Deacon conjured up the incident in the library on Earth when he had fainted due to the sight of blood. She caught that thought but kept it to herself based on the last incident of exposure.

"Now it's time for another demonstration." She started with one tune and then switched to a second, and then a third. She repeated the pattern over and over. Deacon was mystified, for he could not decipher the pattern. She broke the silence by saying, "I guess that you heard only the first chords."

"Right. The first part was easily detected."

"By one as advanced as you," said Schlegar, who interrupted them as an observer.

"I sent the last two tunes to you in an aroused state of mind. In order for you to detect them, you too must arouse yourself. You will not be able to capture these waves from a relaxed state. When I send in an aroused state, you too must be aroused."

"Do I have the ability to receive these signals if I am aroused?"

"Our tests," Schlegar said, "state emphatically that you do."

"So I can go up and down the dial tone, exciting myself to hear certain thoughts and calming myself to hear others. I could put this skill to use for gain."

"That is precisely why we monitor all those who have this power, Deacon." Schlegar then asked, "How do you feel about this affliction now?"

"I am more comfortable with it than yesterday, I admit. But until I experience an incident in a real setting, I am still a little uneasy about what I am being told."

"Come," Schlegar said to him, "rest is prescribed for you. We have other patients to attend to." Gem appeared on cue to escort him back to his quarters, but not before he gave thanks to Schlegar and Lyanna and complimented Lyanna on her efforts. The combination of brain fatigue and travel strangled him. With the two Owlers by his side, he dropped into slumber. His last remembrance before he passed out was the figure of his new female acquaintance. After that, blackness.

Discovery

The next day Deacon worked strenuously, accenting the teachings of the previous day, relaxing momentarily until Lyanna reminded him that these were not games that they played. It was the first time that she had flashed sternness in her tone. Exhaustion arrived sooner for Deacon than it had the day before, the effects of travel combined with her rigorous drills stretching his mind to the limits. Upon awakening, he couldn't recall the stroll from the observation deck to his bunk. He had lost all reference of time. Gem gained his attention quickly and poked him to arouse him. "Master, Jim has discovered a reference to the word *urzel*."

Jim affirmed Gem's comment as he stood beside Gem. "Yes. I found it among the slang used by the early Aralian space traders. Here is the book, retrieved from your own stored data banks." Jim passed to Deacon a small monitor. "Look here, Master." Deacon browsed page one first to read the title, *Aralian Navigational Handbook*. Jim had marked the key page. Deacon fast-forwarded, and on it was the reference to the word *urzelli*, short form *urzel*. It was the ancient code word for the number one.

Deacon was alert instantly. He stretched his arms, donned his shoes, and swiftly proceeded down the hallway, Jim in tow, to Schlegar's office. Before he could present his opinion, Schlegar looked up from his incredibly messy desk to say, "Yes, the Owler visited me hours ago while you slept. I have found that it is derived from the word *oneness*, or *ego*. As best as I can determine, Deacon, the origin is Globianan, not Aralian. I have discovered that some trading vessels still use the term to denote safe harbor, indicating that the ship and the space are at peace, or are at oneness. Peculiar though, that I have never heard this term before."

"I thought about this term immediately," said Deacon. "If it possesses Temisori's mind, as we seem to think it does, then it must have another connotation other than that used in navigation. His condition is anything but safe port, safe harbor."

"If you take the term literally, Deacon, as meaning 'oneness,' it could be that Temisori feels something that we cannot possibly share, perhaps an experience on Nix."

"No, I don't think that it is that simple, Schlegar. Too many connected incidents. Let's consider the idea of oneness or ego as power, the one. Then the chant becomes the result of the encounter." He paced in front of Schlegar's desk. "Perhaps our Aralians were released with their captors knowing full well that they, because of their state, cannot disrupt plans in place; or they were released assuming that anything that we learn cannot be used to disrupt the plans of our assailants. This would be a clear case of ego!"

"Your imagination frightens me, Deacon. I hate to think that someone, or something, released these men knowing that a plan to destroy our worlds cannot be altered."

"I am just thinking aloud, Schlegar. It's easier than trying to spear thoughts, read our minds by expending mental calories. Right?"

Schlegar grinned back. Deacon looked at the aging doctor, the silver mop over his eyes. As he stopped to postulate further, Lyanna entered for her day's teachings. Today she wore a crimson-red gown, a stark change from the drab colors of the day before. Her hem was pleasingly higher, her slender legs showing up to the knees. A graceful, petite figure seemed to fill the robe. Her long hair was neatly pinned back behind her head in a perfect oval bun. A peaceful feeling engulfed Deacon. He was manufacturing a fondness for both of these people.

Schlegar addressed her mockingly. "Mister Coombs thinks that the Aralian crew was purposely released from their ordeal because a power to be out there"—he flung his arms toward the heavens—"knows that we cannot learn anything from these poor souls to counter their plans for further chaos, for universal domination."

Lyanna did not see the humor that Schlegar spoke of. Solemnly, she gave eye-to-eye contact to Deacon. Meanwhile, Schlegar summoned Jim to step forward, by waving his hands.

Upon Schlegar's instructions, Jim opened his torso area to reveal a viewing screen. "Landrew wanted to address us at the proper time.

Proper time being when you have absorbed a better understanding of your skills and when the time for your departure has become imminent. Jim has that recording. Jim, if you please."

Jim strutted forward, bowed deeply, and then stood still as the voice of Landrew emanated, his image appearing on the screen. "Deacon Coombs, with the assistance of Lyanna and Schlegar, my old friend, you now understand more clearly your ability to read other people's minds and how to control this gift. I shall attempt to explain to you why this stop at Brebouillis was absolutely necessary, and is the most critical stop on your mission. Now that you recognize that you have powers beyond your imagination, and now that you have the tools to control them, I hope you realize and admit to the value of such skills on your mission.

"I cannot guarantee that you will use these mind controls in your case. However, I feel strongly that the deaths of Geor and Como were murder. Although they alone held the implements of their own destruction, we, the High Council and the governments of Aralia and Globiana, believe that they may have been mentally programmed, or mentally tormented or mentally influenced, to commit suicide. If this is the case, the unknown enemy is one to be feared."

Landrew raised his voice. "In addition, in case you don't already suspect this, you should know that Travers has these mental abilities and that his are as well developed as yours. That is why you need to understand your powers, Deacon, understand how to use them to the fullest extent! You may be forced to use these powers against Travers to save your life!

"You must use these powers to determine who your friends are and aren't by probing their minds. I trust you to use this advantage at your discretion. We all pray that you can turn your gift against evil to protect yourself. Learn your limitations; learn to survive. I want to see you again. You have the Owlers as your guards. Use them!" Deacon nodded in agreement.

"Plan your moves carefully. Most importantly, your mission is to discover the identity of the enemy, this evil, and then run home to Earth as fast as you can to inform us. I can't emphasize this enough. Once again, run home when you learn the identity of the misdoer. The disappearance of Travers remains unsettling to me, for the Alliance has searched everywhere for him. If you find him, you must be prepared to combat his superior mental abilities. Do not drop your guard! Regrettably, I confess to the misuse of my position to stage his trial, but it was necessary. I will not apologize for it, as nor will Schlegar. Good luck, my friend. The games of the mind play an important role in this unfolding drama. You are not a sacrificial lamb. You are a spy, an investigator, a valuable asset of the Alliance. We are all counting on you. I await your return to Earth with results. Good luck. Our thoughts and prayers are with you." The tape ended abruptly. The room was silent.

Deacon was the first to speak, whispering. "Landrew omitted a grim reality. There could be powers in outer space that could reduce me to that same empty shell that Temisori occupies."

Lyanna took his hand in hers. "Not with my training. Today's lessons are about to commence, so I suggest that you and I excuse ourselves from Schlegar."

Before they left, Schlegar blocked their path and stood directly in front of Deacon. "Not very many have your powers. You must adopt the mental attitude that this power is a weapon, not be afraid to use it, and not be hesitant to invade the sanctity of others. Do you hear me?" Deacon nodded in agreement. "Dismissed."

Lyanna drove Deacon to the brink of exhaustion, changing his moods to change the reception of energy, over and over, until he received and interpreted every message correctly. Deacon was an excellent pupil. The later theme of the day explored the supplanting of ideas into the minds of others, but it was never a certainty, for it depended entirely on the reception of the other individual. The success of such a sortie would always leave an unknown risk.

Lyanna praised Deacon throughout for his efforts and his abilities, building his confidence, boosting his ego. During this short stay on Brebouillis, she had developed an attraction to this small-statured man who displayed an intense dedication to complete his task. "I have a favor to ask of you. You have a visitor who has traveled at great personal expense to meet you."

Deacon was curious.

Quobit

"Deacon, it is my pleasure to introduce my friend Quobit, from the planet of Jabu."

On cue, she entered and gracefully strode toward Deacon, her multicolored gown swaying to and fro, her thick, long crimson hair swaying to the beat of her pace in a ponytail, her four-foot strides closing the distance quickly. Deacon felt intimidated as she towered over him.

"It is a great honor to meet you, Deacon Coombs. I have read with interest most of your works, your mystery short stories, and, of course, the many crimes you have solved. Please excuse my intrusion. I have traveled a great distance, and it is my honor to speak with you." In typical traditional Jabu custom, she bowed first and then they shook hands briefly.

"It is a pleasure to meet you, Quobit." Deacon had never witnessed hands so large, with knuckles the size of peaches, and curled nails at the end.

"Quobit and I met at a science conference on Gastov, and we have become friends. We converse regularly through different media and even vacationed together on the beaches of Globiana last year. I will leave you to conduct your business."

Deacon was curious. "Business?"

"Yes, business," said Quobit. "I have free time, earned by my job as a Vesper engineer on Jabu. With the stress in my job, we are encouraged to use our free time. At my expense, I decided to journey here to meet and talk to you, Deacon Coombs."

"Well, you certainly have my attention. When I entered earlier, I pondered over that rather large chair in the corner, for it was not here the last three days. Now all is clear." Deacon pulled the chair forward and, recognizing the Jabu intolerance for proximity to aliens, positioned it across the room from her. She surprised him after they both sat down, for she placed the chair in front of him, her bony knees protruding through her dress as she came closer. She clasped her hands in her lap, sat erect, and peered down into his eyes.

"With your permission, we shall abandon courtesies and I shall break the suspense."

"Yes, please do."

"I was the engineer on duty at the Jabu Vesper station on that fateful day when the Aralian freighter *Sleigher* disappeared. I want to digress for a moment to tell you that since I was a little girl growing up in the Khackstack desert of Jabu, I dreamed of being a Vesper engineer. I dreamed of managing a Vesper station and making a name for myself in the engineering of Vespering. I graduated at the top of my class only recently and have been assigned to that station since."

"Congratulations."

"Thank you. However, since the *Sleigher* disappeared on my watch, I have felt disappointment and much sympathy for the crew and their loved ones. Imagine my surprise, and everyone else's, when the *Sleigher* rematerialized at the Aralian Vesper station and its crew was declared insane." She paused in a moment of empathic silence with her head bowed. Deacon waited and let her control the conversation, still puzzled by her presence. She raised her head, and her light, sooty eyes focused on him. They were deep-seated and protected by a large, protruding forehead with bushy eyebrows. She noticed his stare into her eyes. "Evolution has played its part in protecting Jabu eyes by setting them deep into our head with long, wavy eyelashes, protecting the eyes from the incessant dust particles blowing every day." She smiled, and then the smile disappeared.

"Deacon Coombs," she whispered to him, "I have replayed that day at the Vesper station many times in my mind, going over each event and fact, and have convinced myself that something was out of the ordinary. I admit they are tiny facts, but so critically important. I am following your sleuthing methods, for you constantly cite that no detail should be considered little in a crime or mystery."

"Did you report these details to authorities at the station?"

"No." Her tone changed. She was blunt. "I am fearful to do so."

"So you journey to Brebouillis to report them to me?"

"Exactly." Quobit shuffled in her seat and leaned toward him. "Lyanna assured me that there are no cameras here and no voice recordings of what I am about to tell you. This lounge is secure. Therefore, I will lay my case before you to judge me."

"And I wish to assure you, Quobit, that you do so with my word that I will repeat to no one what you say."

"Thank you." After a deep sigh, she recited the facts. "In my time at the Vesper station, I have performed admirably. I have not been written up for violations, warnings, any improper actions, or shortcomings. Usually new recruits have a few noncompliances by this time, but I love my job, and the thrill of Vespering and running one of the busiest stations in the Alliance is self-satisfying. I also complete my calculations in rapid time." She leaned toward him further.

"Now for my case. On that fateful day we witnessed some of the worst cosmic energy storms in years, which disrupted magnetic patterns. My routine of guiding ships into the disc to be Vespered elsewhere was grossly upset, and we had delayed traffic up to twenty ships. When my supervisor, Maretz, ascended onto the control deck, he was his usual self, criticizing my actions and throwing his resentment of the new generation my way. Every new engineer has a mentor, and Maretz is mine. I will freely admit that I have learned much from him, but on that day, there was no way I was going to risk safe harbor by Vespering ships through that powerful storm." Deacon viewed her as a very principled woman.

"A window of quietness suddenly appeared, so Maretz and I reacted quickly by successfully Vespering ships out. I never thought anything of it at the time because we were so busy, but three peculiar small things happened." She broke her hand lock to point at him.

"Maretz had never ordered me out of the control chair to take over a Vesper, no matter what the circumstances. Yet that is exactly what he did on that watch on that day. He ordered me out of control for the Vespering of the *Sleigher*." Deacon knew where she was heading.

"When he ordered me out, I didn't think it peculiar, but I should have, for the storm had clearly subsided and there was no further reason for him to take the controls away from me; the risk of Vespering had evaporated as the storm had diminished." Her concern was clear.

"Most peculiar of all, Maretz is a legend on Jabu, having conducted more Vespers than any other Jabu engineer. He knows the intricate details of Vespering, the science and engineering of molecular transformations, and yet for this Vesper of the *Sleigher*, he established a personal worst time of over six units. He has always performed under six. I suddenly shuddered the other day as I sat alone on break and realized the coincidence of his personal bad time with the disappearance of the *Sleigher*. I began to think that maybe . . . the extra time was . . . due to altering the Vesper records. Mr. Coombs, I think that Maretz sent the *Sleigher* to a secret destination—another Vesper station in a remote area determined by him and Travers—and then used the extra time at the controls to revise the records to show that the *Sleigher* had been Vespered to Aralia. I realize that this is blasphemy against Maretz."

Deacon then said, "The implication being that the actions of Maretz are punishable by death according to Jabu law."

"Absolutely. So I could not report my suspicions to him, nor to his superiors, without endangering my career. I felt like they would never believe my suspicion. They would never take the charge of a new engineer over Maretz's gold-plated career."

"Quobit, thank you for entrusting me with this information. I never believed that Vesper rays could be bent, so I was working on the hypothesis that error or sabotage or criminal activity was at play."

"In conclusion, Mr. Coombs, I believe that Travers of Aralia and Maretz conspired to send the *Sleigher* on a secret mission, and that engineers along the route were paid handsomely to cover the *Sleigher*'s trail. Why would they do that? Where did they go? What should I do?"

"All to be determined," he replied, although he would not share with her the evidence that the *Sleigher* had possibly journeyed to Nix, as evidenced by the tape found on board.

"Mr. Coombs, you do not know me as a person. Let me tell you about Quobit. I previously informed you that I graduated at the top of my engineering class. I am very intelligent. I am also a fierce fighter and have been acknowledged by national organizations for my feats of female strength and endurance during national sport festivals. The desert people of Jabu know how to survive in extreme climates, and I have won many survival competitions. These competitions with other planetary inhabitants have allowed me to overcome my fear of proximity to aliens, which is very rare in Jabu people, and is why I sit in proximity to you."

Her tone changed. "I fear for my life, Mr. Coombs. In the days before I departed Jabu, Maretz kept pestering me about where I was traveling for my free time and when I was returning, and I feel like I was watched at the port." Deacon listened to her attentively, already aware of a tough decision that he would be confronted with.

She addressed him royally with supreme confidence. Her voice sounded at times like a feminine soprano, and then like a bold male with baritone inflections. "Please, I have many attributes and raw skills that can be of benefit to you on your quest. Please take me with you. I am smart, a survivor, physically strong, and will be an asset on your voyage."

He returned her pensive stare. Those were the friendliest warming, soft coal-colored eyes he had ever seen. "This is difficult for me to say, Quobit, but I can't. I am in the employ of the Alliance."

"Please reconsider, I beg of you. I'm afraid to go back to Jabu. I think Maretz suspects that I have uncovered his ill deed."

"I will give it more thought but probably will not change my decision."

She rose and bowed and shook hands. "I am so proud to have met you, Deacon Coombs. I will respect your decision. I hope you will solve the case of the vanishing Vesper and protect me in your course of actions." She turned and left Deacon feeling empty about his decision but excited that there was a logical real reason for the malefic Vesper.

Departing

The end of the third day found Deacon and Lyanna in the observatory, where they were laughing together at the humorous anecdotes of the past days.

"Why did you come here?" Deacon was curious.

After a distinctive pause, Lyanna responded, looking deep into his blue eyes. "I came to forget my past. On Earth, I had a rewarding job, a true love, a family. My parents passed away in the same year that I lost my partner. It was my partner's bitter betrayal that drove me into the seclusion of this assignment."

"I didn't mean to be a snoop."

"Don't apologize. Do you have a female companion?"

"Heavens no! My work consumes me day and night." Her eyes told him that she wanted more of an explanation. "Okay, I window-shop. I'm too shy when it comes to love. How many before me?"

She was aghast. "That's a bit too brazen."

"No!" He stood. "No! You know, Lyanna. I'm serious. How many . . . many . . . other . . . guinea pigs have passed through Brebouillis in front of you and Schlegar to be tested on their way to confront this thing, this crisis? I want the truth, Lyanna. Landrew said there were others. No doubt they had mental powers like mine and came here to be tested and prepared. How many, Lyanna?"

Lyanna stirred and then proceeded to the window. The mood had turned solemn. With her back turned to him, she replied, "Five. None of the others have been seen since their departure from Brebouillis. They may still be alive out there, searching for Travers and the evil, but our contact with them is lost."

"Were they as adept as I?"

"Yes and no. You have unusual gifts. I feel that none of them have your powers."

"Who were they?"

She sat down on the ledge facing him, folding her arms about her, heaving her chest. "Two were Aralians, gifted indeed. They departed separately, one a former space trader, one a mentalist. The third was a Mendalgon policeman needing Owler protection and cumbersome life-support systems. It would be a tough task for any Mendalgon, heading out into the galaxy to travel with strange bedfellows, but he was high in spirits last I saw him. The fourth was an Earthling, a reprogrammed derelict—brilliant, severe attitude problem, cocky, immense mental powers similar to yours. Just before you was a Verconian—a member of royalty, a demonstrated survivor, a sportsman, a playboy, a detective."

"And you are sure that they have not made a report to Landrew in confidence that you and Schlegar are not aware of?"

"Yes. I am certain."

"Did they all have Owler protection?"

"The Aralians no, the Earthling no, the other two yes."

Deacon's voice cracked. "So I can read minds. So what? The thing we seek render humans helpless and is possibly responsible for the murders of Como and Geor. With a stroke of a hand it could whisk me away. Maybe that's what happened to those five before me. Whisked away to their deaths."

"Stop it. You have the ability to win. Stop talking like that!" She was visibly upset, with a ruddy face. "Will you take Quobit with you?"

"No. I would need Landrew's permission, and I want to keep my movements secret."

Lyanna moved beside him and placed her arms around his neck. "I don't envy you. Use your gift whenever you can, Deacon. You will find surprises in the minds of others."

"What do you expect of me?"

Very gravely, she spoke. "Discover the true identity of this evil. That is your task. Just as Landrew said. Find it. Flee! I want to see you again, Deacon Coombs."

He risked a chance. "Do you have feelings for me?"

Lyanna inhaled, exhaled. "I've read about you. I know who you are. Deacon Coombs, born with brilliance, uncanny ability to solve complex problems at an early age, long string of scholarships leading to degrees in history, mathematics, physics, until you turned your resources to crime-solving at age twenty. Nickname, The Deacon. Nickname, Moon Eyes. A recluse, a hero, a mystery man, an enigma. What else do people say of you?" She pointed her index finger at him. "Don't tell me that you haven't used your powers to unravel the deeds of sinister beings. You have known of your special gift for years."

"Okay, I admit that I did when I had to serve justice."

Now she was bold to inquire. "Any past loves?"

"On a personal note, I have not had any lasting relationships. My confidence tends to smother people, leading them to believe that I am more arrogant than I really am. I have been nothing more than a curio at parties. As years passed, the number of my close friends has dwindled." In his room, he had rehearsed a speech to give to her now about the feelings he had for her. The timing was wrong; the atmosphere was wrong. Maybe on his return. So, with an excuse of feeling tired, they parted company after Lyanna surprised him with a hug and a sole peck on his cheek.

Back in his room, Deacon longed for Moonbeam and dear Miram. This was crazy, to journey into deeper space, and for what? Tomorrow was the start of a new journey. Perhaps the idea of seeing

Lyanna again would drive his resolve to survive. Should he race back to the observation deck to tell her how he really felt?

He looked at himself in the mirror. The scar on his neck had been strategically hidden with the high collars he had selected to wear. As he pulled the collar back to examine the wound, he saw the red streak that would always be a reminder of his mortality.

Deciding that it was not manly to cry, he wondered if he would ever see her again. To himself, he said, "I am not a God, not immortal, just an Earthling quite capable of dying in space if the circumstances are right."

THE SEARCH FOR TRAVERS

Departing Brebouillis

Deacon watched from the observation deck as a line of Owlers loaded the *Heritage* with supplies for the journey, at the direction of Jim, who waved his arms like a carnival barker while shouting instructions. Schlegar ascended to the observation deck for his last words with Deacon. "I should have known that I would find you here. Have you checked the charts to see where you travel?"

"Yes," Deacon replied, "but I will have to implicitly trust the Owlers to get me there. I couldn't even point in the direction from here."

Lyanna appeared, dressed in a tight black jump suit. "Some reading material that I composed on Travers. Everything that we know about him is here in this disc, from birth to present. It fits comfortably into your handheld device." Lyanna took his hand and inserted the chip and then presented a personal note which he opted to open later. "I hate to say this Schlegar, but how will I recognize Travers, since all Aralians look alike?"

Lyanna giggled and then ran to Schlegar to give him a hug as she said, "I think they are all so cute and cuddly, just like big furry dolls."

"Oh, stop it, Ly!" Schlegar embarrassingly had heard this kibitzing before. "Travers has a scar on his left thigh that he received when he was oh . . . twenty years old. The fur of an Aralian never grows back once removed. He has a powerful, spellbinding voice. Take care lest you come under his trance. The Owler Gem has his voice match. Additionally, he is five foot five, has deep reddish-brown eyes, is somewhat overweight, has stubby fingers, and, yes, is missing a bone chip that was cut out of his left heel. A digit is underdeveloped on his right hand."

Deacon retrieved a photo from the file and studied it. "He looks rather plain and innocent to me."

Schlegar grabbed Deacon's arm. "Make no mistake or you lose your life! This man is dangerous—I repeat, dangerous." His emotional outburst of venom caught them both by surprise. Schlegar turned his back to them. As he whirled back around, Deacon and Lyanna stared back, still surprised by his outburst.

"If I were seventy of your Earth years younger, Deacon, I would relish the opportunity to go with you. But look at me! My silver fur is turning to shreds; I have had five major operations on my vital organs, which consequently restrict my diet. I hobble around these halls. So in the twilight of my many years, what can I do? I can only advise you. And the advice that I give to you is that this man is dangerous. His outward appearance, calm demeanor, and innocent looks have deceived everyone!"

Deacon challenged him, saying, "Your outburst has inbred distinct tones of anger and hatred." The doctor approached him. They were only inches apart.

"Then maybe we Aralians are becoming flawed, as Como suspected. Here are your identity papers. You have the options of traveling as yourself or in disguise as a trader."

"There are other brilliant people who need no training," said Deacon.

"None have your intellect, your imagination, your resolve, your cover. You are a detective first and will question all that you observe. This alone provides a great advantage. You know what to suspect from an arch villain, while others don't. It has been your life. Your cases consistently prove that you possess great instincts."

"Why the hate?" Deacon asked, taunting him.

Schlegar turned away from them again, but as he did so, Deacon could hear him say, "Travers is my son." This confession caught both Deacon and Lyanna off guard. "I am ashamed of him. When the Alliance first came to me to partake in the chance to rid the union of him, I jumped at the chance." Schlegar shook as he spoke. "I even used my influence with Geor to secure a position as head of this project. It was, as you suspected, my idea to plant Mindor close to Travers at the trial. I had to remain out of sight. We could not, however, obtain any valuable information to feed back to the prosecution." Deacon felt sorry for him as Schlegar conveyed his bitter disappointment in himself and shared this confession.

"I have examined all the candidates to fight Travers mentally, and the candidate is you!" His finger and hand trembled as he spoke and pointed at Deacon. "It was I who gave him that scar on his hip during a father/son quarrel. It was an unfortunate accident at the time, but it may now help you to positively identify him. I had dreams that Travers would rise to the political stature that Como did and replace Como in time. These are now the shattered, foolish dreams of a bitter old man."

Schlegar bowed his head in shame. "Let me die in peace. Let me see the day that my son is brought to justice, that Como's death is avenged, even if it means Travers's death." He commenced to weep, and Lyanna moved quickly to hug and comfort him.

Deacon realized what a fool he had been not to have seen the connection between Schlegar and Travers in his previous readings of Travers on Earth. He waited until Schlegar regained his composure, and then asked, "Where should we begin our search for him?"

"Our bodies are so specialized that Aralia is our one true frigid livable home. It is there that you should begin your search. Sure, Aralians are the true great adventurers of outer space, but in reality we love our homeland more than anything else, and other than time on Aralian spaceships, we cannot tolerate climates on other planets. If Travers were to travel by trade ship, he would be uncovered given the tight security at ports." Schlegar had confirmed the findings of Gem and Jim with identical logic.

"But the surface area of Aralia is so vast. The Owlers have some ideas of regions to visit, but where do you think we should start?"

"I have given the benefit of my advice to the Owlers, given them coordinates of towns, districts, areas that are loyal to Travers. The file also includes some of his favorite leisurely locations, his birthplace, the names of his friends. I have also given Gem and Jim the names of persons on Aralia who are faithful to the Alliance. Gem has their voice and skin patterns to confirm their authenticity. With the Owlers' research and my input, you should uncover his path."

"Who am I to be on Aralia?"

"Bothwen, a trader of ten years. I took the liberty to send copies of your identity to all Aralian authorities and space ports."

"But I have traveled little."

"Correct, you have spent your duties on Earth in administrative offices and now travel to see all the planets that you have been monitoring for years. The Owlers will assist you." He looked up. "Now get sleuthing!"

"I am so sorry, Schlegar, for the pain that grips you. I pray that I will be able to relieve some of this burden that you carry by proving Travers's innocence or bringing him to justice." Deacon gripped Schlegar's handshake tightly.

"Keep that translation device in your ear as much as possible. It may be able to interpret critical remarks when you least expect it to."

Deacon stepped toward Lyanna. "I hope to see you again, Lyanna. Thank you for your efforts to help me harness my skills. I won't let you down."

She embraced him hard. Their eyes pierced each other with feelings as she released her hold. "Good luck, Deacon Coombs. My prayers are with you every moment until we see each other again."

It was over so soon. After a short trip down the hall onto the *Heritage*, he was strapped in by Gem. The craft left the dock for the Vesper station as Schlegar and Lyanna held hands on the observation deck until the last remnants of the lights of the *Heritage* disappeared into blackness. Onboard, he whispered, "I will come back for you."

Deacon took to studying his alias, Bothwen. He easily absorbed the facts of his previous assignments, and this was a script well written. He turned to the relationship of Travers and Schlegar as recorded in the files that Schlegar gave to him at parting. It seemed that the souring of their family had occurred recently. The duo had been frequently seen in public together up to that point. Schlegar recorded a vicious commentary that captured the change in Travers's blind ambitions.

Nausea consumed him as they reached the Vesper station. The next thing that he remembered was the arrival at Aralia, at the very station where the *Sleigher* had disappeared. On his viewing screen, the planet Aralia, decked in shades of blue, became visible as they slowly rose out of the purple disc and headed for the frigid planet. Gem assisted him as he selected his winter gear. They would dock at an immigration gate in only minutes, where temperatures thirty degrees below zero awaited them.

On the planet Aralia

The port of Froora was bustling with protracted lines of impatient voyagers waiting to gain access onto the planet. Around him Deacon saw the Jabu, Globianans, Fextwa swordsmen, all walks of life. Not a familiar word did he hear in the congested mob, so he stayed within touching distance of Jim. Aralian security was at a premium with the death of Como. Search stations lined the drab halls before clearing personnel into the city of Froora, Aralia's largest interplanetary port. Every piece of paper was examined, every piece of luggage unpacked, every deck of the *Heritage* searched.

Paranoia was beginning to set in. Deacon's small stature was innocuous in the crowd, but he started to believe that everyone was looking at him. After a lengthy delay in their line, an official appraised his papers. A stern glance from the furry face under the pointed red helmet followed. To his left, a fracas broke out. A Zentaurian was rudely questioning interrogation methods. Numerous police were sequestered as the hall grew silent to watch the confrontation. The agent returned the papers to Deacon, and Gem and Jim motioned to Deacon to return quickly back on board.

As they exited the inner hall to return to the ship, the sounds of laser fire and shouting echoed outside. "Quickly," said Jim, "before they seal the port. We now have permission to land the *Heritage* in any of the sixteen ports on Aralia. First stop, Inglesiss, the hometown of Travers. Here we are to visit a close friend of Dreveney's by the name of I'obo."

"Am I to be Deacon or Bothwen?"

"I'obo can be trusted. You are to be Deacon Coombs to I'obo, Bothwen to the rest of Aralia."

Within the hour they had docked in Inglesiss, and Jim and Deacon were whisked away in a driverless high-speed landsled to I'obo's countryside residence while Gem remained behind to secure their plans for the upcoming days and secure rooms at an inn. Jim constantly fed coordinates to the computer-controlled sled as they skimmed over the snowy landscape at a constant speed. Deacon noticed the furry creatures that dotted the countryside, traveling at high speeds on their naturally polished bare-boned skis on paths that paralleled the sled, changing directions instantaneously as expert skiers on Earth would. Several executed abrupt stops beside the path the sled cut, stopping to gape at the occupants as the swift glass bubble hastily moved by. Along the journey, they saw multitudes of Aralian homes, resembling giant igloos. The colorful, dyed icy exteriors sparkled in the light. The snow and ice they were made of served as a natural insulation over the synthetic domal core of the dwelling. Once, they slowed to pass through a small town where Deacon caught a glimpse of what appeared to be an enormous department store with glossy, alluring advertisements lining all the icy exterior walls.

Their craft slowed as it approached a small structure hidden in rocky, sinewy crags that protruded through the white sheets of the landscape. Because of the absence of shrubbery, the craft made a direct line to the dwelling and was able to park at the doorway. Deacon and Jim each had to crouch down a narrow inlet. Inside, the walls glowed in a pink hue while the air was as fresh as a spring morning in Anglo, though Deacon drew a slight chill from the cold air-conditioning. At least he was now able to stand erect. A chipper silver-haired being intercepted them, introducing himself as I'obo. I'obo resembled Schlegar, with his hobble and hair spewing into his face from above, but I'obo was much taller.

"*Washa-washa*, Mr. Coombs, I am the government agent in charge of local affairs of security. The case of Travers is not within my jurisdiction, but I told Dreveney that I would assist you in any way I can. Come, follow me. It is my pleasure to host any friend of Landrew and Dreveney. It is my honor to host the well-known detective Deacon Coombs." He led them deeper into the dome until they reached a room that sparkled in blue twilight and had numerous hand-painted murals of landscapes dotting the walls. A table setting of juices adorned a huge stone table. Here they sat across from one another.

They conversed for hours, examining each of the potential hiding places on the planet, using the map that Jim unfolded. I'obo marked the last three sightings of Travers on the map, although these were unsubstantiated by facts; they were just rumors. He commented on the priority list that the Owlers had constructed, agreeing with some choices, disagreeing with others. I'obo also explained the safety precautions they would have to take for nature and weather, and also the procedures to obtain security access permits to some of the areas, an issue I'obo could assist with and accelerate.

"If Travers was sighted, why has he not been apprehended, I'obo?"

"Aralians have a great deal of respect for this man, Mister Coombs. Travers has publicly declared his innocence recently, and there are those who believe him. Truth is the bearer of hope in Aralia. Many believe that Travers will recover from this crisis and return to political power and rule Aralia someday. They think this because they believe Travers."

Deacon was not satisfied. "But Como is dead. Surely there are those who believe Travers must at least be detained to prove his innocence? Or to be proven guilty? And why does he not surrender to face charges if he declares his innocence?"

"Coombs, the Aralians are a passive race. We have a love of life and detest and avoid confrontation. If we have a weakness, it is that we forgive too quickly. Travers's past achievements will never be forgotten. Only a few select police officials will step forward to arrest him. And their searches have failed. Very few Aralians believe Travers murdered Como."

I'obo continued to expand on the customs of Aralians in his high-pitched voice, providing Deacon with customary tips for tourists. He stated his firm opinion on the three best leads as to Travers's whereabouts. "Lastly, the hills of Glagn, covered in deep snow at this time of year, make access next to impossible even in sleds unless you have a specific safe destination. The last reports indicated blinding snowstorms in the area, but Travers has been rumored to be there too. Perhaps he just moves about."

A thin, gangly black Owler appeared with food. The colorful synthetic nourishment was tasty, although Deacon found the slimy texture quite repulsive. Deacon forced each gulp down, followed by a swig of spicy liquid. After feeding, they sat, legs bent, on brown fur rugs on the floor, as other furniture was scarce in the room.

I'obo then elaborated on Aralian customs. "Aralians place little value on worldly possessions; instead, our passion is outdoor recreation, which our bodies are naturally built for. We spend money on extracurricular events, either as a spectator or as a participant." He described to Deacon an array of events ranging from an intellectual form of chess on ice to something resembling soccer with fifty players on the field at a time. But skiing on their bare-boned feet was the prime activity, whether downhill, freestyle, or cross-country. "Furthermore, Aralians love their outdoor habitats, so they shop at stores only by physically venturing there. Thus, stores are always crowded.

"I promise help to you should you require it, should you locate Travers. I vow to contact your Owler immediately if there are any additional sightings of the man. Aralian loyalties lie in history, and Travers's family tree is rich in admirable deeds." After some queries by Jim on local police procedures, they exchanged "*Washa-washas*" and departed in the dark.

Meanwhile, in Inglesiss, Gem had secured lodgings. Other investigations by Gem into Travers's whereabouts proved fruitless, and after Gem's report, Jim said, "I shall prowl the streets tomorrow and show you how it is done, Gem!"

Deacon replied, "Too bad your human engrams don't include humility."

Jim snapped his slim form to attention. "Humility. The state of being humble; the absence of pride or self-assertion."

Deacon laughed. "Yes, yes, we know. I am surprised that you do."

The following day, the Owlers made plentiful stops in the morning. The range of the voice detector had limited ability to penetrate dwellings they passed in targeted neighborhoods. In addition, they stopped at inns, recreational slopes, and taverns that I'obo had suggested. With the voice probe on, nothing came close to Travers's profile. That afternoon, while Jim assessed other leads, Deacon remained with Gem throughout in local police libraries until exhaustion overwhelmed him. Back at the inn, he felt bone-weary after forcing down two days' worth of soggy, slithery Aralian fish and undercooked plants. He wasn't even sure what constituted the accompanying white mush always served with the fish. Since the Owlers had no cure for vomiting, he suffered the hard way and was forced to remain at the inn while they continued the search. Deacon had already concluded that I'obo's leads were long shots; finding Travers might have to take a twist. "Have Travers find us," he said.

On the next day, when he arose, the Owlers had departed. It was very difficult for him to venture outside in the slippery streets, but twice he interrupted his readings to go out in the cool, invigorating air. Both times he was cognizant of Aralians standing across the street, examining him. His imagination smothered him as he convinced himself that these could be Travers's spies and the search had already been turned against him. His stomach failed him, so he reached for a refuse container. The long days of forty-two Earth hours were also taking attacking his stamina.

Gem and Jim returned by midday. Important information was gathered by the Owlers on the individuals controlling the traders' union. They checked many local places to hide, but with no encouraging results. Some of the more distant leads were checked by regional authorities with negative results. On the fourth day, Deacon sat inside to read the trial pages while Jim and Gem went on their rounds to verify what they described as a credible lead to locate Travers. After the Owlers departed, Deacon hatched a plan to force the issue of the two Aralians who were possibly sentries keeping vigil on him from across the street. If they were employees of Travers, he intended to verify it.

A dangerous jaunt

Deacon donned his boots and heavy snow gear, wrapping his scarf tightly to fight the biting cold of this gusty day. He was relegated to using the stifling, slow, noisy mechanical lift, as the stairwells were like the toboggan runs he knew from back home. As he laced up his mittens in the lobby, he satisfied a curiosity by conversing with the elderly, husky innkeeper, who smoked a pipe. "Villya, excuse me, sir, but I notice the empty picture frame with the Aralian flag draped over it. Does it have some significance?"

The innkeeper was gruff. Without the flinch of an eyelid or eye-to-eye contact, he retorted. "*Washa-washa*. Each Aralian is asked to remember the departed Como in his own accord. My fondest memories are from when he was not in power as our leader. Como did little for our economy and my business. Thus my flag sits on an empty frame to signify the glory days before Como took political power."

Deacon was stunned. This Aralian had spoiled the image that he had formulated of Como. Deacon had come to believe that all Aralians mourned the loss of Como. And what about hospitality? *Villya* was the recognized universal greeting of respected friendship, but the innkeeper had snapped a *Washa-washa* to greet him instead. Was this rude?

"So you were not fond of Como?"

"Earthman, Aralians do not discuss our sacred politics with outsiders. Your question will not be answered. I speak for many Aralians when I speak of Como's unpopularity." He slammed a ledger shut and exited the lobby area, leaving Deacon alone and uncomfortable. Where was that omnipresent Aralian hospitality he had heard about? *Is the innkeeper's opinion really shared by other Aralians as he stated? First the realization of Aralian dishonesty to try Travers, and now this.*

Deacon paused to take a deep breath before exiting the inn. Pushing the lightweight door open, he descended three steps to street level, where dirty, greasy mush spilled over the tops of his boots. His cheeks stung immediately from the crisp, dry air. It was late in the day, only a few hours of daylight left. Knowing that he should not prolong the exposure of his bare skin to the atmosphere, he paced briskly down the street and into a busy marketplace. A cluster of crude structures selling metal wares provided a brief interlude from the forceful wind gusts. His Earthling frame was taller than those of most of the natives, so he drew sharp glances.

The streets were narrow and slippery, all the dome-like buildings glittering with the last rays of sunlight. Windows were scarce, although the larger department stores each had one window display of goods to lure customers inside. Doorways were tight alcoves to minimize heat loss, so lines were common both outside and inside upon entry and departure. Erected on stone foundations, these structures rose five hundred feet into the sky. The oceans that brought moisture to Inglesiss were more than one thousand miles distant, so the air here was anhydrous.

Deacon looked down the street. It had been patted down smoothly from the intense traffic of Aralians skiing effortlessly by at high velocities. He immediately thought about how fortunate they were as a result of their lack of pollution from fuel-dependent vehicles. For an alien, it was difficult to find footing that would sustain balance, so he hugged the handclasps that were provided at the side of the street for foreigners. The spacing of the clips was inconvenient, and he found himself having to propel himself from clip to clip.

Inside his left mitten he carried a small mirror. Exposing it at eye level, he caught a glimpse of two Aralians walking twenty yards behind him. His heart raced. He feigned an interest in the skin coats in a window, and then, ambling as a tourist, he entered the shop. Inside the upside-down bowl, cherry-red heaters dangled and pumped waves of cool, refreshing air into the hemisphere, obviously an addition for tourists. He raised the mirror again, needing only a second to spy the twosome entering the store behind him.

In his excited state, his mind suddenly became bombarded with unfamiliar thoughts from the Aralians in proximity. He inhaled deeply, relaxed his mind, and set out to find a less crowded counter. A stabbing thought of Como pierced him from an approaching Aralian. He twirled around and saw a group of chatting Aralians heading his way, so he moved to an isolated corner, where he fondled fur balls, a favorite tourist buy of small stuffed animals, available in various colors. His legs ached; his mind was stimulated by incessant incomprehensible thoughts. Another non-Aralian started toward him, so he turned and scurried elsewhere. Over his shoulder was an exit. He shuffled toward it, but it proved to be no less challenging, as another bustling street confronted him. Twice he slipped; twice he calmly arose and spied the duo still in pursuit. Or was it them? All Aralians suddenly seemed to look alike in this congregation. Now his confidence was whipped. Same duo or not? He decided to make a confirming move.

Opposite him, a small shop sold hand carvings made from the soapy rocks of Aralia. Deacon spurted across at a pedestrian crossing for a closer look and entered. Then, as he cast a sideward look toward his examiners heading in his direction, he weaved a path to the back of the shop and exited into a crowded alleyway.

Here, in a mob of strange oxen-like creatures toting wares, he quickly positioned himself behind a shaggy six-legged animal hauling a carriage of goods. The melancholy face of the animal turned toward him, two sorrowful black eyes stabbing from behind a mat of black fur. The long, odiferous coat of the underbelly provided Deacon excellent cover from the Aralians.

The vigil was short-lived, as the two pursuers entered the street and stood in the alley, looking back and forth for him. He had confirmed his suspicions. It was impossible for him to discern male Aralians from females, although Aralians routinely performed this function by smell. Scant cloth covered only the sex organs at the base of the torso, while the more sensitive Aralians wore kerchiefs over the small opening of the respiratory cavity at the neck. These two wore the same black cloth and kerchiefs as the twosome that he had spied previously.

It was time to turn the tables in this case. After long, hard days of receiving no rewards on Aralia, Deacon reluctantly decided that this was worth a chance. Perhaps, one or both would lead him to an accomplice of Travers. Patience was required, as numbing cold penetrated his hands and feet. He jumped up and down behind the bullock to keep warm as the two separated. He checked to make sure he had his signalet in his pocket in case the Owlers required a summons.

A split-second decision had to be made. He chose to follow the slightly smaller of the two, trailing the Aralian cautiously through the dimly lit winding lanes of gummy gray snow. Long shadows began to engulf the sinewy avenues; he was careful to stop and look behind for the other Aralian to ensure that his own plan was not a setup. His heavy, moisture-laden eyelids strained to stay open. Returning to the inn was quickly becoming a problem because of the circuitous series of turns he had captured in his mind.

Voices of passing Aralians squealed curt greetings of *"Washa-washa"* to him, as his bundling could not disguise his true identity as an Earthman. He remained far enough behind the prey to feel secure, though not close enough at each corner. Then panic set in.

As he turned a corner, he found he had lost his quarry. Immediately he retreated into the indented cover of a storefront leading to a closed shop, casting an intense gaze up and down the frozen, deserted, misty purple lane of shop facades. No one appeared ahead; it was eerily silent. Even the incessant squawking of Aralians was absent. With no street lights at this point, the white winter wonderland was suddenly transformed into a ghostly, daunting apparition.

Deacon thought he knew his route back to the inn, so he paused to formulate the series of turns in his mind, bending down to sketch his remembrance in the gritty snow. Then he heard the unmistakable swishing sound of an Aralian's bare-boned feet on ice; it resonated in his ears. Peeking out into the road, he saw that a bluish hue covered the snow; the sound ceased. Farther down the street, shop owners sealed their places with a succession of thuds. With darkness arriving, he had to return to the inn immediately.

Hurriedly, he stepped along, faster and faster, his body not aware of the extended exposure to the climate. As he breathed heavily in short bursts, he found that the streets were familiar to him, the series of turns he had taken was correct to a corner he decided to stop at. While halting to catch his breath, he blew hot air onto his hands and then cupped his mittens to create a pocket of warm air for his forehead and cheeks. The distinct sound of swishing suddenly came close behind him and filled his senses. He halted, and the sound too came to a sudden stop as a spike of fear raced up his spine.

With a surge of courage, he turned. The street was empty except for a couple chatting about one hundred yards away, moving in the opposite direction. He noticed that the street sloped down to a deserted intersection with a multitude of hiding places, so he dashed for the middle of the avenue and squatted behind an ice sculpture, lying prostrate, peeking around the end of the sculpture to look back down the street from where he had traversed. The cold bit at his forehead, his eyes now squinting, straining to see through the frost buildup around his eyelids.

Total darkness was only minutes ahead. A decision was made. He guessed that he was a quarter of a mile from the safety of the inn.

His legs heard the command to run, so he thrust forward, walking at a brisk pace. Suddenly the sounds of swooshing intensified behind him. He had lost his courage to confront his pursuer. Perspiration drenched his body while a hard, swollen lump filled the rear of his throat cavity.

He had to get around the next two corners. Perhaps there would be natives in the street to help him. *Two more turns! Only two more!* He had to reach safety. He pushed himself harder and harder while a swooshing sound now pounded in his head. Shops were closed, streets deserted. The next corner—there it was!

However, just as he prayed to see the orange glow in the windows of the inn about two hundred feet ahead, perhaps even Gem and Jim standing outside hailing him, his heart sank. There was no inn, no familiar sight, no orange glow, no Gem and Jim! He had executed an erroneous calculation. He was lost. He darted from the street and stood stunned, pressing himself tightly against the wall of a shop, not daring to look out into the street. All was silent. The beautiful blues and purples of twilight were turning to the ominous charcoal-and-black night.

Suddenly, as he dared to look where he had traversed from, a hand reached out from behind him and firmly grasped him across his mouth, a second arm strapping his chest. The stranglehold was powerful, unyielding, totally paralyzing. The assailant flung him to the ground, face up. The being was totally wrapped in furs and skins; Deacon could see only a pair of eyes—two sooty peepers. As the assailant relaxed the hold on Deacon, two shadowy figures approached. In the dim lighting, his heart pumped vigorously, but it then returned to normal as Gem and Jim and Quobit suppressed his desire to scream with their motions.

An Aralian passed around the corner in full view. At the sight of Gem and Jim, he fled. The natural skiing artist outdistanced Jim immediately while Gem and Quobit remained behind. "A very foolish move, Master," said Gem. "Trailing the two spies outside our inn was the lead that Jim referred to last night. When you turned the tables on them, we thought for a moment that we could trace one or both to their master. It was not to be. Around the next corner was a trap for you. Our ultimate goal is your safety, so we had to intervene and abandon our plan to capture one of these culprits. When you said that you were going to rest at the inn, we believed you. We took you at your word."

Deacon brushed himself off. Jim returned to join them. Deeply embarrassed, Deacon stood and convincingly spoke. "Thanks for the advice. Thanks for saving me." He continued to flick snow pellets from his parka, and then he eyed each of the others. "Partners?" He extended his hand first to Gem, then Jim, and then Quobit.

"Partners," Gem replied. Jim nodded in agreement. Quobit was silent as they walked back to safety.

In the confines of the inn, Deacon sheepishly felt that his credibility could have been compromised, or even worse. A cocky Jim asked, "Embarrassed?"

Deacon massaged his throbbing fingers, rubbed the cut on his throat from his skirmish on Earth, and then said, "Yes, and I have learned a lesson. Confide in you and Gem."

"Master, we first noticed them when we arrived at the station terminal in Froora. Since I have been recording all voice patterns, I was not surprised when they were observed across the street by my astute partner, Gem. The next day I sent a dispatch to I'obo, who confirmed that they were not his men, and sent a message to local authorities who confirmed the same. After two days of searching files at the traders' office, I found a match with two expelled traders." Jim recited his achievements proudly.

"You held out on me."

"No, Master," Gem said, "it was our intention to tell you tonight. Our reasoning for not doing so was that we did not wish to involve you in any dangerous activity today while you were ill—while you were reading in the comfort of the inn."

Reluctantly, Deacon answered positively. "I'll accept that."

"You have no choice. We made the correct decision. Quobit helped us with our plan. She spied the trap for you and interceded to protect you."

Quobit was sitting in front of the fire, rubbing her hands and arms and massaging her toes. Deacon asked the Owlers to retreat and sat beside her. "I owe you an apology."

"Yes, you do. I saved your life, or perhaps a kidnapping. I could have easily run and outdistanced the Aralian but for the slippery ice."

"You followed us here."

"Correct. I took the next ship from Brebouillis to Aralia and positioned myself across the street from your inn. I observed the two spies on the first day and warned the Owlers. When I saw them follow you today, I laid behind to observe. When I met the Owlers, we decided that I should move ahead of you, and it was then I discovered a trap for you. I doubled back and wrestled you to the ground for safety."

"And you did all of this because you want to prove your worth to me?"

"Yes." She turned to face him. "Did you know that I am in an intern position at the Vesper station and, upon completion, am following in my sister's footsteps to join Alliance Security Forces?"

"No, but I am not surprised. I thought that you were fulfilling a dream as a Vesper engineer?"

"Once again I bring you into my confidence, for potential recruits to security are supposed to remain a secret."

"What is your sister's name? How long has she been in Alliance Security Forces?"

For the first time, Quobit smiled, revealing a mouth full of white teeth and cheeks that pushed upward. "My sister's name is Quobit, and she has been five of your Earthling years in the force."

"Quobit?"

"On Jabu, all sisters in a family have the same name; all brothers have different names. It is you on Earth who have this funny peculiarity of naming sisters different names, as I discovered."

"I must admit that I think you could have crushed me with that grip."

"Yes, I could have. I informed you yesterday about my feats of strength. However, the climate on Aralia is a rude awakening after the heat on Jabu."

"Quobit, I find you to be an enigma. Jabu detest sharing soiled expelled air from aliens, yet here we are doing so. Jabu find the cold climate of Aralia impossible, yet here you are. Jabu are incredibly inward in their thoughts, yet here you are sharing—first your concern about Maretz, and now that you intend to join Alliance Security Forces. What am I to think of all this?"

"I have overcome my fear of proximity to aliens. I am comfortable in these furs and hides to protect me from the cold. I trust you with confidential information. I want to join your team and come with you. I know I will prove my worth, as I did today."

"It is cramped living quarters on the *Heritage* with one bedroom."

"Jabu do not sleep in beds; that is a custom on Earth. We lie outstretched on the floor. And as for the cramped quarters, I am proud to share the air you exhale."

"Gem. Jim. Enter please." The Owlers marched in, and as he stood, he said, "Unless you can find any objection, I am asking engineer Quobit to join our journey."

Jim spoke first. "I believe I speak for Gem and me when I say welcome, Quobit."

She stood proudly. "In the custom of the desert Jabu people, Deacon and I must rub to signify the mutual respect between us. Turn around, Mister Coombs, and stand straight up, elbows bent."

Deacon did so, and she stood back-to-back with him and rubbed her elbows hard against his. When finished, they turned just as Jim said, "My turn." As Gem and Deacon laughed, Quobit and Jim performed the ritual of respect with a little silliness.

"Quobit, I hereby recognize you as a team member, but . . . no more Mister Coombs. Deacon has arrived, and that is what I want you to address me as from this moment on, or you're off the team."

Quobit was all smiles again. "Yes, sir, Deacon."

The mood then turned serious. "I must say that I am uneasy and incredibly disappointed that our presence here has been detected, given all the precautions we took. First the library in Liberty, where safety was breached, and now here. My instincts tell me that Travers has a spy in our midst."

Deacon walked across the room and opened his dossier to pick up a photograph of Travers. As he held it, he said, "Sooner or later, I shall have to come face-to-face with him. I have already decided that it should be sooner rather than later. We have few results to date. Trying to find Travers is going to be frustrating without the aid of Travers, and it appears he has plans to kidnap me. Therefore, if his spies are outside tomorrow, tell them to arrange a parley with the trader."

Gem was quick to respond. "We cannot allow this, Master."

"Gem, this must be done. Somehow, I wish that they had captured me so I could discover their true intentions."

"There are still other leads to be verified. Do not give up. Jim and I will visit the frequented dens of the traders tomorrow, and with Quobit's help we can cover more investigative grounds."

"I am tired, still not 100 percent healthy with these very long days on Aralia," said Deacon. "I will say good night to you. I'm in no mood for arguing."

Jim stood guard while Gem recharged the silicon batteries and Quobit slept in front of the fireplace.

When Deacon arose the next day, neither Jim nor Gem nor Quobit were to be found. He thought about how weak he felt. No doubt the 15 percent stronger gravitational force had caused him to expend more energy than usual, and the strain was compounded by his having to slog through glutinous snow everywhere.

Suddenly the door swung open to expose Jim. "Travers was spotted by I'obo's men in an isolated hamlet six hundred miles from here in the hills of Glagn."

"Can we be sure of this, Jim?"

"A positive voice match by one of I'obo's most trusted men. I'obo communicated this directly to me. He states that this is a believable lead."

With that confirmation, Deacon packed quickly and the foursome fled Inglesiss in the *Heritage* for the nearest port to Glagn.

In Glagn

Leaving the *Heritage* after docking, the foursome traveled into a savage blizzard, the route well marked by fluorescent markers as Jim piloted a steady course, chewing through fifty-mile-an-hour winds that gusted to seventy. The sled was compact, seating for only four. Deacon saw only outlines of occasional rock outcrops and houses as the white curtain from the sled's movements obscured everything. Quobit was cramped in her space, her legs buckled into her chest. They had to trust the autopilot at times to put them back on course as the sled wobbled to and fro, chewing through gales. They made slow time until they changed course and had the breeze at their backs. The sled stabilized.

The wheezing sound of the motor threw him into a deep sleep and a creeping lack of confidence was overtaking him. He dreamed about Miram and Moonbeam. The next event he recalled was awakening as the motor roared into neutral and they parked outside and retreated into a small stone cabin. It was midday, but he was severely depressed by his inability to remain awake as heaviness in his legs slowed him. His afternoon slumber was disturbed by the noise of the Owlers' voices. They were in deliberation. "Never have I heard you two so noisy," he said. "What is the grave matter that should disturb my nap?"

Jim handed him a note. "We left you to visit a local constabulary headquarters. In doing so, we secured the locks to this place, as you and Quobit rested. While we were there, Master, a strange occurrence happened. There was a fracas in front of the police building. We all gathered to observe as some officers raced outside. Peace was restored quickly, except that when we returned to speak to our constable, who had been assisting us admirably, there was a sealed letter on his desk, addressed to Bothwen. Gem took the liberty of opening this correspondence, and we scurried about to find the bearer of this message. But the search was fruitless. We were discussing next steps, and in some disagreement I might add, when you arose."

Slowly Deacon walked toward Jim and took the paper from his hand. He recited the summons. "Travers of Aralia requests the presence of Deacon Coombs." Those were the only words. Deacon grew fearful.

The penetrating powers of Travers and the traders had been firmly established. Travers had found him again with no effort expended. His body tensed when he realized that he must go alone. He also realized that Travers might have found the other agents dispatched before him and disposed of them too. The Owlers approached as he crumpled the note.

Gem was firm. "We cannot let you go alone, sire. It contradicts the prime directive."

"You must obey me, and I say that you will remain here." An argument of logic and counterlogic ensued as Quobit listened.

"Gem, Jim," said Deacon, "Travers professes his innocence to the Aralian public. Follow my logic. If Travers wishes to confront me and eliminate me, how will that look? Cold-blooded murder won't support his plea of innocence. It will only be a confirmation of Travers as a murderer. Plus he has mapped our every move, one step ahead of us. We cannot travel in secrecy on Aralia—perhaps anywhere in this journey. We cannot keep anything privy. If he is innocent, as he proclaims, then I have the opportunity to interrogate him, hear firsthand his proof, and be judge and jury. These can be the only reasons he wants me. Eliminate me, and he will suffer worse consequences."

Quobit was concerned. "Schlegar informed me of the others before you. Their fates are unknown. They may have suffered death."

"I realize that, Quobit. Gem, Jim, what do you know of others before me? Did you and Jim travel with them?"

"No, sire." Gem spoke confidently. "We have no knowledge of the identities of the other investigators. You must understand that we are sworn to perform our duty only to you, so we will not allow you to meet Travers alone."

Deacon took charge. "There is another alternative. I have an idea to deceive Travers and allow you to carry out your mission. Gem, are there any Owlers similar to you in Glagn?"

"Yes, they are in the employ of the Alliance police. Jim and I also observed one such Owler in Inglesiss."

"Then contact I'obo for his assistance. Ask him to find an exact replacement for you and secure it for our team, Gem. Have it arrive soon in identical garb to yours. When Travers or his henchmen arrive to escort me to their hideout, they will see Jim and your identical replacement. They are also unaware of Quobit."

"Deacon, I can ride with Gem and track you using the voice recorder. It has long-range finding capabilities, does it not?"

Deacon nodded to Quobit as Jim piped up. "Perhaps I shall follow too. I will travel behind Gem and Quobit as backup."

"No, Jim. You must remain here with the duplicate Gem to contact I'obo if one of the three of us goes missing, so I'obo can launch rescue operations. This will also give the impression to Travers's men that I have traveled alone." Deacon demanded loyalty to his plan as Jim resisted, so finally he ordered Jim to obey. Gem departed to contact I'obo to secure the replacement and initiate the plan. Then the waiting game began.

Just as Deacon's metabolism fell into a lull the next morning, an Aralian, who could have passed for any Aralian with sloppy hair and naked foot bones, appeared at the doorstep of their cabin. Insisting on a consultation with Coombs, he said, "You and you alone must travel with me. The Owlers stay here under guard to signify your faith in Travers."

Deacon affirmed. The Aralian's comment confirmed that they did not know about Quobit or Gem's replacement.

In the hills of Glagn

When the time came, Deacon descended the stairs into the primitive vehicle, a quiver in his guts and anxiousness in his manner. Meanwhile, Gem, occupying a power sled with Quobit on board, was ready to follow. Deacon knew the risk. In the cruel weather of Aralia, few Owlers navigated, for they were prone to freezing and ruining their batteries should the sled become disabled and the heater disengaged.

Inside his power vehicle, the two Aralians sat in front while he felt jailed in the back. There was no way to determine if these were the same two Aralians that had followed him in Inglesiss. They both required haircuts; he could not see the eyes of either through the drooping hair. It was too late to turn back. They sped to Travers.

The rubbery black pontoon glided on a cushion of air. It wasn't long before Deacon had lost all sense of direction. He tried to probe the minds of these Aralians but found no energy to receive. Eventually they left the flat-lying lowlands to enter a winter wonderland of high-relief elevations. Here in the alpine terrain, he noticed factories with disgusting black and yellow chemical emanations—the first factories he had seen on Aralia. This gave him a good excuse to look out the back for Gem and Quobit's sled and inquire of his escorts what products were manufactured there. Although he tried to perpetuate a conversation, the Aralians ignored him, but he persisted with questions to keep contact with Gem open. Snow flew up from the back of the craft. No sign of any followers.

The probability of Gem capturing his voice diminished as the Aralian silence pervaded.

They soared over hills and gullies for hours, Deacon poorly adjusting to the rolling motion of the craft, praying for a rest stop to relieve his pangs of nausea. Instead the Aralians administered some gum to him to relieve his ill effects. He continued to attempt to make idle chat to provide Quobit with a reasonable chance to follow. The craft decelerated as it approached the mouth of a narrow ravine leading to an escarpment. Then it powered its way up the slope, Deacon being jostled about in the tiny quarters. As the sled accelerated, Deacon became aware of the constant drone inside as he reclined to lessen the jostling. The driver switched into an even higher gear as they passed through a veil of foggy snow. The computer issued a warning just as the sled bumped, and bumped again.

One of the occupants leaned back to Deacon to say, "Avalanche. They are frequent in these hills at this time of year. We must hurry or be buried alive."

Quobit! Gem! he thought. Deacon strained in consternation to see any signs, but outside was a furious white hell. Although his companion was only an Owler, Deacon could not help but fear for Gem's safety. The network of steel and wires and logic had become his closest link to sanity. He had actually developed a fondness for the Owler twosome. *Funny, is this what my life has come to? To having genuine, strong feelings for Owlers? Is this evolution? An excellent question to answer in a future dissertation of my memoirs.* And he cared for Quobit. He silently prayed for their safety.

The computer pilot thrust the carriage in sharp angled turns to the left, then the right, avoiding debris. The seatbelts cut into his stomach and shoulders, momentarily scraping against his neck wound. Higher and higher they climbed, the inclination of the vehicle growing steep, until finally a magnificent view of the scenery was served over a sea of gray and white clouds below as they leveled off.

The sled sped at incredible speeds toward the apex. Then, with no warning, they veered right into thick woods, the first forest that Deacon had seen on this planet. The vegetation consisted largely of contorted trees with spindly branches reaching into the heavens, resembling the pines of Orchardy. The snow was covered with beds of green needles. After more hours of silence, the craft halted in front of an ominous gaping hole in the side of a sheer cliff. Deacon stumbled as he exited, motioning away any assistance for help. But the twosome pushed him forward toward the entrance. Inside the adit, a warm buffer of air hit him. The breeze carried a fragrance that smelled like fresh strawberries. A narrow tunnel led into a massive central cavern with a series of smaller caves around the perimeter. Here hundreds of Aralians gathered to stare at him, a few other alien types in the background. His entrance triggered a silence. He was wobbly after the backbreaking ride, feeling much like a spy among guerrillas as he eyed many of the troops, marching forward step by step into danger. One rather hefty-looking fellow strode forward to greet him. He carried more weight than Deacon had seen on any other Aralian, with a huge gut hanging over his belt. "Villya, Deacon Coombs. So honored that you accepted our invitation."

"What invitation?" Deacon said. He added a reluctant "Villya."

"I am Chebby Eaves, called Chubby by your Earthling trader friends for obvious reasons."

Deacon questioned his decision to come but decided to play it all business. "Thank you. I only came because I was told that I would have a meeting with Travers."

"Yes, you shall, but let us converse first."

As he offered a rebuttal, the portly, pigeon-toed man turned and led Deacon through the crowd of Aralians. It seemed as though he and Eaves were parting a sea, as the onlookers all stood back to let them pass. They entered into another large cavern filled with the odors of food. From here Deacon was escorted to a small, cramped, low-ceilinged cave with only enough seating for six comfortably. There he and Chubby quietly sipped tea. The lighting was dim, provided by a small fire in the middle of the room. A small fan directed the smoke out of the cave.

Travers

In a skittery voice, Chubby said, "Travers is here. He will join us shortly. First I must warn you that his health fails him. We do everything we can to keep him alive."

"How can I be sure that this is really Travers?"

"There is no need to keep a voice scanner secret from us. If you have one, use it! We wish you to be certain that this is Travers before he recounts his tale as truth."

Deacon unzipped his parka and extracted the small device and connected it to his handheld. As he did so, a small, withered, silver-haired Aralian entered. Where the being's skin was exposed it was severely wrinkled, as on the multiple-digited hands and on the top of the head and torso. The eyes were a deep red, protruding abnormally out of their sockets just as Temisori's did. While other Aralians spoke in crisp tones, this one's words were slurred.

"Yourrrr quest for me has ended."

Deacon turned the voice scanner on. He examined this being for the scar on the thigh and found it; a finger was stunted, as Schlegar had described. The chip in his foot was obvious. Deacon initiated the conversation. "It seems that you have the best of me, Travers, since I struggled to find you while you sat back and waited for your moment of contact. Your spy network is very efficient."

Travers chuckled while Chubby roared with laughter. Chubby grinned, his shiny white teeth exposed through fur, and he answered Deacon as he shook the mop on his head. "Quite accidental, my dear fellow. We wish our spy network to be so efficient, but we discovered you quite by accident. You see, Deacon Coombs, it was not you that our comrades recognized at the port of entry in Froora, but rather your traveling companions, the two Owlers. This model of Owler is well known throughout the universe as the ultimate form of security on Earth, the top of the line in quality. They are purchased even by other races, including Aralians. So, naturally, our curiosity was piqued."

Chubby was animated, gesturing with his arms. "Why, their companion must be someone of importance. Who are they guarding? Who is this innocuous-looking little man? Our records showed that the innocent being we unmasked was Bothwen. But why should two Owlers of such weighty credentials accompany an administrator? Imagine our surprise when sources on Earth informed us that Bothwen had only a neoteric history, entered into logs recently. Our investigation into this matter continued. It was the night when you followed our spies that we found you out to be Deacon Coombs.

Up to that point, we thought you to be Bothwen and we planned to capture you to obtain your true identity. So you see, it was quite by accident that we discovered that you are no other than the detective of universal fame Deacon Coombs." Chubby and Travers snorted wildly.

"Then, once we had your true persona, Travers and I assumed whom you are searching for. So you see, we found you quite by accident with some loose deductions."

A great relief fell over Deacon, for if this was the case, he surmised they might not know of his visit to Brebouillis, or of Quobit's presence. Deacon was blunt. "I have been commissioned by the High Council to interrogate Travers with respect to the recent deaths of Como and Geor, and the mishap of the *Sleigher*."

"Ah, can there be no rest for me?" Travers sobbed as he sat down, crossed his legs, and motioned Deacon to sit beside him.

"Let me be honest with you, Travers," Deacon said. "The Alliance has good reason to suspect you of wrongdoings, since Geor was preparing your retrial and Como publicly blasphemed you, and you commanded the *Sleigher*." Deacon addressed him with the firm mandate of the Alliance behind him.

"Not g-g-g . . . guilty!" Travers replied sharply.

Chubby intervened. "The people of Aralia have always respected Travers. He has served as the head of the Union of Space Traders with dignity. He is innocent of all these manufactured charges; he does not support the blaggards who scar the reputation of the union. Travers is bred from a long line of distinguished members of his family."

Chubby moved closer to Deacon. "We traders are a rough lot. You have to be to spend that much time in space battling bad weather, unsavory types, and ruthless traders. We Aralians are a particularly tough breed because the rest of the Alliance depends on us. The union was not designed for weak stomachs and bleeding hearts. We are all a crusty lot. Travers is no exception from his days in travel. But the governing board of the traders' union has never sanctioned killing, smuggling, theft, arms sales, and abetting insurgents. The traders who carry out these acts are in our disfavor, and Travers and I fight this element within. To further accuse Travers of the murders of Como and Geor—this is ludicrous."

"And how will you convince me of this?"

"You are a deee . . . detective. You shall have your prooooof." He paused for effect before adding, "If you d-d-d-d . . . dare." Travers petrified Deacon with the last three words as he raised his head and gazed directly into Deacon's eyes. Deacon used the voice decoder again to confirm Travers's identity.

Chubby spoke with respect. "Travers's speech has been impaired since his last voyage on the *Sleigher*, but the mind is sharp. His health could be better, but he has stamina. He has aged beyond his years because of the trauma of the *Sleigher's* voyage, but Travers will not die until he has proven his innocence."

"What did Travers mean when he said, 'if you dare'?"

Chubby grinned and then whispered in Deacon's ear. "The devil has materialized in our world. Yes, Coombs, the devil. An alien so powerful that we hide here in Glagn in fear from him. However, Travers has seen him and has a plan to free himself of the charges and smoke the devil out of his wretched hiding place." Deacon's eyes were wide as he looked back at Chubby. Chubby smirked. "Yes, yes, I say the truth; he has seen the devil himself. And Deacon Coombs, I know this is ironic, considering your mission, but we desperately require your help."

Deacon felt glacial. "My help? Such a twist of fate. I am employed by the Alliance. Now you offer me employment with the traders?"

"No. You are commissioned by the Alliance to investigate matters of universal disturbance. Travers knows the shortest path to the truth. Join us and discover it."

While Chubby continued with his logic, Deacon decided to read Travers's mind. His thoughts were gibberish; it was difficult to determine what ailed him through his pangs of depression.

"Chubby, I cannot work for both sides. That is illogical."

"On Earth you have a saying that a man is innocent until proven guilty. Are you looking for the facts to convict Travers, or are you investigating this case unbiased to arrive at an unprejudiced decision?"

"The prosecution prepares its case against the accused, and I am employed by the prosecution. That is the employment that I have accepted."

"Then I put it to you again, Coombs. Can you not allow Travers to present his evidence to you? To enable you to judge him?"

The room filled with the scent of burning waxes, released by orange and red flames. Deacon turned to see Chubby taking a notebook out of a pouch. In it were small sketches in crayon. As Deacon stared at it, strong vibrations bombarded Deacon's mind as if Travers were trying to communicate with him.

"To begin with," Chubby said as he shuffled closer to Deacon, "it is necessary to go back six years ago. Since Travers has difficulty explaining the tale, I will assist him."

"I object," said Deacon, "for I have been sent here to interrogate Travers." Chubby refuted, waved his arms, and ignored Deacon's plea. Deacon sized up the paunchy man called Chubby. His eyes, like all Aralians', were hidden in a poorly combed explosion of white hair. His hands moved freely to and fro, gesticulating on cue with every word. A furry pot belly hung out over the cloth of his lower torso. Chubby's voice sounded as one of a great teller of tales, accenting key words for the effect of overtures, an actor overplaying his role.

His attention turned now to Travers. There was little flesh on his bones; his skinny arms and legs stayed clasped by his side. Travers's sorrowful beet-red eyes once again gazed upon Deacon. Chubby was ready to recite the tale. Deacon finally nodded to agree, and he then sat back and relaxed, sipping his drink. *If only Landrew could see me now!* he thought.

Into the
Intriguing Web

Court in session

"Before we commence," said Deacon, "may I inquire what your intentions were with me, if your men had captured me in the city?"

Chubby replied with enthusiasm. "Why, to bring you back here to this place to force you to listen to Travers's tale."

"And what changed your mind to make you think that I would come peaceably?"

"Time."

"Time?"

"Yes. You provided us the time to complete the research on your character. Travers and I decided that you would reason to accept our invitation. Our investigation illustrated integrity, curiosity, and a quest for justice. In short, we trust you."

That was the cue for Deacon to burst out in exchange with "And I trust you." But he remained silent, not providing them the satisfaction. *And how many others have heard the tale?* he wondered. He deferred to ask. Chubby, meanwhile, uncomfortable in the quiescence, began the tale, starting with the story of the trading ship of six years ago that was forced out of the demarcated trading routes. The disabled vessel, powerless in the proximity of fierce electrical storms, glided through great dust clouds to encounter and land on a planet called Nix. Chubby described in detail much of what Deacon had witnessed in the library tape on Earth with Landrew. Travers sat silently verifying Chubby's tale with a frequent curt, stuttered acknowledgment.

"Your detail might infer that you were on that voyage."

"I only quote Travers. He documented this incident very well." Chubby placed a monitor in Deacon's lap.

"A fright-t-t . . . ful experience to see a world so h-h-h-harsh."

"The Alliance informed me of this incident but said that the members of this expedition had received a rehabilitation of the mind and were injected with some mild mind-altering drug to erase what they witnessed."

"Travers is and always will be a loyal member to the Alliance," Chubby said boastfully. "His family is well respected. There was no need to brainwash him."

"I witnessed tapes of Nix that you created. It must have been a shocking experience." Travers affirmed this by bobbing his head up and down. Chubby waited until Travers had completed his gestures. Deacon then entered Travers's mind, shifting gears as Lyanna had taught him. Deacon already possessed an element of fear, but he shivered as terror lunged back into his mind. Discrete thoughts were almost impossible to decipher, but it was the total pattern that seized his brain with a surge of horror.

As he cringed, the paralyzing trance of fear was broken as Chubby shook his arm. "Has the tea had disagreed with you?"

"No. Um, please continue."

Chubby Eaves started speaking again. "Now let me address the rebellious incidents that have occurred during Travers's reign. There have been incited riots, smuggling of arms and drugs, the underground black market, and the holding of goods for ransom. Aralians, by our honest nature, do not participate in such activities, so it is no surprise that all the culprits to date have been non-Aralians. We will lay open our records to you at the Trade Union Headquarters when you return to Inglessis. You and your Owlers can scrutinize to your content."

Deacon felt suddenly comforted by the words "when you return to Inglessis." But what game were they playing?

"The one reason the headquarters of the trade union has been located on Aralia is to preserve the truthful documentation of the history of the trade union. An Aralian has on numerous occasions served as head of this union. We make judicious leaders, you know."

"You do not have to convince me of the truthful nature of Aralians, just the innocence of one Aralian, known as Travers."

Chubby raised his voice. "We all have tried hard to put an end to these disgraceful events. The criminals are usually dealt with from the inside; that is, we deal out selective punishment from within the trade union. In recent times our investigations and policing have failed us. I omit the deaths of Geor and Como, since Travers and I know not the details of these. This was not of our doing."

"Then by your omission I should presume innocence?"

Chubby ignored the comment. Instead he plowed on by elaborating on the self-policing system and how punishments were determined. Then he described each of the infractions, stating how each one had been dealt with by the union. "The charges against Travers caught us by surprise; the verdict did not."

Something was drastically wrong. Why had this vendetta been launched by the Alliance against Travers? Or was Deacon being brainwashed? Manipulated? He catapulted a second sortie into Travers's mind, but it failed to connect. The dark black walls now shimmered in the pink glow of high, flickering flames as Chubby added wax fuel to the fire. Deacon hoped that the burning waxes were not placing him under a trance. Chubby said, "Travers must take responsibility for these irresponsible actions of traders. On that we agree. However, the burden of the trial and his journey to Nix has taken its toll on his health, as you can witness. We cannot turn him over to authorities until his health recovers."

"Tell me about the disappearance of the *Sleigher*." Deacon was anxious to hear about this rather than past treasonable events.

Chubby inhaled and then sighed. "The *Sleigher* and her crew were taken on a torturous journey. Travers is the only sane member who can relate the incident. Even to him, the events are blurry."

"That'ssssactly what it was like—a d-d-d . . . dream. I remember the d-d-disc at . . . Jabu. The neckst thing, I was back at Aralia. Most of that journey is a bu-bu-bu-blur. Though I 'member a derreem. Bad derrrr . . . eam."

"What do you remember of this blurred dream?"

Chubby spoke for him. "Travers remembers visiting Nix, but it was different than the first accidental trip. The inhabitants, according to his memory, were more organized into tribes. They were also armed, as was captured in the footage. That footage also vividly portrays their raw savageness.

"Travers remembers wandering aimlessly alone, in search of his crew. When he finally located them, they were wild-eyed, crazy. He tried to reason with them; then he heard an eerie, piercing laugh that numbed his body. It spoke to him, but he cannot recall the words. The dream repeated itself over and over until he awakened at the Vesper station. It is all in the report that I gave you. Please, Mister Coombs, examine this report as truth."

"Was there anything else different about Nix?"

"Mister Coombs, to Travers the trip to Nix was only a dream until we discovered the tape and realized that he and the others had physically journeyed there. Surely Landrew briefed you on the existence of this tape."

While Chubby was occupied with elaboration of the tape, Deacon blanked out everything to concentrate on Travers. Suddenly he found Travers walking endlessly, searching for his crew amid the omnipresent stench. He was now reading him easily. Travers's thoughts were in sync with Chubby's recital. The landscape was barren of vegetation with few permanent streams. Everywhere he turned were throngs of disgusting beings. No soil had developed, leaving a savage, rocky landscape to traverse—an arduous feat for a bare bone–footed Aralian. The feel of stabbing rocks cut into his bones like red-hot irons, and Deacon experienced this sensation as Travers relived it. The natives began to mock Travers, taunting him as he searched desperately for his crew. He came upon a group in prayer and watched them as they worked themselves into a frenzy with chants that forced him to flee. Deacon felt his despair.

"Deacon, are you ill again?" Chubby asked, disturbing the trance.

"No, just tired. Please continue. I want to know how you rescued Travers from the hospital in Froora."

"Oh, we were afraid that he would be sent to the hospital on Brebouillis, never to be seen again, for the security there is beyond our best rescue efforts. So I gambled at Froora."

"Gambled?"

"Let me only say that we have comrades in Froora, and Travers, well, he does have the ability to plant thoughts in other's minds. We were lucky to catch a shift change where there were no Owlers on duty in his hallway. If you wish, I shall detail the escape in notes for you."

"Thanks. I would like to have the details and the names of the individuals who assisted in the escape. How do you know that Travers is safe here?"

Chubby opened his arms wide. "These caves are proximal to his hometown, where the people don't believe the conspiracy charges. The caves are isolated at this time of year, difficult to find. The insulation prevents penetration by voice decoders and scanners. Avalanches are very frequent, and intruders are few. None get by our posted sentries."

"Did your sentries set off the avalanche?"

"Yes, a necessary precaution."

"And the fate of the sled behind us?"

"It was unharmed but could not pass. This precaution would not have been necessary had you kept your word to journey alone."

"The instructions were not to lead a posse here, but to follow the Owlers' prime directive—to ensure my safety."

"Explanation accepted. Deacon, you see beside you a part of the tale that the Alliance is not in possession of at this time. Travers has prematurely aged—the stuttering, the loss of hair, the withering of the skin, and the deterioration of the bones of the feet. He looks much different than when he was last seen at the hospital."

"Yes, I noticed. What has caused this?"

Chubby was adamant. "The strenuous trip to Nix. Travers experiences mental lapses too. You must help us, Deacon Coombs. The four other executives of the Union of Space Traders arrive within hours, and I want to assure them that you are investigating the incidents with an open mind. I want to assure them that you will not pass judgment on Travers until you have personally examined the facts."

Deacon thought to himself how he had graduated from pawn and spy of the Alliance to respected servant of the traders' union. Was this progress or betrayal?

Chubby extended the plea. "You have top-notch Owlers as security. You have a free passport to travel to wherever you desire. You must relay any information discovered about the deaths of Como and Geor to us. The trade union can help you. If you and I and Travers combine our forces and pool our knowledge, we can catch the devil who is behind these ails. Of this I am sure." Chubby leaned over to grip him on his arm. "Of this we are sure."

Deacon refused to be intimidated. "The information that I gather is for my discretion only. I don't report to you."

"Then do yourself the biggest favor you can."

"What?"

"Take Travers back to Nix!"

"What!?"

"You must discover what happened there. What happened to age the crew? How was the *Sleigher* diverted there? He longs to return but can't with security so tight. You, Deacon Coombs, can arrange it."

"Absurd. And how do you know that I journey there?"

"Where else could Landrew point you? Where else could we point you?" He leaned into Deacon and whispered, "The devil lives there! I swear it."

Deacon grew impatient with references to the devil. "The answer lies here, with Travers. I wish to interrogate him alone, for he alone holds the key to my next destination. Many questions remained unanswered."

"Escort him to Nix and you will have your answers, Coombs. You have the only vessel with clearance to Nix in the Alliance! All others will be denied."

"Chubby, even if I agree, I cannot get Travers through security."

"Yes, you can! Alliance security forces look for a sturdy Aralian, not a withered, skinny weakling such as Travers. The only recent transmissions of Travers still show him as vigorous and sturdy. This aging happened after his escape from the hospital, as I said."

"We may not travel to Nix," said Deacon.

"Then you make a tragic mistake. The devil is there." Chubby arose. "You must go there. You must! Without you witnessing this monster in the flesh, Travers will have no credibility with the High Council, and the High Council will have no proof of its existence."

Chubby waved his index finger at him. "We know this monster lives there."

"Chubby, there is no devil in the flesh. I grow tired of your references to some . . . some . . . some devil."

Chubby grew animated. "Listen, Coombs! Aralians do not commit suicide, so Como did not. He was murdered in cold blood, as you say on Earth. There was on this planet that night a blackness of the heart that Aralians have never felt before. Our spirits were collectively suppressed and shattered. Como was murdered. That is the opinion of Landrew, Travers, Chubby Eaves, Dreveney, I'obo—all Aralians. Oh yes, I know that I'obo assists you. I know of your visit to his abode. I swear the answer is on Nix, Deacon. Listen to me."

"And how do you know? Tell me."

"Travers knows. He told me when he recited his dream, only it is not a dream. Only you have the clearance to voyage there. I beg of you, for the safety of all mankind, take Travers there. It was there that he met up with his worst nightmare. Please, Deacon." Chubby was shaking. "You must believe me that this thing murdered our Como."

"Can the computer recall the exact coordinates of his landing sites?"

"Yes, they are logged."

"I will consider your request but require some answers first." Deacon was growing fearful. How much of this conversation was being controlled by Travers?

His fear turned into shock when Travers read his mind and then leaned over to whisper in his ear, "None of ittt. I don't control yuuuu . . . you." Deacon motioned to Chubby to exit.

"I will question Travers alone."

"No. I shall remain. I am Travers's most trusted advisor, and Travers finds it painful to speak with his affliction. Surely you must feel his pain."

"Then any dealings with you and Travers are terminated."

"You must allow me to remain," said Chubby. "I must remind you that your safe return can only be guaranteed by me."

"Are you threatening me, Chubby? That would be out of character for an Aralian. Good bluff. But I will take my chances that traders do not employ murder. I believe that you will guarantee my safe return since, as you stated earlier, I am the only ticket to Nix and you promised to lay open your trading records to me and the Owlers. I also have you to thank for sparing my Owler from the avalanche. You demonstrated compassion."

"Cocky Earthling," Chubby said under his breath.

"Before you leave, the Alliance dispatched others before me to find Travers. Have you and Travers briefed anyone else on this tale about Nix and your so-called devil?"

"No."

The answer surprised Deacon. He took his word at face value, but not without staring him down. "Please leave us." Chubby delayed and stared at the detective while Deacon relished in this bout of dominance. This was Aralia, light-years from home, and a case of higher authority clearly belonged to him. Chubby eventually broke the glare and departed. "Travers, I will place my trust in you implicitly if you will trust me. To this let us swear before we commence. I will not divulge any information that you impart to me. In return, you swear the same. If you agree, nod your head and hug me in the solemn Aralian custom."

Travers hesitated for a second, so Deacon said, "I am convinced that there is no other way to the truth. I have calculated the risks, and I am prepared to accept them." He had other commentary at the ready, but Travers extended his lean, cold, bony hand to shake. Then the little general stood and hugged Deacon tightly in the Aralian trust hug, one arm around the back of Deacon's neck and the other around his lower waist as Deacon did the same. After signifying their friendship, Deacon moved to position himself across the burning fire from Travers.

"I know of your unusual powers of the mind and that you have the ability to supplant thoughts into others. Did you sway members of the Union of Space Traders to vote for you as their leader?"

Travers pondered his answer, avoiding eye contact, and then he replied, "Shame . . . fu-fu-fully, yes, I now admit tha . . . tttttt I misused my powers to influence members of the union to support me. I d-d-d-d . . . did not want to. I had to." Travers sniffled.

Deacon realized that with all their logic, all their myths, these Aralians were sneaky people. He also knew that they did not consider it shameful or embarrassing to weep in public. Rather, to them it was recognized as a display of emotion necessary to survive. Therefore, it was only Deacon who felt uncomfortable as Travers continued to weep upon his confession. To recommence, he asked, "Why?"

"I thu-thu-th . . . ought that it was I who could res-s-s . . . store dignity and honor to the traders' union. It ful . . . filled a lifelong du-du-dream."

"Does Chubby know?"

"Yes, and three others."

"Did you ever wish Como dead? Wish it in your mind?"

"No. He was m-m-m . . . my hero."

"When you experience these mental lapses, what do you feel?"

"Deep ancks-s-s . . . iety. Light-headedness."

Deacon immediately knew where to venture. "Your father is a doctor, is he not?"

"Yes."

"Have you ever discussed these problems with him?"

"He s-s-s . . . scorns me."

"But you are his only son. Can't you go and beg for help mentally, psychologically, to survive?"

"No. He will not lis . . . ten to me. The Alliance has tu-tu-tu . . . turned him against me."

"Will you attempt to reach your father if I ask you to?"

"No. That door is closed."

"I want to hear from you about the last trip to Nix."

Travers slowly recited his dream at length in his mind, taking over an uninterrupted hour while Deacon relaxed and mentally recorded every syllable. Travers did not recall the landing of the ship as such. His initial memories were of wandering about the planet amid rocks and carcasses. The *Sleigher* was vaguely distant to him, its shape on the horizon. Then he recalled the shouts of the natives, savage beasts, their fists shaking at him, their mouths frothing with foam, many throwing down stones and rocks in front of him to block his path.

"It was so dif-if— . . . ficult for me to move about." He turned the bottoms of his feet upward; numerous chips, deep furrows, and scars dotted the glossy white finish of his underfeet.

He finally found his mates before a group of dancing savages blocked his view. He escaped, only to come upon a group in prayer. The recorder was switched on, and it was this scene that he recorded, of the native firing a modern laser gun. "Fr-fr-frightened, I ran for my

life. It was then that I found my crew, allll . . . lll raving luna . . . tics."
He shook as he spoke.

It was all vague after that. He dreamed of the savages drooling
on him, pressing their horrible, smelly, greasy, matted hair against
his white fur. He remembered screaming as a fire lit in his body, the
depths of his soul aflame in an inferno, him not knowing entirely
what was happening. Then the *Sleigher* docked at Aralia.

"I don't understand how a ship can be transported across the
universe without a Vesper station," said Deacon.

"Nor I," said Travers.

"Who is Maretz?"

Travers seemed puzzled. "I do not know Maretz."

Deacon could not read his mind. It contained undeterminable
thoughts. "Travers, I must know the relationship between you and
Maretz of Jabu, and the plot you hatched with him." Travers was
silent; his mind empty. "I know not of Maretz."

Deacon was confused at this development. *Why do you wish to
return to Nix?* Deacon asked without speaking. Travers paused for a
minute, but it was obvious that his breathing rate had increased.

"I have told you all th-th-that I know and . . . d-d-d what have
you learned? We, you and-d-d I, we must go to Nix. The power to
take a ship is there. The mur-r-r . . . rderer of Como is there. The
devil is-s-s there!"

"The devil. First Chubby and now you. You have seen
this . . . devil?"

Travers froze. His lips trembled. Bolts of fear tore apart Deacon's
mind, the source obviously Travers's thoughts. The translator could
not interpret thoughts, but Deacon did intercept the word *Nix* over
and over. Then a dramatic thought surfaced from within Travers.
"You would really go there without me?"

"The Uscher p-p-p . . . power of Earthlings. We have to stop
exp-p-p . . . pending energy by speaking and bat our thoughts back
and . . . d-d-d-d-d forth instead. I don't stutter in my thoughts. But
yes." Travers increased the volume of his voice and stared back. "I
willlll go to Nix without you! I must do this . . . s-s-s! If you don't
take me with you and your Owlers, I sh-sh-sh-shall make other
plans."

Deacon weighed the odds of whether he would be handicapping himself by taking Travers with him, or if it was a blessing, for a trip with Travers would be the last thing that Landrew or Schlegar would expect. Maybe the last thing that the devil would expect. That was what he had been about to say to Travers earlier, when they were bonding. The path to tough solutions sometimes involves the most unpredictable route. That was the reason to do it—create the unexpected.

Chubby returned, and the first thing that he did was check the health of his dear friend with crude instruments that measured his pulse and bodily functions. Travers hugged Chubby, and as he did so, Deacon admired the caring friendship between the two. When the embrace was released, Deacon confronted them. "I am the only one who can get Travers into the forbidden zone. He has convinced me that we should journey there, but before I commit us to this insane and risky mission, I would like to discuss the arrangements."

Chubby jumped up and down as his belly bounced. "Delightful, delightful! This will be our best chance to solve the murders of Como and Geor. This is our best chance to prove to the High Alliance Council that the devil himself exists and has invaded our space. This is our best chance to prove Travers's innocence."

When Deacon began to speak, he deflated Chubby's enthusiasm. "There are terms. One: Travers travels with me and the two Owlers and my assistant. Two: I have no obligation to you or the traders' union to report back to you of my findings on Nix. I will be the sole judge of who receives my official report. I am in the employ of the Alliance, so for certain it will be received by Landrew and perhaps by the trade union, if I deem it appropriate and believe that you will not misuse the data. Three: our meeting here today must not be revealed to the other members of the traders' union or anyone else. As far as you are concerned, Chubby, from the time that Travers enters my care, you must deny all knowledge of his whereabouts. His life and mine will depend on it. I have had one attempt on my life already, and it is of the utmost importance to keep the whereabouts of Travers and me secretive. My Owlers kill to protect me, and I will issue orders to kill anyone who threatens us. Lastly, you must admit to me right now that the evidence that I uncover may very well incriminate Travers. There still remains the possibility that the periods of blackouts and dreams may represent subconscious criminal acts. Grant all of these terms, or the deal will not transpire."

A surge of self-confidence swelled in Deacon's body as he enjoyed the role of titan here on this distant planet. There were uncertainties that had to be clarified before a final commitment to travel to Nix. As he sat down beside the fire, the warmth made him reflect on Lyanna, but the comforting moments that she provided seemed so long ago. Mentally, he screamed a prayer for her, realizing the futility that it would not touch her. Regardless, it had fulfilled a need.

Meanwhile, Deacon bore the brunt of a long, irritating argument in the Aralian dialect that carried on for twenty minutes between Chubby and Travers. Finally the two looked at him. "Mr. Coombs," said Chubby, "how about taking with you one more voyager, a man who can serve as added protection?"

"I sensed this topic would arise, and the answer is absolutely not. Chubby, you will remain here. I am risking all by taking Travers into my confidence—a gamble that endangers my mission. If the Alliance discovers this, I am doomed, for their trust in me will be shattered. At least I have three other allies who are uninfluenced by emotion."

Travers and Chubby conferred again, and Deacon witnessed Travers invoke his authority as he pointed his finger at Chubby. This time they ended in agreement. "Okay, I will not journey with you. But Travers knows how to contact me, and you must do this if the journey becomes perilous and you need the help of me or the traders to rescue you."

Deacon was pleased. "There is another issue on my mind now that the great debate is settled. Please, let's sit and discuss. The High Council under Geor was preparing a retrial. I have read the transcripts from the initial trial, which deduced that unless new damaging evidence was uncovered it would be impossible to convict Travers. But yet Como spoke to all Aralians of convincing evidence the night that he died. Do you have any idea what Como may have uncovered to publicly announce the premature guilt of Travers? Obviously something that Geor didn't know, for Geor informed his mate, Geolo, that there was a lack of evidence."

The two conferred in ancient Aralian, leaving Deacon at a rude disadvantage until he said, "Ahem. You are speaking too fast for the translator to function."

"I was greatly sur-r-r-r-r . . . prised," said Travers, "that the p-p-p . . . prosecution did not uncover one of the best kept secrets before the fir-r-r . . . rst trial."

Secrets revealed

Chubby spoke to Deacon in a whisper. "Over the past few years, the trade union has lost a number of powerful, important, deadly arms shipments."

"How many?"

"Over thirty."

Deacon was aghast. "What? Lost—is that what you said? Lost? How? Where?"

"Mostly new-technology laser guns, some long-range neutron bombs, a few photon-dextron bombs, caches of small, handheld laser arms, and molecular disruptors—the kind that can go undetected."

Deacon didn't know what to say for a moment. Finally he said, "And these are the very same weapons shipments that the Alliance believes the traders' union has sold to subversive groups and rebel causes?"

As Chubby nodded in affirmation, Deacon probed Travers to feel a blast of deep guilt. Chubby was adamant. "These shipments were not traded or sold to subversives, as the Alliance would have you believe. Rather, they just disappeared without a trace. The traders' union has done everything, examined every possible lead, to locate these arms. It is obvious to us that a conspiracy has evolved within the union to facilitate these crimes. Geor's son was killed while investigating these stolen arms as an undercover member of the security division. Accordingly, Geor held Travers responsible for his death because it was most likely one of our traders who murdered him. The truth, Mister Coombs, is that whoever stole these shipments had Geor's son murdered. Como discovered this fact recently, that these arms shipments were missing, and informed Travers and me that the traders would be further investigated. In a brief meeting that Travers and I had with him, before the last voyage of the *Sleigher*, Como turned against us completely."

"So Geor's son made an important discovery about the shipments or was closing in on the truth? That's why he was killed?"

"Yes, at least that is what Travers and I firmly believe. He had the reputation of being a very thorough investigator. Also, he sent a message to Travers before he died indicating that we had serious conspirators inside our union, although the arms were not referenced in the document."

Deacon turned to Travers. "While on Nix, did you see any of these stolen shipments?"

"No and yes. The hand weapon that the savage f-f-f-f . . . fired probably was . . . s-s-s in the shipment. We have the serial num-m-m-m . . . bers of all the weapons, so we can identify them if we find them."

Chubby spoke up again. "Some have remote locating devices embedded in them. Now you see the importance of Nix. It could be that the savages found the caches. I think an exhaustive search on Nix is in order for Travers, and we believe the weapons cache is there."

"Help me, Chubby, to understand something. These powerful weapons you described are tightly monitored in the hands of local security forces and Alliance forces. They are manufactured at tightly secured plants. Why didn't the Alliance transport these weapons to their new owners? Why didn't the new owners pick them up at the plant? Why did the trade union do this?"

"Until recently, the trade union had a long-term contract to transport all these arms. In transport, we hired consulting third-party security forces with impeccable histories for oversight. That all changed recently once the rumor circulated that arms were being sold to subversive groups."

"Were they stolen from the manufacturing sites themselves, or en route from trade vessels?"

"Stolen from plant sites, en route, at loading docks, and from various points before reaching the new owners by a wide variety of well-planned criminal acts. Travers and his crew witnessed Nicosians with weapons. The weapon that Travers recorded being discharged may well be one from a crewman of the *Sleigher*. Or it may be part of the missing arms. We just don't know. All we know is that it is of recent vintage, and that warrants a return to Nix for further investigation."

"So the possibility lingers that someone might be storing a large arsenal of arms on Nix? That's what you two think? Do you and Travers have any idea who might be concocting this elaborate, ambitious undertaking?"

They hesitated, and Deacon couldn't read their thoughts. After a prolonged pause, they both said no.

"So we are about to walk into the den of evil itself?"

"You need to take the utmost precautions to protect our leader," Chubby said, "and naturally yourself. Travers and I are so surprised that with all effort the Alliance is expending they have not uncovered that the trade union altered shipment records to protect us until we have had a chance to uncover the culprits ourselves. It is possible that Geor's son discovered this, or uncovered a clue to their misplacement and was murdered for it, or maybe discovered the exact rigged records. We suspect that he passed this clue to Como, which may have cost him his life. Understand, Coombs, that the number-one reason we rigged the records was to give the criminals a false sense of comfort while we investigated."

Deacon couldn't refuse the jab. "So truthful, honest, reliable Aralians rigged—that was the word you used Chubby, *rigged*—the shipment records to hide the facts of the missing arms. No. Can't be true. Is it, Chubby? Aralians lying? The entire human race believes that Aralians are incapable of telling a lie."

Chubby did not make excuses. "All in a day's work." He smiled back at Deacon.

"A most unlikely team we make."

Travers rose to excuse himself. "I am tir-r-r . . . ed. There will be time to discuss matters dur-r-r-r . . . ing the trip."

Deacon was irritated. "Not so soon. You both mentioned the devil numerous times in this conversation. What did you mean by that? You seem to have omitted that important part of the saga during your wanderings around Nix. I want facts of his existence, if indeed you have any."

Chubby was offended. "Do not mock us. I am a devoutly religious man, and so is Travers, and our Aralian religious doctrine defines the prophecy of such a mind-bending evil that will descend on Aralia and our universe in this *yarted*."

"*Yarted?*"

"Our religion is divided into clearly defined segments. Each is called a *yarted*. Maybe I let my religion carry me too far, but it is not superstition, it is beliefs. We are in the *yarted* of the Crouse, the one where he is predicted to come, the one filled with disruptive events and evils. Our religion requires us to accept these as challenges and overcome them to become stronger in our faith. You are on Aralia. Please do not mock our beliefs."

"And you, Travers?"

"In my nightmares and du-du-du . . . reams, I see him, the creature of ecks-s-s . . . treme evil with a thirst for blood and conquering. I can only say that he ecks-s-s . . . sists and Nix is a key to his presence! In my dreams, his bone-ch-ch-ch . . . chilling presence comes . . . inside me! Chubby is right. Our *yarted* speaks of him!"

"Where does this thing, this devil, come from?"

Travers turned, and the stare he gave Deacon turned him to stone. Travers turned and hobbled out, leaving the two men alone without answering the question. Deacon confronted Chubby as he intercepted his gaze. "Do not attempt to follow us, Chubby, for I feel that this is your intent."

"You will need help."

"And you will die, for Nix is forbidden to all but the *Heritage*."

"You will need help. Please let me help you."

"Against this thing? The creature from the world of dreams? My Owlers can handle a creature from dreams. If we find the devil, we will shoot to kill. Maybe it can destroy Aralian minds, but the Owlers will be out of its influence, and their weaponry, their technology, is unmatched by any devil."

Chubby's eyes brimmed with intense fear. "This thing is for real, Coombs. I fear that you will need more than two Owlers, a weakened Aralian, your so-called assistant, and your luck. You must believe me, Coombs. Alien invasion is upon us. They killed Como and Geor to create chaos and insecurity as a prelude. The devil leads these forces."

"Spare me your melodrama. This company is somewhat better than I originally thought, for I assumed that I was a solo act. Not a single word of our discussions to your partners, for my instinct tells me that the conspiracy you and I seek has its roots in the Alliance, or more likely is rooted in your beloved traders' union."

Chubby conceded and asked Deacon to tour their facility with him. As they walked around the compound, they crafted a plan to hide Travers on the *Heritage*. Deacon promised that Gem would deliver all the final details of their departure. Deacon knew the biggest hurdle would be the two Owlers. "I want your word that you will not attempt to follow us, Chubby. You haven't sworn this to me yet."

At last Chubby admitted defeat. He stopped dead in his tracks and smiled. "You have my solemn word." Chubby gave Deacon an Aralian trust hug.

"I also want you to acknowledge to me that I shall not be held responsible should anything happen to Travers." These were harsh words for Deacon to spit out.

"Well, I suppose that has to be a part of the plan."

"Yes, it must be. Now that we have a state of unanimity, Travers and you misused Travers's powers to gain control of the trade union to unlock the mystery of the missing arms. I figure it must have been a conspiracy with a number of allies involved in the plot. A neat, tidy Aralian plot by honest Aralians!"

Chubby grunted. "There were twenty of us comrades in arms. At the time, we were apprehensive that if the Alliance discovered the missing arms, they would break the trade union and take over the leadership by force. A quick investigation was required while the Alliance focused on other infractions. There were no leads until Travers returned from Nix with that damning video of a laser gun, and his tale of a dream that contained this devil. It's sad to say, but Como was correct when he said that Aralians are becoming flawed." Ashamedly, on a very grave note, Chubby said, "One man can't possibly fight this cancer. The deterioration is too advanced. We are grateful that you take our trusted member with you."

Deacon was phlegmatic in his response. "I do this because I bet that it would be better to transport Travers with me to Nix than to have him journey there on his own."

In the hours that followed, Chubby provided more information on the escape plan. He also elaborated on the union's efforts to locate missing arms and put an end to illegal shipments. The union was sorrowful over Geolo's two losses—Geor and his son—but the traders were innocent of any wrongdoing.

"Chubby, I want one more promise from you. I will not be in communication with you until our return. I want you to keep your word that you will not let any trade ship follow us. I require your word."

"Much as I want to interfere, I promise. I'll make sure that no other ships follow."

Now they were all part of a waiting game. The pact of the unlikely partners was sealed.

INTO THE NIX

Chubby's revelations

Deacon was led to a small alcove where he was permitted to scan the complete logs of the *Sleigher* on his handheld. Later, he cross-examined Travers's own testimony on his visit to Nix. The details were as he had read them in Travers's mind and as Travers had revealed earlier. There were no new clues, only the confirmation of what he already knew. He was just at the point of boredom when Chubby arrived, bearing food. Following an exchange of pleasantries and hopes, the three partook in a hearty feast. Deacon had never eaten so well before on the planet. Rather than spoil the conversation, he waited until Travers departed and then approached Chubby.

"There was one unusual item in Travers's testimony, and in the travel logs of the *Sleigher*, when the minutes referred to a man named Landrew who visited the ill-fated liner in the Vesper dish at Aralia. Was this our Landrew?"

"Yes."

Deacon was astonished. "Why would he personally travel to Aralia?"

"To investigate the crew and contents of the *Sleigher* after the return from Nix."

"I don't believe that. Landrew has too much else of importance to do; he has officials to represent his interests. He has top investigators at his disposal. Why would he make the effort to travel and Vesper from Earth to Aralia—all the way here—just to inspect the *Sleigher*?"

"He came, and I saw him," Chubby said. Then he gravely whispered, "And he was the first to board the *Sleigher* upon its return. The ship was sealed tight, off-limits to everyone after the engineer discovered its return. No one else was allowed to board, so it sat there at the station for days, a sort of spooky ghost ship, inspiring spectral tales. The Vesper station was closed, and traffic diverted to other Aralian stations. So we all loitered like scavengers at the dock, awaiting Landrew's arrival."

Deacon had lost his appetite. His curiosity was aroused. "Chubby, this is an important clue. Why should Landrew come here? It is indeed puzzling. It disturbs me that he did not inform me of this on Earth. The obvious answer is one I don't like—that there was something or someone on the *Sleigher* that no one other than Landrew was supposed to witness. The question is what? Or who? I don't understand. Landrew did not divulge this fact to me on Earth."

Chubby noisily munched on his food while talking. "The ship sat there for days and became the object of many stories. With the facts around the disappearance and return unknown, it became the investigation of the vanishing Vesper, as reported by journalists. I had my sighting confirmed by one of the other station engineers who also saw Landrew."

Chubby wasn't the least bit interested in continuing this dialogue, although Deacon left the door open. As Chubby focused now on winter fruit delicacies, inspecting each berry, Deacon dared to ask, "Do you know a man named Morris Mydloan?"

He had obviously hit a nerve. Chubby's eyes lit up resiliently as he swallowed his food with a gulp. His expression changed. "How do you know this man?"

"He tried to kill me on Earth before I left." Deacon pulled down his black turtleneck sweater to expose the ruby-colored scar.

Chubby leaned in to inspect and shook his head in disbelief. "That's impossible."

"No, it isn't. My Owler Gem shot him to death on the floor in the library in Liberty City as he attacked me with a length of wire."

Chubby stopped eating and frowned. "Morris Mydloan is an employee of the Special Security Forces of the Alliance."

Deacon was irate. "That, Chubby Eaves, is a lie. I don't believe you. Why should the Alliance hire me to solve a crime and then order one of their own security men, Morris Mydloan, to assassinate me? That is illogical."

Chubby crushed the fruit in his mouth, and the juice dripped off his chin. "I . . . don't know. Why don't you ask Landrew? But Morris Mydloan is a member of special spying forces, and is employed by the Alliance; this I swear to."

"Don't play games with me, Chubby Eaves." Deacon was feeling uneasy and frail.

"I don't lie to you."

"He was a hired assassin! Hired to kill me!"

"He was a spy working on the same case as you, and he came here to this very place to interview me just as you have done. Travers was not here at the time. So there, Deacon Coombs. You dragged it out of me. There was someone here before you, and it was a very thorough interview process conducted by Mydloan." Chubby jabbed Deacon with his finger. "Ah-ha! Ah. Didn't know that, did you? That ole Morris was here. When you asked me previously, you asked if Travers had been interviewed. So I didn't lie."

Deacon was perspiring freely, a tightness knotting in the pit of his stomach. He was at a loss for words until he finally said, "Prove it!"

"Morris—or Madman, as he is notoriously referred to—was hired upon his release from prison because of his unusual mental prowess. He had special mental powers and was able to penetrate the minds of others. He was reprogrammed by Alliance doctors and then joined security to become an agent—one of their agents assigned to investigate the charges against Travers. He was hired to find Travers after he escaped the hospital at Froora and deliver him back into the custody of the Alliance at Brebouillis. Naturally, we hid Travers effectively when we discovered that Morris was on our planet. I'm sorry. It is not a well-kept secret about Mydloan." Chubby became animated. "Why, he strutted right through the grand cavern amid Aralian traders and gloated as he approached me. I found the whole process of conversing with him totally unpleasant. I would never have asked him to do what Travers and I request of you."

"Gossip!" said Deacon.

"No, Deacon, facts. Morris Mydloan had an exceptionally high brain quotient. Morris had the ability to read other people's thoughts just like you. I say again to emphasize it to you that upon his release, he was sent to Brebouillis and was reprogrammed and rehabilitated by doctors there. Then, after a brief stint of training at the academy, he was hired by the Alliance to travel around the universe interrogating and torturing unsuspecting beings. He was a thug of Alliance property. There are rumors and stories of his reign of torture of individuals, extracting information by brute force."

Deacon was petrified, flabbergasted. He suddenly felt insecure, not knowing whom to turn to once more. He suddenly remembered the look Rande had had on his face when the victim was identified. Rande must have been mighty surprised to see one of his official investigators dead on the library floor. Chubby licked the juice from his fingers as he said, "I don't jest, Deacon. We are partners now. Remember?"

Deacon rested in his silence, recalling the words of Lyanna stating that one of the investigators who came before him was a reprogrammed derelict, an Earthling with an attitude problem. His insecurity exponentially grew.

"So Morris tried to kill you. You said with wire?"

Squeamishly, remembering its deadly glitter, he pulled down the sweater top again to give Chubby a second look. "Wire."

"Deacon, I swear. There is a great persuasive evil out there. Trust no one except the Owlers and Travers and me. The last that we heard of Morris, he was traveling planet-to-planet in a small one-man craft, inflicting his authorized wrath of mental torture upon poor, unsuspecting souls in the name of the Alliance. But there was also a rumor that reached my ears only days ago that his torture was in the name of a new lord of evil that he worshipped. Death was not too early for this scoundrel."

"Can you possibly get me the official documents of his stops and of his complete journey since his release from Brebouillis?"

"No promises, Deacon, but I'll try. I have guarded contacts inside the Alliance."

"Can you possibly deliver them to me before I depart Aralia?"

"Okay. For you I promise they will be delivered, for we are partners. I am very sorry that I had to be the one to inform you about Mydloan. I look at you and I see confusion, insecurity, and fear—the same confusion, insecurity, and fear that Travers and I feel. Look at me. You know who your friends are. I keep telling you. It is me and Travers. You will reach this conclusion eventually. Friends?"

Deacon felt more forlorn than ever before. Limply, perhaps even falsely, he shook Chubby's hand; in his mind, there was a new distended vacuum of trust everywhere.

Reunions

Soon good-byes were in order. Over seventy hours had passed since Deacon's arrival. He kept reckoning in his mind that the safest place for Travers to be was with him as he walked into the lair of evil, for Travers's thoughts had betrayed him, and he would definitely venture there with or without Deacon. Over and over he justified his decision while rehearsing his new orders to Gem and Jim.

Hours later, the sled was plowing through fresh-laden powdery snow, the buzzing of the engine making Deacon woozy. He had missed the Owlers. He felt a sensation of security while in their presence. He prayed that Lyanna had not been a party to Morris Mydloan's reprogramming. As the sled barged over hills, eventually the misty shapes of the factories came into sight. The monotonous sound of the motor put him into a trance, where distrustful faces confronted him and unfriendly surroundings pricked him. Then he awakened as the two metallic Owlers shook him, and he was elated. After he gave each one an exceptionally tight hug, they in turn only expressed their concern about failing the prime directive. "The vehicle sustained serious damage, Master," said Gem. "Quobit and I could not continue. It was fortunate that a wayward traveler came by and offered assistance and a ride back to Glagn."

Deacon understood perfectly the coincidence of the wayward traveler. "Another trader, sent by Chubby no doubt, all planned."

"Meanwhile, our search for you was delayed while blinding storms invaded the area. Yesterday, Travers's men informed us that you would be delivered here safely today. We were prepared to invade the Alps if you did not return on schedule."

"Did you inform the Alliance of my brief sortie?"

Gem was firm. "No."

"Nor I'obo?"

"No."

"Good," Deacon said. "Don't."

It took hours to relate the events to Quobit and the Owlers. He did this primarily to have Gem officially document the occurrence and leave a record if anything should happen to them. Secondly, he wanted the Owlers to have the information on Chubby Eaves and the references to Nix by both Chubby and Travers. With Jim gasping in almost human amazement, Deacon related the tale of Travers, emphasizing Travers's innocence as told to him. Gem reminded Deacon of Schlegar's parting words: "This man is dangerous." Her blue eyes looked suddenly cold.

As Deacon finished reciting the episodes, he revealed the surprise traveler who would be joining them. Instantly the Owlers protested, but Deacon reminded them that they, the Owlers, could not be mentally influenced by Travers, so the mission would not be jeopardized. "What better person to accompany us than the person with the exact coordinates of where the *Sleigher* had journeyed?" he stated.

Gem and Jim hurled rebuttals Deacon's way as he gave the orders a third time. Quobit intervened with support for Deacon's logic. Gem said, "Master, your wish will be obeyed, but if Travers poses a threat to you or jeopardizes the mission, he will be eliminated. The directive to protect you will not be compromised a second time." Deacon realized that the directive did not require his approval.

There was silence. The briefing was concluded. The following day, the records of the Union of Space Traders were laid open to Deacon, just as Chubby had promised. Deacon and Jim together reviewed the voyages of the *Sleigher*, and Chubby delivered the escapades and travel plans of Morris Mydloan to Deacon as best as he could reconstruct them from records. Deacon noted that the logs of the *Sleigher* recorded two more passengers on arrival at Aralia than the number of patients at Brebouillis. One of these was Travers. Who was the other one? Deacon decided he had better inquire of Travers as to the identity of the individual. As Jim and Deacon focused on the *Sleigher*'s journey, Chubby provided access to Quobit to record all the serial numbers of the missing arms; Gem traveled to the port to make ready for their departure.

Deacon noticed some items of interest in Travers's recent travels—points of discussion for the trip. Exhausted, he returned to rest on the *Heritage* until their departure. Later, as the last of their supplies and fuel were loaded, he paced nervously inside his quarters, first regretting, and then justifying, this decision to travel with Travers.

"I gather that you are anxious about Travers's arrival," said Quobit.

"Quobit, I have a heavy burden thrust upon me to take Travers with us. I have ignored Schlegar's sage advice and potentially compromised the trust Landrew and the High Council have in me. However"—he softened his voice—"I reason that the traders had many a chance to exterminate me on Aralia with all Travers's resources, but he did not kill me."

"If it makes you feel better, I agree with your thinking. However, Deacon, someone in the Alliance, on the other hand, sent Morris Mydloan after you."

"I am bubbling to disclose this to Rande upon arrival back on Earth. I cannot risk that communication to him now. The Alliance seems to be rife with spies."

Quobit spoke bluntly. "Better to have Travers in our backyard than to not know where he is." The cliché was worn thin, but Deacon was appreciative of Quobit's efforts to reinforce his logic.

Their conversation in the main viewing room was interrupted as a motley-haired Aralian dressed in a smock addressed Deacon. "These discs are delivered to Deacon Coombs for your main recording system, sir."

"Please deposit them on the desk, over there," said Deacon, and he guided him.

Deacon then bounced down to the lower control level, where stood the portal to the outside world. He observed Jim vigorously giving orders, pointing here and there, scrutinizing every activity. Then Jim instructed officials to verify the departure papers. It was then that one of the security officers made a fuss. Waving his arms, he motioned to another guard to proceed on board. Had the plan gone amiss? The officer was speaking so rapidly that Deacon's translator couldn't keep up with the dialogue as to what the problem was.

"You there," the officer said, hailing Deacon. "The life forms on this ship seem to be more than the allotment approved. We will look around." The officer glanced past Deacon. "Hey! Yes, you there!"

Deacon turned to find the old man who had brought the discs on board lingering, bent over in a corner, perhaps hiding. Was this Travers in disguise? Was the plan about to crumble?

"Be off with you. Now! Off this ship! Here is the discrepancy."

The elder Aralian cast a familiar glance at Deacon on the way out. The twinkle in his eye reminded him of Chubby. The guards escorted him off while Jim sealed the hatch. Gem warned Quobit and Deacon, saying, "Secure yourselves; it will be an uncomfortable ride out to the Vesper station with turbulent winds in the stratosphere abounding. The Vesper station we travel to is situated beyond the atmosphere."

Into deepest space

Deacon sat at his usual vigil in the middle seat, staring at the screen that captured the outside images. From here he could also rotate the view through 360 degrees to see what was in front of them and what was behind.

"I spoke to Jim earlier. We will be guided out through the turbulence by the automatic pilot, which is the best chance to minimize the bumpiness. The technology for compensation on this ship is the best technology of the Jabu providers."

Deacon replied to Quobit. "I read that most of the Vesper technology is manufactured on either Aralia or Jabu."

"Yes. There is a very healthy competition between the two planets for sales."

"I apologize that these seats were not designed for Jabu travelers."

Quobit's legs stretched out in front of her as she jostled to find a comfortable position. "Gem has informed me that at our first stop, this seat will be repositioned and designed for my massiveness."

They were momentarily jostled as the ship furtively moved out of port. Deacon rotated the viewing screen to scan the screen for any signs of Travers on the docks they had just left. Then there was a roar and the *Heritage* inclined and soared upward steeply. Dark clouds lay ahead. The tiny vehicle oscillated in the severe turbulence as Deacon gripped the armrests tightly. From the level below, he overheard Jim and Gem deep in banter as the capsule ascended ever upward to free her of the gravity field of Aralia. A voice called his name. Turning in his seat and looking over his shoulder, he saw the uniformed guard who had accompanied the officer onto the ship looking for the weight discrepancy. He removed the uniform first, and then the wig, revealing the thin, distinguished profile of Travers. "Villya, I s-s-s-s . . . still think the ship has eck . . . eckstra weight, don't you?"

Deacon lunged out of his seat and held Travers by the arm, positioning him beside him, laughing. "You crafty one."

"The best way to execute a du-du-du . . . diversion is to be one."

Gem appeared at the entrance of the deck. Deacon felt the cold, steely stare as Gem stoically said, "Villya, Travers." Travers turned and nodded.

"Master, Quobit, Travers, for your safety, please ensure that you remain seated until we have reached the station. We are about to travel through the worst part of the storm." There was a frosty interlude, and then Gem departed.

"Travers," said Deacon, "I would like to introduce Quobit of Jabu to you. She travels with us in secrecy, like yourself."

Quobit confirmed their earlier introductions. "I knew that he was on board and hiding; I witnessed him cagily divert the other officers."

The impact of the severe section of the storm heaved the tiny craft, but the autopilot made instantaneous corrections and the craft turned and sped upward. As they cleared seventy thousand feet, billions of stars suddenly shone back against an ebony background, bold yellow suns of other worlds, beckoning explorers.

"Which way is Nix?" asked Deacon.

Travers waved his crooked index finger to an area to the left but to nowhere in particular. Deacon fixed his stare on the quadrant. Suddenly the Vesper station drew closer.

"According to plan, we Vesper to a v-v-v-v-v . . . very remote mining colony. From there, we clear to t-t-t-t-t . . . travel a frequented path by the m-m-m-m . . . miners and traders to desolate mining asteroids where we then v-v-v . . . veer into a passage to Nix."

On the lower deck, Gem administered the appropriate codes to relieve them of scrutiny by Owler patrols, while Jim set their path.

All the threesome had to do was sit and relax, admire the view, and converse with one another, which they did until the point at which they Vespered.

The Vespering produced the usual anxiety attack in Deacon as Travers tried to relieve the fit by reciting numerous anecdotes of his Vespering experiences. Suddenly, the ship was a faint outline. Then all was dark as gremlins chased Deacon around Moonbeam. Miram grew to the size of the mansion to scare them away. In a haze in front of him, a shapeless being materialized.

Quobit tugged at him. When he opened his eyes, the hot, fiery world of Thous, a colorful volcanic planet, was on the monitor. Sulfur plumes rose into the yellow-clouded skies, while fluorescent lava flows dotted the landscape and bubbling red calderas spewed new lava to the surface. The Vesper station was distant enough to avoid ill effects from the plumes and heat from the eruptions on the uninhabited planet.

Just as Deacon captured a still shot of the dynamic surface, the *Heritage* rotated, leaving Thous and the last Vesper station behind. The thrusters activated at maximum power as the craft accelerated smoothly into blackness. After an hour the sky became aglow as they navigated into a patch of stars ahead. Now individual stars fled by them as flashes of yellow, red, purple, and white, all in an instant passage of time as Deacon was held rigid in his seat by Travers's commentary. This continued for many hours until a sharp maneuver by which the *Heritage* steered into the forbidden zone.

Thin webs of dust clouds came into sight, stretched light-years across the scene. Momentary bolts of red, blue, and yellow pierced the clouds. These were the punishing ion and cosmic storms that prevented this sector from ever knowing a day's peace, ever experiencing a moment's silence. Electrical activity saturated the skies as a multitude of charged clouds came perilously close. Deacon sat mesmerized. He might be the first Earthman ever to see this electrifying sight. Or had Morris Mydloan also ventured this way? Reality hit. He might be the last to view this sight. Exhilaration permeated his body as he sat on the edge of his seat, the ship now twisting and turning amid the myriad clouds.

"Never in my dreams did I ever think I would be accompanying the great Deacon Coombs, or witnessing this incredible sight ahead," said Quobit.

"Quobit, look at those space cloud formations swirling in funnels in the lower left quadrant, riddled by the endless furies of energy."

"Time is a passage of electrical conflicts here. Observe, Deacon, almost straight ahead, those blazing bulbs of crimson firing sheet lightning every second." A turn was in order, and the *Heritage* fled to the perimeter of this activity. Billions of distant stars dotted the heavens in clusters. They were shaped in arms, such as those of spiral galaxies.

The ship veered, this time hard to avoid a rapidly approaching turbulent area. Flashes set the deck ablaze in a throbbing teal turmoil. So engrossed in the sights had they been for hours, that Deacon had not fully heard Travers reciting his other adventures in this sector as the Aralian ranted on endlessly, reveling in past glories. Now it became apparent that they were ominously steering into a disturbing blind spot, a blackness of foreboding somberness.

"We are pointed to the ed-d . . . dge of the Mil . . . k-k-k-k-ky Way."

Deacon saw black patches dotting the sky between strips of twinkling linear mass. Gem ascended to remind them of their need for rest, so Deacon made himself comfortable in his recliner, Quobit lay outstretched on the floor in the corner, and Travers retired to sleeping quarters. Deacon momentarily followed him into the room. He noticed the brown stain on Travers's right hand.

"I have carried a p-p-p . . . passion for Earth's tobacco since my initial tri . . . p-p-p to Earth."

Deacon initiated a sudden change of topic. "Why did you and Maretz take the *Sleigher* to Nix?" Travers remained silent, so Deacon stated his case. "There is no power great enough to bend Vesper beams, and if there is, then you and I and all Alliance forces will bow to such evil creatures and be dead and conquered. We would be hopeless against such a force. The most believable scenario is that you purposely bribed the engineers at Jabu, specifically Maretz, whom Gem discovered is an acquaintance of yours. Quobit confirmed for me her facts about the *Sleigher's* Vesper. She was on duty the day of the mishap. I think you took the *Sleigher* to the Vesper station we just passed, and from there you proceeded down this exact same path—the cold, calculated path to Nix, the same path to Nix we follow. Why? It was planned and executed by you and Maretz with obvious help from an engineer here at that last Vesper station."

"How c-c-c . . . can you be so sure?"

"I researched Vespering in the library on Earth. My background in physics allowed me to comprehend the mechanics of Vespering. As I just stated, either aliens beyond our control took you there or you took yourselves there deceitfully. Also, I felt this astonishing thought in your mind recently back in the caves of Glagn. You briefly betrayed yourself. I am so sorry to invade your privacy, Travers, but it was one of those moments when you reached out to me. Your trip to Nix was no coincidence. I think that you navigated the *Sleigher* to Nix to search for the missing arms shipments as a desperate measure to clear your name and defend the integrity of the traders. Add to that your association with Maretz, and I believe the trip to Nix not a coincidence."

"I feel w-w-w . . . weak. I will sleep."

"Please talk to me, Travers. Why did you take the *Sleigher* to Nix? What did you discover there? Whatever it was, the force weakened you, created the slur you now have, and took the lives away from your crew. You know something terrifying that I don't."

His bent legs unfurled and he lay down, turning away from Deacon, who read the sign to retreat. Deacon slept uneasily; every time he turned around to peer at Travers in the adjacent room, Travers's gaze was eerily fixed on him. From where he sat, he probed into Travers's mind with no success.

The facts to date were perplexing and kept him awake. There were some strange blemishes on the High Council. But in his research on Earth, he noted that the birth date of Brebouillis was very curious. Very peculiar indeed.

Gem suddenly appeared again. "Please, Master, I insist on rest for you."

Deacon's eyes remained riveted on the dazzling sight before him. Black patches spotted the thinly dispersed stars. This was the area of immense dust clouds that he had written a paper on in astronomy class, and now he was to actually enter this zone. Clouds reaching millions of miles in diameter wreaked havoc with the instruments because of their immense and far-reaching magnetic effects. Many a ship had become engulfed by these monsters in the earliest days of exploring before newer and safer routes between solar systems were established. Somewhere in this unnavigable maze was the famous graveyard of trade ships rendered helpless by these storms; somewhere in here was the mysterious planet of Nix.

Arrival

Upon awakening, Deacon was not sure how long he had slept, but he knew that he felt revitalized. Travers was neither in his room nor on his deck; nor was Quobit. The screen looked the same as before as the *Heritage* carefully serpentined though the monotonous, deadly cloud formations. Straight ahead were large, ominous black spots perforated with vicious, twisted lightning. He wobbled around the deck three times to loosen up; performed twenty fast-paced sit-ups, twenty deep knee bends, and fifty jumping jacks; and then, out of breath, descended to the control level, where he found Gem, Jim, Quobit, and Travers poring over computer-generated 3-D screen images on which they plotted their path. "We are much closer to Nix than we had calculated. Perhaps only sixteen hours at top speed," Gem said.

Jim rose to insert a protrusion from his body into the computer controls. A small, narrow tube that danced around and gyrated connected the two machines. Jim blurted out coordinates to Travers, who was now busy shaping a new three-dimensional laser grid suspended in midair over the table, while Quobit gasped in amazement. Deacon felt helpless to assist as he admired the interaction, so he sank to sit on the stairs.

Gem turned to him and said, "You slept fifteen Earth hours, Master." No wonder he felt so revived.

"I overslept too," said Quobit, "sleeping for eight of your hours rather than five."

Deacon watched the chemistry between Jim and Travers as Gem delivered a hot drink and an energy bar to him. Jim commenced to flash numbers on a screen situated in his torso area. Travers digested Jim's data and then maneuvered the three-dimensional grid and began to bark new coordinates to Gem, who steered the *Heritage* onto a new path. The interaction of the Owlers and Travers was warming to Deacon's heart. *Maybe this is the event to win the Owlers over*, he thought.

Piece by piece, Travers constructed a new holographic grid of their current air space, suspending it in air over the table. As Travers held a device on which his fingers bounced without rest for minutes, Deacon realized that Travers was entering and calculating information as quickly as the computer could. A terrible pang hit his head. *Has Travers the ability to have reprogrammed the Owlers while I slept?*

After the ugly idea surfaced, Travers pulled his lips tight before replying with an emphatic "No!" An apology was warranted to the little man later. Deacon climbed back into the upper deck, and the Aralian soon hobbled to sit beside him. Deacon felt ashamed. "I'm truly sorry. Firstly, I keep forgetting that you have the power; secondly, I should have more confidence in you. You work very well with the Owlers."

"No matter. You have more c-c-c-c . . . courage than anyone else I know. Maybe we are both fools." Travers smiled at him. Then the smile vanished. "Evil is near. I feel it."

Deacon reached across the space between their seats and clutched his hand. "Hold on to your sanity."

Travers leaned back in his chair. "S-s-s . . . so tired."

"Rest, my friend." Travers lay back and closed his eyes. Quobit joined them, and Deacon whispered to her, "The woes of the universe have been thrust upon this little Aralian man. Without concrete evidence, his father has cast him out, the leader of Aralia has imparted public shame on him, and the High Council has judged and condemned him."

"He appears harmless as he sits snoozing and snoring. Look at him, Deacon. He looks just as Lyanna describes the Aralians, so cuddly and soft." Quobit smiled. "On Jabu we have only one forested area, where cuddly four-legged silver beings live. I often have speculated that they might be related to Aralians."

"Gem has prepared a brief of the geography and climate of Nix. I can share this with you if you pass me your computer."

As he transferred the data, Quobit said, "If events transpire quickly around us on Nix, whatever you need me to do, just yell at me. I'll respond; you can count on it."

"Thank you. I will." Deacon reviewed the transcripts of the known geography of Nix, preparing himself for the landing, but the worst situation kept stabbing at his mind—his death.

As he looked out into space, pushing his fingers through his hair, he grew fearful. There, dead ahead, was a black spot so deathly opaque that its darkness seemed to reach out and stab him. It was quiet here, with no signs of electrical storms. He strained his eyes to see any trace of light; the entire screen became black. This obviously was the course, as the vessel sailed directly ahead. Deacon ambled down the stairs to the ship's control room, the craft slowing noticeably. Just as he glanced at the large screen in front of Jim and Gem, a black hole materialized with a sparkling yellow veil around it. Was this for real?

"Nix," Travers whispered. As they drew closer, the planet was seen to be marked with red and yellow dots, demarcating the areas of possible volcanic activity.

"Buckle up for landing," Gem said. Travers and Deacon moved to the control table and sat beside each other as the first indications of rapid descent occurred.

The *Heritage* was tossed to and fro as it passed through the first layer of atmosphere. Further chaos ensued as a result of the rising plumes of hot air breaking through the atmosphere, creating high atmospheric winds. Deacon noticed the glowing trails of volcanic ash below. They seemed to be riding on top of one of the fiery thunderheads.

He was well aware of the putrid air on Nix, caused by the presence of sulfur, and the effect that the atmosphere would have on humans; it had been chronicled most definitively in the logs of Travers and the brief by Gem. First it would slow his metabolism down, and then it would precipitate prolonged fatigue, followed by queasiness and disorientation.

On the surface

The spaceship came to an abrupt halt some one thousand feet over the surface and then descended vertically very, very slowly. Six legs protruded from the undercarriage, preparing to bear the brunt of the vertical landing on a possibly uneven surface. The *Heritage* fell and fell. The thrust engines blasted against the rocks until the craft landed with a thud. Deacon felt the impact as a bump hit the base of his spine. Jim turned off the engines while the computer assessed the landing. "On a scale of ten," he said, "I determine a nine point nine for my efforts."

"Such modesty, Jim," Quobit said. "I hope you save some of it for the natives." Deacon treasured Quobit's inclusion in the team. He jumped out of his seat to move directly in front of the screen.

Travers addressed them. "The sun never ri . . . s-s-s-s-ses here. Nix is a bleak, dark world of sp-p-p-p . . . parse vegetation; a warm, dank climate pu-pu-pu . . . populated by slimy primitive beings. Look at the horizon." As a professor, he moved to the screen to instruct them. "It is-s-s-s dotted with smoky sp-sp-sp . . . spires of active volcanoes." To their amazement, a slow-moving massive creature was vaguely discernable against the dim lights of the eruptions. Travers pointed it out. Deacon was not anxious to meet his first Nicosian, remembering the tapes that he had viewed with Landrew on Earth, and recalling the terrifying adventures of Travers.

After each in turn had absorbed the dark, deadly world outside, the Owlers turned on the security system while they scanned, detected, and monitored all the life forms within the vicinity of the craft. The next assignment was to formulate the forthcoming activities in intricate detail. Travers and Deacon pored over the maps on the computer screen, Travers showing Deacon where the crew had landed six years ago, and then the landing area of the recent, fateful second voyage. Quobit worked with the Owlers to plan daily activities.

They decided that Jim should remain on board the *Heritage* at all times to monitor the explorers' whereabouts, executing a hasty retreat or precipitous rescue if required. Gem would take shifts outside to gather basic data on plant life and the planet's atmosphere, and to document activities and observations, while protecting Travers, Quobit, and Deacon. Quobit would act as a swing resource, on board when required, outside as security when needed.

Deacon studied Travers's hand sketches of the natives. The Nicosians wore scant clothing of skins and vines over their greasy, hairy bodies. So to provide proper camouflage, the party spent the following day putting such clothing together. Gem was the most difficult to disguise. The vines were hand selected from a gathering that Jim provided; the skins came from a collection they brought with them. Travers dyed his Aralian fur to dirty gray, while Deacon spent the best part of the day muddying his skin and discoloring other bare parts of his body with metallic dust. He coated his body hair with a repulsive-smelling grease, and he and Travers placed huge false teeth over their own. Quobit would remain out of sight to the natives, as her hulk would draw attention.

As Deacon practiced the grunts and groans of the natives, he drew applause. Prancing around the deck, flapping his head back and forth, Deacon caused Travers to snort hysterically. Quobit laughed and then begged for a mock execution of the savage by Jim; Jim pleaded for an end to Deacon's bad acting too. The bonding of the fivesome was strengthening.

However, their laughter was broken by a bleep of the security system, indicating that an object had moved into the ship's proximity. They all were agape as a large, slow-moving animal lumbered into their encampment and onto the screen. Using magnification, only the mammoth outline was visible, but Deacon recalled for the group a period when creatures of this tonnage with long necks dominated Earth's history. Before the mammoth intersected their force field, the creature moved out of range, so they continued their selection of disguises.

Since some of the natives wore pointed black hoods, apparently made of large leaves or skins, the party decided to wear these hoods to further improve their cover. Both Travers and Deacon were unable to resolve the significance of the hooded beings, although they could clearly be seen on the latest films that Travers had acquired.

During a moment when Travers, Quobit, and Deacon sat to eat, Deacon asked, "Why did you bring the *Sleigher* to Nix?"

Travers sat still. "Who says I d-d-d-d . . . did?"

"I read these thoughts strongly. Trust me. Answer the question."

Travers ignored him. "Did you rea . . . d-d-d-d of Como's death scene?"

"Yes, the hallway monitors showed that no one entered Como's private library and the doors were bolted from the inside. Como alone held the instrument of his own death."

"Suicide is . . . s-s-s-s impossible to us. If the public were to discover that a being drove him to suicide, there c-c-c . . . could be mass hysteria."

"Travers, the tapes that I viewed provided no clues to the murderer of Geor and Como, if they were murdered. I must know why you took the *Sleigher* to Nix. Why? Do you firmly believe that this is the home of your so-called devil? Please, Travers. You must confide in me."

"I find myself unable to r-r-r . . . resist these bouts of s-s-s-sleep. I must rest to have the strength to walk on the surface." With that, he left Deacon with disappointment and went to retire again.

The *Heritage* had set down in a deserted area of the planet where their probes indicated that the population density was low and the volcanic activity was high. Here they would acclimate in their own time and interface with the first savages before traveling to the site where Travers had experienced his last encounter. On the second day, distinguished only by Deacon's cycle of meals and rest, they braved their first exposure to the new world. After donning their native garb, Travers, Quobit, Gem, and Deacon strolled around the ship, braving the putrid air, to indoctrinate themselves with more arduous treks. The gravitational pull was even more severe than on Aralia, so Deacon's legs tired quickly. That, combined with a queasy feeling in his stomach, left him crippled within two hours.

"Gem, why is it so warm on a sunless planet?" Deacon asked.

"Even without a sun, Master, the high heat flow is maintained by the vigorous volcanic outpourings and the existence of molten rock lying under the shallow crust. The atmosphere will become less humid and the temperatures lower as we journey farther from the volcanic hot spots." Gem exposed a monitor in his midbody. "Hot springs and geysers hiss in the far distant hills, with an occasional spray made visible on the horizon by the light of glowing lavas, as you can observe, and fluorescent rock outcrops lay here and there. The local flora consists largely of tough, scrappy, twisted vines that turn around each boulder with hardly a bit of fleshy mass." Gem paused to extract a sole broad, limp leaf, as if it begged to receive moisture.

"Are there temperature fluctuations on the planet's surface? Or just in the atmosphere?" Quobit asked.

"Yes. There are temperature cycles caused by both atmospheric cycles and surface hot spots, Quobit. Look here. Maybe this plant warns us of warmer times as it spreads its leaves open wide."

As Deacon took a step into a puddle, Gem begged him to keep his distance from the streams and standing water in the area because of the acidity. As they walked away from the *Heritage*, minute scaly serpents with sharp ridges on their backs weaved their way through pencil-thin cracks in the rocky outcrop. For a moment Deacon flashed back to dear Miram. What a shock she would have biting into this tough game. Travers intercepted his thought and smiled. "You think of Miram often."

"Miram?" Quobit inquisitively gazed at Deacon.

"Miram is my pet snake and a present from my departed friend Geor. She has a long, sleek, colorful body and is deadly if need be."

"On Jabu, food is scarce, so we eat what you call snakes on Earth. They are bountiful in the desert."

Suddenly, a brief interlude of small, bat-like flying creatures flitted by overhead. "Did you capture that, Gem?"

"Yes, Master." Near a gurgling brook, Gem pointed out to the threesome a multilegged creature of ten pounds soaring low and circling above them. It landed less than twenty feet in front of Deacon, flashing the ten eyes that dotted the head, examining him before jetting into the brook for a rambunctious bath. Then it disappeared into the darkness.

Deacon approached the fluorescent rocks that created a landscape bathed in violet hues. The air in this pocket left his nostrils burning; his appetite had abandoned him. He was feeling weaker by the minute. He forced down the pills that Gem had issued to counteract the gravitational pull and restore proper balance of oxygen in his blood stream; they gave him an inspirational burst of energy, but not enough to sustain the many prescribed hours of exercise required to adapt their metabolisms to the harsher conditions that they would face. Time was precious, so it was no surprise that at the end of the second day, the *Heritage* jetted to their next location.

Gem reviewed the rendezvous points with Jim; Travers explained to Deacon and Quobit the onerous trek overland that they would eventually have to endure to reach the exact landing place of the *Sleigher*. All agreed that the *Heritage* should be left to camp at a more remote place where Jim could monitor their movements unencumbered, and where the landing spots were numerous and smoother for the spaceship. No damage could be risked to the *Heritage*. Quobit, well-armed, would lag behind, within sight of Gem. After they disembarked, panic set in as Deacon watched Jim and the *Heritage* disappear out of sight. Deacon took his oxygen pill and a deep breath.

It was noticeably cooler here than at the first locale. They were in a wide gully devoid of water, but their path was clearly lit by distant eruptions. Gem indicated their direction toward a craggy slope. The top of this mount was not visible in the darkness, while in the other direction the scree ran out onto a plain speckled with campfires.

Each singular pebble presented an obstacle, since the rocks were highly irregular in shape in this wasteland devoid of erosional processes. The saving grace was Gem's extreme difficulty in mobilizing, which kept the gait at a snail's pace, much to the satisfaction of Travers and Deacon. Quobit, meanwhile, displayed her dexterity as she navigated slowly and smoothly. Travers kept pace and thus amazed Deacon with his stamina.

"How old are these rocks, Gem?" asked Deacon.

"These rocks, sire, date at over forty million years old. They are mostly volcanic and metamorphic rocks." Just as Gem proceeded to recite the chemical analysis, a rock tumbled from above to in front of them. Immediately, Gem, Travers, and Deacon scampered behind a large boulder. At the same time, they heard horrifying shouts in the distance. Deacon sat between the two, fondling the trigger of his laser gun. Gem initiated a scanner to identify six hairy creatures about four hundred feet above them on a ledge. From Quobit's vantage point, she witnessed the creatures traversing a thoroughfare and relayed the footage to Gem.

As the three patiently huddled together and Quobit stood in silence like a rock sculpture, no other indigenous forms appeared above or in front of them. Even though his weapon had a finder that could target the hearts of creatures, Deacon was not sure that he had the courage to do so. He fondled the trigger nervously as Gem motioned for them to wait. His heart beat faster just as a Nicosian creature fell out of the sky in front of them.

Gem cast a warning. "He's dead. Don't move. Don't fire. Stay perfectly still. There are still beings in proximity." Bloodcurdling shrills from above filled the air as Deacon examined the corpse in front of him. The creature was six feet tall, about two hundred pounds, and was covered in thick, oily black hair. The chlorine-like odor of it was offensive enough to take his breath away and cause him to turn his head for a better inhale.

Long, sharp, curled claws protruded from the end of each digit on the hands and feet. An oblong oversized head with two terrifying eyes and green mush trickling out of the mouth reinforced the ugliness of the being's appearance. Travers pointed to the long fangs protruding from the gums as Gem crawled closer to photograph the beast from head to foot.

These beings had three major joints from their shoulders to the ends of their fingers. The fingers themselves were long, flexible, one-piece digits. The neck area was devoid of hair, the only part of the body to be so. The eyes petrified him. They were humungous, bulging out of their sockets in death as in life, obviously to track movement in each direction in the darkness. Gem stood up and motioned Travers and Deacon to do the same and follow her. Quobit gave a wave to Gem from her distant position.

"Much as the air s-s-s-s . . . stink-k-k-ks, these beings smell disgusting!"

Gem placed the scanner on alert for any other natives. Luckily for them, the emotional torment of further agonizing shouts was now absent. After three hours, they reached a crest from which they could see fires on the plains below on the other side of the ridge.

"I surmise that with no sunrise and sunset, the expense of energy determines the cyclic lifestyle of the Nicosians. They probably sleep only after all their energy has been used up on the daily rituals." Travers seemed inattentive as Deacon spoke.

From here, there was no starry sky, no sun-bathed moons. Mountain peaks were barely decipherable on the horizon, but Deacon noticed Travers holding his focus on one peak in particular. Deacon stooped to examine some pulpy brown plants that clung to a ledge where a crack had formed in the smooth facing. "With a lack of freeze-thaw cycles," said Gem, "any erosion must be dependent on flash floods, winds, and any contractions or condensations due to the small temperature fluctuations."

The Jabu were known for their keen eyesight, so it was no coincidence that Quobit signaled Gem and alerted them to an enormous outline of a creature perched on a ledge two hundred feet above them. Camouflaged by the bleak scenery, standing statuesque, it stared down at them, an elongated protuberance with a bulbous head stretched out over the cliff's edge. The body was held high above the rocks by an indeterminate number of stocky legs. A waiting game to descend below ensued. Quobit rested, keeping a watch on their rear.

In the campsite

As the din on the plains below died, the trio made their descent down the ridge, Deacon casting an uneasy glance over his shoulder to recognize any movement by the monstrous animal behind them. Once they were on the plains and in the camps, the stench of rotten meat was suffocating. The initial campsite contained about fifty Nicosians resting around a blazing fire. Sentries were posted, so they maintained their distance. Deacon put his hood up while a precautious Gem stalked around the perimeter recording heartbeats, the composition of flesh, metabolic rates, voices, and hair colors and body chemistry. Deacon made some crude sketches of native garb as Travers documented the implements around the fire. Travers clung to Deacon's every move.

Bones and raw meat littered the campsite. Fires were rimmed in stones; plant and mineral matter lay close at hand as fuel. Younger Nicosians slept huddled together in the middle of the site, while the adults slept around the edge of the settlement, armed with bones, wooden clubs, and rocks. Deacon was quick to notice crude cutting and cooking implements.

There were other campsites in proximity, so they chose to visit those too. The scene was much the same except that the sentries returned threatening glances. The closest they stood to a live specimen was about sixty feet.

Deacon could not understand the total lack of curiosity toward them on the part of the Nicosians. He felt confident strutting about with Gem by his side, on alert, treating this walk as a pure scientific expedition. His courage was soon suppressed, as a sentry inquisitively glared at him with razor-like teeth that were glowing from the light of the fires. They saturated themselves with observations and then left untouched. Six hours had passed, so they departed to rendezvous with the *Heritage*. The similarity of each campsite was stunning: the smell of wet hay, rotting flesh, and excrement; the posting of sentries; the huddling of the young; many primitive signs of organized life; the first indications of communities and social structure. As they sat to await Jim's arrival, Deacon shared some thoughts with Gem. "The development of those razor-sharp teeth infers that they are carnivores, as we suspected. The stench of these savages is largely due to the lack of running water to cool themselves and bathe. The bulging eyes provide excellent peripheral vision in the dark and act as a key to defend."

Gem agreed. "The large upper torso has evolved to combat the forces of natural elements. I detect, sire, that tribal traits are just evolving, as seen by the posting of guards, the implements, and the group warfare."

"How do you ec-ks-cks . . . plain evolution on this planet?"

"Perhaps," said Deacon, "the ingredients were transported here undisturbed through space, as we suspect in other cases of evolution in the Alliance. Comets carry the necessary carbon-based compounds. In addition, in this part of the galaxy, there are many carbon compounds in the clouds. Maybe the primordial materials were formed here by the combination of volcanic materials, high heat flow, and the locked greenhouse atmosphere. Maybe this planet had more water in past times."

Deacon rose to collect a soil sample. "This would make an excellent dissertation on Earth. I've sampled both the weathered and unweathered materials. I think I recognize quartz, feldspars, and micas as on Earth. These purple crystals, nonradioactive, are very unusual."

Gem explained. "These components infer a much higher heat flow at one time on the planet's surface, Master."

Travers was taking a sample from a thorny, squat brown bush when Deacon said, "Aha, look!"

A patch of Nicosian hair hung from one of the scraggly bushes. Gem bagged it and sealed it.

"Who knows wha . . . t-t-t-t horrible bact-t-t-t . . . teria may lurk in it?"

"If life began here, Travers, rather than being carried here, with a lack of oceans to brew the mixture, this would make an award-winning thesis," said Deacon.

They departed quickly and climbed up the hills to rendezvous with Quobit, who had also collected plant and animal matter for analysis. The *Heritage* was a welcome sight as she hovered over the nearest mountain, preparing her descent to retrieve them. Deacon hoped her landing would not draw any curious observers.

For another day, the trio wandered around Nicosian campsites, carefully avoiding the peak savage periods and any confrontations. Jim maintained his vigilance while orbiting around the planet, observing the natives, searching for any sign of other alien life forms, and using scanning technology to establish evidence for hidden caches of arms. Instead, all he documented were many diverse animal forms. Jim's data provided an increased understanding of the volcanic and biological activity but no further clues to any peculiar happenings on the planet.

Deacon saw that Travers was losing strength. While he himself gathered a second wind as time progressed, Travers had wilted by the end of each jaunt. Eventually the patches of humidity caused shorts in Gem's wiring system while the jagged rocks scraped the bottoms of the Owlers' feet. As Jim applied a healing plastic coating to Gem, Deacon raised a question to the group assembled in the *Heritage*. "I am curious about the hooded Nicosians and why we have not seen any in these parts. In the tape you acquired, Travers, there were numerous hooded ones." When no one offered a viewpoint, Deacon ordered that it was time to relocate to the exact site of the last landing of the *Sleigher*.

"No need to guess the coordinates; I have them . . . mmm."

The prisoner

Hours later, the *Heritage* was suspended above the surface, plotting extraordinary movements of the population on the surface. Deacon registered tens of thousands of heartbeats in a furious random motion, indicating that the natives were perhaps engaged in battle over territory and food.

Carefully, the ship descended. Perched on a high ledge overlooking the basin of activity, the computer registered no beings within a half a mile of their landing place. Travers confirmed that this was indeed the location where the *Sleigher* had landed, and he also encouraged Deacon to depart to the place he knew that served as an excellent viewpoint of the plains. They carefully donned their apparatuses, and the *Heritage* door opened to lay down a ramp from its underbelly. As Jim tracked the party by zeroing in on Deacon's heartbeat, Deacon, Gem, Quobit, and Travers hiked down a broad gully full of boulders to a perfect observation post where they could vaguely outline thousands of Nicosians lined up like ants about to commence battle in front of blazing bonfires. The sight was bizarre as they shrieked and jumped up and down, working themselves into a frenzy. Deacon saw his first hooded figures; they assembled in front of each of the sides.

He locked his camera on them, magnifying their images to the point at which he could clearly see that the hooded figures were Nicosians, dispelling any idea that they might be aliens. However, they vacated immediately, indicating that they were not to participate in the war scene. What curious immunity did they hold? The four skirted the location by traversing parallel to the edge of the scene while keeping out of sight and maintaining an excellent vantage point.

Suddenly the din grew exponentially as the two sides attacked. The group was not able to see the details of the battle in the dim light, but the shrieks of horror and the sounds of clubbing depicted the grim scene unfolding below them.

Quobit posed an observation: "What a life for the victors—to live to fight another day." Because of the daily battle scenes, Deacon was convinced that the birth rate must be high to replenish the troops, and perhaps the food supply. Within two hundred feet of them, a solitary savage tried to escape before his captors clubbed him to death. Deacon had witnessed enough, so he slumped down beside Travers, who was noticeably shivering. Together they sat, their backs to the large rock, while Gem and Quobit continued to record the events.

Gem tugged at Deacon to get him to resume his upright position as a strange event occurred. Nearby, the fighting halted as ten hooded figures strolled onto the battlefield. Clubs were dropped; Nicosians bowed and then sank to their knees. An eerie silence fell over the spectacle. Deacon felt uneasy about the uncanny nature of the exhibitionists. What should cause them to act so?

As some of the Nicosians retreated, a crazed savage attacked a hooded individual. Suddenly the hood was drawn back, a laser gun was exposed, and the hooded savage fired again and again into the helpless, writhing creature. The sides dispersed quickly as Deacon sat down to retreat from the gruesome act, his eyes afire with fear. Travers looked back at him with this same fright. Gem joined them in a huddle. The strange powers of the hooded ones were no longer a secret; the location of the stolen weapons had probably been uncovered by these natives. Either on their own, or with help, they knew how to kill.

"If each one of those hooded beings has a weapon, it explains why no one bothered us as we made our rounds," said Deacon. "More importantly, where did they discover the weapons? Who taught them to use the laser guns? Enough of this site for one day, Gem. Let's climb up and over the ridge to see what transpires on the other side."

The group clambered up the side to the apex. Hours later, they reached a point where they could not see individual Nicosians in the darkness but could see the bottom of the basin abounding with slithering movements. The sound of sobbing disturbed Deacon's concentration, and he moved to the end of the ledge, where there was an entrance to a cave. Inside he came upon a Nicosian, withdrawn in the dark recess of an adit. At the sight of him, the being retreated farther into the cave, wailing and jumping. Deacon immediately summoned Gem and Quobit, and then motioned Travers to the sight.

"Travers, we're okay in here, in the cave. Gem, turn on your beacon." Travers elected to remain as sentry while Deacon, Quobit and Gem tracked the Nicosian deeper into the recess of the cave.

They turned a corner and found it licking a wound on its arm. At the sight of the towering Quobit, the creature wailed. Deacon withdrew his gun, set it on stun, and fired. The savage collapsed. With medical expertise, Gem quickly disinfected and bandaged the wound before the savage could regain consciousness. Deacon was repulsed by the slimy texture of the hair and the odiferous moisture expelled by the being as Gem treated the injury. Then they sat patiently, waiting for the native to awaken. When it did, it was startled and confused by the bandages, and so it began to grunt and weep and pace about.

Deacon tried to penetrate the being's mind. There were feelings of emptiness, undecipherable garble. The savage jumped to and fro, feigning an escape, only to have Gem block the route. Deacon donned his hood, and then it touched him—the sound of a word. It was so clear, so terrifying, that it seemed to stab his brain with a chill. Astounded, he heard it again and again and again. The word that he heard from the Nicosian's mind was *Urrrr . . . zelll. Urrr . . . zelll.*

Deacon stepped closer; Gem was on the alert in case the creature should unpredictably attack. Deacon took a chance. Sitting on his haunches, twenty feet in front of the savage, he whispered, "Urzel."

The being pranced around, jumped up and down, screeched, and then tried to run from the cave, but Quobit's strength bounced the native off its feet. The Nicosian weighed his options and then crawled into a corner. Without a flinch of a muscle, the two squatted across from each other, keeping their distance, Gem standing behind Deacon, Quobit blocking escape, and Deacon trying once again to establish contact.

Time after time, he failed. Frustrated, he stood to pace and change his mood as Lyanna had taught him. Then it touched him again—a word so decipherable, so important, that he scampered excitedly to only feet in front of the creature, waiting to retrieve it. And it came.

The sound of "Urzel" filled his mind with elation and fear at the same instance. Finally, he revealed his secret to the others. "The creature thinks the word 'Urzel.' I heard it more than once in its mind."

It became important to the group to find the meaning of this word. Deacon wondered if it was the word for the hooded ones, or a command, or a Nicosian god. Before they could figure anything out about the word, Travers disturbed them to say, "A band of N-n-n . . . Nicoshuns coming in our direction."

Deacon wanted to interrogate this specimen further, so he ordered Gem to stun the being, and after Gem did so, the Owler flung it over her shoulder like a limp, inanimate sack and they hurriedly departed. "N-n-n-not wise." Travers shook his head. All the way back to the *Heritage*, Travers attempted to convince Deacon to abandon the Nicosian.

"Overruled," said Deacon. "The Nicosian comes with us. Let's go."

Hastily they scurried to the location where the *Heritage* was parked. Once the creature was inside, the force field around the ship was activated by Jim. Soon the ghastly odor emanating from the Nicosian permeated the entire space inside, discouraging Deacon from eating, and causing Quobit to remark on the contamination of the air. Upon regaining consciousness, the creature continued to wail. Jim gathered some fresh raw meat near the ship and offered it to the captive. Deacon sat intently watching as the Nicosian chewed, its large jaw oscillating up and down, side to side, the sharp razors ripping the flesh into shreds in seconds. The jaw on this creature was one-third of the entire length of the head from top to neck.

The being was strapped into a chair with only the arms free to eat. While Deacon changed his moods frequently to intrude into the Nicosian's mind, Travers retreated to his room, where he opened his door infrequently to spy, watching only from a distance. Deacon washed, disrobed, tossed his hood garment away, and revealed his true white-skinned identity to the creature. A look of inquisitiveness filled the face of the Nicosian as it stared back. It screamed just as Travers emerged, and he threw his hands into the air to signify that he was tired of this routine. Deacon cautiously moved forward to touch the creature's wounded arm, gently stroke it, and observe the being's fangs—cautiously, lest it decide to bite him. The texture of the hair was bristly.

"Urzel," Deacon calmly said.

The return was garbled but understandable. "Ur-r-r-r . . . zel." Even Jim and Gem were now captivated by the bonding.

"Gem, unleash our visitor."

Travers immediately slammed his door, Jim retreated to protect the controls, Quobit blocked the portal to the lower deck, and Gem set the laser gun on high stun to protect his master while standing beside him.

"Deacon," Deacon said, pointing to himself.

"Urzel," the creature yelled in return.

"No, no, no," Deacon emphatically said. "Deacon." As he continued to recite his name to the Nicosian, he pounded his chest. An hour of this prompting led nowhere, so they stunned the creature and bound him once more.

"Master, what do you intend to do with him?" Gem inquired.

"I am trying to have him uncover the meaning of the word *Urzel* for us. He fears the hooded ones, so I am attempting to win his confidence by discarding the hood. We have treated his wound, fed him, and kept him alive. We can now only hope his basic instincts will repay us."

"By doing what?"

"By taking us to Urzel. Uncovering what Urzel is."

"No!" Travers screamed as Deacon jumped. Travers had been standing behind Deacon during his conversation with Gem. He hung his head and whispered, "The l-l-l-l . . . last time here."

"Gem and I will go, Travers. You will remain here on the ship with Jim." This he said to Travers as he placed his arm around his shoulder. "We don't go to confront Urzel, just to locate, identify, and then flee."

Travers shook his head. "I will g-g-g . . . go with you. I know where."

The next day raised further frustrations with the individual until the second feeding time, when the savage, with a mouth full of food, stunned them by saying, "Dak-k . . . k-k-k . . . kit."

Deacon rose and grinned and marched toward the creature, saying, "Yes, me Deacon. Dakit."

"Dakit!" the primitive howled proudly, shaking the air inside the craft. "Dakit," he said again in a resounding, thunderous voice.

Deacon looked at Gem. "Primitive, but effective."

Gem unleashed him after the feeding, and then Deacon reluctantly moved forward to give the bestial, grimy Nicosian a tight hug, detesting every second of the embrace. The claws of the native etched into his back as the Nicosian hugged him back. Deacon broke the lock and took three steps back to say, "Urzel."

The creature went to the corner and picked up Deacon's hood. "Urzel."

Travers interpreted the remark. "See, he m-m-m-m . . . mistakes us for Urzel, the hooded ones."

Even Deacon was confused. "Well, I see we're no further ahead. Urzel could be the hooded ones, the leader of the hooded ones, the hood itself, or the ones who carry the laser weapons."

"All are possible," Quobit said.

Deacon walked to the creature, extracted the garment, and then placed one hood on Gem and another on Travers. Taking hold of the Nicosian's clawed hand, he led the creature to Gem first, and then Travers, each time saying, "Urzel." The savage looked about in the room, puzzled. He stared into Gem's eyes first, and he then stood in front of Travers, his face so close that Travers choked on the beast's putrid breath as it peered deeply into his eyes. Then the native ambled to Quobit to gaze into her eyes. While Deacon looked on in confusion, the native positioned itself in the center of the room, placed his paws over his eyes, and then—slowly spreading his arms open wide—looked away from all three but stood and declared with a yawp that shook Deacon and resounded in his ears, "Urzel!"

Now totally bewildered, Deacon repeated the process with the identical results. The room became silent as Gem, Travers, and Deacon pondered the actions. Deacon spoke first. "I think it is trying to tell us that we do not resemble Urzel. The motion of covering the eyes could mean that the eyes of Urzel are distinctive. The spreading of the arms leaves me at a loss, except that it could be a signal of worship, a godly gesture, meaning that Urzel is a presence, he is everywhere."

Deacon knew that somehow they had to urge the savage to lead them to the meaning of *Urzel*. He looked at Travers. "We leave tomorrow, whatever time tomorrow is. You can remain here, Travers." Travers neither agreed nor objected but stood stoically. The creature was drugged, the interrogation over, and Deacon retired.

However, he found that it was impossible to sleep before the big journey. His body was confused, his metabolism in chaos. Over and over, he mulled the facts. Shipments of arms—enough to equip a small army—had disappeared; then a space trading vessel had been diverted by Travers to the forbidden zone. But why? Records revealed that primitive savages had come into the possession of laser guns. Were they part of the missing shipments? The sole member to retain his sanity on the *Sleigher* was a sickly Aralian whose life seemed to be entwined with this Urzel. Urzel. God or idol or devil? Alien or superpower? Robe or presence? And the creature?

What a case! A father has turned against his son. The trial of Travers was a hoax. Geor and Como are dead. Morris Mydloan of Alliance security turned assassin. Why was the Sleigher released with Travers to tell the tale? Why was Morris Mydloan in the library? To kill Rande or me? Did Chubby Eaves follow us to Nix? Deacon's mind wandered over and over. *Schlegar, Lyanna. Rande, Lyanna, Morris, Gem, Landrew, Travers, Como, Geor, Chubby, Schlegar, Mydloan, Quobit, Maretz, Landrew, Travers, Lyanna, Miram, Maretz, sleep, sleep, sleep.*

The trek begins

The time for the supreme test had arrived, and he had sleep deprivation to fight as well as fear. They bound the Nicosian in chains to Gem, asked Quobit to join them, and left Jim behind as they trekked toward the nearest ridge. Deacon yelled the word *Urzel* at the creature, pushing him harder and harder. After an hour of ambling aimlessly, the savage made a significant move by pointing at a mount barely visible on the distant horizon in front of misty, lit fumaroles.

They weaved in and out of rock cover, struggling to reach the destination that the beast had identified. How much time had passed, he knew not. With Deacon barking the word *Urzel* to remind him of the objective, with Quobit playing vigilant scout at their rear, with Gem constantly on alert, focused on their safety, with Jim in the *Heritage* monitoring their every move, and with Travers spying in all directions for danger, they trudged forward laboriously, impatiently, slowly. As they grew more distant from the ship, Jim relocated the *Heritage* to a locale closer to the party as they confirmed each revised position.

As Deacon was about to abandon the day, the savage became animated, gesturing to the side of a high mount, yelling, "Urzel!" He repeated the ritual of inside the ship by folding his arms, covering his eyes, and then thrusting his arms out horizontally, screaming, "Urzel!"

The beast was hysterical, mocking, jumping, prancing, pointing, and grabbing Deacon.

Gem and Deacon agreed that it would be advantageous for Jim to relocate the *Heritage* to near the base of the destined mount, where they would commence the trek uphill after nourishment and rest aboard the ship. So Gem contacted Jim as they maneuvered behind the mount to a flat spot and awaited the *Heritage*'s arrival. As the bold-colored ship emerged, Deacon felt a security blanket over him—to be close to both Gem and Jim, to be in running distance of the ship. Once on board, Travers was deathly silent. Deacon, however, got caught casting a penetrating glance his way, so Travers decided to retreat. The native was fed and fell into sleep. Gem and Quobit mapped a cross-country path for the journey to the mount. Deacon sat to ponder. He was thoroughly confused about what the Nicosian had told them. Was the mount named Urzel? Did a being live there? Was Urzel a ritual performed there? He knew that they had to answer these questions soon and return to Earth.

Deacon placed his hand in his pocket and remembered that the paper he fondled was the note from Lyanna. Opening it, he read her dearest thoughts about him, warm wishes cast his way. He heard her delicate, soothing voice reciting each word. Warmth crept inside him. It was short-lived, for only moments later Deacon collapsed into a trance. Upon rising, he spied Gem scurrying around, making preparations for the upcoming trek.

Deacon decided that both Owlers should accompany them for this last mission. So the *Heritage* was positioned at the base of the mysterious mount between two high, jagged rocks camouflaged with force fields set to repel all uninvited visitors. A further code would prevent proximity and entry of the *Heritage* if the force field was compromised. The engines were left in an idling state so that a hurried departure could be executed if peril arose. Energy food pills were taken so they could travel lightly. The plan was for Deacon and Travers to wear personal force fields, but the humidity at this particular site interfered with proper functioning on a permanent basis, so Jim's great idea was abandoned. The quest to solve mysteries began.

INTO THE LAIR

Ascending

Deacon assessed the situation. An open route lay from the base of the plains to the location the savage was directing them toward. In the darkness of the plains below, the random motions of torches crisscrossed. Up the slope lay the meaning of the word *Urzel*. Deacon motioned to Jim and Gem to urge the native onto his feet. Onward they pressed, navigating oddly shaped boulders, climbing a treacherous rocky path to the summit some one thousand feet above them in elevation. While Deacon and Travers requested rest stops, Quobit was physically fit for the ascents and thus moved out in front to scout the most ideal path. Once they were within proximity, the Nicosian was gagged by Jim to prevent outbursts of yelling that could give their presence away and to lessen the resistance of the being to their commands.

Deacon presented the hood to the creature every twenty minutes to check their course. Every time, the Nicosian performed the identical ritual of spreading his arms and pointing to the summit. As they scaled the cliff, the loose talus continued to test their tolerance. The uncompacted chips provided many an opportunity to slide backward, and Travers tumbled twice. At each step, abundant pieces toppled down the slope, the sound of the sloughing causing Jim and Gem to pause and observe and monitor any intrusions into their near space.

"Master," said Gem, "nearest beings are over two thousand feet distant on the plains below. The summit we seek appears to be devoid of life." Suddenly Gem slipped, the Owler pulling the weary Nicosian down with him. Deacon prayed to reach the destination soon, before any damage to the Owlers was incurred, before Travers expended all his energy, and before he himself fell from his exhaustion. His knee joints ached; his neck was throbbing. Quobit, meanwhile, was out of their sight.

Finally, Quobit signaled them; a wide ledge was reached about a third of the way up to the apex. The Nicosian, although drugged, became paranoid, breaking into a frantic tirade, jumping up and down, constantly searching in all directions, startling Travers with its ravings. Deacon ordered Gem to subdue the creature by stunning it and then placing the body in a corner where cuffs could be affixed to a large boulder to secure it. Then they set out to inspect the premises.

On the rim

Quobit waved to Deacon. "Look over here. I counted them. There are fifty large torches ensconced at the lip of the ledge, with hundreds of further torches hanging against the cliff face at the back," she said as she turned around to direct Deacon's attention to the facing.

Deacon paced off the dimensions. "Gem, please record that the ledge is about three hundred feet long with a width of about sixty feet."

The Jabu agreed. "The floor and background appear as smooth rock faces, obviously polished. Deacon, someone has gone to a great deal of trouble to polish these faces."

Deacon teetered at the edge with Travers. The front ended abruptly, with a sheer cliff dropping about four hundred feet to a talus-laden slope that tapered to the plains below. "Have you been here before, my friend?" Deacon asked. Travers was silent as he shook his head. "Jim, Gem—please scout the ledge to find any evidence of the inhabitants who could have come here, polished these surfaces, and installed this torch system."

Jim moved quickly to sample the material of the torches and their residues, and then he reported. "Master, the torches are all manufactured of a synthetic substance easily ignited by laser fire; the materials are manufactured on at least six planets. The ashes have been swept into piles at the ends of the ledge"—he pointed—"to keep the polished surfaces clean."

Quobit was busy looking through her televiewer to survey the situation below. Lines of Nicosians were forming to conduct another gruesome sortie, attracting attention as the noise level swelled. Deacon moved to stand beside Quobit and Travers at the lip of the precipice.

Suddenly, Deacon was stupefied. "From this overhang, one possesses a commanding view of the plains below, dark as it is. Volcanoes, miles distant, on the far side of the plains, are visible because of the slow expulsion of glowing, ropy orange lava. With the din on the plains in crescendo, and the savages engaged there, I feel that we are safe in this location while the conflict rages below." He left Travers to help Gem sample the back facing.

"Master, this facing has been treated with arsenic pigmentations in fluorescent paints. Also present are yttrium and flaurium."

Deacon felt the velvety texture. "In other words, Gem, this backdrop will radiate brilliantly when the torches are lit."

"Yes. The chemicals are administered in concentrated doses, so this wall will make use of the light from the torches to become ablaze in gold and yellow."

"Of course," Deacon said as he felt the smooth texture and then moved again to the lip of the overhang. Gem inspected the ends of the ledge, drawing Deacon's attention to a wrinkle in the facing that turned out to be a small crevice. Two steps in, they found themselves in a narrow, elongated cave. Deacon's curiosity was piqued, so he hailed Jim and Quobit. "Gem and I will investigate this cave. Jim, if the creature becomes conscious, you had best put him into a sleep again. If there is any sign of danger, signal Gem." Then he saw Travers. He appeared to be under a trance, wobbling around the edge of the ledge, staring back with misty eyes. "Quobit, keep a close vigil on Travers. Don't allow him to venture too close to the cliff's edge."

His adrenaline pumping, Deacon followed Gem into the fissure. Once they were inside, a warm, humid breeze blew up from the pit into their faces. Gem lit up like a Christmas tree to show the way forward, a red beacon on top casting light in all directions, and white lights on the tips of each finger defining the path in front. There were no markings in this cave, no signs of life. The floor was well traveled, but there were no soft spots where footprints could be observed.

The floor sloped downward, gradually widening from the narrow entrance to over thirty feet as they continued to descend. As the pair entered a large circular cavern, small furry animals squealed as they scurried in hasty retreat from the lights. A slithering eel-like animal cast an ominous look toward Deacon before disappearing into a crack in the floor. Gem's legs expanded as the Owler rose to thirty feet high to sample vines that were suspended from the ceiling, as well as to investigate their position and formulate their next move.

Gem retreated to normal height as Deacon clapped. "You have such hidden talents, Gem."

The Owler smiled back. "Don't tell Jim. He thinks himself last off the assembly line." Deacon had a laugh as Gem pointed. "There are stacks of crates about one hundred feet in that direction, Master, behind those rocks." Furtively, they navigated around fallen chunks of roof rock while encountering slithering snakelike creatures. Onward they navigated, moving steadfastly to encounter the stash of boxes. Analyses of the contents didn't take Gem long. Deacon coiled up against the wall and acted as sentry as Gem disappeared. "My catalog is complete. Food break required, sire—lavish diet, and freeze-dried." Gem extended a limb, holding out the morsels.

"What about the contents of the crates?"

"Origin unknown, sire. Provisions and common carbon-based foods that would be quite healthy for you. No sign of stashed arms."

Deacon stood and ate quickly, munching the tasteless beads.

From there they wound their way downward again over slippery, moist rocks, the breeze sputtering in their face. Ahead, a porthole appeared. It was an exit to an expansive flat area on the back side of the ridge, opposite the plains they had overlooked. Gem scanned for foreign materials and detected soils and metallic pieces not indigenous to the planet. Moving back inside, Gem directed them further. "Master, copious readings of various metallic substances in that direction." Gem extended one limb to over one hundred feet and pointed; Deacon gave the order to advance.

Gem turned on the light system to full white beams, and a tunnel became apparent. Swiftly, the two moved into the entrance. They traveled about four hundred feet before they entered a massive cavern to discover caches of weapons—pile upon pile upon pile, stretching out of view.

"Do not move any closer, Master, as a force field is in effect. I identify it as old traders' vintage, but it is very effective against any mortal intruders, with a quick and painful electrocution. Do you wish me to break it, sire?"

Deacon weighed the options. "No. Leave the scene untouched. We can't afford to let anyone know about our presence here. Can you scan through it, Gem, to read and record the identity of the shipments? And determine the number of weapons?"

"Enough to arm close to three thousand beings."

"What? You can determine all that already?"

"I have completed the scan and recorded the serial numbers on most crates facing us. Do you wish me to travel around to the other side?"

Deacon became edgy. He still couldn't fathom the number of arms. "Yes, but quickly, Gem. I will wait here."

Gem was absent for over ten minutes as Deacon fidgeted, wavered, and paced uneasily in the darkness, disturbed by frequent slithering intruders. He frequently heard Gem scuffling about on the other side of the cavern. Deacon was relieved as the Owler appeared. Gem led the way out. The two moved back to the ledge to join Travers, Quobit, Jim, and the Nicosian. Gem recited their findings. "Yes, these are the missing weapons, according to the documents supplied by Chubby."

Deacon relayed their discovery to Travers. "Inside these caves is a full arsenal." Travers expressed his discomfort. "But who transported and hid them here in this dreadful, godforsaken place?"

Dreams

Deacon and Jim returned to the *Heritage* and hid her twenty miles from the mount in a remote location. Jim put in place a force field pulse to disguise the ship from any alien probes. Necessary goods were transferred to a small shuttle craft—enough for a prolonged campout. Then, returning to the others, they positioned the mobile craft and the camp in an ideal level spot where they could view the ledge, observe activities on the plains beyond, and spy on the back entrance to the cave in the mount, if the owners of the stolen shipments should arrive.

Violent dreams engulfed Deacon during his sleep, with a thousand potential images of Urzel striking at him. Just as difficult a time possessed Travers, as he twice awakened, urging Deacon to abandon any further investigations. When Deacon awoke, he found the Aralian cuddled up beside him, his nose twitching and his eyelids in spasm. He tried to enter Travers's mind, and images of a wicked creature jumped into his mind. He discontinued that exercise but became convinced that Travers had not told him all he knew. Travers had still not answered his earlier query of why he had taken the *Sleigher* to this monstrous place.

Gem completed the full documentation of all the serial numbers on the crates while Deacon and Quobit made use of this opportunity by spending their time at the rear entrance to the cave system, cataloging soils, photographing footprints, collecting bits of plant material, and scrutinizing the site for clues regarding any alien ship having landed in this place.

"Anything t-t-t . . . to incriminate me?" Travers asked when Deacon later returned to the campsite.

"No, my friend. There are signs of radioactive fuels, indications that a small, light ship has repeatedly landed here. I have bagged hair and scales, captured foot imprints, and collected odd bits of metal."

Quobit dangled a bag. "Bits of foreign materials."

Just as Deacon returned to the ledge, his attention was drawn to their captive, who was now aroused in a restless state, as he was constantly denied participation in his daily ritual of battle. The chants from the plains below were stirring a fire within him. Setting him free was a risk too dangerous to assume at this venture of the expedition. Torturous sounds numbed Deacon's mind; he crawled to the edge of the sill to see and hear a bloody fight below him. The victors were soon declared, and the carcasses dragged away. The more he witnessed, the more he wished to complete their investigation and then depart.

As he slept during that period, his dreams took him down onto the plains, where he ran for his life, undefended against vicious Nicosians. He met Landrew, who confirmed that he was an expendable pawn in this chess game. He turned to ask Lyanna for help, but she disrobed to show that she was an Owler. Deacon ran and ran and soon was alone, only to find himself confronted by two beasts. He was breathing heavily, sweating profusely, screaming for Gem and Jim. The landscape was bare. This was to be his fight to the death; he clutched a large bone. He raised the weapon to strike when he felt something touch his shoulder. Jim poked him to signal that his rest period was complete.

Jim and Gem had completed many tasks. They found that the torch material was indeed a substance mined on many planets, but only the planet Prellij, in the Aralian system, was this brand manufactured with these glowing pigments. The markings on the crates gave a perfect match to the stolen arms, to no one's surprise, although Deacon felt less comforted than the others by this fact. It confirmed a conspiracy in the traders' ranks. The supplies of food were from Zentaur; the bits of tin probably from Zentaur too, based on the impurities. The hairs were from an Aralian, a Jabu, and a Centaurian, and the skin scales from Inic'taurians. Until the owners of the booty showed themselves, suspicion could be directed almost anywhere in the Alliance and in the universe.

As the Owlers departed to complete geological and biological tasks and disappeared over a rise, Travers arose from slumber and joined Deacon for a snack. His hands fidgeted as he opened his dried contents. Deacon sat back to firmly ask Travers the question he needed an answer to. "Why did you take the *Sleigher* here? I want an answer, Travers." Travers turned his head toward him with a blank stare. "You can trust me. I will not use your answer against you." Quobit observed them. Still Travers gave no response. "What did you discover here? Answer me, Travers." Travers halted eating and now looked away. He spoke no words to answer Deacon. "Did you find Urzel here? Did you discover the meaning of this word, *Urzel?*"

"I don't know."

"Yes, you do. Have you been to this ledge before? I asked you previously, and you replied no, but I sensed it in your mind the first moment we stood on the ledge. And these caves? Think, Travers. Have you been here before?"

"In Aralian relig-g-g-g-g . . . gion and history, Aralians predict and believe in the birth of the Crawnshee. On Earth, you call him S-S-S . . . Satan. It is he whom I see when I close my eyes. I d-d-d . . . don't know why. I just see him . . . m-m-m. We must be careful. Crawn . . . shee comes. He comes."

Quobit intervened. "Travers, I have not heard or read of this creature you speak of. Where does this Crawnshee come from in Aralian legends? I mean, where does he originate from? And in what specific legend?"

"From . . . m-m-m-m what Earth people would call hell! The land of eternal fire and torment . . . t-t-t."

Deacon looked back in disbelief. "A physical place? Hell?"

"Yes. In Aralian religion."

Travers struggled to stand and then ambled away. "Can't-t-t remember," he said, sniffling as he offered this last remark.

Deacon arose. The routine of arduous exercise was catching up with him; his muscles ached in every part of his lower body. He hailed Jim and Gem and ordered them all to retreat to the shuttle for rest and oxygen—the creature too. Once inside, he decided it was time to vanish from here, as they had made significant discoveries that needed to be conveyed to the Alliance. His mind slipped to thinking of Lyanna; how he ached to see her again.

Discovery

"What is our next step, Master Deacon?" Deacon wondered how the Owler visualized him. Did the Owler have any hidden feelings for him? How did Gem assess his courage, his intelligence, his future? Their future? Gem looked so pretty with a feminine short-cut hairstyle.

"Finish one more scan locally and then around the area for any other hidden shipments of arms, and check for alien life forms too. Then we will make preparations to leave. Our business here is completed."

Travers expressed his opinion that Jim should blast our way out if foreigners should arrive. "Save us-s-s-s-s-s at all costs."

Deacon wandered outside and then drifted into a nap against a cozy indentation of the shuttle at the base of the entrance ramp to the shuttle. His dreams of Lyanna were astonishingly interrupted by someone calling her name. Who could it be? He didn't recognize the voice. He sat up petrified. Where was he? Disorientation followed. Was he awake? In dreams? On Brebouillis? He rubbed his eyes. Looking around, he saw the Nicosian captive scarily staring back at him, eerily whispering, "Ly . . . an-n-n-n . . . ha."

Blood rushed into his burning cheeks. His brain felt singed. What was happening? Crawling closer on all fours to the Nicosian, he spoke the name Lyanna.

The Nicosian smiled. Deacon heard *Ly . . . an-n-n-n . . . ha* in his mind, but the savage spoke not.

Travers had just exited the shuttle and was grasping the handrails for stability. Deacon motioned to him. "Travers, come here." Just as Travers did so, the savage again said, "Ly . . . an-n-n-n-n . . . ha."

"Who is Lyan-n-n . . . na?"

"A dear friend. I was just reminiscing about her in my dreams when I awoke to hear this creature calling her name. I can't believe what is happening. This creature, primitive as it is, can hear my thoughts that I project to it. Let's try an experiment. You sit over there, and I will sit here, and both of us will mentally scream 'Landrew' to the savage."

Before long, the Nicosian said, "Lan-n-n . . . rooo."

Travers wittily said, "Hey, Deacon, he has-s-s-s my stutter too. Bravo."

"That's it! He hears what I send to him. I can transmit thoughts to him. The Nicosians are susceptible to mind implants. Incredible. These specimens are low on the evolutionary scale, but this portion of the brain is advanced enough to capture mental transmissions. What a puzzle. They seem to be surprisingly evolved in their mental abilities, yet so physically beastial."

They tested the savage repeatedly, and the savage passed each challenge. When Gem and Jim returned from their scanning exercises, Deacon astonished them with his discovery. Suddenly, Deacon felt tremors pummel his body. "Travers, I have a theory. Come with me, dear friend. Gem, Quobit—I need you to stay here with the Nicosian but monitor Travers and me. Jim, take the shuttle, ride to the *Heritage*, and bring the *Heritage* back immediately, as close as you can for us to depart, as near as you can to this exact spot. I am taking Travers for one last venture to the ridge." Deacon was in an exhilarated state as the twosome made their way back a short distance to entrance to the caves and then navigated upslope through the connected caverns, emerging on the ledge overlooking the plains.

Deacon took Travers's hand and led him to the very edge of the cliff. Orange hues on the plain below reminded him of a more familiar time of an Anglo spring. A slight warm breeze blew softly in their faces. After a brief interlude, Deacon stood, his hands on hips, to say, "Travers, look at this setting. A ledge high above the plains for all below to see. Behind us and along the ledge's edge, fires are set to accentuate the setting. The lighting of the torches immediately captures the attention of all below as it sparkles in magnificent colors.

"Then"—he hesitated for effect—"onto this sill comes a being—Urzel. Or perhaps whoever is here just gives the command 'Urzel.' Whether it is the name of someone or a command itself, it is effective. The Nicosians hear the word because they are given the word mentally, and they respond with obedience to it. It matters not how distant they are from the cliff. Let us assume that they respond.

"Either the hooded ones represent this being or they enforce his commands. Somehow, in his absence, they are the authoritative figures and are given laser guns to promulgate respect through fear. The hood and gun bring fear into the natives—in particular, the non-converts. Respect is passed from tribe to tribe through fear. Fear, Travers, is the policing agency.

"These people are admittedly low on the evolutionary scale, but somehow they have this advanced area of the brain to receive mental energy." Travers stared back with a curious expression. "What do you think?" He answered not.

Deacon continued. "But the huge question is, why bother to control these people at all? They are so primitive. Our villains obviously thought this an ideal place to stash their booty. They could come and go without being threatened by these savages. Why bother to arm them? These poor savages have not the knowledge to be trained to fight in a space war with the Alliance. Can't navigate ships. And how do the deaths of Geor and Como fit into the mystery here?"

As puzzling as all this was, Deacon stepped to the edge, and chills filled his body. Something evil had stood here; he had a strong sensation—call it intuition, a lucky guess, but it had been here. And Travers was a part of this demon's plan. But how? To be programmed for deadly deeds?

Travers joined him and had read every thought by Deacon, including the part about the deadly deeds. Now the thoughts of Travers turned to sorrow. He started to collapse, and Deacon grabbed him. "I know not what par-r-r-r . . . rt I play in this evil, but I know that . . . t-t I have met it. Please help me, Deac-c-c . . . con. Please. You are right. I know that I have been here before on this ledge."

Deacon was overcome with Travers's grief. "Don't worry, my friend. I will help you with all the strength that I can."

What would Landrew think if he could see them now? Clinging to each other for strength, tears welling in their eyes, light-years from Earth on a planet of savages, awaiting a force more powerful than any known to mortals. Deacon didn't believe in the devil, so with the comforting thought of Jim and Gem and Quobit by his side, he was ready to see this so-called devil exposed before him. However, he worried about Travers. What spell had the devil cast upon him? What power did he hold over him?

Panic

Jim, as planned, had left in the small shuttle to retrieve the *Heritage*, planning to return for their departure. But once back at the campsite, Deacon's heart broke into a thump, as Gem, Quobit, and the Nicosian had vanished. He didn't dare call out for them. Travers too expressed alarm at the situation as he sobbed.

Deacon positioned the distressed Travers next to the embers at the campsite, ordering him to remain there while he scurried around the perimeter in a quick sortie, carefully and methodically covering different areas to locate Gem and Quobit. Using the televiewer as Gem had taught him, he panned the horizon in all directions, searching hopelessly for the pair as pitch darkness set in. Suddenly, a dim light caught his attention at the back side of the mount. Focusing on the shapes, Deacon panicked. "Oh my dear Anglo!"

A small spaceship had landed silently, and it was not the *Heritage* and Jim. It more closely resembled a bulbous fleet spacer of Aralian build. From it, beings were emerging, cloaked in darkness, looking like bugs circling about, indeterminate numbers of them now on the ground, walking clearly upright into the cave by way of the back entrance, walking to where the arms were stored and to where they had just left. He had to take one chance and so used his pager to summon Gem. "Gem, where are you?" No reply. "Gem. Gem." No reply. He waited, slumping and hiding behind a sharp, rocky obtrusion. He typed in an urgent message on his handheld. No response from the Owler; Deacon broke into a sweat. Then he raced back to Travers, keeping in the shelter of the rocks. He had to pray that Gem and Quobit, wherever they were, also saw the craft and were taking the necessary precautions to hide, maybe even too close to the craft to answer. Meanwhile, reality sunk in that the prime directive of protecting him had been violated. He felt naked for the first time. How secure he was when the Owlers were present, and now a false invincibility! Deacon ordered Travers to put a hooded robe on while he clambered up onto a rock buttress for one last search in vain for Gem. He dared not risk contacting Jim at a higher frequency for fear of the risk of interception of the message by the visitors. It was clear that Gem had flagrantly abandoned him. But why? What impactful event had happened at the campsite in their absence? Had aliens secured Gem and Quobit? "No. Eradicate that thought," Deacon said out loud.

Travers became alarmed, increasingly agitated. "Take me home. H-h-h-he-e-e-e comes." Travers shivered and shook vehemently.

"Who?"

"Evil nears, I fe-e-e . . . e-el him." Travers grabbed Deacon by both arms. "Oh Deac . . . on-n-n-n, he comes. We die here."

Deacon had no intention of admitting to Travers that he too was feeling a bout of panic amplifying within him. One of them had to maintain his composure. Deacon knew that having come this far, it would be advantageous to take a peek at this so-called devil. He strained to find Gem and Quobit once more while Travers watched the camp. He was interrupted by Travers's calls.

"Deacon, he is near! The d-d-d . . . devil! Deacon." Deacon flew to his side and then peered from their campsite. Sure enough, it looked like the strangers were making their way uphill toward them; this was confirmed by the path of their torches. Had Gem betrayed them? Or had Travers signaled them quite subconsciously? Had they heard Travers's calls? Deacon's mind spun in confusion.

There was only one saving solution until Jim could discover Deacon by tracking his heartbeat; they had to descend into the throngs below with the use of their hooded garbs to protect them. Deacon was sure this would work. Deacon smeared dirt on Travers's face, bundled the hood and clothing tightly around him to hide his Aralian fur, clutched his hand, and tugged at him, guiding him lower and lower onto the plains. They had to travel rapidly and disappear into the masses at once. Toward the end they lost their footing and tumbled the last one hundred feet to land firmly against a boulder, where Deacon bruised his arm. Travers was sitting upright. "We must flee," he said

"Travers, listen to me," said Deacon. Travers appeared groggy. "Do not let go of my hand. We must hide in the multitude of savages. It is our only salvation."

Travers's eyes brimmed with horror. "No. I can't. I w-w-w . . . won't."

"We must. We will soon be in sight of the people on the ledge. They may have already discovered our campsite. Quobit and Gem and the captive are nowhere to be found. They must have been distracted by an important mission. Jim is retrieving the *Heritage*. We must save ourselves. We must move into the throngs, Travers. Now!"

Deacon was much stronger than Travers in his frail condition, so he found himself tugging and manipulating their path. "Quickly, Travers. To save our lives! Trust me!"

As the pair made their way onto the plains, Deacon continued to take a direction opposite the ledge, not daring to look back, stepping briskly toward the rear of the pack. The hooded clothes had to be their salvation. He stopped to tuck himself better inside the robe and pull the hood over his head tightly. He became frightened when he heard Travers say, "He is he-e-e-e . . . er-r-r-re." At the sound of Travers's mesmerizing whispered voice, Deacon turned to see the little trader's body in total spasms, his hands shaking, his face frozen in fear, his chest heaving, his body breathing in short quakes, a sob following each heave. Tears streamed down his cheeks and fell onto the ground and onto his garment.

Deacon needed a confirmation. "Who is here?" He moved only inches in front of Travers and whispered again. "Who is here?"

"Ur-r-r-r-r . . . zel."

"How do you know this? You have been telling me you don't know the meaning of the word. You have been raving about the Crawnshee and now suddenly you remember Urzel."

Travers's raspy tone scared Deacon. "I am-m-m-m-m remembering now. Remembering him. I feel him near."

"No time to waste, Travers; we must stop conversing. Look at me." He established eye contact. "I am going to drag you into these masses. Do not resist me. We must hide among the savages to save ourselves. Do not let go of my hand. I will walk out in front. Whatever happens, do not look back, do not let go, and hold tightly onto my hand. Do you understand? And don't let your hood fall down." He saw a faraway, glassy look in Travers's eyes. Unfortunately Travers did not acknowledge Deacon's commands.

Travers stunned Deacon as he whispered, "Let me die here."

"No. Listen to me, Travers. We must save ourselves." He was speaking convincingly to Travers but inwardly beginning to doubt his own words. It was apparent that Travers was under a spell of some sort, for he appeared to gaze past Deacon to the mount. If Deacon left him, the Nicosians would surely have him for supper, so he once again grabbed Travers's arm, this time in an armlock, and led him on.

They reached the plains, where the Nicosians were chanting themselves into a frenzy, all directed toward the mount. The chant was not synchronized, and it had no decipherable words. The thought of wall-to-wall Nicosians crowding their every move, and the thought of breathing their expelled breath, repulsed him, but it had to be done. Already the stench permeated his body. Deacon's mind played havoc, for in his excited state he was bombarded with extraneous thoughts from all directions, none of them intelligible.

He halted to catch his breath, daring not to turn, deciding to make their path toward the outside of the multitudes. Deacon cast a look at Travers to make sure that he was camouflaged in the gown.

Suddenly the crowd roared. Deacon slowly turned to see beings on the ledge above that they had vacated, visible only as moving spots, igniting the torches. The crowd roared as the ledge came ablaze in resplendent colors with a fluorescent backdrop. The ledge was transformed into an inferno of brilliant gold. The natives were delirious with rapture. Was this the hell Travers spoke of?

Deacon was mesmerized at the site he beheld. A figure emerged on the mount, standing hundreds of feet above them and hundreds of feet distant. Even at this distance his features were noticeable. A large black robe graced his figure, clinging to the tall form. The head was deep-set in a pointed hood that allowed no facial features to be seen. Deacon was tempted to use the televiewer, but he knew he needed to remain disciplined.

The devil

The figure commenced his ritual. He slowly raised his arms from over his eyes to spread them outright horizontally, the robe hanging from his limbs, just as the Nicosian crowd did. A deathly silence hypnotized the crowd, and a hush fell. Deacon dared to look amid the Nicosians. What he witnessed made him tremble. Every single one was in a trance. A gurgling sound rose from the pits of their bodies as they held their hands clasped as in prayer, all their heads upright, their eyes glued to the ledge where the image stood. This they performed in unison, as if all of them were paralyzed.

Deacon noticed that the ritual had engulfed Travers. He turned his head upright from deep underneath his hood and looked directly at the beast. He made eye-to-eye contact only for a fleeting second, but he quivered when two hot, burning coals from inside that hood penetrated his very soul. His neck twitched; his heart fluttered. *Did I give myself away?* Cowardice surfaced in him while his mind screamed at him to run. He was stricken with horror; feelings of remorse filled his body cavity.

He looked away, turning to Travers to catch his attention, but Travers was in such a deep trance that even Deacon's violent shaking of Travers's shoulders couldn't break the spell. When Travers finally glanced at him, there was no recognition in his eyes. Deacon realized the gravity of the situation. The being up there, whoever he was, whatever it was, held supreme power by holding all the creatures, including Travers, in his spell. He was in complete control of this mob by using the energy from his mind to seize all the Nicosians, penetrating them, gripping them, paralyzing them using his mental commands.

A headache started to split Deacon's skull, culminating with the throbbing of the word *Urzel*. He felt the power of the word overcome him; suddenly his mind was bursting as he resisted. *Change your mood!* he screamed to himself. *Change your mood and resist the force.* He did so as he comforted himself by thinking of Lyanna, temporarily relieving himself of the anguish and pain.

Up on the ledge, the figure flapped his arms up and down as if to fly and vault over the crowd. The Nicosian hostage had imitated this move before. Now the populace commenced, as if on cue, to chant, "Urrr . . . zel, Urrr . . . zel, Urrrr . . . zel."

Louder it grew until it resonated with ear-splitting thunder in the bowl, deafening reverberations bouncing off every outcrop. The crowd was becoming increasingly whipped into an uncontrollable furor, so Deacon felt the need for Travers and him to flee. But Travers remained held in the spell, shouting in unison with the others, "Urrr . . . zel! Urr . . . zel!" It felt to Deacon like a supernatural intervention. As he turned to the mount, the arms of the beast inexplicably dropped, as did the arms of all the Nicosians. The creature paced the ledge. And then, for the first time, it spoke.

The voice was mesmerizing, deep, and mighty. The beast enunciated each syllable in pulsating tones, reciting words foreign to Deacon but familiar to the crowd—or so he judged by their raging reaction. There was obviously an amplification system projecting this fearful message. The creature raced along the edge of the cliff, searching, probing, examining the mob, chanting in a garrulous dialect. Deacon trembled. First he had fought off the control of Urzel. Now he decided to take a deep breath and face the devil.

The burning red eyes suddenly seemed to focus right on the very spot where he stood. He felt as if tens of thousands of Nicosians now looked right to the very place where he and Travers were located, as if Travers had guided the gaze of Urzel to them, but Deacon stood his ground, frozen, staring back, not daring to blink, keeping under his hood. Their eyes met. Such a stab of despair he had never experienced before overcame him. He felt as though two scorching lances had impaled him. He struggled to keep his mind blank. Crouching now behind a taller Nicosian, he took a deep breath and peeked to continue his vigil as the monster maintained his glare, right at their post.

Deacon looked to his side, and his heart sank. Urzel had probably singled their location out because Travers had disrobed, exposing his white Aralian fur for all to behold, including this devil on the pulpit. Deacon's attention was twisted back to the mount as he heard words translated that he understood—the baneful cry of "Infidel! Traitor!"

Then the creature disappeared. Deacon expected the demon to materialize any moment beside him. Goosebumps covered his body; sweat drenched his robe. He dared not signal Gem. He replaced the robe over Travers and bound it tight around his waist. He then grabbed Travers's arm and led him out of the tumult, guiding him through the crowd, not daring to turn back. The Nicosians were still held hypnotized by Urzel, so exposure became a secondary priority for Deacon. But for how long?

Onward they struggled, bumping into many savages and inhaling the thick stench. Behind them the mob fell silent. Shivers slapped behind Deacon's ears, crept down his spine. The chant of "Urrr . . . zel!" rose from out of a disgusting gurgle, again filling the dell.

Suddenly Travers collapsed as he said, "Urrr . . . zel!" Deacon dragged him behind a group of jumping savages, where he hoped to gain a moment's rest. As he looked to the mount, the scene was furious; creatures pointed at them. They had to run for their lives. There was no doubt that they were about to be pursued. Now that they had been fingered, he summoned Jim and Gem with no answer, so he tried again and again.

Confrontation

Travers's resistance to Deacon's pulling grew, signifying the strong spell that Urzel had on him. Now the problem for Deacon was to exit into a hiding spot that was away from the frenzied mob. He turned for one final look before he and Travers ran, and he saw that the mount was ablaze. Urzel looked like the devil presiding over hell, laughing, feeding on the crowd's worship, feeding the fires with his flapping, and defying any God to challenge him, the inferno on the mount growing higher and higher. Travers was still yelling, "Urrr . . . zel!"

It was hopeless. Deacon forced his stun gun into Travers's stomach, fired, and then lugged him over his shoulder and plowed onward. If he left him behind for a future rescue, he would never see him again.

The weight of the Aralian was a huge burden. As the masses responded with more ear-splitting shouts, he dropped Travers. It was useless. He was too heavy. Deacon utilized his last remaining strength to grab Travers by the wrists and drag him behind a large boulder. This place was not safe, but he needed to catch his breath. He strained his eyes to the heavens for any sign of the *Heritage*. No Gem. No Quobit. No Jim. No luck.

In the cliff behind him, there seemed to be a black spot, perhaps an opening to a cave. He left Travers to scamper up the slope, cutting his hand in the process while grabbing a jagged edge of rock to propel him up. Inside he found a warm and deserted cave. Down he went, only to discover Travers on his feet, wandering sluggishly back into the throngs of thousands. Deacon's weary body tackled him from behind, scraping the scab on his sore neck in the process. Once again he stunned the Aralian; he then grasped his wrists and, with infrequent bursts of energy, lugged him up the slope and into the cave, where he collapsed. Deacon stood guard there, only to reluctantly fall into a deep slumber, not one ounce of energy left.

His dreams were disturbing, as the demon Urzel invaded the cave to taunt him and physically torture him with invasions into his mind. Eventually he was interrupted by the sound of talus chips falling from above, some of which landed in his lap. He did not know how long he had slept. This was no time for heroism. He set his laser gun to kill and then dragged Travers deep into the cave with one hand firmly on the trigger. Then he positioned himself with a full view of the entrance, aimed, and waited for the intruder.

More talus fell at the mouth of the cave, and then an eerie stillness followed for minutes. Faint footsteps grew nearer, nearer, closer; then they stopped. It was deathly silent, as even the rowdiness of the savages had subsided. Deacon was drenched in sweat from his emotional trauma, but with his senses still active, he moved furtively to where he could get the best view of the mouth of the cave. *How strange,* he thought, *a man detesting violence, light-years from Moonbeam, about to kill an unsuspecting victim and stranger as the first murder victim in his life.*

A being entered, still in the shadows, and slowly lumbered along until Deacon suddenly recognized the gait. "Deacon?" the being said.

Deacon sighed in relief and then ran to give Quobit a hug that he couldn't find a reason to break. "Never have I been so deliriously happy to see a Jabu engineer."

Quobit smiled. "Gem and I followed your heartbeat here. We have been monitoring your whereabouts for hours. Only now could we circle around the Nicosian rituals to intercept you."

"Where have you been?" Deacon said, venting some controlled anger.

Gem appeared and proceeded to inform him. "Our native prisoner escaped. When the ship landed, it ran toward the craft, so to protect the mission we followed it, caught it, and had to kill it, for it made such a clamor that it jeopardized our safety. However, other Nicosians heard its scream, so Quobit and I had to hide in the rocks, not only from Nicosians but also from the intruders as they approached. We heard your page but could not respond. We waited until the path was clear to come back to the campsite, but by that time you and Travers had departed. I could not locate your trail immediately, Master, but with the heartbeat scanner we realized that you had escaped onto the plains. Quobit and I took to higher ground and followed a circuitous route to avoid the savages and follow your trajectory."

Deacon was excited. "Did you see it? The thing? Did you capture its speech, the ceremony, and the rituals?"

"Yes, Master, I filmed the entire process. The creature and its party are now known to us."

Quobit said, "I was terrified as I watched. I almost regretted coming on this venture. We must escape, Deacon, before the disciples of the creature find us."

"That's the plan. I am so happy to see you both."

"I assure you that you were in no danger, Master," said Gem. "I could have killed anyone who had attempted to harm you or enter the cave, even from the great distance I kept, as I had a direct view. I supervised every movement of you on the plains in the midst of the deranged mob. I watched over you."

"Travers is inside," said Deacon. "He is weak. Can you give him an injection to boost his energy and help him through?"

As Gem entered ahead of him, Deacon's thoughts turned to the poor, helpless Nicosian that they had used and then so coldly disposed of.

Gem examined Travers. "Travers's bodily functions are registering a severely weakened state, probably as a result of the exposure to Urzel's mind." Travers suddenly began to babble, not conversing intelligibly. Gem administered the drug to invigorate him and then repositioned him at the back of the cave. "Our proximity to the Nicosians remains dangerously inconvenient, sire. We cannot risk audio contact with Jim in the *Heritage* from this location. I suggest that I leave you momentarily, move to up to the apex of the hill, and signal the *Heritage* from a safer location. We will have to risk landing the *Heritage* nearby. The shielding devices will prohibit the aliens from detecting it for a short time, but the craft might physically be seen. I recommend that Jim and I chance it." Deacon nodded in agreement. Gem added, "Travers is too weak to travel, so Quobit and you will remain behind."

"I will count every minute of your absence," said Deacon.

"Set your hand weapon to kill, Master; you too, Quobit. I promise a speedy return within minutes." With that, Gem paced out of the cave.

Minutes seemed like hours as Deacon propped himself up onto a rock deep inside the cave's mouth; Quobit fought off sleep and kept vigil closer to the entrance. A short time later, Deacon heard the familiar sound of talus falling over the entrance to the cave again. He hoped that meant Gem and Jim had returned for their rescue, but it was not the case. Two Nicosians, husky in stature, stood at the entrance to the adit. Deacon cursed his bad luck, slithered down, retreated, and pumped up his courage as he fondled his weapon. Quobit repositioned herself behind a large rock ninety feet from him.

Deacon pulled his hood over his face, tied his robe, and aroused Travers and urged him to do the same. Quobit hid and watched as

Travers and Deacon stood to face the intruders while bracing the concealed weapon. Deacon was hoping that the intruders would respect them and retreat. Travers, still groggy, leaned beside Deacon, looking for support.

The tactic didn't work. Six more beings entered, the hairy beings covered in a slimy foam, their fangs protruding, their limbs suspended by their sides, a gurgling sound in their throats. They were not discouraged by the robes of Deacon and Travers. In suspense the Nicosians stood there, about forty feet from Deacon and Travers, until without warning they lunged at Travers. Before Deacon could react, they were dragging Travers outside as he squealed, probably to rip him to shreds. Deacon yelled out of instinct, thinking that as a hooded creature the natives might pay attention to him. It was to no avail, as the claws of one beast tore Travers's garment off and then proceeded to bite into his shoulder as the Aralian screamed for help. Quobit emerged and fired into the masses just as three of them lunged at her legs, trying to topple her massive physique.

Deacon had never killed anyone before. This was it. Even this situation required extraordinary efforts as he witnessed the attack on his friend. But in the one second that he delayed, a Nicosian turned and vaulted on top of Deacon, grabbing him by the back with its claws, knocking the gun out of Deacon's grip. Greasy hair smothered Deacon's face as the tight grip around his chest pressed a rush of air out of his body cavity. Mustering up strength, Deacon chopped with his fingers and hands into the being's eyes, causing his assailant to release his grip momentarily.

Deacon scampered for the gun, turned, and then fired directly into his attacker, only to have the assailants of Travers break their grip on Travers and charge him. The first to reach Deacon butted him in the chest, stunning him. He was helpless as the second Nicosian came at him, mounted him, and readied his fangs for an attack on his head, a look of triumph in his eyes. He commenced to lunge at Deacon's throat.

Deacon grabbed the laser and found the trigger just in time, firing a ray into the creature's neck. The savage rolled over and over, murmuring, until Deacon fired again to put it out of its misery. A Nicosian then tackled him from behind. Quobit, meanwhile, was saved by her tough skin, as the bites of the three Nicosians found no flesh to tear. She fired into the chests of two of them and wrestled free from another to deliver a fatal block across its neck. Then she raced to Deacon's rescue by chopping the Nicosian in the back and kicking him across the cave. The last one lumbered out of the cave as Deacon collapsed rather than follow.

Their sympathies immediately turned to Travers, whose purple plasma was flowing freely from the wounds inflicted on his shoulder and torso. Deacon ripped his hood off and bandaged the cut crudely. The sight of blood, plasma, and raw flesh made him woozy. In an instant, two figures were at his side, and the familiar thin outlines of Jim and Gem became clear to him. "Relax. Master, we are here to escort you to the *Heritage*. We cannot move, however, until the wounds of Travers and Quobit have been properly attended to." Deacon watched as Jim coated Travers's shoulder wound with a gel much like the substance applied to Deacon's neck in the library. As Jim did so, Deacon remained at Travers's side, cradling his head in his arms. The expelled blood stained his beautiful Aralian fur, turning it green as it oxidized. He held Travers tighter, not understanding the severity of the cuts as Jim played medic. "How serious are his wounds?"

"Travers is in critical condition. We must move him immediately to the nearest medical facility for attention, or unfortunately he may die. He is expelling plasma at a rate greater than the efficiency of the gel cover. I am sorry to tell you this news, Master."

"Quobit, are you all right?"

"My arms ache where the savages tried to bite me, but my tough, leathery skin saved me. I'm not good eats on too many planets. I also bruised my knees and thigh."

Jaws

So they left, Gem toting Travers, Quobit assisting Deacon, and Jim locking laser guns on any approaching targets. It was a grueling hike to the *Heritage* as they engaged a long, circuitous route to avoid Urzel's henchmen. The incline was too steep for Deacon to endure, so he stopped to rest with Quobit while Gem, Jim, and Travers pressed ahead and eventually moved out of sight. He required a break, so he lay prostrate with Quobit at his side. "Thank you for saving my life," he said. "You are a ferocious fighter."

"Thank you for the compliment. I will be proud to tell this story to my children. I may ask you to join us remotely for effect." As Deacon lay prone and gazed upward into the heavens, into the shadowy outlines above them, he saw the head of one of the monstrous creatures from days ago. The long neck was extended over the cliff, the peculiar oblong-shaped head bobbing and searching below. He stood to dust himself off and stepped to get a better view. As he did so, footsteps and voices caught his attention below. There was a band of Nicosians gaining on them, heading up the incline. When he turned for one last glance at the creature, two sad, sorrowful eyes looked back at him.

Then, in a split second, the head, jaws open, swooped down to where he stood and continued a hundred feet below. Quobit and he quickly ducked behind a rock as they felt its torrid, hot, stinking breath pass by. As they pressed themselves against the rock face, with the head yet rocketing downward, Deacon witnessed the jaws of the monster lock into an unsuspecting Nicosian who had just climbed in front of them. The Nicosian tried to bite into the tough flesh of the creature's neck to no avail.

With a bloodcurdling roar, the head and neck bit into the lower torso as the Nicosian wailed from his bowels, exhaling his last yelps. Suddenly the Nicosian was bolted skyward in an instant, the jaws still locked into him. The legs of the savage dangled for a second in front of Deacon as the sound of pitiful cries stunned him. Deacon looked at Quobit and said, "I order an immediate withdrawal." Long after, they heard other Nicosians as they became the fodder of the predator. Deacon's desire to see other specimens of this long-necked creature had suddenly diminished.

Once in the shuttle, Deacon raced to the safety of his customary comfortable seat on the observation level. From here he could monitor Travers and inspect their flight. Meanwhile, the Owlers guided the *Heritage* into low altitude until they reached the far side of the planet, where they blasted into outer space. The navigation out of the forbidden zone was once again a difficult maneuver with abundant storms and dust clouds of extreme magnetic intensity causing havoc with the instruments. In Deacon's dreams, he saw the terrible dinosaur-like creature pursuing them.

THE INTERFACE OF EVIL

Into the Sodern and beyond

The *Heritage* shifted lethargically into top thrust as Deacon assisted Gem in applying another sticky lamination of lime-green coagulant to Travers's wound. The Aralian moaned as the stinging agent blistered his skin adjacent to the cuts. Deacon, on his haunches, guided the surficial bandage into place as Gem measured Travers's pulse and biological signs. Then Travers was drugged by Gem, strapped into a reclining position, and attached to a monitor that displayed his vital body functions. With that accomplished, Gem attended to the scratches on Deacon's back. His skin froze and stung as Gem applied a fast-healing glaze.

"Will Travers live?" Deacon asked.

"He has lost a great deal of blood, Master."

"Is there anything that I can do to save him? Perhaps offer my blood?"

Gem wrapped bandages tightly around Travers's chest and applied a gel to his neck wound. "No, Travers requires Aralian-compatible blood. Sorry." While the two mortals lay side by side on the same cot, suffering, the robots navigated the ship carefully through the electrical wasteland. Deacon passed out. Later, as he opened his eyes, a blurry outline of Jim came into focus.

"Master, we are being followed by a spaceship currently two thousand miles distant. It contains five occupants and is matching our every move." Jim used his outstretched arms to signify the distance.

"Are we still in the cosmic storms?"

"Yes, and we shall be for many hours more."

"What type of vessel is it?"

"Master, it is impossible to determine what type of craft it is with all the spatial interference."

"Do you think it was launched from Nix?"

"Most certainly. We are distant from any approved space routes and livable planets."

"Is the *Heritage* equipped with any weapons?"

"The *Heritage* has minimum standard issue for a ship like this. They include neutron guns and electron-radiant torpedoes, all designed to defend and disarm as opposed to fight a battle. The *Heritage* was built to defend and escape, not attack, sire."

Gem joined them and said to Deacon, "We have limited fuel to burn other than what we need to transport us to the nearest refueling dock back at Thous. And there is another problem; we cannot achieve maximum speed."

"Why not?"

"One of the primary fuel engines is blocked, preventing the optimum fuel mixture from being formulated. Perhaps the *Heritage* has taken in too much space dust from the storms above Nix."

"Jim, can our computer guide a repair robot to execute repairs to the engine?"

"The repair robot must be sent outside, but only when the *Heritage* is at a complete stop. One alternative we have is to hide in a dust nebula nearby. Even then, we had better pray that the robot does not malfunction because of the interference caused by lightning and small particulate matter, and that the engines don't take in any more dust."

Deacon grinned. "*Pray*. You said *pray*, Jim. That's a word in your vocabulary, is it, Jim? A logical, unemotional word?"

Jim did not hesitate to reply. "Pray we must, Master Deacon, for we cannot outrun our pursuers with this blockage to the engine's fuel system, so the probability exists that they will overtake us. Thus it seems logical for you, Quobit, and Travers to pray for our best outcome."

Deacon mulled over the situation. They couldn't stop and fight. They couldn't outrun the other ship to escape. "Okay. Hide the ship in the nearest dust nebula. Send the robot outside to make the repairs. Put up our disruptive magnetic shields to try to block their scanners and hide our mass. As difficult as it is, try to plot the track of the other ship."

Jim made a serious overture. "I will spare no effort to reach the nebula. This is a risky venture. And our magnetic shields won't be required, as all instrumentation on their ship and ours will be at a loss in the cloud."

The puzzle

Deacon laid back and faced Travers, who was snoring and mumbling. The short jaunt in the *Heritage* was like the Manchestry rides in Anglo, a delightful, exhilarating experience Deacon had experienced years ago with his parents, in which drops from the sky were simulated. No feelings were untouched as the ship accelerated, decelerated, jumped, lurched, and dropped until they eventually came to an abrupt halt in a pitch-black sector stabbed every sixty seconds with tempestuous lightning bolts. Quobit and Deacon unbuckled and made their way to the console and observed as Gem said to Deacon, "Sire, we have dispatched a robot outside to repair the damage. Now we sit and wait until repairs are complete."

Quobit asked, "Any sign of the other ship?"

"From our last readings, the other ship was drawing closer; we will have to rely on our cover and their inability to navigate inside this cloud to save us. They will be temporarily hopeless to locate our position."

Deacon thought about the term *close. Three thousand miles? Two thousand miles?* He turned to the screen to watch the proceedings outside. The robot appeared as a spindly spider: six huge suction cups ensuring its footing, numerous mechanical arms like tentacles, antennae wavering back and forth.

"Master," Gem said to Deacon, "there is puzzling news for you." His lack of response prompted Gem to issue another statement. "Master." Gem took Deacon by the elbow to gain his attention. "I recorded a strange heartbeat on my instruments while I searched for you and Travers on Nix. I recorded the heartbeat of another Earthling."

Deacon was now riveted. "What? One of Urzel's accomplices?"

A panel opened in Gem's torso and displayed the biological data on the screen. Quobit approached and leaned over to observe closely. "Here is the graph of the heartbeat that I recorded. It is undisputedly that of an Earthman, judging by all the characteristic peaks and troughs. Observe the charted rhythm of the body chemistry too." Gem guided Deacon's glance and Quobit's puzzlement along the wiggles with explanations.

"Are you sure that it was not me that you recorded?"

Gem delivered the punch line stoically. "No. It was he, Master Deacon—the being that stood on the mount to deliver the sermon. The one who ordered the chase, the one who held the savage Nicosians and Travers spellbound. The heartbeat recorded belongs to him."

"Impossible!" Deacon again felt that prickliness on the back of his neck.

"It was he, Master. There is no mistake. My conclusion from data analysis is that Urzel is an Earthling."

"It can't be! No Earthlings have ever been observed to possess the mental powers that you and I observed on Nix! There is no record of such a one as this in the catalogs on Brebouillis. I examined the logs myself. And Schlegar and Lyanna never mentioned an Earthling with powers such as these! They would have informed me of such a . . . being . . . a creature who can project his powers over great distances and hold thousands captive with his mind."

Gem gingerly printed the graphs and presented them to Deacon just as his shoulders twitched from an icy shock. He accepted the evidence, examined it, but was visibly upset. "Damn your graphs, Gem! Urzel cannot be an Earthling. A being born with these powers could not have gone unnoticed. It would have been captured in the records on Earth or Brebouillis for sure. And what about those glowing red eyes? No Earthling has red pigmentation like that."

Then, recognizing the inability of the Owler to tell a lie, recognizing that Gem was not influenced by anything other than facts, and recognizing Gem's furtive, fixed, honest stare, Deacon swallowed hard, gasped, and then sat down in his chair, confused and speechless, as Gem proceeded to tell the baffled Deacon and the puzzled Quobit the significance of each of the peaks and troughs in the printout once again. Gem's digits moved fluently to and fro about the page of data. Deacon peered up into the face of the machine. Gem stared back.

Quobit took up Deacon's cause. "Gem, there must be some other explanation. Earth has monitored all Earthlings born on Earth and elsewhere on other planets. Those who have these mental powers and any extraordinary powers should be known by now, and the exploits would be recorded in medical journals. Deacon told me earlier of your investigations in the library on Earth. I also had the chance to visit with my friend Lyanna about such matters." Turning to face Gem, Deacon convincingly added, "Lyanna and Schlegar told me nothing of such an Earthman! Landrew would have told of his existence. I trust these people. My conclusion is that Urzel cannot be an Earthling!"

"Please consider this, Master. The records do not lie. The heartbeat and the metabolism both support and confirm that Urzel is conclusively an Earthling."

Deacon sighed and sank. "I accept this with great reservation, Gem. However, what we witnessed is a quantum leap above any powers known. How can quantum leaps in evolution occur?"

"Do you wish me to speculate, Master?"

"No. I will debate with you later about the possibilities that this presents. Please assist Jim with the repairs and our new travel plans."

Gem's gait was smoother than Jim's. After the Owler glided down the stairs and out of sight, Deacon sat for a long while. Quobit made some observations, but he didn't hear her. He eventually turned to face her. "This is no assignment for a mortal Earthman like me, Quobit. I am but a pawn in this plot, sent for some deeper purpose still unknown to me. As the plot unfolds, it is becoming clear to me that we must place the ultimate trust in the Owlers to survive, for we have become the hunted."

Tears welled in his eyes. His loneliness, which he so often felt consumed by at Moonbeam, now threatened to wreak havoc on his emotions here. "I was so elated, Quobit, to have escaped from Nix with our lives. But escape to what? The staggering, demoralizing truth that Urzel is an Earthman? The truth that the *Heritage* is now disabled?"

Outside, Deacon heard a thud as the robot clanged against the ship. The robot seemed to be concluding repairs, as its arms retracted, so Deacon moved to the control level.

Jim observed Deacon and addressed him. "Static electricity prevents us from obtaining a confident fix on the trailing vessel. It could be anywhere within striking distance. But something keeps moving out there, as evidenced by space distortions, drawing closer and closer."

"Perhaps they lie in space outside the cloud in an advantageous position, waiting for us to depart."

"Possible, sire. We will have expert detection systems when the dust thins at the edge of the nebula, and an expert race driver—me, naturally—to guide us." Deacon smiled at Jim's confidence. "I suggest you return to secure yourself, Master."

Deacon climbed the steps, leaving the Owlers. He then drifted into a restless nap, starving for the English coast, wishing to put an end to this madness, daydreaming until Quobit sat down.

"How are your wounds?" Deacon inquired.

"The Owler bandaged them well. Jabu mass has very little of what you call blood or plasma, so I don't bleed. It is more the pain of the intrusion of sharp fangs into my muscle and bone mass that causes internal injuries."

Suddenly the *Heritage* was severely jolted. Deacon quickly descended to the lower level, where Jim was guiding the robot into the *Heritage*.

"What was that?" Deacon asked.

"Had to retrieve our robot quickly, disregard the safety measures for demobilization. There are close space distortions that could possibly be the pursuing ship. Certainly there is an unknown object approaching. I dumped the robot into the *Heritage* in the maneuver."

"Can we get a shape to this object?"

"Impossible to determine the outline. It could be a meteorite, our pursuers, just a space density anomaly, or—"

"Okay, I get the picture, Jim."

"One last step."

"Get us out of here now."

"Yes. Calm down, Master."

Deacon decided to join them on their level and strap himself beside Jim, who sat at the main controls, twisting his arm and plugging it into the hardware. Deacon wrapped himself in his arms to curb a chill as a strange shiver navigated from the base of his torso to his neck. On the screen, a gray blob appeared.

"Something's wrong," Deacon said. "It is possible that Travers may have inadvertently led the diabolical creature here? Oh no. Fool that I am not to have seen this! The spell over Travers is too deep. I witnessed it on Nix. Oh my God of Anglo, Travers has led him here, right to us. Get us out of here now, Jim!"

"Master, I am navigating as quickly as I can."

Unexpectedly, Travers hailed Deacon from the deck above. He was standing at the top of the stairs, casting a wild-eyed gaze on the threesome below, staggering, his wounds now spotting blood through the bandages. "He is here. He is-s-s . . . s-s-s-s here."

Quobit corralled Travers's body just as he slumped.

"Gem, you must drug Travers. Render him unconscious as long as the foreign ship nears." As Gem ascended to help Quobit attend to Travers, Deacon, through parted lips, whispered, "My friend, please hang on to hope." Then he asked of Jim, "How long to top speed?"

"Not until we move out of the electrical cloud. It is too dangerous to accelerate now. Secure yourself tightly, please." As Jim directed the ship to the nearest exit out of the cloud, Deacon eyed the monitor in front of Jim in time to see the object change course to duplicate their move. Gem joined them.

"Do they gain on us?"

"Yes, sire, slowly but definitely."

"Even with the repaired engines?"

Jim delayed his response but eventually spoke. "Yes."

"We have to take a chance. Get us out of here, Jim."

"No, sire, the engines are cold and the magnetic and electr—"

"I order you. Do it! Or we perish."

"My prime function is to protect you. The odds of navigating through the nebula at top speed are not in our favor: approximately six thousand eight hundred and five to one. Uncharted meteors and gravity bunches may block our way. The engines could not respond in time to correct the path. Your life cannot be risked."

Deacon was adamant. "Jim, they pursue us to kill Travers and me. Since the ship gains on us and we have only minimal weapon strength, you endanger my life by delaying acceleration. Therefore you are violating your prime directive. I order you to execute your prime directive and save me."

Deacon could not determine whether Jim was engaged in deliberating the logic of his argument or was engrossed in navigational movements. Gem, sitting beside Deacon, said, "Travers grows weaker from his loss of blood. The infection in the wound is growing stronger."

Jim enthusiastically said, "I have recalculated the odds, and there is a slight benefit to attempt escape. As a matter of record, the odds . . ."

Deacon sat back to relax, closing his eyes. He heard Jim's babbling, but his thoughts were focused on their escape.

Jim started the countdown. "Five . . . four . . . three . . . two . . . one . . . rockets!"

Deacon was glued to the back of his seat as the computer took charge and shot them forward at an incredible acceleration. Then the treacherous route started as they dodged obstructions. Deacon's body was thrown about, first left, then right, then forward, and then backward. He tried to steady himself and catch a glimpse of the screen, but he witnessed only blurred images shooting by them. The screams of Travers filled the craft, splitting Deacon's ears with madness, but he and Gem and Quobit were currently hopeless to attend his friend. The path of the meandering vessel continued until the *Heritage* leveled out.

Gem looked at Jim. "We'll have to make our way to the next hiding spot hurriedly before the chasers track us."

Deacon noted the area where lightning ripped apart the space ahead, with red and blue lights ablaze in the heavens. "Jim, what is that area of burning space?"

"That is the Sodern Inferno, so named by the first travelers to enter this region. It is not ablaze. The effects are incandescent lights."

"Can we travel through it to disguise our path?"

"It is out of our way, sire."

"I want us to enter the inferno ahead just as the other craft emerges from the cloud behind us. When inside, accelerate, turn to move out quickly to the edge, then veer to hide in the middle of the Sodern Inferno."

Invasions of the mind

The ship performed the maneuver perfectly. Deacon was proud of the escape that he had concocted. The light show of the Sodern Inferno took his mind from the gravity of the situation, as it provided the most spectacular entertainment he had seen in space, and they were in the middle of it. Blue spots danced about, orange wisps contorted around the heavens, and red and purple shots bolted through the celestial images. After absorbing the light show, Deacon retreated up to the top deck, where he spied Travers, who was resting comfortably in his room. *Did he really cry out or did I imagine it?* Deacon wondered. Sitting in front of the viewer, working the dials in front of him, he scanned the 360-degree view until they left the Sodern Inferno and traversed the escape route.

Quobit was suddenly beside him. "My small wounds ache. I believe I shall find a corner in the same room as Travers and sleep."

"Quobit, before you retire, look at that corner of the quadrant." Deacon pointed. "For a moment, I imagined that a tiny patch of stars blinked at me as I scanned the area." He rubbed his eyes, which were slightly sore from the sting of the air on Nix, thinking of how many hours had passed without a comatose sleep.

"Your eyes play tricks," Quobit said. "Like Travers and me, we all require sleep. Please get some, Deacon." Quobit left, and Deacon closed his eyes, but he shuffled restlessly in his seat for minutes. When he awakened, he strained his eyes again. He adjusted the monitor to calibrate the area they fled, and he unmistakably saw the same phenomenon again—a patch of stars directly behind them blinked out and then came back. In his state, he dismissed it to the gravitational forces in the dust clouds.

Acutely, he maintained the same lookout. To his surprise, the same spectacle happened. This time, however, a larger area was blocked out. It was as if there was a malfunction in the scanner. But there it was—a wave of blackness obliterating stars and then reversing to uncover the stars. He sat stunned.

"Gem," he called down to the lower deck, "does your screen show any signs of malfunctioning from nearby dust, lightning, electricity?"

"No, Master." He vaguely heard the reply, but it was definitive.

"Quobit. Quobit." He glanced into the room; she was sleeping, curled up, a smile on her face.

He focused on Gem again. "Gem, do you see blackness in the sky behind us, twisting at uh . . . one hundred twenty-two point five degrees?"

"No, Master."

"Gem," he said excitedly, "There it is, this time at ninety-seven point six degrees! The stars are blacking out, Gem. Something is causing a spatial disturbance!"

Once again Gem gave a barely decipherable response. "No, Master."

Deacon didn't believe that. The phenomenon appeared so rhythmic, so ominous. As he watched the skies, his eyes only inches from the screen, a wand of black hell started moving, this time on the left side of his screen. It then progressively moved across it to the right. His hands felt the screen, drawn to it. In madness, he pounded on the screen and then summoned Gem again.

"Sire, there is no visible or detectable object registering to cause such an occurrence. In addition, I do not see it."

Deacon persisted with his watch, sitting on the edge of his seat. All was serene as they rocketed through the heavens. After some time, the whole sky began to blacken, again from left to right, only this time the blackness waved up and down as it barreled across the heavens. Now the effect terrified him, causing him to jump. Deacon was petrified and confused. He was a man of science. He didn't believe in fantasies.

He was glued to the screen when it hit him. A face was now barely visible, with two enormous bloodshot eyes looking right into the spot where he sat in the ship. A protruding jaw stood out as wings flapped; a diabolical birdlike monster was about to engulf the *Heritage.*

"Gem!" he shouted, feverishly tried to warn them. "Alter course. Alter course. We are being attacked!"

There was no answer from below. He raced down to the lower level, where the Owlers were calmly going about navigating the ship, sitting at the control panels, warding off Deacon's distractions, focused on the escape mission. "Damn you two," he said. "There is something out there threatening us. I see a ship disguised as a bird! Disguised as a dragon. Look. Both of you!"

Gem looked back at him not with the expressionless, sterile face that he had grown accustomed to, but instead with a demonic sneer that sent him spinning into raw chills. "Gem, what's wrong? What are you doing?"

"Nothing . . . sire." Her answer was dispassionate, but the sneer remained.

He escalated up the stairs to see that the beet-red eyes were moving closer. "Summon the nearest patrol, Jim."

Outside, the wings flapped up and down. For an instant, Deacon even imagined that he heard their leathery movements, like the sound of an ancient pterodactyl. Suddenly, the ship accelerated, knocking him to the floor. But the demon kept pace. The face, with beak open and sharp teeth exposed, hissed at him, threatening to devour the ship, moving perilously closer, snapping.

The flapping now was so deafening that Deacon turned his head away and covered his ears as he lay on the floor. The vessel turned and rolled as he crashed into some cabinet doors. Then someone summoned him. "Deacon Coombs." The voice was the same mesmerizing pitch as the one he had heard on the mount. It was Urzel. And there was no escape. "You are dead. Submit. You are helpless against me." Then the voice launched into a sadistic laugh, first as a gurgle in the throat, moving to a fiendish howl that stuck as a malignancy in Deacon's brain. "You are mine. Submit to me."

Deacon remembered Lyanna. He thought of her and situated her firmly in his mind, trying with all his mental might to expel Urzel from his thoughts. He rose; he walked to the screen to stare at the two fiendish eyes, his body in shivers and a light-headed feeling smothering him. Then he recalled Lyanna's teachings. He stood rigid, his nerve mustered and his calm composure regained, and then calmly replied, "I am not afraid of you." He stood there with his arms folded, wearing a slight smile. Then, in an instant, he pointed at Urzel and screamed, "I am more powerful than you." He waved his arm, his fingers and palms open, and yelled, "Be gone, you snake! You are not wanted here. You are not in control of me any longer. Be gone!" He shouted over and over to admonish the demon. "I exorcise you from this ship!"

With the word *exorcise*, a strange happening occurred. He found himself on the floor of the observation deck, awake, drenched in sweat, his heart pounding. But all was quiet inside and with the heavens. The stars were all in their proper alignment, and the only sound was the murmur of the engines of the *Heritage*. *Was that a hallucination?* he wondered. He scampered to the control level immediately, where the Owlers were engaged in navigational exercises and communications with the real world.

"Where are we?"

Gem replied, "Master, we will be making a refueling stop at a mining colony within the hour, and we will then proceed to Thous, where we will Vesper."

"Did I summon you during the last while?"

"Yes, you inquired about a vision that you saw on your monitor on your deck."

"That is all? Nothing else happened? You heard me say nothing else?"

"You only presented a single inquiry, Master." Gem turned away to assist Jim.

"But did we flee from another ship?"

"There was another ship in pursuit, Master, but we hid in the Sodern Inferno, remember? We lost it as we traveled back into space."

Deacon wasn't satisfied. "Did you not see that giant demonic bird outside? Are there no records in the logs?"

Gem looked peacefully back. "Master, we have been engaged in navigating the *Heritage*. There was no bird or apparition. I do not understand. You did not summon us but once, to ask about a malfunction of your video screen." Gem and Jim began communicating with the docking station.

The bird, the dragon, the flapping wings—was this a dream? he wondered. The feelings of fear were real enough, and he felt a discomforting light-headedness throbbing in his forehead. Every muscle ached. He moved sluggishly to the counter to extract some medicine to relieve the aches. Then he entered the room where Quobit and Travers slept. Faintly, he heard, "Dea . . . con.

De-e . . . k-k-k-k-k . . . kon." He dropped the vial, and the pills rolled on the floor.

The sound petrified him. He moved slowly across the room and saw Travers lying on his cot. He had aged a hundred years. Deep furrows lined his face and his eyes had sunk into his head. Fresh purple plasma stained his beautiful fur, and the wound was bare, leaking more blood and plasma onto the sheets and over his body. "Dea . . . k-k-k . . . kon," he said, stretching his arms out in the direction of the Earthman.

Deacon shouted, "Gem, come here quickly." As he shouted, Quobit stirred and gasped at the sight of Travers's bloody torso. Deacon, on his knees, clutched Travers. The Aralian was convulsing, salivating profusely, and hanging on to Deacon for dear life. Quobit joined them and, sighed deeply, sensing the end of life.

"Travers, does the Alliance know that you took the *Sleigher* to Nix?"

"No. F-f-f-f-f-f . . . find Chu . . . bby. Ch . . . ch . . . ch."

"Where?"

"He has. He knows the s-s-s-s-s . . . secret. He h-h-h-h . . . has-s-s what you want. F-f-find Ch . . . ch . . . ch . . . Chubby. He . . . knows who devil is. Deeeeeeee . . ."

They sat and hugged until the last dying breath left Travers's cavity. In his emotional state, there was nothing better for Deacon to do than silently give praise for this honorable person whom he had come to admire. He held the little giant in his arms as Gem arrived, inspected him, and then pronounced him dead.

Deacon was angry. He turned to Quobit. "He deserved better than this." No one else heard his words.

As Deacon watched the body be sterilized and then bagged by the Owlers, he felt numb and angry. Flashes of their trip ripped apart his mind. He walked back to the control seat, where Quobit joined him, taking his hand and caressing it—a Jabu custom of sympathy. "What has been accomplished, Quobit? The little trader did not find peace from all the charges against him; we found an evil so powerful that millions of beings are obeying it, worshipping it. We have risked the odds, chanced death. And for what? The murders of Geor and Como have not been solved. And about Urzel, what can I say to Landrew?"

"Deacon, I think a quick rout by Alliance forces on the planet Nix is in order."

In silence, Deacon meditated about the events, believing that the terrifying encounter with Urzel had been real. *It had to be real. It had to be. Travers is dead.*

A hair's breadth

Deacon sat at his desk and carefully documented the events of his journey to Nix, his mind churning over the tragic loss of Travers. He'd felt a quiet camaraderie with this inoffensive Aralian, and the two of them had witnessed Urzel's terrifying tirade on the mount. "Quobit," he asked, "could you read this account and please add your observations and the events you experienced while we were separated?"

"Gladly. I am sorry for your loss, Deacon. On Jabu, it is our custom to pray over the dead body and pray that the afterlife of the spirit will exist in peace. Therefore, I shall say prayers over Travers shortly, but I will have to unbag the body. Will you join me?"

"Yes. How could Landrew and Schlegar possibly understand what we experienced? More importantly, how can one individual control so many? And from such a great distance? And reach out in space over thousands of miles to murder Travers? And an Earthling at that? And what possessed this thing to visit Nix? To arm Nicosians?" Deacon sat back. "Urzel cannot be an Earthman, Quobit. There must be another explanation."

Deacon closed his eyes. "The vision of the flapping bird outside the ship had to be the mind of Urzel, reaching in and strangling my brain. It just had to be, since Gem and Jim were totally unaffected by the experience. It bothers me that he reached out from afar in a vacuum. My feelings of horror were so real. It was not an object of illusion. Urzel had meant to frighten me, and he succeeded. Never had I felt so hopeless in my life, until I realized my powers to expel the demonic thoughts from my contaminated mind. My confidence warded off Urzel—a short-term victory provided by the teachings of Lyanna."

Quobit spoke in a firm voice. "This being is to be avoided. This being has to be destroyed quickly by Alliance forces. I fear that we are to be in constant peril, just as Travers, Geor, and Como before us."

"I am convinced that Urzel and I shared a physical state of union. Urzel reached out and desecrated my body, permeated me to share the sameness as I witnessed the giant bird. I point to the light-headed feeling as experienced by others."

Deacon held hands with Quobit as they stood. "It was Urzel that reached into Como's study and willed death; it was Urzel who touched Geor and forced the poison into his cavity; it was Urzel who murdered Travers." He peered into the faint silver light of the room where Travers's body lay, the dark wrinkles in the cover running randomly. "How utterly pointless to have killed Travers."

"Deacon, I will protect you. You have witnessed my physical strength. I know Urzel possesses a brutal and commanding mental strength, but I pledge that together we will defeat him. And don't forget your two trusty Owler friends."

"Our hope now is to run to the nearest station of friends, Quobit, to seek help during these insecure, unsettling times. Brebouillis is close after the Vesper from Thous." They retired into the room where Travers's body lay, and Quobit taught Deacon the ceremonial rituals of the Jabu and included him in them. During her address, Deacon was moved to tears as she cited beautiful poetry and her brief memories of Travers. He fantasized during her chanting, relishing the thought of seeing Lyanna again. He wondered if Lyanna knew of the unusual Earthman who had killed Travers. *Surely she would have warned me if she did,* he thought.

As they refueled, Gem arrived and provided nourishment, and the Owler sat across from Deacon as he revived an earlier dialogue. "Gem, I reluctantly believe your analysis that this thing on the mount that we witnessed is an Earthling. However, speculate on the Earthling that we saw on Nix."

"Master, Urzel is a dangerous specimen, as evidenced by the masses he held in suspension. It is very difficult for any of us to believe that an Earthman could do that, for it involves a quantum leap of mental abilities. There are some possibilities. The Earthman may be a puppet; his control over the masses on Nix, and the deaths of Como, Geor, and Travers, may be created by artificial means, by some machine or other device that we did not discover as we searched the caves. We must consider this possibility."

Deacon thought of a super Mindor machine. "That thought also occurred to me, since there is no evidence of Earthmen with such mesmerizing mental powers."

"However, Master, I recorded no instruments of any kind in the cave when you and I searched, and there was no detection of metallic equipment in the caves or on the ledge as we traversed it, and there was none on the ledge when Urzel spoke. While the evidence is inconclusive, Master, I do believe artificial manipulation is one possibility we should consider."

Quobit spoke up. "Taking your idea, Gem, and moving it one step further, could Urzel be manipulated by an alien? Perhaps the alien does not want to be seen at this time, so Urzel is fronting."

"We now have two ideas to investigate. Quobit's idea is a good one, since again no Earthling has ever been documented with the powers we saw."

Gem then posed a third possibility. "This Earthman could have been trained to perform these mental acts. Exposure to beings or a race could have brought this ability into clearer focus. For example, it is punishable by law for the Medullans to teach their gift of mental communication to aliens. However, power often yields to corruption."

"When we arrive on Brebouillis," said Deacon, "I want you and Jim to conduct a thorough investigation of all library banks to find out which Earthlings have had an unusual interest in Medullan powers. Find out if any Earthman has made frequent stopovers in Medulla recently. Look for evidence that an Earthling may have possibly gained and now misused these Medullan powers. Inspect for any possible regular or prolonged interface with Medullans."

"The records you seek, Deacon, may also exist on the planet Aralia in space trading logs or at the ports. To access them, Jim and I will need the security codes of Bothwen."

"Granted. Can we contact I'obo from Brebouillis?"

"Yes."

"Then ask for his additional help to find who frequents the planet Medulla from Earth, who has visited long enough to be trained and schooled by the Medullans, and which ships of the Union of Space

Traders voyage there on a regular basis. Quobit, perhaps you could assist the Owlers while I keep Lyanna and Schlegar entertained."

Gem then said, "The greatest possibility remains that he is authentic."

In a somber tone, Deacon said, "I doubt it. It is very difficult to hide a being with these supreme powers at any age. It seems as though Urzel is a giant leap forward in evolution for Earthmen, skipping thousands of years, which is why I doubt he is an Earthling. Schlegar and Lyanna praised my ability as superior to that of most Earthlings, and I know I couldn't murder Como by willing it, or keep thousands of Nicosians in a mental grip. Something is defying the laws of evolution and biology in this creature. How can such a creature hide? How could evolution as we know it make such quantum leaps?"

"The recorder does not deceive us, Master. Urzel is an Earthling, as identified by his metabolism and heartbeat. Of all the possibilities outlined, this has the greatest probability."

"Unless," Quobit said, "it is an alien from outside our universe who bears a metabolism similar to that of Earthmen."

Jim overheard them and said, "The chances of that are twenty-two million six hundred forty-one thousand three hundred to one."

Quobit and Deacon smiled, and Quobit then challenged him. "Do your math over, Jim, I think you are off by two hundred."

"I am the last off the assembly line and—"

"Okay, Jim, we believe you," said Deacon. "While we are all engaged in this surmising, may I add that if it is an alien from elsewhere, then we have the unique problem of figuring out where it came from and determining how to defeat it. If he is of Earth, then the records at Brebouillis shall expose his true identity, or the travel records on Aralia shall give us insight. This is the strangest piece of the puzzle. Earth has documented all academic records of those who have such abilities. A man so mentally superior would have been quite conspicuous on Earth. His life would have been observed—as was mine, and as were those of my parents before me—to ensure that his powers were not misused. Why did Schlegar and Lyanna not warn me of such a creature? Why would they not know of it?"

Quobit spoke up. "I like Lyanna, as you do. I am sure you can ask her directly upon return."

Deacon buried his head in the palms of his hands to once again pray that Lyanna was not a party to any deceit played on him. That left Schlegar and Landrew for him to direct his suspicion upon.

Gem looked at each of them. "There is another possibility. May I present it to you three?"

Reluctantly, Deacon said to Gem, "Continue."

"Perhaps he was of Earthling parents but born abroad in deepest space and only recently learned how to use the mental powers from Medullans. That would account for his anonymity. There are segments of deep space whose data Brebouillis has not captured."

"Perhaps."

"Sire, Gem, Quobit, and I do not have complete clearance to the records center on Brebouillis. If you recall, these are accessible by only Schlegar and his staff."

"Then you shall test your skills of breaking and entering at my order."

"We are not programmed to commit crimes. We must follow channels."

"Jim, we don't have time for games. This monster is on the loose. The safety of all mankind is at stake, including your master's life. Time is not on our side. We need to find the identity of the devil before he finds us. The only way to do that is to enter the file banks at Brebouillis. I believe that this should be done without the assistance of anyone else and in secrecy. I do not want any oversight or supervision or files being altered before we view them. I order you and Gem to protect me by finding the identity of this devil."

Quobit stood up to Jim. "You are the last Owler off the assembly line, so therefore you are the smartest. Prove it and find a way to access these confidential files."

Deacon cherished the moment as Jim pondered and replied, "Challenge accepted."

"I am convinced that I may be his next victim," Deacon said. This altered the mood to a sober moment. Quobit and the Owlers stood across from Deacon and pledged to protect him.

"The prime directive is to protect you, so the file entry will be accomplished," said Jim

"Now, that's the spirit." Deacon patted Jim on the shoulder. "I know that this thing, whatever it is, penetrated Travers's mind and killed him on the *Heritage*. I know this devil murdered Como and Geor. I want a complete list of all Earthlings who have passed the rigorous tests of mental communication in the past one hundred years. The list should include pure breeds, mutants, and hybrids. Every possible lead."

Deacon was sure that the search would turn up a number of child prodigies. However, if this was as normal as he hoped, then Urzel could have easily manipulated the files on Brebouillis to eradicate every ounce of incriminating information.

"Just to restate, I also want a list of frequent travelers to Medulla as we said before, and a record of the ships that travel there and for what purpose."

Gem spoke. "I do not feel emotions, sire, but I recognized a respectful camaraderie between you and Travers. Because of this, I wish to express my deepest sympathies toward your loss."

"Yes, I sincerely came to like the old trader. Like me, we are both pawns in a game not yet defined."

Quobit said to the Owlers, "Travers's dying words to Deacon were to locate Chubby Eaves. I shall focus on this. Travers even indicated that Chubby knows the identity of the demon."

As Gem and Jim left, Deacon settled in to examine the physical evidence collected on Nix. The chemical analyses of the hairs, furs, cutins, and scales were fascinating. The soils were documented and positively identified. In the middle of identifying a Jabu, a Bernardian, and an Aralian, Deacon found a piece of evidence so startling that he raced to the high-powered lens. He sat there for an hour, then addressed the computer, and then consulted his own book, *Protecting the Being*. With elation, after they left the mining station, he raced down to the control deck.

"Observe," he said, and he thrust the slide in front of Gem to analyze it.

"Should I check your data banks to identify?" Gem asked.

"That won't be necessary. I already have. I recognize the chemical constituents. The black color, even more so the pith and roundness, the symmetry, the oily coating so characteristic of Asiandans—that is, people from the Asianda region on Earth. The elemental analysis of the follicle is the crowning factor. So, Gem, an Earthman was on Nix at one time, most likely one of Asiandan descent."

"Perhaps Urzel is the Asiandan?"

Deacon asked of the Owler, "How many beings arrived on Nix in that ship?"

"Six. One Jabu."

"The caves are so clean, the cargo so neatly stored and labeled under the care of a Jabu."

"Then I recorded two Bernardians."

"The most unscrupulous race. I'll bet that they were drawn and bribed by greed to become converts."

"Sire, a Globianan was definitely in the crew, and finally an Inic'taurian."

"Right," Deacon said, "a tall, muscular Globianan being to obey orders and stack the boxes—a being of brute strength, the muscle man in the group. The Inic'taurian could be bribed to any task; they are the most unscrupulous traders. They are also great navigators and so could do the planning and provide the familiarity needed of the trade routes around the region of Nix. They most likely distributed well-placed bribes ahead of their journeys. There is no doubt in my mind that Urzel has an Aralian traitor trader somewhere in his troop." He paused. "You must uncover evidence of an Asiandan that may have exaggerated mental powers, and convey your findings only to me."

"Yes, sire," Jim said on behalf of both Owlers. "On Earth we determined that only a handful of Earthlings ever visited Medulla, for it is a harsh, brutal environment for any Earthling to exist in. None of them expressed any unusual mental capabilities, but we will search the files again."

"You already conducted that search?"

"Yes, Master. On Earth you requested such a search when it became apparent that Como and Geor may have actually been programmed to commit their own deaths. We traced all visitors to Medulla since their inception into the Alliance. The Globianans are best equipped to travel there, so naturally there were an abnormal number of them who landed on its moon. None descended to the planet. I determined that five Earthmen visited, all restricted to the orbiting moon and satellites. Interfacing on the planet Medulla is arduous and strictly prohibited by Medullan laws."

"Okay. Let us do the search again. Determine if the findings in the library in Liberty on Earth can be matched with historical logs at Brebouillis. More importantly, is there conflicting data or any discrepancies, and if so, what are they?"

Deacon, Jim, and Gem conversed further to review their assignments for Brebouillis. In addition, Deacon instructed Jim to find and copy the file on Morris Mydloan. While they were busy gaining entry to the files, he would relive the events that transpired on Nix with Schlegar and Lyanna. He would discuss most aspects to keep Schlegar and Lyanna distracted while Jim, Quobit, and Gem completed their investigations.

"Master Deacon," said Quobit, "there is a shuttle from Brebouillis to Aralia departing soon after we land. I suggest that I take it and land on Aralia to inspect trade ship records. Gem has sent a message to I'obo for assistance as you requested, but with the danger of his reply being intercepted, it makes more sense to receive it on the planet. Also, the Owlers are known there, and my investigations will draw less attention."

"Good idea," said Deacon. "In addition, you can locate Chubby Eaves when you are on the planet. You were correct in stating earlier that Travers made it sound like Chubby holds the true identity of the devil. How long will you be absent from Brebouillis?"

"Twenty-four of Earth's hours."

"Complete the tasks and return soonest. I don't want to spend more than two days on the moon. The real pressure is on Jim and Gem to crack the key to access files. We must be very careful in accessing Mydloan's files or else we will attract attention to our missions. Pursue that with extreme caution. On the signal from Jim and Gem that they have accessed all the information of necessity, only then will I raise the issue of Urzel and his identity as an Earthman, and only then will I disclose that Travers accompanied us to Nix. If the Owlers need more hours to decipher priority codes, there will be a definite problem. Quobit, please be careful. Check your surroundings frequently. Trust no one. Use your handheld device to contact me and send any information."

"Understood. We are now friends, Deacon, so may I also say, please be careful."

ESCAPE INTO DANGER

On Brebouillis

Deacon prayed that Schlegar and Lyanna would still be allies as his tale unfolded. Receiving no surprises from them would be a blessing. In the time remaining, he completed his trip report, visited the body of Travers to express his feelings once more, joyfully thought of Lyanna, which caused an infectious excitement to swell within him, and finally pined for Anglo and the comforts of Moonbeam and the companionship of Miram.

He would plead with Schlegar that his task was complete and that this matter should now rest in the hands of Alliance forces. He would tell the doctor that he was incapable of defeating the evil that he had witnessed and that it would be the responsibility of large armies to invade Nix and seize the caches of weapons; that forces more powerful than Deacon Coombs must confront this evil. All these issues created a roller coaster of emotions inside him. What worried him most of all was how the exact identity of Urzel would be determined.

Gem interrupted his thoughts. "Master, we are prepared to Vesper to Brebouillis upon your command."

"And I give it." Deacon sat in silence beside Quobit. As usual he felt ill, but he revived seemingly only seconds later to see they were emerging from the Vesper disc at Aralia and blasting toward Brebouillis.

Gem entered with good news. "We have made contact with Brebouillis. Lyanna is present. Schlegar is absent, gone to planet Aralia."

"Excellent." This twist of good fortune left him gloating. He turned to his Jabu friend. "More time spent with her, alone. However, I'll signal you when Schlegar returns; I think I want you present, Quobit, when we begin the discussion of Urzel. Meanwhile, I am counting on you to find Chubby Eaves."

"I promise I will. I have my contacts within the traders too. I wish Jim best of luck to unveil the security code for files on Brebouillis."

<hr/>

The *Heritage* docked safely. A reception of unfamiliar faces was there to greet them, with no sign of Lyanna. A complete physical was ordered for Deacon by the physician in charge, and the subsequent prescription by the doctor was rest. After his examination, a note arrived from Lyanna requesting a meeting at his leisure. He hurriedly dispelled the rest and hustled around to wash and dress. He then trotted down the hallway to her room. Outside her quarters, he paused to suppress his anxieties.

When she appeared, a nostalgic smile greeted him. There the two embraced spontaneously. Lyanna broke the hug after five seconds. Then she took his hand and they sat next to each other in her sitting area to commence a sincere chat, during which she expressed relief at his safe return numerous times. He accepted her compliments while she basked in his subtle felicitations. Realizing the vulnerability of his thoughts to her, he was careful to suppress his feelings about the mission, the Owlers' search, his worries concerning Morris Mydloan, Travers's death, and the discovery of the devil, Urzel.

<hr/>

Entering the information vaults on Brebouillis was a frustrating exercise. Jim attempted to use every word and combination of syllables in the universal language, but he was not able to gain access. While Jim programmed the complete dictionary again, he also constructed algorithms of names, geography, and history. The procedure was futile. The library remained locked.

⇒◈◈◈⇐

The time for renewing acquaintances had passed. Lyanna demanded all the details of Deacon's adventure, recording the session for Schlegar's benefit. Deacon plodded through the tale cautiously. Interbedded with the facts were his personal feelings of fear, exhilaration, apprehension, horror, and discovery, all of which reinforced the realism of the saga. Lyanna held his hand while digesting every word, expressing her concern when appropriate. Lyanna's feelings soaked proudly into Deacon.

Suddenly an Owler appeared to state that Dr. Schlegar would return early from his business on Aralia on the next flight out. The two repeated their series of embraces. Deacon still withheld the fact that Travers had accompanied them on the mission. This was to be his first revelation in their next meeting after Quobit and Schlegar had returned. He conveniently excused himself and retired, slinging himself prostrate onto his cot, promising a full account of the tale at their next meeting. Lyanna pecked him on the cheek.

Later, in Deacon's quarters, after rest had revitalized him, Jim expressed frustration. "We have tried numbers, alphabets, words, phrases, slang, proper names, places, syllables—every combination imaginable," said Jim.

"When was the code changed last?"

"The new code was entered after our departure. It was entered by Schlegar."

"Who has access to the code?"

"Just the computers, Schlegar, and Dr. Miodo."

"Not Lyanna?"

"No."

"Did you try 'Deacon Coombs'?"

"Affirmative."

"Nix, Nicosian, *Heritage, Sleigher*?"

"Yes. All of them."

Deacon wearied of the conversation.

Jim then said, "We cannot conceal our intentions much longer as I spend inordinate amounts of time on the computer that houses the entry code. Could you ask Lyanna to inquire as to access?"

"No. I won't compromise Lyanna. One last thought: the traders' code book—the one we discovered before we departed—and the file that had the word *urzelli* in it. Have we input all those ancient code words?"

"No, sire. Good suggestion and it is worth a try." Jim skipped out of his quarters, and Deacon felt a sense of pride at his idea just as Gem ambled in. "Greetings, Master. I have stored important files on ship routes, including all those passing close to Nix, landing on the moon of Nix, and using the closest Vesper stations, thanks to Quobit. It was a very successful trip, and the access of Bothwen was valuable to her. Jim and I will have an abundance of data to sift through to find what beings have frequent interaction with Medullans."

Quobit entered. Deacon was anxious and hugged her. "Thank you for all the data. Did you locate Chubby Eaves?"

"No," said Quobit, "Chubby Eaves departed Aralia soon after we left on our mission."

"What flight plans did he file?"

"Here's the perplexing news. He did not file flight plans that can be viewed by Bothwen. Purposely, I believe. I imposed upon I'obo, who is checking now. I could not find which ship he commanded. Rather suspicious, wouldn't you say?"

"I have delayed talking to Schlegar long enough," said Deacon. "His Owler invited us for dinner."

In a droning tone, as they walked the corridor to meet Schlegar and Lyanna, Jim called after Deacon to announce quietly that the entry code had been broken by using the old Aralian trader codes. Now Deacon's enthusiasm and confidence regarding telling Schlegar about Travers and Urzel surfaced. The opportunity came soon as the foursome engaged in a lavish meal.

Travers remembered

"I waited until your return, Schlegar, to disclose a critical decision and the results of our trip. I apologize, Lyanna, for not telling you earlier, but I felt that the events were best discussed upon Schlegar's arrival and between the four of us, since Quobit is witness to some of these events." Deacon exhaled heavily, mustered his boldness, and commenced with his revelation.

"Please allow me to complete my tale before you pass judgment on any decision, react to any event, or interrupt. I ask this of you. Telling the entire tale will answer your questions." Schlegar seemed puzzled, and Lyanna alarmed. Both, however, nodded in agreement.

"On the planet of Aralia, I met Travers." Schlegar's eyes perked up. Lyanna slid closer to Deacon and locked her arm in his. Quobit sat stoically, her arms folded. "I talked with him at length in a secret hideout deep in the hills of Glagn, where he recited to me his story of the trial. He convincingly professed his innocence in the killings of Geor and Como. Furthermore, Travers convinced me . . . he pleaded with me . . . to take him to a planet called Nix to prove his innocence. And I did. We—the two Owlers, Quobit, I, and Travers—journeyed there!"

Schlegar was burning with irritation. His nose twitched, conveying his annoyance. He leaned back and said in a nearly inaudible whisper, "Please continue."

"Schlegar, please look at me," said Deacon. The doctor raised his head. "Travers was guarded at all times by my Owlers on this trip. Our mission was never in danger. There was never a chance of failure or sabotage by Travers, for Travers could not have manipulated the Owlers' minds. He did not influence my decision making in any way, and I will convey the absolute evidence of that in this tale." With a silence from Schlegar, and complete quietness in the room, Deacon proudly added, "I grew to know him and respect him."

Quobit recognized the silent tension and was eager to speak. "Dr. Schlegar, I want to add that Travers was very cooperative and honest in all his assessments of our journey and fought side by side with us against evil, as Deacon will confirm."

Deacon spoke up, sitting vertically, looking directly into Schlegar's eyes. "Travers was a frail, helpless being who had been tortured mentally by the previous ill-fated journeys to a planet called Nix. His crew is here, and Travers's thoughts and sympathies were here with them. He showed us the way there, to Nix, located for us the sites where he had previously encountered an evil, aided the Owlers and me to gather facts about missing shipments of Alliance arms, fought bravely in times of conflict as was required, and showed us the way to safety once our mission of gathering data was complete."

Schlegar was furious. "You have made a grave miscalculation of justice, an error for which you may have to pay dearly. Abetting a criminal is just as serious an offense on Aralia as on Earth as in the Alliance."

"No, Schlegar. Travers became my ally. You must hear the entire story before you pass judgment." Deacon suddenly found it hard to speak.

Schlegar was relentless. "You were sent by the highest authority figure in the Alliance to bring this man to justice, and you dare to call him ally after such a short period of time. Deacon Coombs, you have betrayed those who employ you. You are employed by the Alliance, not the Union of Space Traders."

"Sorry, Schlegar, but he was my friend."

The gravity of the situation eased as Schlegar paused and sat back, his eyes wide. "What do you mean by"—he twitched his ruddy nose—"*was* my friend?"

Lyanna reiterated the same thought.

Deacon bowed his head. It was painful for him to recall that incident of seeing Travers drowning in the pool of his own liquids; painful to recall seeing his body bagged by the Owlers. "I'm sorry, Schlegar. Travers died on the return trip as we were escaping from some great evil that we unmasked. The creature followed us and invaded the *Heritage* and murdered Travers just as the creature murdered Como and Geor. Maybe also just as he murdered Geor's son because he came too close to the truth." With that comment, Deacon slid a disc of his report to him. "It is all documented here in this report for Landrew, written by myself with comments from Quobit. You are welcome to read this copy before I submit it, so you can appreciate the heroism of Travers."

Deacon rose and moved to the other side of the table and placed his hand on Schlegar's shoulder. "I am certain that if you could only have known your son in his moment of heroism, if you could have accompanied us on this trek and seen and heard his actions, you would have been proud of him and regained your respect for your son. Travers performed valiantly. I believe you could have found reconciliation through his actions."

Schlegar was not convinced and stood in anger. "You are naïve, Coombs. I did not want reconciliation. I wanted a reformation of character. I wanted justice."

"Schlegar, he exhibited honor in all his actions."

Schlegar was bitter, seeming distrustful in his glances at Deacon. "This presents a new dimension to your journey. How much was staged for your benefit? Aha, I see you never considered that!"

Deacon grew irate at the ludicrous suggestion that Nix and Urzel had been staged by Travers. He replied, "Travers is dead. That is final. His body lies in your ceremonial cooler, awaiting instructions for his burial."

Schlegar sat down. "I shall attend to it later."

"Are you really disappointed in me?"

"Greatly. You were our one shining hope."

"To do what?"

"To bring justice to this matter."

"And in front of two witnesses, I am disappointed in you, Schlegar. Not just because you cannot come to peace with your dead son, but because I had to venture beyond Brebouillis, beyond the edge of our worlds, beyond Landrew and you, to discover that Morris Mydloan, who tried to assassinate me on Earth"—he raised his voice to drown out Schlegar's potential interruption while pulling down his collar to expose the scar on his neck—"was in the employ of the Alliance and even came here to get, shall I dare say, programmed! Programmed to assassinate me!" Deacon extended his arms to plead for an answer. "Explain to me why I should trust you."

Lyanna was aghast. She placed her hands over her mouth in surprise while coming between them, looking at each alternately.

Schlegar was despondent. "Morris Mydloan was a serious miscalculation in judgment. We all bear the scars of his failure. I carry that burden personally. When he was my patient here, during his authentic bout of mental illness, he was a madman. But time seemed to mellow him as he responded to treatments. His biochemistry changed; his mental state was altered. All the doctors here agreed that a being of his extreme mental capacity could be of enormous value in this case. Even the computers agreed. Morris Mydloan was then sent to uncover this evil."

"Damn your computers!" Deacon shouted, full of rage. "An instrument of the Alliance was turned against me! If not for Gem, I would be dead now."

Lyanna asked, "Schlegar, how did this happen?"

"We conditioned him to travel around the universe to interrogate a specific list of people. The quest started out perfectly as Mydloan transmitted regular reports back to Landrew and me and then . . . Mydloan vanished. Through our security network, we recalled him, but there was no reply, only a deadly, disturbing silence. The next time that anyone saw him or heard from him, I ashamedly admit, was in the library on Earth when he attacked you. Believe me, Deacon Coombs, I deeply regret his actions. I felt that . . . it was my duty to help you to make up for my shortcomings about Morris, so I asked Landrew to send you here, where you could benefit from Lyanna and me preparing you."

"What happened to Morris? Why did he turn against the Alliance? Do you have any guesses?"

"No."

"Well, I do. I think he may have killed Geor's son for his new master. Whoever murdered him got close to him, and the facts from the murder scene infer he was murdered by an ally. He is much more of a suspect than Travers."

Schlegar pounded his fist on the table. "You underestimated my son. He lied, cheated, and deceived—all non-Aralian traits."

Deacon was eager to reply. "There seem to be more exceptions to the rules and history of Aralian integrity, as I learn every day."

Schlegar did not debate the insult. He instead said in a soft tone, "We debated whether to inform you of Mydloan's activities. Landrew urged me to do so before you left. Lyanna is innocent; she had no idea that Mydloan attacked you on Earth." Deacon was relieved to hear this. "However, I wanted you to leave here to investigate on your own accord, to discover facts in your own way and not retrace the steps of Morris Mydloan to find out why he turned traitor."

"Right, like the unbiased facts you fed me about Travers?" Deacon's tone was caustic.

"I knew my son better than anyone." Their eye contact remained unbroken.

"Schlegar," said Quobit, "if I may be permitted, I want to go on record as telling you and the Alliance that we have met the terrible evil responsible for stealing arms and killing Como and Geor, and we fought bravely to save ourselves from his army."

At that moment, an Owler passed by them to Schlegar and spoke in his ear. Schlegar whirled to face Deacon. "What do your Owlers seek by probing into confidential files in our library and without my concurrence? And how did they gain access to these confidential files?"

Deacon waited until Schlegar had concluded another rant about Travers and then calmly addressed him. "We gathered important data on Nix that needs to be analyzed. This cannot be performed without the services of your facility here. The Owlers perform functions under my guidance and at my commands."

"And what gives you that authority?"

Deacon was disturbed and disappointed at the tone of Schlegar's voice. "You mean who gives me the authority? The answer is Landrew."

"Landrew did not give you such authority!"

Lyanna grabbed their hands and pulled them closer. "Deacon, Schlegar, there is a crisis at hand. We must work together. Schlegar, we must hear the rest of Deacon's tale. Please."

Deacon broke the grip and proceeded to wipe his sweaty palms in his pockets as Schlegar stepped away to whisper something to his Owler—obviously something he did not intend for Deacon to hear. A signal suddenly came over Deacon's handheld from his Owlers, notifying him that they had completed their search.

"How did Travers die?" Schlegar asked.

"It is all there in my diary on this chip."

"I will read it later. For now, tell me how he died."

"We encountered a creature with mental powers beyond any ever witnessed before in our galaxy." Deacon sat down; Lyanna and Schlegar and Quobit followed suit. "This thing, this being, reached out and controlled the minds of the Nicosian natives from tens of miles distant. We barely escaped from Nix with our lives."

Quobit was anxious to interject. "Schlegar, in the desert of Jabu are many terrifying wild creatures, but never have I been so frightened. This monster held wild savages in a trance; it worked them into frenzy, and while we were awaiting the arrival of Jim and the *Heritage* to rescue us, a band of savages attacked Deacon and Travers and me. I have never fought so hard, for these savages fear nothing. I sustained bruises"—she showed one of her blemishes to Lyanna and Schlegar—"and Travers received near-fatal wounds, losing copious amounts of blood."

Deacon took over the conversation. "We escaped Nix, but the creature followed the *Heritage* in space and invaded our ship and killed Travers by forcing him to rip off his own bandages, causing him to painfully bleed to death. We found him too late.

"The name of this thing we witnessed, this creature with glowing, devilish eyes, is Urzel, just as Temisori screamed. Urzel is probably still locked in Temisori's mind. Urzel pursued us in space during our escape. As he interfaced with our ship, he bent Travers's mind to self-destruction and forced him to kill himself the same way he forced Geor and Como to their deaths. Travers succumbed easily in his weakened state."

Schlegar said, "I would please ask you and Quobit to remain here with Lyanna. I wish to view the body."

Deacon grabbed Schlegar's arm. "Schlegar, he was a friend of the Alliance. Be kind in your last words. Travers died bravely in defense of the Alliance. We should not seek to incriminate him anymore, for it is this devil Urzel who should be brought to justice." He wanted to say more, but Schlegar ignored him, waved his hand as if to brush away the words, pulled loose from his grip, and left. Lyanna comforted him by giving him a tight hug. Their bodies pressed against each other for an extended period of time, each of them thinking how valuable this friendship could become.

Deacon broke the embrace. "I feel terrible. Travers was tormented by this trip to Nix. He ventured and gambled to prove his innocence, to find peace. Instead he found death. It is my fault that the reunion of father and son will never take place."

"No, no, no. You can't blame yourself. It was fate. It was this demon."

Deacon pulled Lyanna to him and held her tightly again for many minutes until Schlegar returned.

"Perhaps we should discuss this being further," said Schlegar. "It seems to me that this Urzel, if that is what you called him, is the same creature Temisori referred to when he shouted out."

"Yes, Schlegar, I told you, one and the same."

"This creature has my interest piqued." Schlegar's mood had metamorphosed, and he amicably offered after-dinner refreshments as the four sat around a table. Quobit placed herself on alert, as she suspected this change in Schlegar's attitude was a way of manipulating them. Deacon elaborated on Urzel, rambling on about the journey from Aralia to Nix, the rituals that he and Travers witnessed, and the trip back to Brebouillis, omitting very little. Then he came to the startling climax. "On the escape journey to Thous, the Owler Gem divulged a most astonishing fact to me." He paused for effect. "All the bio readings that Gem recorded point to the fact that Urzel is an Earthling."

Schlegar, who was penning his own notes as well as engaging a recorder, placed his pen on the table and stared back in astonishment. "Impossible! That comment is totally absurd. There is no record of such an Earthling with the type of mental domination of which you speak."

"Schlegar, you can review Gem's recordings and decide, for the record speaks for itself. Urzel is an Earthman."

Schlegar was firm in his belief. "I will scrutinize these records, and I will repeat that Urzel, this monster you described, this devil, is no Earthman. I stand on this record."

Lyanna was equally adamant. "Deacon, I have studied and observed all Earthlings who have exceptional mental abilities. I can swear to Schlegar's statement. You are possibly one of the most advanced, but even you could not ever reach into a sanctuary like Como's and murder him, let alone hold thousands of savages in a trance over tens of miles."

"Please listen to me, Schlegar and Lyanna. I was sent with an open mind to identify the villain of recent ails in our alliance. With many questions yet to be answered, and with the deaths of Como and Geor still unresolved, I believe that I have found the source of evil. He is a mighty force . . . and he is of Earth. Believe it and move forward from that fact. Any other assumption may cause us all future failure and embarrassment. Urzel has stockpiled a large cache of powerful weapons on Nix, and as I told you in my summary, he has allies within the Alliance, as evidenced by the leagues of other races following him. He has enough firepower to start and win a war if he can recruit troops, especially millions of bloodthirsty cannibals of Nix who wouldn't know any better than to follow him into a battle, led by his mental fixation of their minds."

Quobit was quick to chime in. "Savages they are; low on the evolutionary scale they are. But they mysteriously have the ability to receive this creature's brain waves and be held by his power."

For long after, they debated the origin of the creature, with Schlegar postulating other theories that Deacon dismissed. Schlegar consistently denied knowledge of any families on Earth who could have bred such an offspring. "I can't believe it. Evolution does not take these quantum leaps, as you yourself said earlier, Deacon."

Lyanna said, "The strong take eons to become stronger, Deacon, as in the Medullans—their mental prowess took millions of years to evolve."

After Deacon and Schlegar and Lyanna had worn thin all the circular arguments and counterarguments, they agreed to prescribe a break, so Deacon visited the Owlers in his quarters and Quobit went her separate way. Deacon instructed the Owlers. "I want the short list of high-priority suspects. Schlegar must not know of our intent if we are to investigate unbiased."

"Sire," Jim proudly said, "while Schlegar and his Owlers know of our entry, Gem and I have ensured their ignorance of where we navigated in the system, and likewise our specific entries and retrievals."

"Excellent."

"It is great work, agreed. It is expected of us. We are programmed, Master, to—"

"Yes, yes, I know, Jim," said Deacon, and he whisked them into the adjacent room so he could drop out of consciousness, fantasizing that he was in the clutches of Lyanna's arms.

The following day's conversation with Schlegar centered on the Nicosians: their physicality, their habits, their patterns, their social structure. Then the stolen arms were addressed, with Gem showing Schlegar and Lyanna the video footage in the caves. Eventually Gem displayed footage from the top of the mount, and Schlegar saw the weakened state of his son.

"When will you have his funeral?" asked Deacon.

"No funeral. Just as in Como's case, we simply commit the ashes into space."

"What? The remains of millions of dead Aralians float around in space?"

"Yes. Aralia at some time in her past became so cluttered with nonproductive burial plots of Aralians that it was decided to convert the remains of prominent citizens to pure energy at Vesper stations and send misguided beams to the edges of the galaxy. Travers's remains have already been sent." Schlegar talked about this subject matter coldly; Deacon and Quobit were dismayed to not have one last solemn minute.

"You should have told me this yesterday so I could have paid my final respects," Deacon said. "It seems such a cruel . . ." he was at a loss as to how to finish his thought.

They soon moved on and completed hours of discussions on the details of the trek, Schlegar insisting on every intricate detail of his version about the sermon on the mount. Later, after Deacon had retired and reread the Owlers' accounts of their investigation, he conversed with the Owlers privately. "We have overlooked a connection somewhere. There are no obvious candidates for Urzel in your report, and no Asiandans." Pointing a finger at them, he said, "Check and double-check every person again. And visitors to Medulla! This list lacks any obvious leads. Jim, we must check all ships that have passed there and their inhabitants."

Before Jim had time to orate his speech about the Owlers' efficiency, Deacon vanished down the hallway, frustrated at their total inability to identify Urzel. Some clue had been overlooked.

Urzel is an Earthling

Back in Schlegar's lab, Schlegar had been waiting for Deacon after conducting his own assessment of Urzel, and he attacked him at the first opportunity, as Lyanna witnessed. "I don't doubt what you witnessed, Deacon; I simply state that there is no Earthling with the mental powers that you described. Outside of the Medullans, who can stretch their mental prowess, all other races who exhibit the power of the Uscher zone have to be in proximity to their subjects, and I have examined our files over and over. This Earthman doesn't exist."

Lyanna added to Schlegar's outburst. "Suddenly, Deacon, you expect us to believe that an Earthman can control thousands of minds at great distances, as you saw on Nix. 'Quantum leap' would be an understatement for what you saw. Again, I don't doubt what you observed; I, as Schlegar, simply question the obvious interpretation. Urzel is not an Earthman."

"Schlegar, Lyanna—let me state the facts. Urzel is not a machine, not an apparition; he is an Earthling. He did manipulate minds at great distances. I can't explain it, but he did it! Gem's recording of the ceremony and his biological analysis support these facts."

"Then he must be a Medullan or an alien in disguise. There cannot be another explanation."

"He is not an alien, Schlegar, for he has the heartbeat of an Earthling. That is exactly how Gem confirmed his origins. He is not a Medullan, for he lacks their profile for metabolism. Check Gem's records."

The debate continued until Schlegar ended it by thrusting his arms in the air to express his frustration. At least Deacon felt comfortable that Schlegar had not withheld information from him. Lyanna was left alone with him and posed a different scenario. "Is there any wild possibility that Urzel was close to you and projected the figure on the mount? Or used Travers to project the bird in space?"

"Gem's opinion is unbiased, and Gem confirmed the figure on the mount as real and as an Earthling."

"How could an ordinary Earthman evolve into this creature?"

"I don't know. But I am losing an extraordinary amount of sleep thinking about it; an inordinate amount of time arguing about it."

"Well, Deacon, believe what you witnessed. You were there. We were not."

"How will I convince anyone of this? It seems that Quobit and the Owlers are my only allies on this. Have you talked to Quobit about this?"

"Yes, she confirmed your entire tale." She tried her best at being patronizing. "As I said, Deacon, you were there."

Schlegar returned hours later with a blatant order. "Landrew wants you to conduct your own investigation on the identity of Urzel. Then you will be released. You will be compensated handsomely."

"Released? *Released?* That is the word that he used?"

"Yes. I spoke with him a few hours ago. Those were his exact words."

"Why does he not speak to me personally?"

"I informed him that I would convey his message. Landrew apologizes that he is engaged elsewhere in important business."

Deacon was irritated, and so he spoke rudely. "I will investigate the identity of Urzel further only if I choose to do so."

"Deacon Coombs, I know that you believe in this heartbeat analysis, but the threat of alien invasion is fast becoming a reality. It may be an alien that possesses the body of an Earthman named Urzel. We don't have time to mobilize other investigators. Our other investigators have failed. None of them have returned except you. You already have come face-to-face with the real enemy. Your account of your adventure made me shiver as you described the evil of this monster. Please, Deacon, I ask you on behalf of an Alliance and their people. Continue your work on this mystery."

As at Moonbeam when Jim first appeared, it was useless for Deacon to argue. "And I have another theory."

Lyanna prompted him. "Which is?"

Theories

"I don't know quite how to express this, but let me try. For a time we believed that Urzel could bend Vesper beams, but I never believed that. From the time that Landrew and I viewed that tape in the library on Earth, I thought to myself that Travers took that vessel to Nix. I just didn't know why, unless Travers had previous evidence of Urzel and went there to destroy him.

"Now we come to Urzel. If he really is an alien with the powers I observed, then we are helpless against him. Urzel has performed immense deeds of treachery, the most dramatic of which have been to reach out over great distance to invade minds and shape thoughts to his demonic ends, and to murder Como and Geor.

"However, he is an Earthman. So the identity of Urzel and his origins are of secondary interest to me. The primary interest of this investigation should be—how did he get this power? We know that the hair found on Nix, coupled with Gem's metabolic analyses tell us that he is an Earthman, possibly an Asiandan."

"Humpff," said Schlegar.

"I think that Urzel has dramatically acquired a way to utilize and transmit his power, to use it in a way that we aren't fathoming. I read a book once about the reactions of disbelief when the Wright Brothers discovered the miracle of flight on Earth; reactions were similar when Vesper revealed to disbelieving Aralians that interspace travel was possible through Vespering and demolecularization. Schlegar, the physicist Vesper died with all Aralians in disbelief of his miracle. Did he not?"

Schlegar nodded his head.

"Do you plan to die in disbelief that Urzel is an Earthman, Schlegar? Do you plan to deny it so that we will always be looking in the wrong place for him? Making the wrong assumptions? It seems to me that if you and I and Lyanna accept that fact and commence an investigation based on the only fact we have in our possession, we can greatly focus our efforts on the appropriate issue no matter what your damn files on Brebouillis say, and no matter what your theories say. How did Urzel become this powerful monster? Witchcraft? Aliens? No, I think not, Schlegar. We just haven't uncovered the answer yet. We have to think as Vesper did. No bounds on ideas. No limitations on our scientific investigations. Consider any theory possible." While Lyanna and Schlegar cogitated on the words of Deacon, he asked, "Do you accept this challenge?"

Schlegar nodded, as did Lyanna. "For the sake of expediency, please continue," said Schlegar.

"I will continue my investigation but never to journey to Nix again. Determining how Urzel obtained this ability will inevitably expose his weakness. That is how I catch other criminals—by finding their weaknesses and exploiting them. No one commits a perfect crime." Deacon recounted the incident in which the projection of Urzel outside the spaceship was in the form of a menacing bird and how it had reached out to touch even his own mind. He explained how Urzel had sparred mentally with him.

Schlegar jumped and broke into a tirade. "You never told me this! You led me to believe that you resisted the incursion of Urzel into your mind."

"It was only momentary, Schlegar. I recovered by standing up to the evil, by threatening him in return. I used what Lyanna taught me—the ability to change my moods."

Schlegar was visibly upset. "Morris Mydloan was perfectly healthy until he met the creature. You may be programmed, just as Morris was, awaiting instructions to perform a dark deed, awaiting a cue to assassinate Landrew. Deacon, this is damaging information."

Deacon was furious. "What paranoia, Schlegar. I am in no way afflicted by Urzel. Hear me out! You asked me only a few minutes ago to accept the challenge of trying to identify this villain, and I said to you that I accept. Now, a second later, you think I'm contaminated and not fit for this assignment."

Lyanna was convinced, so she carried Deacon's argument to Schlegar. "Schlegar, Deacon has witnessed this madman. He must be the one to finish this assignment. You and Landrew agreed on this, and there is no reason to doubt Deacon."

"I am deeply concerned over this development." Schlegar threw up his arms and left the two of them alone.

"You believe that Urzel respects you now that you stood up to him."

"No. Well, maybe—momentarily."

Two security guards arrived at the door with the doctor. "I am sorry, Deacon, but in the name of the Alliance, I shall have to detain you until I have completed some customized tests to provide me the satisfaction that you have not been affected by interfacing with this evil. I desire no confrontation."

"Schlegar," Deacon said, raising his voice, "this is madness. Every minute we delay to continue the investigation brings further advantage to the enemy. I have done nothing to warrant this detention. I am and always will be faithful to the Alliance."

"You went to Nix and escaped from this powerful creature. Maybe he 'let you escape for a demonic purpose. How could you possibly know? Tests are warranted."

"No. I am sane and determined to probe into his identity."

"There is the possibility that you are unknowingly a disciple of Urzel, just like Morris Mydloan." Schlegar pointed his finger at Deacon. Lyanna tried to reason with her mentor. "Please, Schlegar, give Deacon a chance to continue his mission. What has come over you? Deacon is in complete control of his senses."

"That is what I intend to determine. You remain here on this moon until I give you further clearance to leave."

"Schlegar, come to your senses," Deacon said, seeing that it was hopeless. Schlegar was stubborn. As Deacon rose to leave the room, an Owler extracted his laser gun and aimed it at Deacon. "It comes to this. You threaten me? He who ventured and risked his life to find the creature? You will maim or kill me?"

Jim and Gem were proceeding down the hallway to the area where Lyanna, Schlegar, and Deacon were now in a confrontation. The Owlers had completed their survey of all the pertinent files and finished all their master's requests. They were summoned by Quobit as the Jabu saw Schlegar walk furtively toward Deacon with a security Owler accompanying him. Upon entering the room, Lyanna was sobbing, but more distressing was the Owler who had a weapon fixed on their master. Before Schlegar could respond, Gem exercised actions to follow the prime directive by ripping apart the Owler's vital controls with a single strategically placed destructive shot as Schlegar gasped.

Jim stood guard at the door outside. Inside, the scene turned to chaos. As the Owler smoldered on the floor, Schlegar dropped to his knees. "I am sorry, Deacon, but I must ask you not to go. It is my duty to make sure that your mind has not been tampered with. You must understand my position. I must perform these tests. I must detain you."

Lyanna ran out of the room as Deacon aided Schlegar to his feet. "I am not a spy. I depart for Earth. I have an extremely important theory to test there. You must meet me in Liberty City in three days. Do you understand? I believe that there is some important news that I can share with you and Landrew at that time. If not, I will have failed and we all will have failed. Schlegar, my mission on Earth is secretive and dangerous. Do I have your word not to follow me or to undermine my efforts? Do I have your word not to block our Vesper to Earth at the Vesper station? We must have safe journey."

Schlegar examined the disabled Owler and then looked Deacon straight in the eye. "I will have to disclose this incident to Landrew and inform him about your interface with this . . . Urzel. I will not send a squad in pursuit, and reluctantly I will not block your Vesper. But, Deacon, I am sorry that we part under such circumstances. I cannot give you my word that Alliance forces will not pursue you once Landrew learns of these events. You must understand my position. You may be programmed to commit treacherous deeds."

"Can you give us a head start before you report to Landrew? So we can safely land the *Heritage* at a destination on Earth known only to me?"

After giving it some thought, Schlegar replied as he sobbed. "Okay, that much I will do."

"You must also transmit my report on the journey to Landrew, but delay the transmission until we have reached Earth. Do I have your word on this matter?"

"Yes, I swear."

"Then I will say good-bye, Schlegar, and thank you for your hospitality. See you in Liberty City. I will summon you when we require your help."

With Gem and Jim as escorts, they raced down the corridor. Deacon stopped by his room and gathered his gear, all the important documents he had accumulated, and the evidence collected on Nix. He packed his personal belongings and then visited Lyanna's quarters. She did not answer, so he disappointedly raced to the *Heritage* and scrambled up the ramp. As he did so, he noticed Gem checking lift-off requirements and Quobit bringing on supplies.

In a burst, they were inside, Gem starting the engines and Jim fending off unwanted curious Owlers. As Deacon ascended to his personal deck, he was confronted by a mass of computer printouts situated in front of a small computer and a multitude of discs and logs piled high in a spew of sloppiness. To his amazement, he found Lyanna squatting behind the mess. "You will need all this data," she said. She planted a kiss on his cheek and then hastily pranced down the stairs and disappeared before he could speak and say his good-byes. Drowning in disappointment again, he stood there absorbing what had just transpired.

Soon a voice behind him said, "Permission to board, sir?" He looked down the stairs. It was Lyanna. "I have completed my work here on Brebouillis. I understand from speaking to the Owlers earlier that this ship travels to Earth. I can be of more use to you if I am with you than I can here on Brebouillis without you. I have missed Earth. I missed you. I'm not letting you get away without me this time. I want to go with you, and you won't be disappointed in my research efforts. That will be my role—senior research analyst. Quobit has already agreed."

Quobit sheepishly nodded an affirmation and said, "I think this new mate will not easily be discouraged."

Deacon felt warm all over. "I have a very specific mission on Earth. It could be dangerous, perhaps even fatal."

"Permission to board, sir?" she said again, standing at attention.

Jim yelled from below. "Please help her locate the seatbelt, sire. We are blasting off for the Vesper station!"

"Permission granted," said Deacon. "Please come closer." He extended his hand to help her climb the last few stairs. He then led her to a seat beside his, the one that Travers had formerly occupied. The *Heritage* jerked, and they were unable to maintain their balance. In the process, they tumbled to the floor, laughing; Lyanna ended up on top. Sheepishly Deacon said, "I must say, you took my advice to come closer literally."

Quobit grabbed her under her waist and hoisted her up and into her seat. Deacon helped himself.

"Seatbelts, please," Quobit insisted.

"This could be dangerous. I wasn't kidding," said Deacon.

"I am due for a bout of excitement," Lyanna replied. "Schlegar's erratic behavior frightened me. He really is like a second father to me, though. I think he's scared of the unknown. That's exactly what you presented him with—the unknown."

The *Heritage* bypassed local traffic to jump into the basin to prepare for Vespering. Jim appeared with the liquid remedies to lessen the demolecularization. In his usual humorous way, he added, "Aperitifs, anyone?"

Lyanna showed the initiative to hold hands with Deacon during the Vespering process. The ship dematerialized while they held on to each other tightly. At the Vesper station near Earth, the *Heritage* reatomized to produce a chain of events. The recognition of the craft prompted engineers at the station to alert the Alliance as to her arrival, and Landrew personally sent greetings and informed them of his anticipation to meet them soon. Deacon, however, had other ideas.

The *Heritage* rose higher and higher as Deacon leaned forward in his seat. Gradually, the lovely blue colors of planet Earth became visible. Lyanna smiled at Quobit and Deacon in turn as she said, "Earth."

Gem appeared and presented the welcome from Landrew.

"They won't find us," Deacon said.

"What plan have you hatched?" asked Quobit.

"To find Chubby Eaves and Urzel."

"Here? On Earth?"

"Affirmative. Here on Earth. We must follow the only clues that we possess. Travers, in his dying words, whispered to me to find Chubby Eaves, for he knows the identity of the villain. Our Aralian friend I'obo informed us that Chubby Eaves is here on Earth, where he has secretly been since we left Aralia for Nix. So we will follow him. More importantly, he is in Asianda, in the port of Ketapongo, awaiting a new mission. Please excuse me, for I have sleuthing to do in the next hour as we journey. In the meantime"—he spied Lyanna's mess of papers in the middle of the room—"good housekeeping rules may help when we disembark. The *Heritage* has served us well, but we must take the shuttle to Ketapongo because that way we can activate and enter this port of call undetected."

As Jim and Gem were engaged in conversation with authorities to land the *Heritage* in Liberty City, Deacon pulled Gem aside. "You and Jim must arrange to jettison us in the shuttle before the *Heritage* lands. Activate the signal disruption field so we can avoid detection, and then program the *Heritage* to land in Liberty City on autopilot. Make sure you create signals on the *Heritage* that account for two Owlers and three humans."

"Yes, Master, the computer can navigate and then dock the ship successfully. Jim and I will ensure readings disguise our absence. We five, plus the baggage and the computers, will fit in the shuttle snugly to land in Ketapongo."

"You are positive that we can land undetected?"

"On such a small shuttle craft, it would be easy to place a shield around the craft to make us invisible until docking. Then we would need the assistance of controllers on the ground to not report us to Liberty once we land."

"Does the authority of Bothwen override any necessary reports? And do we require identifications to land?"

"We have many identities for the shuttle, you, Quobit, and Lyanna. Jim and I will arrange secure passage."

"We need to buy time to perform some perfunctory investigations on our own. Program the ship to take the longest route to Liberty City by adding an extra day. Construct a tape that cites mechanical docking problems as an excuse to circle the globe. Pass over Asianda on the initial entry route so we can make an early escape in the shuttle."

"Yes, Master. What if officials on Earth want to speak to you or communicate by computer?"

"Tell them I am deathly ill, hoarse with a bronchial infection, and resting to get my strength back."

Lyanna came down to the lower level after prettying herself; she had combed her long brown hair to remove any messy threads. Upon her return, Quobit sparked a new round of questions. "Deacon, I think that Schlegar suffers from Travers's death more than he cares to admit. However, share with Lyanna and me what we hope to find in Ketapongo."

"The evidence that Gem and I gathered on Nix indicates that an Asiandan has visited Nix recently. Thus, on Earth, in Ketapongo, we seek Kam Chuen, a peer, a fellow detective. From all the accounts that Gem and Jim amassed on Brebouillis and Earth, he is the only Earthman to venture to Medulla more than once in the past twenty years. Look." He pointed to a log that fingered Chuen. "Four times in two years. Plus, he is Asiandan, plus he lives in the same city Chubby Eaves visits, Ketapongo. But here is the startling evidence. Chuen is the only Earthman ever to be allowed to land on the planet's surface, which is contrary to Medullan laws. And why would an Earthman venture to such hostile conditions on Medulla four times?"

Quobit then spoke up. "I understand that Medulla's atmosphere has a soupy stench that is quite repulsive to anyone. It causes severe depression to alien minds after even short exposures. No one from Jabu is permitted to land there, since the Medullans themselves are physically repulsive creatures. So, venturing four times in two years, I agree, is anomalous and worth investigating. But are there any other leads?"

"A few; however, the hairs that Gem and I found tempt me to find this human first."

"What if this lead is a dead end?"

"Then, Quobit, I'll turn over the investigation to Alliance Special Forces. We buy only a day, maybe two, before Landrew's security team catches up to us. We only have time to investigate one lead, and that is Kam Chuen."

"You seem so sure about Chuen."

Deacon smiled. "T'obo informed Gem that Chubby Eaves landed in Ketapongo only days after I visited him in the hills of Glagn and has not departed yet. His mission to leave has been delayed three times by orders of the trade union. That represents too much of a coincidence, with Chubby and Kam Chuen both in Ketapongo at the same time. Agree?"

"You are the sleuth."

"I must warn you that this will be a dangerous mission. Urzel made a fatal mistake on Nix: he did not kill me. He made a second mistake in flight, for he missed exterminating me a second time. And he sent Morris Mydloan in his place to exterminate me in the library in Liberty and failed. So I think he revealed to me, inadvertently, that he fears me. I know not how, or why, but he does fear me, and I have to discover why."

"How does Chubby fit into this?" asked Lyanna.

"Travers begged me with his dying words to find Chubby Eaves, and I will. Until I do so, I will be unable to focus on any other candidates from the information we have."

"Do you think that Chubby also knows of Chuen's visits to Medulla?"

"Yes. Not difficult for a space trader to uncover."

"Deacon, I don't get it. Why would Urzel send Morris to Earth to exterminate you while it is highly possible that Urzel himself journeyed to Aralia, and then Globiana, to kill Como and Geor?"

"I wish I could answer your question, Lyanna. There is something more pressing that gnaws at me, but I won't tell you what until my meeting with Chubby." In his mind, Deacon had to live with a terrifying thought of what monster might be awaiting them on Earth.

THE SEARCH
FOR URZEL

Free fall

"Chubby Eaves departed to Ketapongo soon after we left for Nix. According to Quobit, who has been monitoring his activity through I'obo's intelligence, his trade ship has been delayed there, and he and the ship have remained in Ketapongo since. I think that Chubby was bluffing in his requests to accompany Travers and me to Nix. I think he knew all along that I would not permit him to accompany us. His argument with me was a diversion for me to worry about rather than trace his whereabouts after we departed. He pitched a great piece of acting to me. His intention all along was for me to worry that he followed us while he went to Ketapongo on a clandestine mission." Deacon smiled as he recalled how he had been taken in by Chubby's performance.

He continued to address the four of them. "Most of all, the traders' union would never let their most valuable piece of property, Travers, travel to a most dangerous location, possibly never to return, unless it served a valuable purpose. A hero deserves a better fate than to go to Bogeyland and die. I now know that Chubby Eaves needed more time to complete his own investigation for the Union of Space Traders; he needed to buy time. So I served a greater twofold purpose. I went to find Urzel with Travers, and I led the Alliance away from

Earth, while Chubby Eaves traveled to Earth to investigate the best lead in this case. How clever he was."

Quobit spoke up. "I have created this travel log on Chubby with I'obo's assistance." She opened it on the table and displayed it. "Look, he commands the Aralian trade ship *C'oulbaa* to Earth and arrives here, and since his landing, the *C'oulbaa* has conveniently developed engine problems. Chubby has ordered skeleton staff to remain on board. I'obo also informed me that the next destination of the *C'oulbaa* is unidentified. The evidence speaks for itself, as the ship is disabled and its next mission unknown."

Lyanna asked, "Deacon, how can you be so sure that Chubby searches for this Kam Chuen?"

"I can only guess that Chubby knows what we know—that Urzel is an Earthling, that Kam Chuen has journeyed to Medulla an unusual number of times, and that Ketapongo is the residence of Kam Chuen."

"How does Chubby know that Urzel is an Earthling? You seemed to state that conclusion boldly."

"I have a theory . . . thanks to you, Lyanna."

"Me?"

"Yes. You taught me how to penetrate people's minds and read them more effectively. On Aralia, when Chubby recited Travers's tale, he did so with genuine fear in his voice and in his thoughts. I invaded his mind, and when I opened it up, guess what?"

"You felt genuine fear! You think that Chubby was recounting his tale—that he and Travers both witnessed the devil."

"Exactly. The horror in his mind overwhelmed me. At first I thought it to be Travers's mind. But it wasn't. It was the thoughts and fears of Chubby Eaves, and when he realized that I was tapping him, he disturbed me in the cave by shaking me to break the communication. Twice he did this! I have a hunch that Chubby has met Urzel in a former life."

Jim offered another idea. "There was also a discrepancy about the number of patients at Brebouillis and the number of occupants that traveled on the *Sleigher* when it arrived at the Aralian Vesper disc. I think Deacon is also saying that Chubby accounts for the discrepancy."

Lyanna then spoke. "You think that Travers was willing to potentially sacrifice himself if needed and venture with you to Nix to keep, as we say, the scent away from Chubby Eaves."

"Yes. I believe, my dear, that Chubby Eaves is hunting Urzel! And we had better catch up to him soon, for he has a significant head start on us. He may require our assistance."

"Deacon, I am always inquisitive," Quobit said. "If Chubby knows of Urzel's powers, why is Chubby undertaking this manhunt himself?"

"I don't know. However, I will affirmatively state that Chubby Eaves knows a great deal more about this creature than he has led me to believe. He and Travers tried to throw me off the scent by telling me some far-fetched Aralian legend of a monster named Crawnshee returning from hell at this time."

"Deacon," Lyanna asked, totally mystified, "how can Urzel's trail be on Earth when you saw him on Nix? Also, you described a creature whose disguise will not be possible on Earth."

"Questions, questions, questions. I don't have answers yet."

Gem interrupted to announce that all the plans were set to depart. "Master, the ship will automatically dock in Liberty City in two days while we have clearance to land in Ketapongo in secret immediately. You three humans should rest now, for when we dock, we will have to travel secretly over land out of the Ketapongo port area. There is a busy schedule to look forward to."

Deacon leaned over to Lyanna and said, "When we land in Ketapongo, I'll promise that I will confide in you and answer that last question."

Gem issued doses of relaxants and the Owler stood over them until they were unconscious. Given that Deacon was hyper about the upcoming mission, he welcomed the serum to shift his mind into soothing dreams. Mother Earth provided some security; so did Lyanna's presence, so did Quobit as security, and so did the hope of seeing Moonbeam again. The fact that Chubby was here was encouraging to Deacon, for he felt that they could construct an alliance with him—but it would not be easy.

While Deacon slept, Jim and Gem continued to load the shuttle and prepare for their descent into Asianda. Jim was also in haste to recheck the data gathered on Brebouillis to refine the list of potential candidates who could give rise to Urzel. Such criteria in the screening included trips to outer space, parentage, Uscher zone tests, age, and a diagnosis of insanity with brilliance. Jim had earlier tried to tell Deacon that the candidate Chuen really wasn't a match at all except for two of the eight criteria: his voyages to Medulla and the permission for him to land on the planet's surface.

When Lyanna awoke, Deacon was on the floor reading, his back to her. As she rose, he turned and thought how lovely she looked. Her form was strikingly beautiful in the dim rosy lights. She smiled. "I'm flattered."

Deacon had left his mind unguarded for that moment as he admired her. "I'm so embarrassed. I keep forgetting."

"Why are you embarrassed?"

"I never had . . . a chance to say such things before . . . to express my feelings . . . you know, to a lady."

"Say it aloud to me. Right now."

"I'm busy scanning tapes—"

Lyanna cut him off. "And what will your excuse be tomorrow?"

He blushed. "Now? Lyanna, we land soon. And Quobit might overhear."

"Just pretend I am not here," Quobit said.

"Deacon, I want to be your friend. Treat me like your friend and express your feelings to me. Flatter me."

"What do you want me to say?"

"The truth. Whatever feelings you have about me."

"It's difficult. I've never had the chance to converse about these matters."

"I'll help you." She plummeted beside him, turned his face, and kissed him hard on the lips. "Encouraged?" Deacon blushed; she giggled.

"You are so beautiful to me," said Deacon. "My confidence level rises because you're near." His voice reached a crescendo. "You give me a strength that I have never known."

"I am flattered, for you, Deacon Coombs, are an excitement in my life that has been missing. You are handsome, intelligent, and so brave."

"Me? I'm ordinary."

"No. You are exciting."

"I'm a bore."

"Stop it! You are exciting and adventurous. I didn't see Landrew venture to Nix to risk his life for the safety of all mankind, or Schlegar. You are courageous, Deacon Coombs, and Quobit informed me of your bravery during the fight in the cave on Nix."

"I hide fear well."

"Deacon! You need to learn to accept a compliment. If we are to be friends, good friends, then I want to hear you accept my compliments. It makes me feel good."

Sheepishly, he lowered his head. "I am sorry. I didn't mean to upset you. Perhaps, as you have done before, you can teach me."

"Okay. And in return you will allow me to traipse around Earth with you."

"Only to an extent, Lyanna, for I wouldn't want any harm to come to you."

"I accompany you on this mission or you are on your own in love."

He bowed his head to think about what she had said. "You and I, we are complementary, Deacon. You have been hiding behind fame all your life, just waiting for someone like me to come along. I am a bold and confident woman here to win you over."

"Just who *is* someone like you?"

"I am the one who is going to accept all the feelings that are locked inside you. I'm the one who is going to teach you how to unlock them. You have always been a curio, a hero, a legendary detective of our times, and never a lover. Well, here's your chance."

They rose, and Deacon raised his head. "Will you be my little spy?" he asked.

Grinning from ear to ear, Lyanna stood in front of him, her body swaying to and fro with extreme exaggeration, and placed her arms around his neck. "Welcome," she replied. She kissed him, and then sleekly strolling backward, she said, "I'm honored. I'd better finish packing up our notes."

"So should I," Deacon replied.

Lyanna danced across the room toward her friend Quobit, realizing that this detective of high ego had just melted in front of her. Standing in the portal, she watched him go about his business.

Jim was animated as he approached Deacon. "Master, please come below immediately and observe this synthesis you asked us to perform." Deacon followed, and as he did so, he caught Lyanna eyeing him from her recess, so he winked at her as he left the deck and descended.

On the lower deck, Jim had images strewn over all over the monitors. "Master, all the beings born on Earth who have very abnormal powers of the Uscher zone are summated here on these pages. But as you can clearly see, there are two problems." Jim supported the specifics by pointing to three large screens.

"None of these humans have the abilities that you and Gem witnessed on Nix—that is, to reach out and utilize the power over thousands of people not in close proximity. Most disturbing is the fact that all of these individuals can be accounted for on Earth when Urzel was witnessed on Nix, and can also be accounted for on Earth or elsewhere when Geor and Como died. Kam Chuen possesses none of these extreme mental abilities."

"My conclusion, Jim, is that someone has wiped clean the records of our suspect."

"The files have not been tampered with," said Jim.

"How do you know that?"

"These records of the Uscher zone results have an input that does not allow an erasure of records. There exists no overriding code. Plus, even if it was manually erased, according to the commands Gem and I found, it would default to a security file that we have access to. Not even Schlegar and Landrew can manipulate that file and erase the data."

"Here"—he pointed to an example—"is the only copy of a manually terminated file, which defaulted to the top-security files."

Deacon noted that this was the file of Morris Mydloan, rehabilitated—an experiment gone awry. "Thank you, Jim. I would like to peruse the Uscher zone file myself just to see if I recognize any names or patterns." He spent the next hour examining the top-security file, absorbing each detail, but there were no surprises and he gleaned no new information. Later he summoned Jim back.

"Did you absolutely confirm the whereabouts of Kam Chuen when Como and Geor were killed?"

"Yes, Deacon, he was on Earth when Como was killed. Chuen was on Earth for Geor's murder and on Earth while we were on Nix."

"Depressing! I feel that the demon's name is right here in front of us. But where, Jim? He must be an offspring of past generations born off Earth."

"There is no record of two parents bearing such a child of mental superiority."

"Gem, as I inspected these profiles of heartbeats that you recorded on Nix, something peculiar occurred to me during my last examination."

"Yes, Master."

Deacon displayed the data on the screen. "I compared these heartbeat patterns with those of myself and other Earthmen. Look at this strong, infrequent double beat. Here and here and here." Digging into his journal, he checked his previous notes and recited them to Gem. "It occurs in a regular pattern, every thirtieth heartbeat, in no relationship to the normalized Earth heartbeat and the background beats. This pattern you recorded could conceivably be decoupled into two separate profiles. Any thoughts on this matter? Or am I force-fitting the data?"

"I shall investigate further for you, Master. I applaud your observations, but I have already cross-checked this heartbeat against all other races in our galaxy, and nothing comes close to this profile, whether it be one profile or two or three. This being has the biochemistry of an Earthman."

Deacon was deflated. "Well, check again."

"I will, Master."

"When we land, make sure that we bring the heartbeat recorder with us so we can use it to locate Chubby Eaves."

"Master, I will do so. I just want to remind you that Ketapongo is the second-busiest interplanetary port on Earth and that at any one time there are thousands of Aralians in the city of Ketapongo."

"I didn't infer that it would be easy. I know that Aralians have identical or nearly identical heartbeats. It is just one device we will need to employ. Besides, if and when we locate this Kam Chuen, I will be very interested in his heart's profile."

When Lyanna and Quobit joined them in the shuttle, Deacon revealed the plan to them. Jim would accompany him to the docks, where they would commence to track Chubby's whereabouts, discover the status of the *C'oulbaa*, and in particular ask about Chubby's next flight plans. Deacon would use his Bothwen identity. They would take the voice verification machine with them. Deacon asked Quobit to accompany Gem to the municipal offices to determine the current whereabouts and residence of Kam Chuen. "Conduct a criminal and civil background check on Chuen," he said. "Try to verify the times of the trips to Medulla. See if there are any discrepancies between the database on Brebouillis and the flight plans on record. Construct a dossier on his character and determine his habits."

Deacon had no opportunity to be alone with Lyanna anymore. The time for departure was near. The controls were placed on automatic and they crowded into the shuttle with their data. Then, they fell into free fall as they plunged instantaneously into cloud cover with a primitive force field to shield them. A hasty, uncomfortable drop to Earth's surface was in order to make maximum use of their time before the *Heritage* docked in two days, so the capsule turned end over end, causing Deacon to feel his stomach rise into his chest as the tiny shuttle heated up by more than twenty degrees.

The smile on Quobit's face told Deacon how much she was enjoying this ride.

In Ketapongo

The free fall prompted screams from Lyanna as if she were on a precipitous descent on the roller-coaster rides of yore. Soon, they leveled out and followed a smooth trajectory through light cloud cover. In an hour they were at a small, quiet hangar station on the outskirts of the thriving metropolis. A class-one priority from Bothwen gave them private access with no questions asked by the immigration officials. Deacon placed some strong suggestions in the minds of the guards to further their cause. While Deacon, Quobit, and Lyanna stayed out of sight, the Owlers completed the necessary paperwork to allow them entry to Earth.

Meanwhile, the apparently disabled *Heritage* orbited the Earth, regularly transmitting a staticky prerecorded message of its mechanical problems. Gem and Jim had programmed the computer to provide all the physical characteristics of the two Owlers and three humans on board, should the *Heritage* be scanned.

A gorgeous, cloudless sunny day greeted the pentad back on Earth, all of whom had taken up residence at an ancient rustic inn on the edge of the metropolis of Ketapongo. Deacon, with Jim standing in bewilderment, sat on his knees and then proceeded to kiss Mother Earth. Lyanna laughed and then repeated the ritual. Jim was puzzled. "Why anyone would want to come in contact with that dirt?" Quobit laughed. Hand in hand, Deacon and Lyanna walked the first mile through narrow, tree-lined streets, the Owlers only steps behind, Quobit in front, until Quobit and Gem boarded a taxi boat to take them upstream to the municipal offices. Deacon stood watching until the launch disappeared around a bend, and then he addressed Lyanna. "We will rendezvous back here. Signal you when we arrive."

After curt good-byes, Deacon departed with Jim to the heart of the interplanetary space port.

The *Heritage* kept anxious officials at bay with regular transmissions and simulated heartbeats and life functions. Schlegar sent his message to Landrew that Deacon Coombs had journeyed into the forbidden zone of Nix with Travers and had actually interfaced with a powerful evil being capable of brainwashing the human species. Schlegar's message was so blunt and frightening that Landrew immediately conferred with Schlegar by space video to obtain more details. This conversation prompted Landrew to prepare a hero's return but also precipitated an immediate investigation by security forces into the entire matter. Landrew wanted every minute of the *Heritage*'s travel log scrutinized for his personal edification. Landrew's anxiety to welcome Coombs grew.

In the streets of Ketapongo, Jim briefed Deacon. "Ketapongo spews out over the entire island, fifty-five million people in the city and millions more on the outskirts, its inhabitants barely coping with the scarcity of food, fuel, and land. Animals are used for short travels to keep the pollution under control. There are few personal motorized vehicles in the middle of the city. One must leave motor vehicles on the perimeter and travel inland by waterway, or by vehicle with a permit."

Beggars hailed them, cripples lined the streets, and tempting females hugged the corners, soliciting a lonely man's company. Space crews wore the proud colors of the homelands as they patrolled the streets in search of company, good food, drink, or perhaps stakes in illegal gambling games. Some just searched for familiar faces to partake in conversation about the homeland.

The center of the port bore the scars of age. A dirty white discoloration disguised the index boards in front of government buildings, while dusty glass prevented a clear look inside any of the structures' windows. Jim rented a small air-powered vehicle to hasten their travels to the space traders' center and parked the vehicle in a guarded alley. Deacon was amazed at Jim's adept driving skills as they wove among the throngs. They entered the registrar's office and inhaled the stale, papery air of thousands of years. A flash of their credentials, with Deacon as Bothwen, gave them instant access to the space records that they required, so Deacon and Jim retreated to a private stall and commenced their investigation.

"Here it is, Jim. Look. The *C'oulbaa* unloaded weeks ago. She remains without cargo and is detained because of mechanical repairs of valves in the rocket engines. How bloody convenient!"

The list of repairs made to the ship was lengthy. Then he saw it! "Jim, the *C'oulbaa* is departing tomorrow! But without Chubby Eaves! A different captain has been assigned. That means that Chubby has not completed his mission here. This is our good fortune. Jim, I need to secure the list of all the crew members on board the *C'oulbaa* immediately. Make sure and absolutely confirm that Chubby is not on board in a lesser role, even as a passenger." Jim retreated to another room to verify the crew and contents on the *C'oulbaa*. Deacon read on.

The ship had a full load of chemicals bound for Aralia. Then he saw an attachment. Using his Bothwen identity, he opened it, and his confusion was addressed. Chubby Eaves had been instructed to remain behind by orders of the trade union. He was to take the trade ship *G'uillger*, which would be arriving in two days, and guide her to a destination to be disclosed once in space. The communication justified that the mission required an experienced commander for a risky, secretive mission. Deacon thought, *Two days to find Chubby and Chuen.*

Deacon smiled, leaned back, and was elated. Chubby Eaves was still in Ketapongo. The *G'uillger* had a clandestine mission, and they had two days to locate him. *Secret mission. Ha.* Intuition told him that the *G'uillger* was connected to the misdeeds of Urzel. Then he read it again, aloud this time. "Instructions of the Union of Space Traders." It had to be Chubby who had crafted these orders. He and Jim would be the only ones in this metropolis, or on Earth, to suspect any wrongdoing.

Jim returned gleeful. "Deacon, I have confirmed that Chubby Eaves is not on the ship."

"Yes, I know. I have confirmed that he is taking charge of the *G'uillger* in two days. We must move quickly to locate him."

"Furthermore, Master, all interplanetary traders must register their place of residence while residing in Ketapongo. Look, Master Deacon, what I found for you. Chubby Eaves is registered at an inn nearby until the day of his departure."

Deacon checked the address. It was a difficult walk, but better reachable on foot than by vehicle because of the congested streets. So they left the vehicle behind and began brushing against businessmen, rogues, hustlers, and vendors, smothered by the mobs of people in the streets of the port. Deacon walked uneasily but confidently with Jim two steps ahead of him. He kept a low profile with his head bowed and his eyes constantly shifting to and fro to catch a glimpse of anyone following them.

When they arrived at the inn, they were disappointed. "Not here," said the innkeeper with a snarl. "Bin gone 'bout one day. Belongings are still upstairs. What you want with Eaves?"

Deacon passed a few sheckels to the burly clerk to gain entry to the room. Jim protested, but Deacon recalled the usual speech about the safety of the population of the galaxy and billions of lives depending on them. Jim reluctantly stood guard outside as Deacon searched Chubby's room.

It was neat, with everything in place, and sparsely decorated. It confirmed what the innkeeper had said—that Chubby had not slept there in days. Deacon rifled through his belongings but found no clues as to where the trader had vanished to. His clothes were hung in the closet; all the drawers were empty. Then he found a note. It appeared to be from a colleague who desired to share dinner with Chubby in six days. There was no date, so he could not tell what day this dinner was scheduled for. The rest of the search proved fruitless. On departing, he gave thanks and then asked the innkeeper about the time of delivery of the note.

"Don't know. Don't remember. Done enough for you. None of your bidness." They left to randomly travel by a hand-drawn carriage through narrow streets up the hillside to market shops. Weaving amid the carts and the burros, Deacon purchased local culinary delights, and then they returned to the rented air sled and traversed back to the inn that had been secured by Lyanna. By the smile on her face as Deacon entered their suite, he knew that a clue had been unearthed. Lyanna was brimming with news.

"Quobit and Gem found Kam Chuen."

Deacon gave Quobit a hug. Quobit said, "That is Dr. Kam Chuen. He is a rather well known compulsive detective who specializes in missing persons. He is seventy years old, retired recently, lives in a northern part of the city, and keeps a low profile."

Gem handed Deacon some further notes with the information. "He has an unquenchable thirst for high-grade opium and quella. Here"—Gem pointed to a stack of papers on the desk—"are clippings from the local news media that cite some of his more memorable cases."

"And his journeys to Medulla?"

Quobit beamed. "All accounted for conveniently as sabbaticals. Vacations."

"Since when do compulsive detectives take expensive Vespering vacations?"

"And when would any Earthman want to journey to the hostile planet of Medulla for a relaxing vacation?"

Lyanna pointed her finger at Deacon. "Don't knock it, Quobit. Deacon's trip to Nix will be recorded in history someday as nothing more than a sabbatical accompanied by a female Jabu Vesperer." They shared in laughter.

Quobit continued. "Here is what is even more interesting, Deacon. Dr. Chuen has led a full life, traveled extensively all over

Earth. The singular trips abroad off Earth were to Medulla. In his interviews, he says he has no regrets. The interviewer describes him as grumpy."

"Where do we find him?"

Gem unfolded a map, and they gathered around it. "The neighborhood where he dwells is here. It is a great distance from our quarters, but he frequents one of three opium dens every night. These dens are closer to us."

Lyanna then said, "It might be best to find him on leisurely terms rather than intrude at his home."

Deacon was tired. However, this was an opportunity not to default on. He made a decision. "Jim and I and Quobit will venture to these pits tonight, as long as I don't have to sample the goodies. In these neighborhoods, I figure that two security guards are required."

Quobit nodded. "I agree. Gem and I passed through the neighborhood of these opium dens earlier. That's where we aggregated intimate personal details of Dr. Chuen for the right price. We found out that he keeps dangerous company, loves to flirt with the ladies and chat with spacers, and has a passion for playing Vidal Challenge. There was an inference that he associates with the disreputable element who have imparted leads to break his cases."

"You found out all this from gossipers."

Gem spoke up. "The lady Quobit can be rather persuasive, Master."

"Ooh, a hidden sexy side, eh, Q?" said Deacon.

"She even introduced herself as Bitsy to one Jabu trader."

Quobit waved her arms. "Dr. Chuen is a big spender, so I suggest you line your pockets with dockets. The information you seek may not be dispensed freely, and he will seek to cover his expensive habits of gambling and drugs."

"We have all earned our pay today," said Deacon.

"How about your trek?" asked Quobit.

"Jim and I discovered that Chubby Eaves is still in Ketapongo. We located the inn where he is residing, but he is absent. Gem, I want you to go there immediately and act as sentry. On this map, the inn should be, ah . . . here. It is called the Wendovian. When Chubby appears, remove him, forcibly if you have to, but deliver him back here to our inn for questioning. I suggest you take some of the medicine that you used to knock us into a deep sleep. Chubby must be brought back." He turned to look at Lyanna. "You, my dear, will have to mind our base camp alone tonight. Keep it locked up. I'm sorry, but it could be a long, lonely night for you. The rendezvous with Chuen could carry past the midnight hour. Jim, Quobit— excuse me, Bitsy—and I will stay out all night until we find him, even if that means until daybreak."

Kam Chuen

After a quiet meal in which Deacon and Lyanna exchanged frequent glances, good-byes were in order as Deacon, Quobit, and Jim swiftly traveled down moss-laden streets, wandering amid the first signs of the nightlife, deflecting derelicts. They arrived shortly at the first den of Chuen's liking. Chuen had frequented that one recently, so the owner was not expecting him back soon since he made it a habit to sample other drug dens. The host confirmed four other locations.

By the time darkness arrived, Chuen had not appeared at the nearby second bar. After two misses, Jim stood sentry at the third site while Deacon, his stun laser concealed under his vest, ventured down slippery steps into a dank basement of a smoky opium pit where a crowd of approximately thirty had gathered. Quobit followed furtively and sat at the end of the bar.

Putrid orange-and-yellow clouds filled the dungeon, the stains of innumerable years grossly marking the walls and ceiling. Deacon's eyes commenced to water as he wandered through the decrepit chamber of posts and small tables and fire pits, shuffling across a dirt floor, looking for any signs of an aging Asiandan. From the description they had, Chuen had a long gray beard and pony tail. In one corner, Deacon disturbed a group of ill-mannered husky traders sharing crude jokes. Behind a bar, a thin, withered bartender with a long gray beard eyed him suspiciously.

Cautiously, Deacon inquired of Dr. Chuen. The bartender's beady eyes fixed on Deacon as he pretended to wipe a glass over and over with a soiled rag. Then, with an abbreviated gesture, his head swayed only for a split second toward a table in the deepest recess, where Deacon could barely make out the outline of a single person through the smoke. As he moved closer, Deacon saw a low-burning candle faintly outlining the posture of a thin elderly man with deep, sunken, opaque eyes sitting on the dirty floor.

Deacon positioned himself closer for inspection. His fingers fondled the laser gun under his vest, and he felt the signaling device that would prompt Jim's assistance. He looked over his shoulder at Quobit before he took the last three steps, and then a slight barking cough focused his attention on the man. Chuen was distinguished looking, puffing on a long blue pipe of opium. His twiggy frame was outlined in the tight black clothes that he wore. "Excuse me, pardon my interruption, but are you Doctor Kam Chuen?"

"Who is asking?" The doctor's voice was high-pitched and raspy as their eyes met.

"A fellow detective, one representing the Alliance."

Chuen's two dark eyes now penetrated Deacon, opening wider and wider to expose enlarged pupils. Arising from the floor, wobbling on bony legs, the Asiandan reached out and grabbed Deacon's arm sturdily, forcing him to his sitting level on the earthy red floor, yanking him to draw him closer. A whiff of his foul breath caused Deacon to turn his head abruptly to savor fresh air. "The Alliance sends an errand boy? An Earthman? To talk to me? For what possible reason?"

"I regret any inconvenience that I have caused you, but this is an errand of gravity."

Chuen stopped inhaling to size him up, sprinkling his investigation with infrequent darts of eye contact. Sternly, he said, "What do you want of me? I come here to be left alone and enjoy my own company, so make your business brief."

Deacon fondled the signal button to alert Jim, as he didn't appreciate the menacing tone of Chuen's remarks. Then he realized his situation. Chuen was on edge. Quickly he tuned into Chuen's mind. He would listen to him and read him simultaneously. However, the detective's energy thought patterns were unclear, so he initiated dialogue about Medulla.

"Perhaps a smoke while we converse?" Chuen asked.

"No thanks, but I appreciate your offer. I have important matters of business tonight to tend to with you."

Chuen was insulted. "My friends do not turn away from my gainful proposition of a free fix." Deacon noticed that a swarthy Asiandan, was acknowledging Chuen as he passed, and he eyed Deacon with contempt. "All shall be well. Sit and smoke with me." Chuen signaled the host with an encouraging wave of his hand.

Deacon decided to remain and play Chuen's game, as time was short and this was an important lead—and maybe the only lead to play. "You have journeyed to the planet Medulla on more than one occasion during the last few years. In one instance, you were absent from Earth for almost a year, traveling space, reaching Medulla as your final destination. That, I believe, was your first trip; then there were three others. The Alliance desires to know the nature of your voyages."

"Ha! The Alliance is a bureaucratic snoop. I was on vacation. Big deal."

"I don't believe so," said Deacon.

Chuen stared at him with dour, beady, penetrating eyes. "You insult me? You dare to call me a liar?"

Deacon was firm and responded quickly. "The Alliance will reward you handsomely for the names of your clients that you represented during those voyages and also for the purpose of these journeys."

Chuen blew a rancid exhale into Deacon's face. "I represented myself. I took vacation. Who in the Alliance dares to say I did not? You?"

Deacon restated his offer. "Rewarded very handsomely."

Chuen snickered, looked past Deacon, let some awkward minutes pass, and then asked, "How handsomely?"

Deacon knew this was going to be easy, for in Chuen's mind, he betrayed his expectations of drugs and money, and Deacon had deciphered each expectation. So Deacon did not disappoint him as he suggested a value very close to Chuen's wants. Chuen heaved a sigh and boldly upped the ante. Deacon held his ground, for he read Chuen's extreme satisfaction when the initial amount was revealed. Bartering took place lethargically over five more minutes, and the two concocted a deal. Deacon did excite Chuen by adding, "A bonus if you can also deliver the current whereabouts of your client."

Chuen rubbed his chin and then twisted his beard. "Do you have the money with you?"

"Yes."

"What is your name?"

"I am Bothwen, an administrator of the Union of Space Traders and part-time space detective, here on behalf of the traders' union and the Alliance. Here are my credentials." Chuen pretended to inspect the papers and badge, but Deacon's mind read that he was anxious to commence the transaction and obtain the financial gain. Chuen snapped the wallet closed, but instead of passing it to Deacon, he gave it to a swarthy figure who was now towering behind him. Deacon's pipe arrived, and with the deal close to consummation, the two puffed in silence for a few minutes, Deacon taking very short inhales until the brute returned with the papers. Deacon heard a whisper and then read Chuen's mind easily to confirm Chuen's satisfaction.

As Chuen sat cogitating, Deacon relaxed, changing his mood as Lyanna had taught him. Out of the silence, the name Goharn Lok penetrated his mind. *A thought from Chuen?* he wondered. He had to confirm it, since there were other patrons in close proximity. Deacon severed the sereneness. "Come, come, Chuen, let's get on with our discussion, for the Alliance knows that Goharn Lok may be involved."

Chuen was startled. "Why bother me? This deal seems so foolish if you already know of Goharn Lok as my client."

"You lose your bounty if my patience grows thin."

Chuen sighed. He rested his pipe. "Okay. You are correct in your assumption. It was he, Goharn Lok. Lok came to me years ago, asking me to locate his brother, Phendal Lok, who had left Earth years ago when Goharn was but a teenager. He paid me very handsomely to locate Phendal. After a convoluted trail through the farthest regions of our space, which as you noted took one Earth year, I surprisingly located him on the planet Medulla. Apparently Lok's brother resided there for many happy years before he passed away. This is no secret. All the locals know of Goharn's quest to find his long-lost brother, all the locals know that he engaged me, and all know that I found him on Medulla. During my first trip, he was alive."

Chuen moved closer. "So I called it vacation as I journeyed to Medulla. So what? I had not been abroad. It was an exciting adventure, traveling to many planets, following Phendal's trail. It was all exciting except Medulla. Goharn paid for all my expenses—and very well." Chuen stopped to have another puff and faced Deacon. "Maybe I should make sure that you will indeed treat me more than comfortably before I continue."

Deacon was adamant and ignored Chuen's inference. "Where does Goharn Lok reside?"

"Goharn's a recluse, lives up in the hills near here, the hills of Ingkata. He is very popular with the locals. He asked me to journey with him to Medulla. Goharn was very welcome there. He is the only Earthman I know who was allowed to land on the planet's surface except me. During my first trip, when I discovered that his brother had lived there, I was permitted to land on the planet's surface to peruse personal files. What a horrible, disgusting environment exists there. My next two trips were to secure travel plans for Goharn Lok, who was invited to Medulla. When I accompanied Goharn— that was my last trip—I was confined to the moon to conduct my investigation, as are all other life forms. But not Goharn! They actually invited him to the planet's surface as if he were royalty to meet with high-ranking Medullans! Disgusting-looking creatures, these Medullans! I think I would have thrown up in front of them if I had been asked to see them again. Sorrowfully, his brother had passed away by the time I found him." Chuen again put down his pipe.

"Oh my! Excuse me, Mr. Bothwen. Not true. I must correct myself. Goharn's brother was also permitted on the surface of Medulla, for he lived on the surface. Yes! Lived there for many years among these ugly creatures in the disgusting muck and filth on the planet's surface. Goharn too during his trip on the planet actually dined with the Medullans, conversed with them. 'What an opportunity,' some would say. But their physical appearances are completely repulsive, as I said earlier. It made poor Goharn sick to his stomach too. He has many tales to tell about that experience when he interfaced with the Medullans. That is your interest, is it not? Goharn's thoughts on the Medullans and life on the surface? His journey there? To document it for the Alliance?"

Deacon thought that this was all so easy. But he had gained nothing yet except for the Lok brothers' ability to gain access to the planet's surface. "The Alliance does not have to divulge my purposes to you."

Chuen replied sneakily. "He is the one that you seek; trust me. Goharn Lok. I only journeyed to Medulla because of his requests. I am not in any trouble, am I?"

"Did you converse directly with the Medullans, Chuen?"

"Yes. Well, indirectly through an electrical interpreter. They would not allow me to leave the lone shelter I occupied. They were very congenial in allowing me to gather data on Phendal and then piece together the life of Goharn Lok's brother, but it was difficult to look at them. It is illegal to land, you know, on the planet's surface, so I was surprised that they, in secrecy, allowed me. Also, how did this peasant, Phendal Lok, get permission too, eh? That's all Lok's brother was—a peasant." Chuen emphasized the *P*s in *peasant* and *permission* as he spoke. "Kings and High Council members don't have that right, so I was hoping that you maybe have the answer. Why were these brothers allowed to land there? Is that what the Alliance is doing? Investigating the crime of landing there?"

"Well, as I stated before, it is not customary for me to divulge specifics to you."

Chuen inhaled from his pipe—a long, deep invasion of his lungs—and then said, "Goharn Lok and his brother, Phendal, were orphans. No schooling, no future in wealth, no family. It is very curious that this illiterate man Phendal travels in outer space and meets his destiny to reside on Medulla."

"And Goharn visited just once?"

"Yes." A look of curiosity crossed Chuen's face. "What does the Alliance want with me? I am too old to put into prison for breaking a space law. Right?"

Deacon was uneasy. He had the real residence of Goharn. He knew he could get more information regarding Goharn Lok from a prolonged meeting with Chuen, but he decided that this was sufficient. "Anything else that I should be aware of, Chuen?"

"Goharn Lok is well known in the hills of Ingkata. Ask anyone for directions. That is how I first found him. Take the Frendis Road up high into the hills until it turns into cobbles and ruts. Then ask as you continue to make your way to the summit of the hill. The road eventually terminates in a huge clearing, and from there you take the path to his home. The affair belongs in your hands now. There is the matter of gratuities. You will keep your half of the bargain."

"Yes, I shall retrieve it."

"Not alone," he said as he grabbed Deacon's vest. "My friend Chang shall go with you to make sure." Deacon noticed the monstrous shadow in the corner again, which took shape in the light as it advanced.

"One last question, Chuen. You made two trips to Medulla for arrangements. Why did you go there twice for planning?"

"On the contrary, I followed Lok's trail across the galaxy to Medulla during the first trip. Goharn sponsored a second journey for me to get permission for Goharn to land. When I informed the Medullans of the existence of a brother on Earth, the Medullans finally admitted to his presence on my second trip. The third trip was to make arrangements for Goharn; I traveled there with Goharn during the fourth voyage." Chuen looked up. "As we said earlier, maybe Phendal Lok didn't have permission to land so was breaking the law and the Medullans wanted to protect him. I don't know. Not my concern. I was tenacious. I found him. I was rewarded handsomely by Goharn. Go talk to Goharn and leave me alone now, Bothwen."

The tall, husky man stayed one step behind Deacon as he emerged at street level. The henchman crossed his arms and demanded payment. Jim streamed a packet of dockets and a small sack of gems into the man's outstretched hands. They waited until he had counted them and affirmed their safe departure. Then Quobit left the bar behind them, and they vamoosed quickly to secure a motorized vehicle to proceed into the hills. With Jim protesting vehemently as darkness descended, Deacon ordered about what little time they had left to solve the crime and find the villain and validate the safety of the known universe. Most importantly, Deacon was puzzled by Chuen's testimony about the Lok brothers and could not fathom how two peasants fit into the schemes of a devil.

In the hills of Ingkata

Deacon found it impossible to be comfortable as the pathways became infested with potholes, a product of the almost daily rainfall in this equatorial city. They traversed through the forested landscape, winding higher and higher into the hills on trough-laden roads, the roughness of the road creating turbulent air pockets underneath their craft, in turn bouncing the vehicle. Lyanna would have to be patient for his return, as Deacon over and over justified his decision to track down Goharn Lok on this night. He calculated that they were running out of time as the docking hour of the empty *Heritage* drew closer. Landrew would surely initiate an investigation for their whereabouts as soon as the ship arrived empty.

The directions to Goharn's abode became confusing, as an abundance of unmarked intersections now marred their way. Not knowing precisely the next turn, as Chuen had predicted, they stopped to ask directions and corrected their path twice by backtracking. On a hairpin turn, with the lights below providing a grandiose view of Ketapongo, they huddled with natives to once again determine the direction to Goharn's house. An elderly man seeking transportation on his way back from market loaded his chickens and grains into the vehicle and guided them the last three miles.

It became darker and darker as the vegetation closed in around them, the moist, thick jungle canopy blocking out the light of a full moon. The road, which was now deserted, was alive with the harmonious sounds of the creatures of the night. The elderly man departed and pointed to one last steep leg, which he promised would end in the clearing they sought.

The road ended in a large circular glade, with only one marked path visible in the dim light, the track wandering up the slope into the blackness of the jungle. The vehicle was abandoned while Deacon, with Jim's beacon showing the way, trudged up the slope. Quobit remained behind to protect their means of escape and intercept any intruders. On a rocky cliff, Jim positioned himself with a direct view of their vehicle and Quobit and the roadway, as well as a spectacular view of the lights of Ketapongo below. Deacon climbed the last few yards alone, paused to catch his breath and admire the beauty, and turned to spy a thatched hut through the vines.

It was a small, crude structure with cloths strung over the doorway. "Hello?" All was silent. "Hello?" He pulled back the rags to verify that there was no rear exit to escape through. He had just turned to savor the beautiful sight of the city from this vantage point again when a twig snapped. He looked deep into the murky jungle beside him.

"What do you want?" The voice was feeble.

Deacon placed Jim on alert. "Goharn Lok?"

A hush spanned minutes until a diminutive, wiry figure emerged. Shiftily, he looked behind Deacon to spy the Owler keeping watch. Deacon perked up. "The Owler is my bodyguard. He ensures our privacy."

"And who ensures mine? I have no money to employ an Owler. You think that you can intrude into my life? Who are you?"

This was certainly not the voice of Urzel. Deciding that it was a time for truths, Deacon confidently replied. "Please excuse my rude intrusion, Mr. Lok. My name is Deacon Coombs. I am a private detective. I desire a sitting with you. I apologize deeply for this interruption."

There was a lengthy interlude. "Deacon Coombs? *The* Deacon Coombs? And at my doorstep? The detective Deacon Coombs?"

Deacon was amused and proud. "Why, ah . . . yes."

"I have heard discussions of your cases around local tea breaks. I even considered writing you once with a possible case. However, what in the world could possibly bring you to my humble abode?"

Deacon had to gamble, so he stepped into Goharn's space. "I think that you know, Goharn. The time has come for truths, to tell each other what we know. Life as we know it is at a turning point. The crisis we all have feared is at hand."

Goharn once again stared past Deacon to Jim until he was satisfied, and then he extended his hand to Deacon and said, "I know not of what crisis you speak, but please, please, come into my hut, please."

He pulled aside the awning to reveal a modest interior of sparse belongings. In the middle of the hut was a smoldering fire where a heated metal pitcher hung. Sacks of tea leaves were positioned around the rocks of the fire's perimeter.

"Do you desire a smoke? Fresh chontum leaves picked today. Or perhaps a cup of green tea?"

The small amount of opium Deacon had smoked had left his mouth dry. "Tea would suit me fine." As Goharn assembled the ingredients, a small reptile appeared. "Ah, where have you been?" Goharn collected the animal and placed it in a rickety wooden cage. Then he poured the tea out of the metal pot and into small cups as Deacon observed the green eyes of the scaly lizard inspecting him.

Turning his attention to Goharn, Deacon examined his black hair and observed his hands—unusually large hands for one of such a diminutive stature. Deacon placed his age about sixty-five. Goharn's facial features were distinctively Asiandan, with dark eyes and thin lips. Sagging skin hung under his chin, masked by a short tuft of a scraggly silver beard.

"You must sip it slowly, Mister Coombs. Savor its taste. This is a local specialty."

Deacon followed his advice by taking three slow sips and then initiated the dialogue. "Do you know why I am here?"

Goharn seemed distant. "I know not at all why you visit me. Pray tell me. I am at a complete loss. I am especially confused by your previous comments about . . . what was it? . . . life as we know it at the crossroads?"

"I am investigating crimes of the Alliance that have taken place on other planets—crimes so mysterious, so universally encompassing, that my clues and travels have led me to the farthest reaches of the galaxy, to planets where few have ventured. Now a singular clue brings me to your doorstep."

Goharn sipped his tea calmly, emitting an occasional "Ah." Then he encouraged Deacon, saying, "Please continue."

"Your brother departed Earth years ago; you hadn't seen him since your teenage years. Then, many years later, you engaged a detective, Dr. Kam Chuen, to find him."

"You are correct, but I do not understand your interest in my family affairs. I toiled many years to save the funds so that I might finance such a search and finance our reunion. My quest makes quite a story each night somewhere in the Hills of Ingkata. I hired a detective, Dr. Kam Chuen—not as expensive as you, mind you, but nevertheless a capable man, as he demonstrated."

"And Kam Chuen uncovered your brother on planet Medulla?"

"Yes, he did. The search took more than one attempt; the three voyages drained me of my life savings, so I live out my years now here in this humble setting, living in poverty. But I saved all my earnings for such a quest. Phendal left our family under tragic terms. We were inseparable at childhood, as close as any brothers could be. When he disappeared for so many years, I just felt remorse and wanted an amicable reunion before he passed away."

Deacon sipped his tea. "You journeyed there personally. What did you find?"

Goharn peered into the fire and smiled. Deacon probed his mind to encounter jabs of sorrow. "I found the grave of my brother, buried on the planet's surface." Goharn then described the trip to Medulla with Chuen, the excitement of space travel, the welcoming reception that he received from his brother's friends on Medulla. "Apparently my brother was a noted man on Medulla, a popular man who pioneered innovative welding techniques that had great positive consequences in stabilizing metallic instruments and structures on Medulla, a planet with a dearth of welding techniques. Imagine that, would you? My big brother, Phendal Lok, a hero on Medulla because he was a welder."

In the back of Goharn's mind, a fear stirred, but Deacon couldn't interpret it correctly. Deacon concentrated. Goharn continued to talk convincingly about his brother's contributions in welding, but Deacon suddenly recognized an anxiety. The eventual topic of his accidental death summoned tears to Goharn, and he paused to weep openly.

"That's what space travel has burdened us with, Mister Coombs. Relatives, close ones, leave and find work in brave new worlds, never to return to see the ones who care for them, who love them, who worry about them, who want to see them again. What a shame for me to finally locate him after all these years and learn of his death."

"Did I hear you correctly that you spent all your savings to finance three expeditions of Chuen to find your brother?"

"Yes."

"Then how did you finance the fourth journey, the one with you and Chuen? How did you finance that trip to Medulla?"

"I did not, Mister Coombs; the Medullans did. When they heard from Chuen that my heralded brother, Phendal, had a brother alive on Earth, why, they contacted me through Chuen and invited me to Medulla.

Deacon was confused. How did this relate to Urzel? What was it about this saga that didn't make sense? How could an Earthman become so revered on Medulla? There was still a secret to uncover. "Goharn Lok, I have witnessed things not fit for mankind, seen an evil so malevolent that it occupies my every moment when I close my eyes. Two of my kinsmen are dead; another was sacrificed in space. Lok, you must tell me everything that happened during your voyage to Medulla. A path of death and destruction has led me here to your home. I will not leave until I know what you know about the revered nature of your brother on Medulla."

Goharn was silent for many minutes, and during that time Deacon was unable to read a single thought except for the names of Kam Chuen and Phendal Lok and a prevailing sadness. "Goharn, Earthmen are forbidden to land on the planet's surface. It is considered a crime to interface with the Medullans, and there are severe punishments. Yet your brother was permitted to dwell there and live out his life, and in addition, you and Kam Chuen were permitted to land there on the planet in secrecy." Goharn acknowledged none of what Deacon said. "In the halls of records in Liberty City and in the records of the moon Brebouillis, there is no mention of a Phendal Lok living on the surface of Medulla. I find that most peculiar. What did you and Chuen find? You have my complete trust, Goharn."

Goharn wrestled uneasily with himself. "Have another cup of tea, Mister Coombs. I have a surprise for you."

His tone of his voice caused goose bumps to surface on Deacon's arms.

URZEL LOK

While Jim stood as a sentinel in the foliage, Quobit patrolled the clearing below. It was a sultry, humid night, the foliage alive with music from insects. In the hut, Goharn commenced. "Be patient, Mister Coombs, while I tell my whole story. I cannot imagine what his life means to the safety of the Alliance, but I will recite it, and you decide. I am just humbled by your presence here.

"My brother, an expert welder by trade, gained recognition in the ancient forms of welding, which are still required on many planets. But I should begin my tale before that. Phendal and I were admitted to an orphanage at a young age. Our mother died penniless here in Ketapongo. Our father was a rogue, the marriage was not meant to be, and Phendal and I recall very little of our father.

"Upon our release from the orphanage in our teens, I mastered the art of tanning, while my brother commenced his apprenticeship as a welder. We had a very, very unfortunate dispute in which one says things that one later regrets. As a result, Phendal departed Earth, never to return. We communicated for a few years until finally the correspondence halted.

"As I grew older, I longed for him. He was always my big brother. He saved me during all those years in the orphanage when we were rejected from good homes and other children left to find their fortunes with new parents. I remember giving up on life in those days. It was he who told me about our hopes for the future, about how our dreams could come true. It was he who rescued me from deep depression when I was in my teens.

"I made it my quest to locate him, so when I had saved enough money, I hired a detective to find him. Chuen's travels took him to Barnard's Planet, Aralia, Weeropia—many exotic places. Eventually the trail led to Medulla, a strange final resting place with a repulsive people and an even more repulsive surface environment."

"Why is that?" Deacon knew the answer but wanted to test Goharn.

"Oxygen is scarce in the atmosphere. For people like us, heavy air cylinders are a requirement. The culinary cuisine is just plain repulsive. The foods of that planet can be ingested only with great gastronomical punishment, and the surface is covered in dirty orange soup." Goharn paused to look about and then sipped his tea.

"In addition, Medullans are pure intellects; they communicate only by passing thoughts to one another, so conversing with them becomes trivial and unimportant to them. They are spirits and despise other life forms since they exist on a higher evolutionary plane, perhaps the highest in the universe. They deprive themselves of any physical contact with aliens. I can honestly state that the least enjoyable experience of my entire life was the time I spent with them on planet Medulla, when they made an exception to interface with me."

Deacon was growing impatient. "Please continue."

"At this point, I shall convey to you the part of the story of Phendal's life as told to me in strictest confidence by the Medullans. I will rely on you to treat this information with discretion and convey it only to necessary confidants within the Alliance.

"Well, my brother became well known in the community. Initially they sent him chores to accomplish on the moon of Medulla. Eventually his assignments took him to the surface for repairs and constructions of the direst nature. The Medullans constructed an oxygen-rich workshop for him, and he traveled back and forth between the surface and the moon. More famously, he taught them new skills in welding. In time, the Medullans grew to know him, respect him, and love him as one of them."

Deacon's curiosity was piqued. "What kept him there? Why would one, especially an Earthman, want to live in such a difficult environment? I feel that there is an important fact that you conceal from me. Why did he not return to Earth? Why torture oneself on a planet of atmospheric difficulties, disagreeable cuisine, and uncomfortable relationships with the natives? And why was he allowed to stay there permanently on the surface?"

As he threw these queries at Goharn, he entered Goharn's mind to feel the single answer to all of these questions. Deacon was in disbelief when he received the message. "No," he said.

Goharn knew Deacon had discovered the truth. "Yes, Deacon Coombs. You have answered your own questions."

"Love? A female? Love kept him there?"

"Well, I discovered that Medullans are all bisexual, but yes, the love of a Medullan held him there."

"But Medullans are spiritual beings! What you are telling me is physically impossible. Goharn, what are you telling me? I don't understand."

"Medullans as spirits are things of immeasurable spiritual beauty. They change shape, color, and texture frequently. However, in their natural state, as a visible mass apparent to us, they are repulsive, ugly, shifting, quaking, boiling masses. They can refine their corporeal presence to entertain others for very brief periods."

"My God of Anglo. Your brother fell in love with a spirit. Did you, uh, meet her on your trip? Is that why they invited you to the planet's surface? And just how did that work, falling in love with a spirit?"

"Be patient, Deacon Coombs. Yes, I found her to be intellectually stimulating, emotionally pleasing, and exciting to the touch. But they are such a strange race. Here one minute, gone the next. They are fidgety in the physical state, nervous and agitated easily, and as I said, they appear very ugly, as globs of quaking blisters. The being I met was a female, but as I mentioned, Medullans are all bisexual."

"Did you touch her? As your brother did?"

"I kept my visors close at hand to repel her sight. However, for the experience of touching, they must encompass the entire body, and the other must dispel the visors. All races find the Medullans hideous, as I did. All people find them hideous except one, Mister Coombs. My brother, Phendal Lok, did not find them hideous, for you see, Mister Coombs, my brother was blind!"

Deacon was captured by the tale. "So your brother found his peace and happiness there on Medulla by falling in love with a spirit."

"Let me finish. There is so much more to tell. The relationship between the two ripened. The stage of true, deep love evolved."

"Hard to imagine. They did this as she encapsulated him to arouse him?"

After three more sips of tea, Goharn looked sternly at Deacon. "Yes. She encompassed him frequently."

"I thought Medullan law prohibited this?"

"It does. But they performed this act regularly."

"I find it difficult to know why the elders would permit this."

Deacon had no sooner said the word *this* than Goharn blurted out, "They had an affair."

"Now you really have baffled me."

"I will explain, please. There was no sexual contact. That would be physically impossible. However, the presence of the spirit surrounding the body was enough to arouse my brother. This I can attest to, since I also had this experience—a sexual arousal by having my body encompassed by a spirit." Goharn waved at Deacon to keep silent.

"The two spent innumerable hours together, the being enveloping Phendal with her spiritual matter. The physical-spiritual contact is difficult. By way of an operation, my brother's sperm was transplanted into an incubation chamber of the spirit. The egg was fertilized; the spiritual fetus carried the child, and with much glee to Phendal and his spouse, an offspring was born."

Blood rushed into Deacon's cheeks. At the same time, he envisioned a hundred questions about the operation. "Allow me to take a guess, Goharn. The child inherited the physical body from Phendal, the mental abilities from the mother, a Medullan."

"Precisely," Goharn replied as Deacon sewed the puzzle together.

"How could the Medullans permit this? Contact with foreigners is prohibited, and interbreeding punishable by law."

"Yes, you are correct. True love, however, conquers all, and in this case my blind brother and his partner convinced the elders of Medulla to sanction the birth, which contravenes the law. It was a well-guarded secret on Medulla until the birth."

"There are no records in the Alliance of such a sanctioning, and only the Alliance can sanction interracial birth between planets."

"I asked the Medullans about that. I inquired if the sanctioning by the Medullan elders had been approved by the Alliance."

Deacon knew that Goharn believed what he had been told on Medulla. Deacon also knew that this was not the answer. In the back of his mind, some terrifying thoughts were crystallizing about another possible scenario.

Goharn ranted on. "The villagers described it to me as a marriage made in heaven. The Medullan biologists and geneticists had studied this genetic problem for years, realizing statistically that the child would be corporeal."

"Yes. I know that the corporeal gene is a dominant gene in Earthlings but totally absent in Medullans."

"So the child was born with a body, just as predicted." Here Goharn's expression changed. "The experiment went awry. The child was insane from birth. I must elaborate for you. It had brilliance and unbelievable powers of the mind. However, it was declared mentally insane by local doctors. I heard from the mother that its mental powers belittled even hers."

Deacon was animated, his body shivering in the moist night. "I have seen your nephew! I've seen him!"

Goharn laughed. "Please, Mister Coombs. Contain yourself. Let me finish my story. No, with all respect, you have not seen him. Let me conclude. Sit. Be calm. Please." He used his arms to try to calm Deacon down.

"As the child grew, it brought misery to all it touched. It basked in the superiority that it maintained over others and seethed in its glory. It brought shame to its once proud parents as it played malicious, cruel pranks on other children and on Medullan spirits.

"Deacon, the Medullans do not have prisons, or even forms of punishment. They could not comprehend what to do with this malicious child. They wished visions of death upon it. A solution was not easily arrived at."

The sound of Goharn's disappointment filled the room. "Elders met and, unable to resolve the dilemma, eventually concluded that this child, for it was only a child, should be put to death. However, a sympathetic mother came to the rescue and saved it. With the help of friends, the mother abandoned it on a deserted planet where it would have to fend for itself in a savage world. The Medullans call the planet Douso."

"The Alliance calls it Nix!" Deacon shouted. His mind raced ahead to horrible realities. "I have seen the child."

"No, you have not. Before you besiege me again, Mister Coombs, and formulate erroneous conclusions, the tale is not complete. I know you are a great deducer and solver of mysteries, but please allow me the courtesy of finishing." Deacon kept quiet.

"My brother died before the child was banished into seclusion. To this day, I discovered, there are those on Medulla who believe that the child used its mental abilities to crush my brother's mind to death. Snap his mind like a twig. If this is the case, then he died loving his offspring and not knowing he was killed by him."

"Why did the Medullans permit this interbreeding?"

"I can only tell you what they told me. They recognized true love and allowed it."

"The child's name was Urzel, right? Urzel Lok."

Goharn was startled. "Why, wherever did you hear that? That is the name of the child—Urzel Lok. Urzel means *oneness*, in this case referring to the union of Earthman and Medullan to give oneness of the mind and the body. But how did you discover this?"

"It is your turn to listen, Goharn. While you sip your tea, let me tell you of dreadful news. Years ago a trading vessel of the trade union was disabled. It landed on an uncharted, unfriendly planet called Nix, where Urzel Lok had been abandoned. I firmly believe that Urzel, with his mental powers, warped the minds of that crew and escaped from Nix. He could have easily deceived all the crew into believing he was someone else with his mental powers." Goharn waved his hand. Deacon ignored him. "Urzel has escaped and has been among us since that ship returned from Nix six years ago. He has abnormal powers to take many forms, even appearing as you or me."

Goharn was shifting in his seat, and his body language displayed his displeasure with Deacon's comments. "But you said that you observed him recently?"

"Yes, I did."

Goharn motioned for silence. "Mister Coombs, please, enough. Your overactive imagination is stretching facts into fiction!" Deacon decided to listen, since Goharn had raised his voice intentionally to interject and he had no intent to insult his host.

"I know of the deaths of Geor and Como. Who in the Alliance doesn't? I know that you have come here through a series of clues. I know and you know that Urzel Lok is a misbehaved child. But come with me." He stood and motioned for Deacon to follow, and he then led him out of the hut, turned into the vegetation, and walked farther up the slope into the dank jungle, with Jim following closely behind.

"Where do you lead us?"

"I must ask you to remain quiet. We draw near."

Huffing and puffing after a short but arduous steep climb, Goharn asked Deacon to pull aside a sheet that covered the entrance to a tiny hut. Once they were inside, Deacon strained his eyes to see a table in the middle of the room. The shack reeked of human excrement. Goharn lit a candle.

Deacon heard a rustling behind him, and his tingling body vaulted across the room in two steps; there he took refuge behind Goharn. A tiny body emerged into the space he had just vacated.

"Mr. Deacon Coombs, permit me to please introduce you to my nephew, my brother's son, Urzel Lok. Urzel, come say hello to Mister Coombs. Urzel, he is a friend."

Confusion overtook Deacon. Should he flee? Shout for Jim and fire? He could not resist temptation, so he immediately signaled for Jim to join them inside.

"There was no need to summon your Owler, Mister Coombs. The child is harmless. Urzel, this is a friend." Goharn's voice was soft and encouraging. "Come here."

In the flickering candlelight, the being emerged, exposing a five-foot frame, oily charcoal-black hair, thin lips, narrow eye openings, bony protrusions in his exposed legs and arms, and distinct red blotches over his body. Deacon panicked as he remembered the blazing red eyes of Urzel on Nix. This child had those same beet-red orbs. To be safe, Jim extracted his stun weapon. The child retreated.

"That was not necessary, Mister Coombs. I brought you here because I trusted you. Urzel, come here." Goharn extended his hand, and the child moved into the middle of the room for the second time, tilting his head in a pathetic way. Deacon was drawn now to the pitiful sight—two sorrowful crimson eyes crying out for his sympathy. The boy's head bobbed up and down, and then Urzel replied, "Hello."

It was only one word, but it terrified Deacon so much that he extracted his weapon. The child retreated to the corner, frightened.

Goharn was upset. "Why did you do that?"

"That voice. It reminded me of the voice of Urzel when I was on Nix."

"Mister Coombs. I invited you here because when Geor and Como died, Urzel Lok was with me, on Earth. It is time to lay your fears of this child to rest."

"The tone of that voice was strikingly similar."

"It is a pure coincidence. Urzel was here with me. This sickly child cannot harm you. Now let us leave, for I have other news to impart to you that will be of interest."

"Jim, Goharn Lok and I have business to discuss. Stay here and take samples from the boy. Be gentle with him. I want hair samples, cutin, saliva, fingerprints, and, of course, the heartbeat and metabolic energy of the body. I also want a retina scan. Goharn, can you speak to the child to ask him to cooperate?"

Goharn nodded his head and coaxed the child to obey the Owler. "We will provide all the evidence you need, Mister Coombs," he said. Then they left him alone with Jim.

Not a single word was spoken on the descent. Once back in the bamboo hut, Goharn said, "I owe you a further explanation."

"Goharn, how did he get here?"

"The Medullans informed me of what they had done, so I tried to engage the services of traders to rescue Urzel from Nix, but no one could be paid enough to break the law to go there. It was also not a mapped, recognizable planet on trade charts. Then, as you suspected, Urzel escaped on the disabled trade ship from six years ago. Correct you were again in assuming that he duped the crew.

"Older but not wiser, his first step was to go back to—where else—his mother. She had not forgiven him for Phendal's death and warned him to leave before other Medullans discovered his presence back on Medulla. This all occurred after my attempts to find Phendal and my visit to Medulla.

"So Nedilli—Urzel's mother, my brother's wife—informed Urzel of me, and he arrived here on my doorstep. He has been seriously ill for that entire period of time, ever since I first laid eyes upon him."

"What does he purport to have?"

"Not purport. Urzel is deathly ill and is in a weakened state, and has been for six years. Your Owler will discover this and confirm it. He can't even walk from his hut down to my place anymore without my assistance, let alone perpetrate the crimes that you investigate."

"Why?"

"Urzel has been diagnosed with dipholopic fever. There was a time after his arrival here when he lived passively but healthily. I have had a number of medics confirm his condition. He has high fever; a constant soreness of the eyes, which causes the redness; constant urination; some cellular disorder; and infection of the digestive tracts. All these are symptoms of the disease. I want him to be left alone to die in peace. This parade of visitors must stop."

"Parade?"

"You are fourth visitor in three nights."

"Who else has come here?" Deacon asked quickly.

"A pestering trader called Chubby Eaves has come by twice. He too was concerned about my trip to Medulla. I told him nothing. He was arrogant. He's a snoop. I refused any courtesies to him, for he was rude and demanding toward me. I turned him away a second time last night. I told him nothing of the tale that I have told you."

"And the other visitor?"

"Urzel grew enormously strong the other night. No, not strong, furious. Something aroused him. As I sat to comfort him, I swear that there was someone ascending the path. I raced to the opening and cried out, summoning them to appear. Whomever it was decided to remain hidden down the path, but I knew someone was there."

Goharn suddenly seemed to be hypnotized. "Then I heard a strange sobbing, and as I searched in the bushes, drawing dangerously near to the sound, it fled down the hill. Later I listened as the being ran in confusing circles, scurrying around the perimeter of Urzel's hut."

"How many times has this occurred?" Deacon asked.

"Just that once."

"I am educated about dipholopic fever. I know the consequences. I took injections before my travels into space to combat this disease."

"Urzel did not have the luxury of those types of injections, as he was abandoned on Douso—I mean Nix—without any immunizations."

Jim appeared. "I have completed my assignment, Master Deacon. Is there any other data I should gather here?"

"No. I will join you shortly at the vehicle, Jim. Please return to Quobit there." A thought crystallized in Deacon's mind. "How old is Urzel?"

"In Earth years, sixteen years old."

"You mentioned the mother of Urzel?"

"Nedilli of Erestharn, west country."

"The sobbing that you heard—think, Goharn; did it sound like sobbing? What precisely did it sound like?"

"Well, it sounded like sobbing. That is the best word I can think of to describe it."

"Did it sound like Urzel, when Urzel sobs?"

"No, it was not like that at all. It was a strange type of sob, quite a foreign sound to me."

"Were there pauses between the noises?"

"Yes, there were. As I drew closer, it became fainter, but there were definite intervals between the noises. I can't help you anymore, Mister Coombs. I have trusted you with too much of the untold tale. Urzel Lok is a sickly child. He has been in my presence for many years. Please direct your attention elsewhere to find your space demons. And if you see Chubby Eaves, command him to leave us alone."

"Did Nedilli relate this tale of the child to you when you visited Medulla?"

"Yes, with the aid of three associates."

"How many other Medullans know that the child has escaped from Douso?"

"I can't answer that."

Deacon emptied his cup and rose. "Goharn Lok, you have been most helpful tonight. I apologize for any inconvenience. I believe now that Urzel Lok is not the one that I seek. But I must impose two favors on you."

"Certainly."

"Who knows of Urzel's existence on Earth?"

"Only the doctor who treated him, and now you, your Owler, and, of course, me. Urzel has never met any of my neighbors."

"You did not disclose his existence to Chubby?"

"Definitely not."

"It is absolutely imperative that you not tell anyone of Urzel's existence here. Also, here is an apparatus with a subspace code that can reach me instantly day or night. If this noise, this sobbing, reappears, record it by pressing this button, transfer it to my handheld by pressing this button, and notify me at once using this code."

"A reasonable request."

"Goharn, dipholopic fever is fatal. I must know if and when Urzel regresses or dies. Contact me immediately."

"Coombs, why have your clues led you to me? I don't understand. This child is harmless."

"I don't know. I am also confused by the events of tonight. I will return to tell you how this gets resolved. I promise. I have another pressing engagement. I must depart."

They embraced, and Deacon scampered down the cliffs to the clearing below. Not long after that, they were leaving the hilly jungles, the washboard roads more than once sending Deacon's head crashing into the roof of the vehicle. Inside, he was bursting with startling new conclusions that only Chubby Eaves could confirm. He discussed his encounter with Quobit as they raced to the inn.

At the inn

The sight was heartwarming. A relieved Lyanna had sat on the porch all night, swathed in a blanket, awaiting Deacon's safe return, stirring at every little footstep. As soon as she recognized him and Jim, she ran forward and threw her arms around him, kissing him on the cheek twice as Jim said, "Ahem." She broke the kiss and then hugged and kissed Jim too, to which Jim said, "Well."

Once inside, Deacon informed her of the events of the evening, which intertwined the lives of Goharn Lok, Kam Chuen, Phendal

Lok, Chubby Eaves, Urzel Lok, and Nedilli of Medulla but left more questions than answers. Jim stood watch outside and continued to scan for any signs of Gem. Deacon finished his tale long after one in the morning; he was out of breath, and Lyanna was completely enthralled. Then, the mortals opted for rest.

With Jim outside and Quobit curled up on the outside porch, Lyanna decided to teach Deacon his first lesson of love. In her transparent nightgown, she crept into his room and lay down beside him. The cue of snoring told her that this event would have to be postponed. Nudging him gently only brought an exaggerated snort before he tossed, mumbled, and tossed again. Relegating herself to another time, she placed his arm around her shoulders, snuggled up to his chest, and slept peacefully.

Meanwhile, down in the heart of the bars, Gem spied an Aralian slowly and sluggishly approaching the Wendovian. After a brief conversation with the innkeeper, Gem was able to confirm a positive identification. The Owler hid under the staircase as the Aralian slowly started to climb the stairs in a drunken stupor. Outside the room, Gem summoned the Aralian, and as he turned, he received a blow that rendered him unconscious. The master was to have two surprises in the morning.

The pleasant fragrance of Somoan tea wafted up into Deacon's nostrils. Soothing to the mind, it enhanced his comforting dreams until pangs of hunger directed him to breakfast. Upon opening his eyes, his heart jumped at the sight of seeing Lyanna's body turned into him, her left arm straddled across his chest, her left leg curled over his body. While he basked in the moment, a sudden commotion in the outer room seized his attention. Dressing quietly, so as not to awaken her, he stole a look at her figure just as she grabbed his arm to pull him on top of her. "Don't you have even one minute for me?"

As she completed her request, the ruckus in the next room flared to a crescendo, demanding an immediate investigation. "It appears that we have a guest."

With great difficulty, Deacon yanked himself away from Lyanna's grip. When he entered the adjoining room, he saw the arms of the Aralian flailing wildly in all directions. From behind his gag, Chubby blasphemed his captors.

"Well, if it isn't Chubby Eaves! Good morning, Chubby." After making this statement, Deacon ignored him, turned his back to pour a glass of juice, and stood to savor the taste as Chubby fussed. The trader, craving Deacon's attention, moaned incessantly. Lyanna, robed and grinning, sat beside Deacon as they faced Chubby, separated by only a few feet.

"Remove the gag, Quobit," Deacon said.

At the very instant of oral freedom, the Aralian squealed. "Kidnapping is a crime! You hear me, Coombs?"

Gem secured the bonds on his hands and feet. Deacon ignored Chubby to finish his drink, remarking to Lyanna what delights Earth had that he had taken for granted. Then he looked at Chubby.

"I admit to kidnapping," Deacon said, savoring the taste of the fresh fruit.

"What do you want with me?"

He pointed his finger at him. "I ask the questions here. Get that straight." His outburst of temper in an irascible tone surprised Chubby. He turned to Lyanna to flash a smile as Chubby bowed his head.

"Can't you at least release me?" said Chubby. "I can't escape from these Owlers. These bonds hurt. My, who is your monstrous Jabu friend?"

Deacon motioned to Gem to perform this task. The Owler did so, and then the two Owlers stood close by, one on each side of the Aralian as Deacon introduced Quobit to him. There was a silence as Chubby massaged his aching wrist and ankle muscles and then arose to help himself to liquid refreshments.

Deacon, sitting with his legs crossed and arms folded, began the interrogation. "You cleverly fooled me on Aralia. You tried to convince me to take you to Nix, knowing all along that my answer would be no. The Owlers discovered that your flight plans to come to

Earth were filed before I even arrived in the caves of Glagn. As soon as Travers, God bless his soul, and I departed, you left immediately to Asianda to unearth clues about this so-called devil who transformed the crew into a demented lot." Chubby was silent.

"Not having access to exactly the files that we had, I credit you, Chubby, with a remarkable piece of detective work in finding Dr. Kam Chuen and then Goharn Lok."

Chubby was not forthcoming with a response. At the first eye-to-eye contact from Deacon, Chubby said, "Thank you. The trade union has searched for years for the mastermind behind these crimes. The recent clues, including my search for this Kam Chuen, have led me here more than once. I loved Travers like a brother. I was informed of his death only a few days ago. I was drowning my sorrow in drink last night when your Owler intercepted me. I will miss him. Did he die in peace?"

Deacon pondered his response but decided to shock Chubby with the truth. "He died at the hands of this thing, whatever devil it is. It invaded his mind on the escape from Nix and murdered him, just as it killed Como and Geor."

"We in the traders' union owe Travers the greatest debt for opening new routes, negotiating new treaties, establishing safe practices, and providing sound leadership in the union. You said this thing invaded his mind. How exactly does it do that?"

"I don't know exactly. We witnessed a mental power on Nix that paled any I have ever seen. It followed us into space and caused Travers to bleed to death from a wound that he had incurred in battle with a Nicosian savage. I wish I could have saved him. The monster wouldn't let me."

"We all knew the risks of sending Travers to Nix with you. He sacrificed himself so that I could divert to Earth. What did this devil look like?"

"When it attacked us in space, it looked like a giant bird of prey. It was able to project its powers into the ship from a great distance." Deacon's voice descended to a whisper as he continued. "We could not defend ourselves against it. Travers was doomed to die as soon as the energy of the creature tortured him."

"Through space? You say the energy of the creature projected through space? Space is a vacuum."

"Yes, there was not a reading of a life form or a vehicle for thousands of miles, yet it reached out and touched us."

Chubby was saddened. "Travers understood the risks. I actually begged him not to go, but he insisted."

"Chubby, I grew to love the little trader. Our friendship was abruptly terminated. I will pursue the innocence of Travers as long as I live."

"And so will I," Quobit said, "for the Jabu have an interest in this matter too."

Deacon wanted answers. "Tell me, what you are doing in Ketapongo, Chubby?"

"I am a space trader. My line of work takes me here."

Deacon was irate. They were wasting time. "Let me clarify your position. You have just lied. You are in no position to either lie again or bargain with me. Just minutes ago, you mentioned Kam Chuen, and we both know who he is. Let's get to the truth." He stood, hands on hips, glaring at Chubby.

"My trade route brought me here."

"And then the *C'oulbaa* conveniently developed engine troubles so you could stay over and locate Kam Chuen."

"The ship's problems are all in the ship's records. Since my arrival here, my instructions have changed. The *G'uillger* requires an experienced captain of my credentials for its next voyage."

Jim interjected. "Gem and I detected that you have been in Ketapongo three times in the last year. Coincidence?"

Deacon checked the time on his handheld. Only ten hours until the *Heritage* docked and Landrew followed their real trail to Ketapongo. "You delayed your stay here to meet with Kam Chuen and Goharn Lok!"

Excitedly, Chubby danced around the room. "You found them both. Just like me." He began to pace with a broad grin on his face.

"Chubby, I complimented you earlier on your work. I know that for the right price, Chuen talks openly."

Chubby opened up. "I have been aware of this Detective Chuen for more than a year. I could not bargain with him successfully the first two times, so as Jim said, I had to make a third trip. What better time to investigate Chuen than while you were distracted on

Nix." Chubby then eyed Lyanna up and down, and he then stepped forward. "I am Chubby Eaves, my lady." He bowed.

She moved to acknowledge him. "My name is Lyanna, and it is my pleasure to meet you. I have heard a great deal about you." Chubby smiled and kissed her hand. Deacon interrupted his chivalry. "I will bargain with you, Chubby. I will tell you everything that happened on Nix if you will answer my critical questions honestly."

"Maybe."

Deacon whispered in Chubby's ear loudly enough for Gem, Jim, Quobit, and Lyanna to hear. "I know the true identity of Urzel."

Chubby opened his mouth as he was startled. Solemnly, he replied, "Deal."

"It will take the most brilliant efforts of you and me and Lyanna and Quobit and the Owlers and brilliant scientists to devise a plan to defeat him. It will take extraordinary courage from you and me and the Owlers and Quobit to execute the plan. This monster will be upon us soon. We will all die if we hesitate much longer." Chubby was riveted. Lyanna was shivering after listening to Deacon's last words.

"Acting on your own, Chubby, I believe that you are a menace to the success of the mission. I can't afford to take such a risk. So here are my absolute terms." Chubby sat down, attentive. "I will ask the questions. You will answer them truthfully. If you deceive me once, as I believe you and any Aralian is capable of doing, then I shall have the Owlers press charges to tie you up until our mission is complete. I am tired of Aralian deceptions. If we fail this quest, you could be charged with treason." Chubby rubbed his chin. "Furthermore, if you should join and then abandon our cause, then I shall brand you a traitor."

Chubby took a deep inhale and then released his breath and nodded. "I will not betray you, Deacon Coombs. We are deeper allies than you know. Please accept me as your friend."

They both sat down facing each other to commence their conversation. "Why did you seek Kam Chuen?" asked Deacon.

"When the traders' union first detected missing shipments of arms, we did a thorough check of historical records and, to our surprise, discovered that there were previous occurrences. Far too many of them." Chubby thought about the next disclosure. "I was on close speaking terms with Schlegar, Travers's father, so I traveled to

Brebouillis to solicit his assistance in examining criminal records on Brebouillis, with the intent to construct a list of suspects who could perform these injustices. Schlegar gladly agreed to help."

"How did you know that the criminal records of the Alliance were centrally stored on Brebouillis?"

"Schlegar told Travers in confidence. Travers told me in confidence."

Quobit tossed her hair as she shook her head. "Amazing. On Jabu, Aralians are viewed as incorruptible, trustworthy people who can be ultimately entrusted with secrets. Isn't there an Aralian saying? 'Tell an Aralian for safekeeping'?"

Chubby was amused. He smiled back at Quobit. "We are human." He sat back in his chair. "We have fewer faults than most species."

Deacon wanted to complete the interrogation. "Continue."

"Okay. We completed our list of prime suspects and then launched an investigation into the lives of these suspects. Unfortunately, Travers and I made a grave miscalculation. We tried to solicit Schlegar's help to gain control of the traders' union so that Travers and I might take direct control over the investigation of these crimes. The list of crimes expanded to drug trafficking, arms smuggling, inciting riots, and more. But to our surprise, Schlegar turned against us. He was appalled that we would influence traders to gain control and that Travers would use his mental powers to influence voters. That was the start of the rift between Travers and Schlegar, which grew and grew . . . and then grew hateful.

"I begged Schlegar to forgive us. He felt disgraced by his only son. He dreamed that Travers would replace Como one day, but not with the qualities that he had exhibited."

"You carried out your plan anyway?"

"Yes. That turned Schlegar deeper against us when he uncovered the plot. Schlegar believed in the golden days of Aralian pride. He did not understand, as I do and Travers did that to defeat an evil of this magnitude, we must resort to fighting criminals on their own ground. So much for our plan, for we have all failed so far."

Chubby shook his head. "The situation grew worse. Two alarming events took place within a few days after the break of friendship with the doctor. One, our prime suspect, as the mastermind behind these acts, was unquestionably innocent, as he was diagnosed with a fatal disease that had crippled him for at least one year before. This was unknown to us. Two, an alarming number of arms shipments disappeared under our noses again. Right under our noses! Our investigations continued, but only as a diversion."

"Diversion?" Lyanna said.

"Well, whoever the guilty party was, we wanted them to feel secure, so we set up dummy investigations that would lead nowhere. We were counting on the criminal to feel at ease as we created fantastic data and falsified reports. Travers and I were positive that there were spies within the union. Meanwhile, an inner core known only by the leaders of the traders' union was utilized to conduct secret investigations. Believe it or not, we almost solicited you, Deacon Coombs." Deacon failed to see the humor as Chubby's voice reflected joy in this comment. "Our secret investigations backfired."

Deacon stopped him. "How so?"

"Schlegar uncovered our insincere efforts and misconstrued our false documents to the Alliance as a feeble attempt on our behalf to cure our own ails. He seriously questioned the ethics of the leadership, believing that the feeble efforts were an indication of guilt by the union and by Travers and me to profit from ill-gotten gains. He thought that we did not want the culprits brought to justice. He felt betrayed by us. So the rift between the three of us widened.

"Moreover, he convinced Como to propose a motion to place the Union of Space Traders under the administration of the Alliance. When Como addressed his nation before he died and referred to the fact that he had seen evidence to discredit Travers, it was this report of our insincere efforts that he had witnessed. As I stated, we only did this to make the culprits feel safe. Schlegar and Como were childhood friends. It took only this report for Como to turn against us too." Chubby was visibly upset.

"We lost credibility. Como believed that we were covering up our own crimes with this dummy investigation." Chubby opened his arms to plead. "We could not go to him and reveal that the problem of missing arms was more of a crisis than we had indicated. That would have certainly been the end of our careers. We had to keep pursuing our own undercover work.

"Since the Medullans possess the greatest mental abilities in the universe and are forbidden to use them outside their planet, it occurred to me to look on Medulla first, to uncover what had to be a blatant misuse of mental powers."

Lyanna jumped into the interrogation. "Did you venture to Medulla personally?"

"Yes. It was fruitless. I left no clue unturned. Every possible lead I had evaporated. We spent enormous amounts of time on the moons, conducting research in the libraries and files. Depressed, I sent the investigative team home while I stayed on."

Chubby had a glint in his starry eyes. "When I returned to Aralia on a tourist ship, I made the acquaintance of an elderly gent, a Jabu, a man named Stragnnesse."

"I know this man," Quobit said. "He is a worldly potionist. He wanders far and wide around the Alliance."

"Yes, that's him. I spent hours with him, and his tales kept me entertained and lifted my spirits. Imagine my surprise when he told me of his previous excursions to Medulla moons years ago, where he met an Earthling detective who was searching for—"

Deacon upstaged Chubby by saying, "A long-lost brother of an Earthling living on the planet's surface."

Lyanna snickered as the Aralian twitched his nose, which was nestled in his facial hair. "Vesper you, Coombs! If I am to accept the terms of bondage, permit me to tell my own tale to this group."

"I apologize. My enthusiasm for your exploits overcame me."

"Would you like to finish my yarn?"

"Continue, Chubby."

"How surprised I was to hear the gossip from this man that an Earthling had been allowed to dwell on the planet's surface and had mated with a Medullan. The wicked stories that this Stragnnesse spun. He had been personally summoned years ago by the troubled mother and Earthling father to exercise the demons from . . . a child of this marriage, a child possessed. The potionist spent a most unsuccessful time there, only to see the child's maladies grow worse. The detective who later searched for this lost brother was Kam Chuen. Thus, with our current stall, it seemed only natural to locate this Chuen and learn more about this possessed child and the

Earthling father. Also, I had never heard that the Alliance had broken promises to allow interbreeding."

Chubby took a deep breath. "So I found Chuen and, after a few visits, rewarded him enough money to disclose the identity of his client on Earth, who happens to be the uncle of this disturbed child."

"Goharn Lok," Deacon said, beating Chubby to the punch line.

Chubby expelled hilarious snorting sounds. After Deacon extended his apologies, it was all he could do to endure the noises.

"What do you know about this offspring?" Chubby asked.

Deacon spoke politely. "You first, please. I'll say it again. Without the services of research Owlers and an inquisitive mind like my own, you have done extraordinarily well, Chubby."

Chubby accepted the compliment. "I heard all the rumors of how a biological experiment to mate an Earthling and Medullan had been a genetic disaster. The offspring is a beast who feeds on the misery of others. It has performed deeds of treachery. The Medullans tired of the child's crimes and banished it to its own place of suffering. Later I discovered that this was not true and that the Medullans wished death upon it; it was the mother who disobeyed and planted the child on Nix."

Chubby squinted with one eye as he peered at Deacon. "I used my influence on officers in high places in the Alliance to conduct an unofficial investigation, and for years I have searched for this detective and the client." He used body language to accentuate his story as his hands and arms stretched out and his eyes opened wide.

"I scoured travel records. When first we met on Aralia, I still had not visited Goharn Lok. After your departure, I promulgated the rumor that I was on the journey with you to Nix. Sorry, but I needed to buy time. When the *C'oulbaa* was ready to depart, Chuen had still not given me Lok's name. So I took advantage of my position in the union and issued new orders to command the *G'uillger* upon its arrival."

Deacon clapped exuberantly. "Hurrah for the truth."

"I finally found Goharn Lok, but he has not been cooperative in these matters. I think that he can be bought off."

"I wouldn't try that," said Deacon.

"All in the line of duty."

Lyanna said, "I am beginning to understand you, Chubby Eaves," echoing what Deacon was thinking.

"Goharn has information that will help us."

"I thought that I heard the word *us*," said Lyanna.

"Sure. I am a part of the team now. I have been truthful with you."

"Not quite!" Deacon said.

"Why not?"

"Tell me why you and Travers took the *Sleigher* to Nix. What happened there?"

"I don't understand the question."

"I have come to the conclusion that the last trip of the *Sleigher* to Nix was not an act of Urzel bending Vesper waves, as you would have the Tetrad Alliance believe. You and Travers purposely took her there. In his dying breath, Travers urged me to find you. He said that Chubby Eaves knows the truth. Chubby has the secret. Tell us the secret, or you're locked up by the Owlers until our return."

The messenger of death

As Chubby remained silent, Deacon prompted him. "As powerful as any being will ever evolve to, neither Urzel nor any man will ever be able to bend Vesper beams, as you would want us to believe. Travers has already confessed to me that you took the ship there."

"Why didn't you say so?" said Chubby. "The traders' union bribed officials at the Jabu Vesper station—just the two whose cooperation was required to make our scheme . . . I mean plan . . . work."

"Another Aralian skill—bribery. Bribed them to do what?" Quobit wanted to hear it, so she instinctively positioned herself closer to Eaves.

"Vesper our ship to the nearest station at Nix at a time when that station was inoperable because of repairs. It is an obsolete station but served our purposes. Our arrival went unnoticed because there were only two operators there when we arrived. They too were—how shall I say—cooperative."

"Officials there were compensated too?"

"Yes, they were very well compensated. I like that word. The official at Jabu altered the records, and sorry Quobit, but Maretz personally assisted us in our escape to Nix. From the station near Nix, we traveled a route to Nix that led us directly to the planet."

"Travers and you and the crew went there to assassinate Urzel, didn't you?"

Lyanna felt anxiety as she waited for Chubby's answer. Chubby wrestled with his words. "Yes, we wanted him dead. We had a grandiose plan of assassination."

"Did you have proof at that time that Urzel was the creature behind all these problems of the union?"

"We found a missing trade ship in a dormant volcano on Nix. We found the missing arms hidden deep in caves in a mountain." Chubby was uncomfortable talking about this subject. As Deacon let his mind switch moods to intercept his thoughts, he could only decipher one word—*Urzel!*

"What else happened there? Did you unleash the monster?"

Chubby glared at Deacon. It was if he had stopped breathing.

"Right now you must tell us exactly what happened on Nix. Time grows short to capture this creature."

Chubby exhaled. "We landed on a remote sector of the planet. Our plans were simple. Travers and I split the group into three parties. For days, we kept in contact with each other, scouring the planet for him, searching for his hideout. It was my team that found the abandoned ship. It was Travers who found the stolen weapons. We never heard again from the third group. Then Travers lost his crew." His voice began to quiver. "Travers and I sat on a ledge overlooking a campsite, pondering our situation. It was then that we recorded the savage firing the laser gun into the fire. It was then that we realized that either the natives had helped themselves to the discovered weapons or someone was arming them. Stunned, we ran in fright back toward the ship. As we approached, we heard the wailing of Aralians. Travers and I foolishly split up to search for our comrades. After many hours, Travers did not answer his communicator. My crew had vanished too. I was alone."

As Chubby continued, terror flavored his voice. "I pondered about what a tragedy this journey had been. We had carefully chosen our crew to accompany us here, and suddenly they were all gone. We had irresponsibly gambled away top tradesmen to satisfy our revenge on a madman we hadn't seen.

"In my state of exhaustion, my eyes started to play tricks on me. As I stared out over the plains where campfires dotted the landscape, I dreamed that I saw a mountaintop on the far side of the valley rise into the heavens. I furiously rubbed my eyes to make the mirage disappear. It did not. Instead it grew higher and higher into the sky, the outline becoming clearer to me. Now it towered over everything in sight. I was petrified.

"Then"—Chubby had them on the edge of their seats as his voice trembled—"as I feared for my own sanity, I heard a voice. It started as an excoriating gurgle, climaxing in a paralyzing laugh. It overflowed in the dells, rebounded off the cliffs behind me to strike at me, smother me, stab at me, cause me to sink to my knees and cover my ears. The ground shook as it grew louder.

"I dared to open my eyes, and as I did, the mountain slowly, slowly, slowly opened its eyes. Two deep-set, hot-burning red coals looked out from the darkness from the other side of the valley and scorched my soul. My body convulsed into spasms as a crevice in the rock exposed shimmering white teeth. The mountain was alive.

"Deacon, oh my lords of Aralia, it was no mountain. It was he whom we sought. He wore a pointed black hood, with those two hellish eyes and menacing teeth reaching over the plains now to the spot where I stood. He rose hundreds of feet higher, standing over me, laughing. I fainted as my heart went into palpitations."

It was apparent to Deacon that Chubby was filled with consternation. "When I awoke, I was in a small cave. Drained of all energy, too weak to run, I sat and waited. Finally, he came."

"What did he look like then?" Lyanna asked.

"It was difficult to see him in his oversized robe, but he was very tall, slender. That black robe with the pointed hood disguised all his other features. It never leaves him. The only other parts of the body exposed to me were his hands. They had long, slender fingers with a wizard's long, pointy nails. Those haunting red eyes visit my dreams every night."

Chubby took a break and moved to sip some water. Deacon remembered the dreams he had had of late. He recalled those eyes, so he sympathized with the Aralian.

Chubby resumed his tale momentarily. "He paced around me, taunting me, blaspheming me. The voice was so deathly mesmerizing. He told me that he was Lord Urzel Lok, destined for glory, and that he hoped that I had enjoyed his demonstration of mental powers as he towered over me by hundreds of feet. He said that he had encountered Travers years ago when his disabled spaceship landed on Nix; that he had taken the place of one of the crewmen to escape from this horrible place to our worlds. I listened, unable to move.

"Then he sat on his haunches, positioning himself close to me, telling me that he had now hatched a perfect plan to conquer the Alliance and that—here is my terrifying secret—that I . . . was to be his appointed messenger. I interrupted him, demanding to see my crew.

"Whirling around me in his gown with a bout of hysterical laughter, he left to return shortly and parade all my crew members in front of me, one by one. My friends. My dear comrades. They all wore the look of torture: glassy eyes, watery mouths, crumpled bodies. They were all insanely mumbling—mumbo-jumbo. Jonessee, my dear friend, showed a glimpse of recognition, so the monster lifted his arms horizontally and flapped his robe up and down, chanting. Jonessee screamed, and I watched him helplessly roll about on the floor, begging for the pain to desist. I cursed this Urzel. I was afraid, but I was helpless to defend Jonessee. Then Urzel spat at me. 'This is what I do to those who come here to plot my demise,' he said. He hissed this statement at me four times. Jonessee died in front of me. I was powerless to help him." Chubby sank to his knees to cry as Lyanna knelt beside the Aralian and cradled his head in her arms. Deacon sat mortified, wondering if they would ever find Urzel's weakness.

Chubby began to speak again, the words barely decipherable as they rolled out of his mouth during his weeping. "Lord Urzel told me that he had snapped the minds of all of my crewmates, that they were useless humans. He said that . . . that . . . that I would be the only sane one to return from this doomed adventure. I would suffer all the guilt of this foolish escapade."

Chubby stood, regaining his composure. "I am a part of this team. I have a score to settle with this devil. I have the courage to confront him a second time. Lord Urzel called me his messenger of death. I am the chosen one who is supposed to prophesize his forthcoming. Me, Chubby Eaves, who bears more hatred than anyone else in this universe, I am his anointed messenger. I am to be his prophet."

"What message does he want you to spread?" Deacon asked, wanting this information now.

"He is going to rule all life as we know it, for it is all life that has cast him out. He will destroy any race that impedes his path. Rivers will run with blood, just as the Aralian gospel predicts. The skies will turn to fire if we oppose him, just like the Aralian gospel predicts. He is the ruler, Lord Urzel Lok, supreme commander. He has planned this Armageddon for years, and the strike time is soon."

Quobit thought of the weak defense systems on Jabu. "When will he come? What does *soon* mean to him?"

"Don't know."

Deacon and Lyanna held hands tightly as Chubby strained to complete his tale. "So he placed all the crazed crewmen on board the *Sleigher* and rode with us back to Aralia. He thanked Travers for this glorious opportunity; Travers was ill every time he heard Urzel's compliment. Urzel told us that he had mental converts everywhere in the galaxy: some through bribery, some through future promises of ruling for him, some through his mental paralysis and spells.

"We would all bow down and worship him. He spoke of how he had used people to steal weapons for him—the same ones that we searched for, every one of those caches. He talked of how he had mentally controlled individuals in the Union of Space Traders and caused them to incite riots to test his mental competence, to test his powers; he played with both sides as if they were toys. He talked of how he had recently incited rebellion on Barnard's Planet. In fact, he has been responsible for all the sicknesses in our world. He's been playing with us! He kills as if it is a meaningless game with one winner. He murdered Como and Geor too. He reached into their minds and planted their own seeds of destruction."

There was more moisture in his eyes. "We're just toys to him. We are helpless against him. I erred to go there, Deacon, but we have to live with our frailties. I should have been more forthcoming and taken Alliance forces and annihilated him and his followers. And yes, Deacon, he programmed Morris Mydloan to kill Geor's son."

"Why was Travers not completely affected?"

"Travers was strong. His mind was damaged. His body aged by years, but he fought every minute of the invasion of Urzel. He did not escape unharmed, as his speech was severely impaired."

"I am sorry for the rude methods we used to snare you, Chubby. It was necessary for us to talk."

"Apology accepted, Coombs. I avoided him on the return trip, although he sought me out and scared me further with his speeches of glory. He is totally insane.

"The last step was to position the *Sleigher* against the Vesper station. He permitted me to escape before Landrew arrived. If I propagate his coming, I will be tried and convicted of insanity. So I fled here to find Chuen and Goharn Lok to try to unravel what has happened to date. I feel more secure trying to determine what this monster is and participating in its defeat than hiding the rest of my life from it. No matter what happens, I will not be his disciple. I would rather die fighting for justice."

A plan crystallized in Deacon's mind. "There is still much to discuss, Chubby. It becomes clear to me that the only way to defeat it is to exploit its weakness—whatever that may be. Chubby, you said that it rode on the *Sleigher* back to Aralia?"

"Correct."

Deacon smiled. "Hmm."

Lyanna demanded an explanation of the "Hmm." Chubby then said, "His powers are great. I have witnessed them. How will we ever defeat it, Deacon?"

"You must believe, as I do, that this monster does have a weakness, or you wouldn't have signed up for what could be a fateful mission. Travers is dead. That is reality. What was your plan?"

"I don't know. But since I have arrived here, my plan is to . . ." He looked at Lyanna, then Deacon, then Quobit, and then the Owlers, and said, "Join forces with you! Please do not deny me this."

Deacon offered his hand. Lyanna joined to complete a circle with Chubby and Quobit. Deacon said, "I wish to share with all of you that I have already postulated ideas about the seeds of this creature's destruction. I may have also figured out his startling true identity."

Gem and Jim stood close by as the leader addressed them. "The plan I have to beat him is somewhat incredible in nature. But it must be done. It will be disbelieved by many. Therefore, it will require courage that the six of us don't know we possess."

As Jim and Gem joined hands in the circle, Deacon spoke. "The six of us are about to embark on the journey of a lifetime."

THE EQUILIBRIUM
OF EVIL

Revelations

Deacon retired to his room for private deliberation and analysis, leaving the others to converse. Quobit recounted the events that had transpired on Nix to Chubby while Lyanna took advantage of the hiatus to walk with Gem through local markets to purchase supplies.

Later that day, as they gathered for a meal, Deacon was ready to share his findings with them. "The first fatal flaw of any investigation is to look beyond the limitations of what the data suggests. Most certainly, the bending of the Vesper waves has created hysteria in the Alliance"—he looked at Chubby—"and played into the hands of Urzel. Discounting alien invasions, the ship *Sleigher* must have had human help to reach Nix. My early conclusion was simply that the ship was kidnapped; or, more likely, that honest Aralians and Jabu created a deception to travel to Nix for good reasons, which Travers—and now you, Chubby—have confirmed.

"Similarly, we must examine other aspects of this case within the limits of the reality of the data. If we don't, we handicap ourselves." Deacon's blood was flowing. "Let's dine while I recite my thoughts."

Chubby's hands were already sticky in sauce while his utensils lay dormant. Quobit was reciting her prayer of thanks for food. Lyanna and Deacon respected her ritual and waited until she had finished.

"I conversed with Goharn Lok at length about his personal voyage to Medulla. There, with repentance, he learned of his nephew who was banished by the Medullans to a distant, savage planet. He conveyed to me how his efforts to search for the boy, first through the traders, were thwarted. However, Urzel Lok, this offspring of his brother, Phendal, and his Medullan wife, Nedilli, escaped from Nix years ago on a ship commanded by Travers. I discovered from Goharn that the child's first instinct was to return home, hoping all had been forgiven. However, the mother instilled further feelings of rejection into the child, urging him to flee for his life from Medulla.

"Now the story gets complicated; it takes a bizarre twist." Deacon knew the others hadn't figured out what he knew. "There are three episodes that we need to direct our attention to. The first event took place years ago here on Earth, after Urzel's escape from Nix, after he had planned vengeance on the galaxy and had initiated some of his crimes. Urzel Lok knew of the existence of Goharn Lok from conversations with his mother. Soon the creature needed Goharn's help, for he became ill with dipholopic fever. Given that he couldn't return to Medulla, the single person who he could ask for sympathy and help was his uncle, Goharn Lok. So Urzel Lok traveled to Earth to seek his uncle here in Asianda, to seek help with his dipholopic fever."

Lyanna interrupted. "Did Goharn provide a description of Urzel?"

"Better, as Jim will attest to. Goharn gladly accepted the sickly child years ago in his home. Yesterday, I met and visited Urzel Lok, for he dwells up the mount behind Goharn's hut."

"What?" Chubby jumped as he shouted. "You would have us believe this? That Urzel Lok is here in Ketapongo this day? If so, why haven't you summoned the forces of the Alliance?"

As Chubby spoke, Lyanna also felt uncomfortable about the risk that Deacon chanced, and a look of consternation came upon her face. She nodded her head in agreement with Chubby.

"Because you two are jumping to erroneous conclusions. Remember. Honor the limits of the data."

"Damn the data!" Chubby said excitedly.

"Urzel Lok is harmless. I guarantee you, Chubby, and I guarantee you, Lyanna. Let me have the chance to explain." The group directed banter at Deacon as he tried to keep them at bay by motioning with his hands to quiet them down. "When Urzel Lok came here to his uncle, he was deathly ill with the space disease. Dipholopic fever starts with cell degeneration. We travelers get our immunizations in advance of space travel to firm up the cell walls, but Urzel lacked these boosters and contracted the physical ailment.

"His uncle nursed the being and has done so since. As I said, Urzel resides in a small hut behind Goharn's lodge, and Jim confirmed exactly what Goharn said—that his body is infected with dipholopic fever. He suffers all of the consequences and will die soon."

Lyanna put her hand up. "Permitted to interrupt? This story generates a hundred queries in my mind."

"And it will generate more as I continue. If you let me finish, most will be answered. Please. Urzel Lok is deathly ill. Jim's medical examination of Urzel confirmed it tonight. Jim, if you would please, relate your findings."

Jim opened his body screen and spoke. "Let me please present more facts to you. The being Urzel Lok is in his mid-teens, according to the scale used on Earth. He is thin, bony, frail, and undernourished, and his body cannot retain significant amounts of necessary fluids. He is five foot six and weighs a paltry ninety pounds. Irrefutably, the child suffers. His metabolism fights the disease unsuccessfully. He maintains a day-to-day existence, but death is 98 percent certain within a year by my calculations. The cell disruption is too far advanced to be reversed. Observe the deviations from a normal teen on these graphs, and observe the much lower water retention, the lower metabolism, and the erratic brain wave patterns."

"Thanks for the confirmation, Jim," said Deacon. Jim took a bow and stepped back. "I have some surprises for you. This afternoon I determined that the hair specimen of Asiandan that we found on Nix matches Urzel Lok's hair sample that Jim took, proving only that Urzel Lok was on Nix at one point in time. You see, the sickly child that I saw on the hill tonight is indeed Urzel Lok, and he has been gravely ill for years, and he is the child abandoned on Nix by the Medullans."

"Then he could not have slain Como and Geor," said Chubby, "and also be the being I saw and you saw on Nix."

"Wrong, Chubby, for he certainly did commit these crimes."

"How? You make no sense."

"When I saw the bloodred eyes of the being tonight and heard him utter a few words, I was convinced that this was the creature that I saw on Nix. It wasn't, though. I do know now whom I saw on Nix."

Lyanna spoke up. "This had better be good. I am keeping track, and you have contradicted yourself seven times."

"Patience. The first clue to understand what has transpired is the dipholopic fever. It is fatal. When Urzel first escaped from Nix, he made the plans that Chubby revealed to us earlier. Then he grew ill. However, the records of the traders that Chubby laid open to me showed a lapse of activity coinciding with Urzel's arrival here on Earth. I spent the last few hours comparing these records. The reason for this dormant period is now clear to me. He was here with his uncle, Goharn Lok, being treated for dipholopic fever.

"You must believe what the facts tell us. The creature came to Asianda. Why? It felt the weakening of itself, it knew it was losing its life, it needed help, and Urzel was desperate. He sought the comfort of family, his own kin, and pleaded for sympathy from a man unaware of any criminal activities.

"The second important event is here." He slammed the heartbeat and voice profiles in the middle of the table. "Here are copies of data Gem recorded on Nix. Urzel's voice and metabolic patterns are here. Observe: the heartbeat pattern of the being that Jim and I witnessed is remarkably similar to these patterns registered by Gem on Nix. However, the heartbeats are different.

"Gem first noted that the heartbeat of the being on Nix had similar patterns to those of Earthlings. As a matter of fact, the traces most resemble us of Earth except for this subtle yet omnipresent double beat, a deviation from Earthling heartbeats, but not unusual. At first I dismissed this as a unique metabolism, an adjustment to the planet's conditions, or an imperfection of the heart. Now look at Urzel's heartbeat that Jim captured tonight."

Lyanna was quick to respond. "My, they look not exact but quite similar."

"Now the third piece of crucial evidence before I reveal the murderer. The child Urzel is the offspring of an Earthman and a Medullan. Goharn Lok treated this sickly offspring with the intent of aiding kinfolk. Recently Goharn told me that he has heard a strange sobbing sound in the bushes near Urzel's hut. Unsuccessfully, he searched for the intruder. If we operate with the set of facts that I have laid before you, there is only one conclusion."

"There is a twin," said Chubby.

"No!" replied Deacon. "The clues I have given to you are pointing to one conclusion. Urzel Lok retreated to the only hope he had during his bout with dipholopic fever. Here in Asianda, in the solitude of Goharn's hospitality, with cell degeneration in an onslaught, Urzel Lok fought to survive, as all human forms do, and made a most astonishing discovery to survive.

"Urzel is a genetic experiment that failed. The pathetic, sickly creature that I observed tonight did not ask to be created from this wedlock, but it was. Dipholopic fever attacks the cells of the muscles and bones, but it is not present in spiritual Medullans. All beings, whoever they are and wherever they are, will find the will to survive when their lives are threatened . . . and Urzel Lok found it.

"What Urzel discovered in those desperate hours of fighting for his life was that part of him could shed this disease and survive; the other half couldn't. In other words, the spiritual part of Urzel left the sickly body just as the Medullans abandoned corporeal flesh years ago. In time, the two completely separated into spirit and body."

Chubby seemed to be skeptical. "How do you know this?"

"The evidence. Urzel Lok once functioned as an entity with one metabolic rate. The heartbeat that Gem recorded on Nix identifies Urzel Lok the Medullan. Medullans don't have hearts, but they maintain a metabolism, which has a rhythm, like throbbing. That is what we measured on Nix—a pattern of throbbing metabolism occurring within the Earth heartbeats. What I thought was an irregular human heartbeat was really the throbbing of the organic functions of a Medullan.

"When I viewed this thing on Nix, the sickly corporeal child Urzel Lok was here on Earth. Think of it. The creature had existed as one entity for sixteen years. It discovered it could separate into two beings, and the beginning of new energy patterns emerged. I believe that the sobbing in the woods is the spiritual Urzel, come to pay his last respects to his dying other half." He had their attention.

"Imagine," said Quobit, "a child punished through no fault of its own since it was born insane. No playmates. No normal life.

Abandoned among brute savages on Nix. Then, upon escaping, it returns home to suffer humiliation through rejection again. In its will to survive, it realizes it can separate into two entities: one doomed to die, the other a powerful, strong, mad spirit now free to conquer all humanity."

Lyanna decided to challenge Deacon. "How can you be so sure?"

"Lyanna, the matching hair samples, the voice patterns, the complementary heartbeats, the separation to save itself. It makes sense."

Chubby asked, "I know that he murdered Geor and Como. But why?"

"Geor's wife Geolo told me that Geor came to her and surprisingly stated that the case against Travers led elsewhere. He must have stumbled onto some truths about Urzel. Regarding Como, I can't speculate yet." As they contemplated his theory, he said, "Add the murders of Geor's son and Travers, and that makes four counts."

"Five including Jonessee," said Chubby.

"Chubby, here's a thought. It is also possible that if Urzel twisted Como's mind to kill himself, he also could have programmed him to blaspheme Travers nationally in front of all Aralians."

With a note of urgency, Lyanna said, "You were there on Nix, Deacon. You witnessed it. Why hasn't Urzel Lok been able to murder you in two attempts?"

"I don't know, but indeed that must be one of the factors that we must focus on to defeat him. I think he fears me. And it is three attempts, Lyanna. He has had two opportunities to eliminate me— once on Nix, secondly in space—and he failed. He also sent Morris Mydloan to assassinate me rather than perform his own dirty work. This is a critical clue yet to be explained."

Chubby was animated. "I want to know why Landrew visited the *Sleigher*. I told you that he traveled to Aralia and we all sat there waiting until he was the first to enter. You said, Deacon, that this was highly irregular. Imagine, the high ruler himself visiting a demented crew."

Deacon grinned. "I have found the answer. If I tell you, this must be our solemn secret." Chubby hugged Deacon and then shook his hand to signify the oath. Quobit and Lyanna moved closer to complete the oath.

"Often, paths to power are marred with temptation. Thus is the case of our revered politician Landrew. While investigating all the current members of our esteemed High Council, I retraced the past histories of their political careers. Upon leaving Earth, I carried that data in Jim's memory banks. It was only on the return voyage from Nix to Brebouillis that I realized an unpleasant truth that I had uncovered.

"Landrew is a great man. His conquests in making all our lives safe and rewarding are irrefutable. Yet he made one fatal mistake. Slight as it was at the time, I believe that he suffers more than anyone knows. I must journey to Liberty City to test my hypothesis."

"Which is?" Lyanna said, speaking for both herself and Chubby.

"I speculate, so don't jump to conclusions. I believe that Landrew journeyed to Aralia to be the first to view the *Sleigher* because he was looking for evidence of Urzel Lok. As with his conversations with me on Earth, I felt that Landrew knew what I might discover in space. I now know why he thought this.

"When Urzel was born, Landrew was the chief security minister of the Alliance. As such, among his responsibilities were the planet Brebouillis and all the security files. Jim and Gem proved that there is no reference to Urzel in those files, but there should be. It was during Landrew's reign as chief security minister for the Alliance that Urzel was born. His birth, with an Earthling as one parent, should be documented. It isn't.

"Even if the birth was an oversight, tales of this maladjusted child with extreme mental powers are known, and if Chuen and Goharn Lok can uncover them, then surely the resources of the Alliance can. The Alliance must have at one time investigated this creature. Conclusion: the so-called complete files of Brebouillis are incomplete. They do not have any references to Urzel Lok's birth and powers; this has been done deliberately by Landrew.

"I believe that at one time Landrew did recognize Urzel. Medullans are shrewd people. I believe that the Medullans sanctioned this love affair with the approval of Landrew, who again would have been chief security officer when the Medullans approved this affair on Medulla. It was in Landrew's department that all interplanetary immigrations were sanctioned. Yet even the immigration of Phendal Lok remains obscured."

"Can I speculate?" Lyanna asked. "You believe that Landrew knew of the marriage of Phendal Lok to Nedilli, had knowledge of the genetic catastrophe that ensued, and erased all the documentation so that it would not be uncovered by his opponent during the last slanderous political campaign for High Council."

Deacon sighed. "Unfortunately, that may be the truth. Landrew's last election raised bitter pasts for all the candidates. One more blemish and he would have been denied the credibility that he alleged in his speeches."

"Why did he visit the ship?" Chubby asked.

"Landrew fears the mental power that killed Geor and Como and caused the fatal journey of the *Sleigher*. He guessed that the being responsible for the ill-fated *Sleigher* could well be the product of that experimental birth that he sanctioned years ago. He thought the incident of the Medullan child was completed with its banishment to Nix. He now fears differently.

"Only when the *Sleigher* docked back in Aralia did Landrew begin to fear that condemning evidence may lie on the *Sleigher*. He had to arrive first to either erase that evidence or confront it. You said Urzel accompanied you on the journey back to Aralia, right, Chubby?"

"Correct."

"Where is his voice in the voice logs? Where is the heartbeat pattern that we witnessed on Nix? Where is there any evidence of Urzel's presence on the *Sleigher*?"

They stared at Deacon in silence. "The only possible answer, if Chubby is telling us the truth, is that Landrew marked the ship off limits until all that evidence of Urzel Lok was destroyed."

Lyanna shook her head. "These are serious charges, Deacon."

"I realize the consequences if I am right or wrong. However, consider that Landrew may have done us all a favor to prevent mass panic. There is even a more frightening aspect to this case that I will share with you when we reach Liberty City. Our plan from this point on becomes clear. First, we must go to Liberty City in disguise so that Lyanna and I can surprise Landrew and converse in private. We cannot take any chances of having our presence known."

Lyanna nodded in agreement. "I will go with you. Why did Landrew not trust you with this story of the sanctioning of the birth?"

"His political survival. One scandal might be enough to remove him from office. What better way to cover up an unpleasantness than to cover another unpleasantness. Greater politicians than Landrew have misused their power to execute crimes on humanity. I think that Landrew truly believes, just as Travers and Chubby did, that he has a good chance to rectify the situation without alarming the Alliance, and I do honestly believe that he wanted me to investigate without being influenced."

Lyanna continued. "Why did Landrew lie to you about who were investigating the crimes?"

"He didn't. If I remember his exact words, he wanted me to investigate the crimes of the Union of Space Traders independently of all other deployed resources. He desired my unbiased opinion, to direct him to unprejudiced actions. He wanted me to confirm or deny Urzel as the villain. For that, I admire Landrew, for unlike others, he left me alone to uncover the facts."

Lyanna strolled to beside Deacon and placed her arm around him. "No use irritating the boss. I guess you have to go to Liberty City and tell the boss that his suspicions were correct."

"I am certain, Lyanna, that Landrew wants a different answer than the one I am about to deliver. The positive result is that we can now direct all our resources toward beating Urzel."

"I am so proud of you, Deacon." She planted a kiss on his cheek.

He replied, "Thanks for the compliment. I shall accept it while I can. I told you and Chubby that there is a horrible reality that I must hide from you until the time is right to reveal it. It can only be confirmed by Landrew. Until this happens, I can't in confidence share it with you, but I have placed the file in the last Owler off of the assembly line for protection and preservation.

"Chubby, you and Gem must remain here to await the docking of the *G'uillger*. Meanwhile, Lyanna, Jim, Quobit, and I will travel to Liberty City to confront Landrew. Quobit, I must ask you to accept the role of bodyguard for us. Chubby, the *G'uillger* is armed, isn't she?"

"Yes, it is one of a handful of armed trade ships."

"With force fields and subneutro rockets?"

"Yes. And she is mighty fast. Why?"

"The *Heritage* is quick but underarmed for the next leg of our adventure. She has quickness but not protection." Deacon paused and then asked, "Will the *Heritage* fit inside the cargo bay of the *G'uillger?*"

"Ah, I see your wisdom. With your faithful Owler Gem, we could do that calculation."

"If the calculations are favorable, then proceed to Liberty City in two days with the *G'uillger* and get Gem to obtain the necessary papers to load the *Heritage* inside her cargo hold."

"The extra weight will slow us down, and think of the extra fuel expended and needed."

"We will need the *Heritage* to escape with our lives," Deacon said.

"Where are we going?" Chubby asked.

"Medulla."

Chubby chuckled. "Ha, how ironic. I finally get to transport a cargo to Medulla, and it is an empty spaceship that they can't use."

Deacon was aroused. "What did you say?"

"I said how ironic it is that the *Heritage* is the first cargo ever to go to Medulla."

Deacon rose to his feet. "Are you saying that there is no previous record of a trade ship transporting cargo to Medulla?"

"As far as I know, the trade ships travel to Medulla empty."

Deacon beamed from ear to ear. "In the history of trade ships traveling there, there is no cargo transported? Unloaded? Only loaded?"

"Affirmative!"

"Never?"

"For the last time, Deacon, it has never happened. We only ever pick up cargoes there. Medulla provides valuable ores, mostly."

Deacon was flabbergasted. He sat down. "Thank you for that enlightening tidbit of information. So that's the game."

"What game?" Lyanna asked in a demanding tone.

"The last clue to the puzzle, dear. This is scary. Now I *know* we are all just pawns."

"Why wait to tell us what you are thinking?"

"I have to put my hypothesis to the test. Then, if I am right, you shall be told what is brewing in my mind in front of Landrew.

Patience, my dear, I don't quite have the last few chess moves calculated, but Chubby just provided another great clue."

"Let's pray nothing happens to you, for the Owlers can't take up this case."

"Then I will take the liberty of recording my theory in the data banks of both Gem and Jim. Meanwhile, our arrival into Liberty City has to be incognito. We must not expose ourselves, or we will be detained and lose precious time. Therefore, Jim, you will have to succumb to donning a wig, dress, and shoes so that we can disguise you too. Or as on Aralia, you will be spotted."

"Objection," Jim said humorously.

"Place your human engrams aside, Jim. I also want a small, extractable plaster cast placed around your ankle to disguise your walk."

"My gait is elegant."

"Such a problem child," Lyanna said.

"And for me, I want sunglasses, a flowing robe and gloves, high heels, a hat, a shawl, a wig—red hair, I think—and makeup as you please, Lyanna. Gem, I need a force field to alter my heartbeat if the scanners at Liberty are set to detect my entry."

Lyanna was taking notes. "I see that I need to set out shopping. I'll take Gem to assist me."

"Sure. Jim can stay here with Quobit, Chubby, and me to finalize our plans. Quobit, you can travel undisguised and remain within view of us. Lag behind; look for spies on us. After our short visit to Liberty City, I am positive that Landrew will agree that Medulla must be our next destination."

Chubby asked, "Do we travel there to interrogate Nedilli?"

"Precisely."

"Then on to Nix with Alliance forces and fight him!"

"No, Chubby, we would lose. That it is why it is imperative to talk to Landrew. I have a better idea. Design a perfect, devious trap to catch him."

"You can't be serious?"

"All the clues to his demise must be gathered. We don't have them all yet."

"What clues?"

"Who better to know her own child than his mother, Nedilli. Also, Urzel feels remorse toward his counter half. This may also be a clue to his downfall. And consider what I said earlier, that he had three opportunities to exterminate me and failed to do so. We have to find out why. Then there is Landrew, who knows more than I have divulged to you. He owes the truth to me. Landrew must be interrogated in the presence of the High Council to make our plan work. Then there is a terrible thought that I carry as a burden until the time is right to expose it to all. Finally, I believe that you, Chubby, have inadvertently shown me a seed of Urzel's destruction."

Lyanna interjected into the conversation. "Yes. From your return to Brebouillis, I knew that there were limits to the power. Why else would Urzel need weapons?"

Chubby leaped up. "Urzel needs military support to conquer us. Correct. One-on-one he is fatal. Even within certain distances, as evidenced by Travers's death, he is dangerous. But there are limits to his power, and we need to define them. And then we must make him so mad that we push him to the extra step, causing him to spread himself thin."

"Exactly, Chubby. You talked of bribed officials. That means an impermanent mental power. You are absolutely correct. We must stretch his powers to the absolute limits."

As Chubby and Deacon conversed, Lyanna excused herself. "Well, Gem and I must be off. Do I have permission, Deacon, to purchase you something more colorful than the normal garb you wear?"

"I want to be inconspicuous. Just remember that!"

"You will look deeeevine, I promise." With that, she left hastily.

Quobit, Jim, and Deacon huddled to devise plans in Liberty City.

Disguises

After Lyanna's return, that night resembled a costume party, with Deacon and Jim modeling garments that Lyanna had purchased, while Chubby was hysterical at the notion that they would wear these disguises. "A photo of this moment for the records of our adventures," he said, and he snapped a shot, to everyone's objection. "No one will make a pass at Jim, not even a drunken Aralian trader."

Jim chortled. "And what a surprise if they do."

Lyanna slapped extra makeup on Deacon, bringing out a rose color in his cheeks. The dresses were selected while the interest of the audience waned, so they rested for the night in anticipation of the departure for Liberty City the next day. Deacon reminded everyone that this was not a departure but step one of the arduous plan to destroy Urzel Lok.

Later, Lyanna finally had the chance to corner Deacon with her caress. With seductive suggestions and a series of slinky moves, she lay down beside him. "It's just me. Don't be nervous."

"You know me—the last to fall in love. But because it's you, I am nervous."

"Then just follow my lead." She kissed him and proceeded to pour out her love and admiration for him, prompting a response. It was a night for him to remember, for his mind shut down and concentrated on her affections and beauty.

The morning brought mixed feelings as each member of the group in turn pondered over the dangerous passages ahead. Lyanna could not keep her eyes off of Deacon. Chubby noticed Lyanna's gaze and reminded Deacon of the undressing eyes of his friend. Jim recited a poem in which love became the downfall of a starry-eyed general.

"True!" Deacon said. "I read that poem. But, Jim, find me a poem about a strong detective who melts in battle from love."

Jim drew a raucous bout of laughter as he replied, "Just a minute, sire, while I search the literature files."

The comic badgering broke the tension until the time came to leave. The three "sisters," with Chubby snorting up a comic storm, departed. Lyanna was stunning in her sleek red dress, cut knee-high; Deacon was less than beautiful in a bulky, flowery green dress with hints of rose makeup. He held his head high as they strutted to a shuttle to take them into the city. Once there, he was ignored by all male passersby. Jim strolled along as best as possible given the ankle cast, clad in a loose dress, wearing dark oval sunglasses that covered most of his face. Quobit delayed five minutes and took up her position as rear scout.

The trip to Liberty City was uneventful except for Deacon's suggestion to an officer that Lyanna was not as beautiful as on first glance. There were looks in port from curious onlookers. The adventure to date had worn Lyanna and Deacon down, so they slept for most of the trip. Upon arrival, an underground metro car delivered them to primitive secure accommodations, which Jim had arranged. While Jim stood guard inside the door, the little detective lay cuddled up with his desired mate.

"What attracts you to me?" he asked. "It certainly isn't my portly physique."

"I see you as a breath of fresh air, an exciting cavalier, a person who respects me for what I am. Besides, I like the fact that I am the singular person in the entire galaxy that has seen you undressed."

He blushed. "Please. Not so loud."

The clandestine dinner

It was a murky fall day; the sun was totally obscured by nature's summoning of sleet. In the late afternoon, in a private booth, in an exquisite city restaurant, a man slurped down his hot soup, unwinding from a day fraught with impossible decisions. This was the evening of solitude, a time to drown frustrations in culinary delights and gulps of alcohol.

The booth was reserved weekly at this time for him; the staff was acquainted with his rigorous demands; every detail had to be perfectly executed. The manager often sat in anxiety until the weekly visitation had been successfully executed.

Outside, the first howls of a bitter autumn wind chucked strewn piles of leaves into the air. Inside, the restaurant was deserted except for the patron and a line of waitresses standing leisurely around a bar, awaiting their next set of orders, all standing in sight of the drawn curtain. This particular night had brought even more worries to the manager; he nervously sat wondering what had ever possessed him to assign a new hire to the client.

In the booth, daily news was displayed on the televiewer. After wiping his lips and smacking them as a reminder of the outstanding food that he had once again sampled, the man settled back to await the special after-dinner liquor that he knew would be diligently delivered. The silence, combined with a weariness of mind, sent him into a temporary trance that was fractured when the drapes were drawn aside. Through the cracks in his eyelids, he saw the waitress deliver his requested aperitif. She was not as appealing as the regular hostess, although her figure seemed full in the form-fitting gown she wore.

"Good evening," he said, opening the conversation.

She went about her business, first disposing of the soiled tablecloth and then pouring a glass of the dew from the decanter into a small glass. She issued a curt answer: "Good evening, sir."

"I haven't seen you here before."

"This is my first day, sir."

She closed the drapes and abruptly left him to savor the taste of the rare beverage. This time, as the liquid touched his lips, he lapsed into a blackout, the pains of the day fleeing while he slept. The next thing he knew, he was peering across the table, where he saw her sitting there, the drapes closed. In one hand she held a glass; the other rested in her lap. He thought this gesture impertinent on her behalf.

"You might have at least asked permission to join me in conversation," he said. "Although I value my privacy, tonight I might have granted permission."

"I don't require your permission tonight, Landrew. I simply seize the opportunity."

"How dare you!" He opened his jacket and placed his hand inside his pocket to signal the guards. His device was missing. She responded by exposing a pistol which had lain in her lap. "So this is how it ends. I am to be assassinated in this secluded restaurant by an unknown female subversive. Lately, I have often dreamt of my death; that this would not be the site. Damn those guards!"

He tried to stand, but his legs were so heavy, so limp, so paralyzed that he felt glued to the seat.

"Listen to me, Landrew. You have been drugged. It is harmless and will last only for fifteen minutes, enough time for us to conclude our business. You will be unable to move. I suggest that you sit still and don't fight the effect, as no harm will come to you." He looked behind him to no avail. "There is no one to aid you. The servers here are drugged as well. Your bodyguards also welcomed a hot drink on a night such as this. Your only Owler has been disabled by my escort Owler."

"What do you want of me?"

"My name is Lyanna. I am a friend and cohort of Deacon Coombs."

Now Landrew perked up, raising his eyelids. "Your escort, then, must be Jim or Gem. How very effective." Comfort now engulfed him.

"Jim is here. The Owlers and Deacon have journeyed to worlds beyond your intent to solve heinous crimes, as you asked Deacon to do. Their information has identified a sole powerful being whose powers of the mind are so mighty that he truly possesses a threat to all mankind."

She paused to let him interrupt. "Schlegar forwarded Deacon's report to me. I have read it and digested it. I absorbed every detail."

"Deacon Coombs needs your support on the next phase of this mission. You must meet with him tomorrow evening at the library in the same room where you met before. It must be tomorrow night. Can you clear your calendar? Invite the members of the High Council who can attend. Can you make these arrangements?"

He hesitated and then spoke. "Affirmed. But why all this secrecy? I am a reasonable man."

"Deacon could not risk a visit to your offices in daylight, nor contact by any other methods. No one knows that he is in Liberty City, and he wishes that fact to remain a secret. Evil forces are at work all around us, as you shall find out tomorrow evening. The plot against the Alliance runs through Nix, but also Jabu, Aralia, and many other areas of the Alliance, including Earth. It is deeply rooted. I will say this once." She became loud and forceful. "Deacon requires the Council's support, your personal dedicated allegiance, and your sage advice. We must leave for a faraway destination soon with Alliance support, but not before conversing with you.

"Order a metro car for Blenheim Park, out on the island, at twilight tomorrow. Do you know the park?" He nodded in affirmation. "Once there, order the car to park, and wait for us in front of the main fountain. Then deliver us to the chambers in the library, where you and Deacon and Rande and Schlegar and any other members of the Council who are presently in Liberty must hear what Deacon has discovered. I presume that Schlegar has already arrived?"

"Correct."

"If you don't comply, you endanger your political career, even your life, and all peoples of the Alliance. Please call the assembly, but do not risk telling anyone of Deacon's presence at the meeting. It must remain a secret until the chamber is sealed."

"You are the doctor from Brebouillis."

"Yes, I am Schlegar's assistant and I am Deacon's ally." She leaned out of the booth to signal the Owler.

Jim appeared before Landrew saying, "Villya, Landrew!" Jim sounded joyful.

"Sorry for the inconvenience, Landrew, but there are spies everywhere, as you shall learn tomorrow night. Jim and I will clear the tokens from the safe to emulate a robbery. You will confirm this, but with bogus descriptions."

She rose to depart. "Oh, the thieves will drop the bag of tokens by accident just inside the front door. How unfortunate." She then motioned to Jim and fled to the arms of her waiting lover.

Spiritual energy

Deacon emerged from the study the following day with messy hair, rumpled clothing, and a radiant, beaming smile. Lyanna, asleep on the sofa, turned, her arms outstretched, accepting his warmth. "I know that smile," Lyanna said. "You have discovered something."

"Probably, for I have been up most of the night studying the data we collected on Brebouillis and Aralia, especially the tapes of the *Sleigher* laid open to me by the traders' union. You remember the incident of the imaginary bird on my flight from Nix?"

"So melodramatically did you reconstruct it that I still have goose bumps on my goose bumps."

"That incident still puzzles me. Gem monitored space for thousands of miles without a detection of another ship or human. Yet I had the icy feeling that Urzel was so close that I could have touched him."

"Urzel the spirit, correct?"

"Yes."

"Well, maybe you didn't have the proper equipment on the *Heritage* to identify the spirit?"

"Correct you are, sweetie. On the *Heritage*, I commanded Gem to fix the heavens and scan for a proximal ship containing Urzel. It showed a ship distant from us. You are correct, Lyanna. We should have been searching for spiritual energy patterns."

A sorrow engulfed Deacon. "I felt Urzel in my mind. He was so close. I survived; Travers did not."

"You are saying that Urzel surveyed you and decided consciously not to terminate you?"

"Lyanna, when you were young, what did you fear? I mean really fear?"

"Well, when I was five we lived in proximity to cadmium mines. Huge ore freighters landed twice a week in sight of our house. They were ugly planes, the fronts with huge beaks, reaching out to peck you.

"One day, I stood watching the empty yards when, to my surprise, I saw a ship hovering above me, preparing to land. It tilted landward, and I suddenly saw the beak extending to the spot where I stood. Well, I hopped on my scooter and fled to the safety of my bed, where I hid under the covers for an hour. To this day, those freighters scare me."

Deacon sat on the floor, elbows bent, resting on his knees.

"Your turn," Lyanna said.

"That's not the issue here."

"Wait! I just bared an inner fear to you. Call it bonding. Your turn, friend. Come on, just one juicy tidbit to use in my memoirs of you."

He sighed, seemingly irritated, and said, "I remember the first time I invaded someone else's mind. I was six. I didn't realize what this was until an experience scared me."

"Whose mind was it?"

"My schoolmaster's."

"And what was he thinking?"

"How he would like to beat the stuffing out of a little pompous fat kid in class whom he detested. The kid had a secure upbringing; everything the schoolmaster had wanted in life and never gotten."

"Did you ever warn this child?"

"No. I didn't have to." He paused to recall. "It was me that he wanted to beat."

"Oh. I'm sorry, Deacon."

"I overcame him. I outgrew him. I never gave him any cause to get angry at me. You feared the planes, and I feared the hulk Mr. Smithinks; I fear him even to this day."

"You think that Urzel fears you, don't you?"

"Yes. I felt it on the ship. I think . . . he may have reached out and killed Travers to warn me—to try to scare me off."

"Deacon, please don't think that you are responsible for Travers's death." She hugged him. When they released, he addressed her.

"Children do not strike out against those elements that pose a threat to them through fear. They hide, just as you did from the planes, as I did from Mr. Smithinks. Urzel might be insane, he may yield gargantuan powers, but he is still a child. He fears me, and I know it. I am just not sure how to use this to our advantage."

"And you think that Nedilli, his mother, could hold a key to why he fears you?"

"I don't know. But who knows a child better than its mother?"

"Why didn't the *Heritage* and the *Sleigher* detect Urzel's presence? Come on, Deacon. We're soul mates. I'm in this mystery to help however I can. Share with me what's on your mind."

"Both ships, the *Heritage*, the *Sleigher*, failed to detect Urzel's presence. There are gadgets to decipher everything imaginable on both ships—state-of-the-art technology to detect all forms of energy."

"So why did they fail?"

"For the same reason that Urzel was not detected on the palace grounds on Aralia when he slew Como. For the same reason that Urzel was not detected when he invaded the private gardens of Geor. For the same reason that the *Heritage* did not detect the culprit as a bird. For the same reason that Urzel was not detected by systems on the *Sleigher*, even with Landrew's manipulation of the data."

"Which is?"

"I have come to a brave conclusion about Urzel. Either the equipment is faulty in all four cases I cited, or he exists for periods in another spiritual dimension."

Lyanna's eyes bulged. Frightened by this conclusion, she prepared to address her options. Instead, Deacon waved to her to be silent. "Hear me out. All our instruments are calibrated to the dimensions of space that we occupy, plus time. But this Urzel the spirit, the Medullan, is the first Medullan to leave Medulla. We have no comprehension of what these spirits are about. Their energy fields have been studied very little. It occurred to me that these energy fields may not be detected or measured by the calibration of our current instruments and technology."

"So that's why we journey to Medulla, not only to visit the mother of Urzel but to confirm your idea that the Medullans' presence can go undetected by our technology."

"The Medullans are going to have to cooperate."

"This terror that you referenced to Chubby and me back in Ketapongo—you told me that you would reveal it to me in Liberty City."

"It is real. Landrew will confirm it. You shall be present tonight for the unveiling."

Although Lyanna pressed him for additional details, Deacon's moonlike eyes stared into space for hours as he sat silently cogitating the crisis. Once in a while, he rubbed his forehead and then tried to comb his disheveled hair with his fingers. She was content to sit beside him, her arm around his shoulders, her head resting, her eyes closed.

Confrontation

Landrew conveniently dismissed himself from previous commitments that night, ordering his personal driver to Blenheim Park. As the vehicle sat in the shadows, Deacon strolled briskly in the chilly winds, Jim yards behind. He stopped to catch his breath and clap his hands, and a gust of wind almost drove him off balance as crisp brown leaves scurried by.

As he sought the shelter of a bench behind a row of high bushes, he anxiously looked to and fro. Finally, far down the path, amid the large, nude trees, Lyanna approached, signaling to him that the escort was solo. Deacon proceeded over the mound to the black metro car, opened the door, allowed Jim to enter first, and followed Lyanna and Quobit inside. Jim monitored their route carefully.

Deacon had rehearsed over and over what he would say to the audience that night. Lyanna nervously folded and unfolded a piece of paper as Jim conversed with the Owler driver about the sights of the Alliance that he had seen on this adventure. The driver was silent. After emerging from the underground, the metro car halted at the exact spot where Deacon had commenced his adventure weeks ago, in front of the History Archives Library.

In the grand hall, Deacon saw the twinkle in Quobit's eyes that Deacon thought he himself must have had when he first entered. This time Lyanna and Quobit lagged behind to examine statues, admire watercolors, and identify busts. The door to the conference room was slightly ajar. Deacon felt déjà vu as Rande emerged into the hallway on cue, his face fraught with distress. They shook hands as Deacon introduced Lyanna and then Quobit. Then they entered to find Landrew and Schlegar at the head of the granite table, the other members on the sides. Lyanna ran immediately to Schlegar, who did her the privilege of introducing her to the group. Deacon presented Quobit to the audience.

"Deacon Coombs," Landrew mightily said, "I thought that you would have gained twenty pounds by now from Jim's cooking. Instead you look thinner and perhaps more fit!"

"Landrew, there was far too much exercise and very distasteful food on this adventure." The group chuckled. "Travel in outer space has exhausted me but driven me to new physical limits. Hike over here, hike there, up, down, run, leap, jump, worry. Lots of worrying, Landrew. I am so happy to see you again and be able to address this gathering on such short notice." As Landrew and Deacon shared an extensive hug, Deacon gazed over his shoulder to intercept the ominous glare of Xudur. "Villya, Coombs."

"Villya, Xudur."

Landrew said, "I met your bold new companion the other night."

As they made eye contact, Lyanna said, "Sorry." Landrew frisked her mockingly. "My pistol is not here tonight." Landrew breathed a strong sigh of relief to draw a laugh from the others.

Deacon exchanged pleasantries with Schlegar, Dreveney, Eggu-Nitron, and Raal in turn. Finally, he boldly stood before Xudur to say, "I am pleased that you can attend, Xudur." Only Dithropolis had been prevented from attending.

With the meeting declared open, Deacon, with Jim providing videos, recounted their adventure from the time that they left Brebouillis to the arrival back on Earth. This took about forty minutes, and Jim answered the questions posed.

At Deacon's instruction, Jim then retraced the adventure and elaborated on some specific events at Glagn and the investigations on Nix. He then showed extensive footage of the savages. The Council members were riveted at the introduction of Urzel and how Deacon deduced the path to Goharn Lok's abode. This drew a flurry of questions from the Council, which Deacon deflected. "We haven't much time. I must control the balance of this meeting to establish what I believe is our best chance of a planned path to victory."

Omitting the identity of Urzel, Jim concluded with commendations for himself, Gem, Quobit, Travers, and Deacon in the face of danger, and explained how Lyanna and Chubby Eaves had joined the investigative team. Jim ended by asking for a moment of silence for Travers. The group bowed their heads in unison.

Deacon then spoke. "Landrew and members, the creature that Jim referred to is highly dangerous. He must be quickly defeated before he confronts Alliance forces and gains additional allies. Time is not on our side. We must painfully understand the origin of this creature to understand how to defeat it.

"The creature on the mount on planet Nix is named Urzel. More specifically, his name is Urzel Lok. The evidence that Gem, Jim, and I have compiled on Earth, Brebouillis, Aralia, and Nix conclusively indicates that Urzel Lok is the offspring"—he paused to look at each one around the table in turn for effect—"between an Earthman and a Medullan."

The group erupted in disbelief—all except Landrew, who continued to stare at Deacon. Deacon allowed the attendees to vent their doubts for a few minutes, deflecting the vicious taunts of Xudur, who intimidated Deacon with bloody gapes of her mouth.

Deacon stood with arms folded as the clamor finally faded. "Hear me out. I have overwhelming evidence of what I say. You fight me with words. I confront you with facts. The Earthman's father was an Asiandan named Phendal Lok—blind at birth, welder-draftsman by trade, born in Ketapongo. The mother was Nedilli, a well-known Medullan stateswoman." In a soft tone, as they cynically stared back, he added, "This affair was properly sanctioned by both the Medullans and the Alliance."

Xudur roared as she stood to contradict the statement. "Impossible! The Alliance has never allowed such a mating. It is forbidden. It has never been approved by this Council or before me!" Her voice maintained a deep, menacing tone. "Earthman, why do you speak of such falsities? You call this meeting and confront us with these blasphemies." The other members allowed her to speak on their behalf.

"Answer us!" Eggu-Nitron shouted, also rising with objections.

Deacon allowed Xudur and Eggu-Nitron the courtesy to continue as Xudur cited the policies of interbreeding in the Tetrad Auspices. Her knowledge in this area was respectful.

Deacon focused on Landrew. "As I said to you, this mating was sanctioned by the Alliance, years ago, during the reign of your office as chief security minister of the Alliance." Landrew remained stoic at the end of the table. He raised his head and fixed his gaze on Deacon as the other members of the Council waited for Landrew to deny these insinuations.

Xudur stood behind Landrew. "I urge you to eject Coombs and discontinue this conversation. We can easily read the accounts of his investigation. In the interim, please remove him from our sight."

Deacon retaliated. "Tell them, Landrew. Tell them of your knowledge of his existence before he devours all of us. I beg of you. If we are to proceed with the destruction of this very lethal creature, we must begin with the foundation of truths, and you must face your peers with honesty. I know you had good reasons for its birth, but now the time comes to admit your past indiscretion."

There was an interlude of cross-dialogue as Raal quaked and challenged the detective. "Coombs, you do not have the right to conduct a trial with you as prosecutor and judge of our leader." The Mendalgon's colors changed as she became agitated.

At last Landrew arose, walked away from the table, and turned his back to them. He heaved a heavy sigh, preparing to address them. He turned. "I love this Earth and I love the Alliance. How could our ancestors have guessed that history would place Earth in this magnificent Alliance with other foreign races? I have dedicated my entire life's work, my soul, to the safety of the Alliance, for the success of this High Council, for all of us. When I look back at what we have accomplished, I feel so proud. But"—he expelled an ominous burst of air that established a different tone—"Deacon Coombs is correct. There is a political abortion hidden in my past. It is just one." He quivered. "To you, in confidence, I express my deep regret."

Landrew looked at each attendee in turn. "I supported the hiring of Deacon Coombs because I needed to know if my mistake was the current evil. I prayed for you, Deacon, to return with news that the monster we seek is someone else. It was with great enthusiasm, and then deep regret, that I nominated you, Deacon Coombs, for this assignment. I stand here before you, the High Council, to humbly ask for forgiveness. I am consumed with grief."

Sanctioning

With tears welling in his eyes, Landrew expressed further regret. "Coombs speaks the truth. I alone sanctioned the mating of this Medullan and the Earthling after great deliberation during my reign as chief security officer of the Alliance. Later, when I heard about the child's ill demeanor and his horrible deeds against even his own kind, I felt that my political career would be jeopardized, so upon the request of the Medullans, I authorized its destruction.

"Unknown to me until recently, the child obtained sanctuary from the Medullans, who placed the child on a savage planet, the very same planet that Deacon Coombs has just returned from, the planet Nix. However, rumors of its existence in our world persisted and eventually reached my ears. I have lived in deep repentance since the first time I heard these rumors. I have lived in mortification since Como's death."

Now Landrew held his head high. "The Alliance is as strong in peace as she ever has been. I have performed my deeds for the sake of all. You must understand that I erased this singular blemish from the records of the Alliance to protect our people. The laws of interbreeding were broken, as you so rightfully pointed out to us, Xudur. I unilaterally sanctioned the act of expunging this affair from all record bases. It was a mistake to sanction it; it was a mistake to then cover it up."

The room was engulfed in eerie silence. All members of the Council had their gaze fixed on Landrew, and all were contemplating their resolution of this grave matter.

"Now you must understand something else of this chapter. At the time of the birth of this child, I thought this event a new milestone, a brave new step toward unification of the Alliance. It would have brought us closer to the Medullans. Don't you see, all of you, why I did this? Medullans want corporeal bodies as part of our friendship. What a triumph. In their current spiritual state, they do not interface with any of us in the flesh."

Deacon spoke again. "Landrew, please, we all admire your contributions during your reign. I accept whatever mistake you made, more easily than the rest of this group. We must move on to the reality of the situation. There are more important issues to discuss. I recommend that we move forward to an action plan and leave the discussion of your actions behind closed doors with High Council members."

The members of the High Council each stared back. Schlegar and Eggu-Nitron expressed bewilderment; Xudur, disgust; Raal and the Dreveney, sympathy. Deacon broke the stillness. "You, Landrew, journeyed to Aralia to become the first on board the *Sleigher*. You ordered it off limits until your arrival. What did you discover?"

With his head bowed, seated, he said, "I found voice recordings and indirect evidence of his existence on board. I became ill when I saw what had been done to the crew. One trader, named Chubby Eaves, was not present when I arrived. Nor was Urzel, the one that I now fear."

Xudur interjected. "No courage to face him. Confront him only in your thoughts."

"Quiet, Xudur!" said Rande.

Landrew recommenced. "I destroyed all the evidence of an intruder before Alliance security boarded. I ask all of you to understand the chaos among the masses that would break out if word of this demon's powers left this room." He remained stone-faced.

Deacon delivered a message to the group. "Chubby Eaves is now safely part of my team. We encountered him in Asianda, where he pledged his allegiance to our cause. He is to arrive on the trade ship *G'uillger* with the Owler Gem soon. Are any of the tapes of the *Sleigher* preserved, Landrew?"

Landrew seemed to be in narcosis. "What? No."

"Did you note anything unusual about the energy patterns of Urzel? Were you able to find them?"

"Well, ah . . . yes, I found some of them. At times there were periods when the energy presence of Urzel was not there."

Deacon was satisfied. "Exactly as I postulated! Schlegar, you provided me with the first important clue to this mystery."

"Me?" he said proudly.

"Yes. When I arrived on Brebouillis, Jim and Gem noted that top security Owlers were on the moon. When I noticed that they were guarding files rather than inmates, this left me to confront you with the real purpose of Brebouillis—that it served as an Alliance center for criminal files and criminal investigations.

"But you proudly accused me, Schlegar, of underscoring the medical research that was being conducted on Brebouillis, underestimating the contributions of the doctors. In your voice and attitude, I shall never forget the pride that you conveyed. It has remained with me.

"Lyanna, you presented me with selected tapes of criminal investigations when you joined our team on the *Heritage*. I studied these and, as I did so, came to recognize the true identities of those stationed on the planet. They are biologists, geneticists, evolutionists, physicists, all renowned in their fields. In examining the others in the post who had worked on Brebouillis, I find the same host of professionals. So I asked myself, what are all these renowned doctors doing on Brebouillis? And why are Owlers posted at file stations? And what prompted Schlegar's outburst?

"This will come as a shock to some of you in this room when I answer my own questions. I will tell you what Jim, in one of his summaries, transmitted to me. It was a very curious piece of information that we uncovered here at the history library. I noted that the hospital on Brebouillis was opened on the very same date that the planet Medulla was admitted to the Alliance. Coincidence? I think not." Raal fidgeted in her translucency.

Deacon folded his arms and then started to stroll around the room. "Along came Chubby Eaves, who tied my fears together by informing me that all trade ships go to planet Medulla empty. No cargo has ever been transported there, and yet the Alliance extracts valuable commodities. Chubby has dismissed this fact for years as a lack of our understanding of what the Medullans want! Chubby accepted that there is nothing that the Alliance can give to these spirits.

"Think of it, Raal! Think of it, Xudur! Think of it, Eggu-Nitron! The ships go to Medulla empty. We, the Alliance, extract ores, fresh water, gases, and plant and animal matter. So what do the Medullans get in return? Why did they even bother to enter the Alliance if we give them nothing in return for their admittance or for the extracted resources? Have you ever considered that?"

The Council members shifted in their seats as they focused on Deacon's answer to this question. "Chubby Eaves's statement was the great revelation that I needed to tie this all together. I know what the Medullans want. So does Landrew. So does Schlegar."

What the Medullans want

Deacon continued to speak to the Council. "Aralia is the oldest planet in the Alliance. Life evolved on this planet when suns were millions of miles closer to it. Aralia was the birthplace of the Alliance. There was no one else. Just Aralians. But millions of years later, Aralians were dissatisfied so they searched out other life forms and found them. One by one, other races have been admitted to the Alliance through Vespering. Planet Medulla was the entry just ahead of Barnard's Planet and Earth. How odd to me that the isolated distant moon of Brebouillis was transformed from a mining colony to the center of security records on that very day that Medulla was admitted to the Alliance.

"On Earth, I remembered reading that the Medullans are forbidden to teach their mental powers to other races, that they are forbidden to interface with any visitors, forbidden to allow foreigners on the surface of the planet, forbidden—and excuse me, Landrew—to interbreed. Think of the potential misuse of power if the Medullans were to teach their abilities to others. Think of the potential destruction. As each member was admitted to the Tetrad Alliance, friendship was the primary directive. But no one has ever seen a Medullan in its native state. The Alliance admitted a race that they inwardly distrusted."

"What has all this got to do with this monster you described earlier?" asked Xudur.

"The Aralians knew of the Medullans' great mental abilities. They knew and feared that unless they secretly monitored them, the Medullans might conquer us with their superior mental powers. So Brebouillis was also conveniently set up to spy on the Medullans. At the same time, data from other planets was assembled on Brebouillis so there could be one repository to monitor all beings of great mental powers and track the evolution of all the races.

"However, I ask you all to answer. Why did I take this case? Why did Earth enter the Alliance? What is it that all our ancestors dreamed about when the Jabu and the Mendalgons explored outer space?" He paused to allow them to connect with his thoughts. "To travel into deepest space, to meet alien life forms, to make new friends, to share resources with other worlds, to satisfy a craving that there was life beyond the boundary of our worlds and that that life would accept us as friends—friends to love us, to respect us, to become our allies in future quests to probe and expand our worlds again and again and again.

"So we ask, what do the Medullans want? They are no different in this respect than any of us in this room, are they? When the Aralians first encountered the Medullans, the Medullans had but one reason to enter the Alliance. They are spirits. Evolution has prevented them from sharing in newfound friends because of their spiritual state. They cannot interface with us. They cannot experience the warmth of new friendships. They cannot travel to Aralia or Earth. So they made one demand upon the Aralians to enter the Alliance: that in return for the export of ores, gases, and other products, the Aralians dedicate their top specialists in biology, genetics, evolution, and science to reverse evolution and bring the Medullans back to being corporeal entities!"

"Reverse evolution!" Xudur exclaimed.

"The spirits of Medulla want to be flesh and plasma and bones, as we are, to share in the exhilarating experiences that corporealness brings. They want to taste, smell, experience corporeal reproduction—all the sensations that the rest of our races experience. Most of all, I emphasize, they long to interface with the Alliance physically, to have relationships, to bond. They demanded successful unrequited physical contact with alien life forms! And they are currently denied this. Communications with the Medullans takes place from the orbs around their planet. Therefore, the research at Brebouillis has many purposes but its primary goal is the reversal of evolution of the Medullans. Give back their bodies to them! The Aralians have borne the brunt of this request by dedicating their top scientists and doctors to this mission.

"The Aralians are required to provide results on this research to the Medullans on a regular basis, so it was no surprise to me when Jim and Gem investigated the files on travel to Medulla for frequent visitors and the name of you, Schlegar, was near the top of the list as a frequent visitor to this world."

Deacon turned to Schlegar. "Of course, this was why Mindor was developed too, as part of your research to communicate with Medullans. Mindor performed such reporting tasks by descending to the planet's surface to interface with the Medullans because you, Schlegar, were prohibited from doing so, or perhaps repulsed when you did. And of course, Mindor has the added benefit of spying on the Medullans by reading their thoughts as energy."

Xudur glared at Landrew. "So, Landrew, you found out about this commitment to the Medullans by the Aralians and thus sanctioned Phendal Lok and Nedilli to create the protochild of this evolutionary reversal. You sought to undo in a blink of time, in one step, what evolution had taken millions of years to do."

Landrew expelled air as his chest sank. "The research at Brebouillis has continued. This is known, as Deacon has stated, by only specialists on Aralia. When I assumed my post as chief security officer, I received the request by the Medullans for this mating, so I immediately consulted with Schlegar.

"When I confronted Schlegar, he exposed the problem to me. The Medullans were growing weary of the lack of progress to reverse the spiritual phase. We could not believe our fortune when the Medullans asked to sanction this mating of Phendal Lok and Nedilli to advance the project and to unify Medullans with corporeal bondage once again. It was a dream come true for the Medullans."

Eggu-Nitron spoke. His baritone voice was ominous. "So, Landrew, Phendal Lok was an experimental pawn. Did he realize this?"

Deacon stared at Landrew, as they all did. "No. He knew only that he was in love. He did not know the risks of this mating exercise; nor did Nedilli. They did not know of the larger agenda of the Medullans' desire for corporeal flesh and did not know of the egotistical goal of a game-changing evolutionary event. I could not resist the temptation for all mankind to take a giant step to bring the Medullans out of isolation and into our world."

Xudur added, "And to place Landrew in the permanent history records as the man who had the courage and leadership to foster relationships with the Medullans. Imagine the press! Imagine the Medullan vote for you as the next head of the High Council!"

Landrew nodded as he found the courage to look Xudur in the eyes. "Correct, Xudur, on all accounts. Then, when the reports filtered in that a tragic birth had taken place, I had to erase all the evidence of my involvement. As I stated, it was I who sanctioned the killing by the Medullans. However, I did not know that Urzel Lok had been transferred to safe harbor."

Landrew stood tall to face his comrades. "Every day, I walk down the hallowed halls of history. Who is remembered? It is those who made contributions to our successful history, those individuals who had the courage to take risks for results. I thought at the time that it was necessary for a single man to sympathize with the Medullans and take a risk to support them in their time of need. I felt that if I sought the High Council's approval at that time, that I would find myself surrounded by those who would not support my decision!" He turned to Schlegar. "I felt that the more people who knew, the more risk that it would leak out; many would then wait until the birth with great expectations, not recognizing any failure.

"Now I am afraid that there will be widespread panic among the planets if we admit that the deaths of Geor and Como are attributed to a monster that I have unleashed. Schlegar—bless his heart—as I have stated, is innocent in the sanction. He insisted and presented the case that the time for interbreeding had not yet arrived. He thought that I had listened to him. For this, Schlegar, my friend, I am truly sorry." Landrew's voice flowed with sincere regret.

"I granted the request of the Medullans to perform this task. They accepted the hopes of all of us. Phendal Lok may be the biological father of Urzel, but I am the illegitimate father, for withholding the real truth from Phendal Lok, for disguising this birth as a medical, genetic, and political triumph, and for keeping this abominable deed from all of you."

Landrew walked over to Deacon. "I wanted you to find the truth, Coombs. Since Como's tragic death, I have borne a heavy heart and known the guilt that one day I must confess. In front of the High Council tonight, Deacon Coombs has exposed Urzel Lok to us. I congratulate you on your success in identifying this creature. I pray that you will accept my invitation to continue the fight to defeat him."

Schlegar upstaged the conversation. "I accept your apology, Landrew, but still I am disappointed that you sanctioned this without my consent."

Landrew was shaking as if with palsy. "I am so sorry, Schlegar; I overruled thousands of years of research at Brebouillis by allowing the personal gains of the Medullans and myself to interfere."

Xudur's tongue was sharp. "I forgive less easily, Landrew. You showed weakness in your decision. This Council and its officers make decisions without emotional influence."

Deacon diverted Xudur as she was about to unleash again. "Xudur, I need your attention, for there are further chapters to discuss this night about Urzel and the Medullans." She growled at him but reluctantly obeyed.

Deacon shifted his eyes to each of them to ensure their focus and then began to recite his account of the encounter with Urzel Lok on the mount in Asianda. In disbelief, Raal and Dithropolis protested as he revealed his startling conclusion that the being had separated into spirit and body, one a sickly Earthling and the other a power-crazed Medullan spirit. Landrew sat stunned as the room erupted into unfocused pods of discussion.

As before, Deacon allowed them to debate as Jim stood ready to draw their attention. On cue, and in a deep, husky voice, Jim commanded them to allow Deacon to continue. Eggu-Nitron assisted by silencing a displeased Xudur.

"Thank you," said Deacon. "I was deeply disappointed to discover from Chubby Eaves that Morris Mydloan was an employee of the security forces of the Alliance. How came he to be in the library on the night of my departure?"

Rande was quick and forthcoming. "He was in possession of a stolen security card that provided access to the library."

"Yes, he was, Rande. How convenient. Which led me to believe that he had an accomplice, since those passes are issued with top-priority clearance."

Xudur stood to challenge him. "Spies of Urzel in the security forces of the Alliance?" After her outburst, a discomforting calm settled over the group.

Deacon stood tall before them. "When I first arrived on Aralia, I was immediately uncovered by the traders. Travers and Chubby informed me that it was the Owlers that the traders recognized, not me. As Chubby lay open the records at the traders' union on Aralia, I discovered a subspace message sent from Earth to Aralia to ask the Aralian police to cooperate with two arriving Owlers, specifically identified as Gem and Jim, accompanying an administrator named Bothwen. And so it was as the sender hoped that traders and other regulatory agencies would intercept the wire, find Gem and Jim, and then indirectly unmask me."

Deacon turned to Rande. "Rande! You are the bearer of the complete list of investigators on this case, are you not?"

"Well, yes . . . Landrew and me."

"And it was you who distracted Gem while Morris Mydloan entered the library and stalked me that night."

"I made no distraction. I came to invite you to dinner and needed Gem's permission to enter. What are you implying?"

"How did Morris Mydloan know of my investigation if not through you or Landrew?"

"What is happening here? Landrew, Xudur, I believe he is making a rather insulting accusation."

Xudur looked in disbelief at Rande. "Continue, Coombs," she said.

"Rande, two days after we departed Earth, you sent that unsecured subspace communication, hoping to warn the traders of our arrival on Aralia, hoping that Travers would eliminate me and do the work of Mydloan's failure."

"I wanted you to be successful!"

Deacon was furious. "You wanted me dead! You and Landrew are the only ones that could have directed Morris Mydloan to assassinate me."

Landrew intervened by positioning his arm between Deacon and Rande. "Rande, we agreed to complete secrecy of this mission. Why did you send the subspace message to Aralia?"

"Landrew, this is circumstantial evidence. This is a trick. Coombs is baiting all of you. He does not know what he talks about." Rande paced as he spoke.

Deacon moved beside him. "You violated security in the library. You had the opportunity to divert the Owler to allow Morris to enter. You did not announce yourself as you stood on the balcony later. Why?"

Landrew cornered Rande. "My mercy, it was you, Rande, who convinced me to journey personally to Aralia to erase the tapes of the *Sleigher* and any evidence of Urzel Lok, after I shared his existence with you."

"Landrew, as you said earlier, that was for the benefit and security of all. You said it. Surely, you . . . don't . . . don't . . ."

Deacon was insistent. "Rande, you made a grave mistake minutes ago—one that I shall share with this group. As Landrew spoke earlier, he pleaded for us in this room to understand his actions. As I moved purposely beside you to intercept your thoughts, I found that there was no sympathy. In your mind, there was only anger at his remarks. As Schlegar reminded me, I sometimes have to invade others' minds in order to find the truth. Well, I read your disappointment in Urzel being unmasked. I say to you all now that Rande hoped that the traders would have disposed of me, but we fooled him and became allies instead. I will be so bold now, Rande, to ask you what Lord Urzel Lok has promised you."

The veins in Rande's stubby neck were bulging, pulsing. His cheeks turned scarlet. Beads of sweat dotted his forehead. "I am intellectually superior to all of you. I am so tired of being the official note keeper of this sorry, pathetic group, of being the so-called chief administrator. I have talent that has been bypassed by you, overlooked by your egos, but clearly noticed by Lord Urzel. I grow no younger. Who wouldn't want this chance to lead once he conquers Earth?" He surprised them all by slamming his fist and pouting. "And he will!" The chamber fell silent.

In shock, the others looked on while Deacon motioned to Jim to escort Rande from the proceedings. As he exited, Xudur was despondent. "How many other surprises do you spring on us tonight, Coombs? You have devastated this Council with your findings."

"Xudur, I have been commissioned to conduct a truthful assignment by this very group. You shall hear of my discoveries and my conclusions. I insist that we not leave here without a plan to eliminate Urzel. I am sorry, Xudur, but there are more surprises!"

THE DIMENSIONS
OF THE DEVIL

Into the unknown

Deacon was blunt. "Not only are the Medullans spirits who yearn to return to material states, but I firmly believe that evolution has carried their spiritual energy into another dimension. Another way to view it is that they now have energy patterns that cannot be detected by us."

Dreveney reeled and waved his bony arms. "Is this speculation, or do you plan to produce Urzel or a Medullan to testify to this?" He cleared his throat. "My schooling was in physics and I have applied my trade for a lifetime. The existence of dimensions beyond the four that we readily measure, that we exist in, has been theorized and defined in terms of quantum times. No Aralian scientists have ever referenced the fact that other dimensions could be created and defined by energy patterns."

Deacon sat back to present his theory. "Phendal Lok applied for and was accepted as an expert welder on the planet Medulla because he was blind. He was approved because he would be unable to notice when and how these spirits appeared and disappeared. Goharn Lok told me that when the Medullans were present, they were continually quaking, quivering, shaking, presenting themselves as irregularly shaped masses. Those descriptions apply to the Medullans in our dimensions. They are uncomfortable in our dimensions and they return to a more comfortable state of physical energy as spirits."

Deacon looked at Dreveney and Schlegar. "Can you, Dreveney and Schlegar, confirm that there is no record of Urzel's presence at Como's death?"

Dreveney spoke with grief. "It is very curious that Como was found locked in his study holding the instrument of his death. I visit that haunting memory in my dreams. Aralian security forces found no evidence of an intruder in the palace or on the palatial grounds."

"Proving, Dreveney," Deacon said, "that the Aralians don't have the technological means to detect him, because we all know now that Urzel was there in spiritual form; likewise, there is no evidence of his energy at Geor's death. Chubby Eaves rode on the *Sleigher* back to Aralia and informed me that Urzel disappeared at times without a trace. All this tells me that the energy of Medullans has evolved into a dimension, a form, a physical state that we cannot quantify with our current existing technology."

Raal expressed her concern. "This is a dilemma with far-reaching implications that Medullan metabolic energy is imperceptible by us. You postulate, Coombs, that they are under extreme stress when existing in our dimensions, thus causing these wild distortions of their mass as reported by Goharn Lok."

"They probably can tolerate our atmospheres, our dimensions, only for short intervals, Raal, returning quickly to another environment for relief, just as I can submerge myself under water for short periods and then return for air."

"But you did physically observe his bodily form on Nix?" Landrew asked.

"I saw two fierce red eyes peering out from under a hood. That tells me that Urzel did not want to expose himself to the masses, possibly because his shape, his form, his appearance would not be an appealing one. Thus he chose the robe to present an image to quell the mobs. What he elects to do is instill fright into the savages by using his electrifying eyes and invading their minds with hypnosis. I must journey to Medulla to interrogate his mother, Nedilli, not only to learn more about Urzel, but to learn more about the current dimensions of existence of the Medullans."

Xudur said, "I cannot see any reasons for the Medullans to admit this revelation to you, Coombs, with no offense intended."

"I admit you make a strong case for this other dimension," said Eggu-Nitron. "But do we have to define this dimension in order to defeat this evil?"

"That must be his weakness, Eggu-Nitron. Better to trap him in our dimensions and fight him on his weakest foundation, and that's my plan. To my knowledge, there are no sightings of Medullans other than the one by Goharn Lok."

Schlegar replied, "Medullans not only desire to be corporeal in nature, but they also want to halt the evolution that carries their energy patterns deeper and deeper into a cold isolation, into this . . . this . . . dimension, whatever it may be."

Deacon agreed. "Gem and I made a grave error on Nix. We recorded metabolic patterns from the being but did not focus on magnetic moments, electron spins, or detailed energy emanations, just the gross energy patterns. While they did show interruptions, I hadn't pieced together the evidence of a different dimension at that time."

Deacon had their attention still. "The Medullans are lonely in an Alliance that has seen the bond of friendship slip away from them. I will need to consult a certain physicist colleague of mine to confirm what can allow a being to remain undetected by our technology. It will require bringing him into the confidence of our crisis. This I will do tomorrow, unless I hear objections." With an absence of objections, he inferred their agreement.

"Deacon," said Schlegar, "I swear to you that all of the scientists on Brebouillis do not know of this possible existence of life in another dimension by the Medullans. Perhaps that is why we have failed to solve their problem. We do not have the correct database on their metabolism."

Xudur was in agreement with the hypotheses. "How could there be periods of zero energy displayed by Urzel, Schlegar? It is physically impossible unless their energy levels are impervious to our instrumentation, as Coombs suggests. That is what the facts tell me. I believe our detective has performed well."

Deacon challenged Schlegar. "Who gave you the plans to design the evolutionary reversal? Who helped you design Mindor? Put your pride aside, Schlegar."

Through his body language, the others knew it was the Medullans. Schlegar finally confessed. "Yes, the Medullans aided us in the design so we could communicate with them."

Xudur then said, "Zentaur has been a contributor to the success of this Alliance. We have not withheld any information from other members of this Council. Like it or not, Landrew, I will inform the Government Council of Zentaur about these proceedings tonight to warn them of this creature and, regrettably, of your failings."

"Xudur, that is not necessary," Eggu-Nitron said. "We must confidentially focus on this crisis."

The room erupted, with each member pointing arguments at Xudur to keep the minutes of this meeting confidential. It appeared hopeless as Lyanna whispered to Deacon, "You had better take control."

Deacon tapped loudly on the table and said, "Listen to me, please, all of you." The din died, so he arose and circled around the group. "Urzel Lok is not a god, not immortal. He is a spirit whose source of immense powers is not his strength, but his weakness. That is why he requires allies like Morris Mydloan and Rande. Just reason it, as I did. If he doesn't require human allies, he would have swept us away by now. He is an extremely powerful individual on his own grounds and in his dimensions, but"—Deacon raised his voice to fill the room with a thunderous roar—"if his powers are stretched to his extreme limits in our dimensions, I believe that we can defeat him. That is what we must do. This is the condition we must create. Stretch him so thin that he fails to control the situation. Remember who we are dealing with—a child."

They were attentive, and he had the stage, so he continued. "When he is in our dimensions, he plays on our battlefield and by our rules. We must somehow create a battleground where he is forced to confront us, forced to try to defeat us in our dimensions. And most importantly, we must make sure he is alone on the battlefield and isolated from any of his allies."

"He travels sometimes in our dimensions, as on the *Sleigher*, as in Goharn Lok's garden where he was heard, and as when I witnessed him on Nix. Other times he avoids our detection, such as when he was in proximity to the *Heritage* when he killed Travers, and such as on Aralia the night of Como's death. The Medullans, and in particular Nedilli, must help us to understand this phenomenon. My reasoning for traveling there is threefold. One: understand this Urzel Lok better from his mother, Nedilli. Two: plead with the Medullans to help us understand how Urzel uses his energy aura to his advantage. Three: ask for their assistance to design the exact circumstances for his entrapment. If they don't cooperate in all three of these areas, all may be lost! I fear that without their help, we cannot stop him. I am sorry to convey this truth to you, but this monster is on the loose, unchecked, and at present undefeated."

Each member reflected on what Deacon had said. Landrew sat with his head bowed; Raal's transparent form glowed a ruddy rouge; Dreveney and Schlegar stared back stone-faced. "Schlegar," said Deacon, "I would dearly love to invite you to accompany us to Medulla, since the Medullans know you and you have taken Mindor there on previous occasions." Schlegar perked up and nodded.

"Landrew, I request the Alliance's permission to allow Schlegar, Gem, and myself to land on the planet's surface to interrogate Nedilli. Jim and Chubby Eaves and my scientist comrade shall remain in the *G'uillger*, orbiting Medulla to assimilate data on the physics of the planet and the planet's environment and other biological and scientific tasks. Chubby Eaves is currently preparing the flight plans for the *G'uillger* to journey to Medulla. We need approval to transport the *Heritage* to Medulla, as the *Heritage* will be our escape vessel, if needed."

Landrew replied, "I sanction this. I will inform the Medullans. I shall make all the necessary arrangements for your journey."

The greatest challenge

"As I said, there is an acquaintance of mine who can provide us with further clues on the physical state of Urzel," said Deacon. "I need the same privileges that you afforded me previously, to close this library for two days so that he and the Owlers and I can use the resources here to further investigate some historical and criminal data. This must include a residence for Lyanna, my friend the physicist, Gem and Jim, and me. Chubby Eaves shall remain on board the *G'uillger* to ensure her readiness to depart at any minute. All these requests you must grant."

Xudur commenced a monologue of her disappointment in Landrew, but Landrew waved his hand to brush aside her speech and spoke up. "All these things are granted."

Xudur said. "You have demonstrated shortcomings, and now, without consulting the High Council, you grant yourself more supreme powers?"

Landrew confronted her. "There will be no debate. I hereby grant special requests to Mister Coombs." He knew Xudur to be the lone dissenter. "All in favor?" There was unanimity as Xudur abstained.

Landrew moved to Quobit and asked her to stand. "There is a ceremony that must be performed. From the initial disappearance of the *Sleigher*, there have been rumors of misconduct and incompetence at the Jabu Vesper station. The name Quobit has been cited in these rants. I believe that we all agree now that Quobit is innocent of any wrongdoing that day and, from Jim and Deacon's accounts, has performed admirably in her duties on Nix and elsewhere. It is my pleasure to shake your hand and thank you for your allegiance to the mission." Quobit rarely smiled, but this time she beamed purposely at Deacon as the group stood and expressed their support. "Are there any further questions for Mister Coombs?"

Deacon summarized his findings and plans for the group. "The clues to Urzel's defeat are as follows. Urzel Lok feels sorry for his dying other half. He has wept openly, as heard by Goharn Lok. Urzel, powerful as he is, is still a child. He fears me, but I do not know why. The Medullans must help me to understand this. The very fact that he requires weapons and followers is a sign of vulnerability in our world and in our dimension. Somehow, we must provoke a battle with him on our terms, bloody and risky as it may be, stretch his capabilities to the limit, and then assault him with an unknown force. Urzel Lok is not mentally stable and so will probably surprise us with his unpredictable actions.

"If we cannot trick Urzel Lok into fighting us on our terms, then the grim reality is that we may have to sacrifice someone to enter into this other dimension of his comfortably, to slay him there. Wherever this dimension is! But this must remain our last option. I believe that my physicist friend can help us understand our options and risk them for us. Therefore, I will ask Landrew to summon each of you for another meeting to present our options and battle plans."

Landrew stood and offered his support. "I am so sorry that I made this mistake. As I said earlier, I felt at the time that it was the right thing, the moral thing, to help the Medullans become corporeal again, to welcome them to our world. My mistake is upon us. We may decide to plan other courses to defeat this monster, but tonight we must bless Deacon Coombs's stratagem so he can leave here with our support."

Xudur arose. "Your mistake is past history. It is too late to undo your unforgiven sin. The future must be the united coalition of Urzel's death. However, I speak for Zentaur, and I want to state here for the record that Zentaur will not, I emphasize *not*, partake in any scheme by Coombs to control or capture this creature. Your plan, Coombs, must lead to its ultimate destruction. The death of Urzel Lok is the only solution."

Deacon was glad to agree. "You are correct, Xudur. There is a time for sympathy and compassion, but I came to the same conclusion on the escape from Nix that the death of Lord Urzel Lok is the only positive outcome of this crisis. For that reason, the engagement of my friend, the physicist, is an absolute necessity."

Raal spoke. "I gather by your attitude, Coombs, that you will carry the banner for the defeat of the being until the end."

"Correct. I will accept responsibility for the plans. I cannot execute them, but I will design them."

"Even after early round of defeats to this creature?" When Deacon didn't respond, Raal continued. "What inspires you to do so rather than a total attack by Alliance forces?"

"As I said, the creature must be annihilated by a plan yet to be conceived. Call it ego, call it foolish bravery, but I believe that with more information about Urzel, the team can concoct a plan that will defeat him. I will admit to you now that I don't know what that plan is. But my group and I will find it and brief you. I would ask all of you to please attend and invite Dithropolis, if that is possible. Having faced the enemy twice, I will summon the courage to face him a third time."

Deacon paced around the room. During their silence, he sensed their respect in him and their willingness to hear him out. "I personally have seen the results of the experiment for which Landrew now suffers. It is my opinion that you in this room must enter the history books of our beloved Alliance and approve a decision for the good of us all!"

Landrew looked at him in bewilderment; he didn't comprehend. Deacon spoke loudly. "Members of the High Council of the Alliance, when sympathetic Medullans deceived the Alliance and disobeyed Landrew and placed the child Urzel Lok outside the forces that encompass Medulla, on a planet named Nix, they laid unknowingly the first step for Medullan spirits to interface with us, to come into our worlds.

"I am trying very hard not to be a fatalist. It is logical for me, in every case I am engaged in, to believe that there is a solution and I can find it. Why do I believe this? Because there is no perfect crime. Just keep looking for the mistake that the villain has made. In this case, I must insist that this Council consider"—he stared at Schlegar, leaning over a chair from across the table—"abandoning the research efforts for the Medullans that are being conducted at Brebouillis."

Schlegar predictably countered. "You have not the comprehension of the breadth of research that has transpired there. This motion should receive equal time from both sides for a debate in front of the High Council. We just cannot consider a whimsical recommendation from you."

"Let Coombs continue, Schlegar," said Xudur. "I, for one, want to hear his reasoning."

"I am not blinded by the scientific and medical research at Brebouillis and where the results can take us or how it can benefit the Medullans. I have examined the evidence firsthand without bias. The Medullans are mentally superior to all of us, some light-years ahead in their evolution. We are, in my opinion, mental midgets to them. You all must confess that some of the most difficult problems in mathematics and medicine that the Alliance has faced have been solved by the Medullans' intelligence since their entry. You all know this, and I confirmed this in the records at Brebouillis.

"So what will happen to us when we solve their problem to render them corporeal—to finally interface with us as inferior corporeal beings? I have read about the intelligence quotients of Medullans to understand that they are exponentially out of reach from us. And in a thousand years, when we have given them bodies, where will the Medullans be? What will they want? Will they be satisfied to let inferior beings lead the Alliance? Let inferior beings make all decisions which affect their universe? Will 100 percent of the Medullans be law-abiding citizens once they become corporeal? Or will one or two or three, or three hundred, decide to become criminal elements, or rebels, and try to capture power in the Alliance because they know they can—because they judge us as inferior beings and resent us, despise us?

"Urzel is but one misguided Medullan, and a child at that! A child! But look at the damage he has inflicted into our universe and the havoc he has brought to this Council! Will history record that he will be the singular, sole Medullan who tried to conquer the Alliance? Will history record Urzel Lok as the singular instance of a Medullan criminal?"

Schlegar started to object, but Deacon spoke over him with a louder voice. "They will tire of us in less than a hundred years. We will all be a bore. We will all be lower than them, both in class structure and on the evolutionary ladder. Then they will look to new challenges in the Alliance. Perhaps, Schlegar, they will want to replace Aralians as our most trusted advisors as head of the traders' union. Why should this race accept the laws that you, the High Council, construct for them?

"When Earth first joined the Alliance, we were not afforded all the rights of the Alliance until we had proven our intentions to cooperate, listen, and learn to coexist in the Alliance. Landrew is the first High Ruler from Earth after many hundreds of years of testing our commitment."

At this point, Eggu-Nitron interrupted. "Are you finished, Earthman?"

"Yes, Eggu-Nitron."

"There is merit to what you speak, Coombs. I trust you because you speak the truth and it hurts. The Council should debate this issue later, when we have established peace. We engaged you, and I for one want to be recorded as having said that you have outperformed my expectations. Your help is still needed, and I pray that you will not delay. However, as I listen to you, it frightens me that Urzel is not even a purebred Medullan, and look at the power he wields. I support all that Deacon Coombs has asked for, and I ask the rest of you to do similarly. Barnard's Planet is firmly behind you, Coombs."

Schlegar posed his concern. "What if we discontinue this research and later the Medullans discover how to reverse this evolution by themselves or by the assistance of some other species? Or even more frightening, what if they find out how to come out of this . . . this . . . so-called other dimension and come after us and force us to work on this research? They may not forgive our aborted efforts so easily. They could retaliate. I say we continue to minimize these risks. I vote to continue the research at Brebouillis."

Raal addressed Schlegar. "We could explain our lack of success by our scientists. They may decide themselves to abort the efforts."

Xudur snapped her thick lips. "Raal, we do not answer to Medullans. We are not accountable to them. Coombs has made his case. I believe it has merit that we should discuss at some other meeting. As for your concern, Schlegar, the Medullans might be smart, but courage will have to complement their abilities to conquer Zentaur. We submit to no one, not even to this Urzel. If Zentaur should be conquered, it will only be at the death of the last Zentaurian. We pledge our lives to the cause of extinguishing Urzel Lok and will fight him to the death through Deacon Coombs's plan."

"Xudur," Eggu-Nitron said annoyedly, "we do tire of your endless bouts of shows of strength."

"You insult me, little one?"

"I call order to this meeting!" Landrew shouted. "The motion that Mister Coombs has tabled is for our next debate in private chambers. Your comments, Mister Coombs, and yours, Schlegar, are dually noted."

"But, Landrew," Schlegar said, "this motion comes from a detective, not a scientist. Surely you must hear from all the other researchers at Brebouillis." Schlegar disappointedly acknowledged that Lyanna's silence indicated she would be siding with Coombs.

Landrew motioned to draw attention. "Tonight is a night of catastrophic events. My most pious deed has metamorphosed into a nightmare that has materialized a monster. My trusted advisor, Rande, has been exposed to be an aide of Urzel Lok. Then we heard Coombs's plea to discontinue the research at Brebouillis. Earlier, I received devastating news from Jabu, one of the closest planets to Nix." Landrew peered at Quobit as he spoke. "The reason for Dithropolis's absence will be obvious to you. It has begun. Catastrophe has struck."

The war begins

Landrew's voice was growing raspy. "Let me read you a communication received from Dithropolis. I had intended to share this with you earlier, but Coombs's agenda prohibited me from finding the ideal time for intervention." Landrew opened his handheld device and read from the screen.

"'From Dithropolis. Landrew, the dark force army of Lord Urzel Lok attacked planet Jabu. Crazed, fierce, armed Nicosians, hundreds of thousands of savages, landed in spaceships and mercilessly stormed the capital city of Obm. Twelve spaceships mysteriously materialized at the Vesper station and proceeded directly to the port at Obm, where the savages were unleashed under the command of other aliens. They have commenced an onslaught of murdering, pillaging, butchering, and storming the planet's capital grounds, overwhelming the guards by numbers in complete surprise. The events occurred so swiftly, so quickly, Landrew, that we were caught unprepared. As you know, the Jabu are a peaceful race, and we are not equipped or mentally prepared to fight such a brutal army.'"

Quobit was stunned. Deacon moved beside her as he recognized the consternation rising into her gaze.

Landrew took a deep breath. "The Jabu are easy prey for this monster. I will now conclude Dithropolis's message. 'In order to put an end to the slaughter of his dear people, Supreme Donn Vet Ginighties publicly surrendered to Lord Urzel Lok on Lok's terms. At this time, these terms have not been made public. I am privy to one term—that the surrender of the Jabunese army to Lord Urzel Lok has been completed and the Jabu have laid down their arms; I am assured that this was partially done as Jabu commanders succumbed to his mental powers. I will try to dispatch further secretive communiques.'"

The room was eerily silent as Landrew shook and Quobit sobbed. Landrew scanned the room with his eyes. "I support whatever steps Coombs believes we have to take to defeat this monster."

"We will dispense troops from Zentaur immediately to set Jabu free!" said Xudur.

Deacon responded instantly. "No, Xudur. That would be a mistake. We are not prepared to confront him yet. Listen to me. Please." Deacon stood to lecture his audience. "Urzel Lok has conquered Jabu. He has made an example of them, and he knows that fear and panic will follow throughout the Alliance as word of his victory spreads. But as I stated before"—he raised his voice—"he will not be able to hold it without allies and forces as he moves from Jabu to his next quest. We need to formulate our plan to defeat him quickly, and thus I will do so. Any troops you send to Jabu will fall victim to his mental powers and come under his spell and just increase the number of needless deaths. I urge all of you, and you, Landrew, to command all Alliance forces to hold their positions. Do not send troops to Jabu, where their sacrifices will fuel Urzel's honor further. An admirable gesture, Xudur, but please, Jabu was an easy victory for him; we now must surprisingly run interference in his next plans."

Landrew's face was flush with grief. Eggu-Nitron continued to bow his head in his lap. Raal trembled as she spoke. "Mendalgon could be next. We are not prepared for a surprise savage attack, especially if this demon hits with waves of fierce Nicosians who are prepared to die for Urzel's cause."

Landrew said, "I have already ordered Alliance troops to Jabu, Deacon. In light of your comments, I shall retract them."

"I pray that they have not arrived, Landrew, to be influenced by Urzel and then turned against us."

"I will move the timetable up. We will meet in two nights to discuss a united plan. I ask each of you to exercise discipline in the interim. I know it will be difficult, Raal. Discipline will save us."

"Is there anything gained by traveling to Jabu to seek him out," said Raal, "to try to reach a compromise? To buy some time in false negotiations?"

Deacon shook his head. "You are no match for him. I urge the members of the High Council to remain here, where we can meet at a moment's notice, where you should seek secret refuge. Do not travel home. Stay within the force field limits of Earth. I warn you! The Council must remain united. Reach out for Dithropolis, but if he cannot attend, then I understand."

Xudur stood and approached Deacon, and with great intimidation in her tone, she spat her words at him. "So you believe that you are a match for him?"

"I informed you before, Xudur, that he fears me and I have to discover why. I have to find out from Nedilli. I have a hope, a plan; it has to be executed immediately in light of the drastic news from Jabu."

Eggu-Nitron then asked Deacon, "Why does he want to conquer our worlds? What motivates him to do so?"

"Children are programmed early in life by their environment. Urzel was programmed to hate the world around him because as an insane child he was left to fend for himself on Nix with savages, and he found that his superior mental skills were the weapons of defense and offense. He has learned to react only from the environment around him on Nix. And what was that environment? Cruelty. War against your neighbor. No respect for anything, for anyone. His high intelligence combined with his cruel environment has led him on a course of fighting to survive and exacting revenge against all who dishonor him. I suspect that when he found out the instability he could create in our world, he feasted on it and now grows stronger."

Quobit used her experience on Nix to elaborate. "Urzel Lok has decided to make an example of all of us because he knows he can do this! Understand. Urzel was born insane. The entire life cycles on Nix revolve around a struggle for life and death each day. Imagine what this child experienced every single day on Nix, a daily fight to survive. I witnessed this firsthand. As on Nix, Urzel uses his mental powers to conquer any and all beings. With his intelligence, he must have known that an army of savage Nicosians invading Jabu could lead to only one conclusion—victory for Lord Urzel!"

Lyanna agreed and said, "Urzel is spreading fear throughout the Alliance as we speak."

Deacon nodded. "The only life he knows is that of the Nicosians—how to wage battles daily. Therefore, he practices exactly what he has learned and lived."

"You are starting to draw my sympathies," Eggu-Nitron said with sincerity.

"I shall quote Xudur," said Deacon, "who said that compliance to my plan must include the death of this creature. Any weakness by us will cause future regret. We shall all lose our lives if we are not careful."

Xudur looked at Eggu-Nitron. "This savage shall not extract an ounce of sympathy from me. I shall gladly volunteer to partake in its death scene!"

"Since Urzel is on Jabu, trying to strengthen his grasp there, it is time to journey to Medulla. Time grows short. I shall brief you before we depart, as we previously agreed."

"What is his next target?" Landrew asked. "Do you believe it to be Mendalgon?"

"Jabu was easy, as we agreed earlier," said Deacon. "Urzel knew that a surprise attack there could result in only one decision. As I also stated, the risk was small. The results were huge, as word of his glory and victory spread. Unfortunately, Mendalgon—as I fear, and Raal spoke of—or perhaps even Jevnia could be the next targets."

"Why?" Eggu-Nitron asked.

"Because it has a very small population that is unarmed, and it is close to Jabu and would provide Urzel with a second quick-strike, low-risk victory. He has proven that he can navigate in space undetected, so a strike either on Mendalgon or Jevnia is most likely."

Landrew spoke up. "I think Mendalgon. The Alliance is so dependent upon Mendalgon to provide rich ores and spices found nowhere else."

Raal agreed and said, "Tourism abounds on Mendalgon, with our famous landmarks and hallowed prizes of archaeological sites and digs. It occurred to me that Urzel could release all the tourists after an onslaught and let them return to their home planets to spread panic. Two bloody victories would most certainly throw the Tetrad Alliance into severe chaos and cause events that we the Council could not control."

Xudur challenged Schlegar and Landrew by returning to an unpopular topic. "Why has the research at Brebouillis been kept a secret from the rest of the Alliance all these years?"

"We cannot satisfy your curiosity, Xudur," Landrew replied, "except to say that it was held as a confidential arrangement between Medulla and Aralia and the predecessors of the Alliance. It has not been sanctioned as public information by our senators."

Xudur's body language signaled her distaste of the answer. "It is apparent to me that the Medullans want to share our world by us giving bodies to them. However, some moral, ethical, sincere causes have been tainted to produce malefic results. Therefore, we must now answer the question. If basic research continues for the cause of the Medullans, is Urzel going to be the exception—or the rule, as Coombs stated?"

"Xudur, you expect us to believe that?" said Schlegar. "Please let us converse further of the options."

"Schlegar, you are too immersed in the problem. It will take less-biased thinking to resolve this." Xudur hissed the word *this* at him.

Landrew waved his arms. "I have already ruled on a future session to debate this. Schlegar, we will hear you and your scientific team, but at a more appropriate time."

Xudur wasn't finished. "Will they treat us as equals? Will they become annoyed at our ignorance, as Coombs has said? Will they grant us equal rights after we affirm their superior intellect? Zentaurians will not risk this! This issue may risk the split of the Alliance if we tolerate less than discontinuing the research on Brebouillis for the Medullans."

In the silence that followed, Deacon spoke softly. "I have witnessed the powers of Urzel, the first Medullan to transcend beyond the force field of Medulla. He can belittle us just as any other crazed Medullan who decides to follow Urzel's path. So I propose a thought for you. What is the ultimate cost of the continued research at Brebouillis? Is it eternal friendship with the Medullans? Or is it that, years from now, we condemn our future generations to a life of slavery?"

Deacon shook the hand of each of the members, hugged Schlegar and Lyanna, and absorbed Lyanna's compliments. Landrew rose and left the group. He wandered down the hallway to a balcony that overlooked the grand foyer, and here he stared at the statues and busts of all of the great leaders of the Alliance. Deacon took this as a cue to follow, so he excused himself and ambled after the leader. Behind him, Xudur debated with Schlegar while Raal and Eggu-Nitron comforted Lyanna and Dreveney and Quobit.

"I have brought death to all of us," said Landrew. "The blood of the Jabu is only the first drops to be shed."

The detective replied, "History may never know your dark deed, for I will not be the one to recite it in my memoirs. With some luck, Landrew, you may go down in history as the commander of the forces that beat the greatest threat ever to mankind."

"I won't deserve that fame."

"Don't underestimate yourself."

"I want to travel with you."

Deacon was surprised at this remark. "No, your duties are here on Earth and you know this. You once asked me to believe you when you said that I must use my gift to save my life. Now you must believe me when I tell you that your reign is not ended; your days as leader are not over. You have made a terrible mistake, but do not allow that error to let you lose sight of your present obligations. Your day is here and now. You are a monument to the achievements of this administration."

"Tonight I feel as if I do not deserve to adorn these halls."

"I must leave you."

Landrew asked him, "Why do you insist on fighting my battle? I always took you as one who disdained politicians."

Deacon chuckled. "I have a plan to defeat him. I need to locate a former colleague to understand Urzel better. Meanwhile, my friend, you must remain here to direct the activities of the Alliance and prevent anyone else from interfacing with Urzel until we are ready to do so."

The two walked back to the chamber, where groups of discussion were taking place. Deacon clapped to get their attention. "There are many questions to be answered, but we must depart. Lyanna, Schlegar, Jim, Quobit, and I will set up our brief research efforts in the library archives as before. I shall count on top security this time. Who guarantees that in Rande's absence?"

Xudur said, "I will ensure your privacy and security."

Peace offerings were exchanged as the five departed. Quobit touched Deacon's arm. "I will return to Jabu."

"That is not wise, Quobit. We don't even know who is in control of the Vesper station."

"My mind is made up. I also know that we will meet again." Quobit gave him a tight hug, shook hands with the others, and bounded down the stairs and out of sight before Deacon could offer good luck. Landrew stood on the balcony to salute them as they clamored down the stone stairs and exited. Deacon's last words before he passed through the doorway were "Remember, Landrew, your time is not over. You will not pass the way of Geor and Como." After Deacon left, these words still echoed in the great hall.

Landrew stood there long after the High Council had disbanded. He liked this little man of Anglo. He owed his life to him. Suddenly the fears he had been fighting disappeared. Past glories filled his mind, spotted with future imagined victories. He muttered to himself, saying, "Damn, Landrew, we will beat this menace yet."

Toad Roadster

The sign on the gate of the corner lot read "Rodan Roadster." Deacon made his way through the slush of the first snows, leaving the only clear footprints. "Wait here, Jim." Then he climbed a set of decrepit steps to an elevated, one-story white-framed cottage as Jim stood guard sixty feet away at street side.

Deacon reached for a computer portal and placed his card into the slot. The humming electronics verified his identity. However, when the card was released, the door was still bolted. The identical procedure produced the same results, so he descended the stairs, waving at Jim to follow him to the back of the structure.

Jim protested as he pointed out a sign and read it aloud: "No Trespassing." Deacon ignored the insinuation, opened the rusty gate to the small side gardens, and then traipsed to the side of the dwelling. Jim followed while continuing to voice his objections. "We should respect the privacy of this individual. Invasion of private property is a crime."

"Hush!" He turned to signal the Owler to keep quiet. There was an absence of windows until they reached the back side, where two small, round openings displayed light inside. Deacon peered into the dwelling as Jim spoke. "If you must know, sire, I have confirmed a single Earthling inside."

"Behind this wall?"

"Affirmative."

Deacon stepped forward and pounded on the back door. "Open up in there! I know you're there, Toad! This is Deacon Coombs!" Jim proceeded to pound on the wall. "The human has moved to the front of the house, sire." As Deacon retraced his steps to the front and up the stairs, he knocked harder while Jim scanned the street. Suddenly, a crack appeared as a gruff voice saturated with spite spoke to him.

"A man can have no privacy. What do you want? You impertinent being, why I'll—"

The door opened wide to expose a very short, very stout man of about sixty-five. He had a wide, ruddy face; big, bulging eyes; long, taut lips; a floppy belly, a large nose, and no discernible chin. His lips seemed to rest on the bottom of his face. He stared hard at Deacon.

"Deacon Coombs! Oh my goosh! Oh my dear! I have been so rude to you. Oh my chooch! Deacon Coombs, forgive me. Villya, villya, villya." He raced forward to embrace Deacon vigorously with his fleshy hands while a quarter-moon smile graced his face.

"It is I who is rude, Toad, banging mercilessly to disturb you. However, I need your help urgently."

"Oh my goosh!" He danced around his small habitat and then exuberantly replied, "So glad to see you after all these years. Come in. Come in."

Deacon entered and locked the door behind them. "I am so glad to see you again, Toad. You haven't changed one bit."

"Ha, look at you, Deacon, dressed in smart new clothes. However, you still have a small belly compared to mine." He patted himself on his rotund stomach, which hung underneath his drab, baggy pine-green clothing. "Come, follow me to the back room, where we can converse." Deacon spied bits of food on the monstrous table in the dimly lit surroundings. Papers and discs were strewn in every direction, while a thin layer of dust covered the floors except where Rodan had defined his own path of heavy traffic.

Inside the laboratory, the intensity of data was magnified dramatically. They were on the floor, on the counters, beside glass and metal apparatuses. The walls of the entire room were bathed in posters depicting Rodan's heroes of physics.

"Sit," Rodan said to Deacon as Rodan made his way to a weather-beaten high-back green chair and plopped himself down. "Oh my chooch, it is so wonderful to see you. Let me guess. Three years ago?"

Deacon corrected him. "Five."

"Oh my, so long. Five years. Tragic." His lips were taut as he shook his head.

"It was at the convention of astrophysicists at Bristol."

"Aha! Yes." Rodan was very enthusiastic. "Oh, I remember those days. However, times have changed, Deacon, and no one wants to seek my opinion anymore. I must be careful, you know. Pests, they come here all the time. Not as respected as I used to be. No more respect for the aging Toad. I am behind in my debts, as consulting assignments are infrequent."

He bowed his head, seeming somewhat ashamed. "Pests come to collect. Pound on the door and walls just like you did. Roust me out of my sleep. Use phony identifications to gain admittance. Oh, I am a poor host by boring you with my personal troubles. Let me say what a pleasant surprise to see you. What can I do for you? Is this purely social, or did I hear something about an urgent matter?"

"I came here to consult with one of the world's foremost authorities on physics. In my world, you always will be." Deacon leaned into him. "I desperately need your help with one of my cases."

"Oh my, what an honor indeed. Me? Rodan Roadster? You want to engage me? The great Deacon Coombs? Oh my goosh. This is so exciting."

"I wish we had time to reminisce about our memories from college days and the papers at conferences, but that sadly cannot be the case. We must discuss business. If you accept my offer to assist me, then we will have other times to reminisce. Do we have an agreement?"

"Ha, oh yes!" Toad beamed resiliently and sat back, his arms folded across his pot belly.

"Toad, I have been recruited by the High Council of the Alliance to solve the deaths of two great statesmen."

"Hmm. Como and Geor."

"Yes." Deacon knew that he could trust Rodan. "During this investigation, I have stumbled onto what could be a startling idea of how this murderer remains undetected by our modern-day technology. It is of this matter and other conjectures that I come to consult with my old professor. As a great quantum physicist, an expert in laser theories, the author of the fortieth and forty-first and forty-second laws of thermodynamics, I seek your advice." Deacon huddled even closer to Rodan. "Let me commence by asking you a question. What do you think about the existence of dimensions of reality beyond our comprehension and measurement?"

"Oh my dear, the dimensions beyond length, width, height, and time have been studied for a lifetime. Beyond our four dimensions, some scientists have postulated a fifth, sixth, seventh, eighth, and so on, all being theoretically calculated. All of these are not dimensions that mortals such as us can enter or utilize at present, but they are measureable. Ahhmm, yes, these dimensions have been conditionally quantified until the time that a phenomenon is proven to exist."

"Toad, the murderer of Geor and Como went entirely undetected at their death scenes. I have this crazy idea that this villain might have been undetected because the space he occupies is invisible to us. What do you think? Am I crazy?"

"Hmm, you think that the murderer is of another dimension. That is difficult to imagine."

"What? You're the physicist! You always kept your mind open, and you always encouraged your students to do the same. Don't you see the predicament I have? I, as a detective, always look to the facts to solve my problems. I came to you because I need to look beyond the facts and the limits of our physics to catch this evil. You, Toad, always said, 'Believe the impossible.'"

"You are serious, and I owe you an apology. Please present your evidence. How rude of me to dismiss your ideas so rashly." Rodan suddenly felt the urgency of the situation and put on a serious face, realizing he had not heard his guest fairly.

"This must be retained as confidential information. I recite my case as I trust you." Rodan smiled back. He sat on the edge of his chair, his short, stubby legs swaying as Deacon commenced. "Toad, I have witnessed evils that men have only seen in nightmares. Panic would surely grip the Tetrad Alliance if this creature that I corroborated were to expose himself. For the sake of brevity, let us discuss only the aspects of the physical nature of this beast rather than my trip to other worlds." Deacon sat back, and the two were at ease.

"Here in Liberty City and on the moon Brebouillis, my Owlers and I examined confidential files about the parameters of a world known as Medulla."

"Ahhmm, the land of spirits. I have read about them but never studied them."

"They are more than spirits, Toad. Medullans evolved into the spiritual world from the body millions of years ago. Like us, they were corporeal at one time. They severed from their being and reached a stage of evolution unparalleled in our worlds, as they found they could survive without flesh." Rodan was engrossed.

"Let me tell you that it is only natural that the Medullans evolved over time into spirits, and the key factor was not time, as it is in other species. The key factor in their evolution was the physical conditions that existed on the planet's surface. Let me explain. Then I will seek your affirmation, or doubts." Rodan placed his fist under his chin, opened his bulbous brown eyes even wider, and fixated on Deacon.

"On Earth, we have gravity and magnetic fields that we have understood for thousands of years. Our laws of gravity and magnetics, and the laws of physics, are based on the fundamental laws of gravity and magnetics.

"One of the most shocking discoveries that I made in this case is a revelation of the physical and natural parameters that abound on Medulla. They are not the same as Earth's and have little in common with the physics of any other planet in the Alliance. From planet to planet, the physics of gravity and magnetics change. On planet Medulla, we are witnessing an extreme case."

Rodan rubbed his hands in an excited state. "Ooh, I am interested; tell me more."

"Toad, in confidential files at Brebouillis, I noted that the magnetic field on Medulla is entirely unstable. Unlike Earth's poles, which reverse over long periods of time, the magnetic reversals of the magnetic poles on Medulla occur sometimes even daily!"

"Oh my goosh, how did you confirm this?"

"When the Medullans were admitted to the Alliance, they were required to submit basic data about the planet. One of the conditions of admittance was this transfer of data. However, only the Aralians received this information, and they were under agreement to keep it confidential. The Medullans did not want to spark interest with physicists all across the universe. They treasure their privacy."

"I had no idea that the magnetic fields on any planet could fluctuate so rapidly."

"There's more. The core of the planet Medulla, like Earth, is molten. Unlike Earth, while the mass of the planet remains constant, the core and inner parts are in a tug-of war-for equilibrium between liquid, gaseous, and solid states. In other words, there are battles of phase changes within the planet. That means—"

"That the gravity field fluctuates on a daily level too!" Rodan shouted excitedly. "How utterly tormenting for life on Medulla!"

"Exactly. You and I know that all matter consists of electronically charged particles of protons, electrons, and neutrons, down to the smallest nebal. Since all magnetic fields have associated electronic fields, and all electronic fields have associated magnetic fields, imagine the strain of trying to evolve life in that type of dynamic environment where the smallest particles are in constant turmoil because the fields forever change. It was this instability on the planet that caused the Medullans to seek paths of evolution to shed their bodies."

"What a terrible place for life to evolve."

"My observation, Toad, is that their evolution of life took them over millions of years to their current level of spirituality, into a dimension where the dynamic daily changes of the gravity and magnetic fields are now minimal or nonexistent. These life forms, from the very beginning, were directed down paths of nature that would help them overcome the quaking masses of their bodies. They were corporeal at first. But can you imagine the stress of a different gravity field every day? A differently charged ionic body system every day? A different metabolism every day?"

"I understand what you mean. My goosh. You think that these creatures naturally fought the system to retain bodies and discovered that life in the spiritual world was freedom."

"You, Toad, now have what every physicist dreams of—a fully unrestricted pass to the confidential files in the history archives in Liberty City to examine the history of planet Medulla and the evolution of the Medullans. And"—he smiled—"what is not recorded there is brought by my Owlers from confidential restricted files on Brebouillis for your inspection. And you have exactly one and one-half days to examine the fluctuations, construct your own equations, and then hypothesize, to see if what I propose is correct or not."

Rodan stroked his chin. "For an amateur physicist, you have made some startling deductions. You believe that this murderer is a Medullan."

"I know so, for I have witnessed him. The Alliance must know more about the physics of Medulla and how the fields affect human life. We must know if the energy of this creature or any Medullan can exist in domains that cannot be detected. We must know how to contact this evil. However, your most important assignment is to determine how to destroy the malignancy."

"Ahhmm, you seem so confident of what you say. Enough said. My goosh, I will join in your efforts. If this murderer was not detected on Aralia and Globiana, I will find the reason why. I also accept the challenge of finding a way to destroy it."

Deacon reached across from where he sat to grasp Rodan's hands. They shook heartily until Deacon broke the lock to say, "I have had two firsthand encounters with this Medullan. His presence was completely undetected by our instruments, yet he was close, so close that I saw him as a giant bird of prey. If he travels out of our dimensions, how can he be seen but not detected?"

"Oh," Rodan said, "you don't expect me to answer that, do you? I've only been on the job two minutes." Rodan laughed while Deacon said, "Just like the good ole days, Toad and Deacon."

"You do pose an interesting problem, Deacon. Why shouldn't he be detected? There must have been a spatial disturbance?" Rodan then soured. "This sounds like a very dangerous assignment. The murderer can't be seen and can't be detected. It is able to project shapes and able to bend minds. Does he know that you recruit me?"

"Rest assured that you are safe, and I will assign protection every minute from the Owler Jim. Your assignment, Toad, is to additionally identify his physical weakness. Unfortunately, we must devise a plan to kill him, and as I said, we need your help to identify the implement of his destruction. Since I believe that this creature does not conform to our laws of nature and physics, we must uncover those special circumstances that are optimum for his execution."

"Oh my goosh." Rodan beamed waves of respect toward Deacon. "Challenge accepted, Coombs. Beats the chooch of any of the current projects I probe. This sounds so exciting."

"We rendezvous at the library this afternoon. Jim, my Owler, will escort you there in three hours. Pack everything you need for the next three weeks, including any analytical devices. Accommodations for you and me have already been arranged in the archives."

Rodan was shocked. "Three weeks?"

"After our research in the library, we must journey to Medulla."

"Hurrah! Coombs and Roadster to Medulla and beyond!" Rodan's high-pitched voice shrilled in excitement.

Deacon rose and shook Rodan's fleshy hand. "Until later, my friend, for I have other errands before you arrive."

"Deacon, I don't want to appear brash or rude," Rodan said, speaking softly and humbly. "I uh . . . you know, uh . . . how it is these days. There is no more respect for the Doctor Roadster. This new generation, they brush my ideas aside, these young hotshots. They coin new terminology for my past works. My grants have become smaller and smaller. Pests come all the time. I don't want to be impertinent, but funds must be . . . I mean, I can't work for free."

"Toad, I shall have allowances for your time arranged. I never would ask so great a task to go unrewarded. I promise."

"I normally wouldn't have approached you, but—"

"Toad, I am not insulted. What you ask is for fair compensation, and I agree. I confirmed for you earlier that this could be a dangerous voyage, so danger pay will be piled on top of scientific research. I must depart. It was so great to see you again, and so until later, my friend." Deacon departed as Rodan waddled toward the door mumbling about pests and his gratitude to Deacon. Deacon paused at the door to identify Jim for Rodan. They exchanged waves. Then Deacon bolted into the cold morning air to find Jim chatting with one of the local constables about his adventures in outer space.

Deacon hailed Jim. "Do you think that the latest model from the assembly line could find our way back to the library in our shuttle?" Jim saluted the officer and approached Deacon. "Rather nice chap. Chatty though. Master, in answer to your question, the way to the library is trivial. Of course I can find it." Deacon did not have time to ask the officer his impressions of Jim. *Chatty*, he thought to himself.

Deacon was lost in his thoughts as Jim continued to talk to him about the uplifting conversation. Over and over, Deacon replayed the words of Rodan. The same fear that Rodan had visited him in his own idle moments—the fear that someone younger, brighter, would emerge soon to challenge him for the role of esteemed detective, would burst onto the policing scene the way that he had through his own initiatives. Maybe, as with Rodan, this upstart would rewrite and then retitle his treatises for a new generation.

The hum of the engine made him dream, and in his dreams he saw the challenger. He was a tall, muscular, specimen, tanned evenly, handsome, flexing his muscles as his magnetic personality wooed Lyanna. There they were, she in his arms being whisked away from him as the upstart carried her up the stairs of the History Archives Library while he struggled, out of breath because of his weight, and unable to speak over Lyanna's giggles.

"Master," Jim said, shaking Deacon, "we have arrived at the library." Jim shook him again to wake him from his trance and then aided him to his feet. Deacon's muscles were sore; his mind ached.

"Shall I accompany you to your room?" Jim asked.

"No, I want you to check the records, organize files, and set up a research position for Rodan Roadster so all is ready for him when he arrives. Test the monitor and retrieval systems too, and contact Gem and Chubby to find where and when the *G'uillger* arrives and make the arrangements for departure for Medulla. When the ship does arrive, ask Chubby to come to the library to see me. Don't forget to pick up Toad in three hours. Go out of your way to treat him with respect. While his real name is Rodan Roadster, his friends respectfully address him as Toad. I think it appropriate for you to do the same."

After Jim departed, Deacon wound his way through the maze to the back part of the building. There a pleasant scent permeated his nostrils. Lyanna filled his senses. "You approve of my choice," she said.

Deacon was annoyed. "You promised to stop reading my thoughts, Lyanna." He stepped toward his room to find her standing in the doorway.

Puzzled, she stood with her hands on her hips. "I didn't deserve that outburst. I put this scent on to please you."

"Sorry, I'm just on edge. But please stop invading my mind. Don't you find conversation more satisfying?" Striding forward with conviction, he said, "Place your arms around my neck."

"Why should I do that?"

"Please, for me, and hold on." With an extraordinary tug, he hoisted her up, transferred her completely inside the room and then carried her to his bed, where his knees buckled and they tumbled to the floor just shy of the soft covers. She was hysterical.

"I think of you as a gallant knight, but please don't ever act like one again."

"I believe that I love you," he said. His words caused her to crawl closer.

"Do you have time in your schedule to make love to a poor, defenseless scientist?"

"I sent Jim away. Rodan does not arrive for three hours. I consider you to be anything but defenseless. Intelligent, uncanny, resourceful, yes, but not defenseless."

"Why did you bark at me upon your arrival?"

"I'm sorry. I am caught up in the apprehension because I have bet all our lives and future on an aging scientist who I believe can save us."

She plunked a kiss on his lips and then turned away. "I shall return in a few minutes. Let me make a quick trip to my compartment."

"Don't tidy up. I intend to be ruthless with you."

He stood and unbuttoned his shirt to expose his soft belly. "Nothing to disguise that," he said to himself. As he unbuckled his trousers and kicked off his shoes, he heard the door to his room open.

Xudur

Another fragrant odor greeted Deacon. "Ah, that's even more ravishing." He blushed a deep red in his cheeks as he found himself standing almost naked before Xudur.

"Perhaps you did not hear me knock. Why do you blush, Earthman? Do you think me so naive to have never seen a naked male Earth specimen before?"

As she addressed him, he zipped his trousers up and put on his shirt. "Permission to visit these premises must be obtained. I thought that was agreed upon by the Council."

"I do not need your consent. I report to Landrew. And don't forget that I provide security for you and your team. Unlike the traitor Rande, you can depend upon me to protect you."

"Speak, Xudur. I am a busy person. Dr. Roadster arrives in less than three hours, and I have much to prepare. What do you want?"

Her scaly green reptilian hulk slinked around the room, the muscles in her legs rippling with each stride, a small extension at the rear base of her torso wagging, the lime-green scales jostling for position in her legs and torso. "Earthman, your words are impressive, and I have taken the liberty to read some selections by the famous Deacon Coombs, such as the cataloging of soils, your profiles of criminal traits, and your documentation of bacteria." She wandered around the room as she spoke, inspecting his belongings—his books, his computer, his personal effects, and his notebook.

"Put that down," he said as she thumbed through each page of his personal diary about Nix. She spun around to face him and moved into his space. This was the closest that he had ever been to a Zentaurian. Not even Geor had broken the space for same air. Small, irregular, boil-filled troughs existed in the crevices between the ripples of green scales on her face. It was the first time that Deacon had observed that. Xudur, as usual, flashed the inside of her mouth to expose the repulsive bloodred tissue. She knew it would annoy him. Deacon stood his ground and peered into her abyssal eyes.

They were soulless black spots, like those of the face of an ancient form of extinct life on Earth called lizards. Deacon felt as though he was staring into a black hole. He inhaled Xudur's stench in a fight for breath and then asked, "What do you want, Xudur?"

"You speak well and you write well. I admire your efforts to bring this creature to justice on behalf of the Alliance. For an Earthman this is a noble gesture. But . . . you and I must face truths. A truth we both share. Correct?"

"Speak your piece bluntly and leave."

"We know what must be done. Don't we, Deacon Coombs? We know what must be done to rid our world of this monster Urzel." She intimidated him by shaking her head up and down while rubbing the soft, fleshy green crest on her forehead against his face. Deacon backed off.

"I must admit, Coombs, that you have brave, foolish notions." Now her pitch had altered to throw a scare into him.

"But they are only heroic dreams, the dreams of a dreamer—and that dreamer is you. When it comes time to kill this child, what will you do? Will you appeal to its mother to reason with it? Will you appeal directly to Urzel itself? Will you take the glittering razor's edge and rip the flesh and plunge the edge mercilessly into it? Stab it to death? Laser it to smithereens? Will you?" Xudur was afire and answered her own queries. "No, you will not." She was furious as she backed away from him. "You have not the courage to kill it! In the one second that you and other humans delay to think of it as a child, when you feel pangs of remorse, it will have you, and you will have failed. I know you spoke of courage earlier, but those were just words." She raised her tiny, muscular upper left arm and pointed her long fingers at him.

"From the inception of your plan by your physicist friend Roadster, whatever it may be, you know that it is I, Xudur, who must travel with you to this great confrontation. You do not have what it takes to murder, Mister Writer, Mister Sleuth, and Mister Moonbeam Eyes."

In the silence, she strutted around the room again, positioning herself behind him. He felt her breath on his nape. "I, Princess Xudur, have boundless courage and the intelligence of knowing when to strike, and I shall kill this vermin on sight before it begs for mercy. You will mastermind and design the death scenario for me with Roadster. I shall not bother to show pity because it is the unfortunate child of a maligned mating. Do you know what we do to criminals on Zentaur?"

"Yes. I believe that you dissect them."

"Dissect them? Is that what your books tell you? We shred them up into fodder. Failures as humans, we give them a second chance to fertilize the soils and bring new life. We give them a second chance to contribute to society in death."

"That would be inhumane and disgusting on most other planets."

"That is an expected reaction from a fragile, sympathetic little Earthman."

She folded her arms and ambled around to face him again, deliberately breathing puffs of her being into his face. "That is your basic problem here on Earth. You have too many prisons. You spend too much money and time keeping the vermin of society alive, like your friend Morris Mydloan. He was set free to kill again, or be killed." Xudur showed an evil sneer. "Tell me what you will feel when you squeeze the trigger on the implement of destruction to terminate Urzel."

"I will do whatever has to be done. I shared as much with you and the High Council."

"Liar!" she yelled. "You will hesitate, and all will be lost." Deacon jumped as she shook her fist at him. "It is me, Coombs, a woman of conviction, destiny, courage; I must be the one. You know this. Admit this to me now! You must design the death scene for Urzel so that Xudur is the instrument of its destruction!" Her black eyes now bulged from her sockets while she flicked her tongue at him.

"I will consider your request."

"Consider? I just gave you an order to save us all from your bleeding heart. You can save face here and now by requesting my presence to Landrew to accompany you to Medulla and beyond, or else I shall have to work behind your back to join your team and uncover your death plot. Well, Earthman?"

Deacon did not reply, so she smiled leeringly. "Do you know how we make love on Zentaur?"

"I have read about the rituals."

"*Read.* There is that word again. You are so fond of reading, aren't you? I am pleased that you are well versed on this issue. That is what you are—a reader." She placed her claws on his shoulders and came even closer to him to whisper.

"It commences when the female places her hands and claws on the shoulders of the male like this. Then she digs her claws deeper to penetrate the flesh and inject the male with hormonal chemicals to arouse him to the point of simultaneous pain and elation."

They sparred. He felt the spiny claws through his shirt. He lifted his arms and stroked her efforts away just as Lyanna appeared in the doorway.

"Excuse me, am I interrupting?" Lyanna asked.

"No. Princess Xudur was just leaving."

Xudur stared into his eyes. She leaned over to whisper in his ear. "Perhaps we shall dine one evening and I can tell you the invigorating tale of how I made love with one dozen males in an evening. They begged me to stop. On Zentaur, we take pride in our personal conquests. One evening, perhaps?"

Deacon wanted to end this uncomfortable meeting. Xudur did the favor by striding out, brushing past Lyanna. She turned one last time to say, "Your frail little body is blushing again, Mister Coombs. As I depart, don't forget that I can be your single most valuable resource on this mission. It is I, Xudur, who can be trusted and counted on to execute your assassination plan."

"What an irritating woman," Lyanna said. As she approached Deacon, she spotted the slight tear on the shoulder of his shirt. "Deacon, what was she doing?"

"She was taunting me into a favor. The intimidation tactics were not strong enough medicine for me to yield."

Lyanna turned and locked the door. "Now, where were we?" She embraced him, and they went through the motions, but Deacon's mind was infected with her Xudur's challenge. Would he pull the trigger? Was that what he was, just a reader? She had better be wrong, or like Landrew, he would live out the remainder of his life in deep regret. Later that day, Deacon visited Toad in the catacombs of the data banks. Jim connected Toad's monitors directly into monstrous library files.

The plan unfolds

Jim had selected an area on the ground floor for Toad's workstation. As Deacon and Lyanna approached, they noticed that Rodan's own papers and discs had contributed to a messy situation. Rodan took an instant liking to Lyanna and quizzed her on the research at Brebouillis. He also recited the recent incident where he had mistaken Deacon and Jim for pests. Jim, standing beside Deacon, and observing Rodan, replied, "He is a delightful, chubby man, Master. Now we have two chubbies on the team. But he is so messy and disorganized."

Lyanna approached. "When did you first meet him?"

"He was my college professor in physics and laserology. Later, after graduation, we worked on joint ventures at Lambton University. We've kept in touch over the years and even given joint papers at symposiums. It was Toad that influenced me to always work within the limitations of the data but never rule a possibility out."

"He seems so disorganized."

"Jim's thoughts exactly. Ha. Look, Lyanna, Jim is tidying up Toad's mess. This should work up Toad's dander."

Rodan waved his arms for Jim to depart and mind his own business. "Stop that! Leave those discs alone!" However, Jim insisted on organizing the shambles, so Rodan solved the problem by sending Jim away to retrieve some additional data.

Deacon approached. "I am sure that you and Jim will become good friends."

"Did you see what that Owler tried to do? Rearrange my data!"

"Here, Toad, are some helpful files that I extracted earlier for you. They address the evolution of life on Medulla, detailing their biological phases as written by doctors at Brebouillis." Lyanna passed three discs to him. "They will fit your handheld."

Toad was left alone to conduct his research. Deacon, meanwhile, anxiously awaited the arrival of the Aralian Chubby Eaves. For that evening and the next day, Toad concentrated on his assignment with help from Jim. The team had no time for social interactions. Each worked, with only Deacon roaming from station to station to observe their progress. Late on the second day, Toad approached Deacon and stated that he had reached conclusions and was ready to reveal his findings. Deacon dispatched Jim to carry that message to Landrew and to assemble the High Council in the library's chambers just as Chubby Eaves arrived.

"Your timing is perfect. We are ready to review Dr. Roadster's findings to the High Council." Chubby stopped in his tracks.

"Dr. Rodan Roadster? *The* Dr. Rodan Roadster?" Rodan peered around an aisle bookcase with a broad grin, and their eyes met.

Chubby ran forward and hugged him, Aralian style. "Villya, Dr. Roadster. I have read all your articles on Vespering, time travel, and biophysics. There are many hours in space to fill, and reading is a passion with me."

Deacon was astonished as the two immediately bonded with talk of trade vessels and time travel. He sat back and listened to their tales. Chubby later waved Deacon over to join them as they awaited Jim's return.

Later Deacon found himself ambling up the library's stairs again, with his band of Chubby, Toad, Lyanna, and the two Owlers, recalling the turmoil he had created during the last visit. They were the last to arrive. Xudur upstaged Lyanna by positioning herself beside Deacon; Schlegar and Chubby hugged and exchanged pleasantries, which comforted Deacon; Dreveney, Raal, and Eggu-Nitron circled the table as Jim and Gem assisted Rodan. Landrew initiated the meeting with the introduction and biography of Dr. Rodan Roadster, and then he ordered the chamber sealed.

Deacon noted Dithropolis's absence with great sympathy as he stared at the empty chair. His mind wandered for one second to pray for Quobit and that she had found her family safe. The meeting commenced, and Rodan's introduction was sprinkled with his usual "Oh my goosh" and "Oh my chooch," which drew sneers from Xudur and chuckles from Raal, Eggu-Nitron, Landrew, and Dreveney.

"It is so exciting for me to be here to present some findings to you. Oh my goosh, I have heard so much about the leadership and achievements of each of you. I am humbled, but let's move on with the task. After studying the data, I am prepared to offer three points to this group tonight with help of my assistant, Jim." Jim stepped forward to take a bow.

"Okay, the three points I shall address are as follows. One: there exists sufficient evidence in the physical and natural surroundings of Medulla to suggest that these beings can exist in energy patterns and dimensions that are out of our dimensions and therefore undetected by our technology. Two: you are interested in identifying how you can find this creature. This will be difficult. Because we cannot detect it, so I must offer other suggestions, like having the creature find us. Three: Deacon conveyed that you are interested in my opinion on how this creature can be exterminated. What I present to you will be highly conjectural. Reality is the only way to test the validity of my proposed execution methods.

"Let us begin. Jim, step forward and display the first recording, please." The room darkened. Jim opened up the midsection of his body to expose a screen where mathematical equations in numerous variables were littered over thirty lines.

Rodan commenced his recital. "The records submitted from planet Medulla to the Alliance indicate that the gravitational and magnetic fields of the planet Medulla are in a state of constant flux. It is my opinion—and I might add that this opinion was originated by our detective friend, Deacon Coombs—that these fluctuations have provided a severe impediment to the normal evolution of corporeal life on Medulla. So difficult was it to adjust to the flesh that life survived by discovering that the energy fields could leave the body. The biggest strain in evolving in this environment, and remaining on Medulla, is on the cellular structure, so it was only natural to eventually abandon cellular structure through evolution. I might add that the fluctuations must have produced much pain to the bodies remaining on the surface.

"Now, I found that life was not always so difficult. Life on Medulla existed for five million years before the planet's magnetic and gravitational fields commenced this maelstrom. Since it has increased gradually over the last two million years, it has given time for life to evolve and adjust. By leaving the body, the fluctuations are minimized; the magnetic and gravitational disturbances are present to a lesser effect. On Medulla, like anywhere else, life evolved in the direction of the path of least resistance, in the spiritual state."

Rodan grinned from ear to ear. "Deacon Coombs, my esteemed friend, proposed to me that this creature you seek went undetected at the death scenes of both Geor and Como. Being a detective, honoring the facts, he came to the conclusion that his presence was undetected because our instruments are calibrated to the physical parameters of our worlds." A lengthy silence ensued as he sipped on water. "I agree. On the screen, Jim demonstrates additional mathematical equations that represent the energy force fields of the Medullans. It wasn't very difficult to construct this using the files laid open to me.

"In layman's terms, spirits have energy and I determined what activation energy is required to free the Medullans of the detrimental effects of the fluctuations, and thus attain a freedom of uninhibited movement.

"In determining this calculation, I first realized that they would have to be not of the body, as you see in this equation.

"Jim, the next screen, please." In these equations, a shocking truth was revealed. To counterbalance the effects of gravity and magnetism, the spirits moved about in orbitals to counter the forces from the planet. Evolution provided this, just as evolution has provided wonderous aspects in all species. Adapt to survive!" Toad beamed at the audience.

"In time, what evolved are such strong antigravity and antimagnetic fields that complete freedom of movement was achieved."

Rodan was ecstatic. "That is what these last equations illustrate. Given the raw data that I had to examine, it was easy to deduce the required forces for freedom.

"Therefore, Medullans must exist as pure spirits to survive, and any time spent in the solid state, or in the real-world forces of planet Medulla, must be short-lived. The first question was, can the Medullans exist and travel in another dimension unknown to us? In summary, the answer is yes, for if the antifields are as great as I have calculated, then we have no known instrumentation to measure this energy form. Medullans as spirits abide by different laws of electron spin and magnetic moments—so different that we cannot detect or measure them in their state."

Rodan politely requested questions from the audience. Eggu-Nitron asked, "Rodan, are spirits mass?"

"Good question. I agonized over this. Spirit is defined in our world as the feelings of a person as opposed to the body of a being. A spirit is also the soul of life, the energy, the vigor, the disposition of a person. Does all this have to be matter? I say to you that it does not have to be. Therefore, a spirit could be undetected because he has no mass or maybe has minimal mass." There were no other queries.

"The second task is difficult. How do we find Urzel? I strongly recommend that you set a trap to lure him into. In this state of negligible mass and our inability to measure it, the search for Urzel Lok is next to impossible. So I think we must concentrate our discussion on laying a trap.

"Before I address the third problem, let me impart to you an extremely significant finding, which I hope some of you deduced from my previous comments. You look anxious, Landrew."

"Yes. I was sitting here thinking that if what you say is true, that Medullans have these spirits to survive, to be free of the effects of planet Medulla to survive, then it makes no sense to give them corporeal bodies, in which cellular disruption is almost certain to occur."

"Very good, Landrew. Oh my gooch, this is exactly what I deduced too. I spent last night agonizing over this, and I believe that I can state positively that corporeal bodies will be the first step in the extinction of this race. I repeat, the extinction of this race! They see the attainment of bodies as a gift; but the metabolic shock from the instantaneous field effects on the bodies will drive them to insanity, and then to extinction, unless . . . the Alliance relocates them to other planets where forces do not cause these disruptions."

The group announced its dissent. Xudur affirmed, "They will not be allowed to live on Zentaur."

Rodan waited for the outburst of commentary to end. Landrew signaled for him to continue. "Now let us talk about how to rid ourselves of this creature. That is your primary interest. I must strongly advise you that we are dealing with forces that are theoretical. I cannot, my goosh, stand here and swear that what I say to you is real. I cannot guarantee success, because these are untested mathematical models. Rather, based on the data that I have observed to date, I give you my honest opinion."

Jim displayed some new graphs and numbers to support Rodan's theories. "I have calculated the forces that exist inside the creature to combat the exertion he feels. That is, I have translated his metabolic rates into equations. This represents the least amount of energy to escape. Indeed, the atoms of the creature may contain a great deal more energy than this. But there is an interesting principle here.

"To avoid the effects of large gravity fields in space, ships fire bombs of supercompressed mass into space so that they might freely navigate through zones of known meteors, or bypass high-density nebulae. Upon release, the mass instantly provides a body around which they can orbit and then be shot-free. A second later, the mass is dissipated in a billion directions so that its gravity forces cannot cause a permanent unification. The gravitational effects are lost. It is sort of like something we have on Earth, an exploding firecracker, that explodes once into bits, and then each bit explodes into many other bits on a time delay as the bits rub against each other to create a second energy wave. It is during this fleeting second before the second burst that the ship rends itself free of the phenomenon.

"I believe that such a device, calibrated to the forces that hold Urzel together, could scatter his molecules in so many directions, and to such great distances, that the being will be no more, and the chance of gravitational pull to reunite him will become astronomical with a second burst. This method relies upon a key assumption that I have made the correct calculations for the critical energy required to disassemble a Medullan's metabolic energy patterns—enough to blast a Medullan apart forever.

"My second choice is more precise. If this beast could be lured into a chamber where you could compress the molecules, quite simply, the spirit could be liquefied, and then the liquid solidified, and then the solid burned or disposed of in many ways. Or, as in prison, as long as the compression chamber could be maintained, the child would be in solid state and thus immobilized. This obviously would involve a place of safekeeping forever."

Xudur criticized the option. "Total stupidity to keep this Medullan in a place of—what did you call it, Dr. Roadster —safekeeping?"

Deacon pressed Rodan. "Couldn't the spirit pass through the walls of the chamber before we had a chance to solidify it?"

"Lure the creature into the chamber and immobilize it quickly. Xudur, eventually the creature will die, but I don't recommend opening up the chamber to verify it."

"I veto this method," said Xudur. "I have said before that the creature must die. Now! We cannot create, in good conscience, a catastrophic event for future generations."

Landrew asked Rodan to continue. "Lastly, I have calculated that we have the know-how to construct a photon-neutrino bomb, which could blow the creature into irretrievable pieces. However, we would have to exert a significant force—so significant that we would have to capture him in a remote part of the galaxy, or capture him and then transport him to a remote part of our galaxy, before we perform this explosion. The aftermath would create a period of extreme radiation in the sector."

"What do you calculate as the cleansing time?" Landrew asked.

"My guess is five hundred years, to be absolutely safe."

"That option seems destructive and final. Can it be detonated remotely?"

"No. Unfortunately, it can't be imploded by remote operations, Eggu-Nitron. It would require a team to transport and detonate the device. No survivors. On this star chart"—Jim beamed a view of the heavens—"here is a quadrant where life forms are few and the effects would be minimal. You would have to resettle the only occupants hurriedly if this is the choice."

Dreveney asked, "Can you please summarize the risks of each of your options, Doctor Roadster?"

"Option one, the gravity bomb, is risky—very much so. The problem is that the bomb will have to be implanted at close range, and whoever implants it will be sacrificed, or we will have to make the arrangements for shielding at precisely the exact second. We would have only one chance to strike. The device is untested. The damage would be limited to maybe a five-mile radius. It would require sacrifice because it needs to be implanted, and the individual force field for shielding requires a split second to implement. Summary: the problem here is precision, and you need proximity to the being by a sacrificial lamb.

"Option two, the compression chamber, has moderate risks once the being is inside. But as we already admitted, my chooch, how do we get Urzel into such a chamber? Where does this chamber reside for safekeeping until he dies? How do we know when he dies, for no technology can penetrate the chamber? I believe Xudur made a valid point about passing a problem to future generations. However, we can solidify the creature once captured, again by untested technology."

"Option three is the photon-neutrino bomb. This has the least amount of risk. I know that a weapon of this magnitude will be devastating wherever it is fired. It will destroy Urzel. It will destroy whatever is in its path for many miles; it will create a dead zone of radiation for a million miles for at least five hundred years. Summary:

this is a destructive option, but you need only be in medium proximity to your target. The marksman will not survive."

Xudur spoke. "His destruction is a reality. The creature must be exterminated. Or shall we ask Dithropolis how his family is today?"

"Enough, Xudur," Landrew said to curtail her other comments. "The photon-neutrino bomb is an option that requires the discussion of this High Council. This will not be decided tonight. If we use it, it will render a portion of our alliance unlivable and unnavigable."

Deacon rose. "I would speak with this Council now. We—that is, Schlegar, Chubby Eaves, Jim, Gem, Rodan, and I—shall journey to Medulla quickly. There we shall plead with the Medullans for information and assistance to end this matter expeditiously, and with minimal destruction to life and property. We will also interview the mother, Nedilli, whom I hope will cooperate. We must learn everything that we can about Urzel.

"I strongly recommend that the High Council defer any debate on the options that Doctor Roadster has proposed until we return from our fact-finding mission."

Xudur glared at him. "What else do you recommend, Earthman?"

Deacon surprised her. "Landrew, I request that Xudur accompany us to Medulla. The services of a brave warrior are needed for our safety beyond the Owlers, and she can—with your permission—represent the High Council in discussions with Nedilli."

Landrew looked at Xudur, who was glowing in her victory, and nodded. "Thank you," Xudur said.

Raal asked of Rodan, "Isn't there anything else you can tell the Council about finding Urzel Lok?"

"Well, I said already that this is a laborious task. I cannot provide help on this matter. However, Deacon expressed an idea to me earlier that seems as basic and logical as any."

Deacon smiled at his audience. "I believe we have to utilize bait, and there are only two alternatives. The mother, Nedilli, can be offered to attract Urzel, or the sickly other half, the child of Asianda. In the interim, we must all pray that the child lives, for if Nedilli declines to assist us, then our only hope is the sickly child, Urzel of Asianda.

"Urzel Lok is not a god. He is obligated to convert followers to conquer us. But Urzel is a child. He feels for his dying half, or else he would not have risked venturing to Goharn's place. He can be killed by the methods that Toad has outlined, but I fear we cannot accomplish this without the assistance of the Medullans. That is the other reason I have decided that Xudur should accompany the mission. Xudur and I will negotiate a deal with the Medullans for Nedilli's assistance, with Xudur representing the interests of the High Council. We must depart at once, before Urzel uncovers our intent."

Eggu-Nitron was complimentary. "On behalf of the High Council, may I thank you, Dr. Roadster, for your hurried but valuable analyses."

The Council consented, signifying their trust in Deacon's plan and Rodan's efforts. It was their only plan for salvation. "We have not kept the news of the slaughter on Jabu from the populace," Landrew said adamantly. "News spreads faster than I anticipated. I wish the delegation success, and you have my full support to act on behalf of the Alliance to execute the best course of action."

Dreveney was despondent. "I wish you Godspeed, and you have my blessing. In conversation with my dear friend Dithropolis, he described to me the chaos and reign of terror on Jabu. I also wish to report that Quobit has arrived there safely and is with her family, whose desert area is in combat with the savages as a resistance pocket."

Raal did not speak, but Deacon knew of her loyalty to the cause. Landrew solidified the group by saying, "Please keep me abreast of any developments; I in turn will inform you of any movements by Urzel."

Deacon signaled for the others to depart. "We make a speedy exit. The only other issue that I have is to keep abreast of the state of health of the child in Ketapongo. I will leave a communications device with you, Lyanna. It is this device that I told Goharn Lok to contact if developments occur there—either another sobbing in the bushes or a deterioration of the child's health. You must keep me informed."

Landrew looked somber, Xudur stood with confidence, and Schlegar seemed apprehensive. Rodan acted excited as they left, discussing the upcoming journey with Chubby. Schlegar walked with Deacon, expressing his disappointment in Deacon's opinion on the closure of research at Brebouillis.

"I understand your sorrow, Schlegar, but Landrew had to know the options for the future."

Schlegar was despondent. "I heard Doctor Roadster, and we shall spend much time together reviewing his findings on this trip. I am anxious to learn from him."

Back in the solitude of his quarters, Deacon's packing was disturbed by an awkward moment. "I noticed that your plans to Medulla excluded me. I just assumed that I would continue to be part of the group. I can make research contributions on this journey. I really didn't want to remain here just to be a communicator. Or did you make this decision based on emotions?"

"Honestly, yes, I did make the decision based on my emotions. I sense the trip to Medulla could be dangerous. I know that Urzel has spies everywhere, and it won't be long before he finds out that we are at Medulla. I won't risk you, Lyanna. You are the dearest possession that I have in my life. You shall remain here. In addition, I need you here. You are the only link to Asianda if something should happen to Goharn's child or our plans. Events could also transpire here on Earth that I must be apprised of."

She pouted. "I had a penchant for this trip because I wanted to be with you to help you gather facts. I will do as you request though. I accept my responsibilities here—reluctantly, but I accept them."

Lyanna wiped a solitary tear that rolled down her cheek. "Please be careful, Deacon. You have been a short-term event in my life. I don't want to lose you. Please come back."

Deacon responded immediately by hugging her. "Didn't we just have this conversation on Brebouillis?"

She smiled. "I'll help you pack."

"I will return, my dear. This adventure has given me the thirst to live and the determination to close this chapter. Urzel has spies everywhere, as witnessed by Rande's betrayal. Trust no one until I return. I would bet that he has allies on Earth other than Rande."

"Deacon, I thought that while you were on this mission that I would inquire about a posting here on Earth so we could be on the same planet. Schlegar gave me the names of a few doctors to present my credentials to. Would that suit you?"

He embraced her and held her tightly again. "My dearest Lyanna, I took a giant step by saying that I love you, so an assignment on Earth would be a wonderful present for the both of us."

Jim appeared as they were about to kiss. "Ahem, Master, we await you at the metro car. Toad, Schlegar, Chubby, and Xudur have already departed for the *G'uillger*." As they embraced, Jim restated his ahem. The Owler moved forward as Deacon opened one eye and frowned.

"Did you find him, Jim?"

"Whom, sire?"

"The detective who melted from love? The one that you said you would scour the files of literature and history to find?"

Lyanna laughed as Deacon waved good-bye to her. "I also look forward to seeing you again, Miss Lyanna," said Jim. "Perhaps we can play dress up again as in Ketapongo?" Lyanna doubled over and laughed.

"Jim," Deacon said.

"Get out of here, Jim," Lyanna said as the weepiness in her eyes increased. She stood in the middle of the hall until the gray doors had closed and she was all alone with the creaks and groans and loneliness in the abyss of the archives.

On the Planet
of Medulla

On planet Medulla

Deacon used a sharp blade to scrape the gummy orange mud from the sides and bottoms of his heavy skin boots. The entire troop knew that it was imperative to minimize the exposure to the natural atmosphere. Gem lugged the oxygen cylinders as Deacon gasped for more precious air from the hose connected to him. Looking through his protective goggles into the purple fog, he spied more of the same muddy soup. Ahead in the distance, less than two hundred feet away, the dim, massive outline of Xudur was barely visible.

"Gem, signal to Xudur that she must wait for us." As Deacon spoke, he glanced behind to find Schlegar struggling as the smooth bottoms of his feet provided no friction in the slick silt. Twice he tumbled, splashing his fur with sticky, repulsive orange soil. "Schlegar, we are very near the structure."

"Yes, don't wait for me. I will arrive in my own time. Get going. Get us out of this slop. I can't understand why they didn't permit us to land the *Heritage* closer."

"I told you to wear protective footwear."

"It is too late to revisit that error, so move on."

Deacon paused to wait for Schlegar and then the two trudged on together, with Schlegar's arm locked in Deacon's. Xudur was now out of Deacon's sight. *Some bodyguard*, he thought. The incline suddenly became steeper. As Deacon lost his footing, they tumbled and scraped their knees against knife-edged rocks shallowly hidden under the muck. As they fell, the air hose became tangled. Finally, blue lights broke the ghostly mist and a cluster of white-domed buildings came into view, each identified by peculiar blue markings.

Xudur summoned them from the entrance to the largest building. "Here, Coombs! Follow my voice." They had trekked less than a quarter mile, but it seemed forever from where the *Heritage* had docked. As they entered the dome, Deacon and Schlegar discarded the cylinder connections and their helmets to inhale the aromatic oxygen-rich air. Schlegar moved to a foot bath to cleanse his fur and inspect the scrapes on the bottom bones of his feet.

They were in a circular compound furnished only with four benches, a screen, and one very large stone table to seat twenty. There were three bathing units and a foot shower. Liquids to drink and solid brown strips of nutrition lay on the counter. "Gem, have the Medullans initiated the force fields to isolate us from any gravity and magnetic fluctuations of the planet?" asked Deacon.

"Master, this artificial environment is one of three houses on the planet that are immune to the rapid changes. We are safe here, just as Phendal Lok was. Xudur, Schlegar, Deacon, my sensors are registering an incoming energy disturbance that invades our premises. It must be the arrival of the Medullan spirits."

Deacon, Xudur, and Schlegar quickly donned protective eyeglasses to shield them from the hideous sights of the disturbing Medullan apparitions, although Gem had been granted a rare opportunity to capture footage of the alien contact.

Deacon, sensing a disturbance, nervously said, "Nedilli?"

"Welcome, Deacon Coombs," replied Nedilli. "Welcome Schlegar. Welcome Xudur. And to you, Owler, your presence is permitted, and you are allowed to record the proceedings." The voice was soft, soothing, soprano-pitched. It pronounced each syllable succinctly with melodious overtones.

"On behalf of the Alliance and ourselves," said Schlegar, "we wish to thank you for the opportunity for this meeting. We realize and respect your privacy, so are grateful to meet with you."

Deacon waited until Schlegar completed the pleasantries and then expressed his gratitude with "Villya." Behind him, Xudur egged him on to commence business.

Deacon seized the conversation and explained that Schlegar and Xudur and he, with Owler support, were conducting an official investigation on behalf of the Alliance into the deaths of statesmen Como and Geor, and he then elaborated on the details of the invasion of Jabu by Nicosian savages. Deacon had in his possession a miniature energy recorder, and as he cast a downward glimpse to the dials and screens from underneath his hood and opaque glasses, he discovered, as he had suspected, that the presence of the Medullan was not registering as an interruption to the continuous energy phase. Schlegar also had an instrument that showed similar results. When the lengthy tale of Deacon's travels to Brebouillis, Nix, and Asianda concluded, and he had answered all Nedilli's questions about his adventure, Deacon broached the delicate subject of their mission and the power that Urzel was exerting to create chaos.

"Nedilli, Medullans have historically been isolated from the rest of the Alliance. Your son, Urzel, is the first of your kind to venture beyond the planet. By monitoring him on Nix and observing him from the ships *Heritage* and *Sleigher*, we have determined not only that the Medullan race is spiritual, but also that your energy patterns denote that there is a dimension you occupy that we cannot comprehend or detect without your assistance."

Hearing no response, Deacon said, "Nedilli, are you there?"

Gem indicated that the Medullan had departed and then warned of the return. Nedilli explained. "I must apologize to you. There are times when we Medullans have to retreat to a more favorable environment. I shall give you warning when the next uncomfortable episode commences."

Silence prevailed, so Xudur initiated contact again. "Nedilli, we accept your apology as the host. Let us commence into more serious matters. Urzel, your son, has become the most dangerous creature in our worlds. We have confirmed his actions as hostile to the Alliance, as witnessed by the recent invasion of Jabu. We need the cooperation of the Medullans and your personal assistance to arrest his destruction. Please acknowledge this."

Deacon wrestled the conversation from Xudur to diplomatically inform Nedilli of a piece of the tale that was unknown to her—that her son Urzel had decoupled into two entities, one an Earthlike, corporeal, and sickly child residing in Asianda with Goharn Lok; the other a Medullan spirit, insane, vindictive, and powerful, presently engaged in directing the conquest of planet Jabu. He reinforced Xudur's immediate concern for the safety of the Alliance against the unleashed forces of Urzel Lok, the Medullan spirit.

Nedilli finally responded. "We, the Medullans, knew that with the placement of Urzel Lok outside Medulla's environment we were actualizing the risk of Urzel's interfacing with other races. We, the Medullans, also recognized that one day he may escape Nix and venture into the spaces of humans. We, the Medullans, realized that we could not keep secret forever the nature of the unusual dimensions that we now inhabit and that Urzel may ultimately be the messenger of this." Gem was transferring every word and vision spoken to Rodan, who was on the *G'uillger* in orbit around the planet, while also instantaneously translating every word for the group.

The voice faded as Nedilli apologized and receded to her habitat to seek relief from the planet's forces. As she did so, Gem issued another liquid dose of the potion to help the threesome withstand the extreme gravitational rigors.

"Ach! Horrible stuff!" said Schlegar.

Xudur didn't appreciate Schlegar's reaction. "I find the taste and odor quite pleasant, Schlegar. It reminds me of battlefield potions on Zentaur."

Nedilli returned to interrupt Xudur. "Again, I apologize; I am sorry to interrupt our session with these frequent disappearances."

"Understood," Deacon said.

Xudur then said to the Medullan, "We have so much to discuss with you, Nedilli, about your son. We must understand the nature and breadth of the powers of the mind that Urzel possesses if we are to defeat him."

Nedilli unexpectedly left the space and then returned. "Do our physical appearances repel you as well as the natural environment?" Deacon asked. Xudur scoffed at this suggestion.

"Yes, both are repulsive," she replied. "Our spirits cannot tolerate any sustained periods in contact with human forms in which we contact the soiled air that is expelled from your contaminated body cavities. We find this expelled air repulsive. It is also your strange looks, the funny hearing organisms, the beaks that you use to breathe, and your offensive voice tones, but mostly the disgusting habit of allowing the exhaled air to be breathed in again by another body."

Deacon was curious. "Why did you find Phendal Lok tolerable and attractive?"

"Yes, I seem to have contradicted myself. Ah, my Phendal, I never knew such arousal before. I just finished telling you about the repugnant contact with other races, but that is only because of our present state. This is the very dome in which he resided permanently. I visited him many times as he taught me welding techniques, and we spent many hours together, and I grew to respect him. Strangely I found that I could tolerate long periods of his presence, but then he was a humble, graceful creature. Then, accidentally, we interfaced with one another one day when I moved into close proximity to his flesh. My molecules were spread thin, and he found the experience exhilarating and expressed as much to me. I, surprisingly, thought the same and eventually returned the compliment. He wore a recycling mask connected to his cylinder apparatus, so I felt not and smelled not his stench of breath during that interface.

"His feelings for me completely swept away any morsels I had of ill-feelings toward his presence, dispelled all the foul tastes for flesh. Our excitement soon elevated to sexual arousal for each other. Phendal loved me. He told me so often, and I felt the exhilaration of our love. Our love grew so strong that eventually it could not be ignored or reversed. Because of this, I went to our elders and asked permission to become the first Medullan to make love to another species."

After a brief interlude in which she departed, Nedilli returned with joy in her tone. "We asked for artificial insemination exchange, and the elders granted it. Our conception was sanctified by the Alliance quickly, much to the surprise of Phendal and me."

As Nedilli deliberated about her next words, Xudur whispered to Deacon, "I am disgusted at the last comments, as I recall Landrew's ill-fated decision. And now to discover how quickly it was granted."

"Hush," Deacon said to Xudur.

"Our fates were sealed, and I was as happy as I have ever been. My Phendal. My love."

The being departed as Xudur leaned to Deacon to say, "On Zentaur, individual races are not allowed to inbreed."

"Quiet, Xudur, this is not Zentaur. She may still be able to hear your disrespectful comments."

"Xudur," said Schlegar, "love takes many forms. It does not surprise me that you cannot comprehend feelings between two beings of different races. Please, let our hostess dictate the pace of disclosure."

Xudur spat. Then she said, "Such a putrid taste in my mouth. We are in haste. Please convey to her our urgency when she returns."

Suddenly Deacon felt a grip in his stomach and chest. Schlegar expressed alarm. Gem spoke. "There is a strong, sudden quiver in the gravity field. Breathe slowly, all of you. Even though this building has some insulation from the effects, you will still feel slight sensations in your body. It will pass."

Deacon's veins in his arm felt as if they would pop, but just as that sensation culminated, an icy numbness crept up his spine. "I don't know how Phendal managed this every day. And this compound minimizes the effects."

Xudur said, "I ignore these sensations, for they are not life-threatening and are harmless. Be brave like me, Schlegar. Where is that confounded Medullan?"

A different sound paged them. "Deacon Coombs, Xudur, Schlegar, my name is Falthorpe. I am the elder for this region and one of the senior members of the elders. Schlegar, your reputation precedes you, as I have heard of your valiant research efforts. I have overheard all that you have spoken with Nedilli and feel deep regret that Urzel Lok was not put to death years ago as your leaders instructed us to do."

This voice was monotone, sounding much like a mechanical drone. Gem indicated to the group that Nedilli was present with Falthorpe now. Falthorpe continued.

"However, we could not kill this child or any child. Killing is unknown to us. We have had no use for such an act since we left the body, and historical records on Medulla indicate that our ancestors eradicated crime millions of years before we became spirits. Therefore, we planned to abandon the child on the desolate planet that you refer to as Nix."

Xudur asked, "How did you manage to keep the child docile during the voyage? We are interested in how to subdue a spirit."

Deacon complimented Xudur, but there was no reply. Gem said, "They have left."

"Xudur, I think they debate on how to answer your query."

"Force them, Coombs!"

"Not advisable. They will tell us of their own free will and in their own time." As the two conversed further on other issues to raise with Falthorpe, the Medullans returned.

Nedilli spoke. "Urzel is my child. It was I who convinced the elders of this region to disobey the direct orders of the Alliance, and it was I who convinced others in the region to help me transfer him from Medulla to Nix. I located traders who would help in exchange for some valuable materials. We controlled Urzel by placing him in a pressure vessel of a trading ship with a powerful force field around the container. I, as his mother, lured and enticed him into the chamber. As we left Nix, we discontinued the force field and opened the chamber by a timer. We had departed from the area by the time the lock was released."

Falthorpe interrupted. "The love affair between the welder and our own Nedilli brought much joy to our race initially. We, the elders, recognized that this love could represent an achievement that would bring us closer to all the races of the Alliance. The aspirations of obtaining corporeal phase, an aspiration shared by all Medullans, fell on the shoulders of these two lovers."

Nedilli was sad in her comments. "History tells of our proud ancestors who realized that evolution would have to take the path where bodies would be discarded. In those days, the bodies were infested with disease, boils, skin cell deterioration, open sores. The Medullan race was doomed.

"Throughout the years, the energy fields continued to change. We eventually had to have complete escape from the body, and we had to evolve such forces of magnitude to further escape the tribulations of Medulla. But we could not live without some sort of gravitational force, or else we would scatter throughout the heavens, dissipate into ghostly mists of the universe. So we remained in proximity to the planet's gravitational field and to each other to provide self-gravity fields from our own masses.

"Our evolution over time gave us energy fields that provide hiding places from the planet's torturous energy patterns. These places, however, take us into uncharted energy orbitals. If we travel too far away from Medulla, we dissipate; too close, we suffer. So you appreciate our dilemma."

Deacon finally grasped the situation with a new revelation. "Are you in a roundabout way, trying to tell us that even Urzel must return here to restabilize these peculiar electron orbitals?"

Xudur and Schlegar's interests were piqued as Falthorpe resoundingly replied, "You are correct."

An affirmation also came from Nedilli. "When he returns home, we leave him alone, and he ignores us. I never speak to him, but we all know when he is here. Just like human forms, each spirit has uniquely identifying characteristics."

Deacon realized the other important implication and spoke to Xudur and Schlegar. "He needs a uniquely designed ship to travel around the Alliance—one that is especially suited for his molecular structure, one that has proper containment chambers and security."

"Good, Deacon." Xudur actually smiled. "Correct deduction." Schlegar was excited too. Xudur then addressed Nedilli. "How frequent are his visits here? Where does he reside when he returns? By what vessel does he travel?"

"Unknown to me, Xudur," said Nedilli, "since I only hear secondhand of these visitations. He obviously wishes not to speak to me and resents that I abandoned him."

Falthorpe made a bold statement. "The paths that we souls of pure energy travel are now a function of our years of fighting the fields here on Medulla. Life is difficult here for foreigners, but life has now become the most difficult for the primary inhabitants, because sooner or later, we will need to move even farther away from the gravity fields, as the patterns of disruption are intensifying.

"Life as a Medullan is a constant struggle between traveling into dimensions to escape our gravity field, which pulls us into the center of the planet in bursts, fighting the daily fluctuations that disrupt any mass or living being, as we do in front of you in these dimensions, and unsuccessfully fighting the polarized forces. This is not much of a life."

Nedilli spoke again. "Phendal Lok provided a new experience for me. It was so easy to fall in love with Phendal, and he truly loved me and told me so. In his world, sight was denied him and he was shunned; in our world, we accepted him and he was loved. There was always a pervasive peace and calmness inside him that he transmitted to others."

Deacon probed further. "Tell us more about this other dimension."

Falthorpe agreed as Nedilli disappeared. "Our energy sought the paths of least resistance and found them. The rearrangement of energy is done in a manner that is mathematically foreign to you. Our dimensions exist for convenience. We transform and then adapt."

Falthorpe continued. "We wish to locate to a planet where the natural fields won't cause cellular and subatomic disorders. What we hide in is an antimatter, antigravity, antimagnetic field complex. We are doomed unless you discover how to release us. We shall dwell in this tormented house forever. Soon the process of evolution will be too far advanced to reverse it. But Xudur, Deacon, Schlegar, we long to experience your friendship, and the touching, the emotions, the extreme joy of interrelating with one another—what you refer to as social events. We long to travel freely to Jabu, to Zentaur, to see you, to give and to receive. Our only way to travel now is as Urzel does, in specialized compartments that contain and preserve the spirit in space. Thus, we are extremely appreciative of the work that doctors like Schlegar and the physicists on Brebouillis conduct. Thank you, Schlegar, for your efforts to date."

As Falthorpe spoke, Deacon hoped that Chubby and Rodan had captured these comments and were furiously searching the inventory of trade ships for Urzel's possible home away from home. What ship was coming and going frequently from Medulla? What trade ship had specialized pressure compartments to transport the devil? Deacon suddenly had a revelation.

Nedilli took up the conversation. "The time has arrived to leave Medulla. We have conquered the forces here so perfectly that we will soon be absorbed into this dimension forever. Our interfacing with you is convenient only in short periods. We tolerate less and less of these dimensions as time progresses."

Falthorpe said, "Urzel Lok was our only answer to a quick solution. You have witnessed the results, but I hope that you have forgiven Landrew, who displayed compassion for our request. Years of research at Brebouillis by the Aralians, and what do we have to show for it? An offspring who by your own words is unwanted anywhere, who is by your own words a monster. Evolution has not won in this case. There are no quick solutions."

Nedilli expressed sadness in her tone. "Please understand me. I am ashamed of Urzel, yet I love him because he is all that is left of my poor Phendal. I hate him because he . . . he . . ." She broke out in sobs. "He killed my beloved Phendal."

Schlegar, Xudur, and Deacon were not prepared for this development. Schlegar said, "We are deeply sorry to hear this."

Xudur was adamant. "Sympathies play no part in this plot, Nedilli. The child must die. This you must know, Nedilli and Falthorpe. There is only one permanent solution to this crisis. Urzel Lok must be killed."

"He is my son," said Nedilli. "I have mixed feelings about him. I know why you came here, Xudur. You want me to partake in his execution."

Deacon pleaded with them in light of these comments. "Nedilli, Falthorpe, by the power vested in Xudur and by the Alliance, we solicit your sincere help in determining how we can defeat Urzel Lok."

"Tell them, Deacon!" said Xudur. "You Medullans listen to me! We are the Alliance! We command you to help us. Mister Coombs was not entirely correct. The word *defeat* is not strong enough. We wish not to defeat him; I will state again that we wish to kill him!" As Xudur continued to rave and rant, the Medullans left the space. Eventually, all fell silent.

Gem spoke. "I confirm that I have lost their signal, sire."

Xudur couldn't see Deacon's frustrating glare at her through the visor. "Xudur, please allow me to be the one to coax them into this. It won't be easy. I think that you should return to the *G'uillger*."

"When diplomacy fails, orders will be issued to ensure their assistance. Orders by me! Landrew gave me this authority." Xudur pointed her long, scaly index finger at Deacon.

Deacon wasted no time. "Gem, put me in touch with the *G'uillger* immediately."

The voice of Rodan was highly recognizable. "Deacon?"

"Toad, yes, it is me."

"We were worried about you after this prolonged period of silence. Oh my goosh, these data I have captured from the Medullans are fantastic, Deacon. They confirm my suspicions, but there is so much more."

"Toad, listen to me," said Deacon. "Have Chubby and Jim access the data banks on the moon orbiting Medulla. Commence to search the travel logs on the moon to find out what vessels have made an inordinate number of stops to Medulla recently. It is important. Tell them to discontinue everything else they work on to perform this task. I want to find a ship that has precisely controlled chambers for transporting Urzel Lok throughout our trade routes." He paused. "Did you hear me, Toad?"

"Yes, Deacon, you want to find Urzel's ship. Jim and Chubby are on the case. My goosh, as soon as we received the transmission from your conversation, Chubby and Jim hastened elsewhere in the ship to access the records."

Just as he received this confirmation, the two Medullans returned. After a pause, Deacon asked, "Nedilli, I wanted to ask you before you left, did Phendal Lok spend any time in this other dimension, say this fifth dimension?"

"Why do you ask?"

"You said that you loved each other. If you spent time in his dimensions, as you obviously did, then did you take him to yours? Wrap your molecules around him and transport him to yours?"

Nedilli was reluctant to answer. "This is speculation."

"Nedilli, your answer is important. Did you shield Phendal Lok by wrapping your particles of energy around him and transposing him into your world of spirits, protecting him with your molecules as a shield?"

Xudur nudged Deacon while nodding. "Ah, Coombs, I see what you are thinking."

The Medullans left for a brief interlude. Upon returning, Nedilli responded. "I will answer you. Yes, many times I enclosed him within my molecules. He carried his oxygen cylinder with him. Once inside me, he felt the throb of me, the essence of me, and the pulse of my spirit. It was so exciting for both of us and, as Phendal told me, appealing to him. Only tiredness, as I recall, some temporary disorientation, and a strong feeling of light-headedness were the side effects, if that is what you are wondering."

Light-headedness! Deacon remembered the last entry in Geor's diary before his untimely end. He had referred to an inexplicable light-headedness that had overtaken him. Had Urzel actually been bold enough to encompass Geor in his molecules without Geor knowing? Is this how Urzel had forced the Jabu to surrender? Was it how he had murdered Como? Deacon vaguely recalled a light-headed feeling he had experienced on the *Heritage* during the escape from Nix before he changed his mood to expunge it.

Falthorpe was stern in his response. "It is now forbidden to perform this interfacing! You have seen the devastating results." Gem confirmed their absence. It was lengthy.

Xudur asked, "Why do they not return?"

"Their cooperation with us is not an easy decision, Xudur."

"They are fools. It is necessary. It must be done. How can they deliberate?"

Schlegar spoke up. "Quiet, Xudur, for they still hear us. How fascinating all this is, for these regular fluctuations that Gem records and calculates are so close to Toad's theories and calculations."

"Toad is a very bright scholar. I expected him to have a reasonable answer before we departed, and he did!"

There was surge of energy as multiple charges occurred. "It is I, Falthorpe. I have brought with me some of our elders. There is no need for introductions at this time. What do you ask of us? We ask you to speak on behalf of the Tetrad Alliance, Mister Coombs."

Deacon explained. "Falthorpe, if we had the absolute power to bring Urzel under control, your help would not be necessary. However, we are here because we cannot end this terrible reign of evil inflicted on us without your aid. Urzel is on Jabu, maybe in deliberation to attack other planets and races and prey as we speak. He cannot conquer our humanity permanently, but he most certainly possesses the ability to create chaos in our alliance and kill millions of defenseless innocent people. Unless he is defeated quickly, he may be able to hold his conquered prizes by allying with subversives and enemies of the Alliance using Medullan mental powers."

"But what do you ask of us?"

"We respectfully make two requests. What is your advice on how to defeat him? This would involve learning more about your spirit. However, the most difficult request is soliciting your assistance in defeating him, more specifically the involvement of Nedilli."

Nedilli spoke before they all vanished. "I cannot help you."

Gem signaled a quick return, so Deacon issued his plea again. "Nedilli, you must."

"He is the essence of my Phendal. His heart is not pure; his mind is insane. Nevertheless, he is all that remains of my beloved. Please, Deacon Coombs, do not ask me to be a part of your scheme."

"I will be honest with you, Nedilli. We came here to ask you to be the bait."

Falthorpe would not let Nedilli respond. "We will speak honestly with you, Deacon Coombs. We the elders must discuss this request with Nedilli in private. In the interim, your people will find that we have transmitted a great deal more information to your ship, the G'uillger, which will aid in your understanding of our evolutionary traits and our energy patterns. Be thankful for this. We will respond hastily, but I recommend you return to the comfort of your ship."

As the Medullans vanished, Gem instructed Xudur, Deacon, and Schlegar to remove their visors. "The captured footage is excellent quality, sire. They are rather obtuse, ugly characters by your human standards."

Xudur was furious. "Zentaur had no knowledge that the Medullans were withholding valuable information for the research on Brebouillis. Our Alliance scientists are determined to reverse evolution on this planet."

Deacon took up the cause. "From examination of records on Earth and Brebouillis, Xudur, I suspected this. No, I *knew* this. The world of the Medullans is torturous, and as Falthorpe explained, the Medullans will soon be outside the gravitational pull of the planet. The only recourse is to reverse evolution, and my time on Brebouillis made me believe that because our top scientists were working on this problem and have taken so long, they might not be in possession of all the data they require."

"Then why was Zentaur not informed?"

"That," said Schlegar, "is a question for Landrew, Xudur."

JTS H'vington

Deacon commanded a getaway, so they reversed their trek through the mud, which was just as exhausting as the trip to the lodging except they were prepared mentally. Arriving back on the moon of Medulla, they walked to the dock of the *G'uillger* and boarded. Deacon was anxious to confront Rodan and Jim and Chubby, so he scurried down the hallway and found them poring over copious charts and computer screens in the dim, cramped quarters of Rodan. As Deacon entered, Chubby bounced out of his seat and turned to stand before him, arms crossed, eyes bright, smile exaggerated. Deacon knew they had discovered something of interest.

"Okay! Let's have it! I know you well enough, Chubby Eaves. You are bursting with news!"

Rodan arose and said, "Oh my goosh! Wow!"

Chubby pointed to them. "The travel logs on Medulla tell a story."

Deacon looked over the mess. "Which is?"

Toad pulled a printout and placed it on the table. He gleefully said, "Come here, Deacon. This is the log of a transport ship. What a story it tells. It is the ship JTS *H'vington*, out of Melthant, Jabu."

"That's right," Chubby said. "I know this ship well. She was built by traders to transport dangerous chemicals and perishable medicines throughout the Alliance wherever these fragile cargoes are needed. This is in the travel records here, here, and here. Take a look for yourself, Deacon." Deacon perused the highlighted marks. "Guess what we've discovered?" Deacon allowed Chubby to answer his own question. "Deacon, the *H'vington* has docked here on Medulla an unusual numbers of times in the past three years, and her frequent visits document the loading of perishable gases and liquids."

Deacon redirected the conversation. He challenged Chubby and Rodan. "I want concrete evidence that this is Urzel's ship! We can't assume that just based on circumstantial evidence of frequent stops here!"

Chubby reassured him. "The freighter was always delayed, leaving after the same amount of time."

The princess was at the door. "What is this I hear? You have found the bewitched ship?"

Rodan was excited. "It was teamwork. This Aralian Chubby is a gem, Deacon. Chubby discovered that this ship, the *H'vington*, has visited here often, and he has retrieved and recorded the dates and the times. Look, Xudur."

Chubby patted Rodan on the back. "Then my friend Toad investigated what cargoes were being boarded on the *H'vington* and where on Medulla they came from."

Chubby faced Deacon. "I lied to you. I told you that the ships come to Medulla empty. Well, they don't. That is, all of them do except one! The *H'vington*. Look, in every case, in all trips, it carried one chamber of precious gas. One. Only one, Deacon. The transport records don't lie. A single, preloaded precious cargo to Medulla. Take it away, Toad."

"Oh my goosh, the departure of the *H'vington* from Aralia to Medulla with this one precious load occurred just after Como's death. The departure of her from Globiana to Medulla occurred just after Geor's death. The departure from Medulla to Jabu coincides with the attack on Jabu. In that case, one cargo chamber was occupied. It has to be Urzel, stored on board the *H'vington*!"

"We have to be absolutely certain," said Deacon.

"Deacon, these medicines and liquids boarded here on Medulla for transport elsewhere in the Alliance require, my goosh, special compression chambers to prevent spoiling. The settings of these chambers all conform to standard transport practices. However, Chubby discovered that in each case of departure from Medulla, one chamber, the same one every time, had different pressure and temperature settings deviating from standards. This has to be the chamber that transports Urzel."

Rodan hopped across the room. "Then I ran to my calculations that I had been working on. The answer jumped off the sheets." He shuffled through a pile of papers but proudly turned with the solitary display on a computer screen. "Here are the compressional forces needed for the Medullans to exist comfortably. Here are the compressional forces required to transport a Medullan in the vapor state. The parameters of this chamber are set exactly to those settings. Once again, Chubby and I reiterate that the JTS *H'vington* is Urzel's home away from home."

"Why did Urzel or his conspirators not tamper with these records to protect him?" asked Xudur.

Chubby answered. "Thousands of years ago, we Aralians, to prevent smuggling and theft and stowaways, devised the ultimate computer system to catalog all the contents of each trade ship transporting precious goods. Those recordings can't be tampered with. I suspect that Urzel is comfortable with the *H'vington* because no one has unmasked him to date as a stowaway. Who would ever look for a stowaway in a compression chamber? Other than us in this room, who else is searching for him?"

Xudur nodded. "Nedilli and Falthorpe were correct. Urzel returns here to rejuvenate himself in his natural surroundings. He is smuggled on board the same Jabu freighter, which is obviously infested with his coconspirators. But why, Chubby, has no one else questioned the frequency of stops that the *H'vington* makes on Medulla?"

"Xudur, the *H'vington* has proper papers to transport valuable naturally occurring medicines and gases found here on Medulla. The ship has an authorized right of way on every journey."

"So we know where some of Urzel's converts lie," Deacon said. "They exist inside the traders' union to staff his ship and approve trade routes to here."

Chubby looked disgusted. "I will arrest and punish all the guilty after our mission is complete. These files have the list of all the crewmen on the *H'vington*. They are a nasty lot, especially the captain, who has had gross violations before."

Deacon asked Rodan, "How long can Urzel remain in these chambers at these settings? In one journey?"

"The times that Urzel occupies the chamber are for strategic reasons. I suspect that he could remain in the chambers indefinitely, since it is his means of protection at security checkpoints and it enables him to accomplish Vespering without traveling through a vacuum. There are no limits. But someone has to go to the chamber upon arrival at Medulla, decompress it, and release him, or he is stuck there. Therefore, the captain must be a coconspirator."

Xudur said, "Let's find the *H'vington* and blast her to smithereens while Urzel is inside."

"No, my goosh, there is no certainty that Urzel will be destroyed. The methods that I outlined require him to be exposed so we can perform demolecularization. The chamber protects him from the danger of that. My intellectual opinion is that we must lure him out of that chamber in order to kill him."

Deacon added confidently, "We must intercept the *H'vington*, board her with forces to contain his mortal allies, secure the chamber by force field, and then transport the chamber to a remote sector of the galaxy to be the target of a photon-neutrino bomb."

"Don't worry," said Chubby. "I have already sent a message to Aralian Headquarters asking them to track the movements of the *H'vington* and inform us by coded reply of her whereabouts. We will ensure accurate tracking of this ship from this time on. Here's another surprise. Toad and I also verified that the *H'vington* was docked in Ketapongo, coincident with the approximate time that Goharn Lok heard the sobbing in the woods."

"Okay," said Deacon, "I'm convinced that you have discovered conclusive evidence."

Chubby waved a sheet of paper in front of Deacon. "Present in proximity to Nix when you witnessed Urzel on Nix."

"How did the Owlers not identify the *H'vington* as suspicious when she was present on Aralia and Globiana during those critical tragic events?"

"Deacon, I checked Jim's files. The Owler did note the *H'vington*, but for some reason, which we now know is convenient, the crewmen in both instances were quarantined on the ship for the entire stay. Thus the records indicate that the *H'vington* was incapacitated and quarantined and the crew accounted for."

"How many crewmen on the *H'vington* are Aralians?" Xudur asked. "Truthful, dependable Aralians?"

Chubby painfully answered Xudur, not appreciating the satiric accompanying commentary. "The files say about twelve Aralians and three Jabu."

Xudur could not resist. "It seems to me that when this case is resolved, it will be time to examine who is best to rule the future of the traders' union. We seem to be smothered in Aralian deception at every step."

Deacon turned to Xudur. "One problem at a time, Princess, for first we must focus on getting the confidence of the Medullans to help us, and we must find the whereabouts of the *H'vington* immediately." Deacon stepped between the Aralian and the disgruntled Zentaurian. "What else should we know about the *H'vington*, Chubby?"

"Well, she is unarmed, which also deflects suspicion that she might carry a valuable booty. Most of the crew traditionally carry some light weapons."

"I thought," Schlegar said, "that ships with precious cargoes were armed to prevent theft of such valuable merchandise."

"In the past yes, Schlegar, but we decided to destroy the goods or eject them into space rather than have dangerous cargoes fall into the wrong hands. So like the *H'vington*, there are many ships that now roam about unarmed and are prepared to eject their cargo rather than be plundered."

"Which brings me to an interesting point." Deacon asked them all to sit down. "We need to put more thought into our plan to trap Urzel. I think the possibility of luring him to us diminishes each day."

Xudur blurted out and interrupted. "I favor the idea of capturing the *H'vington* and securing the chamber and transporting the demon to the edge of the unpopulated galaxy, as you proposed earlier."

Deacon agreed but waved off Xudur. "The first step of our plan, I believe, is to send a message into space—a message that seeks to contact me, Deacon Coombs, and inform me about the rapid deterioration of the health and almost certain death of Urzel's other half. This message must be subtle but direct enough to capture Urzel's attention, and it must be sent in the line of the *H'vington*. Let's address it from Goharn Lok. I will write the communique and get Lyanna to re-transmit it from Earth by various means. Chubby, I will count on you to propagate some rumor of the imminent death of a sickly, mysterious Medullan child. Let's cover every trade sector."

"You want the *H'vington* detoured to Earth? That's dangerous for all Earthlings."

Rodan objected too. "Deacon, Earth is far too populous to set off any of the instruments that I proposed."

Chubby was suddenly elated, and with his big mouth open, he pounded to get their attention. "Hear me out. I've got an idea. According to the laws of Vespering, one has to turn off manual monitoring devices. Vespering is the time when we should surprise Urzel on the *H'vington*. The response time of individuals concerned about rematerialization will not be soon enough. As the *H'vington* rematerializes in the bowl, we could eliminate the protective cover over the basin early and board before anyone could respond to Urzel's needs. The ship is unarmed, and the crew will be sluggish. The computer will be engaged in other post-Vespering functions, such as checking the safety of the contents of each chamber and clearing regulations for inspection by officials of Earth." The group agreed. "It will only take minutes before the computer recognizes intruders, so we will have to board, disengage security procedures manually, and then storm the chamber to secure its contents."

Then Deacon turned to Chubby. "Hmm. If we already had someone on board the *H'vington* who knew a trade ship, who knew how to shut down security procedures manually within, say, a split second after Vespering."

Chubby trembled. "Urzel knows me! Remember? I would crumble just in proximity to him. What if he leaves the chamber during flight as on the *Sleigher?*"

"Chubby, if our plan fails, he will be unchecked for a lifetime. We have only this one chance. You are a senior executive of the trade union. Don't tell me that you can't find a way to get assigned to the *H'vington* when we locate her, before she reaches Earth."

Xudur piped up. "Use your influence. Practice your skillful Aralian deceit. Get those false papers initiated. Dye your hair. Use lenses to change your eyes. Clip those beautiful nails and lose a few pounds. Change your accent. Are you telling me you can't do that for the future safety of the Alliance?" She then intimidated Chubby by exposing the ruby flesh in her mouth to him.

Jim, with wit, added, "Wear a dress."

Rodan laughed and then said, "I have a remarkable suggestion for Chubby Eaves to go undercover. Fool everyone by acting humble!"

Chubby sneered at the group while they all laughed in a moment of bonding. This time even Xudur bellowed. It was comforting for Deacon to see them as a band of galactic brothers. Xudur's smile was a moment for his memoirs. Deacon issued orders. "Chubby, you and Jim depart before us in the *Heritage* to intersect the next port of the *H'vington*. After you have done so, board her and let Jim steer the *Heritage* back to Earth for our rendezvous. Our business on Medulla is not complete yet, so we will have to follow in the *G'uillger*.

"Only when your papers are cleared to get on the *H'vington*, only then, Chubby, notify me to send the message into space. I will direct Lyanna to dispatch it to all sectors, because if we send it only to the space port or sector where the *H'vington* is docked, it will look suspicious."

Chubby suggested a revision. "Rather than send it to you, Deacon, why don't we send it from Earth to Nedilli on Medulla through numerous space routes but intersecting the route of the *H'vington*? That way we don't tip Urzel off that you are not on Earth. That way he doesn't know that you are in space searching for him."

Xudur agreed. "A great idea from the Aralian. With Medulla's position in the galaxy, no one will be suspicious of multiple routes of a message from Earth to Medulla." Deacon and Xudur grinned at the trader with respect.

As they concurred, Deacon explained the next step. "The message is sent. Hopefully Urzel intercepts and responds. We have to gamble that his allies recognize the names of Nedilli and Goharn Lok and bring the message to him. Now, how to capture him?"

Rodan sifted through his notes. "As I said before, these chambers on the *H'vington* need manual operation to open after docking and Vespering. Indeed, we will have to board quickly even if Chubby delays security procedures for us. The slightest change in docking procedures could arouse Urzel's interest."

Xudur interrupted. "Is there any chance that the chamber has automatic opening controls?"

Chubby sighed, as did Rodan. "Yes, Xudur, there may be controls that Urzel can use to escape." Rodan beamed at Chubby. "That is why, my goosh, we need you, Chubby, on board the *H'vington*."

"When you board the *H'vington*, Chubby," said Deacon, "you will have to locate the chamber, verify that Urzel is indeed inside"—Chubby's eyes were wide—"by checking each control panel"—Chubby swallowed hard—"and then disengage the security controls just before the *H'vington* Vespers."

The Zentaurian placed her arm around Chubby. "A very large courageous feat for a little man. I trust you will complete your task."

Rodan advised the group further. "We must also set up our own force field to contain him so he cannot escape out of the chamber while the *H'vington* is still in the Vesper disc. We must not rely on any force field within the ship."

Deacon was in agreement so far. "Let me explain what should happen next. We have captured Urzel inside a force field in a temporary compressed state inside the Vesper basin. Then we insert the bait, Nedilli, next to Urzel. Nedilli will be transported to our destination in a compressional chamber to control her stress levels, under the same controls as Urzel. However, we have to release Urzel to kill him. Correct, Toad?"

Rodan nodded to signify his agreement.

"Just where do we intend to release him?" Xudur asked.

"We will remain on board the *H'vington*, as I said, and then be routed to the most remote Vesper station in the Alliance. There the force field will be released to allow Urzel to escape from his confines. The very first thing that Urzel will see will be Nedilli, his mother."

We will have to count on the sight of Nedilli to distract Urzel, as Nedilli will talk of happier times with the child. Nedilli will lure Urzel outside the ship. Meanwhile, the marksman, enclosed inside Nedilli's molecules, undetected by Urzel, will take aim. Then she will thin her molecules to permit the marksman to take one shot into the center of Urzel with the photon-neutrino device. Force fields around Nedilli will be automated upon firing. The ship will have to make a rapid escape from their proximity. It will be difficult."

"You, Deacon," shouted Xudur with conviction, "seem to be demanding a great deal from a Medullan who just informed us that she will not cooperate."

"I know what it will take to convince Nedilli."

Xudur's demeanor was unyielding. "I demand to know."

"No, Xudur, it is a private matter."

"Because I would not approve. No doubt some emotional compromise."

"Xudur, you must trust me to make the best deal to save billions of lives."

"Sounds like a conspiracy between you and the Medullans. I shall talk to Landrew privately about this. I demand to know what you will offer the Medullans."

"Listen to me, Xudur. I will divulge to you the deal after it is consummated. If you disagree, we shall talk to Landrew privately to gain support."

"Cocky Earthman. However, you have surprised me so far with your skills and your tenacity, so I will consult with you on this matter later. We all know that time grows scarce. I don't know what you offer the Medullans, but if they take too long to agree to it, then I will assume command of this mission and seek permission from Landrew to take Nedilli forcibly to Earth's Vesper station. I promise."

"I believe you, Xudur, but that will not be necessary."

Xudur puffed out her chest. "Now we should speak of the marksman. We discussed this on Earth. Why hide it? You meant markswoman? Right?"

"It is too early to decide who the bearer is."

"Bearer? What game do you play? Assassin! Say it! Say it is an assassin! I want to hear that word from you!"

"Xudur, it is too early to say." Deacon then uttered the words that he desperately did not want to say. "Urzel will detect any living form inside Nedilli's molecules. Sadly, it will be Gem or Jim—most likely the Owler Gem, based on the specs required." He looked at Gem. *Wires, steel, transistors, computer. No. More than that.* He remembered that night in the library when Gem saved his life. He recalled the icy touch of Mydloan's wire on his throat and thought that to be the end. He recalled the rescue on Nix. Xudur thought that when the time came he would not have the courage to order Urzel's death. Xudur was wrong. It would take all his courage to send Gem to perform this deed, which would lead to the Owler's end. Gem's blue eyes stared back at him.

Xudur was not satisfied. She barked at Rodan for not supporting her position. Chubby ignored her and pretended to gather papers from the floor. Rodan approached Deacon. "When you said marksman, just what weapon did you have in mind?"

"Toad, I was just suggesting a plan whose intent has to be commonly adopted. I did not mean to ignore you. I only assumed that the gravity bomb would have to be fired into Urzel since we have ruled both the photo-neutrino device and the compressional device too risky for reasons previously discussed, although the photo-neutron device is the most certain to be effective."

Toad whispered to him. "The average life span of a spiritual Medullan, ignoring the dissipation of mass and soul, is five hundred and forty thousand equivalent Earth years. I haven't told anyone, my goosh, of this. We can't count on new generations to store this creature."

Deacon and Xudur replied simultaneously to Rodan: "We won't."

"Unless you were referring to a suicide mission, how do you plan to protect Nedilli and the assassin from the blow?" Schlegar asked.

"I was counting on our esteemed physicist, Toad, to design the force field that will save them."

"There is only one risky way, my chooch. The device is fired into the being. One one-hundredth of a second later, a timing mechanism, my goosh, will trigger a small energy field reaching only yards in front of Nedilli. This field will have enough size and strength to protect Nedilli as a gas, since any forces on the gas will cause expansion at no risk. The marksman may not be so lucky, because solids are at risk. There is another problem."

"Which is?" asked Xudur.

"The ideal place to conduct an instantaneous explosion to dispose of the monster is in open space, not in a ship or in any confined area. Therefore, there are two ways to save Nedilli and the shooter. One is to have them adrift in space far from impact of the explosions."

"What is the other?" Xudur asked impatiently.

"The best shot will be to expose the marksman just before implantation of the device."

"It is as we stated before," said Deacon. "We need a sacrificial lamb. You said it, Toad, Nedilli in gaseous state can survive the traumatic shock wave; the marksman cannot." He glanced with forlorn at Gem as he spoke.

"Can't we launch this device from afar with a heat-seeking device attached?"

"No, Chubby, the only way to ensure success, my goosh, is to keep close to the target. Also, we can't fire through Nedilli, so she has to thin her molecules and expose the marksman from close range."

Xudur was curious. "I thought Medullans in the gaseous state were transparent. Won't Urzel see the assassin inside?"

"Good question. I found on the moon some files about the arousal of Medullans and their ability to take on an opaque appearance in the gaseous state. We will have to ask Nedilli to achieve this state and color her molecules to hide the Owler."

"How much space do we need to execute the weapon?"

"About twenty square miles to be sure. Everything in that area will be jostled, hurled, and damaged. However, my calculations are theoretical. I do know that close range is needed for the shot." As Rodan talked, he performed calculations on his hand calculator.

"What about the photo-neutron bomb, Toad?"

"Well, I have new thoughts on that. Any ship releasing Nedilli and the shooter will have to speed a thousand miles away to avoid damage. Both Nedilli and the shooter will perish, even with a force field around them. Any inhabitants of the *G'uillger* are also at risk from the shock wave."

"The bargain I strike with Nedilli involves her living."

"Just as I thought, Coombs," said Xudur. "Your sympathies will be the death of all of us. Remember that. There is always me, who could sacrifice herself for the many."

"You can't, Xudur. Urzel will detect your body pulse, sense something odd on the metabolism. The assassin must be an Owler." Both Jim and Gem stood at attention, as they had from the beginning of this assignment, awaiting instructions from the master, as always.

"You are not the High Council, Coombs." The princess stormed out of the room with Schlegar in tow as Jim and Gem remained attentive in the corner.

Rodan motioned to Deacon to come closer and sit directly in front of him. Chubby joined them after he locked the door. Deacon sensed a mood of secrecy. "There is a serious problem with my calculations, Deacon, that can't be explained. You see, I have calculated the radius of the maximum effects of the current gravity field on Medulla. In order for the Medullans to escape these effects, they must transform further into gases with certain electron orbitals. As I calculated this threshold, oh my goosh, as I calculated the outer effects of the gravity field from planet Medulla, as I . . . oh my goosh, something is very wrong."

Deacon sat up straight and turned to check their privacy. "Which is?"

"Well, the volume and space that the Medullans currently occupy is so great that it . . . ah, ah . . . now exceeds the forces that contain these spirits to the planet."

"I don't comprehend what you say."

"Well, the point is, Deacon, that there exists the high probability that a Medullan can come into our dimensions on a planet anywhere in our worlds and exist as this superior spirit in that world right now. Maybe even dwell on the planet as mass but without the shivering and the quaking right now. They just don't know it."

"So the Medullans have already reached the far exterior and can move into our spaces elsewhere."

Chubby was anxious. "For sure the comfortable way to travel in outer space for Urzel is the chambers on the *H'vington*. Earlier, when I told you that Urzel departed on the *H'vington* from Globiana and Aralia just after the deaths of Geor and Como, I omitted in front of Schlegar and Xudur to inform you that the *H'vington* departed each planet after an event, but in the case of Geor's death, the *H'vington* arrived after Geor's death to retrieve Urzel."

"You are telling me that Urzel found another way to get to Globiana."

"Precisely, my chooch, and I think that he has discovered that he can travel through this new dimension to get to wherever he wants to go. He's found out that the Medullans on Medulla are outside the natural force fields and can use this to travel down paths to . . . travel anywhere."

"So," Deacon said, "there exists the possibility that any Medullan can invade our privacy right now. Urzel is the first to venture beyond, using the dimensions of their space to propel him to us! The Medullans don't know it, but they can at least visit us as spirits anytime they want." His cheeks were riddled with goose bumps as he spoke these last few words.

Chubby was uneasy. "Do you think that they suspect this by observing Urzel?"

"Urzel knows. That's trouble enough."

Rodan explained further. "I have seen wondrous things before in physics. But never have I seen electron orbitals with spins that defy nature and thus occupy space that we can't measure or physically see. These pathways could indeed provide portholes to new horizons, possibly new universes.

"Deacon, this is all new to me. I need time to digest it. All I know is that Urzel doesn't have to take the *H'vington* to ride around the galaxy. I postulate though that it must be inconvenient or painful in this dimension, because Chubby and I were able to confirm that he does travel in the *H'vington* frequently."

"Let us three keep this to ourselves until another time. Agreed?" Chubby and Rodan consented.

"Chubby, you must depart soon to lay your plans to join the *H'vington*."

"My comrades seek the *H'vington*, and Jim has refueled and readied the *Heritage* to depart at a moment's notice. I am uneasy that my fellows have not alerted me to the ship's whereabouts. If it turns out to be Earth, then I suspect we will all be riding on the *Heritage*."

"If the *H'vington* is not on Jabu, then where is it?" asked Deacon. "It could mean that Urzel has Jabu stabilized under his control and is ready to attack his next target. Toad, I need you to investigate if there are any other means to eliminate Urzel without sacrificing lives."

"I think I have exhausted them, but I know your worry. You think that the Medullans will not approve Nedilli to participate unless we guarantee her safety. In any death scene for Urzel, that will be difficult to do."

"Exactly, and I don't think that I can convince Nedilli to enclose her son with her molecules and terminate them both. I might be able to convince her to hide the marksman and save herself. I need to seek out Schlegar and converse with him."

Deacon left Rodan and Chubby behind as he went to search for the doctor. He soon located him in his quarters with Gem, where he noticed the whiteness in his face. "Deacon, wait until you view the footage that Gem acquired on the planet. What hideous creatures, these Medullans. They change shape, color; they look like a mass of open sores and jelly thrown together with discolored moles. They hover, crater, expand, contract, and dart, all with terrible, sickly appearances. To think that this is mankind's greatest achievement in evolution. Disgusting. Thank heavens for the protective visors we wore." He waved his head of hair.

Deacon braced himself with a deep breath and a taste of courage. "Okay, Gem, roll it."

What he saw was worse than he had visualized. It was just as Schlegar had described, as Nedilli and Falthorpe could not remain still. They were ever-palpitating irregular-shaped masses of multiple languid colors, from purples to oranges to mixtures that made him feel queasy. Round protrusions filled and reached the point of bursting. "Enough!" he finally shouted.

"Master, I shall transmit a file to the High Council back on Earth for viewing."

"As long as I do not have to view it again. Tell me, Gem, did you record all the energy patterns?"

"Yes. With copies sent to Doctor Roadster as you instructed."

"Were there any similarities to the person on the mount on Nix?"

"Definitely, sire. I shall summarize the similarities for you in a file. Recognize that not all patterns were recorded, because of our inferior technology."

Deacon gave a thank-you as Jim strode into the room. "Have you completed your assessment of the *H'vington*, Jim?"

"Yes."

"Did you find any evidence of illegal activities being performed on the ship or by her crew?"

"No, sire. Every stop had proper clearance. Every cargo had correct papers. None of the crew was implicated in any wrongdoings, although some of the previous crew members have past criminal records for minor infractions." Deacon and Jim spent the next thirty minutes reviewing activities of the *H'vington* that Jim and Chubby had cataloged. The recently decommissioned ships and missing trade ships were certainly possibilities for transporting the savage Nicosians to Jabu. Weariness overtook Deacon. He wobbled to his quarters, where he found that a transmission from Lyanna awaited him. He was uplifted to see her face on the screen and hear her comforting voice. She was still pursuing employment on Earth, but with no success to date. There had been no communication from Goharn Lok, but Landrew and his wife had invited her to dinner in two nights. "I worry about your safety, Deacon, and I love you. Please find time to reply." As the transmission ended, he pushed the reply button and expressed his feelings, along with a summary of the interview with the Medullans.

His dreams later took him to the planet Medulla, where he ran in the muck from the Nicosians. Then he saw an apparition of Travers, his comrade. Travers. He had forgotten about the little brave warrior with their current hectic pace. As he smiled at Travers, Travers disrobed to reveal Urzel, and the apparition began to shake as a Medullan would. Urzel laughed at him, branding him a fool.

A bargain is struck . . .

"Master." Jim nudged Deacon. "A message has arrived to inform you that Falthorpe and Nedilli await your presence on the planet's surface."

Deacon stretched his arms and yawned. "Inform Gem, Schlegar, and Xudur that I will meet them shortly. How long did I sleep?"

"Four hours." That was not enough for him. In space, it was difficult for Deacon to keep track of time. It seemed as though a great sleep was always four hours; a deep nap, thirty minutes. He washed, shaved, dressed, and departed to intercept the party.

"I have decided to return to the surface with only Gem. I need to negotiate a deal with the Medullans. Xudur, we agreed earlier on this."

Xudur stormed away as Schlegar pleaded his case. "I have spent a great deal of my life working on behalf of these people, trying to rid them of their affliction. What we learn from them on this short trip could prove to be invaluable for my future research. I . . . want to talk to them without visors."

Deacon was emphatic in his response. "No."

"Then for Travers's sake, please, Deacon. I have digested your travel account of the trip to Nix. Your comments were vivid, such as your reference to the poor little brave soul who was shunned needlessly by his father, blasphemed unjustly by the Aralian leader in front of his friends and family. In the end, you said that he deserved a better fate than to travel to Bogeyland and die."

Schlegar grabbed Deacon by the elbow. "After listening to that tale over and over, I agree. Hearing of Travers's bravery on Nix, his efforts on behalf of the Alliance and the traders' union, and Chubby's accounts, I have decided to forgive him. Except that he's gone. So how can I repay him?"

Deacon said it for him. "By bringing to justice the individual who perpetrated the crimes he died for. By reopening his trial so that you might testify on his behalf."

Schlegar's arms hung limp, his head bowed. "I am sorry, Schlegar. If you need any help from me to set the record straight about Travers, you have my allegiance. But I will not allow you to travel with me to the surface this time. You will have to plead with Landrew and the Medullans on another occasion."

Deacon and Gem entered the shuttle. "We will talk upon my return, Schlegar. I have a bargain to strike with these people. I want the success or the failure of this deal to be my sole responsibility. If it fails, Landrew will have only me to blame." As they sped to the surface, Deacon wondered where Xudur had disappeared to and why she had accepted his decision without a verbal assault.

This time, the Medullans permitted a landing spot for the shuttle within two hundred feet, for which Deacon was grateful. It was not long after their arrival in the sterilized dome that Gem urged Deacon to wear the visor in anticipation of Falthorpe and Nedilli's arrival. The pair soon came.

"Villya, Deacon Coombs, we are appreciative of your patience. We have debated your requests."

"Villya, Falthorpe, I am appreciative for the time you took to consider our requests. We also give our thanks for the data transmissions. Time does grow thin, though, in the face of future catastrophes."

"We have talked much with the elders of our region. Unfortunately we have decided that the decision to travel with you must be entirely the will of Nedilli. It is her choice as to the role to play in her son's demise. I know that you find our decision difficult in the face of imminent danger to the Alliance, but we Medullans place highest respect on individual choices in our race. We also condemn killing of other beings. It is not in our nature. The greatest achievements of life are to love and to learn."

"It seems, Falthorpe, that you have led me to a path to converse with Nedilli."

Falthorpe waited until Nedilli returned. "I shall remain to hear your dialogue with our dear Nedilli."

Gem nudged Deacon to commence. "I have a compromise to offer you, Nedilli. You have two children. One we must work together to save; the other we must put to death. So I ask this of you. Come with us on the *G'uillger* to Earth, where we will trap Urzel and transport him to a distant part of the Alliance space. You will not have to be the assassin, but you will have to shield the assassin while his duty is being performed. In return, I will convince Goharn Lok to return your corporeal child to you. He suffers from dipholopic fever and will die if he remains on Earth. He will be much happier in the arms of his mother." He took the pause as a signal to continue. "Here you have a compound where the child can live out its life with you, be loved by you, and possibly extend his life through love and care."

There was a prolonged silence as Deacon paced and Gem stood in the corner. Deacon paused to reflect what a lonely existence Phendal Lok must have suffered before he discovered Nedilli. Suddenly the Owler motioned to Deacon to replace his visor. From the footage he had witnessed, he was not brave enough to contact the Medullans without the apparatus. They returned, and Deacon was anxious. "Have you reached a decision?"

Nedilli spoke. "With great reservation and apprehension, I will accompany you to Earth to try to help you. However, you must also grant me certain terms of acceptance."

"I respectfully will grant your wishes."

"Deacon Coombs, I trust you. Your reputation for fairness and intelligence has been quantified and is known throughout the Alliance. Therefore I will be comforted if you are present wherever I travel. I need your word of that you will not desert me and that you and I will confer and agree on every step of the journey."

"I give you my promise."

"I fear that certain politicians will interfere, Deacon."

"I will ensure your safe condition. I promise to protect the integrity of our joint relationship."

Deacon hoped that the other requests would be so easy to grant. Nedilli continued. "Mister Coombs, I also want your personal Owlers to protect me on this journey."

"My trusty Owlers, Jim and Gem, will accompany us wherever we venture."

"I will not be the assassin of my son. However, if necessary, I will harbor the one whose duty it is to end Urzel's life. But I demand the opportunity to plead with my son first, to beg of him to end this foolishness and return with me to Medulla, to give himself up to the elders of Medulla for trial!"

Deacon suspected as much. "Nedilli, there are many people who feel that the time to negotiate with Urzel is over. Thousands are dead on Jabu because of Urzel's actions."

"No!" she shouted with anger in her voice. "He is my son. My only! I must, as his mother, have this last chance to converse with him, to negotiate with him. Think of what you ask me. Is it not worth this one chance of reasoning? I am his mother. You must be sympathetic to my request." *How Xudur would cringe*, he thought.

"You have asked the ultimate sacrifice from a mother. If I am to subscribe to your request, then please permit me this one opportunity to assure myself that there was no alternative but death. Let me hear from my own son that there is no chance for retribution."

"Nedilli, I cannot promise this appeal. I will champion your cause, but I fear that the High Council will not accept this term."

"Then I do not journey with you to Earth," she replied laconically.

"Nedilli, please, I won't let any harm happen to you. At least journey with me, hear the result of your plea, witness the suffering on Jabu."

She left.

Nedilli and Falthorpe returned together just as Deacon was pacing around the compound, determining how to fix the impediment, worrying that they might not return, creating a significant setback. He was mentally drained.

"Deacon, we have conversed," said Falthorpe. "Nedilli will travel with you to Earth." Deacon gave a sigh of relief. "There are restrictions, as you heard. She must have the opportunity to converse with Urzel before the death scene. She will screen the assassin but allow passage of the death shot only after she is convinced that this is indeed the solution to bring peace back into our galaxy. The other two restrictions must be closely adhered to—that is, your presence and Owler security."

"Thank you, Falthorpe. I must return immediately to Earth. We will make the proper arrangements for Nedilli to travel with us. There is an appropriate compression chamber on the *Heritage*, but you must inform us of the pressure, temperature, and magnetic requirements."

"We will transmit these immediately."

"Good. I am so appreciative of your cooperation. I thank you, Falthorpe, for your support and your trust in me."

"It is a reluctant cooperation born out of necessity."

"We will move into the vicinity of the planet's surface with the *G'uillger* in approximately one hour. We will lower the hatch for Nedilli to board and move her directly into accommodating chambers. Then we will seal the compartment and voyage to Earth."

"Do our conditions have to be divulged to Xudur?" Nedilli asked.

"Yes, Nedilli, I promised this to Xudur. It requires her blessing."

"Xudur will not allow me to talk to my son. I know this."

"I represent the Alliance too. As the supreme representative, I give you my word that your conditions will be honored. Nedilli, these are difficult times, and it is during these times that people, good people, are driven beyond the limits of their reasoning. I want you to assure me that you will not attempt to read the thoughts of others or, more importantly, influence decisions made by me or others—in particular Xudur—regarding Urzel."

"I will not break the laws. I will not intrude into other beings' minds and thoughts. We have sealed our trust, Deacon."

"I must return to the ship to make ready your arrival."

A voice strange to Deacon summoned him with authority. "This plan of evil, Deacon Coombs, intended to fight evil, is foreign to our ways of life. In your care, I place the complete safety of one of our beloved citizens, Nedilli. We cannot conceive of how this will end, what plans you make, but we only ask you to represent the rights of Nedilli on this journey and fight for her rights and safety. We are at the mercy of the Tetrad Alliance. Peace be with you both."

The sound faded, so Deacon and Gem fled to the shuttle, where Gem guided them to the now-orbiting *G'uillger*. As the ship docked,

Deacon wondered what he had just done. Unless he could convince Landrew and Xudor to allow Nedilli to have a chance to speak to Urzel, all was lost. He was convinced the first two conditions were easy; the last condition, impossible. It was clear from their request that the elders did not know of their ability to use the fifth dimension to propel them outside the force fields of Medulla to new planets.

On board, there seemed to be an inordinate amount of hustle and bustle. Jim was in a tizzy; shipmates, recruited by Chubby to assist the readiness of the trip back, were scurrying around like penguins without focus. Deacon sensed panic. *Not another attack by Urzel*, he prayed. He arrived in front of Chubby's room. "What's all the excitement?"

Chubby was breathless. "Shortly after Gem relayed the message to the ship about the results of your meeting, word went to Earth that Nedilli will be our cargo."

Chubby seemed excited and distressed. "I gave orders for immediate departure."

"Why did you give those orders? I told Nedilli we would rendezvous with her in one hour. Rodan has measurements of her pressure compartment to complete. Schlegar hopes for a meeting on the planet if Falthorpe permits. Why usurp my authority?"

Chubby's face flushed. "Because, my dear friend, I did as you commanded me. I checked the logs of the ships traveling to Aralia so that I might flee there on one to intercept the *H'vington*, so Jim could drive the *Heritage* to Earth to save time. I am distressed."

"Take a deep breath, Chubby, and tell me what's happening."

"There is a ship bound from Aralia, and she will be here in four Earth hours. She's Vespering directly in. In the meantime, I suggest that you and Nedilli, Xudur, the Owlers, Schlegar, the *Heritage*, and the *G'uillger* get out of here! Now! You see, she's coming here, Deacon! The *H'vington*! The *H'vington* with Urzel Lok on board."

Deacon felt a shiver.

ON THE *H'VINGTON*

Lookey

Chubby inserted large lenses over his eyes to exaggerate the pupils, hiding the edges just inside his eyelids. The effect changed his eye color to green as well.

Then, sadly, he took a chisel and fiercely slammed it against the beautiful, smooth inner bone of his left foot. Then he smeared brown dye on the roots of his white chest hair to advance his apparent age as an Aralian.

Disinclined to continue, he thought about his mission and opened his medical bag. From it he extracted bandages and wrapped them tightly around his left knee. He practiced the painful hobble that he would fake. Then, with a sorrowful sigh, he shaved a spot under his left armpit and another over his left shoulder, adding a chemical to each spot to present the illusion of a scar with a purple glow.

Finally, he practiced his Yoobian accent, typical of residents of the South Polar Region on Aralia. He decided to leave his hair over his pot belly. When finished, he hobbled to Deacon's quarters. "Aye mate. Where's go ya?" He said when he reached the doorway.

Deacon grinned as Chubby entered. "Green eyes, brown hair, scars, chipped heel, Yoobian accent, burn marks under the arm, gimpy leg. I don't believe that we have met before."

Chubby extended his hand. "Lookey's me name. Tradin's me game."

Gem emerged from Deacon's inner quarters to say, "Don't be fooled, Master. My monitor readings say that this being is Chubby Eaves."

Chubby grimaced. "Damn smart Owlers."

"Lucky for you, Lookey, that this Owler will not be on the *H'vington* to give you away. I gather that you have played the role of Lookey before?"

"I have played him many times, as required to proceed underground to spy for the traders' union. Why, this character is one of me favorites, the rowdy, innocent, fun-loving Lookey! He is a guaranteed snoop!"

"Papers, please?"

"Sure, I will be happy to present my papers to you." Lookey extracted from under his coat a bundled mess of faded yellow and passed it to Deacon.

Deacon was amazed. Lookey had traveled to Circula, Tritaa'ad, Earth, Jabu, Globiana, and twenty more moons, planets, and space stations. "Lookey seems to have been a busy spy. You Aralians are first-class deceivers." Deacon eyed him. "Scars."

"They'll come out with the right dye."

"Green eyes."

"Ah, the ladies love Aralians with green eyes."

"Chip in foot."

"I'll fill it in when I'm finished with the role; knock it out when it's time to play Lookey again."

"Missing hair."

"It will grow back."

"What? Not according to the Aralian biology books I have read."

"That's a myth." He smiled back.

"What? Is there no end to Aralian deception?"

"Oh, it is in the books that I read, too, but my hair grows back. Lookey can't speak for other Aralians, only fer himself. It is and was the old guard, like Como and Schlegar, who believe in those fantastic yarns."

"Travers was missing hair."

"He shaved that same spot regularly when he wanted to be identified. My old friend, Travers, this effort I give is for you. How I miss him in times like these. What else do I need to know about this plan?"

Deacon returned Chubby's identification to him. "Given that your papers are accepted, you will be on the *H'vington*. Before her arrival, we will contact Falthorpe, asking him to spread the word among Medullans that Nedilli journeys to Earth to visit her dying son.

"To ensure that Urzel becomes aware of Nedilli's trip, you must spread the rumor on the *H'vington* of how you overheard that a Medullan named Nedilli journeys to Earth. Don't be overanxious to disseminate the story. Give the rumor a few days to percolate, maybe even a Vesper or two. If Urzel takes the bait, we will need confirmation from you that Urzel still inhabits chamber fifteen, as always. If Urzel remains on board in chamber fifteen, send no message; if he isn't on the *H'vington*, or Urzel is in a chamber other than fifteen, you will have to find a way to get word to Xudur or myself; we will need to know the number of the chamber he occupies before we board the *H'vington* in Earth's Vesper disc."

"Nervous?" Chubby inquired.

"Of course I am. I wanted more time to think this whole scenario out. We get one chance, Chubby. When the *H'vington* Vespers to Earth, Alliance forces will board immediately and set up a force field around that chamber. We will do this before any countermeasures can be enacted on the ship." Chubby remained attentive.

"Nedilli will be brought on board immediately from the *Heritage* and placed beside Urzel's vessel. She will be accompanied by Jim, Gem, Xudur, other security Owlers, and me. Then we will Vesper to the Maxime Quadrant—the farthest leap from Earth, and largely deserted. Rodan and I believe this area is our safest bet to execute our plan."

"Will I have time to disembark?"

"You will have completed your dangerous mission, Chubby, should we get that far into the plan. I suggest you leave the *H'vington*. Once at Maxime, the force field around Urzel will be switched off. The force field around us will be turned on, all except for Nedilli. As the ship moves toward Toad's choice of final destination, Nedilli will be given one last chance to reason with Urzel."

"Once the ship reaches our appointed destination, Nedilli, who shields the assassin, will move outside and coax Urzel with her. We will have to gamble that Urzel follows so we can initiate protective forces around the ship and escape quickly. Then, as the device is fired, the field will be activated at that exact second to protect Nedilli and the marksman. By then the ship will have moved distant from the confrontation. There is no certainty the Owler will be protected; Nedilli's molecules will be spread thin, but it will not be fatal."

Chubby shook his head in disbelief. "I don't believe it. Deacon, I have grown to like you. There are too many variables in this plan. Is Toad sure this will work? Who is to say that Urzel will wander outside the *H'vington* to unite with his mother? Didn't someone tell us that when Urzel is at Medulla, he keeps to himself, and that he has not visited his mother? Why now? Sounds like a ruddy bunch of luck needed. I'll say an Aralian blessing for you. This plan involves accuracy beyond incredible luck. I don't think that you can board rapidly enough to place Urzel inside a force field, let alone activate the force field to protect Nedilli after the shot is fired." His nose twitched.

"This is the only plan we have, Chubby."

Chubby was solemn. "I don't like this. No offense to you and Toad."

"Chubby, I know this is difficult for you, but you need to find the courage to examine the settings on chamber fifteen."

"I'll be a tremblin' all theee way, Cap'n."

"No joking matter."

"Humor sometimes geeets me through these times."

"Chubby, I must warn you. Don't for a single second think of our mission—the *G'uillger*, the Medullans—for if Urzel intercepts one single thought of this plan, we are all doomed and you are a dead man."

Chubby nodded. "It is the plight of my previous crew that drives me."

"Did you make arrangements for the *G'uillger* to be assigned somewhere else?"

"No problem. The skeleton crew will transport her to Aralia for a next mission while all of you flee from here to Earth in the *Heritage*. No doubt she's a faster ship to speed you to Earth."

They hugged. "Nedilli, Toad, Schlegar, the Owlers, Xudur, and I must depart immediately for Earth on the *Heritage* to prepare for your arrival. I must also have enough time to visit with Landrew. Until I see you on Earth, good luck, my friend."

Chubby refused to break the lock. "'Til the Vesper dish on Earth then, matey."

Suddenly Deacon saluted and left. As Chubby trudged down the hallway, Deacon was far ahead of him. He yelled, "Partners to theeee end." Deacon did not hear him.

⟫⟩◈⟨⟪

Four passengers—Xudur, Toad, Schlegar, and Deacon—buckled themselves securely in the *Heritage* on the upper deck while Jim and Gem manipulated the controls to depart Medulla soonest, preferably in the opposite direction of the *H'vington*, which was winging to Medulla. This moment brought back Deacon's last memory of fleeing in the *Heritage* when Travers met his death. Gem announced departure, so the ship proceeded cautiously inside the port on Medulla to connect with Nedilli.

In peril

When Gem signaled that Nedilli had boarded and was safe in the compression chamber on the lowermost engine level, the *Heritage* turned and, in a circuitous route to avoid intersecting the *H'vington's* path, jetted to the Vesper station. As they left, Deacon spied a tiny dot, a shuttle, emerging from the bowels of the *G'uillger* to the docking station. This was no doubt Lookey. His thoughts would always be with him.

⟫⟩◈⟨⟪

Chubby sat in the crewman's lounge staring out into space when, from the corner of his eye, a ship appeared. It was the death ship, and it looked like one ship with two cigar-shaped engines flanking a bulbous, ominous black hulk. On the bottom was written boldly "JTS H'VINGTON."

Chubby's knees trembled. Quickly realizing such a shake would be suspicious, he inhaled slow, deep breaths, recognizing that the moment of retribution for Travers was near. The ship docked, and after a time, he hobbled into the portal. Chubby checked the roster of the *H'vington* and recognized that he had met only one of the crew members before, and only for an instant.

As he ascended the walkway, a voice beckoned him. "You there."

He turned to find a husky young Sorellian approaching. "This ship carries precious cargo. It is off-limits."

"Premission tu board, sir?" he replied gleefully.

"Denied!" The Sorellian was angry. "Be off with you!"

"Papers, sir." Shyly he presented the wad of disheveled orders to the startled officer.

"I am the captain of this ship. I know of no orders to take you or anyone else aboard. No one checked this matter with me!"

"Cap'n, I'm just a loyal Aralian workman of the trade union. I just duz as I am tolds. However, if yee be me off, and take that responsibility, then I'll stay here for the next ship, as I's just met this Aralian hussy in the port office, and she be lots a fun, this hussy."

"Wait here!" He stormed down the corridor annoyedly, leaving Chubby aglow, as he knew that the captain would find that his orders had been approved. Moments later, he charged back. Sorellians are tall, thin, dominant beings, and this one towered over Chubby. "Permission to board based on trade orders, but I'll have you to know that I am not pleased with this and I will have to put you off at the first transfer opportunity."

"Well, I'm not pleased either, Cap'n. As I was sayin', there's this hussy—"

"Silence. What is your name, you crippled slob?"

"My name is Lookey, Captain." Chubby would remember this rude and insolent officer, this potential disciple of Urzel. He exercised discipline by clearing his mind.

"Check with the officer of the daily roster, name of Nurdless, on deck ten. Go on! Get out of my sight!" As he slowly made his way up the corridor, he accented his gimpy gait to annoy the captian. Behind him he heard, "Damn union orders."

Chubby's bout with insolence did not end soon. Nurdless was a surly, tall Aralian, foul of mouth, who barked orders to all within earshot. After reviewing Chubby's duties, Nurdless assigned Chubby to his room, where Chubby happily retreated to the safety of his quarters. There, he temporarily removed the bandages from his knee and sighed with relief. The first step had been accomplished—access to the *H'vington* had been gained! Now the waiting game would begin. At once he thought that he had made a serious oversight. Was this crew all programmed by Urzel to command him? Would Urzel suddenly appear at his door to thrust his will upon him, to brainwash him? Chubby stared at the door and stared and stared. Were these crewmen all soldiers of fortune? Were they aware or unaware of the cargo they carried? Were they under the spell of the demon? "Oh no," he too late realized he had been thinking all these things. "Blank out these thoughts!"

He fantasized about what the saucy imaginary girl in the port office might have looked like. He rested on the bed horizontally, his head on his pillow, until the soft whistle in quarters signaled the crew change. He rebandaged his leg and made his way to the engine room in one of the lower bulbs. As he entered the large room of steel-gray panels and dazzling instruments, someone shouted, "Hey, Lookey, you old sot!"

He turned to recognize his fortune and misfortune. This was a comrade, Warstel, from years ago, when he had been utilizing this disguise to catch smugglers. Warstel would provide any credence he needed as Lookey, but Chubby painfully was reminded of the annoyance that this fellow oozed. Chubby played the role of Lookey to perfection. First he hugged his former mate, criticizing the heap of junk that they traveled in, and then he kidded him about the dangerous cargoes that lay in the holds.

Warstel said, "I'm security! Do you believe it? Me? The biggest scoundrel in the trade, security! Ha ha, if only they knew about me, the captain would be furious."

Chubby did not believe his ears. He did recall what a scoundrel this Warstel was and how he had thieved food from the kitchen and played cruel jokes on those he disliked. How much more incompetence lay in this ship of rogues?

"You? S'curity? Ha ha ha." They laughed together as Chubby resolved to make amends if he ever survived this ordeal.

"I'm off to do my rounds now, Lookey. Later, we drink."

Now Chubby was furious. Traders drinking on a trade ship. It had been so long since he had been in charge of an undisciplined crew that he had forgotten about gross violations.

The ship was docked for what seemed an eternity, obviously waiting for Urzel's return and instructions. Chubby tried to avoid Warstel, but with no luck. It seemed that turn after turn, the irritation was there. It was as if Lookey was unlucky. Suddenly orders for departure came through—for Aralia! Chubby's heart sank. Had Urzel not heard the rumors? Had he not intercepted the communique from Earth to Nedilli? It was up to him.

Chubby did not cherish the thought of being the originator of the rumor for fear that Urzel might want to interrogate the rumor monger. So he devised another plan. He waited patiently for his hourly pain to surface, and surface Warstel did.

Warstel's tale

"Lookey, my Lookey, let's have a drink. I know an isolated spot on the sixth deck. No one will find us there."

"I thoort you'd never ask," Chubby said, chortling. They retreated to a secluded spot and commenced to imbibe, sitting under a bank of stairs, with Chubby pouring his portions down a convenient drain while Warstel was distracted. After overindulgence, Chubby recognized the drunken stupor of the annoying Aralian, who had just spent the majority of their engagement spouting of his exaggerated false heroics.

Chubby initiated his plan. "Tell me more 'bout her."

"About who?"

"You know. This here Medullan, this sorrowful mother who's gone to Earth to see her dyin' son."

"What? I don't know any Medullan."

"Ah," Chubby poked him in the ribs. "You're so drunk that you can't even 'member whats you said to me five minutes ago. You must be a roarin' drunk."

"Oh. Lookey, I'm a-feelin' good, but I can't say that I do remember. I told you 'bout some Medullan?"

Presto, this is it, Chubby thought. "'Course you did."

"Well, what did I say?"

The setup was perfect. This was Lookey's cue. "That 'dullan woman gone to Earth to see someone, possibly her dyin' son. They say that she's got kin there, on Earth. That her son's a-dyin'."

"What? How did a Medullan get kinship on Earth?"

"Yer the one that's told the story to me. How do I know?"

"Oh, well, if I said it." Then Warstel passed out. Chubby gently nudged him, extracted a small knockout pill that Schlegar had said might come in handy, and slid it underneath Warstel's tongue. Now his plan was in place. With security on this floor in a deep sleep, and the seeds of a rumor in him, Chubby rolled Warstel over gently and relieved him of his key cards. Then he stood, spitting out any remnants of the spirits that had passed over his palate, and set out on the most important mission he had ever undertaken.

Chubby summoned courage, although he felt his bodily functions beating inside him. He had to visit chamber fifteen and determine if Urzel was there. Rodan had provided the readings, which would be on the control panels if Urzel was indeed inside the chamber.

He stopped in his tracks. Only the humming of the motors filled his background senses. He looked for security cameras. There were none. Quickly, he went about his business. Down the stairs he limped, his innards churning. He pried opened a steel door and then stepped out into the dead silence on the deck. Beside him the whirring of an elevator signaled its motion, but not to his floor, as the lighted panel indicated.

The area was poorly lit by overhead lights. Lines of containers, row upon row, were in his view. He had memorized the floor plan and knew exactly the number and direction of turns to take him to this devil. He maintained a slight stagger in case a monitor was recording.

Turning a corner, he spied the huge, bulbous, white receptacles of chemicals aligned at the back of the area, so he scooted up a catwalk to oversee the rest of the room and conduct a direct walk to his target. Number fifteen was in his sights from his view above. He quickly returned to floor level as his heart throbbed. He would check all the containers, all the panel boards out in front. He would play the role of security in case he was being watched. Chubby mumbled and sang an Aralian ballad softly.

Oh, say, I'm a rougher, whose travels port to port,
No home, no friends, for I'm never there,
I'm an Aralian trader sort.

He sang the next two verses in his slobbish way as he wound down the aisle, stopping to gaze at all the control panels and observe the readings on each vat. The chambers were about eighteen feet high and round, each with seven steps leading to a window to peer into each unit. The dials were brightly lit in red at floor level with an attached computer.

Chubby leaned against the front of one of the bulbs, noticing from the markings that it was number nine. He sauntered over to the next one, still humming his trivial ballad, still acting unsteady on his feet. This was number eleven, and he could already see the brilliant numbers of thirteen on the adjacent panel.

He let the verses of the Aralian song fill his mind. He dared not pause from his rejoicing in song to let even one foreign thought of the mission permeate his head. He thought about each and every word in the song and slowed down now to annunciate each syllable and repeat verses.

There it was, coming into view. Closer and closer and closer. Number fifteen. What would he do if Urzel were in there staring back at him from the porthole with those eyes? He climbed up the seven steps of unit thirteen to peer inside. "Oh, look at thar bubbling chemicals, Lookey."

Sitting on the top step, he spied up and down the aisle. It was all peaceful except for any sounds that he made. He leaned over and saw the dial on the panel below, noticing that the contents were formaldium. The temperature and pressure were registered in digital red. It was time.

He descended and then hugged the side of the vat to move behind the units. There was knee-high dust and debris blocking his way to the rear, so Chubby sighed and then moved back into the aisle to reluctantly execute the direct approach.

Walking ever so slowly, swaying, thinking not of himself but of the silly traders' song, his head bowed, he counted the paces to number fifteen. Then he stalled, exaggerating his supposed drunkenness with a to-and-fro stagger. Situated on the lowermost step, surveying the situation, he took a swig from a small bottle hidden under his jacket. His metabolism raced as he gulped down the refreshment. Then he stood up straight, moving to examine the dials as Rodan had taught him, while reciting the next verse. He required only that split second to view the pressure and temperature recordings, and in that one second, Chubby's heart froze.

The readings on the dial were just as Rodan had predicted and as the previous records of the *H'vington* had specified. There was absolutely no doubt that Urzel Lok was inside this compartment. Was he watching him from the window? Sleeping? Or intercepting his thoughts of the past three seconds? Chubby ambled away from number fifteen, breaking in a straight line for the end of the aisle but in no hurry. Once there, at chamber one, he sat to rest and hear his heart palpitate. His palms were sweaty, his mouth dry. He needed to gather his composure and head back to the sixth level.

Suddenly, a rustling sound emanated from the other side of the cavern. With courage he stood, slowly walking away from the disturbance, then retreating toward the set of stairs that he had to ascend. A clanging sound paralyzed him. Moving sideways beside one of the elevated bulbs, he sunk to his knees and scoured the floor level for any sign of movement. Darkness met his eyes as he strained to see any images lurking near him.

Cautiously he stood, paced out into the aisle, and, with a fervent stride, counted his paces to the escape hatch. Just as he did so, he heard footsteps behind him. As he stopped in his tracks, so did they. He staggered forward, and they recommenced. Sweat beaded under the hair on his forehead. Now he was concerned.

Chubby moved in the direction of the lifts, and the door opened to an empty carriage. As he stepped forward, a muscular arm grabbed him around the torso from behind, extracting him from the elevator. The brute spun him around to an angry captain. "Who gave you permission to access this deck? Answer me!"

"Why . . . um."

"Who? Answer me, slob!"

Chubby wobbled at the knees and then recognized the necessity for bravery to complete their venture. So he played his role in the act. "I and my bubby had, why we got a wee bit drunken, so I deedn't want him to get into trouble, so I's got to make his rounds for him. So I deed. To make sure he's not in trouble. I am talkin' 'bout Warstel." Chubby delivered his lines with the animation of his arms flinging about and no break in eye contact with the captain.

"Honest. Cap'n, I weren't paying mooch attention to where I was. I was just makin' his routes to make sure that there weren't anythin' harmful happening. No harm, Cap'n. His job got done. I deedn't want Warstel to get into any trouble."

While the captain studied him hard with his stern, chiseled face of displeasure, Chubby heard steps behind him. The voice said, "I watched him; he didn't tamper with anything and seemed to inspect a number of stations on the deck."

Chubby looked over his shoulder to see a tall Globianan, armed with potent weapons, standing at attention. "Why, thank you, mate."

But the captain was furious and grabbed Chubby's fur and tugged him toward him, so close that Chubby could smell his alcohol-laden breath. "You stick to your chores the remainder of this journey. Don't you ever wander onto any deck without permission or I'll put you off this ship by leavin' you, mate, in the cold, dark chamber of outer space. Where is that pathetic drunken mate of yours? Warstel! Where is he?"

In the second he hesitated to respond, he encountered a low blow that knocked the wind out of his cavity, delivered by the husky Globianan blaggard. He sank to his knees, but the assailant was quick to grab him under the arms and hoist him to his feet to face the captain again as he twisted Chubby's arm.

"Where is he?"

"He's hurtin' my arm."

"Speak up or I'll instruct him to break it."

Chubby terminated his false loyalty by responding. "Deck six, at end of large crates, middle aisle, under the stairs."

The captain nodded to the hulk, and the grip was released. "Be off with you, and don't leave your assigned deck again."

"Yes, Cap'n. I won't be of any trouble to you." Chubby hobbled into the elevator as they stood coldly eyeing him. As the doors closed, he breathed a sigh of relief but immediately thought of the worse fate that awaited Warstel. He retreated to his quarters expecting a further punishment that did not arrive. Hours later, encouragement arrived instead, as he received another assignment on deck six.

It was hours before Chubby saw Warstel in general quarters. Chubby suspected by his subdued demeanor that he had received punishment for his delinquency. But Warstel had spread the planted rumor, for suddenly, on their way to Aralia, the orders came to divert to Earth—to Ketapongo! There was a story rampant on the ship that some urgent need was required by this ship and crew there. Shortly thereafter, a crewman confirmed it to Lookey in the mess hall.

"Hear about this Medullan traveling to Earth?"

"Why, yes, I heard it too."

"From Warstel?"

Chubby thought to himself, *Ah, good old Warstel, the blabbermouth. The savior.* Then he addressed his mate. "Why, yes, that's exactly who told me, told me that some 'dullan was goin' to see some sickly relation on Earth."

The conversation was joined by a host of other crewmen as Chubby sat back and basked in his success, munching on his hardened nutrition. The command came. The *H'vington* was preparing to Vesper to Earth.

When Chubby heard it, he felt prickly all over. The moment of truth had arrived. In his belly he was queasy about Deacon's plan, but it was too late to alter it. The final battle was about to commence.

IN THE VESPER DISC

Clandestine plans

There was a note from Lyanna on Deacon's handheld excusing her personal absence on the screen as she was attending an interview meeting at Liberty Hospital. Deacon surfaced a smile as he read it, thinking of how she was relaxing back on Earth, how this could be the beginning of a new and productive relationship for him if she should secure employment there. He read on, growing despondent at a recent communication from Goharn. It read, "Mr. Coombs, the health of the child Urzel is worsening. Unless a miracle occurs, Urzel Lok will die soon, perhaps even before your return to Earth. Goharn."

A miracle, he thought to himself. Was that what they were about to perform? A miracle? Maybe Chubby was right. The details were complex and required precision to accomplish. Leaning rearward in the comfortable high-back chair, he yearned for Lyanna's company at a restaurant, in the park, in the lab, to be with her once again. But Landrew demanded his presence, and it was that meeting that should consume his thoughts. Stretching his khaki-colored shirt over his torso, he departed to the lift, where Gem awaited for him. Down into the catacombs of Liberty to the metro car, they raced through green-lit tunnels, meandering until they were parked in front of the familiar History Archives Library. Gem and Deacon wasted no time bounding up the stairs to meet the Council. At length, Deacon noticed the familiar open door, and he entered to discover Landrew, Raal, Xudur, and Schlegar. The familiar sound of Rodan shuffling down the hall in his cloud of turmoil and scrambled papers was not far behind. Raal seemed particularly colorful to Deacon today in her bluish transparency.

Landrew shook hands heartily with Deacon and then asked him to sit in Eggu-Nitron's chair in his absence. Deacon sensed a taste of success as each member greeted him. After Toad's arrival, the chamber was sealed. Landrew arose and spoke.

"The High Council has met to discuss many issues recently. Since there are important issues on their own planets in these times of crises, the High Council has left the temporary controls with Xudur, Raal, and me. Before we discuss your plan of action, and the requests of Nedilli and her role, there is news from Jabu.

"Deacon Coombs, you are a seer." Landrew leaned forward to praise Deacon further. "Parts of Jabu have been reclaimed by forces of the Alliance. It is as you have told us, that in the absence of Urzel personally, he needs allies to sustain control of his will."

Deacon was anxious to hear more. "What are the details?"

"When you sent word that Urzel was on the *H'vington* bound for Medulla, I ordered Alliance forces onto Jabu to the edge of the capital. The fighting against the savages was fierce, since the savages were well trained from their daily rituals on Nix. They also possessed no fear to fight and die. In time, our modern weaponry and numbers routed the Nicosians until we regained a third of what was initially lost. It is only a matter of time before we conquer the rebels. Not to our surprise, there were other members present in the forces of evil, including Globianans, Aralians, Jabu, Sorellians, Blades, and more."

"Not a single Zentaurian," said Xudur.

Landrew pressed on before Xudur could expand. "Officers of the Jabu forces said that Urzel held their minds for days to immobilize them. But it is as you said, Deacon, that he cannot maintain his stranglehold forever with his mental powers. Nevertheless, many lives were tragically lost; much blood was shed. There is still territory to be retaken. You will be pleased to know that Quobit fought bravely, sustained a minor injury, and has recovered to join Alliance forces to fight again. She sends her warmest regards to you and Lyanna and is anxious to hear of Lord Urzel's defeat by your plan."

Deacon then said, "The only reason that Alliance forces overwhelmed the enemy was because Urzel was absent. He will learn from this lesson in his next attack. He was on Medulla when his troops were routed on Jabu, and that distance is too great for him to maintain mental control."

Landrew sat and nodded. "Xudur has informed us of your exploits on Medulla, and Schlegar has explained many findings. I want to inform you all. You must grasp the fact that Urzel is not defeated on Jabu. He has suffered a setback and lost a third of the ground he held, but I believe that he could easily re-aim his mental abilities to recapture Jabu."

Deacon painted a grave picture to the group. "As long as he is allowed to roam freely, there will be those on our planets who will be willing to follow him for the price of glory, for revenge, for monetary compensation, or for the promise of power, like Rande."

"I totally agree with your synopsis, Coombs!" Xudur said in support. "I think it has become imperative that we dispose of him quickly, for as Deacon has said, he will learn lessons from the experience on Jabu."

Landrew next broached the topic of Nedilli's requests. "Xudur informs me that you have reached a bargain with Nedilli."

"Yes. The first two requests by Nedilli and the Medullans are easily accommodated. I can remain with Nedilli at all times to ensure her role in the plan and ensure that no harm comes to her. It is not unreasonable to go a step further and provide Owler protection, as Jim guarantees her safety at present.

"However, she does not wish to be the instrument of her own son's death. She admits that if there is no other option, she will harbor the assassin." Xudur quickly changed her look from one of support to a threatening sneer. "I am sorry, Xudur, but Landrew and this entire Council need to debate Nedilli's demand." Xudur's stare paralyzed him as her charcoal-black eyes pierced him.

"Nedilli demands to converse with her son one last time, to try as his mother to bring him back to Medulla for retribution, where the elders of the Medulla claim that they will take responsibility for his actions, restrain him if necessary, and even place him on trial."

Xudur rose and addressed the audience. "Responsibility!" she screamed. "Like before? Responsibility? We are talking about an individual who has already committed the most serious crimes in the history of the Tetrad Alliance. This being is solely responsible for tens of thousands of deaths on Jabu. He can, with a whisk of the mind, render all of us disabled." Xudur caught her breath. "Perhaps even me.

"This being is the greatest threat to safety in the history of the Alliance, a worse nightmare than even all the propaganda of alien invasion. Now we hear that the elders of Medulla wish us to turn this child over to them, to the very congregation who initially demonstrated compassion for this beast and are responsible for the dire predicament we are confronted with! My convictions on this matter are a matter of record on behalf of all Zentaurians. We want this child dead! We want the Medullans punished for disobeying a direct order from the Alliance." Xudur exhaled forcefully.

Landrew said to the princess, "I am responsible too, Xudur. I sanctioned this birth. Do you want me done away with? Do Zentaurians want me punished?"

"We are not here tonight, Landrew, to debate your mistakes and your punishment. We are here to take definitive action against this peril that may destroy all of us. I do not promote your death, Landrew. But I promise that I will interfere rather than allow Urzel to return to the custody of the Medullans." As Xudur finished, she growled at Deacon, exposing her ruddy raw flesh in her mouth.

Schlegar spoke next, quietly. "The Alliance has survived many years because we have learned to forgive, Xudur. Landrew, if Nedilli can possibly persuade Urzel to accompany her into the pressure chamber to return to Medulla, this would present a nonbloody solution to a most difficult problem. Diplomacy is a powerful weapon. I remind everyone in this room that Urzel knows only a life of bloodshed and combativeness. If he accepts Nedilli's offer, then I plead with all of you to allow the Medullans to hand out their own justice."

"Your comments are such a disappointment, Schlegar," said Xudur.

Raal spoke up. "If diplomacy fails, there will be no second chance. The demented child will know of our true intentions to destroy him and will be on the alert for attempts on his life. We cannot use Nedilli first for bargaining and then as an aide to kill him. I believe that Nedilli's role must be that of negotiator or assassin, but not both. Therefore, I side with Xudur. We have only this one chance to rid ourselves of him, and Nedilli must be made to understand that she must comply with whatever orders this Council agrees to."

Deacon stated the purposes again. "We can do both, Raal. She has agreed to expose the marksman to terminate Urzel if talks fail."

"If it can be accomplished, Deacon, I favor this approach." Landrew said. "Let us hear from Doctor Roadster on how to accomplish this. Doctor Roadster, you have been patient."

"Oh, my goosh, the photo-neutrino explosive device is such a destructive energy. It cannot be detonated here on Earth. Our plan to take it to outer space is certainly safer for living beings. Depending on the obstacles in the way of the ensuing energy wave, and any meteoric debris and its velocity, this could have a devastating impact as the waves travel through space. I have theorized that the radiation burn will not kill Nedilli as a spirit but will surely destroy the Owler marksman and do damage to the fleeing ship.

"The gravity device is so complicated, but easier to trigger. It could cause enormous damage to the surroundings, and it would require so much more accuracy by a marksman and then the precision to activate a force field to protect Nedilli and the assassin. Then there are humans who will still be in the area. What will happen when the gravity energy wave hits the surrounding environment with projectiles? As I stated before, it requires such precision to carry out this plan."

Xudur turned to Landrew. "I am prepared to perish for the cause."

"The decision will not be easy," Landrew said. "The gravity device, the explosive photon-neutron device—these are risky to human lives. Our plan must exercise precision with the intent to shelter innocent parties. And Xudur, to minimize that loss of life, I sanction Nedilli to speak to her child before we implement more drastic measures. If the plan is executed on Earth, the device will have to be the gravity bomb."

"Landrew!" Xudur shouted.

"Xudur and Raal, I understand your motives. They have weighed heavily in my thought processes. However, I cannot permit mass destruction to be the first consequence of our actions."

"This Council requires three votes to negate your approval."

"I have already spoken to the other members. They are in receipt of your earlier recording, which protests Nedilli's request. They vote with me. Therefore, my action is carried." With that, he circulated a small screen with the consenting votes of Eggu-Nitron, Dreveney, and Dithropolis, for Raal and Xudur to witness.

"If Nedilli is to speak to her child, then it is as Deacon has recommended, with the Owler Gem planted inside her and awaiting the time when talk is no longer an effective weapon and diplomacy is no longer an option. The force field you have designed for the gravity bomb ensures Nedilli's safety. Is that correct, Toad?"

"Hypothetically. Use of the field associated with the gravity device will protect Nedilli, according to my calculations, but not the Owler."

"The plan will be carried out as such," said Deacon, "and I will inform Nedilli of the risks. First we board the *H'vington*, the very second the ship has materialized in the Vesper disc. Then we maintain the force field around Urzel's chamber, chamber fifteen. Thirdly, Alliance forces restrain and subdue the crew, and then, fourthly, we Vesper to the Maxime Quadrant directly from Earth, a difficult Vesper. Toad, will you display the star chart?"

"Oh my goosh, the Maxime Quadrant is sparsely populated. Most of the mining colonies are Owler-operated and in an asteroid belt. The *H'vington* will Vesper to here and then land on the nearest small asteroid, identified by Jim, ah . . . here." He pointed to a spot on the map on the table.

"We will have to lure Urzel outside the ship with Nedilli as bait. We have to hope, my chooch, that Urzel follows. As Gem hides inside Nedilli, we must allow a few moments for Nedilli to converse with Urzel. If those attempts are not productive, then we launch the bomb into Urzel, initiating the force fields around Nedilli and the ship at the precise second the shot is fired."

Landrew, Raal, and Xudur stared back in disbelief. Toad confirmed the obvious. "I know this sounds complicated, but this is our best plan."

"Toad," said Landrew, "the Alliance has used these gravity devices for years and knows the exact area affected for each size of charge. Can't we detonate a gravity charge that destroys Urzel but minimizes damage?"

"I have calculated the minimum charge, and it will be devastating for five miles but must be fired from very close range to affect this Medullan. We need for him to feel the brunt of the charge so that his molecules have no chance for recombination through gravity after the detonation."

Landrew spoke again. "The decision has been made to Vesper this creature away from the civilization of Earth, where too much damage to property and loss of human life is risked if we perform our operations on Earth. It has also been agreed to scramble the molecules of Urzel beyond repair and save Nedilli, as we promised the Medullans.

"I should now call an end to this meeting. I know you have further discussion for the arrangements to intercept Urzel. Raal, Schlegar, and, Xudur, I shall ask you to remain."

"Wait!" shouted Xudur. "Why am I not to be this marksman inside Nedilli? I do not have any human sympathetic element to sway my decision when the time arrives."

Deacon offered his solution. "It is not easy for me to say this, Xudur, but you know that the Owler Gem will not fail us." Deacon had become very attached to the Owler who stood still behind him.

Landrew eyed the Owler. "I agree with the choice."

Xudur protested. "Landrew, you know of my credentials as a sure shot. This Owler is only as good as the programming installed. I, on the other hand, have never missed. I will not fail, Landrew. I am the superior marksperson, not this barrel of tin and silicon and wires." She waved her arm in the direction of Gem.

"Gem is our choice. We voted on that matter earlier, Xudur. Again I have the support of Dreveney, Raal, Eggu-Nitron, and Dithropolis. I am sorry, but your arguments do not go unheralded. I should now ask that the room be cleared."

After Toad and Gem departed, Deacon opened the door to return and say, "Excuse me. Landrew, Raal, Schlegar, and Xudur, I have some final parting thoughts for you. There is a grave discovery that has been brought to my attention by Doctor Roadster. I have known Toad for many years, and I admire and respect his work. His calculations at Medulla have uncovered a serious breach of security." Raal's many pink eyes blinked in rapid succession, a response of interest.

"With great regret and no disrespect intended for the staff at Brebouillis, Toad has calculated that the volume that Medullans currently occupy is considerably larger than the effects of the natural fields in place. It is possible that, like Urzel, other Medullans may very well discover this in the future by accident, or design. Therefore, with great respect, I must reiterate, Schlegar, my request previously that we seriously consider disbanding diplomatic relationships and contact with the Medullans. They are already outside the forces of their fields and could enter at will onto any ship docked at the Vesper station to travel into our worlds." Schlegar shook his head in disbelief.

"Toad has summarized this in this document, which was written entirely by him for your understanding. The facts are indisputable, Schlegar. My esteemed colleague awaits your discussion on this matter. Whatever you debate, you cannot deny that the Medullans are currently capable of coming out of their fifth dimension and into ours as they please."

"How far outside the fields?" Landrew asked.

"By Toad's calculations, currently hundreds of thousands of miles. Enough to interface with a trade ship; and they appear to expand that distance exponentially as time progresses."

"So we use the current treaty to build a new force field," Schlegar said, taking up their cause.

Deacon was ready to depart. "You had to know. I leave you now." As he closed the door, Schlegar argued with Xudur. Ahead Rodan had dropped his discs in the hallway, and as he retrieved them, more spilled onto the floor. Deacon stopped to assist him. "Excellent work, my friend."

"My dear Deacon, it was my pleasure. Now for the hardest part—execution."

Down in the abyss later, Schlegar descended upon them. "Why did you not inform me of this earlier?"

"Toad and I thought that the facts should be divulged in front of the entire group. I apologize, Schlegar."

Schlegar gave an impersonation of Xudur with a Zentaurian grunt, and then wrinkled his nose, Aralian style. As he turned away, Rodan chased him to enter into academic pursuit, thinking that this would appease Schlegar. Deacon, meanwhile, headed to his quarters, where he fell into a rest only to have a familiar odor arouse him. He awakened and rubbed his eyes.

"How long have you been here?"

"Two hours. I sat and read your account of the trip to Medulla in your notebook."

"What time is it?"

"You have slept for ten hours. It is eight o'clock in the morning, Liberty City time. Welcome back." She leaned over his bed to give him a kiss. "I also visited with my second father, Schlegar, who informed me of the details of your voyage."

"Oh, Lyanna, if only Urzel Lok would come to his senses and go away. I dread the experience of encountering him."

"That's why I came. He will arrive soon."

"How do you know?"

"Gem delivered this message for you only minutes ago. I planned to wake you up."

He sat up straight. "Oh no! In twenty hours!" She talked to him, attempting to soothe him as he dashed to the washroom to freshen up. Lyanna prepared some food that he intermittently ate as he sweated and conversed and perused Rodan's notes. "Lyanna, this requires so much to go right: the landing in the Vesper dish, the immediate activation of force fields around the chamber and the *H'vington*, and the escape of Chubby and transport to the outer galaxy. I must see Nedilli at once. My time to remain with her has arrived."

"I saw Xudur doing just that as I entered two hours ago. She was ordering the transport of Nedilli."

"Xudur?"

"Yes. She told me that she was making the final arrangements for Nedilli's positioning in the Vesper station."

"What? That's my job! Now, why would Xudur do that? I briefed her on the series of actions." He knew he had to hurry to Nedilli's chamber to find out what duress Xudur was exerting on the Medullan. In his body cavity, he cramped at the thoughts of the tampering Xudur had done. "I shall eat these last morsels hurriedly, have time for one good-bye kiss, and then I need to find and remain with Nedilli immediately."

"No need," said Gem. "Xudur and Schlegar have already transported Nedilli in her chamber to the moon's Vesper station."

Deacon was infuriated at Xudur's interference. "And Jim?"

"With Nedilli, as you promised, Master."

"Well, I also promised that I would be there at her side throughout. Xudur seems to have violated that."

Gem tried to calm him. "Master, we still have time to depart and reach the moon and converse with Nedilli. We have eighteen hours and thirty-two minutes until Urzel's arrival."

Lyanna agreed. "Calm down, Deacon. I don't think that anyone is bypassing you or usurping your authority. Take a deep breath, my hero." She placed her arm around him and pecked him on the cheek.

"Do you know if Toad has departed?"

"Toad has departed for the Vesper station in a small craft. You and I shall ride in your favorite ship, the *Heritage*. We may even overtake them."

Was he being ignored? What was Xudur up to at this late stage? "I should have been notified like the others."

She placed her arms around his neck. Trying to calm him, she pulled him tighter toward her and then kissed him again and hugged him and walked hand-in-hand with him down the halls to the departing metro car. From the portal of the *Heritage*, she spied the final sight of his brown mop and features before they turned out of sight. Tears welled in her eyes. Deacon had come to the realization that it was his desire to see her again that would keep him alive.

Urzel arrives

The trip on the *Heritage* was excruciating, with every single minute pounding home that this was it—the final confrontation. Could they perform this marvel? The grandness of the glowing disc suddenly came into view. He did not look forward to Vespering again, especially into some distant quadrant of the galaxy. He said to himself, "Never again after this case."

"What, Master?"

"Nothing, Gem." He was strapped in on the control level beside Gem, who had been at his side for this entire escapade. Gem had saved him from the steely clutches of Morris Mydloan. And now he stared at the Owler with the proud red strap. *Is this a sign of evolution that I should feel this way for a machine?* he wondered. He had known for a long time that when the time came to confront Urzel,

Gem would be the chosen one. It was during those early moments after they escaped from Nix that he sketched the plan of attack and knew Gem would be the general. He did not think of Gem as an executioner. And it had been very difficult for him to volunteer Gem as he blurted out the name to the Council, but it had to be done.

"Gem, I appreciate your loyalty to me and what you have done for me. I will never forget you."

"I will never forget you, Master, since every minute of our journey together is recorded in my files."

"How long is your term, Gem?"

"Until I malfunction, until I am injured beyond economical repair, until the Gem Two model is produced in approximately three years." Her taut pink lips pulled into a smile.

Deacon leaned into Gem. "Well, you are a great Owler."

"I wasn't the last off the assembly line. That distinction belongs to Jim. I am proud to have served and protected you." Deacon laughed. "I hope Jim and I are able to serve you again, Master."

Deacon asked, "Have you downloaded all your files to a backup security system?"

"Yes, Master. Jim and I performed that action as soon as it was determined that I shall accompany Nedilli to exterminate Urzel Lok. Jim also has a copy of all my files, including the sermon on Nix and the footage from planet Medulla."

"Do you know your instructions?"

"Yes. While you slept, Toad and Schlegar provided details of my mission. I will hide inside Nedilli until she opens a tiny portal, exposing Urzel to me. At that second, I will fire the device into him. Nedilli will be protected by the force field initiated by Xudur, and I will take the risk of perhaps being damaged."

"Xudur?"

"Yes, Xudur's primary duty will be to place the protective force field around us in one-fiftieth of a second after I have fired. Xudur discussed the timing with Toad, Nedilli, and me earlier. I understand perfectly well, Master, that there is a risk involved. Xudur will have remote access to my program so will know when to activate the fields.

"I realize that I may never see you again, Master. This will require exact timing, and the chances of survival for an Owler are only one in two hundred forty-three thousand six hundred seventeen. Perhaps, it will be me in the two hundred forty-three thousand six hundred seventeen. If not, you still have the last Owler off the assembly line to protect you."

Deacon smiled back. "I will be thinking about you every moment, Gem, and wishing you good luck in your mission."

"Thank you, Deacon Coombs."

They docked, and butterflies swarmed in the pit of Deacon's stomach. The familiar face of Rodan greeted him. "Everything is in place, Deacon. We have the force fields around Urzel's chamber, ready to be fired. I just hope Chubby has had access to the manual security controls. The Owler task force team has confirmed their boarding procedures while we are in the disc. They will escort us. Oh my, I've never Vespered before. Great thrill for me. One last dream realized."

Deacon chastised Xudur as the princess approached him. "You should not have departed without me. I promised Nedilli that I would remain by her side."

"You are," she said. "That is Nedilli's chamber beside you. Touch it. She will sense that it is you."

As Deacon peered inside into a colorless gas, he realized that he was at the mercy of Xudur's word. "I would not have left the moon without you, Coombs, my dear detective. You and I are now intertwined in the future destiny of our worlds."

He picked up his gear, leaving them to proceed to the control center, into the throng of Owler patrols, all waiting for the *H'vington* to land in the disc. They were to be crammed into a small shuttle that would dock onto the side of the *H'vington*; the breach of security would allow access to the ship without warning.

Xudur was at his side. She leaned over and, in his breathing space, said, "You must find me somewhat attractive with my boundless courage and high intellect."

He turned to answer. "Xudur, I am scared to death, for if we fail to execute, this being will have revenge on all of us, you included. Keep your mind on the tasks at hand. Remember, Xudur, you have boundless physical strength compared to Urzel, but he possesses mental powers that belittle you."

"I have no fear. I know Jim is here to protect you, but I too promise to protect you, Coombs. I will save myself, I will see him dead, and I will protect you. These are my three admirable goals."

"The Owler Gem will carry out our orders to the end."

Xudur was persistent and stared at the Owler. "Huh. You may regret your ultimate loyalty to an Owler."

"Why?"

"On Zentaur, Owlers perform menial tasks, which are what they should be relegated to. The most important acts on Zentaur are reserved exclusively for the living beings that deserve them and will ensure their flawless execution."

Deacon ignored her remarks and turned to Gem. "Has there been any communication from Chubby?"

"No, Master, but the time for the *H'vington* to reach here grows near."

Schlegar grabbed his arm from behind as they stood in the crowded glass bulb, looking down into the disc. "We must assume that Urzel is still in chamber fifteen."

A commotion reigned behind as the chamber with Nedilli inside moved on motorized wheels toward the hatch of the shuttle.

"Nedilli will have her space directly in front of Urzel's vat," said Xudur. I personally will activate the force field around Urzel so this vermin doesn't escape. You, Coombs, remain on the bridge with Toad, Schlegar, and Gem to prepare the coordinates for our next stop. Jim will remain with me to escort Nedilli."

Gem said to them, "Xudur, we will Vesper as soon as you transmit to me that Nedilli is in place and the force field is active."

Schlegar's face grew animated. "Look! They are signaling."

Gem turned to confirm. "The engineer signals that the *H'vington* is arriving early."

The group boarded the shuttle while the ionic frenzy outside indicated the Vesper had been activated. In the throngs, Deacon had a clear view of the surroundings, standing beside Rodan, peering down into the disc. A curtain of frenzied purple molecules buzzed around the perimeter of the disc before it appeared as a translucent cover over the top.

"Oh my, oh my goosh, what a sight to see."

"You won't see it anymore. Here. Place these protective goggles on." Rodan reluctantly did so just as the intensity of the motion and the brightness climaxed. There was a flash in the middle of the cover that signaled the penetration of the energy package of the *H'vington* into the disc. "This is it," Deacon whispered to Rodan as a tingle raced around the back of his neck.

With a jerk the shuttle broke loose from its dock high above the Vesper disc, descending slowly, waiting for the split second when it could free fall to beside the *H'vington*. There they waited, directly over the top cover, which had now changed to a blue-and-yellow pattern. Deacon looked over the cramped quarters of security Owlers and police to the elliptical chamber of Nedilli on the far side of the shuttle.

Straight ahead, Jim appeared to break a faint smile. In an instant, Deacon caved at the knees and felt his stomach acid churn into his mouth as they plummeted into the disc, the landscape outside nothing more than a purple blur as they reached the *H'vington* instantly. Outside he witnessed the miracle of Vespering as a shimmering white mass gradually took the shape of a spaceship with vaguely discernible outlines of figures inside.

The signal to disembark sounded. A small, narrow chute extended and connected them to the main deck of the *H'vington*, where life forms were still assembling. As they filed out, they appeared to walk into thin, misty air ahead. Their intrusion obviously indicated that Chubby had manually and successfully disabled the security system, but security patrols would soon be alerted to the presence of the unauthorized visitors.

The noise was deafening as materializing Owlers and crew alike questioned the presence of Alliance forces, with one being asking for the identity of the leader, demanding explanations for this seizure. Nedilli's chamber glided to the elevator bank through the chaos, with Xudur and Jim's help, and was soon gone. The last image that Deacon saw of Xudur, she had her laser gun extracted, ready to disarm or fire into any dissenter.

Deacon took charge on the bridge, continuing to oversee the roundup of the *H'vington*'s crew by Alliance security. Meanwhile, Gem moved to the command center and reprogrammed the *H'vington*'s next route. No time to unload the crewmen. They were taken to an assembly area on a lower deck to be subdued during the next leg of Vespering.

"What is the meaning of this?" The captain shouted at Deacon, his loud voice penetrating the din.

"All you need to know is that, by the power vested in me, the Tetrad Alliance has seized your ship to perform a mercy mission of utmost urgency, and that this ship will be returned to you at its conclusion. Your cooperation is commanded. Perhaps you recognized the Zentaurian, Princess Xudur, from the High Council. Sit down, Captain; there is no time for other explanations. Consume your potion now. We are Vespering immediately."

There were a few dissenters being subdued by Alliance Owlers in the far corner. Unless they consumed the liquid medicine to lessen the shock of Vespering, they would incur severe space sickness upon rematerializing. "I suggest you talk to those three crewmen to point out the situation, or we will have to stun them." The captain complied and strode dutifully to converse with his men. Now Alliance forces had complete control.

Deacon positioned himself beside Gem, his clammy palms sticking to the console, his brow beading, his voice unsteady as he yelled to Rodan. "Don't forget your potion, Toad. We are Vespering any moment."

"Oh my chooch! This is so exciting."

Deacon thought of other adjectives to describe the fear upwelling into his esophagus. The Vesper station crew indicated a clear path as the lights around the circumference of the disc started to blaze. Deacon anxiously awaited Xudur's signal. It seemed to be taking forever. Was something amiss down on the deck?

Then the confirmation came in the form of the previously agreed-upon code on the dashboard. Gem initiated the Vesper process from inside the ship with the contact of engineers in the control center above. Dials twirled in front of the Owler; buttons were pressed. Deacon sat back, closed his eyes, and felt nauseated. The sweat on his back bonded his shirt to the chair.

The countdown began as he pulled his buckle tighter. Through his moist eyelids, he spied the counter. Then he heard that screech that made his blood curdle as Vespering commenced, the sound of the energy particles engulfing and abrading the outside of the ship.

Soon those particles would be here. The computer verified thirty seconds just as he turned to see Rodan, his eyes filled with terror as the sound became deafening.

He extended his hand to Rodan's as the little physicist shook. Rodan's oval face was bleached.

"Twenty-three . . . twenty-two . . ."

"Toad! It's okay." Rodan was trembling. His thick lips were limp and pouty as he tried desperately to spit out words to Deacon.

"Eighteen . . . seventeen . . ."

"Toad! What's wrong?" He looked like he might be having a seizure. Now Deacon was concerned.

Deacon was petrified as Rodan's eyes protruded from their sockets. "Don't Vesper!" Deacon leaned over to Gem. "Can we halt Vespering?"

"Twelve . . . eleven . . ."

Toad squeezed Deacon's hand. "Stop it! Stop it! Look!"

Deacon's heart palpitated and his knees trembled as he shared Toad's concern. The dials on chamber fifteen on the screen were registering zero pressure and normal temperature. Urzel was not in the chamber.

Deacon unstrapped himself and yelled to Gem, saying, "Stop the Vespering! Gem! I order you!"

"Four . . . three . . ."

Deacon jumped a rail and reached a communication device; he summoned Xudur and screamed at Gem. "Urzel's escaped. He's not in the chamber! Stop the Vespering."

"One . . ."

Deacon swallowed hard as objects became mere forms, the desk in front of him hollow but miraculously holding his weight. He expected to awaken, feeling the post-travel effects of Vespering, with those omnipresent associated aches. It didn't happen. They were still in dock. The console was coming back into focus. The bridge was buzzing as Xudur dispatched orders to the Owler patrol. He ran to Rodan to settle him down, made a confirming note of the temperatures and pressures in chamber fifteen, and then descended in the lift with a dozen Owlers to find the activity below chaotic.

As he followed the Owlers down the aisle, he bumped into Xudur coming the opposite way. "Xudur, we have to shut off the force field around the container to absolutely confirm if Urzel is really not inside. We have no choice. We can't waste time by beaming if Urzel is here on the moon or loose on this ship. Where's Chubby?"

"He's okay. I met him on this deck just as I arrived to initiate the field. That Aralian swore to me that Urzel was in that chamber, and according to the readings that Toad gave me, he was still there when we arrived and activated the force field around it."

Xudur drew her weapon, as did Jim and the other Owlers. Jim disengaged the force field, and it whirred to a silence. Deacon's heart jumped as a noise stirred from within the chamber. He grabbed hold of himself to approach and read the dials. He only needed a second to realize that Urzel was not inside.

Jim said, "Xudur, Master, I read a being inside." Just as he said this, the portal to the vat opened automatically, and Deacon's chest heaved as the fingers of a hand grabbed the side for leverage.

The battered face of Chubby emerged into view. Deacon held his head in his hands. The monster was on the loose.

MOONLIGHT SUMMONS THE DEVIL

Surprise

The scene on the bridge was utter chaos. While the engineers in the tower requested directions, Xudur vehemently chastised Chubby for allowing their plan to creep into Urzel's mind, where Urzel unraveled it to now outmaneuver them. "You have failed your assignment, Aralian. To think that Urzel Lok planted the physical form of you to dupe me when I first entered the deck. I thought I saw Chubby Eaves walking toward me, but it was him. He was within our grasp for ten seconds. His mental tricks shall not fool me again."

Schlegar tried to calm a panic-stricken Rodan while the backgound noises intensified as Nedilli's chamber was lugged through the deck for an exit with Jim. Meanwhile, the captain and his crew screamed over the turmoil in the *H'vington*, demanding a meeting with Deacon and Xudur to determine what this seizure was all about.

Slumping in his seat, attempting to clear his head, Deacon felt a blanket of depression over him, so heavy that he couldn't lift himself. Chubby appeared at his side. "Deacon, he was in chamber fifteen as you boarded. I am so sorry that I had a mental letdown that allowed him to read my thoughts. He took control of me at the last second and then locked me in the chamber just before Xudur arrived."

"It wasn't your fault, Chubby. His mind is extremely powerful."

Deacon gazed out into space and back to the blue ball of Earth as Xudur stood beside him and Chubby to say, "This Aralian has exhibited his faults again."

Deacon prevented further arguing. "Xudur, this is no time for disagreements. We have to make for Asianda immediately. We have to make decisions based only on the facts as they present themselves now. If he has escaped to planet Earth, he is definitely in Asianda. We need a new battle plan."

Xudur, Schlegar, Chubby, Rodan, and Gem stood in front of him. He had never been in the position of summoning this much courage before, but this was that moment, and he had to share it with them. "My friends, I have known from my first encounter with Urzel that in the end it could be me who will have to confront him." Xudur growled, but Deacon went nose-to-nose with her. "Don't interrupt me, Xudur. Time is of the essence.

"He fears me, and on this ship as he escaped—to Asianda, I fear—he again had the upper hand against me and let me pass. I am afraid, but this much is known. I know he goes to Asianda to visit his dying other half. That is where Nedilli must be transported; that is where we must go. That is where the death scene must play out."

"To do what?" Xudur asked.

"Xudur, the Owlers will command that shuttle belonging to the *H'vington*. You, I, Jim, and Gem will journey there with Nedilli in the chamber. Toad, you and Schlegar return to Liberty City. Xudur, before we leave, instruct these security Owlers and police to detain all the crewmen until they can be questioned as to their allegiance to Urzel. I don't want any of these beings to leave this ship until our task is completed; I want Urzel isolated from any allies. Chubby, you remain here to assist the interrogation."

Chubby said, "Yes, I have some criminal charges to levy against the captain, and the credentials of some of these traders to check."

"Xudur, before we depart, use your position on the High Council to place the *H'vington* under strict quarantine twenty-four hours a day until all crew are cleared or charged and our business completed. It's going nowhere soon."

Chubby took Xudur and Deacon aside. "I know you want me to remain here, and I agreed. I just had a thought. I have flown one of these exact trader shuttles through space many times, Deacon, and landed in rougher terrains than the hills of Ketapongo. I know you count on Owler navigation, but you will need an experienced captain to put her down as close to Goharn Lok's residence as possible. You will need Nedilli as bait still, and you can't transport that heavy chamber through the rugged, populated streets of Ketapongo. I am that navigator who can land you close by in a pocket of jungle clearing, the clearing below Lok's hut. I think the head of Alliance security quite competent to interrogate all the crew while I journey with you." In this moment of crisis, Xudur agreed.

Deacon did not want to argue as time passed to initiate the action plan. "Okay, Chubby, we haven't a moment to lose. Gem, issue new departure orders and clearance to Ketapongo to the tower. Load both devices, two force fields, and an extra pressure chamber if we need it. We'll talk further on the ship. And load the gravity bomb."

Before Schlegar exited, Deacon pulled him aside. "Unfortunately, Schlegar, I'm not sure what will transpire. You must contact Landrew immediately and inform him to quietly evacuate the hills where Goharn resides as a precaution immediately! You must also tell Landrew to place the entire Earth security forces on alert, for if we fail . . . I don't know what our plan is, except to find Urzel and try to execute the gravity device."

Rodan's face was long; Schlegar's eyes sorrowful. "Good luck."

"Hug Lyanna for me," said Deacon. With that, he left them.

<hr />

The loading was automatic, and they departed in the tiny, cramped shuttle, making use of the double-thrust engines to hurdle them at top speed toward the hills of Ketapongo. "It will get warm in these cozy quarters when we enter the atmosphere," Chubby said. "This shuttle doesn't have the high-tech ventilation system of a new model." Gem assisted Chubby while Jim was positioned next to the cylinder containing Nedilli.

Deacon spoke to the group. "Toad has advised me that Urzel can take one of three forms here on Earth, given Earth's pressures and temperatures. Since he has enormous mental powers, he can supplant the idea into our minds that he is someone else, as he probably did to you, Xudur, on the *H'vington*, when he planted Chubby's image.

That is why we must have Gem and Jim close at all times, since they cannot be influenced by the changeling. We must constantly check with them for verification."

"Perhaps Jim should verify us right now," Xudur said.

"If you are really Urzel Lok, Xudur, then I dare you to strike me down."

"Ha, Urzel will not harm you, detective. I will see to that personally. Neither will he possess me. I will die before I allow him to."

"Business, please. Next, he could be in the phase of a transparent gas, in which case he can surround us at any time. But gases have mass, and we need to equip ourselves with these detectors provided by Toad to measure the atmospheric changes in the density of gas in our proximities, since Toad advised me that Urzel's density is more than the density of air on Earth." Gem distributed the hand-size devices.

Gem explained. "There is one device for each of you. It fits around your wrist, and the dangling screen can be fitted just around your lower arm. Once on Asianda, you will need to take readings frequently to detect his presence. Keep it exposed. Constantly sweep the area. We are looking for an increase in the density reading—a significant, erratic increase."

"For that reason, I will bear the implosive device and turn it on as soon as he surrounds me," a pompous Xudur said.

"You jeopardize innocent lives by doing that, Xudur," said Deacon. "The gravity device remains in the possession of Gem until we assess the circumstances. We must have Nedilli close to Urzel, with her force field activated, to stab at him.

"Lastly, he may, in order to throw us off our balance severely, pose in his natural state—as the ugly life form of a Medullan, with those glowing red eyes. Therefore, we should have these visors at hand. Remember, Toad said that it was the uneven natural forces that cause the ugly quivers of Medullans on their own planet. Earth's forces are more conducive to the stability of Urzel, and he can survive much longer under these conditions than on Medulla. Still, his form will be a quaking sight."

All was quiet except for the purring of the engines as each thought about what Deacon had just postulated. Deacon excused himself and motioned to Xudur to follow to the other side of the shuttle, where they stood in front of Nedilli's chamber with their backs to the wall, across from Jim.

"Greetings, Master."

"Jim, we must converse with Nedilli. Decrease the pressure and increase the temperature slowly." Xudur and Deacon adjusted their visors to shelter themselves from her appearance. The chamber door was unlocked, and Jim stood aside.

"Deacon, what has gone wrong?" Nedilli asked.

"Nedilli, we journey to Earth, to the home of Goharn Lok. Urzel escaped the trap that we laid for him on the *H'vington* in the Vesper disc."

"We travel to Asianda? Now?"

"We are already en route in a shuttle. We will have to agree on a new plan. Nedilli, you will have a brief time to reason with him. Then we must lure him into a chamber where we can transport him elsewhere, or energize a force field around him to constrict his movements, or ask you to . . . help us terminate him by sheltering Gem. Xudur, can we create a dual force field by melding the two fields that we have?"

Xudur's crest on her head waved as she consented. "Yes, that is an excellent idea. That would hold him until we could get an even more powerful field delivered from the security forces in Ketapongo."

"Contact them immediately. Have them meet us in the clearing below Goharn's hut."

Nedilli said, "I will not be the holder of any instrument of destruction."

"That is a last resort. We will try to lure Urzel into the dual force field first. If your talks fail, then you shall retrieve Gem from ground level and hide the Owler to make a strike. Gem will hide inside your molecules. Let your screen down when it is required for the Owler to fire a gravity bomb. Xudur will activate the force field after impact."

Xudur returned. "The authorities have been alerted to our needs," she said. She then asked Deacon to leave. "Xudur, I think that Nedilli's request was that I should stay by her side." Xudur smiled at Deacon.

"I don't think you understand, Deacon. Consider this a mother-to-mother talk, Coombs. I have children too. Please. I want to talk to Nedilli as a female and a mother." Their conversation could be replayed through Jim later, so he granted their solitude, but as he walked away and turned, he saw that Xudur was staring back with a grin. *So unlike her,* he thought. Deacon returned to the group just as Gem informed them of entry into the atmosphere.

"We have high cloud cover on a warm evening in Ketapongo. Chubby will take the controls for the last leg of our journey and set us in a clearing near the base of Goharn's home." Chubby positioned himself in the command seat and shifted the controls into manual landing mode.

The ship permeated the atmosphere with a roar and a bump. Deacon and Gem sat quietly as Chubby adeptly navigated the shuttle toward the island. In one hour he was leveling the craft over thick forests as the thrusters positioned the ship horizontally. Deacon was concerned that Xudur had not returned from Nedilli.

Deacon spied Chubby examining the yellow, red, and gray images on the screen, selecting their location in a convenient flat meadow on the side of the hill below Goharn's dwelling, nearby the same clearing that Jim and he had passed through before. Quietly, the engines were muted to a hiss. The craft tilted and swerved and tilted and dove and leveled as they finally touched down with a thud that jolted Deacon's spine. Chubby turned to say, "Touchdown, as you say on Earth." It would be an arduous uphill hike from here with Nedilli's chamber, but there was less of a chance to signal their arrival that way.

Deacon disembarked to feel the warmth of the evening settling into his bones. Gem cited the time as twenty minutes before eight. The sun was low on the horizon with minutes of daylight remaining at most. Stark gray hues outlined wispy clouds overhead as humidity hung in the air. How could such a beautiful sight precede a bloody encounter? Deacon prayed that nearby inhabitants had been evacuated. He prayed for the safety of their troop. He felt the warmth of Xudur's breath on his neck as she stood behind him. Without turning to face her, he said, "I hope your conversation with Nedilli was not unsettling to her."

"I understand Nedilli's agony more than you do, Coombs. I couldn't imagine abetting the murderer of any of my own children."

Gem took bearings and motioned to the team. "This way." The Owler led Deacon and Chubby, traversing into thick jungle broken by a sole path. Gem lugged the weapon and the two force field instruments. Up and up they climbed for twenty minutes, until Deacon recognized the familiar clearing at the base of Goharn Lok's below them. After checking his proximity for increased gaseous densities and confirming with Gem the absence of more than two beings, Deacon signaled back to the shuttle for Jim and Xudur to commence the trek of carting Nedilli closer. They sat down and waited in silence.

Finally Xudur and Jim appeared, shifted the chamber upright, and made their way to Deacon while Gem departed to plant the ray emitters of a potential force field around the edge of the clearing and likewise deposited the weapon of destruction in an accessible hollow trunk. Patiently, Deacon planted his instructions. "Xudur, you, Gem, and Nedilli remain here. Jim and I will circle around the edge of the clearing and climb the hill to alert Goharn Lok of what might be happening here tonight. Gem, are you sure that you do not register the presence of Urzel?"

"Yes, Master."

"Gem, signal us if you detect the arrival of Urzel. Jim, do not leave even one hundred feet between you and me on this climb. Keep your monitor on to scan in 360 degrees." Deacon looked back at Nedilli, who was emerging from the chamber appearing as a quaking cloud of faint yellowy mist, blocking out vegetation in an irregular, shifting shape. "Xudur, I leave Nedilli and Gem in your care."

Xudur calmly replied, "Hasten back."

With a last burst of energy, Deacon's sore body climbed the hill two steps at a time after they had circled the clearing. His heart jumped into his mouth at every chirp of a cricket, every snap of a twig, every rustle of the underbrush. Deacon stopped yards short of Goharn's hut to catch his breath, and dozens of small green eyes from evening critters peered back at him from out of the twisted shrubbery.

There was an odd, shrill communication between two salamanders behind him. As he turned to look past Jim to the whistling duo, he saw the lights of Ketapongo twinkling below. Just then, the jungle suddenly burst into staccato pulses of the inhabitants. To his left, he noticed the first evidence of a fogbank that was forming and rolling down the hillside. The moonlight was piercing through the canopy and bathing the clearing below. It cut through the darkness of the jungle. It almost symbolized the time for heroism.

He checked with Jim one last time for signs of Urzel. Still negative. He stepped up to the entrance of the hut, where dim lights were vaguely visible from within, and ordered Jim to remain on guard about twenty yards distant. Slowly, he drew the awning aside. As Deacon peered into the hut, his eyes strained to see Goharn Lok huddled beside the glowing embers of his fire—with a startled Lyanna at his side.

"Lyanna! What are you doing here?" He was inside and beside her.

"Deacon, oh, Deacon. You scared us. What are you doing here? You are supposed to be headed away from Earth with Urzel and Nedilli! To the Maxime Quadrant! Off in space. What are you doing here, love?" Lyanna was stunned; she held her hand over her breast, seeming to have been taken by surprise.

Goharn stepped forward to greet Deacon with a handshake, while he continued to fix his eyes on Lyanna.

"Urzel escaped from our initial trap. We believe that he might be making his way here on this night, so we have transported his mother, Nedilli, onto the grounds in the clearing below." Lyanna looked mortified, pressing her hands over her mouth. Goharn appeared to be agitated. Deacon asked again of her, "What are you doing here?" He then added, "You have to get out of here immediately."

"I am studying dipholopic fever firsthand in the child Urzel. I thought it best to visit while you and Urzel were millions of miles away. Also, Goharn contacted me to convey that the child is near death, so I took this opportunity to interview him and take cell samples before he dies." She waved a small cylinder in front of him.

Deacon went outside the hut and asked Jim to move immediately up the hill to the child's hut. Then he reentered as Goharn said, "The child has never been weaker. His body has no fluid retention. There is nothing else that local doctors can do."

He asked of Lyanna, "What is your medical diagnosis?"

"I agree with the local physician Goharn engaged. Urzel the corporeal being will die imminently, and there is no medical treatment to save him. Thanks to Goharn's cooperation, though, we have many more cell samples to study; the child is weak and did not resist my sampling."

"You are leaving right now, Lyanna, for I do not know what scene will play out tonight." He stepped deeper into the hut and tried to grab her under her shoulder.

She pulled away and said, "No."

"I won't have you here when the creature arrives." Deacon continued to try to tug at her. Resisting him, she stumbled toward the doorway. His momentum forced him outside also. He stammered, very upset. "Listen to me. Descend this path to the clearing below and then run as fast as you can. Don't look back! There will be an explosion."

Suddenly, Deacon felt dizzy, as if he were breaking up, as if he was about to Vesper. *That is it. It was all a dream. I was Vespering with Nedilli and Xudur and Urzel and Toad, and we are materializing at the edge of the galaxy. Yes, we were Vespering and are about to rematerialize. I am still in the* H'vington. Why did he think this? Because on his latest attempt to grab Lyanna, his hand seemed to pass right through her arm. *Was I drugged?* He rubbed his throat, his eyes; his temples were throbbing, his head possessed by a light-headed sensation. And then the spinning started.

Deacon knew what had to be done. He was emotional and upset by her presence. He feared for her safety. He stood straight and breathed heavily with long, deep inhales, just as Lyanna had taught him, changing his frame of mind while grasping his head with both hands. He stared at her, her face bathed in a silver shaft of moonlight. Her outline was becoming fuzzy as he reached a calmer state.

Slowly, he took both his hands and commenced a choking grip on his own throat. Harder and harder he squeezed, until he panicked in the confusion. He was on his knees, now visualizing the moon dripping with blood, observing the vegetation nearby with branches as swords, seeing his beloved Lyanna standing before him, sneering at him. As he tightened his grip on himself, she began to hiss at him.

"Yessssssss, tighter! I command it, fool. A fool in love is weak! I knew you would let your guard down for her!" The voice terrified him as he heard it being spat out at him.

Then he regained his composure, changing his mood. Jim had registered two life forms—Goharn and the child. Urzel, as usual, went undetected by their instrumentation in his dimensions and was too distant for them to notice any density irregularities. Deacon's love and concern for Lyanna caused him to overlook that fact. He stood, released his grip, and pointed and mentally screamed at the image, saying, and "You are not Lyanna!"

Using his training that she had taught him, he expelled his anxiety and increased his attraction to her. Releasing himself from the stranglehold by changing his mood and thoughts, he confidently, surely, moved his thoughts to a different gear, his hands now completely free, limp at his sides. He stood erect to defy his challenger. He now understood that his powers could scare Urzel.

He opened his eyes and examined the now-quaking cloud of boils before him. "You won't ever kill me, Urzel Lok! I am your mental match. Come. I dare you! Try again. Come on! Strike at me! Strike at me! Choke me again."

The cloud now magnified in size and began to shiver, expanding and expanding as putrid colors filled the dell. Jim arrived by his side and they heard, "I am Lord Urzel Lok. I will destroy all of you just as I have destroyed the Jabu, Como, Geor, Travers, and all those who have stood against me."

"No." Deacon bravely moved toward the bubbling mass. "You are Urzel Lok, a poor, pitiful child creature. Your reign has been bloody, and it is over. Jabu has been recaptured by Alliance forces in your absence."

"Liar! Liar!" shouted the malefactor.

Deacon stepped forward to the edge of the hill and pointed at him, his body charged with self-assurance. "You are finished! You will die bloody unless you repent." Deacon was furious, but now a strong, sudden gust of wind blew in his face and forced him to grab onto Jim, who stood sturdy.

"We fear you no more. Be gone!" Now the wind reached gale proportions, toppling Deacon as Jim stood firm beside him. Deacon could only hope that with his distraction of Urzel, that Xudur, Nedilli, and Gem had initiated a final assault and readied the force fields for Nedilli and Gem to attack.

"Liar! Liar! Liar!" The form of the cloud faded as Deacon felt a light-headedness. He fought it as Jim stepped forward to warn that Urzel was approaching again and raised Deacon to his feet. Deacon shouted, "I dare you to encompass me so that I can cast you out with my venomous feelings for you!" He stood, arms outstretched, legs together, and his body straight and taut.

"Come, Urzel. Feel the power within me."

Now to his far left, Xudur charged up the hill to catch Deacon as he fell again. The moonlit scene became silent. Xudur and Deacon stood together. "He will return for a final conflict. I am sure of it. He pauses to plan his assault, whatever it may be."

Jim spoke. "The child is on his last few breaths; I checked minutes ago. I should never have left you, sire."

Goharn emerged from his hut. "Why, Deacon Coombs, I feel that I have been under a spell. When did you arrive?" Deacon grabbed Goharn's arm. "No time for courtesies or questions. We must depart the hillside quickly." They scampered down the incline together through the dense brush—Goharn, Xudur, Deacon, and Jim—with Deacon informing Goharn of the Medullan's coming. As they conversed to prepare Nedilli for her encounter, Deacon mentally screamed at Urzel to distract him. "Urzel, you are finished. Your life is over. I will punish you mentally."

As he stood staring into the heavens at the edge of the clearing, taunting a devil he couldn't find, a tempest rose to shake and bend the treetops. Deacon retreated into the forest. "Ready?"

Nedilli was in the form of a glowing orange gas with boils; she signaled affirmatively to him. Deacon addressed the gaseous figure. "Okay, Nedilli, enter the clearing slowly and then summon him to you. If you cannot reach a peaceful agreement, return to camouflage Gem with your molecules and lift Gem into the clearing with your strength. Jim, where is the corporeal child?"

"He is still too weak to move, sire. He registers as still in the hut up the hill behind Goharn's lodge." For a touching moment, all became eerily still, each individual searching the heavens. Then they were directed to the sounds of Goharn sprinting back across the clearing, ascending and relocating the hill. "Let him go," Deacon said to Jim. "He goes to be with the child for his final moments."

Gem and Deacon stood at the edge of the clearing. Xudur and Jim were to their left. Chubby scampered to hide behind a large tree at the entrance to the grove. Nedilli, now a quaking glob of orange, yellow, and green, entered the clearing and hovered about thirty feet from the ground. Then, on the opposite side, Deacon spied a robed figure that appeared on the crest of the hill. Out of the robe glowed those two fierce red eyes that he remembered so vividly from Nix.

The robe grew larger as Urzel expanded. At its sight, Chubby ran into the brush and out of Deacon's sight, seeking deeper cover. Deacon and Gem stood ready just behind the first line of trees. Deacon motioned for Xudur to remain on alert to initiate the dual force fields to encompass Nedilli and Gem. Then Nedilli broke the silence, and with Gem's translator, they heard them converse.

"Urzel, my son, I have missed you."

For the first time, Deacon heard a child's voice from within the robe. "Mother, I have missed your presence too."

"Urzel, it is time to return home with me to Medulla."

"No, Mother."

"Yes, my son. There is so much for you to learn from the elders. There is so much to be taught to you by me. I have been a neglectful parent, and I have failed to give you the teachings and love you deserve. A child should have memories to treasure."

"I will not return to Medulla."

"Urzel, you have brought much misery to many. This is not the Medullan way of life."

Deacon dared to look around the cover and observe the scene. Nedilli was hovering, contracting, expanding, and continuing her plea, rising higher. "You must return to Medulla, where the elders and I will teach you the ways of relating to all forms of life, to respect the right to live by others, to live in true Medullan beliefs."

The voice expressed anger in its reply. "I want to rule. I will bring my friends the Nicosians here to Earth next to teach Deacon Coombs and all Earth people a lesson."

Nedilli became upset. As a mother, she was stern. "Urzel, this is wrong. You are wrong. This is not the way of the Medullans."

Urzel retaliated by saying, "I am only part Medullan. I have the power to choose my own destinies in life. I choose to live as a supreme ruler in these worlds. See my strength, Mama. I have already subdued the entire planet of Jabu! I have followers. Everyone had forsaken me, and now I have risen."

"No!" Deacon heard Nedilli's authoritative tone for the first time. "You have caused death and destruction. This is not the way of any civilized race in our universe. Your followers have already succumbed on Jabu."

"Why do you say this?" There were terrible swirling winds in the glen. Deacon saw Urzel's black robe pulsating with each gusty blast. Then Urzel disappointingly retreated just as Nedilli's molecules expanded to fill the space and move to capture the Owler. Deacon had lost track of Urzel now, as Nedilli had become opaque and blocked him from his view. Deacon turned and sought to find Gem, but with no luck. *Did Nedilli engulf Gem inside her already in that brief second as she expanded? Where is Gem?* The cue had not been given by him, but Gem was clearly missing from behind him. He examined Nedilli's quaking mass.

"Jim, where is Xudur? Locate Gem. Is Gem engulfed by Nedilli? Where is Urzel?"

"I don't know where Xudur is, Master. Gem seems to have disappeared. Perhaps Nedilli encloses Gem and I cannot get Gem's readings. Xudur seems to have left her station to set the force field somewhere up the hill, Master. I can't locate Urzel, as he remains undetected."

"Let's go." The two raced around the edge of the glade until they found Chubby shaking, breathless, and crouching under a wide, low-lying limb. "Have you seen Xudur?" Deacon asked. Chubby was speechless and trembling. "Jim, the gravity device is not where we left it in this log. Gem must have it."

Deacon shivered as Jim signaled to a grove ahead. "We must take cover, Master."

Deacon raced into the spot, but it, too, was vacant. Then a new sight grabbed his attention. He trembled as he saw the sickly child Urzel on the top steps in front of Goharn's place. The child suddenly stood upright, his eyes ablaze, and was strong as he spoke. "See, Mama, we are one again. I am one again. I am Urzel Lok, just as I was at birth."

The child took one step forward into the break of moonlight. His tiny body approached Nedilli. Hallowed as the sight was, it became macabre as he spoke. "Mama, we shall all rule together. I am one again." The child started to cry rivers of tears in a feeble, quavering voice, crying out, "Mother, please join me . . . us."

Both entities now possessed the body, and Deacon wondered if the innocent child could possibly win over the demented spirit and force the spirit out. He turned and then continued his attempt to locate Xudur, keeping an eye on the proceedings in the clearing. He stumbled in his haste.

While on his knees and licking his elbow, he realized that he had just tumbled over the equipment that engaged the force fields. *But if it is here, where is Xudur?* he wondered. Xudur was supposed to be in command of these controls, to activate the force fields instantaneously after Gem fired the blast. Immediately, he arose and examined the jungle. He had an important decision to make. Should he try to affect the force fields once the mother and child were inside the radius? He had not the intelligence to do it. Or should he sacrifice his beloved Owler Gem and Nedilli? This was not the deal.

He needed Xudur's advice. But as he strained to find her, Nedilli moved farther away from Urzel, hovering upward. *What is she doing?* He dared not shout at her, so he tried to invade her mind. Now she moved even farther away and higher as the child Urzel left his feet, possessed by the spirit. *Is she releasing herself from this deal? Is she going to leave me alone to make the decision to destroy Urzel? Is she escaping with Urzel the spirit and the child? Has Nedilli figured out how to retreat them all to Medulla through other dimensions?*

He decided to yell. "Xudur!" He turned to Nedilli. Why would she be hovering like that?

Confusion and panic set in. *What plan is being executed here?* The sight was now mesmerizing as Urzel continued to sob and Nedilli continued to expand even more. Now she opened herself to the child. Deacon saw her shape change to that of a true Medullan, and she projected repulsive, shaking protrusions to coax Urzel to her and cradle him. "Come here, my son."

Jim stood at his side. "Analysis, Jim. What is transpiring? What is happening? Surely Urzel will detect Gem if she opens herself up like that too soon. Go to the force fields, Jim. In Xudur's absence, we will set them on my signal." Jim knelt down beside the apparatus and prepared to initiate the energy field upon Deacon's command. He raised his arm to signal, and as the child became airborne, Deacon realized Nedilli's plan to ensure that the force fields would completely surround all of them. The plan might yet work.

"Urzel, my son, come here. I love you, Urzel."

That's it, Nedilli. he thought. *Lure them into your molecules and Jim can set the force field around you.*

Deacon was glued as the child glided into the outstretched arms, then stopped, and then moved away. Deacon knew that the two entities inside fought for control, the child wanting the caress of Nedilli, the spirit now hesitant and resisting. As Urzel cautiously moved within range, Deacon became further confused by Jim.

"Sire, the equipment has been sabotaged. Observe." He rotated the box for Deacon to see. Deacon was bewildered. *Now what?* He suddenly spied something disturbing the undergrowth. Deacon jumped around the bushes and in the distance saw Gem, disabled. His heart pounded vigorously; he did not know what to think of this. His mind relaxed, and a thought intruded. Then he shouted to Jim. "Run, Jim! Run!"

The scratchy bushes tore at his pants as he made a direct line for Gem. He lost sight of the Owler, so he stopped to catch his breath. In a glimmer of moonlight, he saw Nedilli now only feet from her son. She was continuing to talk to him. Her mass of green and yellow had transformed into a soothing soft red, but her appearance started to metamorphose into the truly repulsive form that he had witnessed on the tapes of Medulla, probably the first form that Urzel had witnessed upon birth.

Nedilli's boils and crevices stretched as she encompassed her son. "Come to me," she said loudly enough for the world to hear; the words reverberated through the jungle. Deacon was riveted by the union of mother and son as the voice of the child cried out, "Mama, Mama."

Deacon's body froze as the union rose higher and higher into the air, carrying them to the top of the glen. With Nedilli now hundreds of feet high, Deacon summoned Jim as his bodily functions performed in terror when he finally realized the grim implication. He tore down the hill farther, summoning Jim to follow. The Owler was slowed down by the obstacles in the terrain, which Deacon vaulted over in a direct line to Gem.

On his way through, he saw Chubby, so he screamed at the top of his lungs, saying, "Run for your life, Chubby. Find a hole farther down the hill! The gravity device is about to explode and scatter debris for miles." Deacon tackled Chubby, and they fell into a deep trench. Together they huddled under the rocky lip as Jim entered and lay down horizontally beside them.

It lasted only a second, but trees, earth, and other debris were uprooted. Dust and soil first screeched by at high velocity before debris rained down on them. Deacon's eardrums were depressed into his canals as nature screamed. His eyes were shut tight. In the dying of the roar, he was sucked out of the trench by an aftershock and thrown twenty yards. Chubby and Deacon landed in a pile of soft debris, which cushioned the blow; Jim landed on both legs but then was crushed by a projectile tree. It was over in seconds. As Deacon rose to his feet, he looked to the heavens, where the stars were blotted out by the aftermath of dust.

After wiping the soil from his face and brushing himself off, Deacon raced up the hill, coughing, passing a damaged, immobile, disassembled Jim who was missing both legs and part of his torso. The clearing had disappeared, and in its place were pieces of the jungle piled and scattered in heaps. He ran around each pile of debris, gasping for clean air, stopping to see the flattened hut hanging over the lip of the cliff. He continued to pant, driving himself to a sheer state of breathlessness until he found what he was looking for.

He raced to Xudur's side as the black plasma of her life was expelled in torrents. Her stench was overwhelming as she lay there motionless, deformed, her belly open, the crest and top of her head missing. Her eyes were wide open, focused on him. "Coombs." He kneeled in her pools of fluids as the end neared. "Hold me."

Disgusted, but obedient, he placed one arm around her mutilated neck and the other across her body in the absence of her protective scales. He now noticed that her left arm was detached. He sat there faithfully as she reached up to his shoulder and dug her claws on her only arm into his flesh. "Please tell my children . . . of . . . my bravery. Please tell them that I love them . . . do this . . . for me."

Her black eyes stared at him, and she flashed a last smile with her cut lips until her bottom jaw dropped and her life left her. He stayed there clutching her—his eyes moist, his body now covered in her fluids, mesmerized—until a battered, bloody Goharn Lok appeared.

Goharn knelt beside Deacon as he closed her eyelids, released her limp head, and covered her with loose branches. Goharn asked, "What happened?"

Deacon could only say, "It's over."

THE TRUTH

Deacon paced around the Council chambers apprehensively for an hour, waiting for Landrew to show. His persistence finally paid off as the distinct sounds of Landrew indicated he was about to arrive. He stopped at the door, ordered the chamber to be sealed by his guard, and sat down in his customary chair at the end of the imposing table. Deacon obliged by menacingly facing him at the far end. They were the only occupants of the room.

Landrew folded his hands in front of him. He recognized the thoughts of the detective by stating, "How long have you known?"

"I suspected it the moment I departed from Medulla. I was so naive. I was caught up in the adventure of this assignment, caught up in survival, obsessed by capturing and mitigating Urzel, and also infatuated by my new love for Lyanna. But then there were some quiet hours on that trip. During the final conflict with Urzel, I truly came to know what the real truth was. You and Xudur planned it this way all along. Destroy Nedilli and Urzel and Xudur as a final solution."

"Correct."

"You struck your own bargain with the Medullans, didn't you, Landrew? In return for the sacrifice of Nedilli's life, you would continue the research at Brebouillis. If Nedilli declined to be a martyr, then the research at Brebouillis would be discontinued. That was the deal Xudur carried to the Medullans."

"Correct."

"You coerced Nedilli to do this when Xudur talked to her privately on the shuttle on our return to Earth. In the shuttle, the two mothers finalized the plan on Earth to sacrifice them both. Nedilli agreed to in order to save the continuation of research at Brebouillis and agreed to sacrifice herself if Xudur would too. Xudur knew that Nedilli's strength would support her."

"Correct."

"I realized the conclusion when Jim informed me that the force fields were inoperative." Thoughts were gnawing in his stomach. "Landrew, I feel that you and the Council may not even keep your word. Correct? You may discontinue the research at Brebouillis even though Nedilli is dead, has given her life for this cause."

"That is for Council discussion and debate. How can I and the High Council ever thank you, Deacon Coombs? We were desperate to have someone identify who was behind the heinous crimes. You found the monster. We needed you to locate Travers. You did. We needed you to smoke out the dangerous Morris Mydloan, who disappeared. You did. We needed you to locate Urzel Lok, to find Chubby Eaves, and—"

Deacon finished Landrew's sentence angrily. "And unite mother and sons to destroy them all, all three of them!"

"Correct. Deacon, please understand that for a lesser cause we would have shared our inner truths earlier, but I had to have you act independently to gather your evidence, to confirm that Urzel Lok was alive. We needed you to engage resources to determine how to exterminate it. You performed admirably when you consulted with Dr. Rodan Roadster. The Medullans would have never released Nedilli into our custody. They did not trust us. But I knew they would trust you. That is your reputation. Only after they released her did we strike this bargain with them as the *Heritage* made its way back to Earth, and then, on your shuttle to Earth, Xudur confirmed the plan with Nedilli."

"But Nedilli trusted me to keep her safe."

"Deacon, please. If you had not performed so admirably, if Nedilli had not given her life, if Xudur had not sacrificed herself, we would all be slaves under the bloody rule of Urzel. Xudur sent me a message in code to say that Nedilli recognized what had to be done."

Deacon was not satisfied. "I demand that my clients inform me of everything they know up front."

"You performed better than I ever dreamed of . . . with the Owlers you had. You solved the murders of Como and Geor for an Alliance populace. You pointed us in the direction of the instrument of Urzel's destruction. You and Doctor Roadster will be handsomely rewarded."

"Were there casualties in Asianda?"

"Regrettably, there were twenty fatalities of residents in proximity to the gravity bomb blast, which collapsed homes and uprooted trees, turning them into missiles; another two hundred were injured. They will all receive compensation from the Alliance. There was much property damage, but the new construction has already commenced. I depart tomorrow for the funerals of the unfortunate and to approve new dwellings for all who lost their homes."

Deacon conceded a point. "We have fought a hard battle and won. Urzel was a threat to the safety of the Alliance. Perhaps what I have learned from you, Xudur, Urzel, the Medullans, and the Aralians is that the greatest weapon of all is deceit."

Landrew was not pleased. "It had to be done, lest we all perish."

"How is Gem?"

"Xudur disengaged Gem's defense system in order to take her place with Nedilli as the assassin. The Owler suffered great damage in the ensuing blast. Gem will be assigned to a role with top-security Owler forces here in Liberty. The repairs on the Owler afford us a chance to install new technology in the Owler. I think I will have Gem assigned to me personally on occasions as a valuable reminder to me of what has happened, and of my luck to hire you and our good luck to have won this battle."

"What about Jim? The last time I saw the Owler in Asianda, the blast had crushed critical parts."

"Too much damage." Landrew sounded disappointed. "It will not be cost effective to repair Jim. He will be deactivated and replaced with a new model. Unfortunately you are correct; his torso was crushed and many of his functions destroyed."

Deacon was disappointed. "Will you compensate Goharn?"

"Compliments of the Alliance, he now has a new lodge with modern conveniences—except for his fireplace to make his herbal teas, which he will build himself, as he stated to me. His wounds and broken bones will heal over time."

"Have you remitted to Toad his compensation?"

"I ordered a handsome stipend and dispatched it today. A most peculiar man, but I must admit he designed an effective weapon to scatter Urzel's molecules. Unfortunately, as a result of her trying to protect Xudur during the explosion, Nedilli was sacrificed; her molecules too were scattered beyond recognition."

"I know. The dual force field was never an option for you and Xudur."

"Xudur and I realized that Urzel may detect the field upon initiation so went to battle nude, as planned."

"How long had you suspected that the research at Brebouillis must be discontinued?"

Landrew rose and proceeded to sit beside Deacon. "You and Toad brought this to our attention. You are a marvel, Deacon. I knew that if we could just find Travers, he might hold the key to unlocking this mystery. Your reputation for tenacity preceded you."

"Did anyone else really know that you had sanctioned the mating of an Earthman and a Medullan?"

"Other than the Medullans, no. I alone sanctioned it. I alone carried the burden. The other members of the High Council discovered it that evening when you revealed it to them. I felt embarrassed and humiliated that night. Xudur expressed her deep disappointment in me privately and explained that a chance for redemption would give her satisfaction. You can guess what she wanted from me. The chance to be the assassin. She had the confidence in herself to see the mission to its conclusion. Dreveney defended the research at Brebouillis, naturally; Raal wanted a solution foremost; Eggu-Nitron and Dithropolis both approached me late to say that while disappointed in me, I had their full support to resolve this crisis before we all fell victim to Urzel.

"Rande's betrayal only reinforced to all the members that we must have the resources and commitment to see the crisis to the end. By betraying us, Rande actually dispelled some of the animosity toward me and united us in our cause. I never suspected Rande to be a traitor."

"When will you stop all communications with the Medullans?"

"Ironically, the last ship to dock at and leave Medulla was the *H'vington*. Ironically, the last cargo was Urzel Lok. There is no need for any trade ship to journey there again. We will have to live without the valuable ores they have afforded us."

"What is the current state of disorder on Jabu?"

"The Jabu government has been reinstated, and all the Nicosians have been transported back to Nix. Final casualty toll was sixteen thousand dead. Planet Nix has been scoured, and all the caches of weapons are back in the hands of Alliance Security. We also have arrested all known subversives and allies of Urzel who were fighting against the Jabu. Your friend Quobit, played quite a significant part in defeating the Nicosians on Jabu and has been rewarded with a promotion to director of Jabu Vespering Security with a future design to bring her into Alliance galactic forces."

"I am so pleased. She will be visiting Earth to see Lyanna and me soon." Deacon rose. "My work is over. I leave you with my record of this adventure in this disc, and a second copy will reside in my files at Moonbeam and be protected. Jim and Gem recorded most of what transpired. I hope you find these records in suitable condition and detail." He walked very slowly toward Landrew and passed him his discs. "A tribute to Xudur is enclosed."

Landrew stood to heartily embrace him in handshake. "I shall never forget you, Deacon Coombs. The compensation you received is only part of what I can offer. If you ever need the assistance of the Alliance, or if you require my assistance personally, please do not hesitate to contact me. The Tetrad Alliance still owes you a great deal of gratitude.

"May I remind you that these memoirs should not be published. I have already reminded Chubby, Toad, Quobit, and Lyanna of this."

"The Case of the Vanishing Vesper shall go to my grave with me. You have the only other accounts."

Deacon heaved a sigh. "Good-bye, Landrew. In these troubled times, you are a most respected leader, and you still have much to contribute. For me, I long for Moonbeam, Miram, and not to Vesper again for a few years." He made a decision to leave abruptly after a firm handshake.

As Deacon made his spirited exit, he passed the works of Vergotti—classic art, the busts of those historians he admired—while

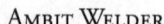
bouncing down the stairs to floor level. Landrew stood on the balcony overhead, watching him, step by step, admiring him. Deacon Coombs looked back and knew what Landrew was thinking, that he had given Landrew that chance in history. He smiled.

MOONLIGHT BRINGS A VISITOR

Visitors

The old oak door opened fully to reveal the Owler Jim dressed in an apron, beater appliance in hand, beaming with a smile. "My," Jim gleefully said, "Master Chubby Eaves and Schlegar." As they entered Moonbeam, Jim continued to greet them each with courteous remarks and to speak about his extreme satisfaction with his new assignment as servant and guard to Deacon Coombs. "Master Deacon will be delighted to see you both. Please wait here in his lounge."

The Owler strutted away after he had seated Chubby and Schlegar in the room, which overlooked the far reaches of the straits. Upon Jim's announcement, Deacon excitedly hurried to them; once there, he received the usual tight Aralian bear hugs.

"Villya, Deacon," they said in unison.

"We depart from Anglo port tonight to Vesper to Aralia," said Chubby. "We had free time, so what better to do than pay homage to our dear friend Deacon Coombs." Chubby accompanied his remarks with exaggerated body language conveying his delight.

Schlegar looked slightly confused. "I was told that Jim was sent to the junk heap to be recycled as used parts. Is this a similar model?"

Deacon paused before answering. "I know this sounds crazy, but I became very attached to Jim and Gem. At one point in the case, I felt that they were my only two true friends, the only ones to trust. That was before I met you two, naturally. Landrew once said to me to trust the Owlers. I did. He also stated that if there was anything else I needed, I should just ask."

He looked over at Jim, who was now dusting the bureau in the hallway. "I couldn't just let them trash old Jim, so I paid out of my compensation to make him fully functional again, and when Landrew discovered what I had done, he reimbursed me."

Chubby shook his head while Schlegar found it humorous and snorted loudly in his laughter. Schlegar then stopped to speak. "I didn't need to convince Chubby to come here. I wanted to tell you in person that I didn't hold it against you for recommending that the research at Brebouillis be terminated. Continuing our efforts posed an even greater danger. I now believe it firmly."

They engaged in spirited chatter, with Jim attending to their every need for food and refreshments, even providing his fleeting humorous anecdotes. They reminisced about the journey to Nix, Chubby's tribulations on the *H'vington*, and the comic interventions of Lookey. They also relived the final battle scene and discussed the outcome, each admiring and saluting Xudur for taking the final bold step. Schlegar was despondent in his comments about Travers. "Too late did I heed your advice about my son, Deacon. As I read and reread the accounts of his attempts to lead the traders' union, and your records of his heroism on Nix, I felt so stupid, so ashamed that I never reunited with him before his death. It was so foolish to let my obstinate ways stand in the way of forgiveness. Being humble is not an Aralian trait, as you discovered, Deacon."

Schlegar moved to beside Chubby and placed his arm around him. "I have adopted a new son. Chubby's parents are both deceased. My only son is deceased, so it made sense to increase the size of both our families. Right?"

Chubby grinned and said, "He has already put pressure on me to run for the vacated position of head of the Union of Space Traders, with support from my dad, the campaign chairman."

"My son, the rightful heir to the throne of the traders' union. He would make a fine leader. Don't you agree, Deacon?"

Deacon felt a warmth creep through him as he saw them together. "I shall never forget you two. Whatever you do in life, call on me for my support. And yes, he would make a fine leader, Schlegar. He has all the great deceitful traits." Schlegar and Deacon laughed as Chubby objected vigorously.

After further banter, Schlegar said, "Take care of her. She is like a daughter to me. On Brebouillis, she was one salvation. I know you don't see her as much as you like with her job in Liberty City, but Lyanna is my special person, as she is yours. We just visited her and gave her our regards in Liberty yesterday. She kept me company during those long, lonely nights on Brebouillis."

"I will take care of her. I promise."

Chubby said, "Let's use the Earth custom this time on departure. I am referring to handshakes of sincerity. No Aralian hugging."

After the ritual, Deacon stood at the door with Jim as Schlegar and Chubby sauntered down his lane to their vehicle. Chubby turned to yell, "Partners fer life, matey!"

"Aye, Lookey," Deacon replied. He stood there until the craft disappeared, and he then returned to pen a note to a barrister he had engaged as a client. Miram cuddled up in his lap as he finished the lengthy correspondence. As was the case each night since he had returned to Earth, he found that his eyelids became heavy early in the evening as the cool night air descended.

A visitor

Deacon moved to his deck to rest on a recliner as the waves crashed into the rocks below. The moon cast intermittent beams on the hissing white tide as Deacon Coombs lay prostrate over two hundred feet above the sands. The rhythmic crashes placed them into a deep sleep. Miram had missed her master so had spent many hours by his side since his return. This evening was no exception.

Hours later, the moon was high but repeatedly blocked from view by streams of clouds racing across the heavens. Miram was awakened by the sound of a rock chip tumbling down the chalky cliffs. Slithering over the dew-laden deck, she spied a stranger approaching and ascending to the far end of the balcony.

She immediately hissed in Deacon's ear to arouse him. As she did so, he heaved a deep sigh and stretched his arms outright. As

Deacon arose and then gazed out over the paradise of surf and sea and stars, Miram continued to hiss. He suddenly shared her concern as a hooded stranger ascended the steps at the end of the balcony and, piece by piece, step by step, came into view. The scene was tense as Deacon struggled to understand who the intruder was; Jim was too distant to summon. Miram perched behind a beam, awaiting her master's signal.

An arm extended and pointed to him as a deep, husky voice said, "Deacon Coombs. I have traveled far to reach your residence. Your presence is requested immediately to resolve a very urgent matter."

Deacon strained to see inside the hood as Jim now moved onto the deck and stood beside him. He felt confident as he returned the comments. "I have a front entrance."

"And I come as a friend."

"What do you want?"

The tone was firm but changed its pitch. "You are a wanted man. I want you on the beach below immediately. Now!"

Deacon smiled in elation as Jim positioned himself beside Deacon and whispered in his ear what he already knew. "Master, that is the voice of Lyanna."

"You sneak. Miram might have bitten you."

"Doubtful. When you were in Medulla, I visited here, and Miram and I became very good friends. Right, Miram?" The slinky orange asp wound itself around Lyanna's ankle and looked upward with a smile. "I just couldn't resist a look inside Moonbeam while you were absent."

With that comment, Lyanna and Deacon raced through the rocks to the beach, he in pursuit of her, until finally he caught her and they tumbled into the shallow surf. She pointed to the rocks behind them where Miram stood guard. Then she pushed him off and ran farther in the sand in her bare feet. As Deacon approached, she discarded her robe, revealing her elegance to him in her bathing suit. "Come warm me up."

Deacon said, "I am still very shy."

"Not for long," she said as she approached him. Miram sat among the cold, mossy rocks, eyes wide open and thin mouth in a taut smile.

That same evening in Anglo, Maisie Pitchford and the Alliance-renowned actor Dymenttt were giving a command performance for the royalty of Europa. As the audience watched, Dymenttt stunned the small group by clutching his throat and slamming to the stage in another one of his award-winning performances. The death scene was precise, riveting, and as the curtain closed, the audience expressed their appreciation for the arts with a thunderous standing ovation.

But on this night, Dymenttt did not rise for his normal curtain call, and the tears that Maisie Pitchford shed were genuine. As Lyanna and Deacon lay down as one soul, cuddled up on the beach, little did they know that this tragic death of Dymenttt would bring them closer together and drive them farther apart as they launched into the depths of space again.